The Nightmare

and Other Tales of Dark Fantasy

Francis Stevens

EDITED AND WITH AN INTRODUCTION BY

Gary Hoppenstand

ILLUSTRATIONS BY THOMAS L. FLOYD

University of Nebraska Press
Lincoln and London

⊗

First Nebraska paperback printing :
2004

Library of Congress Cataloging-in-
Publication Data
Stevens, Francis.
The nightmare, and other tales of
dark fantasy / by Francis Stevens ;
edited and with an introduction by
Gary Hoppenstand ; illustrations
by Thomas L. Floyd.
p. cm.—(Bison frontiers of imagination)
Includes bibliographical references.
ISBN 0-8032-9298-8 (pbk.: alk. paper)
1. Fantasy fiction, American.   2. Horror
tales, American.   I. Hoppenstand, Gary.
II. Title.   III. Series.
N54 2004
813'.52–dc22   2004009710

For Karl Edward Wagner—
Master of Dark Fantasy

From Kane's #1 Fan

Contents

GARY HOPPENSTAND

Francis Stevens: The Woman Who Invented Dark Fantasy

One of the most influential authors during the development of science fiction and fantasy in the early decades of the twentieth century was A. Merritt (1884–1943). An American writer who first appeared in the pulp magazines during World War I, Merritt wrote such classic fantasy novels as *The Moon Pool* (1919) and *The Face in the Abyss* (1931). He is considered one of the first writers of speculative fiction to combine narrative elements of science fiction with fantasy and horror. *The Encyclopedia of Science Fiction* defines his contributions as being "influential upon the SF and fantasy world . . . because of the genuine imaginative power he displayed in the creation of desirable alternative worlds and realities" (Clute and Nicholls 1993). By successfully blending science fiction, fantasy, and horror fiction, Merritt helped establish the foundation for that twentieth-century literary hybrid known as dark fantasy, but he was not alone in this endeavor.

Dark fantasy is defined as a type of horror story (possibly containing science fiction and fantasy elements) in which humanity is threatened with destruction by hostile cosmic forces beyond the normal ken of mortals. Within the larger genre of horror fiction, dark fantasy expresses a macabre existential variant, one that envisions a desperately bleak worldview in which stereotyped notions of courage and heroism fail when confronted by the overwhelming presence of ancient and unfathomable evils.

An acknowledged master of dark fantasy was H. P. Lovecraft (1890–1937), a contemporary of Merritt's and an American writer of pulp fiction. Critic Donald R. Burleson articulates the standard appreciation: "H.P. Lovecraft was not only a writer of highly worthy and unique stories, novels, and poems; he was a philosopher of genuinely incisive perception, an essayist of much persuasive power, a literary critic, and an epistolarian whose equal is scarcely to be found" (1983, ix).

The thematic linking of Merritt's and Lovecraft's fiction is an obvious one. Lovecraft certainly admired Merritt's work. Noted science fiction critic Sam Moskowitz states that Lovecraft regarded Merritt's short story "The Moon Pool" (which was, in part, the basis for the novel of the same title) as "one of his 10 favorite stories of fantasy" (1985, 21–22). Lovecraft, however, extended his vision of horror beyond Merritt's fantasy stylings to create a more terrifying type of story, best illustrated in his famous Cthulhu Mythos cycle and seen in tales such as *The Case of Charles Dexter Ward* (1927), *At the Mountains of Madness* (1931), and "The Shadow Over Innsmouth" (1931). The traditional scholarly emphasis on the importance of Merritt's and Lovecraft's early impact on the creation of the dark fantasy genre is certainly correct to a point, but such an assessment fails to closely examine the work of other, lesser known but equally significant writers who published at the same time and in the same pulp magazines. In my own monograph, *In Search of the Paper Tiger* (1987), for example, I argued that Lovecraft was the inventor of modern dark fantasy (51), but I was wrong. I have since discovered a relatively unknown writer who was a contemporary of Merritt's and Lovecraft's and whose work certainly influenced their own efforts.

The person who may stake the best claim at creating the new genre of dark fantasy is Francis Stevens (1883–1948). It is readily apparent to those who survey Stevens's pulp magazine novels and short stories that her fiction was greatly admired by Merritt and Lovecraft. Both authors expanded and reworked in their own fiction the dark fantasy narrative elements that Stevens first developed and employed in her writings, published in the pulps between 1917 and 1923.

The American pulp magazines were among the most ephemeral forms of mass entertainment during the first half of the twentieth century. They evolved out of the nineteenth-century dime novel and, like their dime novel predecessors, they were printed on inexpensive pulpwood paper and sold for a dime (or perhaps even a quarter). Regarding the early development of the pulps, Tony Goodstone states in his edited collection of pulp fiction, *The Pulps: Fifty Years of American Pop Culture*:

> In 1893 . . . a severe economic recession began [in America]. Taking advantage of technological advances, *McClure's*, a magazine of superb quality, dropped its price from 15 to 10 cents. The middle and educated lower classes responded enthusiastically. Other magazines soon followed suit, and circulations climbed to staggering figures. In 1896, with the population at 76 million, *Munsey's* peaked at 700,000. Frank A. Munsey was inspired by its success to transform his boy's magazine

Argosy and the first Pulp was born . . . By 1907 *Argosy* had 500,000 readers. (1970, xii)

The early pulps, such as the *Argosy* and *All-Story Magazine*, featured a wide selection of diverse genres—from the love story to the western, crime fiction to the scientific romance—in each issue and were intended as "family friendly" magazines, offering stories of interest to the father and mother as well as the children of the working-class household. These earliest pulp magazines typically presented several short stories, a novelette or two, and at least one serialized novel to ensure that readers who had become engrossed in a novel-length story would purchase the subsequent issues in which the story was serialized.

Popular culture historian Ron Goulart, in *An Informal History of the Pulp Magazine* (1972), remarks that Frank A. Munsey, the man who helped to create the pulp magazines, was called a "meat packer" of fiction by his critics. But Goulart notes that Munsey's artistic tastes (or lack thereof) did not diminish his critical role in the development of popular fiction in American culture.

[E]ras and movements, like people, can't pick their fathers and so a history of the pulp magazines has to begin with the ruthless and un-likable Munsey . . . who at the end of the 19th century invented the pulpwood fiction magazine. If it had not been for him there might never have been the pulps and, consequently, no Tarzan, no Sam Spade, no Dr. Kildare, no Doc Savage, no Zorro, no Shadow and no Tros of Samothrace. Zane Grey might have stayed in dentistry and Charles Atlas might still be a 97-pound weakling. (1972, 9–10)

There also would be no Francis Stevens, as her first story, along with the bulk of her work, appeared in the Munsey pulps. Nevertheless, everyone who was involved with the production or consumption of the pulps—the writers, the editors, and the readers—understood the ephemeral nature of the medium.

No one at that time expected the stories that appeared in the pulps to be of so-called lasting quality. Pulp fiction was, literally, "disposable fiction." For the contemporary reader, the irony here is that a handful of authors who wrote for the pulps became established and critically successful (and thus remembered) outside of the medium. For example, Tennessee Williams's first story appeared in the pulp *Weird Tales*, while a few others, includ-ing Dashiell Hammett, Raymond Chandler, and Lovecraft, became quite famous as pulp authors and were celebrated by the mainstream literary community. Their pulp fiction continued to be reprinted over the years; however, the vast majority of pulp magazine "hacks" simply disappeared from the historic literary record. Their contributions to the pulps and their larger contributions to popular fiction crumpled into obscurity along with the yellowing and flaking pulpwood paper their stories were printed on.

Francis Stevens is one of those forgotten authors, who appears to us as a shadowy outline at best, indistinct and lacking important details. Little is known today of her early life, and even less is known of her later life. The real name behind the "Francis Stevens" pseudonym was Gertrude Barrows, though her family liked to call her by her middle name of Myrtle. Most sources incorrectly list her date of birth as 1884, but after locating her birth certificate, pulp fiction scholar R. Alain Everts identified her actual birth date as September 18, 1883. Everts learned that she was born in Minneapolis, Minnesota, to Charles Barrows and Carrie Hatch. She had a brother, Clarke, who died at age twenty-four (2000, 29–30). In his introduction to the Polaris Press reprint of Stevens's *The Heads of Cerberus*, critic Lloyd Arthur Eshbach stated that Stevens

> married an Englishman named Stewart Bennett; they lived in Philadelphia. Eight months after the birth of her daughter Josephine in 1910, her husband was drowned in a tropical storm while on an expedition seeking sunken treasure. He had been a newspaper reporter, a fact which probably led his widow to contribute feature articles to the newspaper.
>
> Faced with the necessity of supporting herself and her infant daughter, Gertrude Bennett worked for a time as secretary to a University of Pennsylvania professor, increasing her income by typing theses for students at night. With the death of her father, several years later, her invalid mother became an added responsibility—and since it now was necessary for her to spend most of her time in her third floor apartment, she turned to fiction writing. (1952, 14)

Pulp historian Robert Weinberg suggests that Stevens ceased to write following the death of her mother around 1920, as she then had the opportunity to return to full-time employment (1984, 8). Weinberg published an autobiographical statement written by Stevens in his introduction to the 1984 reprint of *The Citadel of Fear*.

> Born in Minneapolis, Minnesota. Parents both of literary tastes and I was brought up in the midst of books, though I had to leave school

at the end of the grammar grades and go to work. I had a little talent for drawing, and wished to become an illustrator. Studied nights for some years but finally gave it up. I wrote my first story when I was seventeen and working in the office of a department store. I had just one merit, as I remember it, and that was a rather grotesque originality. Of course, in the writers' estimation, it was a very wonderful story, but nevertheless, I was more than surprised when the *Argosy*, the first magazine to which it was submitted, accepted it. (6–7)

Eshbach, however, provided the first known biographical portrait of Stevens in his introduction to *The Heads of Cerberus*. He wrote that she spent a considerable amount of time doing background research for her plots. She then composed her stories rapidly in longhand, taking about seven months to complete her novels. She preferred to be alone when she wrote and often locked herself in a room of her apartment for isolation. After she finished a story, she read it aloud to her daughter who critiqued it before the manuscript was sent to the publisher (1952, 14).

In some ways, Francis Stevens is reminiscent of Mary Shelley, the young author of *Frankenstein; or, The Modern Prometheus* (1818). Shelley was not a polished writer but instead was a genius at generating truly important concepts and ideas. *Frankenstein* itself is a shaggy-dog story, creaking under the burden of four narrative framing devices and regrettable lapses into sentimental romance and travelogue formulas that diminish the more important development of suspenseful gothic horror. Nevertheless, Shelley wrote the most important novel to come out of the Industrial Revolution. With *Frankenstein* Mary Shelley invented modern science fiction, just as Francis Stevens's pulp fiction, which is at times ungainly and at times brilliant, invented modern dark fantasy a century later.

So far as we know, Stevens published only a handful of novels and short stories. Her known fiction is uneven and not without serious narrative flaws. For example, she seemed to have an awkward time getting the plots started in her novels. Nevertheless, after a chapter or two, when she finally established her characters and story, her narrative pacing was often exceptional. Pulp historian Will Murray identified at least two novels that were purchased by the pulp magazine *The Thrill Book*, but they did not appear in print before the magazine folded. The manuscripts were subsequently lost (Weinberg 8).

Stevens's first major novel-length work, and perhaps her best, was *The*

Citadel of Fear, published as a serial in the *Argosy* from September 14 to October 26, 1918. It opens in central Mexico as a lost world adventure, somewhat in the tradition of H. Rider Haggard's African romances, but midway through the story as the narrative moves to the United States, it quickly changes its form (and formula) into a tale of dark fantasy. The hero, Colin "Boots" O'Hara, is suitably heroic, and the villain, Archer Kennedy, who learns to master the forbidden Aztec black magic, is as nasty as they come. Stevens's descriptions of the lost Aztec city Tlapallan early in the novel feature a brilliantly realized fantasy setting that is comparable to Edgar Rice Burroughs's settings in his Martian adventures. In his introduction to the 1970 reprint of *Citadel*, Moskowitz addressed the connection between *Citadel* and the work of Lovecraft. Moskowitz quotes extensively from a letter written by Lovecraft to the *Argosy*:

> *Citadel of Fear*, if written by Sir Walter Scott or Ibanez, that wonderful and tragic allegory would have been praised to the skies. . . . Underlying its amazing and thrilling scenes was the sad but indisputable lesson that once a man gives himself up to evil and to evil deeds only, resulting from selfish greed, that man's soul is lost. I find also in it a very strong suggestion that real evil does not lie in the so-called personal peccadilloes, but rather in black treachery toward one's own kith and kin and country, an unmoral endeavor to harm all those who stand in the path of selfish purpose. . . . I feel so much interested in the motif of that curious tale that I should like very much to have my curiosity gratified . . . would like a sketch of the life of Stevens and particularly the source and development of *The Citadel of Fear*. That story would make one amazing moving-picture drama, if taken up by the right moving-picture manager. . . . Stevens, to my mind, is the highest grade of your writers. (5)

In the above passage, Lovecraft gushes his obvious admiration for Stevens's *Citadel*, using the novel as a sounding board for his own larger philosophical discussion of the nature of evil. In fact I would suggest that Lovecraft later adopted and refined Stevens's use of settings and characterizations in his own dark fantasy fiction.

The Heads of Cerberus, published serially in the *Thrill Book* from August 15 to October 15, 1919, was Stevens's second novel to see print. A dystopian tale set in a future Philadelphia, it is the closest she came to writing pure science fiction. *Heads of Cerberus* features Stevens's reworking of Edward Bellamy's novel, *Looking Backward, 2000–1887* (1888), transforming Bellamy's urban utopian narrative into a bleak vision of tomorrow. It anticipated the type of story reworked for the cinema; for example, Fritz Lang's *Metropolis* (1926) as well as the films it inspired including Ridley Scott's classic, *Blade Runner* (1982). Science fiction critic and author P. Schuyler Miller also argues that *Heads of Cerberus* was possibly the first story to "envision the parallel-time-track concept" (Eshbach 1952, 15).

Stevens's next major novel, *Avalon*, was a four-part serial appearing in the *Argosy* from August 16 to September 6, 1919. Though the *Argosy* touted the story as being "written with all the power of incomparable imagination and character-drawing which gave you *Citadel of Fear*, that weirdly compelling masterpiece which lingered so terrifyingly in the memory," *Avalon* is actually vastly inferior to both *Citadel of Fear* and *Heads of Cerberus*. Burdened by a confusingly large cast of major and minor characters, it unfortunately fails in its attempt at being a thriller. The promising supernatural elements hinted at in the story at various times are, regrettably, never fully developed, and of all her longer macabre fiction, this story is her most mundane and muddled. It is undeniably Stevens's weakest novel, yet despite its many flaws *Avalon* is not without its merits as a work of romantic suspense. Its gothic setting is well developed and appropriately atmospheric, and its narrative pacing, as with all of Stevens's longer work, is fast and furious.

Stevens's last major novel, *Claimed*, published in the *Argosy* from March 6 to March 20, 1920, is my personal favorite. It tells the story of a small "casket" discovered by a sea captain and his crew on a mysterious island that was raised to the surface by underwater volcanic activity. The casket eventually finds its way into the possession of an old, greedy collector named Jesse Robinson who would rather die than relinquish his possession. When it is learned that the casket actually belongs to a dark sea god who wants it back, a horrible conflict ensues that embroils young Dr. John Vanaman, who is treating the old miser, and Robinson's niece Leilah. Stevens hit her stride as a storyteller in this short novel, developing scenes of weird horror that rank with the best work of Merritt and Lovecraft and no doubt influencing Lovecraft's own dark fantasy.

Take the opening scene, for example, when the sea captain first encounters the volcanic island:

> The formation [of the island] is a dark, chocolate-colored rock, striated with metallic-red. . . . Near the center the rock has been flung up in ridges, forming rectangular and other shapes, quaintly reminiscent of the ruins of old buildings. . . . From where we stood the illusion of ruins was nearly perfect . . . we may today have looked upon the last surviving trace of some ancient city, flung up from the abyss that

engulfed it ages before the brief history we have of the race of man began. (1966, 8)

This excerpt is emblematic of two essential dark fantasy motifs: the ancient monolithic city and the disquieting sense of history that predates the arrival of humans. These motifs appear again later in Lovecraft's "The Shadow out of Time" (1936), which first appeared in the science fiction pulp *Astounding Stories*. Note the striking similarity in Lovecraft's story to Stevens's passage above in the following description of his reworking of the dark fantasy motif of the prehuman alien city:

> In certain places I beheld enormous dark cylindrical towers which climbed far above any of the other structures. These appeared to be of a totally unique nature and shewed signs of prodigious age and dilapidation. They were built of a bizarre type of square-cut basalt masonry . . . [and] there hovered an inexplicable aura of menace and concentrated fear." (1963, 381)

In comparison to *Claimed*, Lovecraft's crafting of his setting is obviously more elaborate and detailed and the depiction of the ancient city expanded and better developed, but it is readily apparent that the images in both tales, and the ideas behind those images, are closely related.

Following the appearance of her two-part novella, *Sunfire*, in *Weird Tales* in 1923, Stevens seemed to have disappeared from sight as a writer and as a person. She moved to California, where she eventually lost touch with her daughter, and was apparently not heard from again. In an attempt to explain this period of Stevens's life, Everts wrote "The Mystery of Francis Stevens (1883–1948)." For this critically important essay, Everts researched the specific facts as they related to Stevens's birth, marriages, and death. He first established her correct birth date as discussed earlier. Investigating various city directories, Everts learned that in 1901 a Gertrude M. Barrows was identified as a stenographer residing with her mother, and in 1904 she is listed as a stenographer with the Security Bank of Minnesota. While in 1902 a Gertrude L. Barrows is listed as a stenographer for the Powers Mercantile Company. Everts notes that Weinberg discovered Gertrude Barrows Bennett had remarried following the death of her first husband and had lived in Boston and Philadelphia in the 1920s. Everts spoke with fellow researcher Douglas Anderson regarding the contents of her final letter to her daughter dated 1939. The letter identified California as Bennett's residence. Following this lead, Everts obtained her death certificate, which listed California as her residence since 1936, twenty-two years before her death in 1948. Everts, however, could not confirm her Boston connection with this information. It is possible that Bennett moved to California in the mid-1920s, perhaps traveling between the East and West coasts, or that the actual time periods identified in her death certificate may have been estimates. Her second marriage to a man named Gaster, Everts notes, has never been confirmed (2004).

No one knows for sure why Francis Stevens decided to become a fiction writer, and certainly no one knows why she aimed her work at the pulp magazines, which were then a decidedly "male run" and "male read" operation. When women published in the *Argosy* or *All-Story Weekly*, they wrote traditional romantic love stories. With the publication of "The Nightmare" as well as her subsequent macabre tales of imagination, adventure, horror, and suspense, Stevens subverted the stereotypical expectations of editors and readers regarding a woman's proper role as a writer for the pulps. She instead opted to publish a unique blend of fiction that would eventually be admired and imitated by her male pulp-writer counterparts. It has been suggested that "Robert Davis of the Munsey periodicals disliked using female author's [sic] names, and consistently tried to persuade them to use a masculine pseudonym" (Everts 2000, 29–30), hence the androgynous-sounding "Francis Stevens" nom de plume.

It was no secret that male writers dominated the adventure and fantasy genres in the early twentieth century. The French novelist Jules Verne created the science fiction adventure story, or scientific romance, in 1863 with his first novel, *Five Weeks in a Balloon*, thus inspiring a legion of male-written and male-centered scientific romances for the next fifty years. British author H. Rider Haggard refined Verne's "extraordinary voyage" narrative and developed a more specific literary formula—the "lost world" adventure—in popular novels such as *King Solomon's Mines* (1885) and *She* (1887). American writer Edgar Rice Burroughs then introduced the lost world adventure to the pulps in 1912 with the publication of *Tarzan of the Apes* and *A Princess of Mars*. With the single exception of Francis Stevens, female authors were not publishing speculative fiction in the early twentieth century.

In fact for a number of years readers and critics thought Francis Stevens to be the pen name of A. Merritt. Both Stevens and Merritt appeared in the pulps at nearly the same time, and it was a commonly understood practice for prolific writers of pulp fiction to publish under various pseudonyms to allow them to sell more than one story to the same issue of a magazine. During the 1940s, after Merritt had achieved notoriety as an innovator of science fiction and fantasy and was involved in the promotion of several pulp titles based on his "style" of speculative fiction, Stevens was one of the authors he championed to a new audience. He suggested to the editors of several pulp magazines that they republish Stevens's best stories, including her finest novel, *The Citadel of Fear*. *Famous Fantastic Mysteries* did just that and reprinted it in the February 1942 issue. Noted science fiction editor and historian, Moskowitz, wrote in the introduction to the 1970 reprint of *Citadel of Fear*:

> The reprint of her [Stevens's] short story *Behind the Curtain* in its January, 1940, issue . . . evoked memories in the mind of the great fantasy writer A. Merritt, who was then still alive. He called [the] editor . . . of that publication and urged her to reprint *Claimed*, a short novel by Francis Stevens. (6)

Merritt was more than just nostalgically fond of Stevens; he "borrowed" liberally from her ideas, incorporating them into his own work. From *Claimed*, Merritt (as well as Lovecraft) worked the similar dark fantasy motif of an ancient and hostile sentient evil that threatens humanity with destruction. From *The Heads of Cerberus*, both Merritt and Lovecraft successfully adopted and adapted Stevens's critical thematic revision of the science-fiction horror story, which became a part of the interweaving of speculative fiction formulas typically found in dark fantasy.

Just as Shelley's *Frankenstein* grew out of the historical context of the Industrial Revolution, Stevens's dark fantasy grew out of the horrors experienced during World War I. This event was unlike any that preceded it in human history in its apocalyptic sense of global conflict and destruction.

The horrors of world war helped to reshape the field of art, as illustrated by the development of the Dadaist movement; the war also helped to reshape popular fiction, as illustrated in the supernatural tale. The popular British, Edwardian, antiquarian ghost story as written by M. R. James (1862–1936) or E. F. Benson (1867–1940) became less dominant in popular fiction by the 1920s and was supplanted by pulp fiction dark fantasy. In America, near the turn of the twentieth century, the satiric humorist Ambrose Bierce (1842–1914?) created a new type of bitingly cynical horror story, as represented by Bierce's collection *Tales of Soldiers and Civilians* (1891). These macabre tales certainly explored effectively the horrors of the American Civil War, but Bierce's tales of terror about civilians tended to be centered at the personal and immediate level, not at the level of collective social disquiet found in dark fantasy. As with Bierce, Robert W. Chambers (1865–1933) was an important and influential force in the evolution of the American horror story, with the publication of his collection *The King in Yellow* (1895), but Chambers's horror fiction tended to be thematically obscure, overly atmospheric, even obtuse and thus possessing less dramatic impact with readers. Dark fantasy possessed a greater punch that was decidedly more terrifying for an audience desiring an escapist, entertaining fright.

The Nightmare and Other Tales of Dark Fantasy is the first book collection of Francis Stevens's shorter fiction, thus demonstrating her mastery and range in writing groundbreaking speculative fiction. The link between Stevens's writing to the war is obvious in the plot of her first published story, "The Nightmare." She was influenced by the German sinking of the British ocean liner *Lusitania* on May 7, 1915, off the southern coast of Ireland, a tragedy that helped draw America into World War I, which is an important plot device that opens Stevens's narrative. The story appeared in the April 14, 1917, issue of *All-Story Weekly*. Stevens was announced to the readers of *All-Story Weekly* in the April 7, 1917, "Heart to Heart Talks by the Editor" column. Prefaced by the statement that many readers "still have a love, somewhere deep buried within us, for accounts of the 'giants and witches and elves, and squidgi-cum-squees that swallers theirselves' of our youth," it is noted that Stevens's forthcoming story, "The Nightmare," is a tale of the "convincingly impossible." As proclaimed in this blurb, it was apparently important to the readers of *All-Story Weekly* that the fantasy fiction have some type of rational explanation. The announcement continues "and yet in the end [of "The Nightmare"] you will find that you are *not* merely being fed a hodge-podge of untrammeled imagination, but that there is a reasonable explanation for everything." Stevens's initial literary effort at undermining fantasy's rational dénouement, which was the readers' formulaic expectation of that period, ultimately led to the establishment of dark fantasy. Stevens, in fact, initially seemed to provide a clichéd resolution for the aptly named Roland Jones in the story, only to undermine the cliché at the conclusion. In addition the astute reader will note her treatment of radical political thought as her story expresses the American readers' social paranoia of that time for villains who were Russian and who advanced extremist, or revolutionary, leanings.

Stevens's novella, "The Labyrinth," serialized in *All-Story Weekly* from July 27 to August 10, 1918, is characteristic of the romantic suspense popularized much later in motion pictures such as Alfred Hitchcock's *North by Northwest* (1959). As such, "The Labyrinth" is similar to *Avalon*, but Stevens is more successful with her treatment of the formula in her short story. The title is descriptive of the unique setting, which is wonderfully realized, and the convoluted love entanglements among the major characters, which are stilted and artificial. Although considered one of her less engaging efforts, "The Labyrinth" is not without its charm. At one level it offers a moral critique of American politics and political leaders, such as seen in the behavior of Stevens's love-stricken Gov. Clinton Charles. At another level, it explores the problematic nature, from Stevens's point of view, of social class in America. Her decision to employ several negative racial stereotypes is unfortunate, though at the time it was a common practice among writers for the pulps to use such stereotypes. For me, the most interesting feature of this story is Stevens's characterization of Veronica Wyndam, who appears as an idealized representation of the author herself. The protagonist, Hildreth Wyndham, is more amusing than inspiring; as a hero he often behaves most unheroically, though he tries to play the detective and Veronica's rescuer. The finest dimension of the story, however, is the bizarre labyrinth setting itself, which is decidedly macabre in origin and function. As an insidious device of revenge (for the deceased character, Daniel Mason, even from the grave), it is reminiscent of the tales of psychological horror by Edgar Allan Poe. This was fertile soil for Stevens, and she later returned to Poe as a source of inspiration in her story "Behind the Curtain."

"Friend Island," published in the September 7, 1918, issue of *All-Story Weekly*, is peripherally science fiction. Set in the year A.D. 2100, the narrative features a future world of airships and the women who flew them. More directly, "Friend Island" is a feminist fantasy, a story in which women are the dominant gender and men are depicted as being rather boorish in an ongoing battle of the sexes that even extends to the environment. The tale possesses an ecological dimension, exploring the social-biological relationship between humans and their environment. It thus anticipates Arthur Conan Doyle's Professor Challenger adventure "When the World Screamed" (1928) in anthropomorphizing nature; Stevens's variant gives an island a female personality. Last, and most important, "Friend Island" is a story about shipwreck and survival in a potentially hostile yet exotic land and, as such, draws reference to the first great novel of popular adventure fiction in the English language, Daniel Defoe's *Robinson Crusoe* (1719). With Stevens, the Robinson Crusoe protagonist is a crusty "sea-woman" aviatrix, telling of her fantastic adventures on a living island, while the Friday character is a man who doesn't know how to behave properly around a woman, even if that woman is a "living" Pacific island.

"Behind the Curtain" was first published in the September 21, 1918, issue of *All-Story Weekly* and is written in imitation of Poe's classic tale of revenge, "The Cask of Amontillado" (1846). As with Poe's story, "Behind the Curtain" is also concerned with revenge, though Stevens is much more specific than Poe in providing the protagonist's motivation for revenge: romantic infidelity. However, "Behind the Curtain" is most concerned with the readers' exploration of suspense through the use of imagination. Stevens fully understood that the tale of terror is most effective when the elements of horror are not graphically described. In his study of the horror genre, *Danse Macabre* (1981), Stephen King recognized this essential quality of terror—the ability to depict something scary without having to resort to visceral descriptions of blood and gore—as achieving the most artistic level of horror writing. He suggested W. W. Jacobs's classic tale, "The Monkey's Paw" (1902), as a good illustration of how terror can function in a story (34). Stevens's use of the door in her story as a metaphor of hidden horror is particularly apt. As in Jacobs's tale, Stevens masks the visual images of horror from the readers' eyes, thus enhancing the development of suspense. Her tale also works nicely in the tradition of the mummy horror story, especially the type practiced earlier by Doyle in "The Ring of Thoth" (1890) and "Lot No. 249" (1892) as well as by Bram Stoker in *The Jewel of Seven Stars* (1904). In spite of its many virtues, "Behind the Curtain" disappoints a bit in the end with its decision to adopt the cliché of the dream sequence to explain—and dismiss—what transpired earlier in the story. Yet even in her use of a creaky and melodramatic clichéd plot device to wrap things up, Stevens once again subverts her readers' expectations by ever so subtly alluding at the conclusion to the protagonist Santallos's disquieting necrophilic sensibilities. Poe would have loved it.

Stevens's short story, "Unseen—Unfeared," first published in the February 10, 1919, issue of *People's Favorite Magazine*, is an update of Fitz-James O'Brien's seminal science fiction tale, "The Diamond Lens" (1858), about the existence of a miniature world beyond human sight. O'Brien biographer Francis Wolle called "The Diamond Lens" "an excellently executed and absorbingly interesting short story" (1944, 153). This concept of the unseen world is essential to dark fantasy, and Stevens's subsequent reworking of this motif, making this world extremely hostile to human existence, fundamentally defines dark fantasy. "Unseen—Unfeared" also explores the image of the mad scientist. This character type is one of the oldest stereotypes in horror and science fiction and film, and according to Roslynn D. Haynes in her study *From Faust to Strangelove* (1994), over time it has created "archetypes that . . . have acquired a cumulative, even mythical importance" (3). Stevens uses the stereotype to suit her thematic intent. Arguably, the first significant mad scientist appeared in *Frankenstein* as the protagonist Victor Frankenstein. His dark obsession to discover the secret of life and death in his quest to create a new type of human being unnaturally divorced him from the love of family and friends and distanced him from the therapeutic effects of living a life in harmony with the natural world. Frankenstein's failure to control his obsession, coupled with his inability to assume responsibility for his creation, caused him much grief, literally pushing him beyond the brink of sanity. Stevens's variant of the mad scientist is Dr. Frederick Holt, "a tall, lean man, somewhat stooped, but possessing considerable dignity of bearing." He is well dressed, and despite his "dark" complexion and "coal-black" eyes, his hair is "almost silvery-white." He is a visual contradiction, a character of black and white. His appearance is unique, but his behavior is even more unusual. He is a flatterer, proclaiming that the narrator, Blaisdell, is "different," not one of "these timorous, ignorant foreign peasants" that dominate the neighborhood (thus anticipating the xenophobic racism found in the dark fantasy tales of Lovecraft, such as "The Horror at Red Hook" [1925]). Holt is also a seducer, and he entices Blaisdell to witness his strange presentation, engaging the narrator's curiosity in spite of the character's sense of dread. He is a scientist, explaining in meticulous detail how he achieved his miraculous discovery of an unseen world of invisible creatures. He is, finally, a showman, mesmerizing his audience of one with a fantastic special-effects display. And, ultimately, he is quite insane.

"The Elf Trap," published in the July 5, 1919, issue of the *Argosy* is Stevens's most lyrical tale. The story opens with the death of the central protagonist, the academic Theron Tademus, and then proceeds, in the form of Tademus's diary, with the professor's last summer spent in the Carolina Blue Ridge to recover his health. Most important, it recounts the week he mysteriously disappeared in the region. It is a transformational story in which the scientific and highly pragmatic Professor Tademus, a person of no artistic sensibilities who holds little sympathy for gypsies and other artistic types ("Why, the hills are fairly swarming with artists, gypsies, and Lord knows what else."), alters his life—and death. Tademus becomes infatuated with a magical girl named Elva, and by losing his way in the mundane world of actuality, he discovers the mystical and beautiful world of the elves in turn. By this process, he comes to better comprehend the artistic sensibility, admiring the literal and figurative magic of the authentically magical artistic life. Such a realization grants Professor Tademus a newfound youth; the man who never danced—and never wanted to learn to—now danced with abandon with the enchanting Elva, until he "was mad with the music and her voice." Offered a home in this elfish paradise, Tademus's tragic love for science overwhelms his need for magic, and he makes the fatal decision to leave. He has thus denied the bounty of the elves and returns to the gross human world and to his own mortality. But once caught in Elva's elf-trap, Professor Tademus, in death, returns (the reader assumes) to the magical realm and to his love. Stevens gives us an elegant and wonderful modern fairy tale that anticipates the gentle fantasies of American humorist, Thorne Smith (1892–1934), author of the famous Topper novels.

"Serapion" is, to my mind, Stevens's best story among her shorter fiction. This novella appeared in the *Argosy* between June 19 and July 10, 1920, and is her most sophisticated tale. Its treatment of psychic occultism nicely undermines the Victorian and Edwardian conventions for this type of story, and the warning, stated early in the narrative that "there are entities and forces dangerous to the human race outside of what we call the natural world," decidedly confirms the fundamental ideology of dark fantasy. As a tale of demonic possession, "Serapion" harkens back to J. Sheridan Le Fanu's "Green Tea" (1869), one of the finest tales of terror published in the nineteenth century. I actually prefer Stevens's treatment, as she concocts a marvelously problematic ending for both the possessed and the possessor. Neither evil nor good wins in the end of her morally ambivalent tale, nothing that simple here.

With "Sunfire" the author returns to the heady mixture of adventure and fantasy that hallmarked "The Nightmare." In "Sunfire," however, Stevens follows a more traditional lost world/lost race formula, as developed by Haggard. Appearing as a two-part serial in the July/August and September/October 1923 issues of *Weird Tales* (the most important pulp magazine to feature fantasy and horror fiction) the lost world setting for "Sunfire" is appropriately uncanny. What makes the story unique, I would suggest, is Stevens's unexpected incorporation of humor in the plot. The (at times) comical interaction among the major protagonists is written with a deft hand. If not done correctly, the story would quickly descend to the level of mere camp, which it does not. Stevens manages to balance adventure and humor quite well, so that the one rarely interferes with the other. The result is one of the best stories to appear in the early issues of *Weird Tales*, the pulp that would later help make famous the names of Lovecraft, Clark Ashton Smith, and Robert E. Howard.

In "The Nightmare" and "Sunfire," Stevens charted the intersection between lost world adventure and horror, while in "The Labyrinth" and "Behind the Curtain," she revised and upgraded the psychological tale of revenge originated earlier by Poe. "Friend Island" pushed the formulaic boundaries of science fiction into new feminist areas, and "The Elf Trap" postulated a new variant of the classic fairy tale, one with a charmingly stylistic sense of melancholy involving the loss of paradise, and its subsequent rediscovery through death. "Unseen—Unfeared" created a powerful sense of unease in its portrayal of an alien landscape existing beyond the normal experience of humans, a hostile world that is made even more frightening in her ominous tale of possession, "Serapion," in which the hostile intelligence infects and affects the mundane world. This is the primary stuff of dark fantasy, a new type of horror and fantasy story that evolved out of the apocalyptic calamity of World War I, one that posits the danger of forbidden knowledge and an ultimate lack of human understanding (and control) over such banal concepts as "good" and "evil." Dark fantasy is nihilistic fiction in its prediction (directly or indirectly) of a terrible end to our world that we inhabit in blissful ignorance.

Though Stevens's total output of short fiction was quite small, her contributions to the development of dark fantasy cannot be overestimated. It is impossible to make the claim that without a Francis Stevens, there would have been no A. Merritt or H. P. Lovecraft. But it is entirely fair to argue that Stevens had an undeniable impact on the work of both and thus had a critical role in the establishment of dark fantasy as a new expression of the tale of horror. Both "The Nightmare" and Merritt's first story, "Through the Dragon Glass," appeared in print in 1917, a number of years before much of Lovecraft's important short fiction. Stevens's work was featured in the same pulp magazines that Merritt and Lovecraft read and published in. And both Merritt and Lovecraft made direct comments in print about their tremendous admiration for Stevens, thus establishing, without any doubt, an undeniable link between the three.

It is my sincerest hope that with this collection, *The Nightmare and Other Tales of Dark Fantasy and Adventure*, Stevens's innovative and engaging storytelling talent will entertain a new generation of readers. As did Merritt and Lovecraft, perhaps you too will fall under Stevens's literary magic. Moskowitz called Stevens "the most gifted woman writer of science fiction and science-fantasy between Mary Wollstonecraft Shelley and C. L. Moore" (1970, 9). To that assessment, I would add that she was also the woman who invented dark fantasy.

WORKS CITED

Burleson, Donald R. 1983. *H.P. Lovecraft: A Critical Study*. Westport CT: Greenwood Press.

Clute, John, and Peter Nicholls, eds. 1993."Merritt, A(braham)." *The Encyclopedia of Science Fiction*. New York: St. Martin's Press.

Eshbach, Lloyd Arthur. 1952. Introduction. *The Heads of Cerberus*. By Francis Stevens. Reading PA: Polaris Press.

Everts, R. Alain. 2000. "The Mystery of Francis Stevens (1883–1948)." *Outsider* 4:29–30.

———. "Re: Stevens." E-mail to the editor, 2 Feb. 2004.

Goodstone, Tony, ed. 1970. *The Pulps: Fifty Years of American Popular Culture*. New York: Bonanza Books.

Goulart, Ron. 1972. *An Informal History of the Pulp Magazine*. New York: Ace Books.

Haynes, Roslynn D. 1994. *From Faust to Strangelove: Representations of the Scientist in Western Literature*. Baltimore: Johns Hopkins University Press.

Hoppenstand, Gary. 1987. *In Search of the Paper Tiger: A Sociological Perspective of Myth, Formula and the Mystery Genre in the Entertainment Print Mass Medium*. Bowling Green: Bowling Green State University Popular Press.

King, Stephen. 1981. *Danse Macabre*. New York: Arlington House.

Lovecraft, H. P. 1963. *The Dunwich Horror and Others*. Selected by August Derleth. Sauk City: Arkham House.

Moskowitz, Sam, ed. 1985. *A. Merritt: Reflections in the Moon Pool*. Philadelphia: Oswald Train.

———. 1970. "The Woman Who Wrote 'Citadel of Fear.'" *The Citadel of Fear*. By Francis Stevens. New York: Paperback Library.

Stevens, Francis. 1966. *Claimed*. New York: Avalon Books.

Weinberg, Robert. 1984. "A Forgotten Mistress of Fantasy." *The Citadel of Fear*. By Francis Stevens. New York: Carroll & Graf.

Wolle, Francis. 1944. *Fitz-James O'Brien: A Literary Bohemian of the Eighteen-Fifties*. Boulder: University of Colorado Studies.

The Nightmare

CHAPTER I.

MR. JONES, CASTAWAY.

"Philip, did you notice that tall, thin man in the gray ulster, who was walking up and down the boat-deck just before dinner?"

"Yes, sir. I observed the gentleman. Very haristocratic appearance, if I may say so, Mr. Jones."

"Exactly. He never bought that ulster in New York. When we reach London I want you to look around and see if you can find a tailor who will make me one of the same cut."

"Very well, sir. Very good taste, if I may say so, Mr. Jones."

"You may. And—let's see—I need a few new

golf sticks, and—a dozen new shirts. Why did you pack this automatic in this trunk, Philip? Put it in that suitcase."

"Yes, sir. I 'ardly thought you'd require it while on board the Lusitania, sir, if I may say so, Mr. Jones."

"Certainly you may. No, events requiring a pistol as stage-property are not frequent on a liner. By the way, you never showed me how to work the thing, Philip."

"No, sir. The shopman from whom I purchased it declared it simple of hoperation, but I 'ave not found it so, sir."

"Well, find out in London and show me. I never met a burglar, but if I ever should it would be embarrassing to point a pistol at him and not be able to fire it off. I admire the heroes of burglar stories. They're always such efficient people."

"Hunder exciting circumstances, sir, one becomes much more efficient. They bring it out of a man, if I may say so, Mr. Jones."

"By all means. Well, golf is exciting enough for me. Merridale and I are going to run over to the St. Andrews links. It's been the dream of my life to play the St. Andrews, but something has always come up to prevent."

"Nothing is likely to hoccur, I am sure, sir. Shall I repack the steamer trunk now, Mr. Jones?"

"Yes. And call me a little earlier, in the morning, Philip. I have an idea it's going to be fine weather, and since it's the last of the voyage I want to make the most of it. What time is it? Eleven, eh? Well, I'll go to bed early for once and get a good night's rest. Thank Heaven for a quiet life, Philip. Cribbage and the *Times* for you, golf and—"

"Beg pardon for hinterrupting, sir, but do you want this book packed in the trunk?"

" 'Paradise Island'? Yes, pack the thing away. Did you ever read it, Philip?"

"No, sir. I don't care for them himpossible stories, if I may say so, sir."

"And welcome. Now, I'm thirty-two years old, I've yachted, ridden, mo-tored and been about the world a good bit, and I've never had a real adven-ture in my life. People don't have adventures—unless they're gentlemen in the filibustering line, or polar explorers, or something like that. This modern world of ours is as safe as a church, barring accidents, and they are never romantic. End in a hospital or a beastly morgue. Anybody I suppose, can find trouble by looking for it, but that's not exactly in my line."

"No, sir. Very bad form, sir, if I may say so, Mr. Jones."

"You may indeed. Here, I'll help you with that strap, and then—bed."

Ragged fragments of cloud raced across a sky where great, brilliant stars beamed fitfully. The wind hurled the wave crests through space, so that the air was almost as watery as the wide waste of billows and creaming surges in the midst of which Mr. Roland C. Jones, of New York City, found himself most unexpectedly struggling.

How it could be that he was here, battling for his life, with the stars, the wind and raging, tumbling seas for his sole companions, did not immediately trouble him. He was too thoroughly engaged in trying to get a breath that was not half or all salt water to concern himself about either past or future. The mere physical present was a little bit more than he could comfortably handle.

But the fight between man and sea was too unequal. Mr. Jones was a fair swimmer, but not being provided with gills he found it impossible to get a living modicum of oxygen out of the saturated air, even when the waves did not go clean over his head. Thoroughly exhausted, more than half drowned, he had just decided that he might as well throw up his arms and let the sea have its will of him when he found himself rising upon the shoulder of a particularly mighty billow.

For an instant he caught a glimpse of something dark and huge looming above him. Then he was in the trough again, but only for a moment. Up, up he was borne in a long, swift, surging motion. The water seemed to fall away from under him. He was on his knees in sand and the receding breaker was trying to drag him back with it. The next wave, however, carried him much farther up the beach, dropping him with a vicious thud when it was done with him.

Barely conscious of his own efforts, Jones dragged himself along on hands and knees until he was actually out of reach of the ocean which had been so unappreciative as to spew him up.

For a time he lay still, gasping the water out of lungs and stomach, then rolled over and sat up. He felt like a man in a dream, yet the pain he suffered informed Mr. Jones that this was no dream, but a grim, incredible reality.

It was not alone the question, where was he, although that seemed pressing enough. But how had he gotten into the water at all? The last thing he remembered was a little, pleasant, white-finished room—a state room—ah, that was it. He was in his state room on board the liner. He was on board the Lusitania, and he was going to London to visit his cousin, the Hon. Percy Merridale. And he had—let's see, he had been going over the things in his steamer trunk with his man, Philip. And then—then he was going to bed. He must have gone to bed, and then—

He cudgeled his memory, but failed to beat out one single further recollection back of that dazed, strangling moment when he had found himself struggling with the waves.

Where was the liner? While in the water he could not recall having seen any lights, receding or otherwise. Stare earnestly as he might now across the sea, there were certainly no lights visible, other than the stars, which storm-clouds now obscured at ever-increasing intervals.

Where was the Lusitania? And how had he come to part company with her so inexplicably? If the huge ship had melted away from about his slumbering form like a dream thing, instead of the vast solid steel hulk she was, she could not have vanished more thoroughly or mysteriously.

Only one explanation occurred to Mr. Jones, and even that was inadequate to explain the liner's total disappearance. When a boy he had been given to the habit of sleep-walking. He had usually slept locked in, in those days, but had thought the habit long since dead and gone. Nevertheless, he must have risen in a dream, gone on deck, and in some way fallen over the rail without being seen by any one.

What an extremely awkward predicament. Where could he be? What land lay near enough for him to have reached it undrowned? In view of the approximate position of the liner, so far as he knew it, Ireland seemed the only possible answer to that question. Had he been cast upon some portion of the Irish coast? Certainly the only thing for him to do was to get up and walk along this lonely, God and man forsaken beach until he came to some place where he could get dry clothes and cable his friends in London.

His clothes! He was fully dressed, and he examined the garments as well as he was able by starlight. They seemed—wrong, some way. They were not *his* clothes, at all, but the clothes of a stranger. Had he, in his sleep, wandered into a neighboring stateroom and robbed some innocent stranger? He recalled that he had been talking to Philip about burglars and pistols; lightly, it is true, but perhaps the suggestion of that conversation had led him into such an astounding exploit.

Mr. Jones searched this hypothetical other person's pockets, but all he brought to light were some wet, useless matches, a small penknife, an unmarked handkerchief, and a little loose change. There were no letters or anything by which the rightful owner could be identified.

By a mighty effort Jones forced the problem of the clothes out of his mind and fixed it upon the greater one of finding shelter and means of communication with London.

While he sat there the sky had completely cleared, and even by starlight he could make out that he was on a long, bare stretch of sand, which curved smoothly away on either side. From the inner edge of this strip a black wall of rock rose sharply, looming to the stars above Jones's head. This enormous cliff also curved away on either hand, following the line of the beach.

Selecting a quarter from the small coins he had found, Mr. Jones flipped it into the air. "Heads to the right, tails to the left," said he. The coin fell with the eagle uppermost and the castaway obediently started off in the direction indicated by Fate.

Walking was easy on the smooth, wet sand. The night air was so warm that even in his wet clothes Jones was not uncomfortably cold, and although the interminable breakers still roared in almost to his feet, the storm had evidently blown itself out. These rushing seas were only the aftermath.

Presently the beach dwindled away to nothing, and the cliff extended itself into the sea in a sort of long, sloping foot of jagged rocks. Mr. Jones managed to feel his way around this point, drenched again with spray, and wading through shallow pools of water. He tore his clothes and scraped his hands raw, but at last achieved the place where the beach began again.

"Halt!" commanded a stern, uncompromising voice.

Before him loomed the dark bulk of a figure which seemed to be pointing something at him. The figure came closer and the "something" developed into an unpleasant-looking rifle, along whose leveled barrel the starlight glimmered. Behind the figure, a hundred yards or so, Jones saw a yellow gleam of lights, and not far out to sea, on the comparatively quiet waters of a little bay, some sort of vessel lay at anchor.

"Halt!" the man of the rifle again exclaimed in yet harsher tones.

"I have halted," replied Mr. Jones mildly. "May I ask—"

"None of your lip!" said the stranger ferociously. "Who are youse, and what do youse want around here?"

"Nothing—nothing at all. I was just walking along the beach—"

"Ho! Takin' y'r evenin' stroll up Fift' Avenoo, was youse? Well, just stroll along ahead of me now, and no more of your lip. I'll turn youse over to the captain, see? Now, march!"

Perforce Jones marched. He was unarmed, but even if he had carried the automatic pistol (and known how to use it) he could not see what would be gained by opposing this determined and ruffianly person . He stumbled along ahead of his captor, who occasionally hastened his footsteps by prodding him in the back most uncomfortably with his rifle-muzzle.

Luckily it was not far to the lights, where Jones presently discovered that three small tents were erected on the sand.

Another man came forward to meet them. He was a tall, well set-up figure. Even by the dim light of three ship's lanterns, set about in the sand, Jones could see that he was handsome, after a dark, foreign manner, and

generally rather aristocratic in appearance. Neatly attired in white ducks
and of a fairly amiable expression, he seemed to Jones far preferable to his
first acquaintance.

"What is this, Doherty?" inquired the gentleman in white.

"Youse c'n search me, y'r excellency," replied the man with the rifle. "I
found it up there by the point, and I brung it into camp for yous fellers to
cut up or keep, just as you please. I don't—"

"That will do, Doherty," broke in the other, a shade of annoyance in his
even, cultivated voice. "You may return to your post. And now," turning to
the castaway, "who are you, sir, and how did you come here?" He spoke
courteously and with the slightest trace of foreign accent in his otherwise
faultless English.

Several other men had now gathered about them. They were rough-
looking fellows, unshaven, and with dull, uneducated faces. Their costumes
were not elaborate, consisting mostly of a shirt and a pair of more or less
ragged trousers, the only exceptions being the man in white and a tall,
powerful-looking brute of a fellow who was dressed in a blue serge uniform,
like a ship's officer.

The moment had come for Mr. Jones to relate the tale of his strange
misadventure and receive the aid and sympathy to which he knew himself
entitled and which he fully expected to get, since rough clothes are by no
means the natural insignia of unkind hearts.

"My name is Roland C. Jones," he began. "I am an American, and during
the storm I was cast up on the beach over beyond that point. By the way, is
this the coast of Ireland?"

"Is this—*what?*" exclaimed the man in white with a look of intense astonishment.

"Oh, isn't it?" stammered Mr. Jones, rather taken aback by the stranger's
amazement. "Well, you see I couldn't very well know what place it was. As
I said, I was cast here by the storm, and of course I am very glad indeed
to run across you fellows. That's a yacht you've got out there, isn't it? I
thought so by the look of her. I'm a yachtsman myself. My craft's the little
Bandersnatch, New York Yacht Club."

These words should have been an open sesame to instant solicitude and
hospitality, for to own a yacht is to belong to a sort of freemasonry, extending over the whole wide seas; but this stranger only stared at Jones with
increasing coldness and suspicion.

"Exactly," he commented briefly, his lips curling in a curious little smile.
"And how did you come to be cast away? Has your yacht been wrecked?
Did no one else come ashore? Where are your companions?"

In the teeth of this fusillade of questions Mr. Jones launched once more into his explanation.

"My yacht was not wrecked. I was not on my yacht. I was on board the Lusitania, and Heaven knows where she is now."

"Heaven probably does," interrupted the stranger, smiling coldly. "The Lusitania was torpedoed by a German submarine early this morning. We have but just received the information by wireless. If you were one of the victims you are indeed to be pitied. You have been forced to swim a very long way—several thousand miles, I think. Did you come around the Horn, or through the canal, my friend?"

Jones stared at him blankly. Was the man insane? Torpedoed—by Germans—thousands of miles! He clasped his head in his hands and groaned. It must be he himself who was mad. Then raising a very white face he spread out his arms in a gesture of despair.

"I'll have to admit that I don't know what you are talking about. I—I am afraid something has happened to my head—or I don't hear you correctly. No one could possibly torpedo the Lusitania—unless it were an anarchist, and I can't imagine what you mean by several thousand miles."

"That is sad. Yes, your brain must be affected, sir. You recollect that you are an American, and that is much, but I think you are mistaken about your name. Well, we will keep you with us. I do not really think it would be safe for you to stray about any longer alone in your pitiful condition. Captain Ivanovitch," he turned to the tall man in blue serge, "I will turn this young man over to you. You have heard him and will agree with me that it is wise to guard him carefully—against himself, of course. Do you understand?"

He still spoke in English, and it was in broken English that the captain replied. He spoke with a grin.

"Excellency, I und'stand. He have forgot his name. He have forgot even that there ees war. Have you suggest a name which he know perhaps better than that one he say?"

"Not yet. My friend, if I should address you as Richard Holloway, would it arouse no recollections in your mind?" The words were pleasant enough, but the voice was keen and cold as a winter wind.

Jones looked at the man in increased bewilderment. For the sake of peace and until he could escape from these madmen, had he better accept this now cognomen? Before he could make up his mind, "his excellency" turned aside with a short laugh. "Take good care of Mr. Holloway, Ivanovitch," he flung back over his shoulder. "It is just possible that we may arouse his memory and make him useful."

"Ah, Meester Hol'way," said the captain, with deceitful politeness, "eet is great pleasure to entertain you. So leetle we theenk Reechard Hol'way come to us so, free of weel. Weel you accept shelter from one of our leetle tents? Yes?"

Some inner instinct informed Mr. Jones that this Holloway personality was a dangerous one to assume. Playing himself off as another man did not appeal to him, anyway.

"I am not the person you seem to think I am," he said rather doggedly. "But I'd go anywhere to get something to eat. I'm nearly starved."

The captain grinned again, mockingly, hatefully. "At once, Meester Hol'way. We are all humbly servants. Dmitri—" Here he turned to one of the seamen who stood by staring stupidly and launched a command in some language which was unfamiliar to Jones, although, judging by the captain's own name and that of the man addressed, he assumed it to be Russian.

The sailor sprang to obey, and Captain Ivanovitch led Mr. Jones to one of the small tents. "Here," said he, "weel Meester Hol'way permit to lodge himself. The tent, he is leetle, but you not mind that. Eet is more better than the ocean, no?"

"Humph! Perhaps," grunted Mr. Jones. He had taken an immediate dislike to the amiable captain. "By the way, you people seem to be very chary of introductions. Who is that gentleman I was just now speaking to? Your owner, I presume?"

"You not know? But of course. I forget you have jus' been sheepwreck. That ees his highness, Preence Sergius Petrofsky. The name also—it call nothing to your mind?"

"Nothing but Siberia and—er—Russian cigarettes. So, he's a connection of the royal family is he? Now, tell me, what is all this fuss about this man Holloway? There's no particle of use in calling *me* Holloway any longer, you know. I never even knew any one of that name."

"So sad, Meester Hol'way. Perhaps you receive the blow upon the head—from wreckage, you und'stand? Eef you will show the place, we try to play the good part. We weel put upon eet the bandage."

"My head is all right, I tell you. My stomach is the only part of me that is in need of attention."

"Ver' good. Here come my man now weeth the good food. We shall not starve you, my friend. Also comes once more hees excellency."

The prince indeed came up at that moment. His features were set in a haughty frown, and he addressed himself immediately to Mr. Jones in a domineering tone.

"See here, Holloway, I have been considering this matter carefully and can see no reason for your continuing the farce. How you came to fall into our hands is your own affair. But you must not rely upon the fact that your face is unfamiliar to us. There can be no question of your identity. You are the only man on the island—at least on the outside of it, for you yourself are the only person who knows what is inside,—who did not come here in the Monterey. Which places you beyond the shadow of a doubt as Richard Holloway. Now, answer me, yes or no. Will you tell me where lies the entrance to the caverns? If you help us we will make it well worth your while."

"What caverns?" queried Jones impatiently and with rising anger. These Russians were intolerable.

"Your feigned ignorance will not help you in the least, my friend," replied Petrofsky sternly. "I mean, of course, the caverns that lead beneath the cliffs. Out of all the caverns, the one which leads to that inner valley of yours. It was your story and yours alone which brought my brother across half a world to seek it.

"Come, sir, it is true that all of us here belong to the Brotherhood, and Paul has poisoned your mind against us. Also, by American eyes, I know that the great cause of nihilism is regarded askance. That is because you have experienced nothing of the evils which we plan to correct. But at least you know that I am a gentleman. If I give my word, I keep it. My brother has your trust."

"I am glad to hear it," murmured Jones wearily.

"What is that? I say that I, too, am a Petrofsky, and I swear to you that neither Paul nor those with him shall suffer the very least harm if you will help me. Nay, I will go further and promise that he shall receive his full share of the gains. The cause will not begrudge him that, although he has done his utmost to thwart our participation in this venture. But he and his little party can do nothing now. They have scarcely any provisions, hardly any arms or amunition. We could sweep down and annihilate them at this moment if I did not always remember that Paul is indeed my brother. Come, Mr. Holloway, save him against himself and for the time at least cast in your lot with us. Will you give me your hand on it?"

Jones hesitated. To him this long rigmarole of nihilists and caverns failed to carry any meaning whatsoever.

"How can I convince you, sir," he said at last, "that I know nothing whatever of these matters? That all I desire is to get away from this place and continue my quiet, respectable journey to London. And last and most emphatically that my name is certainly not Holloway, but Roland C. Jones, of New York City. You are making a serious mistake, Prince Petrofsky, and a most absurd one, if you will pardon me."

The Russian's eyes flashed angrily.

"Ho! You are yet stubborn? We will see if we cannot loosen your tongue a bit. Now, listen to me, and remember that I pledge my word as a Petrofsky that this promise will be kept. If you persist in your present attitude you will be taken on board that yacht and triced up to the signal-mast. Then you will be beaten as they beat criminals in Russia. With the knout. Do you know what the knout means? I can see by your expression that you do. Well, make up your mind which it is to be. You may expect either our gratitude or—the other! You have until morning to decide. While making up your mind you may remain in that tent. Ivanovitch, set a guard over this man and see that he does not escape. Mr. Holloway, I give you a very good evening!"

Sergius Petrofsky turned his straight white back upon the dismayed American and stalked off down to the shore. There he got into a waiting dingey and was rowed out to the yacht.

Jones started, shivering slightly, as the captain touched his elbow and said in a soft voice, "You are foolish man, Meester Hol'way. But do not be so foolish as try leave us to-night. You und'stand?"

And Mr. Jones was left with his guard of two bearded sailors.

"Good Lord!" he muttered to himself. "What a crazy mess! Is knouting any worse than drowning, I wonder? I'll bet it is!"

Chapter II.

THE ADVENTURER ESCAPES.

Midnight found Mr. Jones sitting in his prison tent disconsolate. There was a neat cot and blankets, but he had never felt less like sleeping in his life. He clung to his wakefulness and the few hours intervening between him and the morrow, like a sick man anticipating an extremely painful but inevitable operation. For something told him that Sergius Petrofsky was not the man to make empty threats.

Mr. Jones could see no way out of his predicament—unless he might anger the Russian into shooting instead of torturing him. The man certainly possessed a violent temper behind those haughty eyes of his.

While the captive was still revolving in his mind this desperate expedient, he suddenly felt something poke him sharply in the back. At the same instant some one said "Sh!" in a sharp, sibilant whisper.

The pain of the unexpected jab made Jones spring to his feet, crashing into the tent-pole and shaking the whole tent so violently that one of his guards appeared in the entrance. He thrust a large hirsute countenance into the aperture and said something that sounded like the name of a Russian province.

"Get out, get out!" exclaimed Mr. Jones, gesturing violently to make his meaning clear. "It is nothing at all. Nothing. I bumped into the pole. Go away!"

The guard stared at him suspiciously for a moment longer, glanced about the little tent, which was dimly lighted by a lantern, and at last withdrew himself.

Once more the prisoner sat down, close to the canvas wall, and cautiously whispered, "It's all right. He has gone. Who are you and what do you want? What did you poke me like that for?"

There was a moment's silence, followed by a slight ripping sound. Through the canvas close by his shoulder Jones saw the point of a knife appear. It deftly cut two sides of a small triangle, then the flap so made was lifted and a face appeared. The face looked familiar. Then Mr. Jones recognized Doherty, the man who had captured him.

"Say, where are youse from?" The question was barely breathed in a voice which could not possibly have carried beyond the walls of the tent. Jones replied in the same bated tone:

"New York. Why?"

"That settles it, bo. Wait a jif."

The face was withdrawn, and the knife came into use once more. This time, however, it sawed out an aperture about three feet square near the bottom of the canvas wall. "Come on out, bo," whispered the rescuer.

Mr. Jones obeyed, moving as stealthily as he could, and having first made sure that the lantern would not cast the shadow of his escaping form upon the side of the tent. The situation required caution if ever a situation did.

Once outside he straightened himself, and felt a powerful hand grasp his arm. "This way, bo," came the whisper, and rescuer and rescued crept softly across the sands, behind the tents, and away, keeping close to the cliff. Glancing seaward, Jones saw the riding lights of the yacht, otherwise a dim, black bulk upon the quiet waters of the bay.

His guide led him away from the camp, not in the direction of the point where the two had first met, but onward along the beach. As soon as they were out of ear-shot of his Russian companions Doherty halted and said:

"I don't go no furder wid youse, see? G'wan on along until youse comes to a ravine. Go up there, and pretty soon youse comes to where dis other prince guy is, see? I don't know whether youse and this Holloway feller are the same guy or not. If you are, then youse don't need no more help from me. If youse ain't, then take a tip and hold your jawr about comin' straight from this camp, see? Now, beat it!"

"But see here!" exclaimed Jones, laying his hand on the other's shoulder to stay him. "Why have you helped me out this way? I'm everlastingly obliged to you, and—"

"Aw, forget it!" snapped the other, shaking off the detaining hand roughly. "I ain't no friend of youse, neither—see? But no Russian dook ain't my boss when it comes to beatin' up another N'York feller with that knout thing. See? Now, *will* youse beat it, or d'youse want t'go back there and get what's comin' t' youse?"

"I'll go. But—thank you, just the same. Say, can't you tell me something about all this business—"

But already Doherty had disappeared in the darkness, and with a slight sigh Roland C. Jones turned his face in the direction he had been instructed to follow. At any rate, the knouting was indefinitely postponed, and he could think of nothing much worse which could befall.

A short distance beyond the place where Doherty had left him the beach again ended in rocks. The man had spoken of a "ravine," so Mr. Jones again climbed and scrambled, coming at last to where the cliff seemed to be split in two parts. How far this split penetrated into the rocky wall, he had no means of knowing, for it was all as dark as a pocket.

He discovered by stumbling into it that a little rill of water flowed down the middle of the split and into the sea. His best chance of exploring the ravine was to walk up the bed of this stream, which was no more than ankle deep. The water, he found, had the bitter chill of a glacier stream, and his feet were soon numb with cold. He had been offered no opportunity to dry his clothing, and it was still very damp and uncomfortable. He hoped that the extreme warmth of the night might prevent him from getting pneumonia.

Mr. Jones was not accustomed to such privations and hardships, and he found them extremely annoying.

Having no means of making a light, he stumbled along in the darkness, alternately cursing himself for having fallen overboard and the Hon. Percy Merridale as the (however remote) cause of all his misfortunes.

At length, however, the watercourse made a sharp bend, and rounding it, he beheld, a short distance ahead of him, a reddish glow upon the rocks. Then a black figure appeared in silhouette against the glow. He was considering how he could best make his presence known, for this he correctly surmised to be the place of that mysterious other encampment, when a voice exclaimed, "Hands up, there, or I'll fire!"

"Twice in one night!" muttered Jones rebelliously.

"What's that? Stranger, you've strayed onto the wrong range. Come into the light, and don't make no false moves, or you'll sure get perforated."

The voice had now come close to his side, and Mr. Jones felt the hard muzzle of some sort of weapon pressing against his ribs.

"I assure you that I am not armed," he said.

"I'll assure myself in a minute," responded the unsympathetic voice. "March, now!"

And again Jones marched. The light which Jones had seen reflected upon the cliff was cast by a fire built between two huge boulders in such a manner as to obscure its radiance so far as was possible. Emerging into the full glare, the unfortunate halted again, obedient to the pressure on his arm.

About the fire, which they were probably maintaining for the sake of illumination, since they were cooking nothing, and the temperature of the night was so high, several figures were gathered. All save one of these persons were men, the exception being a slender young girl, who at that moment turned her face and stared straight into the eyes of Mr. Jones.

"By Jupiter!" he murmured. "What's a girl like that doing with this crowd?"

The young lady was attired in a somewhat dilapidated white yachting costume, which looked as if it had been soaked more than once and not pressed in a long time. But she was not of the type whose social standing or personal attraction would ever be judged by her clothes, however she might be dressed. Her crisply curling hair gleamed almost red in the firelight, though in daytime it would probably be no more than auburn. Her skin was of that clear, transparent whiteness which sometimes accompanies such hair; her features clean-cut and firm to a point which would have been almost masculine had they not been relieved by a pair of blue eyes so pure, childish, and innocent that looking at them one could only be reminded of the eyes of a suddenly awakened baby.

For the rest, she was slight of figure, with small, tapering hands and feet, giving an impression of physical weakness which Mr. Jones later discovered to be deceptive.

He did not, of course, absorb all these details of appearance in that first brief meeting. At the moment he saw only that here was a beautiful, well-bred girl in the midst of surroundings entirely unsuitable—unless she happened to be a movie actress, which seemed improbable.

Of her companions, one was a tall, rather good-looking man with a sensitive mouth and slightly receding chin, also in yachting costume. Another was a rangy, lanky sort of fellow, attired in nothing more formal than a shirt and shabby trousers. The two remaining men were plainly of a lower class, probably seamen from their general appearance.

With a look of astonishment the girl glanced from Jones to his captor, who stood slightly behind him, and said:

"James, who is this person? How did he come here?"

Yes, she said it exactly as if she were standing in her own drawing-room, inquiring of the butler how some unknown vagabond had penetrated into her domain. Something humorous in the whole situation smote Jones abruptly, so that he laughed aloud, and she stared at him more haughtily than ever.

"I beg your pardon," said Mr. Jones, hastening to correct his involuntary rudeness, "I have had a rather trying evening, and—er—I did not expect to see a young lady in this place."

"And why not, pray? You are one of Prince Sergius's friends, are you not? Paul, this must be one of your brother's men, although I for one have never seen him before. Do you know him?"

She addressed the handsome man with the weak chin, and Jones knew this must be the brother of the Russian who had imprisoned him.

"No," he replied, rising lazily. "I have never seen the fellow before. Do you know him, Dick Holloway?"

"Not yet, but I've no objection. What is your name, anyway?"

So the man in the shirt and trousers was Holloway. Jones looked at him with considerable interest, since it was in his name that he had nearly suffered so much, and saw that he was a young man with a keen, rather strong face. Dressed differently, he might have been either a reporter or an automobile salesman—or a member of Jones's own club.

"My name is Roland C. Jones," stated the castaway, somewhat weary of reiterating that face. "Some hours ago, early in the evening, I was cast up on the beach by the storm. I—think I had fallen overboard in my sleep. I was on my way to London. Then I—" He suddenly remembered Doherty's warning. He decided that he owed it to his benefactor to keep faith. "I came on up the beach and stumbled into this ravine and walked up it and—and here I am, you know."

This simple statement was met by dead silence for a moment. Then the Russian asked: "You were going to London, you say? That sounds a little peculiar. And you say you were wrecked some hours ago? Where were you, pray, in the interval? Do you mean you have met no one since that time?"

"Yes," admitted Mr. Jones, realizing that his story lacked strength. "I met one man—or, rather, I saw a man; but as soon as he caught sight of me he made off. I chased him, but he was too quick. Then I wandered around a while, until I found my way here."

"H-m! What ship were you on?"

Jones started to reply, "The Lusitania," but checked himself. He was actually afraid that these people, too, would insist on that nightmare tangle of German torpedoes and impossible distances. Then he would know that something had gone wrong in his brain. He did not want to know it just then. There was too much to attend to without that.

"I was on my own yacht, the Bandersnatch. We were just cruising around, you know. We had thought of running over to the Azores." (Jones was not at all sure by this time where in the Atlantic he might be, but the Azores, as occupying a fairly central position, seemed safe.) "I must have walked in my sleep, for first thing I knew I was in the water, and the only wonder is that I was not drowned. I am a New Yorker, but we sailed from Savannah." He was rather proud of this touch of realism, but Holloway burst out laughing.

"First London, and now the Azores," the latter remarked in a tone of good-natured amusement. "You seem to have put out on a remarkable voyage."

"For my part," interposed the young lady, who, despite her infantile eye, seemed of very determined and decisive character, "I don't believe a word of your story. If you were on a yacht, which I don't doubt, it was the Monterey, and she lies in the bay now. I believe you were on board at the same time we were, although we didn't see you. That about London and Savannah and the Azores is merely ridiculous. I can't imagine your object in making such absurd statements. Paul, this man has been sent here by your brother to spy upon us and find out the secret of the caverns."

Paul nodded his head, saying: "Holloway, do you not think that Miss Weston is right?"

"It's a one best bet she is, prince. All that gas about his yacht and the rest of it was probably planned to make us think he's a bit light in his upper story."

"What?"

"Bats in his belfry—nobody home—you know."

"Oh, you mean insane. But why should he wish us to think that?"

"So we won't take *too* much pains to keep our cards face down. If you'll take a tip from me, prince, you'll keep this angel-faced little castaway tied right to mama's apron-strings till time's called."

The prince laughed amiably, but the amiability was for Holloway, not Mr. Jones.

"Your expressions—your idioms—they are so very charming, Dick Holloway. But you are right. We cannot afford to be betrayed. James Haskins, you will kindly remain close to this gentleman's side. Take him with you and return to your post. And now, my friends, we have already sat too long talking. Let us sleep for the two hours that remain of night. Remember, we start at dawn."

Chapter III.
A TALE OF TWO PRINCES.

As if stricken dumb, Mr. Jones obeyed the guiding hand of James Haskins, as it steered him back to the point whence he had first sighted the camp-fire. It seemed as though something even stronger than Fate were against him. Whatever he said was turned back upon him; whatever he did, it merely led him into fresh disaster. There was no use in fighting the tide. Henceforth he would keep still and permit events to shape themselves, unhelped or hindered by his efforts.

Perhaps, presently, he would wake up. Yes, this must be some unusually vivid nightmare which had him in its clutches.

"Squat right down on that rock, stranger, and make yourself at home." Of course, it was Haskins who broke in on his reverie. "If any more mavericks stray off your range up this way, I'll be right here to throw, tie, and brand 'em. Have a cigarette?"

"No—yes, thank you, I believe I will."

For a few moments the two smoked without speaking. The night was silent, save for the low, distant murmur of the sea and the occasional squeak of a bat. Overhead the great, brilliant stars, which hung so strangely low and near, seemed to wink at Jones, as if they were sharers in some huge joke of whose nature he was not yet informed, but of which he was unquestionably the butt.

"Strange," he reflected. "I can't remember ever having smoked in a dream before. I can taste the tobacco, too. And my hands hurt like the dickens where I scraped 'em on the rocks. I wonder if I ever will wake up. That girl is a winner for looks, all right; but, oh, mama; I don't like her disposition one little bit! Seems to have it in for me, all right. I wonder—"

"Pleasant dreams!" It was James Haskins again. "Say, did you really get washed ashore like you told the bunch?"

"I certainly did," said Jones with convincing vigor and promptitude. "Look here; if I should tell you the whole story about what has happened since I reached this place, would you believe me?"

"Fire away!" the other replied non-committally.

Jones obeyed, and his jailer listened patiently and in silence to the full tale of his misadventures. Barring the fact that it was a liner and not his own yacht from which he had fallen, he adhered closely to facts; for, in the light of his reception, it seemed it was only for his own good that Doherty had warned him not to speak of the other camp. And in this opinion his listener presently confirmed him.

"So this man Doherty told you not to tell you'd been in his camp, did he?" was Haskin's comment at the end of the recital. "Well, he was dead right, friend castaway. Prince Paul has got just the same love for Prince Sergius that a grizzly has for a rattlesnake.

"But me, I think you're straight. For one thing, you haven't got the map of a bunco-steerer; and for another, I think you are because *she* thinks you ain't. Do you get me? I never saw anything in skirts yet that you couldn't copper her guess and be on the right trail. Only your swim seems to have twisted your geography some. It isn't the Azores you mean—it's the Philippines, or Hawaii. Now, if you and me should swap yarns, will you give me away to my outfit, or will you keep it under your hair?"

"Prince Sergius's knout wouldn't extract it from me," sighed Mr. Jones, with the happy sense that here again, where least expected, he had found a friend.

"Well, to commence with, me, I'm riding a long way off my own range, which is Colorado, by rights, though I was born in Arizona. Arizona Jim, that's me. Well, this prince fellow come along when I was on my uppers in Frisco, having gone up against a few large doses of red-eye and an outfit of card-sharks some simultaneous. But, say, you fellows started from Savannah, you said. Did you get into the Pacific through the canal?"

The Pacific? Jones's brain reeled again, but he managed to keep his voice steady and reply: "Yes, of course we—we went through the canal."

"I asked because I know a fellow that runs a café in Colon. Did you stop there?"

"I didn't go ashore there. But how did you meet the prince?"

"Oh, yes. Well, as I was saying, he met up with me, and he offers me a job. Says he's goin' on a big trip and wants a guy with a good gun-eye. That's me, all right; so I joins the outfit immediate. Then's when I meet this brother of his, they bein' on good terms then, just like an owl and a prairie-dog.

"So brother Sergius, it seems, he's gone right ahead and chartered a yacht without waiting for brother Paul to approve the deal. This annoys us some, but not half so much as when we get way out on the broad, be-yutiful, lonesome Pacific Ocean and finds that the captain and the crew are all 'brothers' of his, too. Yes, little Annie, Sergius is in with the anarchists, saddle, bridle, and spurs, and the great and noble cause has got to get its share in the profits, even if brother Sergius has to knife brother Paul to do it. Oh, yes, it was some rotten deal, take it from me."

"But where does this Miss—Miss—"

"Weston come in? Not yet but soon. We picks Miss Weston up out of an open boat, along with a couple of half-dead sailors. She's a Boston young lady that's been taking lessons in nursing. She aims to join the Red Cross, but she's some foxy, so she comes clear across to Frisco and takes a boat for Japan, figurin' to get into the festivities by the back gate, so to speak. No German torpedoes in hers."

(Jones gave a mental groan. Again!)

"And right then was when the lid blew off the kettle for keeps. I never did see two brothers take a shine to the same girl quite so simultaneous and sudden. Gee, they ought to have been twins, their tastes are so similar. Was she going to be Princess Sergius or Princess Paul? I suggests to Paul, casual-like, that they cut her in two and divide her up, it being my idea that there ain't any female woman born that's any real good in a round-up like this one. But he didn't seem to take to it.

"So brother Paul, he reveals to her the perfidy of brother Sergius, and right away that swings her. No nihilanarchists for hers. In which she shows more sense than I'd expected.

"Right about then we sights this here Joker Island. Some name, Joker; but she's some Island, too, believe me. There being considerable hard feeling, what with one thing and another, me and Prince Paul and this Weston girl and her two sailors, we thinks it wise and becoming to withdraw ourselves from evil associations, and we drops off the yacht the first dark night. Then Prince Paul, he says there's a guy on the island expecting him, which is the first I heard of Holloway. As near as I can make out, this is Holloway's island, by right of being wrecked here and finding out some darn thing about the inside of it. These cliffs go all the way around, you know, but there's a cave runs under 'em, and Mr. Holloway, he's the only one that knows where it is."

"I shouldn't think it would be very difficult to find a cave in a wall of rock like this, if one hunted for it," suggested Jones, deeply interested in the narrative.

"Oh, no, it's dead easy—like three guesses at which is the right hole in a colander. There's about fifteen hundred other caves, and they all run back under the cliffs, and there's only one that goes clear through. And if you get lost in a blind lead—good night!"

"But what is there inside, anyway?"

"Me not being Prince Paul's confidential secretary, I don't know, nor I don't know how Sergius thinks he's going to get there without dear brother Paul and friend Holloway. But it's plain he knows something about Holloway, or he wouldn't have made that nice, kind offer to persuade you when he thought you was Holloway. One thing, it's clear he don't know him by sight. The way I figure it is that when Holloway was wrecked here, after he comes out of the inside again, he was taken off by some ship, and then he hikes right after Prince Paul, who, it seems, is his dear old college chum. It must be some secret, all right; for Paul, he gets leave immediate from his regiment by the Czar's special permit.

"But brother Sergius, who's some unpopular at home, he don't need no permit, because he's in America already. I don't think Paul was lookin' to run across him; but when he does, he takes him in on the deal for the sake of them old days back on the farm. Well, while Paul is rustling this outfit together, friend Richard gets himself put on the island alone again, with provisions, and stays right on the claim to wait for Paul. Paul comes along with a brother and a aggregation of nihilanarchists and a Boston schoolmarm girl, and now the only way out is in."

"What?"

"Just like I says—in. We're going through the caves at daybreak. Holloway says even he might get the wrong one at night."

"Good Lord!" murmured Mr. Jones softly. From boyhood he had suffered from a dread of dark, shut-in places, running parallel, perhaps, with his habit of sleep-walking. Even now he never slept without a light in his room, and he would not have explored the Mammoth Caves with a guard of fifty guides for all the money in the world. "Are you—are they going to take me along?"

"What's the matter? Don't you want to sit in? Take it from me, you're better off with Paul than you would be with Sergius, and you've only got Paul and Sergius to choose between."

"What sort of lights are you going to use?" queried Mr. Jones anxiously.

"Oh, we have some electric torches. Stranger, I've talked myself into the finest thirst outside of Arizona. But it's wasted—absolutely wasted. Ain't that a sad thought? By gracious, I'd almost go over and take up with this naughty Sergius party, if I thought he had anything stronger than water to give me. But, alas! The Monterey is like Russia—she's gone prohibition. Don't you notice a different feeling in the air? What time's it getting to be?" He glanced at his watch.

"What time were you intending to start?" inquired Jones.

"Half an hour. It's three now. Here comes Holloway."

Chapter IV.
THE ADVENTURER ESCAPES AGAIN.

"Did you catch any more bugs, Jim?" called Richard Holloway cheerfully as he approached. "No? Too bad. Hoped we could start a collection. Say, Mr.—er, what did you say your name was? Something unusual, wasn't it?"

"Jones," replied the castaway rather stiffly. He was a trifle tired of the disdainful attitude which every one except the cowboy had so far assumed toward him. "Roland C. Jones."

"Mr. Roland C. Jones, I salute you." Holloway bowed very low and straightened with a laugh. "Did you leave any last will and testament with his serene and nihilistic highness when he sent you over here? Because, you know, it's just possible that something might happen to you inside. You've no idea how wonderfully exciting 'inside' is, Mr. Jones. Don't let me alarm you, though."

Jones laughed almost hysterically. "It can't be much more exciting than— than everything else," he said. "And as for getting killed, I'm beginning to have a suspicion that that's the best thing which could happen to me."

He was thinking of his own mental condition, but Holloway understood him differently.

"So bad as that?" he asked with mock commiseration. "No home? No friends? Somebody cooked your chestnuts for you? Never mind, sweet child. We'll buy you some more—if we ever get off Joker Island. Coming, Prince?" he called back, as a voice hailed him from the little camp. "Come on, Jimmy; and you, too, Rolly! You don't mind if I call you Rolly? I feel in my heart that we're going to be friends, Rolly, and what's a name between pals?"

"I don't care what you call me," replied Mr. Jones, smiling in spite of himself. After all, there was something very likeable about this impertinent, good-natured fellow. He felt that he could get along very nicely if he had nobody but the cowboy and Richard Holloway to deal with.

They found the rest of the party eating a very informal breakfast, consisting of hardtack, a few rashers of bacon, and some really excellent coffee. Jones received his share thankfully. He could not remember a time when he had been so hungry, or hungry so often, as in the few hours since he had come to Joker Island.

Then the fire was extinguished; what provisions were left and some simple impedimenta were divided equally among the men, and the expedition started with only Miss Weston unburdened. She tripped lightly along beside her Russian admirer, apparently as merry and light-hearted as if they were bound on a picnic.

Dawn had come upon them with extraordinary suddenness as they ate, it seemed to Mr. Jones. There had been a few moments of ghostly twilight. Then the sun leaped into the sky, like a tiger springing from its lair, and flung at them his first rays with an ardor which promised insufferable heat later on.

Now that it was light, Jones perceived that the ravine, or split in the cliff wall, ended abruptly just beyond the camp. There the precipice towered as forbidding and unscalable as it hung above the outer beach. The little stream sprang from a mere crevice in the otherwise solid wall. There were certainly no caverns in that direction, and he was not surprised when Holloway, in his capacity of guide, led the way back down the ravine toward the sea; but he did wonder how they could emerge upon the beach without being seen by the nihilists.

They had followed the watercourse only a short distance, however, when Holloway turned aside and led them into a yet narrower crack in the rocks which branched off from the main ravine. The going became more and more difficult, and Paul Petrofsky was obliged to almost carry the girl over some places, while the rest of the party scrambled and sweated and swore *sotto voce*.

At last the crack widened; they caught a glimpse of blue beyond, and in another moment they came out upon a part of the beach which was cut off by a jutting promontory of rock from the small bay where the Monterey lay anchored. Jones thought that a bird's-eye view of that island must show the cliff to be fairly scalloped with little bays and promontories.

And here the black rock was honey-combed with dark holes, bored out either by the sea or by volcanic agency; some of them no more than a foot or so across, a few large enough so that a motor-truck could have been safely driven in.

"This is only the beginning of 'em," declared Holloway, addressing Petrofsky, but in loud enough tones to be heard by all. "Half way 'round the island the rock is fairly perforated. Some place for a tribe of cave men, no?"

Then, suddenly assuming the manner of a tourist guide: "Just step this way, lady and gentlemen. Here you may behold the finest—oldest—most dog-gonedest aggregation of black holes—"

His voice died away and became indistinguishable, for he had dropped to hands and knees and crawled into one of the smaller caverns.

Petrofsky, pausing only to draw an electric torch from his pocket, immediately followed, and close upon his heels crept Miss Margaret Weston. To Jones's amazement, the girl was laughing just before she disappeared. He could not have laughed himself to win a medal. However, Jim Haskins and the two sailors were looking at him expectantly.

There was nothing else for it, so he, too, dropped to his knees and crawled into the hole, pushing ahead of him the small bundle which had been assigned him to carry. He wondered bitterly if they were to crawl all the way through the cliff.

Ahead of him he could see a moving black mass against a dim glow of light, which he knew to be the intrepid Miss Weston, of Boston, Massachusetts. Jones had no light himself, and was too far behind the leaders to get any benefit from theirs. The rock was wet and a trifle slimy. He thought of snakes, but remembered gratefully that if there were any they would have a good chance to bite three people before they got to him.

Behind, he could hear a grunting and scraping, and knew the other three were following.

Then the glow ahead abruptly disappeared, and there was a scrambling, thumping sound. Had Holloway and the Russian fallen into some abyss? He halted, but immediately after heard a voice calling, "Come ahead! It's all right! Oh, what a perfectly lovely, splendid place!"

It was the voice of Margaret Weston, and a moment later Mr. Jones scrambled out of the narrow hole into an enormous, scintillating cavern. The lights of two electric torches were reflected dazzlingly from a million fiery points.

"What perfectly gorgeous stalactites!" exclaimed the girl rapturously. "Oh, Mr. Holloway, I'm so glad you found this place! It's worth *anything* just to have seen it. Why, if it were not so hard to reach, this would be one of the show places of the world, would it not?"

"It would," admitted the flattered Mr. Holloway. "But I only wish I could let some sunlight into the hole for you. I've taken some pieces of this stuff out, and in daylight they are all colors of the rainbow. Look like stuff out of a jeweler's window. The colors don't show up in this light."

"Thank you, but it's quite beautiful enough as it is."

Even Jones had to admit to himself that Miss Weston was, in a measure, right. Above their heads was a black void. The roof was too high and probably too dark in color for their lights to show it, but all about them, depending almost to the floor, hung a thousand icicle-points, which reflected the electric rays as if they had been encrusted with diamonds. From the floor, also, rose points and mounds of brilliant crystals. This lower forest of stalagmites seemed to extend itself indefinitely, certainly beyond range of the torches.

"Dick Holloway," said the prince, "this is fairyland to which you have brought us. The air, too, which I had thought would be almost poisonous, it is fresh. It smells of the sea. There must be many more openings into this place than that by which we entered."

"There probably are," agreed Holloway, "but I'd hate to hunt for them. I was lost in these caves once—that was the way I happened to locate the way through—but I'd hate to risk it twice."

"But tell me," continued the prince, gazing, upward curiously, "is there no danger from the falling of some of these huge masses from the roof?"

"Sure thing there is. But—Jiminy, there goes a beauty right this minute!"

There was an ominous crackling sound, the mild forerunner of a thunderous, deafening crash. The air was filled with a cloud of choking white dust, through which the torches gleamed faintly as through a fog. The noise was followed by a series of lesser crashes. Then came again the calm, unagitated voice of Holloway.

"Did that hit anybody? If it did, farewell to the dear departed. Is every one here?"

One by one the little party answered with their names, Jones last, and in a voice which he rendered steady with some effort. He had always known that caverns would be just like this. For a moment he had been deceived by the treacherous beauty of this one, but no more. Surely they would turn back now. Nobody could expect to pass through this place where at any moment a thousand pounds of glittering stalactite was liable to drop on him—

It was the voice of Miss Weston which answered his unspoken thought.

"Well, there is no need of our standing here, is there? How in the world can you find your way, Mr. Holloway?"

"Been here before," replied that gentleman cheerfully. "Know it like the streets of Hometown. Come along."

By this time the white dust had somewhat settled, and Jones could see his companions clearly. They were starting off single file between the innumerable stalagmites, apparently careless of disaster. On an impulse he crouched down behind a white mound.

Jim Haskins passed within hand's reach, but did not see him in the shadow. The two sailors were a little behind, and on a sudden thought Jones cautiously pushed his bundle of miscellaneous camp articles out from behind his mound.

An instant later one of the sailors stumbled over it, and as Jones had craftily foreseen, imagined that it had been dropped by one of the men ahead. Grumbling, the man picked it up and added it to his own load, and with no thought for a possible escaping prisoner, passed on.

In fact, nobody gave Mr. Jones a thought. He was alone, neglected and forsaken, and the fact gave him supreme relief. He had looked carefully, while there was still sufficient light, and had seen a black hole yawning, the hole by which they had entered this place of terror. Having honestly restored to his captors the goods with which he had been entrusted, Mr. Jones felt no scruples about deserting them.

Just before the last gleam of light from the electric torches faded and disappeared, Mr. Jones plunged back into the small tunnel and began rapidly wriggling his way toward open air and the blessed light of day.

Somehow or other the passage seemed much longer than when he had come that way at the heels of the Boston girl. Jones crawled and crawled, until his knees and elbows were sore, but still he could see no gleam of light ahead. It seemed to him that he had been crawling for hours. What could be the matter?

Suddenly the horrifying explanation dawned upon him. This was not the tunnel by which they had entered, but another of the labyrinthine system of caves to which Holloway had referred!

Mr. Jones stopped crawling and tried to turn himself about. There was not room enough, however, and he only hurt himself still more upon the slimy rock. There was no use in trying to wriggle backward, for he knew that he would become exhausted before he could ever regain the cave of stalactites by such a laborious process. Besides, he reflected, even if he did get back there he would be no better off. Surrounded by impenetrable midnight darkness, how could he hope to rediscover the passage he had been unable to identify while there was light?

With a sinking heart he contemplated the many hours of mental and physical suffering which lay before him if he should fail to extricate himself. He must go on. What a fool he had been to desert the party of adventurers! After all, they were kindly, honest folk and it would have been far better to have died suddenly by the fall of a stalactite, or in some merciful abyss, than here alone in the darkness of the damned.

He *must* get out! And when "must" drives, a man will do a great deal more than appears possible. Roland C. Jones did. He crawled literally for hours, turning, winding with the tunnel, like an unhappy and desolate angle-worm in the black bosom of Earth.

Once, exhausted, he let himself subside, and despite all the terrors of darkness went to sleep. He had not slept for a long time, and when he awoke, though he ached in every limb, he felt refreshed and took new courage to crawl on.

Crawling is a slow process—at least, for a human being—but if a man crawl far enough, and encounters no obstruction, he is bound to get some-where sometime, and that is what happened to Mr. Jones. He had long since given up all hope, and become a mere, dogged crawling-machine, when it happened. It was a tremendous thing and an experience which in all his after-life he never forgot. He saw the rock beneath him!

Then he raised his head, hopefully, prayerfully, and there, far ahead, beamed a glorious star of light!

Then did Mr. Jones perform prodigies of crawling. As if he had just started, he wriggled and scrambled along, and at last actually emerged from the black womb of death into the adorable, intolerable brilliance of day. Also into the very arms of Doherty, his former rescuer!

Behind Doherty stood Captain Ivanovitch, and beside him was Sergius Petrofsky. Mr. Jones had crawled windingly through the rock, all the way from behind the promontory, around the end of the ravine, and back to the little bay whereon the Monterey still lay at anchor.

He had expected anything—but not this. In the eternity which had elapsed since entering that black rat-hole he had forgotten that such a per-son as Sergius Petrofsky existed. His clothing was ripped to slimy rags. In a dozen places his body and limbs were scraped raw, he was faint and sick for lack of food and drink—and before him stood the man who had promised to torture him that day. The villainies of Fate were too prodigious.

Mr. Jones slipped suddenly from the sustaining grip of Doherty, and dropped in a wretched heap upon the sand.

Chapter V.
Allied with the Enemy.

When sense at last returned to the castaway, he opened his eyes and stared blankly about for a moment. He had dreamed that he was in his own bed-room in his own New York bachelor apartment, and these walls of brown canvas, that strange face bent above his, seemed incredible, far more vision-ary than the dream itself.

Then the whiff of an agreeable odor reached his nostrils. Food! Mr. Jones sat up and reached out his hands in one single motion. Doherty placed the bowl which he carried with them.

"I've brought youse your scoffin's," he said. "Gee! Youse was a sight when youse fell out o' that hole. His nibs is waitin' to see youse."

"Let him wait," commanded Jones in a determined voice. "Keep him out, can't you, till I finish this? This is the first thing I've had to eat for—for weeks, judging by the way my appetite feels."

Doherty laughed and seated himself on the side of the cot. "I'll tell him youse was pounding your ear so hard I couldn't wake youse up."

"Thanks, old man." There was an interval of silence, then Jones handed back the polished bowl with a great sigh, swung his legs to the floor and sat up. "Where are my clothes?" he asked.

"Your clothes? Gee, youse ain't got no clothes. There was a couple of old rags hangin' to youse, but if dat Anthony Comstock guy ever seen youse he'd t'row a fit, sure. Them things youse has on now belongs to the captain."

"But what am I to do? I can't walk around in these pajamas."

Doherty grinned. He seemed in an uncommonly good humor.

"Dat's all right. His nibs has came across wit' dese here glad rags. Climb into 'em and look sharp, or I'll get the hide tore off me for keepin' him waitin'. There's a basin over there if youse wants to wash some more, but gee! they sure had to give you one bath before they could put youse to bed even."

"Well, I guess a little more water won't hurt me."

Jones also found a safety razor and a mug of luke-warm water beside the basin, and was glad enough to shave, although his beard was by this time a very stiff one to get rid of.

Then he dressed in the "glad rags" indicated by Mr. Doherty, which he found consisted of a suit of thin silk underwear, breeches and tunic coat of khaki, socks, puttees, and a pair of heavy, but well-made shoes. In fact, as good an outfit for a tramping or hunting expedition as Jones could have bought anywhere in New York.

Very gratefully he donned the garments, which to his joy fitted him quite passably. The shoes were a little loose, but that was much more satisfactory than if they had been too tight.

He thought, as he dressed, that if they intended to abuse him they had made a peculiar beginning. Sleep and food had done a great deal to bring him back to a normal outlook on life. His limbs still ached, but that was hardly strange in view of the strenuous character of recent experiences. Mr. Jones presently announced his readiness to go to or receive the waiting Sergius.

"Youse c'n wait here. I'll get him," said Doherty, who all the time preserved the same astonishing amiability. He did not even question Mr. Jones in regard to how he had come to return there, and not only return, but return in such a singular manner and condition. Some species of relief or joy fairly radiated from the man's every glance and word.

Mr. Jones did not have to wait long after Doherty's departure. He had gone to the entrance and stood looking out. The sun beat down from almost directly overhead, and he correctly surmised that this was the day following that on which he had emerged from the cave. He must have slept the clock fairly around.

Some distance up the beach a number of men were gathered about a large object which was partly obscured by an intervening tent, so that he could not quite make out its nature. In a moment he saw Sergius Petrofsky coming toward him alone.

"My friend," said the nihilist, glancing him up and down with a smile, "you have a much improved appearance."

"Thanks to you, Prince Sergius," assented Jones, wondering yet more at the apparent friendliness of every one.

"You are entirely welcome, Mr. Holloway. But come inside, please. We must talk together."

They seated themselves, Jones on the cot, Sergius on the camp-chair.

"And now, Mr. Holloway, perhaps you will explain what has become of my brother and—and the young lady, Miss Weston."

So that was it. They had discovered that the other party had vanished into thin air and looked to him to recover the trail. Jones determined in his own honest mind that he would never discover to them the location of those caves. Besides, they might try to make him enter them again! But he could not feel that any loyalty to a party which had, after all, treated him only as a spy and a liar, demanded further sacrifice than this.

"In the first place, Prince Sergius, I am not Richard Holloway. When you found me I had never seen or heard of such a person, but since that time I have met the man himself."

Without reserve, save as regarded any implication of Doherty, Jones proceeded to tell his story, to which the Russian listened with an impassive face. At the end, however, he rose and extended his hand to his involuntary guest.

"I was mistaken, Mr. Jones, and I have to ask your forgiveness. We must have seemed to you not only inhospitable, but boorish in the last degree to so threaten you who deserved only our help and kindness. But your story of the Lusitania you yourself will admit was—well, let us speak no more of that. Perhaps some day you will entrust me with your full confidence. Now, however, you are in a position to extend to me a very great service.

"No—" he raised a protesting hand as Jones started to speak, "I do not longer ask that you reveal the cavern entrance. Your own experience shows what is the most likely fate of those attempting it without good guidance. We have done all in our power to make you forget our past unjust treatment, even while we still deemed you Richard Holloway. May I expect your favor in return?"

"Why, of course," replied Jones in some surprise. "But I don't exactly see what I could do—"

"You will see," said the prince, with a rather peculiar smile. "Will you be pleased to follow me?"

Together they left the tent and walked across the sands toward the object of which Jones had earlier caught a glimpse. Now he saw what it was. It was an aeroplane. The nihilist was again speaking:

"I had planned to take with me the man, Doherty, but he is an ignorant fellow, entirely unsuited to such an undertaking. Also, he was afraid to go. None other of the men are suitable. Ivanovitch, he must remain to look after our crew. My mechanic is ill on board the Monterey. The others are too stupid. They are fellow Russians and brothers in the cause, but you see I speak frankly. You, on the other hand, are young, intelligent, and—"

"You want me to go up in that thing with you?" gasped Mr. Jones.

"Of course. I am a good airman. You need feel no alarm, for in the air you will be in no danger. It is when we descend to what is within that I desire with me a reliable companion. Are we to be comrades?"

"You give me a choice?"

"But yes. Unless you come willingly, I would better make my flight alone."

"All right. I'll go."

Yes, it was really Roland Chesterton Jones, the coward of the caverns, who said these words! As a matter of fact, Jones was not a coward at all, but a victim of subconscious terror of the dark. Given a fair chance and the open air, he had always felt perfectly willing to face danger, although his life before coming to Joker Island had not been an adventurous one and he was by choice a young man of quiet life and manners.

The prince gave him an approving nod.

"I am not a bad reader of features. We will meet everything like comrades, eh? And you will not be tempted, if we should come upon them, to return to my brother and his people?"

"I will not," said Jones firmly. He had nothing against any of them, but he possessed a natural predilection toward any one who treated him courteously, nihilist or not.

Moreover, there was something about Sergius Petrofsky which had attracted him from the first, in spite of his brutal threat that first night. Fanatical, cruel even, when thwarted, there was yet about him that invisible aura which we term personality, for lack of a better name. If he had been an actor he would undoubtedly have been an idol of the matinee girls. Jones wondered, when he thought of it, that Miss Weston had turned from him to his less attractive brother.

They had now reached the group of sailors gathered about the mono-plane. Captain Ivanovitch was nowhere in sight, and they were lounging about in the sand, but all sprang to their feet at sight of Sergius. He said something sharply to them in Russian and all save two went off toward the tents. Then he turned again to his guest.

"I have been obliged to do almost all the work of assembling the plane with my own hands, because of this unfortunate illness of Thoreau, my mechanic. Are you in the least familiar with this sort of engine? It would be too much to hope that you know anything of the science of flight."

Mr. Jones hastened to disclaim any knowledge on either subject. He had always left even the mysteries of his own motor-cars, and his big power-boat, the Bandersnatch, to the expert attentions of their respective chauffeurs and captain. The most he knew about gasoline was that it sometimes exploded, and was used to drive automobiles, power-boats, and aeroplanes. Of the dark secrets of spark, ignition, carburetor, and so forth he was as innocent as a child.

"Then it is of no use for me to try to instruct you in the brief space which lies between us and departure. Your part will be to sit quiet in that seat which you see behind the pilot's place, and if we come to any grief I will endeavor to play the part of driver and mechanic also. We are taking with us no provisions, save a slight luncheon in that hamper, but these rifles may prove convenient. It is my purpose to make, as it were, a reconnaissance, and we may not even descend into the inner valley or crater until a later flight."

At this moment Captain Ivanovitch came up, accompanied by Doherty. The captain entered into conversation with Sergius in Russian, and as Mr. Jones waited for the next move, Doherty said in a low voice, "Gee, ain't I glad youse showed up? I ain't got no use for them flyin' things. If ever I gets to be a angel I suppose I'll have to flutter me wings—but till I gets 'em I sticks right to the ground floor."

"You may be right," Jones admitted.

"I thought we'd butt into the valley by the subway after all when I seed youse come out. But, gee, this lets little Willie out complete. Youse is wel-come to the job."

"Mr. Jones," interrupted Sergius, "will you put these things on? It is not so warm up above there, you know."

He was holding out a heavy coat and a sort of hood, which Jones donned while the nihilist put on a similar outfit. To the hood was attached a pair of large goggles which could be pulled down over the eyes. It was not a regular aviator's costume, but near enough for the short flight contemplated.

Then the two strangely assorted companions climbed to their places. Needless to say, it was the first time Mr. Jones had ever been in an aeroplane. He had attended meets, watched the daring evolutions of the dragon-flylike things against the sky, and had one or two opportunities to go up himself, but he had never experienced any desire to rise higher above solid earth than the top floor of a skyscraper.

Yet now he found himself strangely cool and unperturbed. Sergius Petrofsky inspired him with a great deal of confidence in his ability as a man of action.

Now Ivanovitch and a seaman had grasped the monoplane, one on each side at the rear, and were standing with feet braced as if expecting some great strain upon their muscles. Sergius did something with a lever and the engine burst forth into a roar which startled Mr. Jones extremely. He had forgotten what a racket the things make.

Then he felt a slight jerk and the plane was rolling swiftly along the sand. He was thrown back in his seat, as the machine tilted upward, and a moment later shut his eyes, for he had seen the beach dropping away from under them, and it seemed as if a violent wind had suddenly arisen. Remembering the goggles he reached up and pulled them down over his eyes before opening them again.

Glancing downward he saw the sea, rocking and swaying beneath them, had a moment of nausea, and realized that it was the plane which was rocking. They were up, they were actually flying through the air. The wind of their flight was beating upon his fate. The experience was different to anything which he had ever imagined, and yet it was strangely exhilarating, too. For the first time since he had found himself adrift in the sea, he was glad that he had fallen off the liner.

No matter what might befall, nothing could ever rob him of the memory of this moment when he learned the real meaning of man's victory over the air.

Sergius turned slightly and shouted something over his shoulder, but the roar of engine and propeller drowned his voice. Jones shook his head and shouted back something equally indistinguishable. He had meant to say "Grand! Glorious! Splendid!" but the wind seemed to hurl the words back down his throat.

He looked down again and saw to his amazement how high they had already climbed. The island lay beneath them, with that maplike appearance which one notices in bird's-eye views. The black cliff which had appeared so awesome and forbidding was now no more than a huge, irregular oval line of black. And this line surrounded—what? A sea of green, it seemed, probably the tops of trees, although the foliage was indistinguishable from that height. Moreover it all appeared to be swinging in vast circles, for they were ascending in a steep spiral.

Jones began to wonder how high they were to mount. He had imagined, in the brief time given him for thought, that they would simply rise above the cliff and immediately descend upon the other side.

Then, abruptly, the steady roar of the engine slackened and died. The nose of the plane dipped earthward and they were sliding down the air, swiftly, but so smoothly that the sensation was one of pure delight. The circles of their descent were so wide that, as they came nearer, Jones had plenty of time to study the strange valley which lay shut off from and unsuspected of the outer world.

That the island had been one huge volcanic crater at one time in its history, there could be no doubt. Now, however, there was nothing to suggest a volcano save the wall itself, and within was a wide expanse of the greenest verdure. The great oval was about ten or twelve miles long. Its floor was of a slightly undulating, parklike appearance, the upper, darker green being broken here and there by lighter patches which Jones presumed to be little lawns and open glades in the forest.

The engine roared out again, but this time Sergius did not ascend. He turned so sharply that the plane "banked" at what seemed to his passenger an alarming angle, and shot straight across the valley. Then he once more cut out the engine and shot downward swiftly and steeply.

Suddenly Jones perceived what they were aiming at, a broad, smooth space of green, about a quarter of a mile in length, which the prince in his circlings had picked out for a landing place. An instant later dark masses shot upward on both sides, the pilot deftly straightened out the plane, and with a stiff jolt they had struck the earth.

The lawn, which had looked so smooth and even from above, proved to be an expanse of villainous hummocks, over which they bounded and sprang for fifty yards or so, and at last came to a creaking, swaying halt.

CHAPTER VI.
VERY NEARLY EATEN.

"Ha, my friend," cried Sergius, turning a beaming face, "that was a good landing, no? Coming down in such unknown country something is always liable to break, but we have better fortune."

"What funny-looking trees!" exclaimed Mr. Jones, paying no heed to the Russian's self-congratulations. "Why, they look like—like cabbages! And what a horrible smell!"

The word "horrible" was none too strong to describe the intolerable odor which permeated the air. Descending as they had done from the clear, clean, fresh upper atmosphere, it seemed at first almost impossible to breathe at all. It was a sort of concentrated, well-nigh visible stench, suggesting nothing less than decayed slaughter-houses or open graveyards. Even the prince lost his smile after the first moment of delight over his successful landing.

The "trees" to which Mr. Jones had referred, were indeed not trees at all, but some sort of vegetable growth entirely unfamiliar to either of the men. If they had really been the cabbages they resembled, they would have made the everlasting fortune of the market-gardener who grew them, for the smallest was as large as a fair-sized hen-house, and some of the larger ones must have measured at least a hundred feet from root to crest, with a diameter at least one-fourth as great. They were a dark purple in color, shading upward into a sickly green. None of them grew very close together, and the spaces between were filled with an astonishing variety of mushroomlike things, whose vivid coloring, red, yellow, violet, and orange, jarred upon the eye in a disharmony of which nature is very seldom guilty.

Like a giant's vegetable garden, these monstrous growths entirely surrounded the glade where they had alighted. But even though they towered so high over the heads of the aeronauts, they caught glimpses between and above them of other and different growths, yet higher.

There was no wind in the glade. The sun beat down and the stench rose up. Mr. Jones had a strong feeling that if they did not get out of the place in a short time he was going to be very ill indeed.

"This is awful," he said appealingly. "Can't we go up again?"

The Russian, who had been looking about with much interest, shook his head. "Of what use to rise now when we have just made such a very nice landing? Another time we might not be so lucky. The odor is certainly unpleasant, but after all it is only a smell. It is only the vegetation. I knew that here in the crater valley we would find some very peculiar things. We must not be too easily deterred. Let us penetrate past these vegetables and find what lies beyond."

Sergius undoubtedly had the final say-so in regard to their leaving or remaining, so his companion followed his example, unstrapped himself from his seat in the monoplane, and descended to earth. The prince handed him a rifle and cartridge belt and took one himself. They discarded their coats and hoods and advanced toward the nearest passage between the "cabbages."

As they approached the dreadful charnel odor became more intense, if that were possible. Shoulders thrown forward, eyes half-shut and smarting, they pushed through it as through some tangible obstruction.

Then the first of the many-hued mushrooms were crunching beneath their feet. They crushed and squelched, with a semi-liquid sound, sending up a sort of acid gas into the faces of the two adventurers, somewhat like the fumes of hydrochloric acid. The prince took out his handkerchief and bound it over his mouth and nose, signaling to Jones to do likewise, for both of them were past speaking. With these improvised and inadequate gas-masks, they waded doggedly on through the fungi.

They were within fifteen feet of one of the smaller cabbages, when with a sort of swishing sound it began to move. Its outer sheath of purple and green leaves, twenty-five feet long and five broad, began to open out and descend.

Jones caught a glimpse between them of a huge, scarlet, writhing mass, and tried to turn and run. The crushed mushroom things held his feet. It was like trying to leap or run in a quicksand.

Then the rough, thick, sawlike edge of the nearest leaf struck him a glancing blow on the shoulder, and he was down in the mess of fungi. A long, writhing, bright-red thing, like a nightmare fishing-worm, lashed out above him, curled back and encircled his neck in a strangling grip.

"Help!" he tried to shout. "Sergius—help!"

Then his shoulder was seized and he was being pulled away from the giant cabbage. The tentacle which held him straightened out and actually stretched as if it had been made of india-rubber. A knife flashed over him, severing the tentacle, and a moment later he was out of reach of a dozen more which were shooting after him. That was the last thing he remembered until he came to under the shadow of the plane, to look up into the anxious face of Sergius Petrofsky, who was fanning him with a handkerchief.

Mr. Jones sat up and felt of his neck gingerly. Luckily his collar had somewhat protected it, but it felt very stiff and sore.

"I thought you were gone, my friend," said Sergius, standing up and wiping his perspiring face with the handkerchief.

"So did I. What I can't understand is why the thing didn't get you, too. Look at it now—ugh, the horrible, nasty, writhing beast!"

The "death cabbage" (as they afterward named the interesting vegetables) had not closed its outer sheath, and its inner hideousness stood fully exposed to the sun. Straight up from the center sprang a sort of slimy, blue-black stalk, terminating some twenty-five feet above the ground in a wide plume of green fronds. Surrounding this stalk was a dense, intertwined mass of the long, scarlet tentacles which had nearly dragged Mr. Jones to his doom. To be eaten by a vegetable—and *such* a vegetable! Jones shuddered and looked away, feeling very sick and disgusted.

"Look!" cried the nihilist. "It is twisting itself about like a thing in agony. I wonder if the brute has eyes and sees us here and still hungers after its prey? But that is curious. See, it is becoming of a bright orange color!"

Jones looked again, rather unwittingly, but what the Russian said was quite true. The wriggling scarlet mass was rapidly changing to orange, and from orange it faded to a sickly yellow. Moreover it was wriggling more and more feebly. The outstretched sheath-leaves lifted themselves spasmodically two or three times, then wilted limply among the fungi at its base. The central stalk began to droop over to one side, and the green fronds hung dispiritedly down. At the end of five minutes all motion had ceased. Even the now pale tentacles writhed no more. The death cabbage was itself dead.

"Do you suppose it perished of a broken heart?" asked Sergius whimsically. "You resisted its ardent caresses, and it died of disappointment! But rather, I think it possible that another than either of us has killed this monster, my friend."

"What do you mean? Have you seen anybody else?"

Sergius pointed upward solemnly.

"I mean *him*," he said, and he was pointing at the sun. "There is but one explanation. These are creatures of the night, and they get their—their food in the night, whatever it may be. They are not accustomed to grasp their prey by daylight. This one was tempted, and he opened his protecting sheath, and he was slain by the sun! But he would have killed us first, if I had not been able to spring back more quickly than you, my friend, and escape his first gropings."

"I owe you my life," said Jones earnestly. "I never knew anybody before who would have had the courage to throw himself within reach of that—that thing, and drag another man away from it."

"It is nothing," Sergius demurred, looking very much pleased nevertheless. "Now we will be comrades, indeed—no? I think, however, that we have done and seen enough for one day. Mount again to your seat and we will leave this valley of death. But we will return to-morrow and alight in some more favorable spot."

"I'm with you," Mr. Jones assented joyfully.

But first they cleaned themselves as well as they could of the pulpy fungoids with which they were both plastered; Jones from head to foot. Then they started to put on their heavy coats. Mr. Jones was buttoning his and

Sergius had just slipped his arms into the sleeves, when a voice behind them said sharply:

"Stand perfectly still, please! If either one of you moves a finger I'll kill you first, Prince Sergius Petrofsky!"

Chapter VII.

CAPTURED AGAIN.

Startled and amazed, Jones and the nihilist yet obeyed, for there was a certain sincerity back of the command which was not to be denied. Their rifles lay on the ground a few feet distant and Sergius himself, with his arms half into his coat, was peculiarly helpless.

Both looked over their shoulders, however, and there behind them, rifle pointed at the middle of the Russian's back, stood Richard Holloway! He was still attired in his simple costume of shirt and trousers, now very ragged and dirty, and his face wore a grim smile.

"Who are you?" asked Sergius, although he may have guessed.

"It's Holloway," supplied Jones in a whisper.

"You don't need to murmur it in his ear, sweet child," interrupted the newcomer. "I'm *so* glad to meet you again, Rolly. You know I said I was sure we should be friends. But we thought after all a stalactite must have dropped and crushed out your innocent young life."

Mr. Jones could think of no reply. Of course, now, the other party would never believe that he had not been lying when he said that he had nothing to do with Sergius Petrofsky. Even Jim Haskins would no longer believe him. Then he forgot his own troubles in wondering how this unexpected meeting would affect his new friend, Sergius.

"Move farther back from those rifles," commanded Holloway. "That's right. And just remember that I don't love either of you one little bit. The only pity is that my dear little vegetable garden didn't succeed in getting both of you for its luncheon. It's a lucky thing for you that you didn't try conclusions with one of the really big fellows. That one was a mere child— poor innocent thing!"

He shifted his rifle to the hollow of his arm and came toward them.

Sergius, his face white and strained with anger, still stood with his arms half way in the coat. "May I—have I your very kind permission, Mr. Holloway, to finish putting on my coat? I give you my word that we are neither of us armed, except for the rifles."

"In just a minute, prince. Sorry about your word, but if you did happen to get careless about it, where would I be? Rolly, I've got you covered. Just go over and turn your friend's pockets inside out for me, will you? And now your own? That's right. No, I wronged your serene highness. You can put your coat on, though you must be a cold-blooded fish to want it in this sun."

"We were just about to ascend," said the Russian stiffly.

"Oh, I see. Well, you're just about not to ascend now, so you won't need it. We saw you fluttering gaily about over the valley, and saw you drop into this place. Paul (he really seems to retain a regard for you, for some reason), your brother, asked me to come out and pick up the remains, if there were any, which I doubted myself, knowing what sort of place you had landed in. He asked me to extend to you his apologies for not coming himself. He sprained his ankle in the caves, but Miss Weston is looking after him so well that really it can't be much hardship."

Sergius's eyes narrowed, and Jones remembered that Jim Haskins had told him both brothers were seeking the girl's favor.

Holloway picked up the two rifles from the ground and tucked them under his other arm. "So nice of you," he murmured. "We're rather short on arms and ammunition. But I know you're anxious to be welcomed in camp. Turn to the right, please, and straight ahead. Don't be frightened of the little cabbages. I won't feed you to them this time."

Jones was beginning to detest the young American as much as he had formerly been inclined to like him. His mocking banter, in this place that smelt like the tomb and was the home of detestable death, seemed as out of place as the tinkle of a pianola in Purgatory.

However, the man must know a safe way out, or he could not have appeared there himself, so the two prisoners turned their faces in the direction indicated and started off, with Holloway close behind.

They crossed the glade obliquely and came into view of a broad road, or trail, which had apparently been trampled over and through the fungi and several of the young and comparatively small death plants which lay crushed and broken. Two of them, each well above ten feet from root to crest, had been actually torn up by the roots and tossed to some distance from the place where they had been growing.

What power or agency had been strong enough to perform such a feat with such victims?

As they involuntarily paused, staring, Holloway's mocking voice answered the unspoken question:

"That's the work of another of my lovely island's children. Don't get scared. He doesn't prowl around much by day-light, but when he does take a walk, and things get in his way or annoy him, he just pushes them gently to one side—as you see. He's a foul brute, but not foul enough to feed upon such carrion plants as these. He was probably hunting something."

The nihilist was too proud, and Jones too overcome, to question Holloway in regard to the mysterious "brute" to which he referred, and after a moment of hesitation they marched on through the sickening mess of broken fungi and wilted, blood-sucking tentacles. But first, at Holloway's own suggestion, they all three again bound handkerchiefs over mouth and nose as a partial protection against the thrice-vile fumes rising from beneath their feet.

At last, however, a breath of purer air reached their nostrils, and raising his head, Jones's watering eyes beheld a scene of weird and unearthly beauty. Behind them lay the field of death cabbages, in all its foul ugliness. Before them was a forest—but such a forest! The trees were mere slender, graceful stems, shooting up to an unbelievable height, where they branched out into a feathery tuft of graceful leaves, resembling palms.

But these slender stems were all wound and garlanded with gorgeous blossoms, like glorious floral butterflies swaying and fluttering to every breath of air.

Here and there huge balloonlike growths had forced their way upward between the palms, bending them aside and so making their own path to the sunlight. These, however, unlike the cabbages, had nothing horrible or loathsome in their appearance, but were of the most delicate shades of pink, shading into lemon yellow at the summits. They, too, were overgrown in the riotous embrace of a thousand blossoming vines.

Underfoot the ground was thickly carpeted with moss in wide patches, like rich rugs of velvet-green, starred all over with little points of brilliant blue and scarlet, which were also flowers. Between the butterflylike blossoms of the vines innumerable real butterflies were flitting. Their colors were so similar to the flowers that it was impossible to tell if a blossom one's eyes rested upon were really such or a butterfly, unless it suddenly spread its wings and flickered away through the slanting sunlight.

Moving forward slowly, like men in a dream of fairyland, they came at last entirely out of the zone of vile odors; and, the more delightful by contrast, their nostrils were filled by the divine fragrance of this unlegended Garden of the Hesperides.

Again Holloway had his comment to make.

"You like this all right, now—but I just invite you to take the trip by moonlight!"

"By moonlight," said the Russian softly, forgetting for the moment his animosity toward the speaker. "I should think by moonlight this place would be—ah, celestial!"

"H-m! Well, I've been here, and take it from me it was more like the other place."

"Impossible!"

"In the bright lexicon of Joker Island, there ain't no such word, dear child. Your imagination needs exercise—or you wouldn't have come here, so I'll just permit you to exercise it on this. But I'll give you one tip: You've seen the flora, but you haven't seen the fauna—yet. Straight ahead, now, through that little lane between the vegetable balloons. No, *not* that way. Halt! Good Lord, man, if you'd gone down there you'd have wished you was safe inside one of those mild-tempered little cabbages back yonder!"

Sergius, absorbed in gazing at the wonders about them, had started to go to the left of the balloon in question instead of the right. The ground sloped sharply downward there, and as he drew back his foot in surprise at Holloway's evident agitation, there was a sudden rattle and slide of falling gravel.

Both he and his fellow-captive looked keenly down the incline, but could see nothing out of the way. A tangle of gray, leafless vines formed a veil across the bottom of the slope, through which they could see nothing.

Then the perspiration sprang out on Sergius's forehead, and for the first time since Jones had met him the prince looked really frightened. For over that tangle of vines something was moving. It was a leg, and it had come out from between the vines. It was jointed in two places, the space between the upper joints being about three feet long, and at the end of it was a single, great, curved claw, black and gleaming like polished ebony.

Another similar leg followed it into visibility. Then two eyes came into view, round, black, and fastened upon the ends of stalks like those of a lobster.

"Good *God!*" breathed the Russian. "What is the thing, Holloway?"

"Just a little spider," responded their captor cheerfully. "But plenty big enough to make three mouthfuls of you. That's its web it's sitting in, wondering why you don't come on down to dinner. I'd shoot the old devil, but what's the use? He's only one. Shall we go on now?"

With cold shivers running up and down their spinal columns, Mr. Jones and his companion stepped carefully back from the entrance to the giant spider's den, and entered a little path or trail which led windingly away through the lovely, treacherous forest. Jones, for one, heartily wished that their guardian would march in front instead of the rear. The death cabbages had been bad enough, but they had seemed such vast, unnatural prodigies that already his memory reproduced them dreamily.

That spider was another matter. He had heard of spiders as large as dinner plates, and shuddered at the thought of them. This spider had been as large as—well, judging from its forelegs it could better be compared with an extra large dining-table.

And Holloway had spoken of it as "only one." How many more such fiends lay hidden, waiting for the false tread of a foot, or the careless speed of some hunted jungle thing? He began to be careful indeed to look where he trod, and suspicious of even the supposedly harmless flowers and butterflies. Beauty becomes more horrible than frank ugliness when one has learned that death lurks behind it.

Fortunately, however, for their peace of mind they saw no more of the "fauna" of which Holloway had hinted, although once in skirting a dark morass they heard distant crashing sounds, as if some large beast were threshing about somewhere in the depths.

"This place is like a Broadway café," Holloway informed them. "Nothing much doing in the daytime—but oh you midnight suppers! Eat and be eaten, that's our motto after sunset."

"You seem to know a whole lot about the place," Jones ventured.

"Yes, indeed. Regular old homestead to little Willy. You see, I lived here for two years, and got real well acquainted with the inhabitants. Maybe we'll let you and your dear friend Prince Sergius try it, when it comes time for us to leave. You'd learn a whole lot you never knew before, believe me. That is, if you survived the first week or two."

Mr. Jones looked at him hopelessly. Was the man in earnest?

But Sergius laughed scornfully. "I should not particularly mind," he said, "so long as we were relieved of your company, Mr. Holloway."

"You don't say! How very rude and unkind you are, prince. But never mind. I'd be sore, too, if I were in your place, so I forgive you like a true Christian. And here we are, home at last, all safe and sound."

For the path, turning sharply, passed out of the jungle and into the full light of day. Half a mile away, across a broad expanse of green meadow, the rim of the crater raised its black height, hidden from them until now by the forest. To the right, in the distance, some unidentifiable animals were grazing, and ahead, close to the wall, a pillar of smoke was rising, almost white against its dead blackness.

"There's our camp. Keep right on going. Don't worry, they're expecting us."

That they were expected was presently evidenced, for the figure of a man appeared coming toward them across the meadow. In a few minutes

Jones was able to identify him, for it was Jim, Paul's cowboy retainer. He met them with a grin, which suddenly faded as he recognized Mr. Jones. He looked from him to Sergius and then back again.

"Well, of all the—snakes!" he exclaimed, and his hand dropped suggestively to his hip-pocket. "So that yarn of yours was just a string of whoppers, was it? By jiminy, I've a notion to drill you right now, you—you low-down horse-thief! Lettin' me get the notion that you was layin' smashed back there in the cave, and me mad as thunder because they wouldn't let me hike back to look for you. An' all the time you pikin' around with this here nihilanarchist bunch. Say, what kind of a low-down, lyin' cattle-rustler are you, anyhow?"

"Shut up, Jimmy," interrupted Holloway at last, although he had listened to the arraignment with a grin of pure enjoyment. "Rolly's nerves are all upset as it is. How is Prince Petrofsky?"

Jim's face relaxed again into a grin. "Doin' fine," he answered. "I know now why he brought that female woman along. Gee! I wouldn't mind sprainin' a leg or so to get nursed that luxurious."

"He'll get well for pure joy when he sees who's here. Forward the array! We'll be right behind you, gentlemen. Sorry the hotel bus wasn't running, so as to save your walking all this way, but you know what these summer resorts are."

His cheerful nonsense bored Jones wretchedly, as they went on toward the camp. What sort of a greeting were he and Sergius likely to get? Not a very pleasant one, judging from the sample offered by Haskins. He heartily wished that Sergius had stuck to his original intention of "a mere reconnaissance." They would have been back with the nihilists by this time, and at that moment the nihilist camp actually seemed like home to Mr. Jones.

What could there possibly be in the crater valley of sufficient value to make all these people so very anxious to reach it? Unless they were seeking the rather morbid pleasure of being killed and eaten, he could conceive of nothing liable to be there which would repay the extreme trouble and risk attendant upon obtaining it.

A gold mine? How could anybody work a gold mine in a place like this? Diamonds, perhaps? He himself would have cheerfully forfeited a full ownership in Tiffany's just to escape from the place.

He had never had any opportunity to question Sergius Petrofsky, and as that gentleman stalked along moodily by his side now he did not look in a good humor to answer such interrogations. Both men had long since removed their heavy coats and were carrying them, but even so their clothing was saturated with perspiration. Hot, weary, and disgusted, they neither of them looked, as they came into camp, as if they had been upon any pleasurable expedition.

A fire was snapping and crackling cheerfully in the cliff shadow, and about it lay scattered various paraphernalia, but no one was in sight.

"All in the cave," said Jim, in an explanatory tone. "Some cliff-dwellers, our bunch, ain't we, Holloway?"

"First-class apartments," corrected the other. "Dry, airy, cool, but dogs and children barred. Hey, there! Anybody home?"

At Holloway's hail a woman appeared in the entrance to one of a large number of the dark openings which perforated the crater wall. It was of course Margaret Weston.

"Oh, did you find them, Mr. Holloway? Why, who is that with the prince? Isn't that the man we lost in the caverns?"

"It sure is, ma'am," grinned the cowboy, not giving Holloway a chance to reply. "He ain't crushed none, not so you could notice it. I take off my hat to you, ma'am. You was dead right about the snake, but I was too plumb pigheaded to know it."

"That is all right, James," said the girl, smiling sweetly. "A woman's intuition is sometimes correct, after all, is it not? Prince Sergius," with a sudden severe formality, "your brother would like to see you as soon as it is convenient."

The nihilist bowed with a dignity equal to her own. His face was sternly set, but Jones, watching curiously, saw a look flash up into his eyes as they rested on the girl which confirmed the cowboy's statement in regard to his feeling toward her. He could hardly be blamed, either. Miss Weston looked a good deal more than attractive, standing there with one white, shapely arm extended to support herself on the precarious foothold of rocks at the cavern door. She looked very young, girlish and utterly out of place in that nightmare valley. Her smooth cheeks were slightly flushed, her scarlet lips were set just sufficiently to bring out their exquisite lines, and her big blue eyes were shining with some emotion, but one hardly favorable to Sergius, if Mr. Jones were any judge.

In fact, Miss Weston was angry, and Jones felt vaguely sorry for Sergius Petrofsky. He wondered again at the girl's ardent dislike for his friend.

"I am grateful to my brother," said Sergius slowly, "for sending such a charming messenger!"

"Thank you. But kindly reserve your compliments for some one who will better deserve and—appreciate them. Mr. Holloway, will you kindly accompany these gentlemen? The sailors are in the other cave, and I hardly think it safe for Prince Paul to receive them alone—"

Sergius flushed deeply. The thrust evidently went home.

"Certainly, Miss Weston," assented Holloway, with a smile of amusement. "But I was just going to start cooking supper."

"I am not myself such a bad cook as you seem to think," laughed the girl. "What use is a woman in camp if she can't do the nursing and cooking?"

"You're dead right, ma'am," commented Jim, but in a most respectful voice. Jones reflected sadly that even this woman-hater appeared to have been converted to admiration for the girl. Probably he regarded her diagnosis of his, Jones's, character as a symptom of most unusual wisdom.

"Go right in, gentlemen," commanded Holloway. "Here, Jim, will you take these rifles? And lend me your little popgun? Thanks. A rifle is no good at close quarters."

With a disdainful shrug Sergius turned his back on the voluble American and entered the cave, Mr. Jones close at his heels.

Chapter VIII.

TOMATO SOUP.

In one of the dark but cool chambers in the rock a rude couch of blankets had been laid. Beside it, upon a flat-topped stone, stood an electric lantern of the type which, using large batteries, will burn for eighty or ninety hours, and which illuminated the place quite brightly. Beside it a bottle of arnica and some carefully folded bandages were arranged.

Upon the couch lay Paul Petrofsky, the lower part of one leg swathed in more and beautifully adjusted bandages. As the two captives entered, however, he sat up and gave utterance to an exclamation of joy as he recognized his brother.

For the first time, seeing them together, Jones realized the strong resemblance between the two men. There were the same broad, intelligent brow, the same high-bridged symmetrical nose, the same thin-lipped, sensitive mouth, and pleasant, dark eyes. The only real difference between the two faces lay in the expression and in that slight inclination of Paul's chin to recede.

Sergius's eyes were keen as well as pleasant, his mouth was set in firmer lines, and his chin was of a squarish and very determined shape. Also, at time, his face wore a haughty and somewhat domineering look—a look which Paul's countenance never assumed.

If, knowing neither of them, Jones had been asked to choose, he would have unhesitatingly named Sergius as the supporter of aristocratic government, and Paul as the man to be easily led, particularly into any scheme, however wild, for the betterment of his fellow Russians.

"Sergius!" exclaimed the man on the couch. There was pure relief in his voice. "Then you are safe. I was afraid—".

"That some of your friend Holloway's pets had made a meal on your dear brother? I should not have thought that would have appeared to you as a great trouble, Paul."

His brother shook his head impatiently, with a slight frown.

"That is absurd, as you very well know. Because you have been misled by these murderous, bomb-throwing companions of yours is no reason for me to forget that you are my brother."

Sergius flushed and straightened himself.

"My companions are not bomb-throwers, and you very well know the difference between nihilism and the madness of anarchy, although you choose to pretend that there is none. You are in a position to say what you please to me, Paul, but you know my feelings on that subject and it seems hardly generous—"

"It is not a question of generosity, but of common sense," the other broke out. "Some day you will thank me for standing out against your fanatical views. Russia will never be saved by such mad dreamers as your so-called friends. It is I who truly serve Russia in her hour of need. How long, think you, will the war which is slaughtering our people continue after I turn over to the government the—that which we have come to seek?"

"Long enough, I hope, to destroy every member of the cruel beaurocracy which holds her in its bloody grip. Yes, it is your friends who are bloody, Paul, not mine."

"There is tyranny in every fixed government. Moreover, it is not the rulers of Russia who suffer most. It is the very peasantry which you profess to love so much. Turn your face from the mirage you are pursuing, my brother, and cast in your lot with us!"

"I will not desert my brothers," replied Sergius briefly, but with evident sincerity.

"Then," said Prince Paul with some firmness, "you will not be allowed to return to them either. Dick Holloway, I had hoped that after all I might persuade my brother—I have no *brothers*—to ally himself with us. Since he is not yet ready to do so, I must ask that you and James Haskins see to it that he remains in this camp. As for his companion, the spy, it would be no more than right if we should shoot him outright."

Jones started slightly. This amiable-looking Russian seemed to be even more arbitrary than his nihilist brother.

"Oh, I wouldn't go that far," counseled Holloway, with an amused grin. "I'll be responsible for it that he doesn't leave us so easily as he did before.

By the way, prince, I left the aeroplane where they landed. Do you want the thing brought into camp?"

"No, I think not," said Paul, after a moment's hesitation. "I fail to see how it could be of any use to us. If you or Jim chance to go that way again you might see to it that it is rendered useless for any one, however." He gave a significant glance in the direction of the plane's rightful owner.

Then he dropped back upon his couch with a little grimace of pain. "Sergius, will you remain here with me? I should very much like to hear of what befell when you descended into the valley. That is, if you don't mind telling me. Dick Holloway, please take this man Jones out with you and set him to work about the camp. We may as well make him useful since you are set on keeping him."

Holloway looked doubtfully at the two brothers. Sergius saw the look and laughed bitterly.

"You had better assure your friend, Paul, that I am unlikely to murder you in his absence. Also you are mistaken in regard to Mr. Jones's relations with me. I never met the gentleman until night before last, and we parted then because he managed to cut a hole in the side of his prison tent and escape. I will admit that I do now regard him as a friend, but that is because of his very excellent qualities. We are friends, however, and any treatment which you accord him I must beg you to offer me also."

He looked very haughty and dignified has he uttered these sentiments, and Mr. Jones's heart went out to him more than ever. The man had not only saved his life, but now he was defending him from undeserved oppression. Somehow, he determined, he would endeavor to repay Prince Sergius.

Paul shrugged his shoulders and smiled rather dubiously at his brother. "Of course, if you say he did not come to our camp as a spy I shall have to take your word. You are in a position to know if any one is. Holloway, we will have to treat the gentleman courteously, since my brother is determined to share his fate." He laughed. "I really don't care to make you wash dishes, Sergius."

Holloway and Mr. Jones went back to the camp fire, leaving the two brothers alone together. There was no exit to the cavern chamber, save that by which they had entered, and even Holloway did not really believe that the nihilist would harm his brother for mere revenge.

Jones longed to ask some questions in regard to this mysterious war which had been again hinted at, but he still suffered from a deep-seated dread of what the answer might reveal, and also of being regarded by these strangers as hopelessly feeble-minded.

"Let it wait. If I'm really crazy I'm bound to find it out soon enough," he thought bitterly.

In a short time supper was prepared, consisting of canned goods and the fresh meat of some animal, probably one of those creatures which still grazed quietly in the distant meadow. Jones, for one, was ravenously hungry. He had eaten nothing save the bowl of stew brought him by Doherty for thirty-six hours or more, and did full justice to Miss Weston's cooking, which was excellent. She explained this by saying that she had taken a course in domestic science to supplement a brief hospital training, preparatory to her work as a Red Cross nurse in the European battlefields.

The European battlefields! How much of Europe then was involved in this mad, chimerical war of theirs? Whoever the fighters might be, he felt that they had missed a very beautiful and determined young nurse when Miss Weston was side-tracked into this equally mad island affair. Mr. Jones was feeling more and more as if, having slept a single night, he had awakened into a new and entirely unfamiliar world.

Paul had managed to hobble out of his cavern retreat, supporting himself on the shoulder of his brother, and the whole party, including the two sailors, ate together without regard to caste or rank. Paul was glad to sit down at once, but Sergius first wandered about for a few moments, apparently inspecting the arrangements. Jones wondered if his reckless companion had designs on the rifles, three of which lay together close by; but if this were so he resigned them as impracticable, for presently he came and seated himself between Holloway and his brother.

As he did so he leaned across, behind Holloway's back, and whispered something to Jones, who had taken his place just beyond. Jones, however, did not catch the words, and he thought best not to attract the attention of the company by asking for a repetition.

The upper rim of the sun was just disappearing below the western wall as they finished, and only a few minutes later the sudden tropic night was upon them, with its wonderful stars and refreshing, fragrant breath of coolness.

It brought something more than coolness in its wake. It brought a rising wave of sound from the jungle beyond the open meadow. The valley of the day was no more, and the valley of night had swung wide its doors for all the creatures which crouched, awaiting the liberating touch of darkness.

The first intimation of this other valley, which none of the party save Holloway really knew, was a deep-throated roar from the jungle immediately opposite. This was followed by a sort of wild, bubbling shriek, as of a creature suffering from nightmare. The sound ended so abruptly that one

could only judge the shrieker to have been swallowed by the roarer. Next
there was a great snarling and yowling and crashing of branches, as if two
enormous tom-cats were engaged in a combat to the death. The noise of
battle was soon drowned out, however, by the full rising chorus of night
life, the separate notes of which all blended as into one mighty, discordant
cry, rising harshly toward the white, indifferent stars.

Only Holloway remained entirely unaffected by the uproar. Miss Weston, the intrepid, actually trembled and shrank toward the protecting shoulder of her Russian lover—that is, of the Russian lover she favored.

The two sailors sprang to their feet and looked longingly in the direction
of the caverns. Arizona Jim reached casually over and drew his rifle up beside
him. Sergius also gazed desirefully in the direction of the rifles, forbidden
to him and Jones, while the latter, shuddering inwardly, remembered that
they had actually walked through the midst of all *that* only a couple of hours
ago.

"Some opera, isn't it?" remarked Holloway, with an amused glance about
the little circle of white faces. "When I first came here I used to lie all night
and shiver and shake and try to make up sleep in the daytime. I had a gun, but
only a little ammunition, you know. I found that a good-sized fire would
keep all but the really big fellows away, though, so I got in the habit of
building one in front of a small cave and sleeping behind it. If a little fellow
came along, he was afraid of the fire. A big one couldn't get in the cave.
Great Scott! For a while after I got taken off the island I couldn't sleep at
all. Missed the noise, you see."

"Great Heaven! What was that?"

The whole party, except Holloway, sprang to their feet and stared wildly
into the air. Something huge, black, monstrous had flapped out of the darkness and into it again, passing so close that the wind of its flight scattered
burning brands right and left from the fire.

"Guess we'd better be going to bed," said Holloway, rising but with no
undue haste. "I don't know exactly what those things are, because I've never
caught a glimpse of the brutes by daylight, but the fire really seems to attract
them instead of keeping them away. Once one of 'em made a grab at me
in passing. Made a nasty gash on my cheek. I just dodged into my little
boudoir in time."

"It looked like a—like a great, impossible bat," cried Margaret Weston,
and there was a hysterical note in her voice. "Oh, why was I brought to this
frightful place? Why did we not retire into the caverns before sunset, as we
did last night?"

"Poor little girl," said Paul Petrofsky gently. "I never would have brought you here, if there had been any other way. Come. You shall sleep to-night on that nice, soft couch you prepared for me, Miss Margaret, and Dick Holloway and I will sleep in the cave entrance. Nothing shall come near you that can harm."

"There's really no need for you to be frightened," interrupted Holloway in a more serious and considerate tone than one usually heard from his lips. "There are five men of us, at least, who are well-armed, and any one of us would die before we would let harm come to the only girl in Joker Island."

Sergius bit his lip, but said nothing. By his "five men" the American had carefully left him and Mr. Jones out of the number of Miss Weston's protectors.

"You and Rolly," continued Holloway, addressing the nihilist, "can sleep in Room 5, Suite A. Here it is, and here's a torch. Be sparing with it, for we haven't many more batteries."

He pointed out the cave which he humorously dignified with the title of "Room 5." "Jimmy boy will be right at your door in case you want anything in the night," he added significantly.

The prisoners entered, Sergius leading the way with the torch. They found it to be a small but dry cavern, and as they spread down their heavy coats to sleep on, it seemed as decent a bedroom as could be expected. It also formed a very efficient jail, since, like the other where Paul had lain, it had but the one exit, and that way led past the presumably wakeful Jim Haskins.

At least he had enough to keep him awake in listening to the wild night chorus of Joker Island and keeping his little fire going at the entrance.

For a time the two companions in misfortune lay silent, listening to the uproar which was somewhat muffled by the rocky walls about them. It was Jones who spoke first, voicing a question which had been all along in his mind.

"Prince Sergius," he said, "what on earth are you and the rest of them after in this place? I mean, why did Holloway want to come back, and why did he persuade your brother to fit out a yacht and come after him, and why did you—" He paused suddenly, wondering just how sensitive the prince was on that subject.

But his companion laughed softly in the darkness.

"That American—that Jim—he did not tell you everything, eh?"

"I think he told me all he knew. But of course, if you don't want to trust me, just say so. I'm only curious, that's all."

"But I do trust you." Sergius reached over, caught Jones's hand, gripped it hard, and then dropped it as suddenly. "Really—do not laugh—you are the only friend I have within two thousand miles at least. Those men of mine? They are of the rough peasant type whom I pity but cannot love. My Captain Ivanovitch? He is—well, to be frank, I do not like him. He has not the least refinement. My brother? Ah, yes, I love him, but we are not friends—not now. He is my elder, the head of my house since our father died.

"Paul was educated in America, and our father sent me to Oxford, for he was a man of broad, splendid ideas. He thought thus we two should share the education of two continents, but instead it was so we grew apart. At Oxford I met other Russians, thinking men, one of whom—alas, he is now in Siberia—changed the whole course of my life. But I cannot now tell you of all that. Paul, in your free America, clung still to the old, I call them the cruel and tyrannous, ideals.

"But you I liked, even when I thought you were that beast, Richard Holloway. It is true that I threatened you, but then I was angry, because I wished you to do something reasonable and you would not. But when we met again and I asked you to come with me into this place of hell, you did not even hesitate. You came like an old friend—a comrade."

"But you saved my life afterward, prince," said Jones, amazed at this tribute and the evidently sincere feeling which lay behind it. "I am in your debt for that and for standing up for me to your brother."

"And why not? Comrades must not desert one another. And I do not like to be named prince. Such titles stand for all I most abhor. Call me Sergius and I will call you Roland, as friends should. Tell me, would you go yet further and accompany me upon a greater adventure than any of these dogs that hold us dare attempt?"

"What do you mean?" asked Mr. Jones, somewhat startled.

"I mean," the other replied, lowering his voice to a whisper, "that tomorrow they will destroy our only means of escape—the aeroplane. Tonight it still stands there, safe unless some night-devil has trampled it. In half an hour we could be on board the Monterey. Is it not worth some risk to attain that? And we could return, but next time we would not be trapped so easily. We would be upon our guard."

"Good Lord," groaned Mr. Jones. "What you propose is impossible, prince—I mean, Sergius. We should be killed before we had gone fifty yards into that nightmare out there."

"You hesitate? But I have not yet answered your question. Listen. In this island—this island which contains so many strange and unaccountable surprises—in its soil is a substance more valuable a thousand times than gold."

"Radium?" hazarded Mr. Jones.

"Radium—bah! No, it is a strange, secret substance, which for ages has been sought by science until it has been termed a vision of fools and madmen." He lowered his voice yet more. "It is that which was once named the Philosopher's Stone—and it will change the nature of what have been called the elements. My friend, this substance will transmute common lead to gold!"

"Oh, is that all?" sighed Mr. Jones. "I thought it was probably something about gold, but believe me, it isn't worth it, prince—it really isn't."

Sergius sat up, and Jones knew that he was staring at him in amazement.

"You are a very strange man, my friend. Has gold no temptation for you?"

"Not a bit—not that sort of gold, anyway. Do you realize that if this mythical stuff of Holloway's proves what he has claimed to you people, it will upset the financial systems of the entire world, and become itself of no more value than—than mud?"

"Not at all. Do you think we would be so mad as to flood the world with gold? No, we will give out that we have discovered a very valuable mine and we will only release it in such quantities as may prove judicious. For myself, I desire it only for the cause. Russia shall be freed from herself and become a blazing lamp of liberty to enlighten the whole world. Paul, he desires only to help the government in overcoming the Germans. I desire to make the Germans my brothers."

So, it was really Germany that Russia was fighting! It all seemed very strange. If it had been England, now—

"As for this Holloway," continued Sergius, "who discovered it, he thinks only of himself. He says he wants to be a 'captain of industry.'"

"But why didn't he bring some of the stuff away with him in the first place?"

"He could carry only a little, and that was used up in demonstrating to us its value. But there is a great deal more here—the whole soil is impregnated with it, and he discovered it by the chance of a leaden bullet falling into the fire. The heat melted the bullet and it sank to the earth beneath. And in the morning, when he swept away the ashes from before his cave, there lay a splash of gold upon the ground. He is a bright man, this Richard Holloway, and after thought he experimented with another bullet."

"Yes, he would," sighed Mr. Jones. In spite of Sergius's assurance, the effect on himself and all his friends, if this improbable tale proved true, was staggering to contemplate. "Now I know why I dislike the man so much. Isn't the air in here frightfully stuffy? I can hardly keep my eyes open."

"A little smoke from the fire at the entrance perhaps. Or—my friend, do not tell me that you ignored the warning I gave you!"

"Warning? What warning?" Jones felt himself growing drowsier and drowsier. He wished Sergius would shut up and let him sleep.

He realized that some one was shaking him vigorously. "The soup—the tomato soup! Tell me, surely you did not eat of it?"

"Yes—sure. Good soup. Mighty nice soup—nice girl—too—"

His voice dwindled away. He was drifting comfortably off upon a sea of the softest down. Then something hard, unpleasant, was thrusting itself against his teeth. His mouth filled with fire—liquid fire. Coughing, strangling, he sat up and recovered sufficiently to push his companion's hand away from his mouth.

"Wha'—wha' you tryin' to do?" he asked hoarsely. His throat and lips felt stiff and numb.

"Trying to revive you, my friend. Here, drink some more of this."

"No. 'S horrid stuff. Take—away."

"Drink. You must."

Again something was forced against his teeth in the dark, and his mouth was flooded with the fiery liquid.

It *was* "horrid stuff," but it was effective. Jones felt the numbness going out of his vocal organs, and his brain cleared.

"What's the matter with me?" he gasped. "Have I been poisoned?"

"No, no. Just a harmless drug, but it would have been disastrous had you succumbed to it, though I pray Heaven the rest have done so. I warned you not to touch that soup. Why did you do it?"

"Was that what you whispered to me? I didn't understand. But do you mean to tell me that you have—that you have—"

"I've put them all to sleep, that's all. The stuff is a perfectly harmless soporific, but it tastes a little, and that is why I put it in the highly seasoned soup, which all would be most likely to eat. But it is fortunate I had with me also the antidote, or my plan would have surely reacted upon myself, for I would not leave you here to meet their anger."

Jones staggered to his feet.

"I can't say I like the idea, my friend, but I suppose from your point of view you were justified. What are we to do now?"

"Get back to the aeroplane. It is useless for us to attempt the cavern without a guide, and even if I could awaken Holloway, I doubt if he could be induced to help us."

"You would leave them here—in a drugged sleep—defenceless? Why man, what are you thinking of? It would be worse than murder! And the girl, too. Why, the idea is criminal!"

"For what sort of devil do you mistake me, Roland Jones? No, I have thought of everything. We will place them all in the cavern chamber where Miss Weston now lies. Then we will block up the entrance with large stones, build before it a great fire, and they will certainly be as safe until morning as anyone can be in this perilous place."

"I see. Well; perhaps it could be done. But first, hadn't we better find out if every one is really asleep?"

CHAPTER IX.

ABDUCTION.

Having first lighted the electric torch, the two men crept stealthily through the narrow passage. In the doorway the fire had burned low, and beside it lay sprawled the figure of Jim Haskins. The nihilist stooped over him and felt cautiously of his heart. Then he straightened himself. "All right," he murmured, and they passed on out. At each of the two other inhabited caves they made a similar examination, and in every case Sergius's little dose had done its work. Every one of their captors lay helpless.

"Let us begin with Paul," said Sergius, in his natural voice, since no need of caution seemed to now exist. But he received an unexpected reply. There was a sudden rustling, a sound of footsteps, and there behind Paul's outstretched form appeared a slender figure.

"You here!" exclaimed Miss Weston. "What have you done to Paul? Have you killed him? Oh, you—you anarchist!"

She dropped on her knees and felt anxiously for Paul's heart.

"My dear Miss Weston, certainly I have not killed my brother." Sergius's voice showed not the slightest agitation at this discovery by the girl he so much admired. "He is only asleep. They are all asleep. We grew tired of seeing so many people asleep, and we are therefore about to leave."

She sprang up and faced him with flushed cheeks and blazing eyes.

"You have drugged them all! How did you accomplish this dastardly thing?"

"The tomato soup, Miss Weston. You did not eat of it?"

"Of course not. I detest canned tomato soup. Well, I—I hope you are proud of yourself. I hope—I hope something will *eat* you! So, you were going away, leaving your brother and all of us to be killed, were you?"

"By no means. We were just about to provide against that little contingency. But your being awake alters matters."

"Oh, does it? Perhaps you are ashamed of your work, now that a woman has seen you at it?"

"Not at all. But on the other hand, I cannot leave you here, awake, to be terrorized all night. Asleep, it would not have mattered. When you awoke it would have been daylight and the others would have also awakened with you. Mr. Jones, the aeroplane will easily carry three passengers. We will have to take Miss Weston with us."

"Oh, I say," protested Jones, "do you think that is really necessary?"

"But yes. She will be far safer on the Monterey than here, under any circumstances. You need not fear me, Miss Weston. I am a gentleman and Paul's brother. Later, when we have settled our differences, you may return to his side, if that is your choice."

He looked at her a trifle appealingly, but she flung back her head defiantly.

"You dare!" she stormed. "I will not go a step and leave *my friends* to be devoured."

Sergius took one stride across the body of his brother and seized the young lady in his arms, holding her firmly, but as gently as he could. She did not scream, but she fought desperately, and with an amazing strength.

Jones's gorge rose at the sight. This was going much too far. He sprang forward and seized his companion by the shoulder.

"Here, this won't do," he exclaimed. "You can't force the young lady in that way, Sergius."

The Russian turned a disgusted face to him and said over his shoulder, "Do you prefer to leave her here to be frightened into insanity? Is that your idea of chivalry?"

"Let me go—let me go!" cried Miss Weston, beating fiercely at him with her hands.

And just at that moment something black, monstrous, hideous shot down upon them out of the blackness beyond the fires. There was a harsh, grating scream, and the shoulder of a giant wing struck Jones, knocking him down, and grazed the rock wall. He was involved in a swirl of beating, struggling pinions, there were two more screams, one human, the other quite the opposite, and the thing, whatever it was, was gone.

Jones picked himself up, bruised and trembling from head to foot. The girl lay limp in Sergius's arms, her face white, arms and head hanging. Sergius himself was pale as a ghost, but he had not moved from his position.

"I don't know what it was, Roland Jones," he said with a rather stiff-lipped smile, "but do you still think we ought to leave her here?"

"Great Heavens, how can we take her? How can we go ourselves? Sergius Petrofsky, I believe that you have gone mad!"

"Not quite," said the prince patiently. "We have the rifles and the electric torches, and I really believe we can make the trip safely. I have myself passed through an African jungle in the same way, and never received a scratch. We will carry Miss Weston as far as the outer edge of the meadow, then we will revive her and go on. Later we will open negotiations with my brother—he will not then have so much advantage—and Miss Weston, for whom I have great reverence and respect, will be far safer on the Monterey. Come! In the midst of so many perils, the boldest course is best. You say that I saved your life. It was a very ordinary deed, but for this one night let me claim your gratitude!"

Jones was in a quandary. His innate chivalry revolted at the idea of forcing a woman into accompanying them, yet the arguments of Sergius seemed very plausible. And he loved this daring, fanatical, imperious new friend of his as he had never loved any man in his life before.

"All right. I'll do it. But afterward Miss Weston is to be free to return here if she chooses."

"Very well, if you wish it. I give my word."

With no more talk they hastily dragged the insensible members of the party into the selected cavern, and with considerable labor blocked up the entrance. In the morning the imprisoned ones could easily pull it down from within. Then they gathered all the fuel together and made one enormous bonfire, that leaped and roared skyward. Some of the logs were of very satisfactory size, and they felt sure the fire would burn for some hours. It was then nearly midnight and dawn would break shortly after three.

While they worked Jones found himself casting many apprehensive glances upward, but the flying monster did not return and they completed their task unmolested. Miss Weston, fortunately or otherwise, had not awakened from her swoon.

Their own two rifles and amunition belts, together with an automatic pistol and cartridge clips belonging to Prince Paul, and a heavy, old-fashioned .44 revolver looted from Jim Haskins, they had kept outside the cavern, together with two of the most powerful electric torches.

With one last anxious glance skyward, Mr. Jones picked up the two rifles, both torches and their heavy coats, which he was to carry until they reached the place where Sergius's remarkable scheme involved reviving the fainting lady. Sergius himself carefully raised his scornful idol in two muscular arms, and so burdened they started out across the meadow.

How they were to find their way along that thread-like trail, between the hidden dens of impossibly large spiders and past the other roaring, screaming, bellowing natives of Joker Island, remained to be shown.

Chapter X.

THE ADVENTURER PROVES EFFICIENT.

They had reached the first of the scattered outer-sentinels of the forest of slender palms. Dimly beyond it, by grace of the tropic star brilliance, they could see the looming mass which they must penetrate to reach the aeroplane.

So far they had met with nothing alarming. Everywhere, in and out, giant fireflies danced in a mystic saraband, very beautiful to behold, but also quite confusing to the eye. They had not yet used their torches, fearing to attract more of the terrible flying monsters, of which they had already seen quite enough to satisfy any morbid curiosity they might have felt.

"Here," whispered the prince, although he could almost have shouted without fear of being overheard above the general uproar, "we must awaken Miss Weston."

Jones saw his dark form bending over at the foot of the slender tree, and knew that he had laid his burden down.

"Shall I light up?" inquired Jones in an equally low tone, and speaking close to his companion's ear.

"On no account. Not yet, that is. Will you hold up her head, please? That is right. Now—this liquor would well-nigh rouse life in the dusty veins of an Egyptian mummy."

"If it's the same you gave me, you're right. Look out—there's something behind you—*look out*, I say!"

Over Sergius's shoulder he had caught a glimpse of two green eyes glaring, balls of fire set in the black velvet of night. Sergius, with the swiftness of a prestidigitateur, replaced the stopper in the small flask he had been holding to Miss Weston's lips, reached with unerring grasp for one of the rifles laid across Jones's lap, rose from knees to feet in the same motion and—laughed softly and lowered the weapon. Stooping, he picked up a small stone and flung it straight at the glaring eyes. There was a startled snarl, a fiendish yell, and the eyes vanished, accompanied by a scuffling and crashing in the underbrush.

"A hyena," commented Sergius, resuming his interrupted task with unruffled composure. "No use wasting a shot on that sort of vermin."

"Good Heavens, man, have you the eyes of a cat? How could you tell what it was?"

"Oh, I can see better than most in the dark, I will admit. I should never have suggested this venture if it were not so. Now—ah, she is awakening."

There was a cough, a little, strangled gasp, and Miss Weston sat up very suddenly. Unlike more ordinary people, she did not exclaim "Where am

I?" although the query would certainly have been excusable, but seemed to spring instantly to full consciousness and knowledge of the situation.

Without a moment's hesitation, she reached up in the darkness and delivered a slap in Sergius's general direction which would have been splendidly effective had he not sprung back with the same speed he had shown in dealing with the hyena. A second later she was on her feet, panting and sobbing, but not, Jones feared, with panic.

"Oh, you did it—you did it! You cowards! You left them there and carried me away when I was helpless. Oh—if I live till morning you shall be punished for this. You shall, I say!"

Gently, but with irresistible strength, Sergius took her small hands in one of his, and placed the other over her mouth.

"Be silent," he said softly and sternly. "You must not endanger your own life because of your anger against me. Paul and the rest are a thousand times more secure at this moment than we, unless you control yourself and use your splendid vigor and determination to a better purpose than recrimination. If I release my hold, will you come with us quietly and softly?"

A miracle occurred, for Miss Weston yielded—on that one point, at least. She must have nodded her head, although Jones could not see the motion in the darkness, for Sergius released her and stepped back.

"Do not imagine that you have greater concern for my brother than I, Miss Weston. We placed them all in safety, barricaded the entrance, and built a fire which will burn until morning. And now, you will please keep between Mr. Jones and myself. If we run, you must run also; and if we should crouch suddenly down, you must do likewise. Do you understand?"

"I understand," came the answer in a tone of suppressed rebellion.

"Very well. Will you give me one of those torches, Roland? You have your rifle ready and cocked?"

"Yes—but I'm a darned bad shot."

The nihilist sighed. "One cannot expect everything," he said: "If I tell you to shoot, aim between the eyes—you are likely to see them, at any rate. And now, forward!"

Two long, white beams sprang into being, and by the shifting rays Mr. Jones saw the narrow, trodden trail from which they had emerged in the afternoon. More than ever he marveled at Sergius's almost supernatural abilities. How had he managed to strike that one single place where they had a bare chance of entering the jungle successfully?

The Russian led the way, followed by Miss Weston, and Jones brought up the rear. And now they had entered the very center of pandemonium itself. Roars, shrieks, grunts, bellows rent the air upon every side.

"Don't be frightened!" Sergius called back over his shoulder. "These torches will keep most of the brutes off—but, good God, not *this* one!"

Jones caught a glimpse of a mighty bulk rearing itself high over the head of their leader; there were three sharp, rapid reports; then the thing, whatever it was, with a terrific snarl of rage, had lurched forward and downward upon the unfortunate nihilist. Miss Weston, with remarkable presence of mind, had turned, run back to Jones's side, and then turned again to face this midnight terror, without a scream or act which could have impeded her sole remaining guardian.

He, staring with horror down his little, wavering beam of light, saw only a monstrous black head with snarling, savage jaws and two red eyes that glared like coals of fire.

"Shoot him—shoot him!" It was Miss Weston's voice, and she was shaking his arm viciously. "Shoot him—or give me that rifle!"

"Between the eyes!" gasped Jones. " 'You're likely to see them!' "

He had no idea of what he was saying, or that he had spoken. Then, as he stood there, shaking in every limb, he suddenly reached the extremity of terror, and passed beyond it into that unnatural coolness and calm which is so efficient and, sometimes, so hard to reach. The trembling palsy passed, and every nerve and muscle tautened to abnormal firmness. From numbed quiescence his brain leaped to lightning action.

He knew what he, "a darned bad shot," must do if he would save the friend who lay invisible somewhere under that dreadful head.

With a sure swiftness of which none of his acquaintances would have deemed Jones capable, he handed the electric torch to the girl, darted forward to within ten feet of the monster, raised his rifle and fired, aiming at the center of the forehead, and pumping one cartridge after another into place as fast as he could work the level.

Undoubtedly the fact that the brute had paused at all in its attack was due to the dazzling effect of the electric torch, and if it had not been for an unusual piece of luck Jones would probably never have lived to marvel at his own feat. For at the first report the light-blinded brute snarled again, started to lift itself, failed, drooped, and sank slowly down upon the path. Jones, however, emptied his magazine before he realized that he had actually killed the creature with that first fortunate bullet.

Then he called back masterfully to the girl: "Come quick, Miss Weston; we've got to pull it off from Sergius!"

She ran up, still bearing the light, and the two looked down in consternation at the mighty bulk which lay like a monstrous black tombstone over the body of Sergius Petrofsky. It was a great, hairless mountain of flesh. The dropped head looked like the face of some gargoyle carven in unpolished ebony. Its fore legs were invisible, doubled under the body. Move it? They might as well have tried to move an elephant.

Nevertheless, catching hold of the upstanding, rounded ears, they tugged and heaved with all their might, but could only succeed in shifting the head a little to one side.

"Sergius! Sergius!" cried Miss Weston, dropping suddenly in a little heap of pathos beside that mountain of brute flesh.

She was answered by a moan. To their amazement, it did not come from beneath the monster, but from some little distance to one side of the path. Yet it was certainly a human moan, for it was followed by a voice: "Over here. I'm—I'm coming."

Miss Weston sprang to her feet and accompanied Jones in a wild rush toward the voice. There, sprawled out among the flowering, tangled vines, they found the nihilist himself; and as the circle of light struck his face, he sat and stared back at them with an amazement equal to their own.

"What—what hit me?" he gasped.

Jones laughed aloud in his relief. "*It* did. How in the name of all the saints did you get here?"

Sergius passed a bewildered hand over his head. "I—I begin to remember. Something seemed to come right up out of the ground. I—I fired at it—and then—and then—"

"It must have struck you with its paw and knocked you clear away from the path," interrupted Miss Weston in a calm, indifferent voice. Jones glanced at her in astonishment. Was this the girl who had been sobbing out the name of Sergius a few minutes before? "If you are hurt, you had better get up and go on with us—although I would suggest that you let Mr. Jones take the lead, as he seems much the better shot."

Jones helped his friend to rise, and as he did so Sergius laughed without a trace of annoyance. "If you actually killed that brute, my friend, Miss Weston is right. Did you kill it?"

"I must have, because it's certainly dead, although I can hardly believe it myself. What on earth is the thing, Sergius?"

They had recovered the narrow path and stood beside the black hulk which blocked it entirely, overlapping on both sides into the underbrush.

Sergius examined the huge head with interest. "I never saw anything exactly like it before. Where did you hit it?"

"Between the eyes. You remember you told me to fire between the eyes, so I did. I fired about ten cartridges into it, but I think it died at the first shot."

The nihilist looked up at him with a curious expression. "It did? That's rather odd. The beast has a frontal bone as thick as a rhinoceros's, if I am any judge. No; here are three bullets embedded in the bone, but not a sign of a hole. Ah, that was it, eh? My friend, by very well-deserved good luck your first bullet did not strike the forehead at all, but penetrated this left eye and went straight into the brain."

"Great Scot!" exclaimed the American. "And I was about ten feet away! It's a good thing the brute has a head as big as a barn-door, or I'd have missed it entirely."

Sergius smiled. "Nevertheless, you deserve great congratulations. If your first bullet had not gone a few inches astray, we should perhaps none of us be alive at this moment. But what a strange brute it is! I should say it was a monstrous bear, from the shape of the head, if it were not so hairless. I wonder, now, if this is the creature that pulled up the death cabbages there by the plane?"

"Prince Sergius," again interrupted Miss Weston, with a slightly impatient note in her voice, "would it not be better to come back in daylight to continue your zoological researches? If this creature has a mate, and it should come this way, Mr. Jones might not be able to kill the second one."

"And you are quite sure, after what has happened, that as a protector I am an entire failure, eh? Well, perhaps you are justified, but still I had better continue to lead the way. What do you think, Roland Jones?"

"Don't be absurd. I'm a rank, bungling amateur, and you both know it. Shall we climb over this thing, or go around it?"

"The underbrush is thick here—and there might be snakes, though we have seen none. I think we had better use your victim as a causeway."

The two men helped Miss Weston up to the gigantic shoulders, and they walked the length of the huge creature, more and more amazed at its bulk. From nose to hind quarters it must have measured a full fifteen feet, and in his heart Jones wished that he might have transported the head to his rooms in New York. How he could have gloated over the surprise of a friend of his who was a big game-hunter and very proud of certain rhino-heads and lion-skins, trophies of African expeditions.

He reloaded his rifle carefully and resumed his position as rear-guard with a new confidence in its powers which took no heed to the fact that only by a lucky accident had his shot struck a vulnerable spot.

Many times as they marched silently ahead, the underbrush by the wayside swayed and bent, crackling, to the passage of animals of which they caught not even a glimpse. Once a lynxlike beast as big as a large panther dropped silently into the middle of the path ahead of them, glared for a second into the bull's-eye of Sergius, and with another spring was gone before he could fire at it.

This incident, however, encouraged the three, for it seemed as if most of the jungle inhabitants shunned the blinding electric lights as they would have shunned a camp-fire.

And at length there came to their nostrils a whiff of noxious odor which told the two men that they had successfully passed the first barriers to their escape. Vile smell though it was, it came welcome enough just then, for it was the odor of the fungi that grew about the roots of the death cabbages.

Jones realized with pleasure that they had passed the great spider's trap without even being aware of it. He had subconsciously dreaded more than anything also going past that dark incline, at the foot of which waited the thing of long, black, shining legs and protuberant eyes.

But as the full force of the stench enveloped them, Miss Weston stopped dead, so that Jones almost collided with her in the narrow path.

"Stop—I can't go on into this—this horrible vapor!" she called after Sergius. He heard, for he turned back immediately and returned to where they stood.

"What is the matter?" he asked a trifle impatiently.

"This dreadful smell. I can't—"

"Miss Weston, a smell won't kill anybody. At least, this one will not. Mr. Jones and myself were in the midst of it for nearly an hour, and we were not harmed."

"But—"

"Do you wish to be left here, then?"

The question was brutal, but it served its purpose. A moment the girl was silent; then she threw back her shoulders and smiled contemptuously. "I presume you would not hesitate to do that, either. No, I will not oblige you by relieving you of my hampering company. I can certainly face anything that you can.

Sergius looked at her with plain admiration on his face.

"Believe me, Miss Weston, this charnel odor is no worse than that of the battle-fields to which you were going. I have been there, also. Will you take my arm now? For we must walk through a very disagreeable place."

"No, thank you!" she—well, she snapped, although it isn't a nice thing to say of a heroine. "I am sure Mr. Jones will offer all the help I may need."

"Very well." The prince shrugged, and without more ado they passed from the forest of slender palms into the safe way, broken, perhaps, by the very creature which they had encountered and ungratefully slain that night.

Chapter XI.

A DANGEROUS MOMENT.

As the three staggered out, one after another, from the acid-fumed fungi onto the wiry grass of the central space, their ears were rent by a sound of hideous and continued screaming which drowned out all other noise entirely. Startled and shuddering, both Sergius and Jones directed the rays of their lanterns toward the sound, and a most extraordinary picture leaped into view.

The scene of the tragedy was one of the larger death-cabbages. Its seventy-five-foot leaves were spread almost flat, and all the inner tentacles were writhing and squirming upward, so that at first glance it looked as if this vegetable flesh-eater were all on fire with slim, scarlet flames. Then, as they moved their search-lights upward, they saw what it was that screamed.

Clinging with huge claws to the upper stalk, just below the tuft, was a dark, winged thing, and all about its body and head the tentacles were wound and fastened. So wide were its frantically beating wings that even where they stood, a hundred yards away, the wind of them struck their faces in heavy gusts. The stalk swayed and bent under the strain, but the tentacles had firm hold, and continually new scarlet cords shot upward to aid in the binding of the captive, until its body was no more than a bundle of flaming red.

The screaming grew weaker; the wings fluttered spasmodically for a few moments longer, then drooped down helpless. The tentacles took hold upon them, also. Into the field of light a pointed, serrated thing rose slowly, followed by others upon all sides. The death cabbage was closing its doors to feast in sacred privacy.

A moment later the vision of trapped prey was shut from their eyes.

With a long, shuddering sigh, Sergius turned his own light slowly about the grim ranks encircling the glade. Everywhere it fell upon spread leaves and living, ready tentacles. Only one or two other of the cabbages were closed. Doubtless their dinner had come to them earlier in the evening.

"What are they? What is this place you have brought me to?"

It was Miss Weston. Both men turned to her with a guilty start, realizing that in their fascinated absorption they had for the time forgotten her.

"I am so sorry," apologized Sergius, as if he and Jones had invented the vegetable horrors, as her tone implied.

"It is like—it is like a circle from Dante's Inferno!" exclaimed Jones, laying his hand pityingly on the girl's arm, and wishing with all his heart that he had never acceded to Sergius's wishes—that they had left the girl at the caves, or stayed there themselves. What might not the effect of having witnessed such a scene be upon the mind of a delicate, high-strung woman?

But she drew slightly away, and spoke again to the Russian. From first to last she gave Mr. Jones no more attention than one grants to a supernumerary—a necessary adjunct to the play, but scarcely of more human interest than the furniture.

"You are sorry!" she repeated scornfully. "Your sorrow is rather late, it appears. Where is the aeroplane?"

The nihilist bowed gallantly to her contemptuous tone.

"As usual, Miss Weston, you speak directly to the point. The aeroplane is—why, where in the name of Heaven is it?"

For his light, flashing up the glade, encountered only empty space. The aeroplane, which they had left not far from where they now stood, had disappeared.

Jones felt his heart begin a slow, systematic descent toward his toes. If the machine were actually gone, what would they do? Then he gave a joyful cry as his own light, dancing spritelike over the grass, flashed upon something broad-winged and motionless over near the wilted death-cabbage which had so nearly made a meal of him and Sergius.

"There it is! It's all right! It's there!"

"Thank God!" breathed Miss Weston, again frightened momentarily out of her attitude of disdainful indifference.

"But how did it get there?" frowned Sergius. "Miss Weston, you must not go so near as that to the—cabbages. Will you wait here with Mr. Jones, while I go after the plane?"

"I will not," she replied instantly. "We will either all go, or none of us will go, whichever you please. Oh, I'm not troubled for your safety, Prince Sergius. Don't imagine that. But if you should be killed or injured, who is to pilot the plane?"

"I am overwhelmed by your solicitude for me," murmured Sergius, bowing again. "If you must go, keep behind us. Here, take this light and one of the rifles. Yes, please, I want my hands free. Come on, then."

He set off at a swinging stride, followed by Jones and Miss Weston, who looked pale by the reflected light of her lantern, but very determined indeed.

The plane, they found, was fairly in the midst of the many-colored fungi. But worse, and more important, it was quite near to a thirty-foot vegetable which, they had just had good testimony, would make no more than a good meal on all three of them. In fact, as they approached, it seemed to sense them, and stretched out a dozen hungry tentacles in their direction. Two or three of these, feeling blindly, encountered a rear strut of the aeroplane and curled about it. Then the tentacles contracted suddenly, and the aeroplane rolled backward an inch or so.

"*That* won't do," cried the nihilist, and seizing a forward strut he braced himself and pulled, but with no apparent effect. More tentacles reached toward him as he stood there, but he was partly shielded from them by the plane itself.

To his credit be it said that Mr. Jones, without an instant's hesitation, dropped his rifle, handed his torch to Miss Weston, and springing to Sergius's side flung his weight also into the tug-of-war. But it was evident that the strength of the vegetable was greater than their combined efforts. The utmost they could do was to hold the machine where it was.

After several muscle and nerve-straining minutes, the nihilist said to Jones in a low voice, not to be overheard by the girl, "My friend, there is only one thing to be done and that is creep back there, over the tail, and cut some of those tentacles."

"Impossible! Why, the others would get you in a second."

"I don't care if they do. I will cut them also. They are strong, but a knife goes through them easily. Do you not remember yesterday afternoon? Miss Weston, will you keep both lights trained on the rear of the plane for a few moments, please? I am going to try something."

"I won't let you do it—" began Jones, but with a spring Sergius had mounted upon the plane and was working his way toward the rear.

The withdrawal of his strength was accompanied by a surge of the aeroplane backward, and Jones had to use all his muscle and attention to keep it in place. Sergius was now out of his sight, but by a sudden swaying and jolting and a scream from Margaret Weston, he knew that his too-daring companion must have been found by one or more of the questing tentacles.

The machine swayed again violently, then he heard Sergius's voice.

"Hold those lights steady, Miss Weston. Ah! two at once. Roland, we needn't have been so worried—one might as well be afraid of a stick of celery. You devil! Would you?"

There was a strangled, gasping sound, another scream from the girl, then the Russian's voice again, somewhat hoarser but still cheerful. "He almost got me that time—but not twice! That is right. Send me a few more feelers—Pull! Pull, Jones, with all your force!"

Jones obeyed with the strength of desperation, as a sudden lightening in the weight and a renewed swaying told him that Sergius had jumped to the ground. Slowly at first, then with gathering ease and speed the plane moved. In a minute it was out of the fungi and rolling clear upon the turf.

The second that he dared, Jones let go and ran around to the rear. To his great relief there was his nihilist friend, leaning against a strut and wiping his forehead. Miss Weston joined them with the lights, and they all stared at one another in silence.

Then Sergius dropped his handkerchief, and brought his hand down upon his thigh with a resounding slap.

"What a fool I am!" he exclaimed. "What an utter fool! All I had to do was to climb into the pilot's seat and start the propeller. Even that brute could hardly have outpulled the engine. And my neck would have been saved a very unpleasant experience." He felt of it tenderly, then laughed.

"Well, it is over now. Some inquisitive beast must have come by here and given the plane a push, so that it rolled down that little incline."

He began a careful examination of wires, struts, taut varnished canvas, propeller blades and last, and most important, the engine itself and its tank. In a few minutes now their very lives might depend upon the thoroughness of that examination.

"I can find nothing wrong," he said at last, and his announcement was greeted with an involuntary sigh of relief from both his companions.

"Miss Weston," he continued," I think you and Mr. Jones can manage to occupy that seat together. At any rate, in a few minutes we will be out of this intolerable odor. Here, Miss Weston, put on my coat, since you will find it cold in the upper air. If you will be so kind as to cover your face with your hands when we get up, you will not need goggles. Are we all ready?"

"I shall certainly not take your coat," said the girl indignantly, waving the garment away. "Not that your comfort is so important, but I know a little about flying, and if you became numbed by the cold, what would happen to us?"

Sergius laughed. "There is no danger of my becoming numbed in the few minutes that we will be in the air. Your dress is a great deal thinner than my tunic. I am sorry, but you will have to take it or we cannot start."

"Let her take mine, interposed Jones. "I have nothing to do but sit still, and it really doesn't matter whether I get numb or not."

"You are very kind, Mr. Jones." Miss Weston smiled sweetly upon him. "Yes, since you insist, I shall be glad to borrow your coat."

And suiting the action to the words she took it from him and slipped into it. Sergius frowned and looked as if he were about to say something, then checked himself and turned away, putting on his own coat without any further protest. But Mr. Jones caught what looked like an expression of amused triumph on Margaret Weston's beautiful face. It was the first time that she had really succeeded in annoying Sergius Petrofsky.

A few minutes later, having pushed the machine to the extreme end of the glade, turned so as to face the open run, they all took their places and strapped themselves in. The rear seat was a tight fit indeed for both Jones and Miss Weston, but it was only to be for a few minutes, and the girl murmured that at least she was glad she did not have to sit so close to Sergius.

Mr. Jones might have felt more flattered if she had not put in the "at least."

The Russian started his engine, the propeller began to revolve, and a second later the plane rolled forward across the uneven grass. They did not gather speed very quickly, however, and it looked as if the machine would refuse to rise in the limited course. Twice Sergius raised the elevator, and twice the plane continued on its rough and bouncing course up the glade, refusing to leave the earth.

They were now perilously close to the further end and the plane was running at a speed of about sixty miles an hour. To stop was impossible, and for a time it seemed as if their career was to end in the maw of a particularly wide-spread and hungry-looking death cabbage, when just at the last minute he again raised the elevator, the plane tilted slightly and took the air beneath its taut canvas wings.

They barely cleared the crest of the deadly vegetable, and with their hearts still in their throats found themselves shooting onward and upward, away from the valley of death.

Yet even as they drew in their first full breaths of relief and clean, cool air, Death itself, though in another form, rose after them.

The first consciousness that they were the object of attack came as Sergius banked his wings and swung in a wide circle, preparatory to straightening out on the seaward course. As the machine tilted against the light breeze, a large, dark thing shot by its nose, just missing the plane by a foot or so, and causing even the iron-nerved Russian momentarily to lose control.

The plane dipped and shot downward at a dangerous angle. They had risen scarcely four hundred feet, and there was not much room for evolutions. He just saved them from destruction, and rose again, casting anxious glances about in the darkness, for they had extinguished the electric torches before rising.

The girl was not aware that anything had happened, for she had covered her face with her hands to shield it from the sharp wind of their flight, Jones stared about as anxiously as their pilot, but could see nothing. Sergius's eyes must have been, as he had said, of an unusual kind, for presently he shouted and pointed into the darkness.

A second later something huge came up from below, actually grazed the left wing, and was gone again.

Jones knew that the dark thing must be one of the flying monsters, of which this was the third they had encountered, and he earnestly hoped that its interference was purely accidental. He said nothing, fearing to frighten Miss Weston, but on a sudden impulse he loosened the strap that held both of them, with a vague idea that if they should be flung to the earth they might have some chance of jumping clear.

That Sergius was fully aware of the danger was made evident, for he began to climb in a swift, steep spiral. Birds of the night hardly ever fly high, and if they could reach the upper levels of the air, so easily accessible to them, they would be safe.

But the evil genius of Joker Island had no idea of permitting them to escape so simply. Again, with a wild beating of vast pinions, the winged peril was upon them. This time it struck downward from above and even the skill of the nihilist could not save them.

Of what happened next Mr. Jones was never able to give a coherent account. Probably the weight and impact of the creature partially stunned him. At any rate, his next conscious memory was of finding himself swinging and dangling over empty space, his arms and hands firmly buried in something that felt like warm fur, and that he was being carried along in great swoops and lunges, so that it required his utmost strength to keep from being jerked off.

Chapter XII.

A MODERN SINDBAD.

Wide, frantic wings were beating on either side of him, and even in that desperate moment he realized that he must have grasped the flying monster at the instant it struck the aeroplane. Doubtless much against its will, it was now carrying him along as an equally unwilling passenger.

As a matter of fact, he was clinging to its fur and the skin of its breast, which was fortunately very loose, affording an excellent handhold. But Mr. Jones was no acrobat, although he was certainly playing the part of one. Already his hands were numb and aching. He wondered if he could manage to climb around and up to the creature's back, but gave it up as a feat too great for his weakening muscles.

Suddenly he found himself laughing wildly. He had remembered the story of Sindbad and the Roc, which had carried him into the Valley of

Diamonds. But the Roc bore the sailor in its claws, and this creature was not half so obliging.

Looking downward, Jones was sure that they were far higher than when the beast had struck them. He should, even swinging so dizzily through the air, have caught a glimpse of light where the fire must still be blazing by the cliff, or perhaps, if they were very high, the lights of the other encampment outside the wall. But all beneath was a black void, under what seemed a swirling, dancing firmament of stars.

Then, sick and giddy, the moment came when Jones knew he must shortly let go his grip upon skin and fur and whirl down, breathless, helpless, into the waiting arms of death. Suddenly he began to kick violently, and swing his body from side to side. If he went he was determined that his involuntary captor should go with him.

Came a harsh scream from above, a few mad circles, and then, though the wings still beat, he knew that they were dropping with dangerous speed through the empty blackness of space.

The fall, however, ended a great deal sooner than Jones anticipated, and not upon the earth but in the sea. There was one terrific splash, as beast and man struck the water.

Mr. Jones, being of course underneath, had decidedly the worst of the dive. In the first place he had expected to be hurled into the maw of a death-cabbage, perhaps, or to be dashed to pieces upon the earth, or, if he were lucky, that they might break their fall upon the crest of one of the tall, slender palms. The one thing which he did not anticipate was to be plunged into a cold bath. His mouth was open, and his lungs nearly empty of air when it happened, and the consequence was that he nearly drowned before recovered sufficient sense to let go of the fur to which he was still clinging with the tenacity of the dying.

Even then it was more by good luck than presence of mind that he reached the surface, for all the water was in a whirl with the flapping struggles of the creature which had brought him there. Fortunately, although evidently it could not swim, its convulsive efforts pushed it along, so that Jones came up at last a few feet clear of the worst of the turmoil.

The sea was running in long, smooth, oily swells, nearly as kind as quiet water to the gasping swimmer. He cleared his lungs, then turned on his back and floated, drawing in the air in huge draughts.

As his blood became reoxygenated, he began to feel a certain curiosity. What had become of the enemy? Turning again he swam slowly and quietly, reserving his strength, and looking anxiously about from the top of each swell as it came under him.

The sea, which was free that night from the phosphorescence that often characterizes those waters, reflected very little light from the stars. He could see nothing—no land, no monster—nothing but the stars above and beneath—blackness. He felt as if he had been dropped into a sea of India ink, a sea where no man or beast had ever come or sun shone upon.

Then he remembered the possibility of sharks and hoped devoutly that no company of that sort would arrive.

His clothes dragged him down, and he determined to be rid of them, at least. He kicked off his shoes and at last, by working carefully, got rid of his khaki tunic. The puttees were hardest to deal with, but he finally got them off, followed them with his breeches, and even shed the thin, loose-fitting silk underwear, as a last slight impediment to what he intended to be a fight to the finish for life and the chance to get back and finish his voluntary job of helping Sergius, or find and bury his remains. The latter contingency seemed the more likely one.

The water was warm, the slow, even swells friendly, and Mr. Jones felt sure that he could keep afloat till dawn, which could not now be far off. What he would do then depended upon circumstances, but he did not really believe the flying monster could have carried him far out to sea, and he hoped that when day broke he would see Joker Island within easy swimming distance. Until then it would be folly to strike out, perhaps in the wrong direction, so he floated a great deal, only swimming enough to keep his blood in circulation.

In one of the periods when he was on his back, his ears in consequence being under water, there reached them a peculiar, vibratory, explosive sound. He had heard it before, while floating in the quiet reaches of Long Island Sound, and with a great rush of hope Jones turned over and trod water raising himself as far as he could above the surface and staring from right to left through the blind veil of night.

Nothing.

He turned himself slowly, waiting for the rise of each successive swell to look long. Then he gave a wild shout and letting himself drop back struck out with frantic strokes.

Very small, very far away, he had seen two lights which were not stars, for one was red and one was green.

Had his mood of exultation lasted long he must have perished even on the threshold of salvation, for such a pace as he had set himself would have exhausted the most expert swimmer. Fortunately common sense returned in time, and he realized that since he saw both the red and the green it must mean but one thing. The vessel, whatever it was, was approaching him, probably at a far greater speed than he could possibly attain even if he could have kept it up.

He "loafed" again, rising on each swell with the deadly fear that this time one of the lights would have disappeared, sinking again into the trough with the blissful assurance that both lights still shone.

There is nothing much harder than to estimate distance at night across water. Knowing this from his own yachting experience, Jones floated several times, listening for the engine beat which the sea carried so much farther than the wind. And each time he fancied that it was louder, more distinct.

At last he raised himself again upon the crest of a swell and sent a long, anxious hail across the waste. To his inexpressible joy it was immediately answered.

Ten minutes later Mr. Roland C. Jones was picked up out of the watery vastness of the Pacific Ocean by his own power cruiser, the Bandersnatch, which had for three days been cross-quartering those waters in the vain, despairing hope of picking up some trace of him or his body.

Chapter XIII.
A PROMISE EXACTED.

Although the fact was not included in the extensive notices which later appeared in the New York papers in regard to the loss and rescue of the well-known millionaire yachtsman (his own friends told nothing, but one of the sailors talked), there occurred a peculiar psychological phenomenon as Mr. Jones came over the rail of the Bandersnatch.

It was as if a dark veil, which he had scarcely known existed, had been suddenly swept away from his mental vision. It had torn a trifle when he recognized one of the men in the dingey which rescued him as his old friend, Henry Martindale. He had sat in a silent, stupid-seeming daze as they were rowed back to the yacht by the sailor who accompanied Martindale, and listened to his friend's exclamations of joy, amazement and congratulation.

But as he stepped, barefooted and naked, upon the white deck of his own, familiar, beloved Bandersnatch, that veil split asunder from top to bottom and vanished forever from his brain.

In plain words, Mr. Jones remembered. He remembered how for two years, since the moment when a small, heavy clock, carelessly placed upon a shelf in his stateroom on the Lusitania, had fallen at a lurch of the vessel and struck him upon the temple, he had been the victim of that queer mental disease amnesia. Cared for by the best doctors in London and New York, they had not been able to restore the delicate equilibrium of his brain.

The loss of his memory had been accompanied by physical deterioration, and this winter the physicians had ordered a long cruise through Southern seas in the hope of improving, if not curing, his condition.

They had, exactly as he had informed Jim Haskins, come around into the Pacific by way of the Panama Canal, and were bound for the Philippines when one night Mr. Jones actually did get up out of bed, dress himself, not in yachting clothes but in a gray morning suit, walk out on deck, straight across it, and over the rail, before the men on watch could stop him. In the sea that was running they had been unable to find him, but, although they had from almost the first, given him up as drowned, still his good friends Martindale and Charles Laroux could not bear to leave the spot of the disaster, but cruised up and down, back and forth, for three whole days and nights, ever on the lookout, ever hoping against hope that they might at least bear his body back to New York for burial.

Upon falling overboard the shock of his sudden immersion in the sea had, by one of those little jokes which Nature sometimes perpetrates, started his mental machinery going again at exactly the place where, figuratively, it left the rails. The equal shock of finding his rescuers to be his friends, and the rescuing vessel the Bandersnatch, completed the good work, and that deep abyss of two forgotten years, wherein had been lost the great war and many other memories less vast, was filled.

Once again he could spread out before him the pages of his past life and find not one leaf missing.

Curiously enough, his first thought, after the sweeping realization of it all came over him, was of his cousin, the Hon. Percy Merridale, whom he had been going to visit on that unlucky voyage across the Atlantic.

"Poor old Percy," he said, paying no heed to the flood of questions which were pouring from the lips of both his friends, "why, he was killed along with half his regiment at the very beginning of the war. And here I have been wondering what he would think because I did not arrive in London on time!"

"You have, eh?" asked Laroux, looking at him keenly. "Then you remember that you did start for London?"

"Oh, yes. I remember everything now. Lord, what chums you fellows have been, putting up with the crazy whims of a man with only half a mind! But by Jove, I'm cold. If you'll have the steward get me something hot to drink, and let me get dry and into some clothes, I'll be glad to tell you all about it."

With bitter self-reproaches at their own neglectfulness, Laroux and Martindale fairly hustled him below and to bed. They would hear nothing of his dressing, but on one thing he held out. He was perfectly willing to go to sleep—he had never felt so utterly tired out in his life—but they must promise to hold the Bandersnatch where she was, or at least near to it, until he awakened.

To this his friends agreed, and Jones slept the sleep of exhausted but perfect health for eleven straight hours.

It was three o'clock in the afternoon when he appeared on deck, and he immediately sought his two friends. They greeted him eagerly, for they were more than anxious to know how he could possibly have kept afloat for nearly three days, and settling comfortably down beneath the awnings on the breezy after-deck, they all lighted their excellent cigars and the story began.

Before he had progressed very far their interest became other than that of curiosity, and as he went on two of the three cigars were allowed to languish and die unheeded. From curiosity they passed to amazement, and from amazement to carefully suppressed incredulity.

This, however, caused Jones no uneasiness, for it was about what he had expected. Finishing the incident of the flying monster with the utmost complacence and indifference to their more than dubious glances, he called for Captain Janiver.

"Captain," he said, "I want you to locate for me an island which I know to be in this immediate vicinity, although beyond the horizon in some direction. What land is there hereabouts?"

The captain shook his head: "The only island I know of within a hundred miles is hardly worthy of the name, Mr. Jones. It is nothing but a high, barren chunk of rock sticking up out of the sea. As far as I know it has never even been named."

"Oh, yes, it has," smiled Jones. "That island is Joker Island, and I want you to put the old Bandersnatch's nose about and take us there just as fast as she'll slouch through the water."

"Very well, sir, but—"

"Why, Jones, old man, we were at that place ourselves, and there isn't anything there!" This from Laroux.

"You were there?"

"Of course. Janiver remembered the place and we went, on the slim possibility that you might have been washed ashore. We cruised all around it, and even landed wherever there was a beach. We found some footprints and a few old tin cans, but there was certainly nothing else."

Jones grew suddenly very white. He had a sensation of sickness in the pit of his stomach, and an overwhelming consciousness of some dreadful disaster impending, he himself scarcely knew what.

"Captain Janiver," he said between his teeth, "put this boat about and do as I directed."

The captain touched his cap and obeyed, not without a curious glance over his shoulder. He was familiar with the idiosyncrasies of his owner, all developed, however, within the past twenty-four months, and he sighed as he gave the necessary directions.

"Too bad," he murmured, shaking his gray head sadly, "too bad. Such a good-natured, quiet young fellow as he is, too."

As for Jones himself, he resolutely declined to speak another word on the subject until he had himself visited the scene of his recent adventures. Clinging passionately to the belief that they had actually occurred, he forced his mind to dwell upon the question of what might have happened to Sergius and Miss Weston after he left the aeroplane in such an unexpected manner.

He was possessed by a really loving concern upon this matter, although the love was not for the Boston girl but for Sergius Petrofsky, who had in the short space of three days won a place in his heart never before occupied by any man, even his faithful friends Harry Martindale and Charlie Laroux.

The two latter let him alone, when they perceived that he no longer wished to talk. Like the captain, they were accustomed to some rather strange moods in their friend, although they had hoped for better things with the recovery of his memory.

About five o'clock the rapid little Bandersnatch raised a blur upon the southern horizon, which soon developed into a dark blot, then gradually took shape as the familiar black outline of the crater-wall of Joker Island.

With the sight all Jones's courage returned. He could not sit still, but paced back and forth across the deck, and when at last they came to anchor in the very bay where the Monterey had lain, he fairly tumbled into the small launch which was lowered to accommodate Jones, his two friends and a couple of sailors.

Of course the Monterey was gone, but there was the place where the nihilists had been encamped, though now no tents raised their brown canvas against the cliff. Springing from the launch Jones rushed up the beach and examined the place where they had been. There were, as Laroux had said, a few tin cans scattered about, a good many footprints, and the ashes of a fire, but these might have been there for any length of time.

He ran down the beach, hoping to discover the marks left by the aeroplane's launching, but this had been upon the smooth, hard sand near the water, and the tides had obliterated them, if they had really ever been there. If they had been there! But they had been—it *had* happened. It was all so indelibly imprinted upon the tablets of his brain that it was clearer than any other event in his whole life.

The caves, then. Beckoning to Laroux and Martindale to follow him, he pressed on to the rocky promontory hiding the cleft, or ravine. Well, that was there anyway. And there were caves, too, hundreds of them. Into which of them had he crawled, following Prince Paul and Miss Weston, followed by Jim Haskins and the two sailors? This one surely, or—no, it might have been this, or any one of a dozen others.

He felt the touch of a hand upon his shoulder.

"Look here, old man," said Martindale with a gentle indulgence which seemed to Jones well-nigh intolerable by reason of its implications, "you must not take this so hard. Now listen. Charlie and I know you are absolutely all right now—absolutely all right. Don't let there be any question in your mind of that. Your memory has returned, and you can go on to the Philippines, or back to New York and take up your life exactly where you were before it—that accident on the liner—happened.

"But just now you are suffering from the memory of a particularly vivid hallucination. If we didn't think you were all O.K. we wouldn't tell you that, you know. We'd humor you, and say we thought it was all real. But you wouldn't want us to do that now, would you? You'll believe, won't you, that while you were here on the beach, thrown up by the storm you—well, dreamed a whole lot of things that couldn't possibly have happened? Then, still dreaming, you started to swim out to sea again, thinking you were pursued by these impossible monsters, and so we picked you up, by about one chance in a million. The currents are very strong about here, Janiver says, and they carried you a long way—clear out of sight of the island. Can't you believe all this, which is the truth, and let the rest go along with the last two years?"

He spoke earnestly, with a deep and loving tenderness, which made Jones extremely uncomfortable. How could he convince these men that those things had really happened? That there, within the island, was at least one other friend of his, possibly in dire need of help, if he yet lived? Then Holloway, Prince Paul, Haskins, the beautiful, sharp-tongued girl—

Suddenly the mental defenses which he had raised gave way and went down before the flood of damning, almost unendurable conviction.

"Harry," he said hoarsely, staggering a little where he stood, "will you and Laroux get me back to New York? Just put up with me till—till we get back to New York, won't you?"

"Don't be a fool, Rolly," cried Laroux, springing forward and actually shaking him, but with a roughness that was all friendship. "You aren't crazy—you never have been crazy—you've been in a sort of delirium, like you have when you're down with fever. You're right as Harry or me. If you weren't you wouldn't be ready to believe the truth. It was nothing but plain, ordinary delirium, I tell you."

"Well, maybe it was," conceded Jones, with a somewhat sickly smile, "but whatever it was, I know I want to get away from this place and back to New York. I want to see brick buildings, and ride on every-day street-cars, and eat dinner in a Broadway café. You boys have been the best, most patient friends a man ever had. Will you promise me something?"

"Of course," broke in Laroux, "but look here, Rolly, just to satisfy you entirely suppose we stop in at Frisco and find out if such a yacht as the Monterey was chartered recently by a bunch of Russians, and—"

Jones held up his hand. "No," he said. "A man who's been off his nut for two years, and knows it, doesn't have to go around hunting up evidence to support the facts. I want to get back to New York just as fast as the old tub will travel. What I want you to promise is this. Don't ever mention any of this—this crazy dream of mine to me again. I know you won't tell it to anybody else. But—I just don't want ever to hear anything about it—again."

Chapter XIV.
A HERO AT LAST.

Three months had elapsed, and Mr. Roland C. Jones remained, to all appearances, a well and mentally sound man. Back in New York he quietly resumed the peaceful pursuits of his easy-going, pleasant, bachelor life. Laroux and Martindale adhered strictly and honorably to their promise and never mentioned to any one the singular delusion which had marked the termination of their friend's illness. Indeed, they themselves had practically forgotten it, thinking of it only as the overheard ravings of a sick man, not to be regarded as indicating mental unbalance since the man had regained his health.

Mr. Jones's first act on reaching New York had been to consult an eminent specialist in diseases of the brain, and have himself examined for insanity. The report was reassuring. Whatever he might have been in the past, this worthy physician declared him to be now free from any taint of the disorder he so feared.

Jones went to the theater, danced, golfed and made brief cruises in the early spring, but an invitation to a flying meet was instantly and firmly declined. He never wished to see another aeroplane in his life. In fact, he did all that a man could to banish from his memory that dream which he had dreamed while cast upon the barren beach of an unnamed—absolutely an unnamed—rock in the Pacific.

If in visions of the night man-eating vegetables writhed their flaming tentacles, or strange yet familiar faces smiled or frowned upon him, he at least never spoke of the matter to any one.

So the three months had drifted by, and it was the latter end of March. One morning Jones slept later than usual—he never was an early riser—and when he sat up in bed, yawning, his window was a gray expanse against which sleet drove with a continual desolate rattling.

"Darn!" exclaimed Mr. Jones, at the end of his stretch. "Another day of 'indoor sports,' I see. How I hate a sleet storm! Philip!" he called.

Instantly his English man servant, an elderly but intensely efficient individual, appeared bearing coffee, newspapers, and the mail.

"You can get my bath ready. Now, let's see. Who's going to be married, and who desires the extreme boredom of my company—hello, I wonder what this can be?"

"This" was a small flat package, wrapped in white paper and addressed to himself in a small, perfect hand. Unlike a woman, he did not pause to contemplate its exterior, but untied the string immediately. Within the paper was a white pasteboard box, and inside that another box of Morocco leather, unquestionably a jewel case of some sort. He pressed the catch and it snapped open. What—in—the—world—

The whole room seemed to reel and sway about him dizzily. It vanished, and before him stretched a little glade, all dark save where two white beams of light flashed and danced. Sergius—Miss Weston—the aeroplane—the flying monster! Was this some cruel joke that his friends had perpetrated against him?

For within the box, upon a bed of white velvet, rested an exquisite affair of gold, encrusted with blue-white diamonds. It was a tiny aeroplane, and enmeshed with it, its wings and the plane's inter-locked, was a golden bat, with two tiny rubies for eyes.

Who had sent him this thing? Who had been so cruel as to taunt him with such a reminder of his time of madness? He raised box and jewel in his hand and was about to hurl it across the room when his eyes fell upon one of the letters scattered before him on the counterpane. The writing upon it was in that same small, yet distinctive hand that had appeared on the box-wrapping.

Dropping the leather case Jones hastily seized the letter and ripped it open. He read:

"My dear friend Roland:

"Two weeks ago I read in an old newspaper of your rescue and of your return to your native city. Until that moment I—we all—believed you to have been drowned in the sea, as was the enormous bat which carried you thither. We found its body washed up upon the shore, and believe me, my friend, I wept over it for sorrow at your loss and for such an end to such an heroic deed as yours.

"I know, however, that you must have been far more overcome by your terrible experience than the newspaper account indicated. You will not need to explain to me that otherwise you would have taken your yacht back to Joker Island and, if necessary, risked death in the cavern labyrinth seeking to return to aid me, if I needed aid. There are some friendships which spring into being without the need of years to build them up, and though few words were spoken, I know that ours was such a one."

"Well, the old son-of-a-gun," murmured Jones, "and he means it, too!" The eyes he raised to Philip, coming to announce the readiness of the bath, were perceptibly wet, to that worthy Briton's great, though unrevealed, astonishment.

"Get out, Philip," was Jones's only reply. "I'll bath after a while." Alone once more he eagerly resumed his reading:

"But enough of that. I am coming to New York soon—this is written from Tokio, where I have caused to be made a small remembrance which I am also mailing you—and then we can talk together.

"After you had so courageously and with incredible presence of mind flung yourself upon the great bat—

Jones grinned, remembering the actual state of his feelings in that moment.

—and been snatched away into the air, I managed to right the plane and we went on across the wall. I did not even know that you were gone. Miss Weston tried to tell me, but you know how great is the noise in flight. We came down upon the beach and I was overcome with dismay and self-reproach when I discovered that you were missing. I could perhaps have pursued the bat and rescued you from the sea, but then it was too late.

"Well, the yacht—the Monterey—was gone. I afterward learned that the traitorous and rascally Ivanovitch, believing that I had been killed or captured in the valley, and wishing to make off with the yacht which he afterward successfully sold, had deserted me early in the afternoon of the day you and I took flight.

"And, of course, Laroux and Martindale had to wait until the Monterey was gone before they looked up the island," muttered Jones.

"There was nothing else to be done, so I took Miss Weston back into the valley. We arrived there a little after sunrise and found things at the cave just as we had left them. I pulled away the rocks and we applied my restorative to my brother and the rest. They were considerably annoyed at my little strategy, but Paul was, I am sorry to say, so rejoiced over the desertion of my companions that he forgave me and persuaded the rest to do so.

"After making one flight in vain, I crossed the course of a tramp steamer and succeeded in dropping upon her deck a letter wrapped about a stone. It was fortunate that I succeeded, for there was barely sufficient petrol left to take me to land. The captain of the tramp, more I fear for the reward which the letter offered than for humanity, turned his vessel to the island and took us all off, together with our possessions.

"I have little more to tell you save that in the month we spent in the valley Holloway, Haskins and I (Paul never cared for hunting), killed off most of the more dangerous animals. They are a peculiar collection. Over on the eastern side we discovered a cavern, or grotto, much bigger than any which Holloway had before explored. In it— it was, of course, daytime—we found scores of those enormous bats hanging, asleep.

"They are nothing but bats, although they are so big. They are fruit-eaters, subsisting upon the fruit of the palm-trees, something similar to a large date. I do not believe that it is their custom to attack other creatures, but that they were simply actuated by curiosity. Still we thought it best to kill them, and their skins are really wonderful pieces of fur.

"Two of the best are for you, my friend, and also the hide and head of the hairless bear-creature you killed. We bagged two more of them, and I think they were the last of their kind.

"After we killed off the bats the death cabbages began to wither and decay, and now they, too, are all dead. It is evident that they lived almost entirely upon the bats, which they attracted by their palmlike crests. I do not thinks the bats could have had any sense of smell, though, do you?

"And now, I come to my conclusion to a very long letter. Mr. Holloway was mistaken in regard to the quantity of the substance, of which I told you, to be found in Joker Island. We were able to obtain altogether only about a pound of it, enough to make perhaps a million rubles' worth of what I told you it would make.

"This is not sufficient for the purpose of which I spoke, so, as both Paul and myself are fairly wealthy, we agreed to divide it among our companions: The largest share was received, of course, by Holloway. We gave him our portion as a wedding present. Did I tell you that Holloway and Miss Weston were married two weeks ago here in Tokio?

"For the love of Pete! First I thought it was Paul, and then I thought it was Sergius, only she didn't want him to know it, and all the while it was Holloway! I'll bet Miss Weston had Jim Haskins wondering if *he* wasn't the lucky one, too. Guess I was the only one not in the running. Well—"

"They have, of course, my very kindest wishes for their happiness, but Paul—perhaps you knew of his hopes—he felt very badly. He has returned to Russia and is now fighting at the front, having, I fear purposely, obtained his transference to a very dangerous position. And why am I not at his side? Because, although those men with me proved traitors, such a thing would hardly turn me against the cause. And it is upon a mission for the cause that I am now about to engage, after visiting you in New York.

"Hurray!" ejaculated the reader. "Just wait until I introduce you to Messrs. Cocksure Martindale and Laroux! Oh, when will I forgive you two for the last three months?"

"It is a mission of some danger, perhaps, but also I think that it might interest a man of your adventurous disposition. I will tell you more of it later. Until that moment, my friend, believe me ever and always your friend and comrade of the past, perhaps—who knows?— of the future,

"Sergius Alexius Petrofsky."

It was a long letter, but Mr. Jones read it through twice. Then he laid it down carefully, picked up the little box and stared at the golden bat and aeroplane with shining eyes and exultant face.

The sleet still beat upon the window, but it didn't bother Mr. Jones, for he was far away, on a little rock-walled island in the Pacific Ocean, which did have a name after all, and a most appropriate one—Joker Island!

The Labyrinth

CHAPTER I.
BAD NEWS
BEFORE BREAKFAST

Rising to the extent of a supporting elbow, I viewed my early caller with one eye—the other was still asleep. Rex Tolliver had the entry of my rooms at all hours, but it didn't seem nice in him to take advantage of that fact to break my sweet slumbers in the early dawn. So far as I am concerned, that is any time before 11.30 A.M.

"Great Scott, Hil, haven't you any heart at all?" demanded the ruthless one. "I thought she was just about the same as a sister to you."

I shook my head sleepily.

"Numberless booful ladies have promised to be sisters to poor little orphan Hildreth. Which she is it? And why the excitement?"

Rex dropped into a chair.

"Then you haven't heard?"

"I heard that chair. If you love me, spare my furniture. No man of your weight and temperament ought to—"

"Hil, for Heaven's sake!" It's Ronny I'm speaking of—your cousin, Veronica Wyndham!"

My eyes opened suddenly.

"What are you talking about? Ronny's all right."

"She is? Then you know what has become of her? Where is she?"

"At home—or at the office, more likely. They have such unearthly ideas about early rising."

"Oh, is she? _Is_ she? Well, just glance at those head-lines and then—go back to sleep, since you're so darned indifferent."

He flung a badly rumpled newspaper on the bed and stalked gloomily over to the window, where he stood looking out, his back expressive of condemnatory scorn.

But I was not in the least indifferent to anything concerning the only cousin I ever really loved.

Those head-lines, in which her name appeared in letters of glaring size and sinister hue, got me out of bed and into my clothes quicker than anything else in the world could have done.

VERONICA WYNDHAM VANISHES SUDDENLY.

———

Former Secretary of Governor Goes and Leaves No Trace.

———

FIANCEE OF SOCIETY MAN.

———

Feared She Has Been Spirited Away—Police Search Vainly.

I cast a hasty glance down a whole column of "It is saids" and "Supposed to haves," but having known a few reporters, I had no desire to waste time in acquiring misinformation. I reached for my clothes with one hand and my shoes with the other, not stopping to ring for Billings. As I projected myself into them I shot a series of Sherlockian questions at Tolliver which disabused him of any idea of my indifference.

His answers were not particularly helpful. The last time he had seen my cousin had been three days previous—that was Monday—and he had taken her to the theater. He went on for five minutes before I realized that what he was saying had nothing to do with her disappearance, but was in the nature of self-reproach because he had disagreed with her about the play. She liked it and he didn't, and it was too Ibsenesque with the Ibsen left out, but now he wished he'd kept still about it, and—

I was dressed by that time. Shaving could wait.

"Never mind Ibsen," I broke in. "Did you see her home that night?"

"Did I—say, Wyndham, would I be likely to leave her in the street? Of course I saw her home, and she was so annoyed over that confounded argument that she would scarcely say good-night. That's what hurts most. We parted in anger, and now—"

"That's how you and I will part, if you can't come down to brass tacks and tell me exactly what has happened. You saw her three days ago—no very long time. How do you know she has disappeared? Maybe she has gone off on a visit or something."

"No, she hasn't. Do you think *she* would leave her work at loose ends, that way? Carpenter kept it dark—confound him! Only phoned me last night, and said he thought she and I might have eloped. The blamed fool! Why the dickens should we elope? It seems she didn't go to the office Tuesday morning."

"You're sure she reached home all right Monday night?"

"Look here, Wyndham, do you think I had her kidnaped? If you do, come right out and say so; don't beat about the bush."

I stared at him.

"No; I don't think you had her kidnaped. I want to know if you left her at the street entrance or went up to the apartment with her."

"Oh! Well, I've been talking with 'steen detectives who have all asked the same question—where did I leave her. It's got on my nerves. I took her up, of course, but Mrs. Sandry had retired, so I didn't go in. Besides, she didn't ask me."

Mrs. Sandry was the nice old lady who shared Ronny's apartment and played chaperon. For all her independence, Ronny was a great little stickler for the conventions. Hence, when she went on her own and acquired an apartment, she also went in partnership with Mrs. Sandry.

"Carpenter called up her place," continued Rex, "when she failed to show up at the office or telephone. Mrs. Sandry told him that Ronny wasn't there—that she had not come home, and was supposed to have spent the night at Anne Lacroix's house. Ronny had told Mrs. Sandry that she and

I were to meet Anne and her husband for supper after the show, and that she might go home with them. So Carpenter took it for granted that she had done that, and that something had delayed her. He never called up the Lacroix house till late in the afternoon. Of course she wasn't there. Anne was ill, and they never kept their appointment with us.

"Then, instead of notifying the police, Carpenter went up to see Mrs. Sandry. They talked it over and made up their fool minds to wait another day before starting anything. That is, Carpenter made up his own mind and the old lady's, too. I know what ailed him, and I'll square that account before the finish. He was afraid of any scandal in connection with his precious office.

"Then yesterday afternoon—*yesterday afternoon*, mind you, two whole nights and nearly two days after she had disappeared—he had the nerve to call me up and ask me if we had eloped. Oh—"

"Forget Carpenter. Have you told the police?"

"Have I—say, isn't it in all the papers? Didn't I tell you that I have been badgered by detectives ever since?"

"Well, why didn't you come to me last night? I was here—got in on the 5.10. And why haven't any enterprising journalists been around to look me up? Every one knows Ronny and I are related, and—yes, there it is, head of another column. 'Beautiful young woman is a cousin of the well-known millionaire clubman, Hildreth Wyndham.' Whenever I am dragged into print it's always in the millionaire class. Those boys are so generous. But why haven't any of 'em been around?"

"Hang your egotism! You'll find a dozen reporters drifting about the corridors. That man of yours wouldn't wake you for them."

"Good old Bill—but this time I wish he had. What have the police done?"

"Talked—talked—talked! And hinted things, and asked things, and made insulting insinuations. The only wonder is I didn't turn loose and murder a few of them!"

"Detectives are supposed to ask questions—just like children. I'm going to see Mrs. Sandry."

I had reached the conclusion that nothing useful could be extracted from Tolliver until he had calmed down a bit. In vulgar parlance, he was "rattled," and badly.

"They won't let you see Mrs. Sandry," he asserted with bitter gloom.

"Who won't? Don't tell me they've arrested Mrs.—"

"Of course not. She is in bed with a nurse in attendance. When I went there this morning I met the doctor coming out, and he said her blood-pressure was two hundred and her pulse—some outrageous speed, and if she isn't kept perfectly quiet there is danger of cerebral hemorrhage."

"Poor old lady! Ronny was as dear to her as a daughter."

"Don't use the past tense that way. She isn't—she isn't—"

"No, certainly she isn't. Come along, old man. We'll begin with Carpenter, then."

"You may, if you like. If I go near him just now, there'll be bloodshed."

"I see. Don't suppose you slept much last night? Not at all? I thought so. Your car outside? Lend it to me; I'll drop you at Hanready's, and be around again after you in a couple of hours. Then you'll be fit to help make use of any news I run across meantime."

Naturally my plan, being a sensible one, didn't appeal to Tolliver's mood of frenzy. At last I told him frankly that if he wouldn't fall in with it, I should have nothing more to do with him—at least, until I found Veronica. Then he yielded to reason.

It was not that he had any deep respect for my sleuthing ability. That was an unknown quantity, since never before had I suffered the loss of anything more dear to me than a sleeve-link. No, it was the fact that I was Ronny's nearest living relative. We three had chummed around together a lot ever since he made her acquaintance, which was, by the way, through my friendly and cousinly offices.

So he saw reason at last, and we went down to the street, besieged all the way by the cohorts of Misinformation Row. Their pleas for attention were pathetic. Knowing, however, their imaginative powers, I wasted no time nor sympathy on them. Even if I had had anything to tell, they could have invented something much more exciting.

We reached Tolliver's big touring car at last, and five minutes later pulled up in front of Hanready's. Rex went in to the Turkish baths with the air of a man walking into the mausoleum of all his dearest dead, but I hoped for the emergence of a saner man when I should return that way.

I hadn't stopped for breakfast, and didn't intend to. "Carpenter first," I decided, springing into the driver's seat, for Tolliver had been driving his own car. "After that—we'll see."

CHAPTER II.
TWIN COUSINS.

My frenzied friend spoke not beside the mark when he said that Veronica occupied a sisterly place in my affections. She and I had played and quarreled and gone about together ever since our romper days. For anything to happen to Ronny hit me just about the same as if we had been twins, instead of first cousins.

Our fathers were two English brothers, who came to America in their hopeful youth. They drifted part way West, married and settled down in Marshall City at the mining-camp stage of its career, when it looked as much like the future State capital as a two-mustang-power buck-board looks like a De Luxe-Rollinson Eight. They came in with the "first families," and grew up with the city.

My mother died at my birth, and my aunt mothered Ronny and me without partiality, until she, too, was taken. We were both the only children of our parents, and by the time of which I write, both orphans, though with one more or less important difference.

Dad left me enough of the indispensable to keep me indefinitely from the sorrows of toil. Ronny's father, however, died a bankrupt, a deed of which no one had suspected him capable. My cousin was left with nothing but a heritage of brains, from which not even the bankruptcy courts could separate the poor girl.

Naturally, I went straight to her and offered to divvy up, but all she would take was a loan. On that capital she started to make her own way in the world. Fortunately she had learned stenography and played private secretary to her father for a year before he died. Carpenter & Charles, real estate, took her on at a salary of ten per. One year later she was dragging down thirty, and old Carpenter wondered how he had ever run the business without her.

Charles wasn't around the office much then. He had just been elected Governor on the People's ticket, and before that his duties as State Senator made it necessary for him to leave the business in his partner's hands, to a great extent.

A while after he had taken his oath of office, Charles blew into the real-estate emporium with the melancholic complaint that there was no such thing in the world as a personal secretary who could do one hour's real work in less than three hours time. He played on his poor old partner's sympathies so that Carpenter offered to "lend" him Miss Wyndham until some one else showed up. Charles had already "hired and fired" six ambitious young men.

Ronny appeared five years less than her reverend twenty-two, and of the ornamental rather than the useful type. Mr. Governor looked his doubts, and of course that settled it for Ronny. She's a thoroughbred. Just tell her, "This is past your abilities," and she'll fly the hurdle or break her neck attempting it.

So a young and fair Wyndham was installed in the executive mansion at the desk six times vacated, and I fancy Charles's doubts were dissipated before the end of three days' tenure. After a while Carpenter wanted her back, but Charles put him off. For nearly a year her successor failed to materialize, and at the end of that time she quit of her own accord.

I was glad of it, for all that year she owned few idle hours to waste on little Hildreth, and I missed her confoundedly. I took it for granted that she left to save herself from nervous breakdown. Clinton Charles was a notorious slave-driver, and that he drove himself harder than any one else must have been small consolation to those around him. So back she went to the real-estate office.

Carpenter was delighted, I was delighted, Ronny herself seemed pleased. Every one was happy, except, probably, the Governor, who had again to take up the elusive trail of an efficient secretary.

During that year I had joined the "Idle Sportsmen." It was the "Idle" which attracted me, I suppose, but the name was a fraudulent misnomer. I was the only member of that club who didn't rise at least an hour before eight o'clock, breakfast, and perform a lot of acrobatic stunts with dumb-bells and exercisers and things. And they all shot, and rode, and boxed, and fenced, and set up physical prowess as their little platinum idol.

Of course they soon found me out. In fact I was such a *rara avis* in their set that they took to me as a novelty. I remained a member and made quite a number of friends among the strenuous ones. However, the only man with whom I became really intimate was Rex Tolliver, and that was after I presented him to Veronica.

Since she was back with Carpenter, who closes his office at four, gaieties were resumed among the Wyndhams. That is, she accepted my escort to dance, opera, or play; blew around the country in my car, and generally conspired with me to make sad the hearts of a number of young chaps not lucky enough to be her near-brothers—and wouldn't have been if they could.

Veronica did not remain a poor working-girl for lack of matrimonial chances.

Then Rex met her, and that was his immediate Waterloo. The Idle Sportsmen saw him no more, except on such occasions as he could not bestow his company upon my cousin. This did not surprise me, but Veronica's own behavior did. I had seen her pass out charming indifference to so many of my sex that I had begun to think her matrimony-proof.

From the first she seemed to take quite a kindly interest in Tolliver. He was a hale, good-looking young fellow, who took out his surplus energy in athletics, and had so clean a record all around that my brother-cousinly watchfulness could find no fault in him. I had always supposed that if Veronica should marry, she would pick out some human dynamo like Charles, with lofty brows and a fatal inability to loaf. However, opposites, etc., and it wasn't six months after meeting that their engagement was announced.

In Marshall City a girl does not necessarily lose her social position just because she has to work for her living. We are not New York. About fifteen hundred miles far from it. Marshall City society took just as much interest in Ronny's engagement as if her father had never lost his grip, and old Tolliver was delighted. Said he had heard of Miss Wyndham's abilities from Carpenter, and a girl who could handle Clinton Charles's work, not to mention Carpenter's, ought to be an ideal housekeeper.

I don't follow his analogy, but he said it.

My cousin gave notice at the office. Carpenter was heart-broken, but resigned. The minister was chosen. The trousseau was preparing. I was to give away the bride, and Rex Tolliver was the most fatuously happy young dub in Marshall City. That was the prospect of last Saturday, when I had left town for a few days' fishing up-river.

Exactly what were the prospects of this Thursday had yet to be discovered, but as I sailed up Chisholm Street in Rex's car I felt like a very determined little discoverer. Lazy I may be, but there are circumstances which can prod me into desperate displays of unsuspected energy. I was going to find Ronny, if I had to search every home in Marshall City from cellar to garret, and I knew that Rex Tolliver was fully as determined.

Chapter III.

DESPAIR AND SUSPICIONS.

As a giver of clues, Carpenter proved a barren failure. I had always thought him a kindly old boy, who regarded my cousin with almost paternal pride and affection. Now I discovered that his pride was that of a man who owns a unique and efficient machine, and rejoices in the envy of his fellows.

He welcomed me with bitter complaints about the "scandal," and how embarrassing it would be for Governor Charles to have such a scandal come up in connection with an employee of his business firm, who had also been his secretary *pro tempore*, and how this scandal would never have got in the papers save for Tolliver's impetuosity.

At the third repetition of the word "scandal" my well-known good humor forsook me. I reminded Mr. Carpenter that Miss Wyndham was my cousin, that she was just about the finest and straightest girl who ever wasted her abilities on the work of a money-grubbing, land-grabbing, soulless bundle of moral cowardice who walked on two legs like a man, and that he had best be extremely careful what he said about the matter. Otherwise the firm of

Carpenter & Charles might find itself facing notoriety of another sort in the shape of a libel suit.

Somewhat breathless and distinctly warm under the collar, I emerged from the Real Estate Trust Building and turned next to police headquarters.

There they were civil enough. When the police have no news and the family come around inquiring, they are always civil. Of course they don't need to go so long on politeness if they have something practical to show for their efforts. I know this now, but then I was at first quite pleased.

The chief was all consideration and assurances that everything possible was being done. They were already, he said, in possession of several promising clues. The nature of these clues he would not divulge, however, lest some one be "put wise" who at present regarded himself as entirely unsuspected.

I did not quite like this talk of a mysterious "some one" in the masculine gender. It hinted at suspicions and innuendos of which I wished, above all things, to keep the case clean and free. I suggested to the chief, somewhat dolefully, that Veronica might have gone down again to the street after Tolliver left her, perhaps in order to post a letter. Then she might have been murdered for her rings and purse and her body weighted and dropped in the Hawkeye River.

Or (and this I considered a rather brilliant inspiration) she might have been kidnaped in connection with some political matter. Governor Charles was at that time engaged in a bitter fight, in which he and the "Reform" party were lined up against the railroads, backed by a coalition of Senators who disgraced the State. Politics are a bore, but no man who read the papers could avoid knowing that much. Might not his former secretary have possessed information which, if it could be extracted from her by terrorization, would be a weapon in the hands of Charles's opponents?

The chief eyed me pityingly. Then he replied that either hypothesis was of course possible, but that they were about equally improbable.

The Aldine Apartments faced on Farragut Place. The street was boulevarded and lined with trees, like almost every residence street in the city. But it was well lighted, and there was a policeman on that beat who swore that no deed of violence could have taken place there between the hours of twelve (when Tolliver left her) and eight, when the patrolman was relieved.

As for political intrigue—well, the chief laughed outright. Acts of violence attributed to low-grade politicians and the "Ring" were mostly worked up by the boys of newspaper row. There was nothing to it. Besides, it was six months since Miss Wyndham had left the Governor. Anyway, was it likely

that he would put very important State secrets in the hands of a young lady
of twenty-two or three?

Knowing Ronny, I thought just that was possible. And ignorant though
I was, no one could hang halos over the heads of our railroad magnates and
expect me to believe those halos more refined than pure brass.

However, I saw that to persuade the chief of this would take more time
than I had years to live, and would hardly be worth while at that. So I bade
him farewell and went straight to the Aldine Apartments.

Tim, the elevator-boy, knew me—naturally. He had seen me there often
enough. He reminded me that, since the Aldine did not boast two shifts of
employees on its elevator, and since he, Tim, went off duty at 10 P.M., you
after that hour walked up—or down, as the case might be.

I had known this, but it had slipped my mind. I might have realized that
so important a witness as the elevator-boy—supposing him to have been
present—would not have been overlooked by the police.

Common humanity forbade my trying to see Mrs. Sandry. I retired from
the Aldine and started the car, just in time to evade attention from an alert-
looking young man whom I recognized as Brownley, of the *Evening Bulletin*.

Discovering that my two hours had expired, and not wishing to keep
poor Tolliver in suspense, I ran straight back to the baths.

As I swung into Chisholm Street, from its termination a few squares
distant the Capitol stared me in the face. It is not such a big building, but
beyond doubt it is beautiful. The charm of its gleaming white pillars and
the exquisite curves of its dome held little appeal to my anxious sensibilities
just then, but the sight of it reminded me of Charles.

Would it be worth while, I wondered, to try for an interview with the
Governor? Could he know of anything which might account for his former
secretary's murder or abduction?

While not enjoying his personal acquaintance, I had of course more
than once seen him, and even attended a couple of banquets where he was
a guest. Clinton Charles had not impressed me as a person who would like
to be bothered by anxious young men seeking their kidnaped cousins. He
had the broad brows and the deep-set eyes of a dreamer, but the squarish
chin and firm mouth of a man of determinative action. He fairly irradiated
personality, but it was of an energetic sort. I felt that unless a man had
business with him very pertinent to the Governor's own activities, he might
better keep off and let Charles alone.

Besides, now I came to think of it, the Governor must read the papers.
If he knew anything that would be helpful in tracing Veronica, he would

surely come forward with it. That would be common decency, and by reputation Clinton Charles was personally a model of all the virtues. Even
his muck-raking opponents had never succeeded in "getting anything" on
the Governor. No man of that kind would allow his one-time assistant to
languish in captivity, when a word of his might free her; or, if she had been
murdered, bring vengeance on the criminals.

Not a bit of use bothering Charles, I decided, and just then arriving at
my goal, I saw Tolliver coming down the steps to meet me. He did look
more himself, but when he heard the negative result of my efforts his face
fell. He climbed heavily into the seat beside me.

"I went over all *those* places," he growled scornfully. "When you left me
I thought you had something different up your sleeve."

"What could I have?"

"Well, you really know her better than any one else does. Hasn't there
been anything in the past which could account for this?"

"Meaning anything, or any one?" I asked in a very quiet, even voice.

"I mean either." Tolliver looked straight ahead of him with a sullen set
to his jaw that I did not like. As he said, I knew Veronica; but I had made
Tolliver's acquaintance less than a year ago. There might be qualities in his
disposition of which I was ignorant. For instance, unreasoning jealousy.

"You had better tell me just what you mean, Tolliver, if you wish an
intelligent answer."

"You know what I mean."

"Perhaps—I—do." And with that I stopped the car and jumped out.

"What is it? Where are you going?"

Rex forgot his sullenness in dismay.

"Going it alone," I retorted quietly. "I believe I'd rather, since your
affection for my cousin is of that quality."

"Why, Hil, old man, what did I say to start you off like that? Ronny
is everything in the world to me—you know that. For God's sake, don't
misunderstand me. Get back in the car here."

I did, for his protests were so excited that people were beginning to stare
at us.

We went on, and Rex proceeded to explain in detail. He had meant only
that Veronica might in the past have known some one who was sufficiently
crazy about her to abduct or even do away with her, driven to it by her
impending marriage.

"That's very unlikely," I pointed out. "If you are going to set the police
on the trail of every man who has wished he stood in your shoes, you'll
have half the male portion of our set in jail. Don't you realize that such a

thing mustn't even be hinted at? Do you want *that* sort of surmise circulated through the papers—about your future wife?"

He turned rather pale.

"No!" he gasped, and I knew that I had shut him up effectually on this score.

After all, Tolliver was reduced to the point of desperation, and having reached that stage a man can't be held responsible for his thoughts. A lover out of the past would be just the torture conjured up by such despair. I forgave Rex, and set my mind at the task of thinking up new coverts wherein might lurk some news of my missing cousin.

CHAPTER IV.
ANOTHER FORMER SECRETARY.

Well, we skated around all day in Rex's car, both spreading and imbibing gloom among various friends and acquaintances. All of them were considerably excited over the news.

One girl—Janet Williams, it was, daughter of Harrison Williams, who owns every taxicab in Marshall City—had given a sewing-bee for charity on Tuesday night. She had expected Ronny to be present, and when she did not appear Janet "just knew that something awful had happened to her." Wonderful thing, these after-the-event premonitions.

But at least Janet had done something practical toward finding her friend. She had instructed her obedient father to interview every one of his taxi-drivers and question them. If that brought forth no information, each of them was to keep his ears wide open to pick up any scrap of conversation which might be let fall by his passengers in transit. The idea was that the criminals might be run to earth among the giddy patronizers of such vehicles.

I foresaw an alarming series of taxi collisions. A man can hardly drive circumspectly and at the same time keep one ear firmly glued to the little window behind him. Also that if I had to ride in a taxi I was going to be careful what I said.

Her father had consented to offer fifty dollars reward to the man who brought him any valuable information. Tolliver and I looked at each other in disgust. The disgust was for ourselves, not Williams. The obvious wisdom of offering a reward had neither occurred nor been suggested to us.

With a hurried commendation for Janet's enterprise, we hastened to put that matter right at once.

In the last edition of the evening papers any crooks interested might read that "the family" of Miss Veronica Wyndham would be glad to pay one thousand dollars for information which should lead to the discovery of her whereabouts. I, the family in question, wanted to multiply that niggardly sum by at least twenty-five, and Rex was with me to the limit of what he could extract from father.

But just after we left Janet's we met up with one Harvey Jenkins, who discouraged our munificent intentions. Jenkins was chief advertising man for Farlingham, Inc., the mail-order people, and an old friend of dad's.

"You boys have the right idea, but the wrong method," he said when we had told him our plan. "There's a psychology of rewards just as there is of selling stoves and furniture. If a man thinks he can earn, say, five hundred dollars by sleuthing around a bit and investigating his own neighborhood, he'll do it if he has to suspect lifelong friends. But twenty-five thousand, or even ten, will paralyze his imagination. It's like offering to sell him a dining-room suite for fifty cents. He can't see it—thinks there's a trick somewhere. You offer five hundred, and you'll have 'em all working for you."

"But," I protested, "we weren't thinking of amateur sleuths. We were driving at the criminals themselves."

"In the first place, these criminals of yours are supposititious. In the second, if any one is holding her to ransom, then they'll certainly let you hear from them. And if you offer anything enormous to start with, you'll never get off with any twenty-five thousand. Take a tip and start with five hundred."

We couldn't quite agree on that, but compromised on the thousand aforesaid.

Then there wasn't anything to do. The only private detective agency in Marshall City is a joke, and not even a practical one. They couldn't find a lost dog if the unfortunate canine came and howled outside the agency door. We didn't bother with them, and so, after offering the reward, as I say, there seemed nothing more we could do. It was horrible, intolerable, maddening, but for the life of us neither Rex nor I could think of a next step.

We had seen all her friends. They knew nothing. An impertinent, prying plain-clothes man had gone through poor Ronny's private correspondence. It was innocent of clues as so much blank note-paper. Mrs. Sandry was still in a critical condition, but she knew nothing. If she had, she could never have concealed it from Carpenter. The dear old lady was no secret-keeper.

Two interminable days dragged past. By Saturday, however, we could have kept busy enough if we had followed up every one of the "clues" which were turned in to me and to the police by those ambitious to acquire that thousand.

Jenkins was right. We began to think that every man, woman, and child in Marshall City was working for us, and also that we dwelt in a city of imbecile optimists.

Some of those clues—but the people were no worse than the police, and I can prove it. Sunday morning Rex came around in the early morn, as had become his habit, and informed me with deep disgust that he was being "shadowed." At looking out the window at said "shadow," I agreed that he was an unmistakable plain-clothes man.

I agreed with Tolliver that this was too much, even though he was the last person to see Veronica. He and I went straight to the chief, and Rex produced so many alibis to account for his every movement after leaving her, and for the next two days, that the shadow was withdrawn—without apologies, for, said the chief:

"You yourself admit that you quarreled at parting. Sorry, but you know we have to suspect every one. Our business. It's the respectable ones who do the craziest things—sometimes."

"Cheer up, Rex," I consoled him later. "At least, he said you were respectable—by inference."

"How the deuce can you make a joke of it?" complained Tolliver. "It seems to me, Wyndham, that you take the whole business very light-heartedly."

That was unkind and not true, but one must make allowances for a man in Rex's place. I let it go at that. Anyway, I could appreciate his feelings.

That was Sunday, and already excitement had calmed down too much to suit me. If Tolliver thought me light-hearted, I accused the world of positive jubilance. Who, except Rex and I, and—yes, probably Mrs. Sandry—really cared about Ronny? To whom else was she indispensable, or who felt that her loss was so intolerable that life might as well stop short because of it? Answer: Nobody. Popularity is all very well, but—

With such melancholy meditations did I while away two hours of Sunday afternoon in my own rooms. Rex was off investigating one of the innumerable clues which our offer had brought forth. The police sorted out a few, and cast the rest aside with professional scorn. This was one of the outcasts. Rex was looking it up more to keep busy than for any other reason, while I stayed at home to receive that longed-for phone call from the chief.

At last it occurred to me that some part of my hopeless depression might be traced to another cause than the indifference of a cruel world to my sorrow. I rang for Billings.

"Bill," said I, "you are letting me starve to death. Is that right?"

"You never eat luncheon here, sir."

"And so, quite naturally, you supposed that I never eat it anywhere. Next time—if there ever is a next time—that I remain with you for any considerable period, you may serve luncheon exactly four hours after breakfast—whenever that may be."

"Yes, sir. I'll have it ready in—"

"No, you won't. I am deeply hurt, and I'm going to the Blue Thimble round the corner. If any one phones while I am out, you may call me there."

Billings looked not the least impressed by my displeasure.

"I'll attend to the phone, sir," he promised. "It certainly is dull waiting around this way. Wish there was anything I could think of to help you find the poor young lady."

"So do I. If Mr. Tolliver comes in, send him around to the Thimble."

The Blue Thimble is a little café where the food is as good as the name is ridiculous. The name suggests sewing circles and tea parties, but as a matter of fact it is a strictly bachelor resort, with a grill and a chef who graduated from the best hotel in paradise, and descended upon earth to bless it.

I found my favorite table vacant, and seating myself, considered the menu. The little café was almost empty, as I knew it would be at that hour of Sunday afternoon, and I was glad to see that none of my acquaintances were present. I was tired of shallow sympathy and unmeaning condolences. "It's a shame, old fellow. You thought a lot of her, didn't you? Have you heard that Jim is entering Peterkin III at the bench show? Some bull-pup, Peterkin."

Of course they weren't all that bad, but the spirit was there. They had passed through their brief spasm of emotion over Ronny's disappearance, and now they wanted to be done with it and get on to something interesting and really vital.

So, when I saw Fred Dalton entering, saw him observe me with a happy smile, and then bear down upon my table, I felt less pleased than I should. Of course by the time he reached me said happy smile had been modified to a doleful grin. Good of him to consider my feelings.

"Any news?" he asked, as he seated himself and accepted a menu from the waiter.

"Yes, they say the Governor will veto the Gratz bill."

He looked at me with pained surprise.

"I meant about your cousin—Miss Wyndham."

"Oh! No, we haven't heard anything."

He gave his order, then turned again to me.

"Too bad. But nothing ever hits you very hard, eh, Wyndham? Wish I had your happy disposition."

At least I had headed off the "You thought a lot of her, didn't you, etc."

"Nothing ever hits me at all," I retorted. "I thought you'd be more interested in the Governor himself—having worked with him."

Dalton flushed slightly. He was one of Ronny's six predecessors at the secretarial desk.

"I lasted a month," he said defensively. "I wouldn't have kept on if he had wanted me to. Say, that man ought to have forty personal secretaries, instead of one. Your cousin must have been a wonder to stick it out so long. I hear he almost wept when she left him."

"Yes—the same as Carpenter. Hated to lose a first-class machine. Fine firm, Carpenter & Charles."

"What's the matter with you to-day? It's not like you to carry a grouch. As for Charles, you can't blame him for regretting one person who could keep up with his infernal energy."

Dalton laughed suddenly.

"Tell you what, Wyndham, if any one has kidnaped your cousin, I'll bet it's the Governor. He's probably got her hid away somewhere in durance vile, making her attend to his correspondence."

That was too much for me. I gave him leave to be indifferent, but not to make a joke of it. I beckoned the waiter and asked for my check.

"You haven't finished," protested Dalton reproachfully. "Why, Wyndham, am I driving you away?"

"Certainly not." Dalton's nothing but a good-natured, harmless kid. His reddening face made me feel like a brute. I told him that I was half-sick when I came in and worse now, asked him to dine with me next week at the Sportsmen's, and returned to Billings and the happy occupation of awaiting a message that never came.

Rex didn't show up at all. About ten o'clock he phoned me that he had followed his clue clean out in the country, and run it to earth in the Park View Asylum. The "abducted" lady turned out to be a person of large avordupois and few facial charms, who had gone mad over the death of a cherished pug-dog, her companion of fifteen years' standing.

While touched by this sad episode, I agreed with Rex that the police were right. The clue had been hardly worth following.

Chapter V.

A CALL ON THE GOVERNOR.

That night I dreamed outrageously, perhaps because I had eaten so little. I hunted for Ronny through enormous houses, whose corridors had no ending, and whose doors possessed a nasty habit of swinging open to disclose heaps of wormy skulls. I ran miles after a huge black motor-hearse, which I knew contained her corpse; but when I caught up with it there was nothing inside but a crazy pug-dog, with a ticket on its collar: "Consigned to Governor Charles—a first-class working machine."

At last, after other equally charming adventures, I did find Ronny. She was concealed in a secret chamber under the dome of the Capitol and was hammering furiously on a typewriter. Documents and unanswered correspondence were stacked about her to tottering heights, and beside her stood Governor Charles, brandishing what looked like a Herculean club.

I, however, knew it to be the Power of Veto.

Veronica's cheeks were hollow, and her eyes, as she turned to look at me, enormous. She said: "Hildreth, come soon, as I can never finish all these letters."

Just as I was about to spring upon the Governor and wrest away his Power of Veto, without which I knew him to be helpless, the energy summoned up for the attack awakened me. Ronny's words were still in my ears, as if she had been in the room and spoken them. "Hildreth, come soon, or I can never finish all these letters." The sentence repeated itself over and over in my brain with maddening persistency.

At last, in desperation, I got up, took a hot shower, and dressed. Then, lying down with my clothes on, I slept until nearly eight. In my boyhood, when I suffered much from insomnia, I had learned that trick and it almost invariably worked.

No sooner was I awake, however, than that absurd dream recurred to me.

"The 'Hildreth, come soon' part is all right," I observed to Billings, as he served my coffee and omelet, "but the rest is mere nonsense."

"Yes, sir. Mr. Tolliver called up a while ago—"

"What?" I nearly upset the coffee. "Why didn't you wake me? Confound you, Billings—"

"He said not to disturb you, sir. Only to say that he would be at home until noon, and after that you could reach him at the Sportsmen's."

So, even Rex had deserted me. That was the self-pity of nervousness, of course. Aside from our mutual loss, Tolliver and I had little in common. Ronny was the connecting link between us, and if he fancied other society than mine for a change, it was not astonishing. But that morning I was in a mood to find fault with the whole of creation.

My mind has one peculiar faculty—weakness rather. It will occasionally seize upon some trivial idea or notion and proceed to go over it and over it, to the point of madness. Poe wrote about a fellow with a brain like that. Only he was worse than I. He ended, as I recall it, by fastening his attention on his sweetheart's teeth, and when she died he went out and dug her up and pulled 'em all out. Something like that. Cheerful, pleasant fireside companion, Mr. E. A. Poe. I was never *that* bad, but when I read the story I knew what Poe meant.

In this case it was Freddy Dalton who had started it. His fool joke about the Governor's kidnaping Veronica to make her go on with his work had camped right down in the back of my mind, and there it intended to remain. Hence the dream. What Dalton said, and what I dreamed Veronica said, was repeated to the point of nausea. That there was no possible sense in it made no difference. I couldn't get away from it, and I knew I couldn't.

There was only one cure. I had found that out in previous cases. To be rid of the idea I must translate it into action. Just as the poor dub in the story had to go and pull out those ghastly teeth, so I would have to go to Clinton Charles and ask him—but no, there reason rebelled. I could *not* ask him if he had my cousin shut up somewhere writing his letters.

Still, I could go to him and—oh, inquire if there were any way in which the search could be officially encouraged by him, as Governor. At the worst, he would only think my brain turned by grief. I was going.

Calling up the executive mansion, I found that Charles was in, but would be leaving in twenty minutes for—I didn't wait to find out where. I hung up in a hurry, and a few minutes later was beating it out Central Avenue in my roadster. Since little Hildreth had to make a fool of himself, let him get it over with as quickly as possible.

By good luck—or bad—I drew up at the curb just in time to see Charles coming down the steps. He had two men with him, important-looking dubs, but my impatience did not propose to be thwarted. Just as well to be snubbed here as anywhere else, I thought. Jumping out, I waited on the sidewalk in front of his own limousine.

As the three came abreast of me I stepped forward, lifting my nice, pretty Panama.

"I beg your pardon, Governor Charles—"

He never even looked at me.

"I'm not giving interviews this morning," he threw me, and went on talking to the man on his right.

"I'm not a reporter," I protested, realizing his mistake. "I want just a moment of your time on a matter of private business."

At that all three turned and glared at me. That is, Charles's companions glared. The Governor never found that necessary. There was something of the magnificent about Charles—something big and overwhelming. As if one should meet one of those giants of old romance, "over twenty cubits high." I don't know how high that is, but I presume it is a great deal more than the five feet nine of Charles's actual stature. No, this largeness was not physical; but every time I had seen him I received the same impression. That he was so much bigger than I that my own insignificance had no right to trouble him. And yet, with other men, I'm not famed for self-effacement.

"I have no time just at present, Mr.—"

"Wyndham," I finished for him, and got out a card.

"Oh, Wyndham, is it?"

His eyes left my face, and he stood a moment looking down at the card, and tapping it against the fingers of his left hand. One of his companions— a fat, fussy, side-whiskered individual, whom I now recognized as Senator Comstock, a leading member of Charles's own party—stirred impatiently.

"Can't we go on, Governor? Fairchild will—"

To my complete amazement Charles raised his head and cut the Senator's speech short with: "It is not necessary for me to be present, Senator. You are fully acquainted with my views and, I am certain, can convey them with greater eloquence than myself. I find that I shall be detained for a short time, but I may join you somewhat later."

"But—"

"I ask it as a favor, Comstock. I know that you are more than competent to handle this for me."

Charles possessed a voice as remarkable as his personality. It had a vibrant and at the same time velvety quality. He could, when he chose, give it an almost caressing note that was in some queer way personally flattering to the man or men whom he addressed. Flattery is hardly the word, either. It was something nobler than that. But every one who has heard Charles speak from the platform will know what I mean.

The Senator swelled visibly.

"All right, Governor. I'll do my best—but Fairchild will be disappointed."

"Oh, I think not." Then to the other man: "Good day, Mr. Berger. It was kind of you to come to me so frankly."

"Not at all, sir—not at all." Mr. Berger beamed upon the Governor as if he had never hurled verbal tin cans and bad eggs at him from the political stump.

I knew Berger, too. He'd been caricatured often enough. "Rotten politics" stuck out all over him like bristles from a porcupine, and he was the acknowledged tool of our dear old "railroad ring." I was rather surprised to see him here—that is, I should have been if I had retained any astonishment in stock. Could it be possible that Governor Charles was dismissing these men in order to attend to me?

It was not only possible, but true. As the limousine rolled off, bearing the virtuous Senator and his blackguardly companion, Charles turned to me.

"And now, Mr. Wyndham, if you will come into the house I shall be glad to hear whatever you have to say."

"Thank you. You're very kind."

He led the way, walking a few steps in advance, and I followed meekly behind. Ha! I had it! He had mistaken me for some one else. Some other Wyndham, some important, expected Wyndham, should have been going up that walk at the gubernatorial back. Once inside—my real identity established—well, fireworks were due.

I set my teeth. Before I was thrown out I would ask him one question, if I had to barricade myself behind chairs and tables.

He took me straight to his private study, a large, somber, book-lined room on the first floor. There, having closed the door, he laid his hat, stick, and gloves on a table littered with papers, and faced me, still standing.

"Now, Mr. Wyndham?"

Often when most embarrassed or excited I am outwardly most calm.

"I won't detain you but a few moments," I began in the coolest and most leisurely manner. "I came to see you about my cousin, Miss Veronica Wyndham."

"Yes?"

The word came curt as a knife-stab. Nothing caressing about that. But at least he was not astonished, and therefore could not be receiving me under any false impression.

"Yes," I continued, still very leisurely of speech, and increasingly embarrassed under the surface. "You know, for a while she was your private secretary."

What an asinine thing to say! Of course he knew it. But instead of snapping me up as I expected, Charles half-turned away and indicated a chair by the window.

"Won't you sit down, sir?"

He seated himself in a chair facing me, and pushed a small humidor across the table.

"Smoke?" he asked briefly.

In a sort of daze I took a cigar, he helped himself also, and not another word was said until the two Havanas were cut and lighted. Then he answered me, as if there had been no interruption:

"Yes, as you say, Miss Wyndham was for a time my secretary."

"He had a queer way of speaking, I thought. Quite rapid, and yet every word distinct and some way—tense. I had never before noticed it was a mannerism of his.

"She has disappeared," I observed.

"I know it."

"She is—very dear to me."

That was inane—sentimental—oh, for Heaven's sake, why couldn't I ask my question and get away? Those deep-blue, visionary eyes of Charles were fixed on my face. Beneath them the contradictory mouth and chin seemed to grow even firmer and more stern.

"Yes?" Again that cutting monosyllable.

"We are trying to find her," I continued, "and I thought you might be able to help us."

"And why, Mr. Wyndham, should you think that I can help you?"

He leaned across and shook the ash from his cigar into a tray on the table.

Suddenly I gave up. I was making a fool of myself with a vengeance. I rose from my chair so abruptly that Charles started.

"Governor," I said, reaching for my hat, and my absurd embarrassment leaving me in the act of defeat, "I had no right to come here and take up your time. Since my cousin went, I have naturally been under a heavy strain, and everything else having failed, I recalled her connection with you. I thought you might be willing to use your influence toward pushing the inquiry. It was most kind of you to grant me an interview, and I fear you put aside important matters to do it."

"That was nothing—a meeting from which I could easily be spared."

Charles rose, too, and I thought he looked much less stern. Probably my apology had softened him. Then he actually smiled.

"Miss Wyndham was a very unusual young woman. I can hardly blame you for being grieved over her disappearance. I read of it in the papers at the time. I fear there is little I can do to help, but if an opportunity does arise, be sure I shall take it. Nothing else you wished to ask?"

"Why, one question, if you don't mind."

"Certainly not. What is it?"

"Do you know where she is?"

Yes, I asked it. The question slipped out of ambuscade and off my tongue before I could check it. What I meant to say was, did he know of anything in connection with her work of that year which could have any bearing on the case. But my subconsciousness tricked me, and loosed the most amazingly insolent query I could have possibly devised.

Charles started again, and like a flash all the geniality left his face. He looked cold as an iceberg, and unapproachable as the Grand Lama of Tibet.

"Mr.—Wyndham!"

I was quenched—obliterated. And my deadly calmness of embarrassment returned.

"It's a question I ask every one." I drawled. "Sort of habit I've acquired during the last week. Good day, Governor—and thanks, ever so much."

"Good day, sir."

I left the room with a dignity which I knew to be awesomely ridiculous— and left him standing there, staring after me. Somebody—or something, I was too flooded with chagrin to know which—showed me to the door. That was the end of my call on Governor Clinton Charles.

All the way down the walk, as I got into my car, started it, and drove on out Central Avenue, I was conscious of nothing but a rising tide of white-hot rage—a most unfamiliar sensation.

Why—why—why? Why should I allow myself to be so overwhelmed by the mere presence of a man that I could not speak to him intelligently? Why did I care in the least what he thought of me, one way or the other? But why, above all other whys, did I ask that last impertinent, altogether outrageous question?

Chapter VI.
MRS. SANDRY READS A LETTER.

Rex never came near me that morning, nor did I seek him. I had nothing to tell him, except a humiliating episode which I wouldn't tell to anybody.

The more I thought of it, the less I thought of myself. Clinton Charles, recognizing my name, doubtless, as being the same as his former secretary's, had put off attendance at a meeting in order to grant me an interview. Of course he remembered Ronny, and of course he remembered her kindly. No one could do less.

Then, instead of taking advantage of his courtesy and putting my case to him frankly, I had stumbled and dawdled along, said nothing that I wanted to say, and generally given him an impression of total imbecility. And crowned the effect with an impertinent insult.

What if Charles *were* an important man, of an unusual and dynamic personality? Ronny was just as wonderful, in a different way. Just as important, too, and a darned sight more so, where I was concerned. I had behaved like an awkward schoolboy. Worse, I had lost a possible chance to enlist in the search a man with some real brains and intelligence.

I avoided my friends all morning, but finding my own society intolerable, decided at last to go around to the Aldine and call on Mrs. Sandry. Every day I had sent her flowers, and made telephone inquiries, and I knew that she was sufficiently recovered to see me.

The nurse met me with a professional smile and the information that Mrs. Sandry was out of danger, though still weak. I found her sitting up in bed, a lace boudoir-cap on her snow-white hair, and my last flowers on a table beside her. She welcomed me with tears, and I was so glad to talk with some one (besides Tolliver, of course) who was really afflicted by the same loss as myself, that I found myself enjoying the call.

We talked, and agreed, and discussed possibilities (I had to be hopeful there, for Mrs. Sandry's sake), and eulogized our lost one, quite in the manner of the family when they meet after the funeral. Of course, Mrs. Sandry was not related to Veronica, but if they had been mother and daughter the old lady could have felt no worse over her disappearance.

Finally she pointed at a little desk.

"There's a bundle of letters in there, Hildreth. Letters that she wrote me while I was in the sanatorium last winter. They are so dear. There is one where she speaks of you, Hildreth, and I want to read it to you. Will you bring them over here?"

I was by that time in a condition of maudlin sentimentality where I knew I should weep outright if Ronny had said anything very touching about me—though how she could have done that was a matter for curiosity. However, I went to the desk, selected the bundle referred to, and as I pulled it out of the pigeonhole by the ribbon it was tied with, the ribbon gave way. It had been tightly bound, and its sudden release caused a sort of explosion of letters. Ronny's missives flew right and left, some on the floor, and a couple in Mrs. Sandry's ivory-finish scrap-basket.

I gathered up those on the floor, and reached in the basket after the other two. My hand came up with not only the enveloped letters, but a torn half-sheet of note-paper. There were only a few lines written upon it, and they were in my cousin's upright, firm hand, always clear and legible—so legible, in fact, that my eyes took in the meaning almost without volition.

It was a letter which she had begun, sitting at Mrs. Sandry's desk instead of her own. But instead of finishing it, she had torn the sheet across and cast it aside, doubtless dissatisfied with her opening lines. The detective who, while Mrs. Sandry was too ill to protest, had explored my cousin's private correspondence, had stopped short of raiding Mrs. Sandry's own desk. The nurse probably played dragon at the door. The torn sheet had not been emptied from the basket, because there was practically nothing else in it.

For some obscure reason, as I looked at my cousin's writing, my mind seemed to come to a dead halt—to stop thinking. I knew that those few words were laden with a meaning which was not innocuous; some dreadful import which loomed up like a huge black wave, poised, frozen, held motionless by the momentary numbness of my brain. There was in me a gripping sense of evil—but no thought at all to tell what the evil might be.

"Hildreth!" It was Mrs. Sandry's voice which set my mind going again—and released the black wave. " Is there anything the matter? Are you ill? What have you there in your hand?"

"Nothing—or rather, your letters. Won't you read them to me?"

I walked over to the bed, laid the letters on the coverlet beside her, and myself sat down in a chair. The little table with my flowers was between us.

She searched among the letters for a moment, drew one out, and began to read. What it was about, I have not the slightest idea. My eyes were fixed on that torn sheet of note-paper held on my knee, and concealed from Mrs. Sandry by the table.

While the old lady read, and I sat there very quietly, the black wave was flying over me—choking—strangling.

Said the bit of paper on my knee:

My dear Clinton:

Your description of Asgard Heights was charming, but in the spirit of your letter I prefer to think that you wrong both yourself and me. Should I do as you have asked for such an incentive, surely we should have little regard for one another after the first glamour had worn off. I tell you frankly—as I have always been frank with you—that the very least of your personal arguments carries more weight than all the splendors and luxuries you could devise to tempt me. You must understand—

There it ended. "You must understand—" and there it broke off, was torn across, and cast aside. I did understand—understood with an ever-increasing and abominable lucidity; understood beyond the reach of blessed and merciful doubt.

"My dear Clinton," and "Asgard Heights." There, in my hand, I held the key to the whole mystery of the disappearance of Veronica Wyndham. And I would have given anything—my life gladly—to hurl that key back into oblivion.

Asgard Heights. That was the famous estate in the mountains which

Charles had purchased within the last few months. Until that time he had never been wealthy in any large sense—merely prosperous. Then an uncle of his died, and in pride for his nephew's successes and great aims, left him nearly the whole of a reputedly enormous fortune. When Charles's first act after receiving this inheritance was the purchase of Asgard Heights, his supporters shook their heads and his enemies rejoiced.

Here at last was a handle, a dangling rope, by which Charles could be pulled down from his popular pinnacle. No man, they said, could own Asgard Heights, with its vast palace of a house, its wonderful gardens, and its square miles of fenced-in game preserves, and go on playing the game of People *vs.* Plutocracy—at least, not on the people's side.

When it became known that not a single American citizen was employed by Charles on the large staff of servants required by the scale of house and grounds, his opponents pounced on that also and exploited it with vicious joy. They ignored the fact that in our State Chinese servants are a commonplace in many households.

The Governor, moreover, though a native of Marshall City, was the son of a missionary. He had spent most of his boyhood in China, spoke two or three dialects, and was known to have played patron saint to more than one strayed Celestial in our midst, fallen into difficulties born of the white man's prejudice against the yellow. He had reason, then, to look among them for loyalty and service, though perhaps I alone now knew the reason behind the reason for this choice.

He ran not one-tenth the risk of gossip-spreading from his probably well-bribed Chinamen that he would have run from servants of any other nationality.

Despite the strenuous efforts of his detractors, what actual effect the Heights would have on his career remained to be seen. I had heard it said that Charles was an exception to the common rule; that he held the people's attention, fascinated them, by his sheer brilliancy and magnetism; that he was not a common man raised by his fellows to be their representative, but a master who commanded and was obeyed by all.

That, of course, was gross exaggeration. But, at least as yet, his popularity throughout the State seemed unaffected.

So, "dear Clinton" had described Asgard Heights charmingly to my cousin? Now, a great many people call me Hildreth or Hil. But who called Governor Charles by his given name? His most intimate friend, perhaps—if he possessed one—and, it seemed, his former secretary. That she should call him so was to me almost evidence enough in itself. Why, he hadn't even a nickname among his enemies or friends. He was Governor Charles—

Clinton Charles—damnable, hypocritical, woman-betraying Charles, as I named him now.

I recalled the man as I had seen him that afternoon, with his beautiful eyes, and his fine, strong face and noble forehead. Recalled the charm of his voice, and the enchanting flattery of his manner—when he chose it to be flattering. Recalled the magnetism of his personality, attractive or repellent, as he wished to make it; his amazing abilities, and his immense capacity for concentrated work.

There was the very picture of the man whom I, before Rex stepped in, had prophesied that Veronica would marry.

Yet she had never dropped a hint, even to me, that Charles had offered her any personal attentions. His name and hers had never been connected in that way. Certainly he had never paid her open courtship.

No—open—courtship! But secret, secret—"My dear Clinton—" "Asgard Heights," "Should I do as you have asked for such incentive—" "The very least of your personal arguments carries more weight—" The words of a woman prepared to yield, but striving still to hold about herself some few rags of self-respect. No, I wronged her there. If Ronny had sold herself, it had been for love, and no more ignoble inducement.

But that she—my cousin—my little chum—a Wyndham—

No wonder that, when he heard my name, saw my card, he dismissed his companions, and led me into his house. No wonder he eyed me with the stern expectancy of a man who faces a cocked and leveled pistol. And no wonder he was courteous, and at he same time strained of voice and manner.

He thought that I knew! And when I asked him outright, "Do you know where she is?" his indignant "Mr.—Wyndham!" was no more than the final bluff of a man who is at the point of throwing down his hand.

And I had walked out of there—left him—never pressed the question. But, thank God, there was time enough yet for that.

Carefully folding that scrap of Veronica's writing, I put it in my pocket and rose. I realized that all this time Mrs. Sandry's voice had been sounding in my unconscious ears, and that now it had stopped.

"It was very good of you to read it, mother," I said, "and now I've tired you enough. Good-by."

And, to what must have been her acute amazement, I bent over and kissed her.

"Why, Hildreth!" she exclaimed, and began crying again.

You see, I wanted to bid an affectionate farewell to somebody who loved Ronny and liked me, because I intended to go out and kill Governor Charles.

Chapter VII.

A CHANGE OF HEART.

I am just a common, ordinary, quite indolent and usually optimistic sort of a dub. Certainly cut on the lines of neither an assassin nor a hero. High tragedy and little Hildreth have never been team-mates. At least they never had until intuition, deduction, and general information made me aware that the Veronica I knew, the beloved, comradely Ronny, bound to me by ties not only of consanguinity but the most sympathetic understanding—that this girl had indeed gone from me forever.

That the person who had destroyed her, more surely than by murder, was the man who, above all others, should have held himself straight, firm, true, as his face would have me believe him, even without his puritanical reputation.

And why shouldn't he have married her? Was a Charles so much better than a Wyndham? Snobbishness is a quality I despise, but a man has a right to defend his name when another man casts mud at it, even by inference.

Had Charles been a married man, this thing would have been equally atrocious, unworthy, but at least understandable. But he was not. Somehow, despite his matrimonial desirability, he had reached the Governorship and the age of thirty-five and remained a bachelor. Every one knew that he had no interest in women, though (or perhaps because of it) he was as popular among the feminine voters as among the men.

Oh, no, he had no interest in women! How many others beside Veronica had yielded to that magnetic charm of his, thrown away their happiness, and kept it secret for love of him—to save his accursed reputation?

I had left the Aldine Apartments, and next thing found myself walking into my own rooms, though how I reached there I had no idea. Billings met me, took one look at my face, and the next instant was beside me.

"Lean on me, sir. I'll get you into bed. You're all right, sir. I'll have Dr. Meadows here in—"

I flung his arm off angrily.

"What's the matter with you, Billings? I don't want any doctor."

He hovered around me with the anxiety of an old hen over its solitary, sick-looking offspring.

"I beg pardon, sir. You're white as a ghost and look worse than when you was coming down with typhoid. It's all this strain and worry, sir, and you ought to take care of yourself—you ought, really. If the poor young lady should come home to-day and find you looking so—"

"Never mind the poor young lady, Bill. And don't worry about me. I'm going out again in a few minutes, and if Tolliver calls up—"

I stopped right there. Until that moment I had forgotten all about Rex Tolliver. Should I tell him? If I did, vengeance would be taken out of my hands. I could be sure of that. During the past week the cheerful, somewhat opinionated, but always fun-loving boy who had won Veronica had changed into a sullen, grief-ridden man, irritable, ready to fly into anger at a word or look. I could imagine the red rage into which this news would throw him; and what form would that anger take?

I had thought to force Charles privately into admission of the truth, then kill him, and take the consequences. No need for the world to know any reason. Let them think what they liked. But Tolliver—how well did I know him? Would not his hatred turn upon both betrayer and betrayed?

To Clinton Charles mere exposure would be a worse punishment than death. In our State such an intrigue would not be tolerated for an instant. Charles was taking a terrific risk for the sake of his selfish pleasure; yet no one could doubt that to him ambition was more than life.

Would Tolliver's vengeance take *that* form?

And thinking of it put a new aspect on my own determination. Was this my boasted loyalty to Veronica? She loved the man, loved him so that, yielding at last to his entreaties, she had been willing to forget honor, friendship, all that had made up her life till then, and go to him in shame and secrecy. And for the satisfaction of my own anger, she was to be cut off from any possible return to the respect of her world and, more important still, herself.

I was ashamed. What worth is a protector who protects by unreasoning violence? I would go to Charles, but instead of assassinating him out of hand, he should have a chance to make such reparation as still lay in his power. Veronica must go away for a time. We would fix up some sort of plausible story to account for her original disappearance. What it would be I could not conceive, but hard-driven invention will work miracles. Then she must openly return, break off her engagement with poor Rex Tolliver, and openly receive the attentions of our honorable Governor. The bitter comedy should end with their marriage.

I no longer stood the least in awe of Charles. It had been fear, not contempt for my insignificance, which had enveloped him in an atmosphere of strain and caused my own unreasonable embarrassment.

And yet, to make my weapons invincible, did I not need evidence a trifle more complete than the scrap of letter in my pocket? I knew, and he would know that I knew. But he might barricade himself behind his great and virtuous reputation, have my cousin spirited away, close the mouths of the Oriental servants with the wealth he now possessed in such plenitude, and laugh at me for a suspicious, presumptuous fool.

The simplicity of my original intention had its virtues. His denial would be small good to me if he died next moment; this other plan involved complications, difficulties.

I had driven poor, worried Billings from my sitting-room while I thought the problem out. Now I called him back.

"Bill, I'm going out. It's four now, and I may not be back till late this evening. If Mr. Tolliver phones or comes here, tell him there's nothing new. That I'll see him in the morning—or to-night, if he cares to wait."

I was going to have my hands full with Rex Tolliver. I pitied him from the bottom of my heart, but Veronica's happiness came first. If I could possibly prevent it, Rex was never going to guess the shameful truth.

Half an hour later I was speeding out the Charlevoix Pike, headed for that charming mountain retreat from the cares of office, Asgard Heights.

CHAPTER VIII.

AN UNEXPECTED COMPLICATION.

Marshall City, as you may know, lies on two sides of the Hawkeye River and in the center of a wide valley, around which sweeps the curving Père Marius Range. The iron and copper district is somewhat to the southeast, and Charlevoix Pike runs westward, ascends Kennett Mountain, and on to Charlevoix beyond the range. It is a hard, broad, well-oiled road, a great favorite with motorists, and that day there were plenty of cars out besides mine.

The afternoon was sunny, but not too warm, and as more than one acquaintance gave me a passing hail, I was sick with memory of the many times that my little roadster had carried Ronny out this way.

Three miles from Kennett I turned off the pike into the branching road which led to Governor Charles's splendid and isolated domain. Since he bought it he had never entertained there.

I knew why now.

Ronny would have plenty of time to be alone with her reflections, for Charles doubtless deigned to visit her only at such odd hours as he could conveniently spare from his political occupations.

I ground my teeth. Yes, I did. Exactly like the regular villain. Indifferent, was he? Charles, the magnificent, with the world and my cousin at his feet! Well, just wait a little—till I had seen her, talked with her, had the evidence of my own eyes to support my story. Then we should have the spectacle of Mr. Clinton Charles on his knees to little Hildreth, begging for a chance to bestow all public honor upon the neglected resident of Asgard Heights.

A picture of him in that attitude came to me, with myself, arms folded in masterful scorn. There was an incongruity about in which brought an unwilling grin to my lips. Nevertheless, something pretty near that was going to happen, or the State would find itself minus one perfectly good Governor.

Just as I reached this interesting stage in my reflections, a loud bang, followed by a whistling sound, brief but ghastly, apprized me that my left rear tire had given up its ghost.

I stopped the car. For a moment haste tempted me to run her off the road, leave her, and walk the remaining distance. Common sense, however, reluctantly assured me that thus I should arrive much later than if I stopped and adjusted the spare tire. I was yet nearly four miles from my destination. Moreover, to arrive on foot, dusty and warm, would give me an appearance which scarcely fitted with my purpose.

So I descended, got out my spare tire—and discovered that the jack was missing. I recalled then having loaned it to a fellow motorist on the road, who had broken his, and who had promised to return it "in a couple of hours, old fellow, when I pass your place on my way back." He might have turned it in at the garage, but it was certainly not in my car.

I glanced back along the road, and was somewhat dismayed to see another motor approaching. It was still about a quarter-mile distant. This road led nowhere but to Asgard Heights. If that were Charles coming, the situation might develop with more speed than I had anticipated. But every one knew the Governor's brown touring-car; this car was bright-red, and I at once determined to hail it and borrow a jack.

It was traveling at considerable speed, but I stepped in the middle of the road and waved my arms. He had to stop or run me over.

He stopped.

"Hello, Tolliver!" I said. "You're just in time to lend me a hand. Tire's busted."

Yes, indeed it was Rex. I'd a good deal rather it had been Charles, or Lucifer, or some one else whom I wouldn't have minded meeting just then. But we have to take what is handed us in this world, and so I had to take Rex Tolliver. Of course, my visit to the heights was off.

"Out for a spin?"

Tolliver sprang to the ground and came toward me. I thought the amiability of his tone excessive. Since last Thursday amiability and Rex had been perfect strangers.

"I was," said I off-handedly. "Will be again, perhaps, if you'll lend me your jack. Howard Trumbull has mine. Why a man who will spend three thousand dollars for a car should carry a cast-iron jack beats me. However, he's got my good steel one now."

"You don't say so! So your tire blew out, eh?"

"You can see it," I retorted impatiently. "Come, hurry up with that jack, won't you?"

"Sure—in a minute. Say, Wyndham, why are you going to call on Governor Charles?"

"Governor Charles!" I repeated it as if I had never before heard the name. It was bad acting, but he took me by surprise.

"Ye-es. Or didn't you know this road leads to Asgard Heights?"

"Of course I knew it. But you needn't infer that little Hildreth is going to call on the Governor. In the first place, he hasn't been invited, and in the second—"

"In the second, having seen him once before to-day, why should you bother to come 'way out here this afternoon?"

That made me angry. My own amiability had been worn pretty thin by recent events, and besides, Rex's tone was insufferable.

"What do you mean, Tolliver? Have you been spying on me?"

"I've been trailing you around a bit."

He pushed up his goggles, and I saw that he was watching me keenly, eyes half-shut, suspicion in every line of his tanned, handsome face. My irritation vanished in alarm. If Tolliver had learned anything to make him suspect Charles, then that morning call of mine, together with my presence on the Heights road, was plenty to start something which I might have hard work to stop.

"That's a little bit beneath you," I said with an air of dignified reproof. "I hardly thought you'd do a thing like that."

"No? Well, I don't mind telling you, Wyndham, that I've known all along you had something up your sleeve that you were precious careful to keep me out of. You shut me up mighty indignantly, didn't you, when I suggested—"

I broke in on him sharply.

"Don't say it! I won't pretend that I don't know what you mean. I'm not likely to forget that the man who is supposed to be the most jealous guardian of my cousin's honor insulted her by the basest sort of insinuation. Believe me, Tolliver, I haven't forgotten it at all."

That took him aback. My heart was sick in me, and there was no real spirit behind the words, but he thought differently. He flushed, and looked from my face to the yard of dusty white road between us.

"I'm not—altogether responsible, I think." Then his eyes flashed up and met mine again. "But why are you going to Asgard Heights? And why did you call on Charles this morning? Good Lord, Hil, if you knew all I've suffered, you'd not blame me for suspecting things. Be frank with me. All those months she was working for him—alone with him half the time. Carpenter had no right to send her there, nor Charles to take her. He's not married. No other women in the house but servants. Wyndham, if I'm wrong, kill me for a jealous fool. If I'm right—for God's sake, tell me!"

Nice position for Hildreth, yes. Said Hildreth pulls himself together and remembers that, not being of the G. W. family, he can artistically lie.

"My friend, if you were any one but the man whom my cousin has seen fit to choose for her prospective husband, I'd take you at your word—or try to. But you are Veronica's choice—and besides, I haven't a pistol handy.

"Now I'll tell you something that I had meant to keep from you until I had proved whether there was any truth in it. Thought you had had enough of false hopes and bad clues. Really, though, you've hardly proved worthy of so much consideration."

"What d'you mean? Don't stop like that! If you've run across something that may lead to Ronny, tell it to me. I'm a dog—a beast—anything you like. But *tell* me!"

I wanted to tell him, all right, but for a minute my inventive powers failed. At last, in desperation, I pitched on the "political secret" idea which I had suggested to Chief Brennan, and had meant to ask Charles about— before I learned the truth. Only I turned it inside out, and hoped that to Rex's keyed-up imagination its extravagance might sound plausible.

"Well, I called on Charles this morning."

"Yes, I saw you."

"You said that before. I called there because I had a notion that in Ronny's work with him she might have been given some information which could be used by the Governor's enemies. I wanted to ask him straight out if that were so."

I stopped again: Drama—also invention—is helped by artistic pauses.

"Yes? And he said it was possible?"

I might have assented, but that would not have accounted to him for my presence near Asgard Heights.

"He didn't admit it, but some of the things he said aroused my suspicions in another direction. Rex, I shouldn't be at all surprised if she is being held at the Heights to keep her from telling something she knows about Charles— something which would ruin him politically. I came to find out that, and if you'll kindly go back to Marshall City I'll finish the job. No, my dear fellow, one can do it better than two. I'm going up there and say that Governor

Charles has sent me out with a message for Miss Wyndham. The very fact that I know she's there will gain me admittance—if she is there. Once her presence is proved, it will be easy enough to get her away, and—"

"Yes, it will!" Tolliver viewed me with gloomy contempt. "First thing they'll do will be to telephone the Governor and ask him if he's sent out a messenger."

That was true enough. But anyway, Tolliver had swallowed my bait—or appeared to.

"I never thought of that," I confessed with a melancholy air. "Then the best thing we can do is to go back to town. I'll have another interview with Charles—"

"You mean *I* will!" Rex's hazel eyes flared with a sudden reddish tinge.

"No, you won't." What with excitement and the strain of impromptu false-hood, my coolness was by this time ice-bergian. "That is my privilege as her relative, and besides you'd simply go in there, get in a tearing rage, and spoil everything. Let me handle this, Rex. For Ronny's sake!"

It seemed he was going to yield. That "for Ronny's sake" was a nice touch of sentiment—and applicable enough, in all truth. He hesitated, and I thought to clinch his decision by saying: "This is a case for diplomacy, not brute force. The police would laugh at us if we went to them, and if *you* see Charles in your present mood, it will end by her being removed to another hiding place. She's already been somebody's prisoner for a week. You don't want to risk lengthening the time, do you?"

That clinched his decision, all right, but at an unexpected angle. He took one stride forward and grabbed my shoulder.

"Hil, if she's at Asgard Heights, why in the name of sense should we wait to go through all that 'diplomatic' rigmarole? She's your cousin and my promised wife. Aren't we men enough to go up there, find out the truth and take her away—by force, if necessary?"

Yes, we probably were—if she were being held by force. Even at that moment my opinion of Rex's mentality dropped ten degrees below normal. He really believed my story—thought that Governor Clinton Charles had violently kidnaped his former secretary to prevent her revealing some dark secret of the Reform Party. However, the main consideration was not Rex's credulity, but to get him away from this vicinity.

"I think you're wrong, Tolliver. We can't do anything now, just the two of us. The whole estate is fenced in with deer wire—and probably patrolled by his Chinese servants. And they'd never let us in at the gate."

Again he eyed me steadily and long. I saw by the look in his face that an idea was about to spring into brilliant being, and braced myself to squelch it if I could.

"We may not be able to enter by the gate," he said slowly, "nor over the fence. But what if I should tell you that I know a way to get in those grounds without meeting any such obstacles?"

"Airplane?" I suggested intelligently.

"Airplane! No. You and I can go in there, Hil, and no one be any the wiser, unless we choose. Here! The first thing is to get your tire fixed."

He was back at his own car as he spoke, and opening the tool-chest.

"But, Tolliver—" I stopped. What "but" could I advance?

What his plan was I could not imagine. Something wild, no doubt, that would end in our arrest for trespass, and in no glimpse of Ronny. On the other hand. Fate might not be half so kind. If he did get in—found my cousin, perhaps in the very company of her lover—heard from her own lips that she was there by choice— He mustn't go—he *must—not!*

"Man," I said, "don't be a fool. Whatever your scheme is, it's sure to end disastrously for all of us. Come back to Marshall City and let me talk to the Governor."

By that time he had the jack in position and was working the old tire off the rim. He glanced up with a flash of renewed suspicion.

"It seems to me, Wyndham, that you're darned anxious to keep me away from Asgard Heights. What's the idea?"

"No more than I said. Oh, well, if you want to take the risk, go ahead. Perhaps, after all it's the best way."

For now I realized that my unlucky "inspiration" had landed me where further protest would only confirm Tolliver in his original suspicion. All I could hope was that Charles's Chinamen were alert, intelligent watch-dogs—or, if we did find Ronny, that I could get a word with her ahead of her desperate *fiancé.*

Chapter IX.
"jacob's ladder."

It was then after six o'clock and, as Tolliver cheerfully remarked, by the time we were within the boundaries of Asgard Heights darkness would lend its concealment to our visit. I thought it also increased the chance of Charles's presence there, which would lessen my opportunity for a solitary talk with my cousin in advance of Tolliver by about ninety per cent. I could hardly advance that as a reason for delay, but I did ask to be informed immediately of the mysterious means by which we were to enter undetected.

"Never you mind, Hil. I've something to show you which will make you sit up. I don't believe Governor Charles knows there's a back door to his new estate—of course, if he does know and has had it blocked up, then the game's off—or rather, it can't be played on the same lines. No, I won't stop to explain here. Take too long. Climb in your little go-cart now, and follow Uncle Rex."

The prospect of immediate action had produced a remarkable change in Tolliver. His old boyish spirit had returned, and if to me his cheerful impetuosity appeared like the enthusiasm of a maniac, rushing headlong over a cliff, that was because I knew the cliff was there and he did not. And the worst of it was that the least word of warning would only precipitate disaster.

Seeing no way out of it, I followed the dust of Rex's touring car, one minute cursing him for a credulous fool to believe so wild a yarn as I had told him, the next praying that his credulity might not give way again to his original and, as Ronny's letter informed me, correct suspicions.

He did not, as I had expected, drive on along the road to Asgard Heights, but started back toward the pike. In a short time we had joined the scattered procession returning cityward. For the life of me I could not reconcile this with his avowed intention to make his investigation that very evening.

A short distance beyond Salvator's, a road-house at whose pleasant open-air tables I had often dined with my cousin, Rex turned aside. Turning after him I found myself invading what might have been considered a road by a pre-Columbian-American of unexacting requirements, but he would have deceived himself. It was not so much a road as a series of hummocks traversed by ravinelike ruts. The natural forest began here, which spread out toward the pike from a spur of Kildaire Mountain, and this road-thing struck inward and upward between the trees.

Tolliver's car is like a traction engine, or one of these armored "caterpillars," that they use in trench warfare. It might refuse to climb a vertical stone wall, unless the stones were rough enough to give tire-grip, and then it would probably go right along up. But my roadster is more delicate and ladylike. At the end of the first forty yards she plunged her left fore wheel in a rut she thought was a bottomless crevasse, gave one panic-stricken sob, and quit. Rex came back on foot, in response to the yell I sent after him.

"If this car walked on stilts," I said, "she might be able to toddle along here. As it is, she's done. Is it necessary that we invade the wilderness?"

"Of course," he retorted impatiently. "If you would only drive a real motor instead of that wretched— Say, I can't tow you. The grade is too steep, and it's too rough. You'll have to ride with me."

"And leave my car here? She'll be stolen. Come on back to town, Tolliver, and let's go at this thing from a sensible angle—"

"Any man who would steal *that* would deserve—deserve to own her. However, if you care more for your car than you do for your cousin, go back by all means. I can get on alone, I imagine."

I imagined, too. I imagined Tolliver coming upon Ronny and Cl—

"I'll go with you. Give me a hand, though, and we'll put her in the underbrush."

We did, and covered her over with boughs, like a forlorn, deserted babe in the wood. Rex begrudged the time spent, but worse than futile though I knew delay to be, I could not resist holding back as much as possible the hour of our début at Asgard Heights.

Once in Rex's juggernautal machine, however, matters were out of my hands. We went. I spent most of the time in the air, as we negotiated the slight inequalities of the way—in other words, bumped the bumps—for Rex drove as if he thought he were on the Harlequin track, which is the pride of Marshall City's racing-car owners.

Dusk was laying its gray soft veil across the summer world. Naturally, it got laid first in the forest. Rex lighted his lamps, and by their spreading, rut-exaggerating radiance, we penetrated where foot of man may have trod before, but not the tire of an automobile—I'm sure of that. At last, when I was certain that in ten more cataclysms the inside of that car would drop out and give the "road" its hard-won victory, Rex jumped a ditch—I thought he did, though there may have been a plank or so over it—and we came to a halt.

The lamps showed a rocky, treeless slant directly ahead, ascending at an angle of eighty-five degrees.

"Why don't you go on up?" I inquired. "Run out of gasoline?"

My friend disdained to reply. He sprang out, took off his dust-coat and goggles, bundled them under the seat, and began searching for something in the car.

"Now, where's that torch gone?" he demanded. "Oh, by George!"

The hunt stopped and he straightened up. "Trumbull has it. He borrowed it one night last week."

"Wanted it to look at my jack with, maybe. Now we know why friend Trumbull can afford a three-thousand-dollar car. What did you need it for? Torch-light procession?"

"Never mind. Come along," was his sole reply.

I meekly obeyed, as he started off through the underbrush at right angles to the rocky slant which had, apparently, ended our connection with the automobile.

"Don't you think the mystery could be decently canned now?" I pleaded, as I caught up with him. "I'd like to know what we're doing."

"Going up Jacob's ladder."

"I believe you *are* crazy."

"Thanks. I call the place Jacob's ladder because only an angel could use it conveniently. An angel or a small boy."

As he spoke, Rex ducked and plunged beneath a dark mass which, on following, I identified as the low-spreading boughs of a balsam pine.

Emerging into yet blacker shadow, a match flared in Rex's hand. We seemed to be standing at the bottom of a narrow fissure in the rock. Above the walls drew together, ending far up in a threadlike slit of stars. There were loose pebbles underfoot. Some time a stream had flowed here from out the stony heart of Kildaire Mountain.

"What do you think of the Asgard Heights back hallway?" my friend inquired.

"You'll have to show me. Name the big idea."

And at last Rex condescended to explain. Years ago, it seemed, his people had owned a summer cottage located some two miles distant. Julys and Augusts Rex used to play happy barefoot kid, and in that capacity he joined a band of desperate brigands (heirs of several neighboring cottagers), to whose captaincy he won by discovery of this very rift in the Heights stronghold.

"I don't believe old Mason ever had an idea where some of his best fruit went to." (Mason was the "iron and copper king" from the heirs of whose estate Charles had acquired the Heights.) "Brigands, you know, are bound to be unscrupulous. He trusted his fencing, but there's a sort of plateau above here and my Jacob's ladder leads up inside the fence. It's not conspicuous at the top, and that good old balsam hides all the lower part. If our mothers had ever guessed the broken necks we risked and the forbidden fruit we got away with, they'd have seen visions of undertakers' wagons or criminal futures for us all right. Gee! We were some desperate bandits!"

I was feeling very sorry for Rex just then. Blindly, almost joyously, he was approaching that before which this folly of secret stairways and stolen apples would be scorched and shriveled to nothing. He evidently proposed to rescue his promised bride after the best style of any serial "movie." How would he face the sordid truth of his betrayal?

If Rex observed in me any lack of response to his own enthusiasm, he made no comment, but turned and led the way yet further into the yawning depths.

Stumbling after, I wondered if I had cold-blooded nerve enough to pitch him off the top of this mysterious "stair" once we were up it. Some such drastic method was needed, it seemed, if I wished to prevent a great disaster.

But the actual sight of Jacob's ladder, as he had named it, jarred me out of my murderous meditations and recalled to me that I had a neck of my own to break.

The crevice had narrowed sharply, till further progress along the stream bed became difficult. Suddenly I collided with Rex, who had come to another halt.

"Where do we go up?" I inquired.

"Right here."

By the light of another match, I saw that he had seated himself on a projection of the rock and was calmly unlacing his shoes. He stopped to wave an airy gesture toward the converging walls above.

I craned my neck and groaned.

"Jacob's ladder is right. We'd be merry little angels before we ever finished that stunt. You're dreaming, man. Come home."

"Did you expect an elevator?" His tones were injured. "Stay here if you're afraid."

He fastened his shoes together by the laces and slung them round his neck. Then with a straight upward spring he caught at a jutting ledge, found invisible foothold for his stockinged toes, half turned and a moment later was braced diagonally across the chasm just above my head.

"So-long," he called tauntingly. "I'll tell Ronny how anxious you were for her."

Which reminded me.

In a moment Rex was again on his upward way, yielding me room to follow. He shouted down a few words of encouragement and approval, but he needn't have bothered. So long as I had breath in me, I had simply got to stay in the rescue business. It wasn't Charles, though, from whom I expected to save Ronny once we found her.

The ascent proved slightly less difficult than I had expected. After the first the walls were a fairly uniform three feet odd apart. It was rather like going up the inside of a black chimney, where innumerable ledges and projections made foot and hand-hold possible. In my troubled state of mind I had neglected to remove my shoes, and in consequence slipped more times than was pleasant. But though my muscles may have been softer than Rex's, my weight was considerably less. When he achieved the final edge, I was not far behind.

Climbing by touch is not a method I should recommend to any other amateur mountaineer, but at last Rex caught my wrists and I realized that even Jacob's ladder had an ultimate top rung.

The narrow crack through which we had emerged was closely bordered by underbrush; prickly, brambly underbrush, as I discovered when we began to push our way through it. As Rex had said, there was a sort of plateau here on the mountain slope, along whose outer edge ran the high deer-wire fence whose winding miles of length surrounded the entire estate. Far down and to the northeast Marshall City glowed against the sky. Ahead there was only the darkness of trees rising against a starry heaven.

"Come along," urged Rex in a low voice. "Don't make any noise. We might run into a gamekeeper."

I hoped we should. A gamekeeper or a grizzly bear or any other formidable being who might check our progress Veronica-ward.

"No one," Rex continued, "shall stop us now. Are you armed, Hil?"

"Lord, no! I didn't leave home with any idea of playing bandit."

"Well, I am," he said with satisfaction. "There are ten good little persuaders in the clip of this automatic."

"Oh, Lord!" I said again, and then—I think—I groaned.

CHAPTER X.
THE STOLEN LADY—A MELODRAMA.

It took us over an hour to traverse the distance between our point of entry and the formal park immediately surrounding the residence.

I'm no socialist, but I don't think any man has a right to own nearly two entire mountains. If he does, he should be forced to landscape-garden the whole thing and make the going a little pleasanter for trespassers. I fell down gullies, was detestably scratched by briers, and became convinced a number of times that we were hopelessly lost.

Since breakfast I had been living on anxiety and nervous excitement; good stimulants but poor nourishment. An empty stomach added its plaint to my physical discomforts. By the time we caught a gleam from the first ground-lamp, I was hating Charles and Tolliver so impartially that it would have been a real pleasure to see them meet—provided my cousin could have been left out of the consequences.

Having crossed the valley between Kildaire and Kennett, and negotiated a breath-taking slope on the other side, the aforesaid first lamp welcomed us. Tolliver, who had been cursing and grunting along, suddenly assumed the manner of a noble redskin sleuthing it round the teepees of his hated foe.

I had no objection to dropping full length in the underbrush. In a few more minutes I should have dropped anyway, for I was all in. But on his announcing that in that attitude we would snakily writhe the balance of our way, I rebelled.

"Tolliver," I said, "chloroform the boyhood reminiscences and recall that you're over ten years old. You're not going to rob an orchard. You're going to be shot for a burglar. You're an adult, little though one would suspect it. Let us flit from tree-trunk to tree-trunk like sinister shadows, if we must, but this slinky sliding idea of yours doesn't appeal to little Hildreth. I'm no snake—not even a caterpillar."

I think his reply hinted a third alternative—a worm, in fact—but I carefully missed its personal application. In the end he rather sulkily yielded, and it was on our pedal extremities that we proceeded toward where he said the house was.

In the natural forest we had met neither man nor beast, and it seemed as if the more ornamental part of the estate were equally deserted. I was too occupied by my thoughts to appreciate the beauty of those famous grounds. Electric lamps were frequent among the trees and along the graveled walks, but glimpses of level pools agleam with lotus blooms, of blossoming bowers, of fantastically clipped yews and flower-starred vistas bordered by trees like slim green guardian damsels, left me unenthusiastic. In fact, I quote that description from a tourist's guide-book, written when the place was Mason's and occasionally on exhibition. Trees like slim green damsels must be worth looking at, too. To diverge back to my story, we tramped unmolested through about a mile of aforesaid scenic triumphs, and then Rex began to get cautious again.

"We're close to the house," he said. "You'd better stay here, Hil, while I go on and reconnoiter."

"As a reconnoiterer, I'm it," I countered. "You stay here, give me that automatic and let me go ahead. I'm slimmer than you and can hide behind anything from a lath to a beech-tree."

"Not on your life! I'd look nice hanging behind while you rushed to the rescue of my promised wife."

"Your promised wife, but my cousin and chum since birth. Don't be so conceited, Rex. She'd welcome a rescue from me just as gladly as from you."

I thought it probable she would, too. Her dismay at seeing either of us was likely to be considerable.

"All right," growled Rex. "Then we'll go on together, but for Heaven's sake drop that careless air of owning the place you've been striding along with. Remember that we can't afford to be caught. If Veronica has really been brought here and forcibly detained, they'll stop at nothing to prevent discovery."

By "they" I presumed he meant those desperadoes of the Reform Party who had committed the supposed crime. Torn between pity for his mentality and dread of impending revelations, I followed on. In my own mind, however, I had determined that Rex was going to lose his little pal soon after we came in sight of the house, which was still concealed by trees. I should slip away from him, go straight to the door and demand to see my cousin. Beyond that foresight halted, but at any cost Veronica, and Charles, if he were here to-night, must be warned.

We were sneaking along in the shelter of some shrubbery that bordered a broad drive, when with a roar and whir a large car shot past us. Rex had grabbed my arm and pulled me flat on the turf.

"Did you see him—did you see him?" he whispered excitedly in my ear. "That was Charles himself in the tonneau."

"Of course it was," I responded with bitter calm. "He'd naturally come home to welcome us. Rex, can't we choose another night when Charles isn't around—"

"I never thought you were such a—baby, Hil." He had started to use an unkinder term than baby. Well, if I seemed a coward to him, he seemed a fool to me, so matters were equal.

"Duck!" I whispered sharply. Rex had risen again to his feet, and my ears had caught a slight clinking and rustling sound some distance to the left of us away from the drive. He heard it, too. We crouched very still on the dew-wet turf, peering into the darkness of a group of small fir trees on the lawn.

Then a yellow glow silhouetted their Japanesque trunks and boughs. Beneath, peering straight at us, it seemed, we saw a hideous saffron face. It was not five yards distant, and every detail of the features was clear as some grotesque painting—the slanted, slitlike eyes, wide grinning mouth and yellow, hollow cheeks.

We both gasped, caught by the same eery feeling of spectral horror.

The face turned away, and we caught a glimpse of a shining black coiled queue above a dull blue smock. There was a sound of shuffling, retreating footfalls.

"Hmph!" sniffed my companion. "Keep your nerve, Hil. That was only one of Charles's servants lighting up the gardens."

"Is there a lawn fête coming off? Most of the place is bright as daylight already."

"It makes no difference," said Rex impatiently. "It's the inside of the house that interests us. I think now that the best plan will be for us to conceal ourselves until later in the night, when things quiet down. I know the very place."

He was off again and I after him. I couldn't afford to lose him till I knew the whereabouts of this newly proposed ambuscade, so that I could locate him again—after my mission of warning should be accomplished.

We crossed one green alley of trees, at the end of which loomed a majestic portico, a side entrance to the house, I judged. Its imposing size gave one a chill hint of power and grandeur, but the main body of the mansion was merely indicated to our eyes by the gleam of lighted windows through foliage.

Rex approached no nearer. Turning to the left he led me down a steep terrace, round a laurel hedge, and so to the level of a sunken garden that might have been the pleasance of a wealthy mandarin, rather than a supposedly democratic American.

In the midst was a pool nearly big enough to be called a lake, with a fair-sized island in the center. A steeply curving bridge led across the lotus-starred waters to the door of a scarlet pagoda, whose curved, overlapping roofs, scalloped and fringed with tiny bells, answered the winds' soft breath with a faint and elfin music. (See guide-book aforesaid.) The faint and elfin music didn't attract our consideration half so much as a sound of swift, chattering human speech, emanating from the pagoda, and bearing news that yet others of Charles's Mongolian myrmidons were about.

"Quick!" snapped Tolliver. "We mustn't be seen!"

Soft-footed, he dashed back toward the terrace, but this time on the hedge's inner side. I was at his heels when he dodged beneath a curtain of some kind of yellow-blossoming vine, and I followed him.

We had entered what proved to be an ornamental grotto, though it was darksomely damp enough to have been the mouth of a cavern or cellar. I knocked my shins on a box of gardener's tools, sat down on it to recover breath—and realized that I ought to have dropped my would-be cousin-in-law outside. Now I was going to have the deuce of a time framing up an excuse to leave him.

"Three of us kids," said Tolliver, "foiled old Mason's head gardener by hiding in here one whole afternoon. We got home around 11 P.M., and the neighborhood was out hunting us through the woods with lanterns."

"Those were the happy days," I said sarcastically. "Too bad you ever grew up, Tolliver."

I heard him turn in the dark.

"What's wrong with you?" he demanded. "If we're here on a fool's errand, it's your fault. If we're not, I can see nothing shamefully kiddish in what we are doing."

I couldn't tell him that the kiddish part was in suspecting the Governor of forcibly abducting his former secretary. At the first hint that she was here of her own free will fireworks were due. So I pivoted and said:

"Your way is more dashing than mine would have been, but possibly it's the best, I'm more concerned than I seem, old man. I haven't your patience to lurk here in the dark. I'm going out and—"

"You are not!" His big body barred the way. "Sh!" he added sibilantly. "Some one is coming!"

Close to the grotto a flight of marble steps cut the terrace, and it was a click of heels and slight scrape of descending feet on these which he had heard. Intuition informed me who was approaching. Had it been any other two people, intuition would probably have sounded the same alarm in my then state of mind, but for once the inner monitor was right.

Tolliver had parted the vines which partially screened our retreat and was peering out. I followed his example.

Two figures, a man and a woman, came into view and strolled a few paces along the shore of the pool. They halted directly beneath a great lantern of painted silk, one of the many which lent the sunken garden so Oriental an appearance. It cast a ruddy glow downward upon them. I could feel the eager tremor which shook the man beside me as recognition became sure.

The woman was Veronica and Governor Charles was the man. Fate, which might so easily have been kinder, had led them as directly to us as if by intentional appointment.

My cousin looked very slim, innocent and young, standing there in the rosy light beside her lover. She was dressed in a blue, droopy gown of long, soft lines, with a filmy scarf flung loosely about her shoulders. Hers was a face of tender, almost childish curves, crowned by hair like soft, pale gold. Her brows and lashes, however, were very dark, shading slate-gray eyes— the kind of eyes that give one a fresh little thrill of pleased surprise every time one looks at them. With those eyes, and with her red little mouth, dimpled chin, and Dresden shepherdess nose, no man would at first sight ever pick Ronny Wyndham for any task more intellectual than choosing a trousseau suited to her charms.

Yet packed in that small round skull under its fluffy adornment were brains of a quality to be respected. Good sense, too, or so I had believed until to-day.

To me, with that scrap of letter burning my pocket, Charles seemed to tower over her, to dominate her. Like a malignant jinnee of the fairest outward seeming, his personality had engulfed that of my poor little cousin and swept her helplessly from home and honor.

As I stared with tingling hatred at the face of Veronica's successful lover, I forgot the cheated man at my side. Reversing the situation as I had foreseen it, it was Rex's hand which restrained me from rushing out to force a precipitate reckoning. His grip brought me to my senses, and at the same moment Ronny spoke.

Throughout the dialogue which ensued, we in the grotto stood just so, and as I listened I realized that for the second time that day all my ideas must be astonishingly reversed.

Well-nigh too astonishingly, in fact. Though I could place but one construction upon the words uttered, all the while I had the oddest feeling that what I heard could not be true. Or that some other truth underlay it, as the real life of an actor underlies his stage presentation. Perhaps the theatric background of colored lamps and reflecting pool played a part in that impression.

"When is this folly to end?" Ronny turned with an impatient gesture from contemplation of the scarlet-pagodaed islet. Her tone was as unsentimental as the question. "You have held me here for a week. Don't you yet realize the hopelessness and the madness of what you are doing?"

"The end rests with you," Charles responded quietly.

"It won't rest with either of us soon. Every day increases your risk of discovery. And when you are found out, don't you think I have friends who care enough for me to see you punished? Haven't you any regard left for your own—I won't say honor, but for your ambitions? Why, the very position that saves you from suspicion—"

"Will make the crash bigger if I'm found out," he broke in, with grim acquiescence. "And the love that risks a sacrifice like that means nothing to you!"

"Love and sacrifice! Those are beautiful words. They're not fit for a man like you to use! What happiness can you imagine would come of it, if I should surrender? Do you want a wife who hates and despises you? Why, when I was walking beside you just now I wondered how you could endure the company of a person whom you have so wronged."

"Yet you came out with me to-night."

"You said you had something to tell me. I was foolish enough to hope that at last your manhood had awakened and you meant to let me go. I won't be your wife—no! And if you don't free me soon, you will have to keep me cooped up here the rest of my life—if you can succeed in doing it. Let me go now, and I'll keep still—that's the price I offer, and you will be wiser to accept. You are behaving like a Chinese mandarin, who wishes a slave, not a wife, and I would as soon be married to one." She glanced scornfully about the garden. "These surroundings are very suitable to your idea of love."

He laughed, but with no amusement.

"I didn't design these gardens, though I heard that Bartoli regarded them as some of his best work. I did think that their beauty would please you. As I've said often enough, I only bought the place for you, Veronica. Till you came into my life I never knew the purpose or need of beautiful lands and flower and jewels. I would like to give you every beautiful thing there is in the world. You don't really hate me as you think. You cannot—must not! No other man could care for you as I do."

"I hope not." Her tone was icily unresponsive. "To have seen the beast and tyrant aroused in one man is more than sufficient."

"Stop!" That controlled, flexible voice of his quivered slightly. His face went suddenly darker in the lantern-light. "Have I harmed you? Have I so much as touched your hand since you came here? If you really believed me beast and tyrant, you would not dare call me so!"

Ronny's dimpled chin went up in that defiant fearlessness which was so incongruous to her appearance and so exactly expressed her inward spirit.

"At heart you are precisely what I said! You are afraid to touch me because you are afraid to drive me through the one door of escape you have left open!"

He drew back, with a slightly ironical bow. "Aren't we verging the least bit on melodrama, Veronica?"

"A courtship that includes a kidnaping can hardly escape melodrama." Suddenly she laughed, and her mirth had a ring of sincerity. "The situation is so preposterous that I can hardly even yet believe that it's real. You—the Governor of this State, a man of your reputation and standing—"

"To love so deeply that nothing counts beside. No doubt it is amusing."

"But you don't love me. If you loved me, I should be at home this moment. The simple truth is that you set your will against mine, and when I declined to be mastered by you, you resorted to trickery and violence rather than have your will crossed!"

"You can put it that way, but—"

"It's true. If you really want me to believe differently, let me go home!"

"I can't do that. Will you walk further? Or do you hate the night and the flowers for my sake?"

"Let me go!"

"Not yet—never, if I can hold you so long."

"Now!" whispered Rex in my ear, and the two of us, one in purpose at last, burst through the curtaining screen of vines.

CHAPTER XI.
FLIGHT.

When Rex insisted on invading Asgard Heights, I had dreaded some startling denouement. I had accompanied him in such misery of mind as I had never before experienced. The tale he had swallowed seemed to me so absurd that I called him a fool for believing.

Yet his very credulity had prepared him for a fact more amazing than my fabrication. Having accepted the idea of Governor Charles as a kidnaper for political reasons, to find him in the same guilt for a more romantic cause only stimulated Tolliver's indignation.

A psychologist might have read in Charles's visionary eyes and determined chin the capacity for some such enormous folly as that conversation had revealed, but to me the discovery came as a shock.

It was in a hysterical mood between laughter and relief that I followed Tolliver from the grotto, no longer fearing anything. In the bare fact of discovery, Charles was lost, and at that moment I almost pitied him.

But Tolliver, seeing not the victim of a gigantic folly, but an unscrupulous and dangerous enemy, ran truer to form.

When the grotto disgorged its rescue-party, Veronica cried out, and instinctively, I think, for he could not have recognized us at first glance, Charles sprang between us and the girl.

His hand dropped toward a coat-pocket, but Rex caught his wrist, at the same moment jamming the muzzle of his own pistol against the Governor's vest.

"One struggle or shout for help, and you're a dead man, Charles!"

"Hildreth!" cried Ronny. "You've come at last!"

And running past the other two she threw her arms around my neck and frankly hugged me.

That was all right, and I was glad enough to return the embrace. It didn't strike me until later that Tolliver might not like her greeting me with enthusiasm and ignoring him.

"Yes," I said, "and it's time, eh? Why, Ronny, everybody in Marshall City has been hunting for you. This last week has been—"

"Hil," broke in Tolliver, in a somewhat strained voice, "will you kindly take this scoundrel's pistol from his pocket? Both my hands are occupied."

At the words, Charles, who had stood perfectly motionless, very rigid and white of face, came unexpectedly to life.

There was a swift flurry of action, too quick for my eyes to accurately follow. I think that Charles tried to knock aside the automatic with his left hand and wrench himself free. Had Rex remembered his safety catch, that attempt would have finished the Governor. But the catch was on, the trigger of course resisted all pressure, and what might have been prompt tragedy ended in a rough-and-tumble fight.

They went to the turf with Rex upper-most, rolled over a couple of times, and, still locked in an energetic tangle of legs and arms, slid off the bank and splashed resoundingly down among the lotus blossoms of the pool.

Then Veronica, for the first time in her life, so far as I know, really screamed. I had forgotten the voices we had heard earlier from the pagoda, but as her shrill woman's cry cut the night, two men came flying out of the pagoda and across the bridge toward us.

Seeing Rex's pistol where he had dropped it, I snatched up the weapon and went to meet them. Rex was an A-1 swimmer and his plunge into that fancy pool didn't alarm me, but I thought the arrival of those Celestial gardeners superfluous.

They seemed to agree. Having faced for one second the pistol's threatening muzzle, they beat an agitated retreat back over the bridge. I let them go. In fact, I couldn't have stopped them. I tried to fire a shot in the air after them, found the catch down, and by the time it was released they were out of sight in the pagoda, whence their shrill voices rose to heaven in frantic yells, addressed, I assumed, to such of their fellows as might be within hearing distance.

It seemed a good idea to leave before any saffron-skinned horde should rush to their master's succor.

I ran back toward where I had left Ronny, and found her down at the pool-edge, tugging at somebody's collar.

"Leggo!" came Rex's voice, half-strangled. "Y're ch-choking me!"

"Let him alone!" I dropped on my knees beside Ronny and caught her well-intentioned hands away. Released, Rex's head and shoulders subsided under water, but promptly reappeared in a complicated swirl of lotus stems. Another head came up close by. Rex dived for it and they both went under.

"Oh, they'll kill each other—they'll be drowned!" sobbed Veronica.

Knowing Rex's pertinacity, I thought it possible myself. Though a poor swimmer, I was kicking off my shoes preparatory to joining the submarine struggle, when the two rose together within arm's reach. They continued to rise until they were no more than chest-deep, and I perceived that Rex, at least, was standing.

"Lend me a hand, can't you?" he said crossly. A minute later I was helping Rex to scramble out on the bank, dragging with him a very limp Governor.

"It's shallow; all mud below—and these confounded weeds!" Rex disgustedly removed a pink lotus-bloom, draped coquettishly over his ear, and flung it from him. "I ought to have let him down in the mud, if he wanted to."

Though conscious, Charles lay gasping helplessly on the turf, while Ronny still sobbed and the pagoda-hid Celestials continued to split the night with vociferous appeals for aid. The whole affair could not have consumed more than four minutes' time.

Stooping, Tolliver half jerked, half lifted his unscrupulous rival to his feet. With a beautiful continuity of purpose, he plunged a hand into one of Charles's dripping pockets and removed the automatic which reposed there. That the Governor should carry one was not surprising, under the circumstances.

"Let's get out of this, Tolliver," I said. "All the Chinks on the place will be down on us in a minute."

"They'll do anything *he* says." Ronny nodded at Charles. "They'll never let us out unless he orders them to."

"He'll give the order all right," I said with conviction.

"He tried to drown us both in the mud there." Rex seemed to be still indignant. "He's desperate. We'll go out as we came in, and it won't be necessary to trust him."

"Have your own way," I yielded hastily, "but let's move! Come, Ronny!"

The ululations from the pagoda were being answered by shrill shouts from the houseward direction. A distant slap and patter of flat-shod feet announced the approach of reenforcements.

With two pistols and the Governor for hostage we might have stood them off, but heroics come easier in theory than practise. There is something curiously alarming in the swift approach of many inimical feet through the night.

I won't speak for Rex. His actions may have been the result of sober judgment without a trace of panic. But the instant I took Ronny's arm and started to run I felt like a scared rabbit. All the stories I had ever heard of Chinese knives and Chinese disregard for life lent me energy, and, as panic is contagious, Ronny caught it. She flew along beside me at a pace to discount all claims that skirts are a hindrance to speed. I am recording an unheroic retreat without apology.

In five seconds we were out of the sunken garden and scampering lightly across a wide expanse of open lawn. There were too many lights. Our shadows fled about us in every direction, expanding and contracting, flat-black monsters on the dew-glinting grass.

Ahead some kind of high level barrier loomed darkly. It proved to be an unusually high hedge of clipped yew. Running beside it a few paces we came to a break, like a gateway, dodged through and—another similar wall faced us with no gateway.

It was dark in the shadow of those parallel hedges, and we came to an uncertain halt. The night was warm, and fragrant with the scent of flowers. Somewhere men were running and shouting, but the sounds were far away. We had fled like two frightened children, and a sense of acute shame overtook me.

"Where is Rex?" Veronica's question brought home my guilt. Conscience smote me yet more sharply when I found that Tolliver's pistol was still in my hand. Then I remembered having seen him commandeer the Governor's, so that was all right, but why had I run at all—and from a pack of cowardly Chinamen?

"I supposed he was following us," I muttered. "I'll go back."

"Where are you, Hil?"

Tolliver was calling, low-voiced, from outside.

"Thought I'd lost you," he complained as we both appeared in the hedge-gate. "We can't afford to get separated."

"My fault," I admitted. "But it is necessary to drag *him* with us?"

Rex was not alone. At pistol-point, evidently, he had brought his rival along, and I suppose that Charles, his fighting impulse cooled by the underwater struggle, and realizing that his world was tottering to a fall, had not cared enough to resist.

"I presume," said Rex sarcastically, "that you would have left him behind to direct his servants in pursuit."

Charles spoke, for the first time since our emergence from the grotto.

"You have no need to fear my servants," he said in a low voice. "Come back to the house and I'll send you home in my car. I'm—finished, of course."

"Don't trust him!" warned Ronny, with what I recognized as a deliberately retaliatory note. He was down and I was a bit sorry for him, but my cousin seemed not inclined to mercy. "Governor Charles believes in the right of force and considers himself above the law."

"I don't mean to trust him," responded Rex matter-of-factly. "We'll go home in my car, not his. Quick! Out of sight! They're coming!"

Several figures had burst into view on the open lawn's far side, but I doubt if they even glimpsed us. We bolted into the dark alley between the hedges, Ronny and I again leading, and Rex still dragging his unresistant captive.

CHAPTER XII.

AN IMPEDED RESCUE.

The path between was not of gravel, but carpeted with grass, in which our feet made little sound. For light we had only starshine and what faint trickles of radiance pierced the thick wall of yew from the bright lit lawn beyond. However, within ten yards I sensed a blacker blackness to the left, which proved to be another opening, this time through the inner hedge.

The other two close at our heels, Ronny and I turned the corner and went straight ahead, walking now, for it was too dark to run.

The shrill, excited yelps of our pursuers sounded more distant every moment. It occurred to me that those Chinamen might be none too anxious to run to earth a quarry armed and desperado-like, as the ones I had driven back at the bridge no doubt reported us.

Walking straight on in the dark, we violently encountered another hedge at right angles to the path. Ronny and I retired as gracefully as might be from the collision and, yielding to the hedge's compulsory guidance, we again proceeded, though in a new direction. When the same incident was twice repeated, with variations of angle, I began to weary of the eccentricities of our journey.

"What is this place anyway?" I inquired at large, rubbing a twig-scratched face. "There's more hedge than path."

"We're in the maze," volunteered Charles, and added gloomily: "We'll spend the night here if you go much further."

Then I recalled my guide-book informant and his reference to "the pleasing revival by Mr. Mason of that old-fashioned fancy, a bewildering series of paths and lanes shut in by hedges, called a maze, and once so popular on the more pretentious estates."

"Know the way through, Tolliver?" I asked hopefully. Heretofore he had gone as one carrying an accurate brain map of the Asgard Heights grounds.

But he failed us now. "These hedges weren't here a dozen years ago," he explained.

"Go back," advised Veronica sensibly. "We might wander here for hours."

In perfect accord for once, the four of us volte-faced and executed another retreat, but the tangled alleys in which we had entrapped ourselves proved less easy to escape than one would have supposed.

In entering we had turned four times, twice to the left and twice to the right. I was sure of that, but to my disgust the others disagreed. They followed my lead without argument till the second turning, which Ronny insisted came too soon, and Rex said was in the wrong direction. Charles ventured no opinion, having relapsed into melancholy and indifferent silence.

Rex got his way at last by sheer persistence. He may have been right, for all I know, and the next may have been the fatal turning that lost us. After that, however, we turned and turned, wound back and forth, found ourselves in unexpected culs-de-sac, and generally enjoyed the "pleasing fancy" of the diabolically clever person who had planned those hedges.

By this time, as if by conspiracy, the sky had clouded over, and the many electric lights, of which I had once foolishly complained, seemed to have been obliterated with the stars. No least gleam of them now penetrated the mad tangle of leafy walls in which we were involved. I had a few matches, but they were soon exhausted. Of course, it was no use for Charles and Tolliver to search their drenched pockets.

Sounds from without, even the most blood-curdling yells, would have been welcome now, for we had reached that point of confusion where we were no longer sure that even in a general way we were moving toward the circumference of the maze. Save, however, for the occasional cry of a bird, or chirp of insects, the silence and darkness were equally complete.

Charles, I am sure, was free to have departed our company a dozen times over, for even Rex had lost interest in everything but a passionate distaste for overgrown yew hedges. But, perhaps in the love of misery for companionship, he seemed more inclined to cling to us than leave us.

Recalling his existence at last, Rex demanded information as to exactly how many square miles the maze covered.

"About a quarter mile across, I believe," replied its owner. "I've never been in here before."

"Any one who came here intentionally would be— Why didn't you warn us what we were getting into?"

"That's unfair," broke in Veronica unexpectedly. "He did warn you, Rex."

Her fiancé muttered something undistinguishable, then added aloud: "We'll have to break through these hedges in a straight line till we're out, if it's a quarter of a mile or ten miles. Come on, Hil, get to work."

We tried it.

Did you ever attempt to break through a hedge of healthy, well-cared-for yew? With a machete, or even an ax, that mode of progress may be possible, if not expeditious. We had no machete and no ax—and very little temper by the time we made up our minds to desist.

By another inspiration I climbed on Tolliver's shoulders and peered across the tops of the hedges. The lights of the house were not visible, nor were any lights visible anywhere.

The discovery gave me a queer sensation—like returning into a room one has left brightly lighted a moment before, and finding it in pitch darkness. There was a flashing suspicion that I had gone suddenly blind without knowing it. But that was absurd. Climbing down I reported.

"This is some of your doing!" snarled Rex. I assumed that he was addressing the Governor, and it was Charles who answered out of the darkness.

"I wish it were," he said with a sort of depressed humor. "If I could turn off the lights from here, I could certainly turn them on again, and we might get somewhere. Do you suppose that I am enjoying this—this prolonged agony?"

"Please let's not waste time quarreling," put in Ronny's sweet contralto. "Li Ching may have turned off the lights."

"Who or which is Li Ching?" I asked.

"The butler. He's the funniest old Chinaman. He does almost everything backward, and it would be just like him to think that throwing off the lights would keep us from getting away."

"Well, it is keeping us, isn't it?" Rex seemed to be in an extraordinary irritable mood, quite different to his temper just before the rescue.

"So it appears." The contralto was now a bit more cool than sweet. "Hildreth, won't you take my hand again? I'm afraid of being separated from you."

"Wow!" I thought. "There's a hint to moderate your tone, friend Tolliver!"

Since the alternative to playing blind man's buff with those hedges was standing still, the game proceeded. There was not even the slope of ground which one might reasonably expect on a mountainside to guide us. Asgard Heights itself was built on an outstanding shoulder of Kennett Mountain. The surrounding lawns and gardens were by no means level, but the maze was an exception. It's turfed ground throughout was as flat as a tennis-court.

At least it seemed so until my trustful foot descended into vacancy, and I saved myself from pitching headlong only by a quick reverse which made me sit down with violence, dragging Ronny along.

"Look out!" I ejaculated. "Here's a precipice or something!"

On investigation the precipice proved to be a short flight of descending stone steps.

"We've reached the center," Charles observed. His voice sounded oddly tremulous. Both he and Tolliver were dripping wet, and Charles, at least, had reached the shivering stage. "There is some kind of pavilion or rest-house here," he added shakily. "You go—go d-down these steps to it."

"Thought you'd never been here," growled Tolliver the suspicious.

"I d-did not say I had never seen the gr-ground plans."

"No, but we don't put much value on what you say, one way or the other."

"Oh, let up, Tolliver," I broke in. For the last half-hour he had been flinging similar remarks at the unhappy Governor, and I was sick of hearing them. Too much like nagging at a condemned man. "If this is the center, let's cross it and start fresh on the other side. Where are you, Ronny?"

"Here." Her firm, slim hand met mine. As we went cautiously down the steps I thought what a good, satisfactory little pal she was. Not a word of complaint from her yet, though as rescuers Tolliver and I had made rather a mess of it.

To our eyes, inured to the blackness of the hedges, this central space was almost visible. I could make our Ronny's white figure and face moving beside me, and ahead something dim, big and solid, which must be the pavilion. An idea struck me.

If this building, I said, were wired for lights—as it probably was—and if we could find the switch, and if it were on a separate circuit from the rest of the grounds—why couldn't we light up the pavilion and gain a point of direction?

A lot of "ifs" as Tolliver unkindly remarked, but Ronny supported my suggestion. Still hand in hand, we felt our way up some more stone steps into the pavilion.

I heard Rex and his inseparable antagonist following just behind.

Exactly what form of structure the place had, darkness forbade our knowing. It seemed to be built of marble, or some other smoothly polished stone, and in entering we passed between round, thick pillars. Within, the blackness was impenetrable.

Ardently I wished for those wasted matches now. Still, there was a hit-or-miss chance that we might find a switch-box by feeling along the walls.

In ten minutes we had determined that the pavilion was round, the walls formed of polished stone panels set between pilasters, and that it had no windows nor entrances save the one we had come in by. This not particularly helpful knowledge was our sole reward.

We met at last in a discouraged group near the center. There was a thing there shaped like a sun-dial—or a very thick broken-off column. It rose from the floor to about the height of my chest. The top seemed carved in deep relief, and, leaning wearily against it as we talked, my fingers strayed over the carving.

"If you would sh-shout for help," shivered Charles, "or allow me to, we might be heard. W-won't you take my assurance that I've given up all hope of—of—have given up all hope? What can you fear? That I would have you m-murdered—in c-cold blood?"

"How do we know?" came Tolliver's inevitable retort. "It's no great step from kidnaping to throat-cutting."

I heard a sound suspiciously like a hysterical giggle, but the voice that followed from that direction was sweetly dignified.

"Governor Charles can hope to deceive none of us as to his true character, but—I think perhaps it would be best to shout. You see, Rex, even though *he* may deserve to perish of pneumonia, you're both equally drenched. I think we've been lost long enough. Governor Charles has a chill now, and you'll have one soon, unless you get dry clothes."

"Anticlimax for hero and villain," I thought with an inward chuckle.

My fingers, which had been half unconsciously tracing the raised carving of the pillar-top, closed on a piece that was loose. Being very human fingers, they tried to loosen it some more. It wouldn't lift, but it slid along smoothly for about an inch, as if in a groove.

"I'm hard as nails," Rex was saying impatiently. "Thanks for—"

I don't know what he was going to thank her for, because just then something happened.

It was sudden as lightning, and as disconcerting as an earthquake.

With a horrible, shuddering vibration and a sound like the groan of a cracked iron bell, the solid stone beneath us tipped, sank away, was gone. In one sliding, struggling heap, the four of us were unceremoniously dropped through the treacherously yawning floor of the pavilion.

Chapter XIII.
THE RESCUE PROCEEDS UNDERGROUND.

The unguessed abyss into which we had been precipitated wasn't very much of an abyss, and its bottom had been considerably padded. My sprawling and astonished self landed unhurt on a soft, feather-cushiony surface some eight feet below.

Overhead there came a recurrence of that metallic groaning, followed by a sharp click.

Almost more amazing than the fall itself was the fact that we had dropped out of midnight darkness into a place filled with light. I realized it dazedly, though, of course, till my eyes had time to get adjusted, I couldn't see a thing.

"Ronny!" I called, scrambling up anyhow. "Ronny! Are you there? Are you hurt?"

"Oh!" said a small voice close by, and "Oh!" again, as if that covered the situation.

"Yes, oh! But are you hurt?"

I staggered forward, my feet sinking deep in the cushiony floor, collided heavily with another bedazzled staggerer, and then a pair of steely hands closed on my throat.

"You devil!" hissed Tolliver's voice between set teeth. "You sprang that trap—but you'll pay for it!"

I'm not so big as Rex, but the footing was uncertain and I easily tripped him. We went to the mat together, his hold was broken by the fall and I wriggled away.

"What the *deuce* are you trying to do?" I gasped angrily.

"Hil! I thought—thought you were that scoundrel, Charles!"

"Well, I'm not. Look who you're choking next time. Ronny, where are you anyway?"

But even as I spoke my vision cleared, and I saw my companions and the place we had been tumbled into.

It was a white-walled chamber, round like the pavilion, and some twelve feet in diameter. The floor was covered by a tufted padding, upholstered in forest-green, very thick and soft. As I had already surmised, the ceiling, which was, of course, the floor of the pavilion, had closed again after letting us through. Its under-side was covered with a layer of elaborately embossed metal, painted in brilliant colors, and so designed that it would be almost impossible to say where the piece or pieces which opened were joined.

Four narrow archways led out of the circular room, and over each of these was an electric globe and some kind of motto painted in black on the white wall.

As for my fellow victims, Rex still crouched, blinking at me, while a little way off Charles, for whom I had just suffered as proxy, was helping Veronica to her feet.

My cousin's pale-gold hair was tumbled about her shoulders. She was staring up into Charles's face, her lips quivering like a child's about to cry.

Tolliver and I reached them at the same moment. After glaring at us as if he intended to dispute our right to take her away from him, the Governor turned his back and moved off. Veronica looked after him with an expression which we interpreted as amazement that he had dared touch her.

While Rex scowled threatfully at the Governor's back, I cooed over my poor little frightened cousin like a sentimental maiden aunt till she began to laugh at herself and me.

"I'm not a bit hurt," she protested, twisting up her fallen hair. "But where—what is this place?"

"Ask the owner!" Tolliver still glowered. "He dropped us down here—this is a regular trap."

"He fell into it himself then," objected Ronny.

I had a startling recollection.

"If you want to see the real villain," I modestly observed, "look at little Hildreth. No, I mean it." I related how my fingers had closed over that loose carving on the sawed-off column. "It slid along, and this is the result. Plain as a pikestaff. That carving controlled the mechanism of a trapdoor."

"Maybe," Rex skeptically admitted, "but I still think it was his doing and that he only came down with us by a slip."

Charles had been standing hands on hips, head thrown back, staring as if reproachfully at that treacherous ceiling. Now he turned again and came toward us across the yielding floor.

Recalling my interview with him that morning, I thought what a vast difference a few hours and emotions can work in a man. That he should be white, even haggard was not surprising; but more than that, Charles looked as if he had been sick—sick a long time with some devastating fever. Yet he had regained control of himself. For all the misery his eyes reported, he was managing to face us and smile, which must have required some moral courage, of whatever quality.

"Old M-Mason," he said, "seems to have b-been a pr-practical joker."

"You'll have to check that chill in some way," announced Ronny irrelevantly. "Whisky would do. Doesn't any one of you carry a flask?"

It appeared that Rex did, but obviously he objected to Ronny's concern for his fallen rival, and it was equally obvious that carbolic acid would have been as welcome to Charles as a drink of whisky which he had to accept from Tolliver.

I admired Ronny's calm indifference to the sentiments of either. The drink was given and taken under her inflexible direction, Rex had one himself, I did not refuse my share, and then consideration of Mr. Mason's "practical joke" could be resumed.

By Charles's story, in the plans of Asgard Heights there was shown at the center of the maze a small, round building, of more or less Grecian architecture. As for a trick opening in the floor operated or controlled by a movable bit of carving, there was no indication of it on the plans or in the written descriptions, and he swore he had never heard any hint of such a place existing beneath the pavilion. Personally he had never explored the grounds to any extent—he had no leisure to waste in that manner. No, he had never heard a word of it from any servant or employee. Every one knew what an eccentric old fellow Mason had been. This must be some device of his, built secretly and designed for a purpose as unknown to him, Charles, as to us.

Certainly the place was an elaborate and intentional trap, but the wherefore of it remained to be discovered.

Tolliver was inclined to sneer at the Governor's claim of ignorance, but those four archways were beckoning to my curiosity. I proposed exploration as more profitable than holding impromptu court to try Charles's veracity.

As I have said, over every arch there was a light, which we surmised might have been turned on by the same mechanism that sprang the trap. This assumed Charles's story to be true. They certainly couldn't have been burning ever since Mason died, nearly a year previous.

Beyond the archways four flights of stairs curved downward out of our view, and we could tell by the reflection on the curving, white-painted walls that there were other lights. All the stairs turned in the same direction—to the right as one faced them.

Hoping to find some clue, we read the mottoes painted in old English characters just below the electric globes. They left us more puzzled than before. The four inscriptions had been culled from the Old Testament, and not only did they offer no guidance, but the selections had been made from the more vengeful utterances of the Prophets, and every one of them read depressingly like a threat.

" 'Rejoice not against me, mine enemy,' " Veronica read aloud thoughtfully: " 'when I fall I shall arise.' That's not quite so—so unfriendly as the others. Let's try this 'Rejoice not' one first."

She set foot boldly on the first step of her preferred stair. Tolliver and I started after her, but to my surprise Charles caught at my sleeve detainingly.

"Wyndham," he said earnestly, "she ought to wait here and let us explore. We don't know what those stairs lead to. It maybe something—unpleasant."

For a moment I hesitated, wondering if he might not be right. Or was he trying to split our party?

"We'll stick together," I said, "and, if you don't mind, I'll bring up the rear."

I stood aside for him to pass me. He looked at me, opened his lips, then compressed them firmly and went ahead without argument.

We had fallen into this peculiar situation because of one almost incredible act on the part of our esteemed Governor. Tolliver's suspicions since the rescue might be exaggerated, but I myself had no mind to let Charles be tempted to any further novel extensions of the gubernatorial power.

He shouldn't leave us, and he would bear watching while with us. Ronny was an inspiration to care which I didn't intend to forget.

Chapter XIV.
ALARMING DISCOVERIES.

The stairs led to a straight, narrow passage ending in a blind wall. Three other passages, similar to the first, branched off from it at varying angles.

Our first impression of these underground corridors was an extraordinary one. They were decorated with half-inch stripes of black on a white ground. The stripes ran up from a dead-black floor to the ceiling, across, and down the opposite wall. It gave an effect like the bars of a cage, and a perspective that was bewilderingly tiresome to the eyes.

The small electric bulbs placed at intervals were unfrosted and without globes. This so increased the dazzling effect that we only discovered the branch passages as we reached them. Adventuring a few paces along one of these branch ways, we came on yet another zebra-striped corridor opening from it.

"I believe," declared Ronny, suddenly inspired, "that we are in an underground duplicate of the privet maze—and we'd best be careful. This is precisely the way we lost ourselves up there."

"It looks so, but read that." I pointed out another inscription, set in a lozenge of white on the end wall of the passage we stood in. " 'Arise ye and depart, for this is not your rest.' Invitation to proceed. There must be something down here besides these futurist corridors."

Tolliver got out a pencil.

"If this is a second maze, we don't have to get lost." He made a cross on one of the white stripes of the wall. The pencil was soft and the mark stood out well against the painted cement. "We'll blaze a trail, and in that way can always return to the center. The hedges were a different proposition."

"Hello!" I said. "Some former victim had your bright idea, Rex. See his mark?"

It was a small, lop-sided cross that looked as if it had been smeared on the wall by a finger dipped in thin, reddish-brown paint. A few yards further along Veronica pointed to another white stripe.

"There's a red mark, too. But it's a circle instead of a cross."

With an impatient shake of the head, Rex made his own symbol, bold and black, just under the circle.

"Silly game for a man like Mason to waste money on," he commented. "The old fellow must have reached his second childhood."

Still hoping for something more interesting than empty passages, we followed the new angle, passed a couple of corridors, turned into a third, chose another intersection, another—and brought up at a blind wall, which announced the inevitable inscription:

> That Which Is Crooked Cannot Be Made Straight;
> and That Which Is Wanting Cannot be Numbered.

"Oh—rot!" exclaimed Tolliver irreverently. "What a *fool* game!"

Retracing our steps, we felt ready to cease exploring and try what could be done toward reopening the pavilion trap from below. A child-minded person with time on his hands, well-fed and dryly clothed against the damp chill of the corridors, might have enjoyed losing himself here. As for us, we had had enough.

Following Tolliver's black crosses we—reached another blind wall. Yet there was the pencil mark, five feet from the end and directly beneath a light.

"That's queer, I said. "That can't be your cross, Tolliver. It's an old one that somebody else marked up."

"It's mine. See how each line ends in a hook? I did that purposely to identify my own mark—and besides, I remember putting it there."

His insistence gave one a sickish, unnatural feeling—like meeting a blank impossibility and being forced to believe in it. One does that sometimes in a dream.

The end wall announced unconsolingly:

> He Hath Hedged Me About That I Cannot Get Out;
> He Hath Made My Chain Heavy.

Our eyes sought each other's faces.

"That's not my mark," Rex contradicted himself suddenly. He hastily scribbled his initials, "R. T.," beside the hooked cross. "There. I shouldn't have used a cross, of course. Everybody makes crosses—or circles. We've passed a dozen red ones, and there are probably plenty of pencil crosses scattered about. Luckily we haven't come far."

Had we retained any faith in Tolliver's hooked crosses as guidance, we should have been quickly disillusioned. It seemed best to follow back along what must be a false trail to the point where it diverged from the true one. But instead of success in this, we met only another cul-de-sac, ominously inscribed:

I Also Will Laugh at Your Calamity;
I Will Mock when Your Fear Cometh.

At that we laughed a little ourselves. These sententious quotations were so plainly meant to inspire terror that they overshot the mark. Yet they angered one, too. They had begun to take on an air of vicious and personal attack.

"You—you *mean* old man." Ronny shook her head at the painted taunt, as if it directly represented Mr. Daniel Mason. "Your joke is so ill-natured that it isn't the least bit funny!"

Nobody thought of even hinting that it was funny when a line of "R. T.'s" *plus* hooked crosses brought us straight to a blocked passage and the mocking statement that:

As the Fishes That Are Taken in an Evil Net,
so Are the Sons of Men Snared in an Evil Time.

"Were we here before?" demanded the owner of the initials dazedly. "I don't remember—"

"There's been *nothing* said about fishes in any place we've gone!" Ronny declared positively. "We aren't alone down here. I've been certain for some minutes that I heard footfalls and a kind of rushing noise in the corridors we had just passed through, but I thought the sounds might be echoes. They weren't. Some one is following us about and writing up copies of your mark, Rex. Listen!"

We did listen, with the strained alertness of people who have agreed to spend the night in a haunted house—"Such a lark if one really should meet a ghost, you know!"—and are suddenly very much afraid that the ghost has audibly materialized.

Not that we were superstitious. If any one but ourselves were present, the person was a flesh-and-blood human, to be hunted out, captured, and forced to explain himself. But why—well, what malevolent sort of a human would it be who dwelt mysteriously in a secret labyrinth, and trailed us to forge our blaze-marks?

We listened. There was no sound but our own breathing, and very little of that.

Yet Ronny had not been alone in hearing "echoes." They had been troubling me for ten minutes past, and I had seen both Tolliver and Charles cast an occasional startled glance backward as we passed from one corridor to another.

Suddenly the Governor, who had been straining his ears with the rest of us, gave a muttered exclamation.

"What's that?" Tolliver turned on him with quick suspicion. "*You* know all about this!" he accused.

"I think I do." The Governor's smile was half-bored, half-amused. "The explanation is staring us in the face. A small boy of average intelligence might have guessed it earlier."

Still smiling, he walked to the dead-wall that ended the passage. Raising one hand he struck it a sharp blow with the heel of his palm. The "wall" gave out a hollow, metallic clang and rattled slightly in its place.

"That's a door," said Charles. "We did pass here before, only then the door was open, and subsequent to our passing it closed."

"But," cried Ronny, "that's worse than having our mark copied! Who closed it?"

"You possibly, or any of us." He laughed outright. "Please don't be indignant with me. It's amusing that four supposedly intelligent people should have been so easily deceived."

"Suppose," said Rex with ponderous sarcasm, "that in the majesty of your intellect you condescend to explain."

Ronny cast him an annoyed glance. Such persistent discourtesy seemed needless.

"You mean," she said, addressing Charles, "that they are trick doors? They close themselves by a spring?"

"By springs or weights. Very likely pressure on some part of the floor in another corridor released this door so that it either slid across or dropped from a slot in the ceiling. The former, I'm inclined to think. If it slides horizontally, it might be opened again by similar means from another point. The sounds which reached us were the rattle of these doors, the faint thud of dropping weights, or the swish of ropes within the walls. Now we have only to slide the door back in its groove and pass on."

Probably he was right. That was all we had to do. But unluckily we couldn't do it. There was no means of getting a grip on the thing. At every side its edges entered floor, walls, and ceiling, and, of course, there was no handle or knob to grasp. Had the barrier been of wood we might have cut into it with a pocket-knife and secured finger-hold; but it was of thin iron or steel; and impregnable to any attack in our command.

Giving up at last we went back, investigated two or three other corridors, and soon found another of the trick doors which stood open.

A new meaning was given to the striped walls and black floor by our discovery. To the eye there was no difference between a half-inch black stripe and a half-inch hollow slot, while across the jet-colored floor the slot was equally indistinguishable.

There was no sign of a door-edge, the slot running all the way around, and having a depth past probing by the longest pencil in our possession. We, however, had cause to assume that door there was, no matter how deeply hidden.

"Our problem," said Charles, who seemed to have temporarily assumed command, "is to prevent this and any other such barriers which we may encounter from entirely closing."

Removing his wet coat he ruthlessly tore it into halves, wadded one half into a rough ball and laid it against the wall across the slot. From whatever direction the door might appear, it would become involved with the wad of wet cloth, which, acting as a buffer, would prevent the journey being completed. Given a grip on the edge, doubtless we might push it back without trouble, while, with the three coats among us, we could, if necessary, stop six doors.

The scheme seemed good, and to test it Veronica remained to watch while we three men walked here and there in neighboring passages. Of course we had no means of knowing exactly what it was that released the panels, but assumed that it was the weight of a person passing over some part of the floor. Taking care to keep within calling distance of each other, we walked with fingers running along the walls and eyes alert for the telltale slots.

I had just found one, and was about to sacrifice a garment at its alter, when I heard a swish, a dull thud, and then a call that was almost a shriek from Ronny.

Being nearest I was first in the rush back. There had been terror as well as surprise in that call, so that my first thought was of unmixed relief to see her standing unhurt where we had left her.

Then I perceived that she was staring downward with a white, horrified face.

"Look!" she ejaculated as I ran up. "And—and, Hildreth, think! I had laid my hand over the slot at the side. If I hadn't merely happened to put it up to my hair—"

She stopped, her voice still shaking, and I didn't blame her. The others had come up now. Charles stooped and picked up a dank wad of cloth. Part of a sleeve fell to the floor. It wasn't half a coat now, it was the quarter of a coat. The soggy, wet material had been sheared through cleanly, as if by a tailor's cutting-knife.

"That door fairly shot down!" said Ronny. "It whistled past my face so that I felt a wind on my cheek!"

"With an edge like a razor." Charles dropped the fragment of cloth, and, hands on hips, frowned thoughtfully at the new inscription which our experiment had brought to view. It briefly and murderously declared:

Here I Will Make Thy Grave, for Thou Art Vile.

Thinking of poor Ronny's hand that had so nearly shared fates with the Governor's coat, I shivered.

Chapter XV.
A DEAD MAN'S LAUGHTER.

With hope resigned of blocking doors that dropped like butchers' cleavers, we rather disconsolately sought out the ways which remained open. None of us cared to voice the impression of senseless and, therefore, insane malice produced by our surroundings.

I have been told that there is no experience more terrible than for a sane man to find himself in the hands of a lunatic.

To deem oneself grasped by a lunatic dead months past, a man with not only the genius of insanity, but vast wealth to execute its malevolent devices, is, I can assure you, equally appalling.

By tacit consent, further speculation as to the labyrinth's purpose was avoided. Neither did we care to speak any more of the crosses, nor crosses and circles, smeared here and there on the walls. I suppose we shared the thought that reddish-brown paint was an odd convenience for a man trapped as we had been to carry—unless he carried it in his veins.

Who had wandered here, desperate, cut off by barrier after falling barrier, each offering its threat more virulent than the last, among endless vistas of painted bars whose illusion became ever more distressing as the eye wearied, with the echo of his own feet and the rush of the trap's machinery for sole companionship?

How had he finally escaped? Had he escaped? One of those knife-edged panels, dropping inopportunely, might end a man's wanderings with frightful ease.

We turned no corners now without a quick glance ahead that feared the thing it might encounter. We made carefully sure that we passed no deadly slot unaware, and when we crossed one, did it swiftly and with discretion.

But so far the panels dropped only behind us, always out of sight in some comparatively distant corridor. That they were driving us on in one general direction was apparent. Yet we must let ourselves be driven, since the only alternative was remaining in one place, an inactivity that none of us cared to face.

We must go on, and we must keep together. Let one of those panels isolate a member of the party, and assurance that we should ever be reunited was disagreeably uncertain.

Occasionally, to leave no hope untried, we shouted or banged on the metal panels till the infernal racket deafened us. And all the while we knew our efforts in this direction to be utterly futile. Above there were many feet of heavy, sound-deadening earth. Had we been lost in the depths of a mine, the world could have been no more cut off from us. Moreover, we in our hearts knew that this had been so designed.

Charles and I were both in our shirt-sleeves now, for I had insisted that Ronny take my coat. She was thinly clad in a gown whose V-shaped neck and quarter-length sleeves offered scant protection from chill.

Physical discomfort was heavy on us all, and a sort of sickening distress caused by eye-strain. The black-and-white bars stood out, receded, wavered and danced in hypnotic revel till the mind was dizzy and sharp pains shot to the back of the brain.

Our progress was by no means commensurate with the distance covered. Again and again we traversed a series of ways which ended in a wall that was not a panel, but solid concrete. In each such case we observed that the motto was the same, though this was the only quotation repeated. The movable panels presented an astonishing variety of invective.

Its reappearance became irritating beyond belief; it was like a shouted taunt, echoing a dead man's mirth forever:

> I Also Will Laugh at Your Calamity;
> I Will Mock when Your Fear Cometh.

We made flippant variations on the phrase; we cursed it under our breath; we laughed loudly at facing it again—and ceased to laugh, because of the far-running echoes.

And then once more we must return on our steps, always to find panels where we had left open ways, and at last choose another corridor yet untried, and emblazon a fresh series of black "R. T.'s" beside those ghastly red-brown naughts and crosses.

By what means such a multitude of lights could be supplied with current was in itself a riddle.

Asgard Heights, as its owner informed us, had its private power-plant operated by turbines from a high waterfall within the estate. There was power enough and to spare for the house and grounds, but in this subterranean maze we had already passed hundreds of lamps. They were small, it is true, being mostly tungsten filament bulbs of low wattage, but the total current consumption must have been enormous.

I tried to trace a connection between the disappearance of the lights behind us while we were among the hedges and this underground illumination. The only basis on which I could do it was the assumption that, half an hour before our descent, some one had knowingly thrown all the power from the upper circuits into these lower ones.

This, unless we assumed a complicity on Charles's part which seemed far-fetched, was improbable. It implied a foresight of our actions nothing short of miraculous.

The question was suddenly dropped in the fact of a thing that affected us much more practically.

Our wanderings had ended.

Oh, no; we had not reached a broad, beautiful stairway labeled, "This way out"; nor a man-size rat-hole, that we might crawl through into open air, and which we would have welcomed with equal joy.

Our wanderings had ended, because there was no way to go on.

We were, in fact, safely shut within a small area of short-corridors, blocked, every one of them, and each presenting that silent shriek of maniacal mirth:

I Also Will Laugh at Your Calamity.

First we made sure that the "calamity" was as bad as it seemed. That did not occupy us long. Then we strayed aimlessly about, on a pretense of making sure all over again, but really because we were afraid of a certain minute that was coming.

I mean the minute when we must look at one another and admit: "Here is an end of action. From this on we have to rely on a rescue from outside. Waiting is our part, and as we have neither food, drink, nor proper covering against cold—in this damp, cellarlike place—the wait is going to seem very long and hard to bear. We three men can stand it, but how about you, little Ronny?"

Of course that a rescue would finally come was inevitable.

No matter how secretly Mason had caused the labyrinth to be built, it had taken workmen to build it. Skilled workmen—electricians and artificers of various sorts, all men of intelligence. They might have been brought from far and paid well for silence. But such a man as Clinton Charles could not vanish into thin air without news of it being flashed all over.

Probably quite a lot of people would come forward then with the information that would send us help.

True, past denial. And, nevertheless—what if no help ever came?

Your fellow man is such an uncertain creature to rely on—when you can't do one thing for yourself.

We were cut off. We were shut under the ground, in a place concealed with just that devilish intent.

Nobody said much. We strolled around a while, and came to a halt beside the last panel that had closed, ending our perilous journey.

The chill air breathed heavy, laden with hopelessness and discouragement.

We looked at the panel. Tolliver kicked it, gently and without spirit.

The inscription upon it seemed to glare at us vengefully; terse, ruthless in its use here; insane:

> Thou Shalt not Live, for Thou Speakest Lies
> in the Name of the Lord.

Suddenly Ronny began to laugh. I asked her why. She explained that the accusation of that particular panel struck her as quite amusingly mad.

As soon as she mentioned it, we could see for ourselves that it was funny. Several very witty jokes were made on the subject. I don't now recall what they were, but at the time they appealed to my sense of humor so that I laughed till my head hurt severely.

Strange how stiflingly heavy the air had become since the dropping of that last panel.

There were weights on my feet, too. Wondering how they had got there, I looked down and discovered the explanation. I was dressed in a sea-diver's costume.

It was, of course, the great, heavy helmet on my head that made everything dark except in two round circles before my eyes.

The figure of a girl drifted slowly by. Turning jerkily with the current, it faced me for a moment. I recognized Ronny's drowned face, strained, bluish-white, with gasping, open mouth and drooping lids. In spite of the old-fashioned cork-jacket buckled round her body, she had sunk to the very bottom.

Though I knew it was too late to save her, I stretched out my arms. Those lead soles wouldn't let me move, and she drifted out of my sight.

The round windows of the helmet began to cloud over, and the heavy air failed. They had ceased pumping air to me. The windows darkened—I sank—

Chapter XVI.

THE RESCUE LOSES ITS HEROINE.

My awakening from that dream is to this day a most unpleasant memory.

The odorless and insidious gas which had caused it must have been drained off soon after consciousness departed. Otherwise I should never have awakened at all.

As it was, I came to abruptly, leaping in one instant from insensibility to life. I was lying on the floor, but started up like a man roused from sleep by some loud alarm. My head, though it ached slightly, was almost unnaturally clear and memory took up its normal function as if there had been no break.

Huddled against the wall lay Tolliver, a dark, careless heap that did not stir.

Ronny was nowhere to be seen. Neither was Charles.

There were with me only silence, and that motionless heap of flesh and clothes which might or might not be a living man.

I didn't stop then to find out.

Some inhaled poison had robbed us of sense for a while. Though it had dropped two of us in our tracks, the others might have withstood it longer. They had perhaps staggered a little way off; they were lying insensible around this corner or that. The space of our prison had many corners to be searched.

Back and forth I went, running, anxious, like a lost dog questing its master. Where was Veronica? Charles might have gone to the devil in a cloud of brimstone for all I cared. I must find Veronica.

The unwelcome knowledge forced itself on me at last that the only people in this section of the corridors were Tolliver and myself.

Then I realized that I had known it from the first moment of awakening.

All that elaborate ignorance of the Governor's had been feigned by him and swallowed by us with the simplicity of children. Granted that our being entrapped was sheer accident. It was an accident of which he had taken eager advantage. The labyrinth was Mason's, but its new owner had found good use for it.

If Tolliver and I showed up missing, who would ever look for us on the Asgard Heights estate? The only clues we had left were the two motor-cars, one hidden by the road, the other standing at the foot of that steep, apparently unclimbable slope on Kildair Mountain.

It would be another mystery as baffling as that of my cousin.

And Charles—the damnable hyprocrite—would follow his ambitious way with a smiling face, not so much as breathed on by suspicion. Oh, a perilous road to walk, no doubt, but he had already given proof of reckless daring.

Honest, straightforward Tolliver, whom I had secretly deemed boyish and crude, had been possessed of clearer vision than myself. "But a short step from kidnaping to throat-cutting," he had said. In the dark I had smiled incredulously and Ronny had laughed outright. Poor little Ronny! She deserved sympathy.

Slowly I went back to Tolliver. He must be roused, and between us we must hunt out the trick by which this prison opened. Charles knew it, so the trick was surely there.

It surprised me rather than he hadn't smashed the light bulbs before going. Darkness would have left us no chance whatever. Well, that would come later. I could almost see the sardonic smile curling his fine mouth as his hand should close over the switch that threw off every light below here.

Death muffled in the dark for us; for him, safety—and my cousin, Veronica.

Stung by the thought, I fell upon Tolliver's inert form in a rage of determination. I hauled him away from the wall, straightened him out and, as an afterthought, felt for his pulse. It was faint but regular.

All right; since he was alive he could wake up and help me.

Some whisky had remained in his flask, which we had carefully refrained from using. I hunted through his pockets for it. They were empty. The pistol he had taken from Charles was gone, too.

There was something petty and sneaking about this rifling of a helpless victim! I smiled scornfully and plunged a hand in my own trouser-pocket, whither I had transferred Tolliver's gun when I lent my coat to Veronica. To my surprise the weapon was still there.

He had overlooked it, or else been frightened off by some move of mine that threatened returning life.

With a contemptuous shrug, I shoved the gun back in its place and set to work on Tolliver. The healthy tan of his face hid a sallow paleness, and his lips were a faint bluish-purple. The nostrils, too, looked thin and pinched.

I am ashamed to say that his condition aroused in me more of impatience than pity. In my fervor of anxiety for Veronica, Tolliver seemed less a human being than a means to help get out of here and find her.

And he wouldn't rouse. I tired of pumping his arms and rolling him back and forth, the only means of resuscitation my inexperience could recall. Finally I sat back on my heels and scowled at him.

Then I bent over, took him by the shoulders and shook him savagely.

"Tolliver!" I shouted. "Wake up, man! You—wake—up!"

"Do you think you are going about it in the best way, Wyndham?" inquired an anxious voice from behind me.

I whirled like a shot.

There stood Governor Charles, with the missing flask in one hand, a small liquor glass and a silver spoon in the other.

Where he had got the glass and the spoon didn't at once interest me.

To have the black-hearted villain you have been cursing show up suddenly is always disconcerting. To have him show up bearing the utensils and the considerate air of a hospital nurse is fearfully upsetting to one's nerves.

It upset me, physically as well as mentally. In turning so quickly I lost my balance and brought my hand down full weight on the midst of Tolliver's helpless person.

He showed his resentment by a deep groan and a kick.

"After all, perhaps your method is the best," said Charles, "though I should never have considered trying anything so violent."

Chapter XVII.
SAVED BY THE VILLAIN.

"I brought this spoon and glass," he continued, "because it is easier to give liquor to an unconscious person from a spoon. Without spilling it, that is, and we have only a little left."

If I hadn't been through quite so much I shouldn't have given myself away. I would have accepted him and his spoon and his glass, inquired politely where he had the rest of the hospital concealed, and, in a casual way, if he had happened to see my cousin.

But the breaking point and little Hildreth had come together at last.

My thinking apparatus took a vacation. All the dark criminalities I had believed of him came tumbling out of my mouth in a jumble of heartfelt accusation. If I didn't accuse him of murdering Veronica and burying her under a corridor, it was only because my breath gave out suddenly. I sat down on the floor beside Tolliver, who hadn't even stirred again since that one kick.

The next I knew, some one was giving me whisky—out of a spoon, I think—and there was a supporting arm around my shoulders.

"You'll feel better shortly, Wyndham," a grave voice was saying. "I took that pistol because it was mine. I really have no use for it, however, and since you feel so unsafe in my company you are welcome to carry it."

I felt something cold and heavy thrust into my hand.

"Where's Veronica?" I muttered.

"Not far off. Are you better?"

"I guess so. Tired. Empty stomach. Haven't had a thing to eat in ages. Silly way to act—I know it."

"Not at all. Are you able to walk a short distance?"

"Tolliver?" I said.

"Oh, we won't desert him. Just lean on me—shall I carry you?"

"Cer'nly—not."

That one drink had got control of my tongue with surprising ease.

I suppose I walked, but I don't remember much about it. Next time I felt any interest in proceedings I found myself lying on something soft and springy, and my face was being bathed with a wet cloth. I opened my eyes and looked straight up into Veronica's face.

"Poor dear," she said softly, and then, over her shoulder, "Hildreth hasn't been strong since he had typhoid. If this leads to a severe illness, I shall never forgive myself."

"My fault entirely."

That was the Governor's voice. Evidently he had got me safely installed in his private hospital.

"Isn't that coffee nearly made?" Veronica asked.

"Just done. Shall I pour in the cream?"

"No. Hildreth likes it black."

Things seemed to be coming Hildreth's way. Into my range of vision stalked the Governor, looking solemn and anxious over a laden tray.

"I hope the bouillon will be right," he said. "I'm not much of a cook."

"It will be if you fixed it the way I told you."

I wondered if she were training him for a chef in case he lost his job as Governor, and just stopped myself from asking. I was recovering.

I had recovered enough to sit up by the time Ronny had fed me half a cup of bouillon—out of another spoon—and some coffee that possessed more strength than flavor.

"The coffee was ready-ground, and it stood too long in the can," explained Ronny deprecatingly. "Clinton did the best he could with it."

"Clinton is a jewel," I said. Then something struck me. "Clinton?" I repeated.

She flushed to the very tips of her ears.

"Governor Charles," she said stiffly. "I think you are better, Hildreth."

"Much, thanks to you and Cl—Governor Charles. In the language of the poet: Where am I?"

The room of my quick convalescence bore no resemblance to the black-

and-white striped horrors of our recent surroundings. It was a long room, not very high-ceilinged, but furnished in a taste that amounted to barbaric splendor.

It had, however, two characteristics which prevented me, after the first glance, from thinking it a room in the Governor's residence.

One was a total absence of windows. The other was the extraordinary condition of mildew and mold which existed everywhere, and rendered the absence of windows or other ventilation decidedly unpleasant.

I lay on what had once been a magnificent brocaded divan. Before putting me there, Ronny had thoughtfully covered it with a silk rug in rather better condition. Where the brocade showed, however, it was green with mold and the other furniture was similarly afflicted.

Extravagant expense and extravagant ruin appeared on every side.

The once highly polished floor looked dull, warped and spotted with moisture. The tapestry with which the walls were hung was stiff and cracking with mold, and in a trophy of Eastern weapons above my divan, the spear and sword-blades, were a red lace-work of rust.

Down the room's center extended a table. It had been laid with a lace and damask cloth and set out with a regular banqueting service, crystal and silver and a great silver urn near each end filled with dozens of roses. But the silver was tarnished black, the cloth eaten by mildew, and the roses had died long ago. They and their fallen petals were black as the silver urns that held them.

If they had only been a few skeletons sitting around the table, and a coffin or so set up for decoration, the scene of merry festivity would have been complete.

However, there were no skeletons—except those in use by ourselves— and the scene did well as it was.

Ronny, who had been putting dishes back on the tray, remembered to answer my question.

"We are still underground. I can't tell you any more than that, but it's something to have escaped from those miserable corridors. Lean your head back, poor boy. Would you like some creamed codfish?"

"Help!" said I briefly. "Why bouillon, coffee and codfish in the midst of decay? And where's your Clinton Governor gone *now?* He's vanished again."

"Hildreth, I wish you would please not tease me about what was merely a slip of the tongue. Governor Charles and Rex have both gone to put on dry clothing."

"Haberdashery establishment next door. Old Mason was thorough. I hope the tailoring department is in better repair than the dining-saloon, though. Say, Ronny, don't tell me I've been eating things that came off that table!"

"No, indeed. Governor Charles found an airtight chest with some canned provisions in it. There were an electric percolator and chafing dish and a few dishes there, too. And we found a case of bottled water.

"I don't understand anything. Governor Charles says that one of those 'calamity' walls was a door, and he woke up before any of us and it was standing open. He's been keeping it closed since, in case of another rush of gas. He carried me in here, and when I came to he was feeding me whisky—"

"Out of a spoon."

"How did you know?"

"Oh, I know. And then he went back and rescued me, and then he rescued Tolliver, and then he cooked dinner, and now he's arranging for a new suit for Tolliver, to replace the one spoiled in his lotus pond. Dear Clinton is absolutely indefatigable."

"Hildreth, you are horrid! It's not like you to make such ill-natured fun of—of people. If you didn't look so s-sick I w-wouldn't talk to you any m-more! What if I did speak of him as Clinton? M-mightn't anybody do that by mistake?"

"Yes," I conceded, "especially if it were a habit. May I get something from the pocket of that coat you're wearing?"

I felt like a brute, for there were tears in her eyes, but I thought the "Clinton" business had better be finished now. It might save trouble later.

She jerked off my coat and extended it with the very tips of her fingers. What I wanted was in the breast-pocket.

"Here's your letter, Ronny," I said, handing her a fragment of note-paper. She didn't faint, though she appeared pretty near it. Instead she sat down on the divan, put her face on my shoulder and began to cry.

Finished. Nothing for Hildreth but capitulation and wild promises of anything—the earth, the moon, the stars, Governor Charles's head on a salver—oh, anything in reason, if she would only be consoled.

None of my inducements were accepted, but the sympathy they conveyed had its effect. First she forgave me; and, second, I learned at last the real facts in connection with her disappearance from the Aldine Apartments.

At the tale's end I realized what an utter brute I had been. Her familiar use of the Governor's given name had led me to the verge of another error. I had again doubted that Ronny might bear a portion of blame and Charles be to a certain extent excusable. I learned otherwise.

The tale, of course, began with my cousin's secretaryship. Her new work, which touched on interests so much broader than anything in the real-estate business, fascinated her. Charles had found a fellow-worker rather than a mere clerk; they pulled together beautifully, and Veronica might have graduated to a full-fledged stateswoman if the inevitable had not occurred: Charles, who had never paid much attention to women—except those with votes in their hands—fell hard and far.

Over this portion of her story Veronica passed hurriedly, but I inferred that she threw Charles in with the work and allowed herself to be fascinated by both. They became engaged. In our rather democratic community there was no reason why such an engagement should not be announced, except one. The work. Once the romance was published Ronny could hardly go on as his secretary. The Governor's position demanded a betrothal of due length and a full-size wedding. Ronny suggested that their engagement be kept secret till he could find an efficient man to take her place.

Touched by her devotion, Charles accepted.

A week later their interest somewhat diverted from the mutual fascination of toil, two strong wills clashed violently. The clash's object was unimportant—as always—but Ronny didn't propose to wed any man who meant to be her master.

Charles was adamant; Ronny was flint. The romance was smashed by the impact, and my cousin returned to the welcoming realm of Mr. Carpenter.

Wisely determined that her young life should not be wrecked, Ronny allowed herself to be wooed and won by Rex Tolliver. He appealed to her, I inferred, largely because he was in every way Clinton Charles's opposite.

But this, too, turned out a mistake.

"*What?*" I ejaculated here. "Why are you marrying him, then?"

Her slate-gray eyes opened wide; her brows arched.

"I'm not," she said simply. "It was all over between us that night when he took me home from the theater. I think Rex realized that it was best. There was hardly a subject in the world on which we agreed. Anyway, he took his ring and left me without a word."

CHAPTER XVIII.

A WARNING.

"I—see!"

What Ronny had just said explained a number of things. Why, for instance, Tolliver was so concerned over a petty disagreement about the play. It was the why of his overdone jealousy, and of the sullen air he had worn ever since we found Ronny at the lotus pond. He had repented of letting her break the engagement, and had hoped that as a rescuing hero she would take him back with open arms.

The welcome, however, was bestowed on my unworthy self, and, come to think of it, she had not showered endearments on Rex anywhere along the line. In fact, she had most of the time kept close to me.

While these reflections raced through my agile brain, the story continued.

Charles, moved like Tolliver to repentance, had sought to reestablish the entente. A little thing like her engagement to another fellow didn't deter him. With the wise knowledge of Veronica one would have expected from a man who had never met her, he baited his line with Asgard Heights. There entered my fragment of letter. But the letter she actually mailed to him said only that as she was soon to be married, she preferred that his attentions should cease.

Crushed, Charles retired from the field—to the side lines, where he proceeded to cook up a daring and nefarious scheme.

The only excuse I could make for him was that on this subject he must have been as mad as Mr. Daniel Mason.

Rex, after his final disagreement with Veronica, left her at the apartment door. Finding Mrs. Sandry asleep. Ronny took pains not to wake her. She was removing her hat in the sitting-room when the bell of the apartment rang. From the speaking-tube Ronny learned surprisedly that Charles was below and wished to speak with her on a very important matter.

With childlike faith—having then no idea of his true quality—she told him he could have three minutes.

The elevator had stopped two hours before. Charles walked up, met Veronica in the sitting-room and related his tale of woe.

Here again Veronica somewhat slurred her story.

"He told me of a great misfortune which had come upon him and explained how I could help him. It was all a trick—a miserable, contemptible trick—but I believed him implicitly. His car was below, and as I meant to return inside an hour, I didn't leave any message for Mrs. Sandry. I put on my hat again and went with him and—and he wouldn't let me come back! He brought me out here and ever since he's been doing nothing but argue—in what little time he could spare from his work. I've been alone all the rest, with no company but a lot of miserable Chinamen. Well, old Li Ching is rather a dear. I've spent hours talking with him—he speaks beautiful English—and he used to tell me long stories about the old Chinese gods and heroes. You've no idea—"

"Yes," I said, thinking the subject had rather strayed, "but why did you go out with Charles at that time of night? How did he persuade you? Are you quite sure, Ronny, that you don't still—well—care for him?"

"Don't be horrid again. I despise him. He appealed to my pity and sympathy. I'll tell you the whole conversation another time. He and Rex will be back here in a minute. But I simply detest Governor Charles."

"Then, of course, you won't marry him."

"I—I can't."

"You don't have to. What's more, he is going to pay for this high-handed outrage with everything he cares for in the world. We'll force him to resign under threat of—"

"You won't do any such thing!"

She faced me, a high color in her cheeks, her dimpled chin well raised.

"But he deserves—"

"You don't understand. Governor Charles personally would neither deserve nor receive from me any consideration whatever. But it isn't fair to the State. He is the first decent, straight Governor we've had in ten years. You don't realize the work he's doing, Hildreth—"

"I realize that—never mind We won't talk of it any more now, Ronny. Plenty of time for that when we're above ground. Did I hear you say creamed codfish?"

"Yes. I'll fix some more. This is cold."

I let her go, for I wanted to think, and the more I thought the more provoked I became.

Charles's recent amiability could be due to but one cause. A man as clever as he could not but have seen wherein his safety lay. Having lost the game, he threw down his cards with a great show of frankness.

"Here am I," he posed, "meek as a lamb and ready to take any punishment you choose to hand out. True, if you publish the story it is going to injure Miss Veronica Wyndham. You may depose me—send me to the penitentiary—I offer no resistance. Miss Wyndham has spent a week alone in my house with not so much as one woman for company. By all means publish. Certainly, take this pistol back. Do you think I would resort to such crude means of self-protection? I am yours to command!"

I saw that Charles had left the pistol in question laid conspicuously on top of a tabouret close to my hand.

Picking it up carefully, I weighed it thoughtfully.

Just then a door at the other end of the long room opened and two figures entered.

Among the first symptoms of that poison gas had been delusion. Had some more of the gas leaked out and penetrated here? One of the figures was clearly a swashbuckling Charles I cavalier. The other was Hamlet, or the lord high executioner, or somebody that wore black tights and a long black cloak.

They approached nearer. Veronica, who was hovering over a chafing-dish, glanced up and said casually:

"Oh, you did find some things you could manage to wear. I'm so glad. Are they dry?"

Hamlet drew the conspirator-like cloak around him a bit more closely.

"Drier than those we took off, at least."

The cavalier swaggered over in my direction.

"Get in style, Hil," he grinned. "You can be anything from a pirate chief to little Bobby Shafto."

"Tolliver," I said, "let me be Haroun al Raschid. Which of the thousand and one tales is this?"

"The one, I guess. There's a roomful of giddy garb back there, but most of the costumes are in bad shape. They're the real thing, though. Look at these doeskin thigh boots, and this gold lace on the cloak is real. It's hardly tarnished at all."

"You have patches of mold on your doeskin boots, and your cloak is full of moth-holes. You look like a resurrection from a seventeenth century grave."

"Don't find fault. The conspirator there," he waved a lace ruffled cuff toward Hamlet, "has a hole in the back of his doublet as big as my hand. That's why he's a conspirator. The cloak covers it up."

"You're on friendly terms with him now?" I asked tentatively.

There was something in Tolliver's manner that puzzled me. An indescribable air of swaggering indifference. Though his rival was talking to Veronica across the chafing-dish, the cavalier seemed not in the least concerned.

"Oh," he said, "there's no use fighting all the time. He's a good enough fellow in his way. You see, Hil—"

He broke off with a gasp, biting at his lip, and all the swagger was gone.

"I'll talk to you about it later," he choked, and strode off—in another direction from the chafing-dish.

His sudden emotion hit me hard. I knew the reason for it. Tolliver had given up hope of Veronica for himself, and had noted those same little reminiscences of intimacy between her and Charles which had deceived me. With a boyish generosity as headlong as everything he did, Tolliver had withdrawn from the field.

Well, I could protect my cousin without his aid.

I got up, a bit shaky, but strong enough, and meandered over to the chafing-dish party. I touched the conspirator's arm.

"Just a minute," I said. "You'll excuse us, Veronica?"

"If you'll hand me that can of cream—and the salt, please. Thanks."

The conspirator and I withdrew. He looked at me questioningly.

"Charles," I said, and the prefix was purposely omitted, "I have learned the full history of your proceedings in connection with my cousin."

"Oh! Did she tell you?" he murmured.

"Yes. Your cleverness will have informed you that for her sake you will go scot-free of the law. Her reputation is your shield. I congratulate you. There will be no publicity, but—here, take your pistol."

I thrust the automatic into his hand. He stared down at it with a very red face, saying nothing.

"I want you to have it," I continued, "in case I should catch you annoying my cousin any further, or speaking one word to her beyond absolute necessity. Should that occur—I wouldn't care to shoot an unarmed man."

Turning on my heel I walked back to Veronica. When I reached her he was still standing there, staring down at the pistol.

Chapter XIX.
"exit."

The finding of this decrepit but once splendid banquet-hall cast a different light on the purpose of the labyrinth. Multimillionaires in search of novel entertainment for their guests sometimes produce strange fancies.

The misuse of scriptural quotations to give a deadly thrill or so in advance of pleasure was an irreverence which would not have troubled old Dan Mason. He was scarcely of the church-going type.

Guests of the sort he affected would have stood for the deadly thrills if they got their fun out of it afterward.

I could picture a gay party gathered about that table when the black silver was bright and the roses were fragrant. How they would shriek with laughter as each new arrival stumbled in, sick with the fear that he had been inveigled to death in a madman's trap. How they would shoo him over toward the master of the wardrobe, to be invested with fanciful trappings and emerge as gay a masker as the rest.

The threat of mocking death—the rush of asphyxiating gas—the awakening—an opened door, and all to end in wine and merriment.

Rude play, it is true, but Dan Mason had risen from ranks where rudeness is a synonym for mirth.

How he had so pledged his merry victims to secrecy that not a word of the device leaked out was a question we did not try to answer. One suspected that the revels were of a kind not to be bragged of publicly.

However it was, the hard-faced old master of the mask lay quiet now, while mildew and mold ate up his pleasure hall.

I had a great longing to escape from all this dank decay and breathe clean air again.

I had resumed my coat, Veronica flung about her the white wool outer garment of a crusader's costume, and, heartened by food and drink, we set out to find the exit provided against the ending of the mask.

At first sight the banquet-room had but two entrances, one of which led in from the wardrobe, the other from the labyrinth proper. Above this latter door, on the inside, was written in letters of gold:

> If Thine Enemy Be Hungry, Give Him Food to Eat;
> and if He Be Thirsty, Give Him Water to Drink.

Mason's "enemies" had probably been served with something a good deal stronger than water, but the quotation was apt enough to pass. We left that and hunted along the walls, behind the rotting tapestry.

Our search soon met reward. Charles, who had been very silent, apparently taking my warning to heart, called out, and as I was nearest I reached him first. Tolliver and Veronica were then at the room's upper end.

He had drawn aside a cloth-of-gold drapery, and there, sure enough, was a door. It was an ordinary-looking door, with a brass knob and mahogany panels, and across it was printed in large welcome letters the one word: "Exit."

Charles took hold of the knob, but it wouldn't turn.

"Pull it sidewise," I suggested. "Most of these doors either slide or drop."

This one slid. It drew aside easily and revealed, not a passage or stair, but a small, square, bare chamber with another closed door at the far side.

Charles crossed toward it and I stepped in after him. As I did so I heard a sharp crash behind me and, wheeling, saw that the door had slid to automatically.

There came a rap on the outside and Tolliver's voice shouting:

"Hey! You in there! Open this up! I can't stir it."

I would have liked to oblige him, but I couldn't see any knob to take hold of. The word "Exit" had confronted the banquet-hall. This side was more voluble. It observed:

> The Simple Believeth Every Word,
> but the Prudent Looketh Well to His Going.

"This other door is only a dummy, I fear," Charles sadly remarked. "It won't move."

"We're the dummies," I retorted savagely. "Now what are we to do? Tolliver," I raised my voice, "can't you find an ax and smash this confounded door?"

There was no reply.

"Do you hear the groan of machinery?" demanded Charles.

"Of course I do. And the place is shaking like a factory. We've got to break out of here. Come on, put your shoulder beside mine and push."

Comrades in dismay, animosity was forgotten. He sprang to do as I asked.

And just then the noise and vibration stopped with a kind of jolt, there was a snapping sound and the door opened as it had closed, voluntarily.

We emerged.

The banquet-hall had magically vanished and confronting us was a curving flight of white stairs.

With a contemptuous bang the intelligent door had shut again and didn't even offer a motto for our edification. There was merely what looked like a recess in the wall, covered with those eternal black and white stripes.

"I trust," said I, "that the lift or sliding car, or whatever the darned thing was, has gone back after the rest of us. It seems to me that Mason carried his jokes to the point of banality."

Chapter XX.

THE VILLAIN CONQUERS.

Hoping that "Exit" had meant what it said, though after a tricky fashion, we ran hastily up the stairs. They led to the padded chamber beneath the pavilion.

Disappointed, but not despairing, we surveyed the ceiling. Presently, as the lighter man, I accepted the use of Charles's shoulders to examine that ceiling more intimately.

The embossed metal was worked into highly involved patterns, and I couldn't so much as find a crevice to mark the trap-door's boundaries. It wasn't thin stuff either that one could cut into and strip off with a pocket-knife.

After a fruitless hunt for some kind of knob or projection that would slide like the carving on the pedestal, Charles politely asked me to descend.

"I'm going back," he announced when I stood beside him again. "If Veron—your cousin and Mr. Tolliver were able to follow the route we did they would have arrived by now. They are imprisoned in the banquet-hall.

You can stay here, if you like, and try to get the trap open, but I'm going back."

"You don't say! And may I ask why I should let you go to her—you—and myself remain here? She is in safe company now, but—"

"Mr. Wyndham, you choose to be extremely insolent. Whatever her feelings toward me, Veronica is my wife, and—"

"Your what? That's a—lie!"

I jumped for his throat, but he caught me and held me off by the shoulders at arms' length. My strength had by no means returned, and anyway he was the more powerful man. I struggled. Anger had robbed me for the time of reason. The blood surged through my brain, and his face loomed hatefully through a scarlet mist. Staggering about, our feet sinking deep in the green upholstery, I felt myself jammed tight to the wall, and the pressure drove Tolliver's pistol hard against my hip. Ceasing to try for his throat, I reached for the gun.

It was in my grasp. His hand slid down my arm, but before it reached the elbow I had brought my wrist up and fired.

An automatic will shoot as fast as one can press the trigger, but I had time to press this one only twice. Then I was caught in a bearlike hug and fairly lifted off my feet. Half-smothered in the folds of the conspirator's cloak, I was swung round, and next thing found myself flat on the padded floor, staring up into Charles's face.

He had tripped me, twisted the weapon out of my hand, and now knelt triumphantly on my prostrate person. The two bullets fired had found a mark only in the voluminous folds of that cloak. I noticed that instead of reciprocating my effort to kill he had tossed the gun aside.

"Do you often go crazy like this, Wyndham?" he demanded.

I didn't answer. The first red mist had passed, and it was occurring to me that I had been foolish. I should have used the automatic to start with.

"If I let you up," he said, "what will you do?"

"Let me up and find out!"

"Thanks, no. Now, Wyndham, won't you be reasonable? You think me an utter scoundrel, and I'm not sure you are wrong. Still, you were calm enough before. What did I say that—"

"You lying hypocrite!" I snarled. "You referred to my cousin as—as your wife!"

"But why shouldn't I? I assure you the marriage was perfectly legal and in good form. She told you everything, so she must have told you that she entered into it willingly, even though under a misconception. Of course I lied to her—I've been bitterly regretting it ever since—and, of course, I did an unpardonable thing in bringing her to Asgard Heights against her will; but you must know—"

I went suddenly limp from head to foot.

"I don't know anything," I admitted. "Let me up, please."

"You won't?"

"No, I won't. It's all over, I'm subdued."

He courteously assisted me to rise, and again we faced one another.

"I don't at all understand you, Wyndham," he complained, and there was a certain pathos in his voice.

"The Wyndham family are not to be lightly understood. When I said that Veronica told me all, I exaggerated. Comparatively speaking, she told me nothing. If you won't consider it impertinent on the part of an utter stranger to Veronica and yourself, may I ask when this marriage took place?"

"Monday night—or rather Tuesday morning. About 1.15 A.M."

"*The* Tuesday morning, you mean?"

"Yes, the fifteenth. I hadn't supposed that Veronica would wish it kept secret from you, or I should have said nothing. Too bad. I told Tolliver, too."

"Of course. Friend Tolliver was about to impart the glad news, but he was overcome by emotion and desisted. You have such a casual way of announcing your weddings, Governor Charles."

"You are bitter over it, but that's hardly strange." He sighed. "I made a great mistake," he added sadly.

"It does seem that a slight error has been committed somewhere. However, as you suggested a while ago, we may as well hunt up the lost bride. Shall we try and open the door of that sliding car and make it slide back to the hall?"

He acquiesced and we did—try.

Like every other device in these lower regions, the door followed some sweet law of its own being, and was obdurate to all persuasion.

"I was afraid of this," said my companion gloomily. "We can only return by following our original path."

"Those closed panels," I reminded.

"That would be provided for. As the guests arrived they would pass through, as one might say, in series. Therefore, as one panel drops, another nearer to the entrance must rise. In that manner any number of people could journey through, and the trap remain perpetually in readiness. I shouldn't wonder—" He paused reflectively.

"Well? I queried.

"That would explain the lights. The same mechanism that controls the panels may throw off one circuit and turn on the next. In other words, only a comparatively small number of lamps would be in use at any one time. Light follows the victim's wanderings about the labyrinth at a very slight expenditure of current."

"No doubt you are right," I conceded rather impatiently. "I'm no electrician. By the way, how about those other two archways? One of them may lead to an easier road."

"Impossible. Mason would not have offered any real choice, or the joke would have been spoiled."

"Nevertheless—"

"We can look, if you wish."

A hasty glance from one of the stairways in question showed that it led into the same system of corridors as our original choice. The other ended similarly, but to our surprise we observed, set on the lowest step, a number of objects.

They proved to be several bottles of fine wine, Chablis and Madeira, two jars of anchovies, three of pâté de foies gras, and six tins of French sardines.

"The butler grew weary last time he went to provision *Bluebeard's* chamber," I suggested. "His burden was left by the wayside."

"Put some of these in your pockets," advised the conspirator, as he stowed away a couple of boxes of sardines in the front of his medieval doublet. "We ate most of the provisions in the banquet-hall."

I complied.

"You are intending to live there indefinitely?"

"It is well to be prepared for anything. I am not sure," he continued, "that I should take you with me, Wyndham. Veronica was greatly worried when you fainted. She says your health is poor; the fatigue of the return journey might be too much for you. Rest here, and let me go alone, and if I—er—shouldn't return, you can come on later."

Such anxiety was touching, but not so personal as it might have been. I could see in his eye that to him I was only a treasured possession of Ronny's—something she would hold him responsible for if harm came to it.

"My health," I said grimly, "is better than yours will be if you try to prevent my going. I'm not afraid of Ronny, and you are. I can hit you and you daren't hit me. Forward!"

Charles eyed me strangely. Either he thought I was crazy, or he was embarrassed that I had discovered his secret. No matter which.

The continual reversal of all the ideas I could gather concerning him and Ronny was enough to drive any man to mental irresponsibility.

Chapter XXI.

A TALE OF TOTAL DEPRAVITY.

To prevent mistakes, we indited a message on the wall in three conspicuous places. Should Ronny and Tolliver arrive here it would be well for them to remain stationary. Otherwise, in seeking to be reunited, the lot of us might circle the labyrinth indefinitely, like a kitten chasing its tail.

Then, with the "Rejoice not" archway for a starting point, we once more essayed Dan Mason's tortuous entrance halls.

My just-revealed cousin-in-law had been right about the panels. We encountered no obstruction to losing ourselves, and in a few minutes were safely cut off from return to the padded cell.

It was too bad that on our first journey in we had been quite so thorough about blundering into every blind alley the labyrinth boasted. Rex's initials formed no guide to a short cut. In fact, we found it best to ignore them, and an intricate system of beautifully interlaced "C.C.'s" was soon added to the interior decoration of the corridors.

No longer did we shudder at the pathos of red-brown noughts and crosses. If some poor dub had used his heart's blood for paint, we knew that he had been consoled with champagne at the finish, and sympathy would be wasted.

As we strolled, laden with hope and sardine tins, Governor Charles laid bare the shameful story of his crime.

In Ronny's narrative I had been vaguely conscious of something important missing. It was just a little thing—merely the hinge on which the whole preposterous adventure turned. I could scarcely blame Charles for himself halting and stumbling over it, for his was indeed a weird tale to fall from the lips of a rising statesman.

It seemed that, made desperate by the approaching marriage of his escaped secretary *fiancée* to Tolliver, Charles determined that for the first time in his life he would resort to wicked subterfuge.

Offerings of luxury beyond the dreams, *et cetera*, having been declined with thanks, his astute brain suggested trying the opposite. He would do two things. Rouse the generous sympathy which was one of Ronny's strongest characteristics, and then rush her off her feet.

"What I wished," he explained, "was to show her the mistake she had made in allowing a trivial misunderstanding to separate our lives. I believed—I still believe—that in every important respect we are suited to one another as few people are."

Suddenly his rather spiritless manner dropped away. His face flushed, and his fine voice quivered.

"Wyndham, I love her. I loved her so. I couldn't forget her. Even work failed me. Day and night she was before my eyes and—I couldn't forget her. Then one day it came to me that ambition and the power to do are empty, fruitless things, that bring a man nothing but loneliness. It seemed to me—I was wrong, of course—but it seemed that, having labored so long and hard to safeguard the happiness of people with insufficient intelligence to guard their own, I had earned the right to take, if needs be by trickery, this single joy that I wanted for myself.

"It was false logic. Happiness can't be based on a lie, and if it doesn't come by free will it cannot be forced. I knew that, but I pretended otherwise. Still, if there really remained no love for me in her heart, my scheme must fail. On that basis I excused myself and carried it out."

With a nice sense of drama, he chose midnight for his début as a deceiver. That Ronny had broken her second engagement the same evening, and been left at her door five minutes before his arrival, was mere coincidence. One of those little helps of fate offered the ingénue on the downward path.

"She allowed me to see her, and I told the story I had devised. Experience on the speaking platform is not so different from an actor's training. I think my manner was convincing, and she consented—"

"Look here," I broke in ruthlessly, "just what was the wonderful yarn that you told Ronny? It was carefully deleted from her story, but I'll be hanged if it's going to be deleted from yours without a protest. *What* did you tell her?"

He flushed again, and stammered like a boy.

"If you must know—well, to be perfectly frank—I believe I hinted that— you see, it was this way. I wanted her to marry me that night, before she had time to think about it or change her mind again. I told her that—"

Suddenly he plunged desperately, and managed to get it out of his system.

"I said that years ago I committed a crime in hot blood. That there was only one witness, a friend, who had kept silent, but that of late he had taken to drink and gone to the dogs. I said that Louis Berger got hold of him on a drunken spree, and by the offer of a large sum induced him to make a sworn statement. You know, by the way, Berger has played turncoat and thrown his railroad princes to the lions? He's a soiled tool, but Comstock agrees with me—"

"I *beg* your pardon. Would you mind finishing your other story first?"

Interrupting a Governor is bad taste, and not always safe. But this was a thoroughly tamed Governor, and besides he was used to my interrupting him. He meekly returned to Ronny.

"I said that this friend of mine—this witness against me—had repented when sobriety returned, and warned me of his betrayal. It was too late, however, to save me from ruin. Not only my political career, but even my status as a citizen was lost. To save myself from a prison term, or worse, I must leave the country, and for the rest of my life play the part of a hunted criminal."

"But *what* did you say you had done?"

His embarrassment increased.

"I could think of only one crime that a man wouldn't dare stand trial for."

"Good Lord! Murder?"

He looked relieved at not having to say it.

"Yes. I had killed the man in hot blood, however," he added hastily.

"That undoubtedly saves your character. And as a murderer, Ronny of course welcomed you with open arms."

"Mr. Wyndham, no doubt this seems amusing to you, but for me it is serious."

"Yes, one would expect that. Pardon my levity. And Ronny?"

"As I had dared hope, she insisted upon sharing my exile. After demurring insincerely, I yielded, and since every hour's delay increased the danger of my apprehension, the marriage must take place at once. Then she could return to her apartment, pack a suit-case, and meet me at the Nicollet Street station."

"And I thought Ronny was intelligent!"

He looked resentful. "She is the most intelligent woman I have met. And just at this moment I can recall no man of my acquaintance who is her equal."

"Thanks. So the wedding took place instanter. But—why, Governor, who performed this ceremony? How is it that with the police on the trail, not to mention a hungry horde of reporters—"

"I'm coming to that. In a way, it is the most regrettable part of the affair, for it has involved an honorable and highly conscientious man. The Rev. Dr. Theodore Crowell, in fact."

"Ah! Well, why not? Yesterday I should have said—but we diverge. Dr. Crowell, then—"

"Understand me, he knew nothing until later of the duplicity that I had practised. While amazed at the suddenness and strange hour of the ceremony, I assured him that if he would not perform it, Miss Wyndham and I would only seek another clergyman. As an intimate friend of my dear father's, he consented, and we were married."

He ceased speaking.

"And then?"

"I told her the truth," he said heavily.

"She was not pleased?"

"She was—greatly annoyed. In fact, she expressed a desire never to see my face or hear my voice again."

"Naturally. Ronny could tolerate a murderer in distress, but not a man who had made her feel foolish."

"Was that the trouble? I hadn't meant that she should feel foolish. I merely tried to show her that her love for me really existed, and that, in the face of misfortune, she would go any length for my sake."

"You showed it. And then—"

"Then I lost my head. Instead of taking her home, I brought her here, and instead of relenting, she has every day grown firmer in her desire to leave. The moment that I heard your name, when you stopped me on the street outside my house, I knew that the end had come. I have never found surrender easy." He smiled rather forlornly. "I tried to carry it off, but I suppose I gave myself away pretty completely."

"You nearly scared your caller into suicide, if that's what you mean. It wasn't till three hours afterward that I had the remotest thought of connecting you personally with Ronny's disappearance." I explained about the fragment of letter which had put me on the trail, saying nothing, however, of the ignoble character of my suspicions. They were not the kind to feel proud of.

"So you knew nothing at the time of your call?" he queried. "I believed otherwise. In fact, I came home to-night prepared for anything."

"Even murder in earnest."

The words slipped out before I could check them. The moment they were uttered I would have given a good deal to recall them. In one clear-sighted flash there came to me the true meaning of that pistol he still carried. And Tolliver's angry expostulation at the pool—"I ought to have let him drown if he wanted to!"

Ronny had certainly made one beautiful mess of an originally fine and courageous character.

And yet—it wasn't really fair to judge her. It was not—fair.

"No," said Charles, as if he had read my thoughts, "all the wrong was mine. I had no intention to defend myself by violence. In fact, I had decided on a peculiarly cowardly way out—of which I should prefer not to speak."

"Unworthy," I dared, in a very low voice.

His teeth came together with an audible click. "No—cowardly." After a moment he continued, "The cold plunge I shared with your friend may have washed a few cobwebs out of my brain. The—the nervous tension had been running pretty high. I'm not apologizing—only explaining. You won't understand, but I *couldn't* let her go. Not till the very end was reached. And it's a rather queer sensation to feel your world sliding from under your feet. This is the full confession they say is good for the soul, Wyndham. I think that now you have the whole miserable story."

"Not quite. Dr. Crowell?"

"I went to him on the day following and told him everything. I appealed to him on the ground that should Veronica leave me in anger and tell her story my political career would be ruined. That was not my reason. What I really feared was that once away from me she would never return. Dr. Crowell, however, while deeply distressed, hesitated at injuring the son of his old friend. He consented to keep silence for a few days, while I tried to persuade Veronica. Fortunately, no license being required in this State, only Dr. Crowell, his daughter, and an old servant of theirs, whom he positively assured me could be trusted—"

"One thousand dollars reward!" I gasped.

"What did you say?"

"I said that the day of miracles has not passed—maybe. If I were you I'd go and hand a thousand-dollar bill to that remarkable servant. I'd do it first thing—the minute you're out of here, I mean."

"It might be a good idea," he conceded thoughtfully, "though it savors a bit too much of bribery. However, as I was saying, only Dr. Crowell and these two witnesses were conversant with the facts, and he has not recorded the marriage at City Hall. That is, he had not done so the last time we talked."

A look of startled recollection flashed across the Governor's face.

"Do you know," he observed, "just after your own morning visit, Dr. Crowell called me up. He said it was imperative for him to see me. I made an appointment, but was prevented from keeping it, and I have heard nothing at all since. I wonder—"

"That would be fine," I remarked. "I can just see to-morrow's papers."

There was a pause.

"I personally don't matter," he said at last. "My moral code gave way under the first real strain, and I should be forced to take the consequences. I suppose, too, that some other man can—will carry on my work as well as I. But Veronica—it is going to be very unpleasant for her if any of this comes out. What would you advise me to do, Wyndham?"

"The only safe way would be to destroy the record, strangle Dr. Crowell, his daughter and miraculous servant, knock Tolliver and myself on the head, drown Veronica in the lotus pond, and bury us all in the labyrinth. If you want any less drastic advice, you will have to give me time for deep thought."

There was a long, silent interim, in which both of us were plunged in reflections. Mine were curious.

As a scoundrel he had been startling but comprehensible. As *Sir Galahad* he was irreconcilable. And yet, after some strange fashion, I knew that it was *Galahad*, not *Gawain*, who walked beside me. I wonder if *Galahad* could have found the Holy Grail if he had been burdened with a sense of humor?

Chapter XXII.

THROUGH THE LOOKING-GLASS.

"Come to think of it, she said she couldn't marry you, but I believe that's a mistake. It isn't bigamy to marry the same person twice. Any law against it in this State?"

He looked at me sharply. "No. What do you mean, Wyndham?"

"Under no circumstances can you afford to let this secret marriage business leak out. I doubt if Dr. Crowell has made it public without telling you of his intention. Ronny must go home and frame up some kind of yarn—or rather I will—so that the baying kiyoodles of the law will drop the matter without a scandal. Then you can be remarried with all the correct flourishes—"

He stopped me off by seizing my shoulders, whirling me around, and facing me with eyes that literally blazed like blue fire.

"Wyndham," he demanded, "are you on my side?"

"No," I said very coldly, "I'm not. I'm on Veronica's side. First you made her fall in love with you, then you drove her away by bossing her—except in a business way, Ronny cannot be bossed—you nearly forced her into a loveless marriage, played the mean trick of letting her make a great sacrifice, the meaner one of showing her that no sacrifice had been made, and crowned all by trying to force her forgiveness in ignominious captivity. The initial fault, however, was making her love you. With two people like you I suppose the rest was inevitable. You may repeat that I choose to be extremely insolent, but I've been through enough to justify—"

His attention had halted two sentences back.

"On your word of honor, Wyndham," he said slowly, "do you believe she loves me?"

"She says she detests you—and will take horrible vengeance on any one who dares cause you inconvenience over this incident."

"Oh, that's for the work's sake."

The light went out of his eyes, and his hands dropped from my shoulders. Again we walked in silence.

"By the way," I said, "have we passed any 'R. T.'s' lately?"

"What? I don't know—we were talking."

"And walking—an unsafe combination down here. It seems to me we've come a very long way."

"Remember, you were tired at the beginning."

"I was tired so long ago that I'm rested again. We've come too far. And—I say, don't you hear some one shouting?"

We stopped in our tracks.

Silence, then from far off, muffled by many intervening walls, there reached us a long "Hal-loo-oo-oo!"

"Sounds like Tolliver," I ventured. I raised my voice in reply, Charles joined me, and we got an answer after a moment.

To set out in the direction of the hail was impossible. In the first place, it was hard to know where that direction lay, and in the second, our peregrinations were governed not by will, but by where we could find a way. Reaching Tolliver was a long and tedious business.

One thing we discovered with surprise. We had become so accustomed to falling panels cutting off the rearward road that we had ceased to note whether a passage was blocked by what Ronny had named a "calamity wall," or one of the steel panels.

Earnestly conversing on matters of grave import, we had given attention to nothing but Charles's liberally bestrewed "C.C.'s." Were a passage bare of these, we followed it. And thus, it now appeared, we had wandered into a region panelless, "R.T."-less, and even nought-and-crossless. Only Tolliver's voice, echoing through the waste, indicated that we were still in the region of the banquet-hall.

Our education, it appeared, was not complete.

Tolliver's voice indicated something entirely different, as we learned when at the end of a half-hour's steady hallooing, that gentleman met us at the turning of the way.

It was a distressed and mentally disheveled cavalier who followed his voice into our presence.

"Have you seen Ronny?" was his first casual greeting.

"What—do—you—mean?" Charles's voice was softly sweet—like a tiger's growl.

"I say, have you fellows seen Ronny?"

Then I perceived that Tolliver's casual manner was deceptive. He was speaking between clenched teeth in a desperate effort at self-control.

More or less in unison we explained to him the improbability of our having recently looked upon the lady in question.

"She was left in your care!" accused the Governor. "If you have allowed any harm to happen to Veronica—"

He didn't finish, but his tone implied all the lingering deaths of a medieval torture-chamber.

Tolliver, however, was too genuinely distressed to care for our opinion of him. It appeared that after we had been shut off by the so-called "Exit," Tolliver fled in search of some implement to break through. Failing to find anything better, he snatched up one of the great silver rose-urns, with which he meant to smash out a panel.

With Ronny urging him to haste—for they, too, had heard the grind of machinery—he had done that little thing. In fact, he demolished the door so thoroughly that it fell in splinters before his knightly arm.

"But the door went with us!" I objected.

"Double door!" snapped Charles. "Go on, Tolliver."

Disclosed by the smash, they beheld a concrete wall rising some six or eight feet beyond a black and yawning abyss. There was not so much as a rail visible for a sliding car to have run on.

"Overhead rails," interjected Charles, who must have had a leaning toward mechanics in his youth. "Electric motor automatically connected, self-starter, and automatic brake. That's all simple. *Where is Veronica?*"

Veronica, it seemed, had displayed unusual symptoms of hysteria. I believe that her remaining guardian had to restrain her by force from flinging herself into said abyss, whither she insisted that Charles and I had fallen to our deaths.

"You see?" said I to the Governor.

"You are very dear to her, Wyndham," he retorted with a melancholy shrug.

"Oh—rot!" Good little pal though she was, I couldn't see Ronny committing suicide on my grave. "Well, for God's sake, Tolliver, I hope you didn't let her jump in?"

"What do you think I am? Certainly not. I told her I'd make a rope of something and go down there myself."

So he got her to a chair, rushed to the wardrobe-room, and was back in three minutes with an armful of gaudy cloaks and garments from which the rope was to be constructed.

Then came real tragedy. Ronny had vanished. Cursing himself for a fool, the unlucky cavalier flew to look down the horizontal shaft. Nothing doing. A blank white panel presented itself, which when he assaulted it with the urn gave answer with a steely clang.

"That," explained our mechanical genius, "was the inner half of the door. The car had returned as it went, and if you had waited you could have opened it as we did and joined us under the pavilion. As it was, I supposed you had smashed the mechanism?"

"I don't know," mourned Tolliver. "There was nothing to take hold of. I battered both urns flat trying to break it open."

This explosion of energy exhausted, it occurred to our hero that after all Ronny might not have flung herself down the shaft.

Running along the wall, he jerked down tapestry to moldy billows, till he did actually uncover another doorway. It was an open arch. Hurling himself through it, he found himself once more in black-and-white stripedom. Frantically seeking Ronny, he rushed along, not troubling to R. T. his path, shouting her name and hallooing from time to time.

As a result of this impetuous proceeding, the devious ways had soon swallowed up friend Tolliver. Therein he had wandered disconsolate, till our answering hail assured him that others than himself yet lived and moved in Daniel Mason's too labyrinthine labyrinth.

"Maybe when the car came back Ronny got aboard and was carried to the pavilion," hazarded I.

"Now, you must know that's impossible, Wyndham." The Governor was wearily patient. "We were there at least half an hour. The white panel that he saw was the car. If she'd been inside, she would have called to him through the door. What I fear is—"

He broke off, and we didn't ask him to finish. Had Ronny, in her temporary insanity, done the thing that Tolliver meant to prevent her doing? While he was in the wardrobe, before the car returned—

"Nonsense!" I ejaculated. "Here we stand like three fools, while Ronny is straying about somewhere all alone. Come on and find her!"

Brave advice, and eagerly taken up. Where we should look, however, was a matter beyond our choice. We could only—wander—and wander—and wander some more, shouting, hallooing till our throats were hoarse, and one would have thought that Ronny's name had echoed clear to Marshall City.

Let it not be imagined that the variety of the inscriptions had ceased with the falling panels. We met them continually—little, cheerful reminders like,

Terrors Are Turned Upon Me;
They Pursue My Soul as the Wind.

Or—

Their Flesh Shall Consume Away
While They Stand Upon Their Feet.

Oh, lots of variety, though we hardly bothered to read them any more.

It was a vile and twisted use for the Great Book, but the mind that had spent millions for such a purpose was too primitive to be judged by ordinary standards.

A suggestion that we separate received the gubernatorial veto. Charles had command now, and neither of us thought of questioning it. Seemed a bit strange, too. We weren't hunting for my Ronny, or Tolliver's Ronny. We were looking for Mrs. Clinton Charles—and I hadn't got used to the idea any more than Ronny herself.

In spite of us, we returned again and again over the same territory, making, I suppose, a vicious circle, or quadrilateral, or some villainous geometric figure.

"This is a hell of a joke!" our cavalier complained. "I hope that old Dan Mason—"

But it isn't necessary to say what he hoped for old Dan Mason. I hoped an unrepeatable thing or two for him myself.

Charles, however, didn't waste breath on anathema. As it was, though he had a fine voice to start with, it was pretty nearly worn out by the time we came to the place where we met ourselves walking along a corridor.

The device is as old as the hills, and wouldn't frighten a child. Naturally, it wasn't calculated to frighten three grown men. That's why we all stopped as if we'd been shot, Tolliver reached for his gun—which he hadn't got—and I heard the funniest little sound, like a gasping sob of panic. It come out of my throat.

Then we grinned for the first time in ages, and our reflected selves grinned sheepishly back.

"A mirror!" sniffed Tolliver. "Say, that's stale. By George, I do look like a specter of the Merry Monarch, don't I?"

"No—the Pretender after hiding all night in a tree."

"Veronica!" The cry was so sudden and sharp that it made me jump.

"Clinton!" came a faint little wail from somewhere. "Oh, Cl-linton, where are you?"

"I'm here! Where *are* you, Veronica?"

It seemed to me that Veronica and Clinton really ought to be reunited.

"Rap on the wall, Ronny," I called. "We can't tell from your voice where you are."

There came one violent thump. The mirror swung out and back.

Our reflected selves vanished into the all-where, and in their place stood none other than the Lost Lady of the Labyrinth, Veronica Wyn—I mean, Mrs. Governor Clinton Charles.

CHAPTER XXIII.

A HIDEOUS DISCOVERY.

Did this romantic couple, reunited after hours of terror, fall upon one another's necks?

Veronica cast about one-half of a beaming smile through tears in Clinton's direction; she swayed a similar fraction of a sway toward him.

I held my breath.

Next instant Ronny's arms were around my neck again, and her tears of relief were bedewing my shoulder.

I felt rather like a tailor's dummy—one of those wax figures that wears another man's coat.

Still, after all our years of comradeship, I could hardly shake her off rudely, and say: "Here, this is all wrong—you go and weep on Clinton. Can't you understand that you're tearing the very heart out of the man you love?"

No, it wouldn't do. Ronny must walk her own road as she'd always done, and if Governor Charles got stepped on—well, he would have to "learn about women from her," that was all.

I looked up. The back of a cavalier was just disappearing through the mirror doorway. Tolliver had gone to see where Ronny had been hiding. The back of a conspirator was moving slowly off in another direction. Charles was going to look for—oh, anything—his lost self-respect, perhaps.

"Ronny!" I said, in a voice I'd never heard speaking to her from my lips before. "Brace up! We've tramped two hours looking for you. Where have you been?"

She drew away, and her eyes had the reproachful, amazed brilliance of a baby's, that has been slapped when it expected to be consoled. Her rosy mouth quivered.

"*Poor* little girl!" said Hildreth, coming down with a dull, sickening thud. "Were you very much frightened?"

"I've had a horrible experience—perfectly horrible! If I hadn't found you again, I should have died, I think—where did Rex go? He didn't go in *there*, did he? Call him back quick, Hildreth! Quick!"

Fearing I knew not what dreadful trap, I sprang to the mirror door and shouted Tolliver's name.

He was not more than a couple of feet from the entrance, and my yell startled him considerably. He leaped through the door with the wild expression of a man called upon to defend his lady against dragons, saw that Ronny had not been assassinated, and turned on me in exasperation.

"For Heaven's sake, Wyndham, isn't there enough to get on a man's nerves without your yelling like that at him? What do you want?"

"I don't know. Ronny said you mustn't go in there."

"There's a dead man in there! He's sitting at a table, and he's dead! He poisoned himself—he read a letter—and Mr. Mason—the labyrinth—"

Suddenly Ronny pulled herself together, drew a long, quivering breath, and when she spoke again it was in the perfectly controlled voice which she reserved for matters of importance.

"You must not think that I gave way to fright because the man is dead. I've been conscious since the first moment of our entry here that something was utterly wrong. I don't mean the knife-edged, murderous panels, nor the malice written on the walls, nor any single thing that a person could see or touch. I mean a sense of something intangible and—and ferocious. It's lurked around every corner we turned. It fairly brooded over that horrible, musty old banquet-table. Do you recall how after a while we couldn't bear to speak of or look at the marks painted in—painted in red on the walls we passed? And how—"

"Ronny, you've been too long alone. There's nothing down here but our four selves."

"And a dead man—and a letter. Here—or no, I don't want you to read it yet. First you must see what I have seen—and then you—you'll know what I know."

Another quivering breath, and she caught at her under lip with her teeth. Charles had come back.

"Wyndham, you stay here. Tolliver and I will find out exactly what is wrong."

"No," demurred Ronny with an abrupt return to firmness, "we'll all go together. For just a minute, when I first came out, it seemed as if all the—the horribleness were shut in that room beyond the door. But it's not. It's everywhere, and from this time on none of us must lose sight of the others for one single instant. I tell you, there's a vicious *intent* against us because—we've discovered his secret."

Ronny was talking so wildly that I feared her mind had suffered by whatever experience she had met in those two lonely hours. From the look in Charles's eyes I knew the same fear was on him. She was so bent, however, on our accompanying her that it seemed best to give way.

Crumpled in her hand were three or four sheets of paper, which we assumed formed the letter she had referred to.

Having examined the mirror, and made sure that it was simply a swinging door with no catch or provision for self-locking, we passed through. On the other side was a curving passage, painted in red for a change, and rather dimly lighted.

As Ronny's sole acceptable guardian, I brought up the rear with my arms in hers. Her little cold fingers locked themselves nervously around mine, but aside from that she was now rigidly calm and self-possessed.

We had not far to go. The passage made almost a semicircle and in the midst of it was an open archway.

"Don't go in," whispered Ronny. "I went, because I saw the poor man, and I thought perhaps he might have got lost here, and been half-starved, and tired, and fallen asleep sitting there. But I can't bear that any of us should cross the threshold again! Look!"

We had been looking while she spoke.

We saw a dim, circular room, finished in a shade of pale, greenish-gray. Around the wall, here and there, was fastened up a peculiar ornament—a sunflowerlike thing, of which the petals were dull-black with lighter patches of gleam.

In the center of the room was a round table, with a lamp hung just above it that cast a steady, downward glare, the only bright place in the room. Just under it stood a strange little rack of bottles. There was a partly filled water-carafe, too, and a dingily fogged empty tumbler. This latter was set close to the quiet, waxlike hand of the man.

That hand fascinated us. It was long, thin, fragile, and half curled stiffly, as if it had released the emptied glass and frozen so.

The man's hair gleamed white against the dull black of his sleeve. An old, weary man, who had dropped down in the chair at the table's far side, laid his head on one extended arm and fallen asleep. So it had appeared to Veronica when she first stumbled upon this hidden chamber.

Yet how had she ever been deceived? That hand—and the side of his face where it showed, with its slightly greenish, waxen pallor!

"The letter lay scattered in sheets," whispered Veronica, "on the table and floor. I was going to speak to him. Then I—I saw."

"And you gathered up those sheets and read them?" I gasped.

"Yes. First I ran away. I couldn't get far. I didn't know about the swinging door. It looks just like the wall on this side. I was shut in with—it. I kept going back and peeping through the doorway. I couldn't think what was dragging me there. I didn't want to go. Then it was just as if a voice spoke in my ear. 'The letter!' it said. 'The letter—the letter!' After a while I knew. *It* wanted me to read what was written on those sheets. I—I went in, on my tiptoes—very softly. It would have been so horrible, you see, if I should have—have waked him."

"Veronica, stop!" Charles spoke in his ordinary voice—a startling thing to hear when every one else had been whispering. He seemed to think so himself, for he lowered it before speaking again. "It's not like you," he continued, "to give way to fancy. There is nothing here to harm us."

"But there is—there is! Read the letter and you'll know. Read it!"

She thrust the sheets into Charles's hands, and we other two couldn't wait for him to finish and pass it along. We stood under the small electric bulb that lighted the passage.

Rex and I read with one eye apiece what the Governor had the advantage of holding straight before him. But we got on very well. The writing was in a large, bold hand, as easily legible as print.

At the top was a date five years old. The paper was commercial bond, with the letterhead of the Corporate Iron Companies, and in one corner the name of Daniel Mason, president.

As we read on, the rough, violent personality of the writer seemed to thrust itself out from every line like a discord jarring on stillness—the stillness of death.

It was addressed, "Bradley R. Fern, Esq.," and began without further preface:

> You'll never read this letter till I've got you where I want you, and that's sitting right at this table in this room I've got ready for you, and with the fear of God—and me—in your heart at last.
>
> And the best of the joke is that I'll be looking over your shoulder as you read, though you won't see me—or will you? Maybe you will. I hope so. I should like you to see me peering and laughing at you—as you laughed at me one time, do you remember? I see you do. Oh, yes, I'm standing here, looking right over your shoulder while you read. I'm laughing you down to hell, old man, do you understand?
>
> You stole her neatly, with your butter-mouthed Bible talk, and

telling her how she, living open and honest with me, would go to hell sure, because some other butter-mouthed Bible quoter like you hadn't said words over us and called us man and wife.

We'd get to that likely, too, in a year or so. Those were rough days. It hadn't seemed to her and me to make such a lot of difference— till you drifted into camp and turned my wife against me. Yes, she was my wife, and all the preachers from here to Jericho couldn't have made her more so. But you took her away, and made her a thief in the bargain.

Mary and me had saved that two hundred together, and it was ours together. If I'd taken that money and drifted off with some other woman, wouldn't I have been a thief? Yes, I would, and that's what you made of her when you got her to take it and sneak out of camp with you.

But you "made her an honest woman" afterward, didn't you? You *married* her—and *she* knew she was my wife, and all the preachers couldn't change that and let her be yours. You didn't make her an honest woman; you made her a thief and a— I won't say the word about Mary.

You was smooth and sleek and educated, and you sure knew your Bible those days, didn't you, old man? You know who they say can quote Scripture? Well, the regular devil didn't have a thing on you that way.

You used to fire off Scriptures at me; all the while you was plotting to do the meanest sin in the whole Book—steal another man's woman away from him. But I'll bet you've got enough of Scripture quoting about now. I've spent a lot of study and trouble digging out a few bits to keep you interested.

And you won't read this till I'm dead, so I can stand and look over your shoulder and read with you. I thought about it some before I planned this out. I wanted you to suffer like the damned, before you was dead and damned forever. And a man can't do that right unless he's alone. *You* showed me that. I've been alone ever since, and if I had all the money and money-bought women in the world, I'd be alone.

So I wanted you to be alone, and, just the same, I wanted to be right with you, seeing you suffer, and enjoying every minute and every hour of it.

And how could I be with you and you be alone?

Why, just the way we've been ever since you sprung the trap I fixed for you. I'll be dead when you read this—and I'll be *standing right behind you, reading it with you over your shoulder.*

When you and Mary went off I tried for a while to find you. I'd got two bullets in my gun, both of them hungry for a mark. But I was broke—you'd seen to that—and I had to work, and you got off and hid pretty clever. It wasn't till three years ago that I saw you again, sitting up on a platform in the town-hall at Rochester. You was changed some. Your hair's white, and I suppose you know how good it goes with that sanctimonious, silly face of yours. But I spotted you in one minute.

Select councilman then, weren't you? Left the pulpit, and gone into politics—rotten politics, where you belong. I don't know what you've done with Mary—my woman that you called your wife. Dead, I guess. Or maybe you deserted her and left her to starve, or worse. That's what seems most likely to me. Anyway, you've got another wife now; I found out that much.

I just read in the paper yesterday that you're going to run as candidate for mayor or Rochester. That's good. I hope you get elected. I hope you get to be just as high as you'd like to be, even if it's President. The better off you are, the more you'll have to lose. Can you see me standing here laughing at you?

I didn't know exactly what to do about you till I got talking with Signor Guido Bartoli. He's an Italian and he knows a lot. He's a devil, too, though not *your* sort. The *signor's* a big man, and a big artist in his way—that's landscape gardening—but the first time I met him, I saw in his eyes what sort of devil he was. So I out pointblank and told him about you.

He helped me—for money, but he put something in the work that money couldn't buy, and that's pleasure. He enjoyed planning this underground maze for me, and setting in that silly, innocent hedge maze over it—the solemn yews that shade the secret tomb, he called them.

He got the workmen, too, a lot of dagoes, his own countrymen, who couldn't speak a word of English to tell tales, and thought Signor Bartoli was a little god on wheels. Bartoli and I worked together like brothers. I did it for hate and he for love—love of my hate, that could wait such a long time and take so much trouble.

Bartoli killed a woman at home, he told me—that's how confidential we got—and he's been mourning ever since because her lover escaped him by shooting himself when he heard the news. Nobody ever suspected Bartoli of that girl's death, and I should be surprised if they had. He's something more than an artist—he's got brains. And he's a devil—the sort of devil you taught me to like by stealing my woman.

When I'm dead you'll get a letter. Bartoli has it now. He'll post it from wherever he happens to be when he hears of my death.

It's a very clever letter. Bartoli wrote it, and you'll believe every word of it. And you'll sneak up to the Heights all alone—I know you, with your gold-greedy, woman-greedy fingers. And you'll spring the trap. You *have* sprung the trap, or you wouldn't be reading this, would you?

You've had your fun, and now I've had mine. Can't you hear me laughing over your shoulder?

You've been looking for a way out of here a long time, haven't you? Now I'll tell you the truth, you dirty dog.

There is no way out.

I've been in and out here many times, coming and going by the door you fell through, and *being mighty careful to leave that door open behind me.*

The only way you could get it open—from underneath—would be dynamite. Do you see? That's the way it's made. And no matter how loud you yell and screech, nobody 'll hear you.

How do you like being alone with riches, and splendid rooms, and fine, fancy clothes, with food that drops to dust in your fingers, and wine that looks fine in the glass and tastes bitter as loneliness and death?

Alone? *You* haven't been alone one minute since you fell down here—into hell.

Now drink your poison or cut your throat—do I care which? I've had my fun. Look up! Look over your shoulder! Do you see me—

DAN MASON.

Scrawled half across the page, the signature came like a savage, triumphant shout, or the crash of iron on iron. Though audible only in our minds, it echoed there as he had meant it should echo in the ears of Bradley Fern.

We didn't look over our shoulders. Our backs were against a wall, and I, for one, preferred it that way.

Governor Charles suddenly crumpled the sheets together in his fist. He stood very straight, and said in a loud, stern voice, the voice of a judge:

"Daniel Mason has committed a crime more worthy of a devil than a human being. That he committed it after his own death does not excuse him. He is a murderer in his grave, and every man shall know it!"

I don't know whether he was speaking to us, or to the presence that was heavy on us all—the presence of the year-dead Master of the Labyrinth.

I know that his stern, slightly defiant voice shocked my strained nerves like the touch of an electrified wire, and that Ronny cried out softly: "Hush! Hush! Don't speak so loud!"

And then the horror happened.

The dead man stirred.

First his waxlike hand quivered, and the long, thin fingers straightened.

Then the whole upper part of his body lifted, the white head rose, and the face stared straight across at us with terrible, wide eyes.

It was a thin, rather ascetic face, with the greenish pallor of death in every line. The mouth opened.

"I saw you coming in a dream," it said. "I am very glad, for it has been lonely enough down here, with only the unrepentant dead for company!"

Chapter XXIV.

A BENEVOLENT VICTIM.

There are occasions when it is difficult to keep the calm poise a man should hold in face of any humanly possible event.

In the first place, for a greenish-white corpse to raise its head and speak is only inhumanly possible. In the second, we had all got our minds "set," so to speak, on this particular corpse being the sad remains of a stranger.

To see a ghost is bad. To see the ghost of a man you have supposed to be alive, and he, moreover, a person you have known all your life and thought a lot of, is infinitely worse.

It was Charles again who broke the tension. He strode into the room as boldly as if it had been the commonplace library of his own house.

"Why, Dr. Crowell," he said, "how long have you been down here?"

The "corpse" viewed his approach with a benevolent smile.

"Long enough to become thoroughly weary, Governor. I fear I am no longer young enough to enjoy such an adventure."

The old clergyman rose stiffly from the table. Charles grasped his hand, and as they stood together under that lamp I saw not one vivified corpse, but two. When the rest of us had somewhat dazedly joined them, I saw four. I suppose I was another myself.

But, of course, like every one else, I was so familiar with the ghastly effect produced by a nitrogen lamp that I wasn't the least bit frightened.

I hadn't been exactly *frightened*—well, to get on with the story, greetings were exchanged with relief on both sides. If the ghost of old Dan Mason was really present, it must have retired in disgust from such an uncongenial atmosphere of joy.

Ronny behaved like a good little sport. She laughed at herself unmercifully for the inhuman horror which she had conjured from Dr. Crowell's sleeping form, but we were not inclined to make fun of her. We recalled too clearly a few of our own emotions.

"I knew, though," said Charles quietly, "that the man was not Bradley Fern."

He must have caught a skeptical gleam in my intelligent eye.

"No, really," he smiled. "I was acquainted with Fern in his lifetime. He died last year. Yes, he passed out within a week after Mason himself. And I think we all remember about Bartoli."

Of course we did. Last spring's papers had been full of it, for the *signor* had been well known in Marshall City. Dan Mason had set a sort of fashion with his Asgard Heights landscapery, and we have enough millionaires of the sudden and splurgeful type to have kept two Bartolis busy following it up.

Then with sad abruptness the artistic Italian had been wrested from our midst. Extradited, in fact, and hurled back to his native land. The murder of the girl had not been quite so cleverly covered up as Mason fancied.

"Ah, the hopeless futility of revenge!" mourned Dr. Crowell. "The wasted wealth and genius expended on this underground horror might have given pleasure grounds to ten thousand play-starved children!"

That is Dr. Crowell's special mission—getting playgrounds for children. I sympathized with his grief, but the imaginative picture of Dan Mason and Signor Bartoli gloating together over the design for a merry-go-round was too much for me.

"How did you come to get caught?" I inquired hastily.

"Through my own inquisitive nature, I fear." He turned to the Governor. "You will recall that you invited me to dinner."

"I did." Charles admitted. "But I phoned the Heights around five to let you know that I should be detained in town and couldn't reach here before nine or ten o'clock. Li Ching said you had gone to walk in the grounds. Later on he telephoned that you had returned to the city."

"I see. But Li Ching was mistaken. I came out early, as you asked me to do, but the—the person with whom you wished me to talk declined to see me."

Ronny looked him straight in the eye and smiled sweetly.

"I sent word that I would see you at dinner when Governor Charles should have returned."

He nodded.

"Yes, I believe that was the message. Having dismissed my hired car at the gate I strolled about the grounds for a time, enjoying the sunshine and the fragrance of the flowers. I fear that with old age absent-mindedness is creeping upon me. Being engrossed with a—a certain question which has been deeply troubling me of late, I raised my eyes to find myself walking between high walls of impenetrable hedge. I had become involved, it seemed, in a maze of endless extent and infinite convolutions."

Tolliver grinned.

"That's the best description I've heard for it, Dr. Crowell."

"Yes, I wandered there for some half-hour, calling out from time to time, till I reached a small, round building, beautifully constructed of white marble. Curiosity led me to enter. Within was a single chamber, and set in the midst of it, an empty pedestal.

"Carved upon the top of this pedestal in high relief appeared a quotation from the Book of Proverbs. I could see no aptness in its presence here, nor could I surmise for what purpose the pedestal itself was intended. The quotation, moreover, was incorrect. It is a very familiar one, and I could not be mistaken. It should have run, 'The heaven for height, and the earth for depth, and the heart of kings is unsearchable.' For 'kings' the word 'man' had been substituted, and its misuse, moreover, emphasized. 'Man' was not only carved in deeper relief than its companion words, but the letters composing it were of greater size and more elaborate design.

"Intent upon this singular deviation, I laid my finger upon the word, idly tracing its letters. To my astonishment it moved slightly. Here, since I was meddling with the property of another, I should have desisted. Instead, curiosity led me to see if it could be entirely lifted away. It moved again, but in a horizontal instead of vertical direction. A small sheet of copper was disclosed, but before I had time to investigate further, the pavement fell away from beneath my feet, and to my intense dismay I was precipitated into an underground vault.

"I need not go into the details of my wanderings since that hour. You, I presume, have with you a chart of these regions. I had none. While deeply distressed by the evidently malevolent use which had been made of sacred writings, I soon came to take a certain consolation from their presence. They formed, indeed, a perpetual reminder that, whatever the ill intent of man, I was, as always, in the safe hands of my Creator.

"Later, when I passed from the musty and desolate banquet-chamber to this smaller room, and when I had read the missive there in your hand, I felt more inclined to pity than wrath against Daniel Mason. Consider it, my friends! He must have studied the Testament through and through, and out of those wonderful pages he could extract nothing but evil and a means for cruel revenge!

"I sat thinking of this." He smiled again. "It may have been childish, but I received the most vivid impression of his personality about me and—I talked to him as if he had been here with me in the flesh! I'm afraid I preached quite a sermon to Daniel Mason's ghost. If God lets such things be it may have done him no harm. Then, being very weary, I fell asleep. Your voice must have reached me, Mrs. Charles, for I dreamed that you were beside me in this room. I awakened, and it was very pleasant to see not one friend, but four, standing in the doorway watching me."

"Dr. Crowell," demanded Veronica suddenly, "did you find that box of canned food in the banquet-hall? You didn't, of course. It hadn't been touched. And you missed your dinner–why, you must be nearly starved! We'll have to get back into the banquet-room right away."

"There's nothing there to eat," reminded Tolliver. "We cleaned out the ice-chest, I'm afraid."

"Sardines!" I remarked dramatically. "Dr. Crowell, did you ever dine on sardines, minus all fixings?"

"I believe I could dine on sardines in their natural state, at the present moment, young man!"

"No, this is real luxury. Cooked and served à la can."

The conspirator and I stacked our spoils on the table.

"If we had only included the foies gras and Madeira!" I mourned.

"Never mind," consoled Ronny. "We may need those later."

This was the first hint Dr. Crowell had received that our presence here was as involuntary as his own. As minister to one of the largest congregations in the city, his acquaintance was wide. Though Tolliver and I had not met till six months ago, he had known us both since boyhood. Naturally, then, Tolliver's engagement and my relationship to Veronica were facts with which he was familiar.

What import he at first drew from our presence here, I don't know. Dr. Crowell's thoughts could not be too easily read. He had the tact of forty years' successful ministry in Marshall City and elsewhere, and so far, aside from a curious glance at the anachronistic costumes among us, he had refrained from asking questions.

The time, however, had come when some explanation must be made.

Charles felt it, for he began abruptly:

"We haven't a chart of the labyrinth, Dr. Crowell. We fell down here by an accident."

"You don't say! All of you together—why, how very unfortunate! Hildreth, would you mind opening this can?"

They were French tins, without any patent openers. I got out my pocketknife.

"I'm the guilty man," I confessed. "My arm was resting on top of that pedestal, and in the dark my fingers happened to close on the fatal word. Guess you'll have to eat 'em out of the tin, Dr. Crowell."

"Yes, certainly. You'll lend me your knife? In the dark, eh?"

Suddenly Charles gave me one half defiant, half appealing look, turned his back and strolled over to the wall, where he began examining one of the sunflowerlike ornaments.

I looked at Ronny. She smiled sweetly and said nothing. I looked at Tolliver. He scowled; then he muttered something about finding out how Ronny got in here, and disappeared through the arch.

Clearly, it was up to Hildreth.

"Yes," I began. "In the dark. You see, we ourselves were lost in the hedge maze."

"A very easy thing to befall one, particularly in the dark. I understand."

"Yes. Tolliver and I came out to call on Veronica. Of course you are aware that there has been some—ah—misunderstanding in regard to her marriage."

"Yes, Hildreth. I am fully acquainted with the facts. The ceremony was performed by myself."

"So I was informed. Well—the Governor felt that he owed us some slight explanation, and while we were walking about the grounds talking it over, we blundered into the maze. In trying to find a light switch at the pavilion I played fool, as I've told you, and since then we've been straying happily from place to place. Rex and Governor Charles had to change their clothes for what they could find in Mason's crazy wardrobe, because just before we reached the maze they fell in a pond—accidentally. Quite a chapter of accidents, but you know these things will happen. Have another can of sardines?"

"Thanks, no—though you open cans beautifully, my boy. And now all that remains to be done is for us to extricate ourselves."

"Just that one little thing," I agreed, "and our troubles will be over."

Chapter XXV.

A HEALTH TO VERONICA.

The titanic revenge of Dan Mason had misfired utterly, so far as Mr. Bradley Fern was concerned. It was a pity that the old iron king had not troubled to consider that innocent people might receive the punishment intended for Fern. During his lifetime he probably saw to it that the pavilion was not meddled with. Or did he?

Dr. Crowell denied that any of his life blood had stained corridor walls in anguished noughts and crosses. He explained that the idea of marking his track had not once occurred to him. Mere chance guided his steps to the banquet-hall, which he entered, not through the gas-chamber, but by the open arch of Tolliver's later discovery.

Who, then, was responsible for the red-brown symbols? The question has never been answered, and possibly it was only another device of the Italian's subtly fiendish ingenuity.

The air-tight chest of canned goods, not to mention the delicacies Charles and I had found on the stairs, were not explained by the letter. Mason's "food that drops to dust in your fingers, and wine that tastes bitter in the glass," hardly applied to this assortment of really excellent provisions. The letter, however, was dated five years back. In the interim he might have decided that agony would be prolonged by a slightly more sustaining diet. Or it may be that Mason had them to refresh himself on gloating expeditions to the scene of his proposed post mortem revenge.

The elaborate completeness of the entire scheme reminded one of that famous bombardier who "took a cannon to kill a lark." Bartoli had certainly grasped the opportunity to make a very good thing out of the twist in his patron's mind.

The "death-chamber," as we named the gray-greenlit room where we found Dr. Crowell, was well calculated to inspire a desperate man to suicide. The sunflower ornaments were formed of knives, their red-rust black in the greenish rays, but once keen-edged and bright. In the table-rack were bottles containing a charming assortment of deadly chemicals.

"Cut your throat or drink your poison," commanded Mason. "Do I care which? I've had my fun." Then the final fearful suggestion of his own invisible presence, and, as he had hoped, the end.

But the Rev. Dr. Theodore Crowell was not Fern. The kindly old man wore coat-of-mail not to be dented by any weapon in a monomaniac's armory. He spoke gently to the restless, cruel genius of the labyrinth, and dropped quietly asleep.

We had no doubt that, did we care to explore further, we would find other rooms than the banquet-hall, but any curiosity we had started with had perished some time ago. Our whole desire now was centered on escape.

"Wither away?" I inquired, stowing the remaining sardine-tins in various pockets. "If we play *Alice Through the Looking-Glass* as you did, Ronny, we'll only be lost all over again."

Just then our energetic cavalier came tramping back.

"The door to the banquet-hall," he announced, "had jammed. I've wrenched it open."

This was good news, so far as it went. Following the red, semicircular passage, we returned to mold and mildew. It appeared that Ronny, driven by an anxiety which she insisted was for me, had leaped up the instant Tolliver disappeared in the wardrobe. Seeking another exit, she found this one, it closed behind her, and, the wood being sadly warped, stuck fast.

She said that she rapped, pounded and called Rex's name, but he was too noisily engaged in flattening silver urns on the car panel to hear her.

It was obvious to us all that the only quick, safe way to regain the pavilion was by the car.

Tolliver and Charles set themselves to seek out the mystery of its working, but my assistance was declared unneedful. In fact, I found that a reclining position on the dear old divan suited my energies better. Dr. Crowell went to encourage the toilers. Ronny sat down by me. I was touched by her loyal attachment.

"Ronny," I said, "don't you think you've punished him enough?"

"Don't be horrid again," she retorted placidly.

"I'm not horrid. I'm tired. We're all tired. I think your Clinton Governor is tireder than anybody else. You are ruining one perfectly good man, and the worst of it is, you love him."

Her gray eyes softened, became almost transparently brilliant, but she shook her head.

"Not any more now. He killed my love twice over, and it can't ever live again. He lied to me—deceived me in the most cruel and treacherous manner. I can't forgive him! Oh, Hildreth, I want to forgive him! I do—I do! If he had let me go of his own free will, I—I might have felt—differently. But he wouldn't—and now it's too late. I said I hated him, but that's not true. I'm so—so sorry for him that—that it hurts me—here!"

Her slim little hand—with the fingers that from babyhood wouldn't bend back the fraction of an inch—covered her heart.

Charles's words came back to me: "You won't understand, but I *couldn't* let her go. Not till the very end was reached." It seemed to me that there was a certain unfortunate similarity between their natures.

"And yet," I observed, "you haven't appeared even annoyed with Dr. Crowell. He kept silent when a few words would have brought you help."

"Dr. Crowell did exactly as I asked him," she retorted surprisingly.

"What!"

"He telephoned me as soon as Clinton left him, Tuesday morning. I told him on no account to betray Clinton to any one."

"But, Ronny—say, if you could use the phone that way—by George, you're the most remarkable *prisoner* I ever set eyes on!"

"You don't understand. Clinton took advantage of me in—in every possible manner. He said the only way I could go was to ruin him by telling the police. That's just one more of the things I can't forgive."

"Well, as I remarked once before, Clinton is a jewel. He has a knowledge and an ignorance of you which are simply stupendous—both ways—and why were you so overjoyed to see me? If you had phoned, or sent me an 'at home' card, I'd have run out any time."

"I wish you wouldn't be sarcastic, Hildreth. You don't act like yourself."

"Part of me got lost somewhere in the labyrinth, maybe. I'm doing the best I can with what's left. Why did you accept a rescue by force with joyous relief when you could have had all the cops in Marshall City out here any time in the last week?"

"If you and Rex had been policemen," she said stiffly, "I should have sent you away without allowing you to interfere with Clinton. But I knew you would both do as I wished and keep silent."

"I see. Dr. Crowell, and Hildreth, and Rex, and I haven't a doubt, old Li Ching, the butler, would all do as you wished—everybody in the world, in fact, except dear Clinton. Isn't that the idea?"

"I shall leave you alone. Perhaps when you are rested, Hildreth, you may be in a better temper."

She left me with the dignity of deep offense. I knew she would probably never forgive me either, but somehow I didn't care. I was too tired.

I went to sleep for a while, and when I woke up Charles was standing over me, shaking my shoulder.

"The car is working again," he announced. "By bracing open the door, when it's at the other end, we can go back and forth as we like. Tolliver is trying his hand on the pavilion trap-door, and the others are with him. I came back after you."

"That was kind," I admitted.

"Veronica wished you to sleep as long as possible."

To his great amazement I rose and shook hands.

"Comrades in disgrace," I explained. "She's angry with me now."

"Is that possible?" In his eyes the final calamity had befallen me. "I hope you haven't quarreled with her on my account?"

"No; entirely on my own. What's that under your arm, Governor?"

"Madeira. I brought a bottle in case you needed some restorative."

"You have my vote from this moment. Shall we split the bottle?"

"Thank you, I rarely touch wine."

"Just one small glass," I implored. "For your soul's sake—a toast to Veronica?"

That corrupted him. I knew the mention of her name would.

And so we stood there in the decayed midst of Dan Mason's futile revenge, and drank a health to the fairest, most lovable woman I ever knew; and the most unforgiving.

Chapter XXVI.
RESCUED AGAIN.

Once more the scene changes, and we find ourselves in the well-known padded cell. It was as good a place to rest as any other, and a lot better than some. We could sit or recline comfortably on a cushion of forest green, imbibe, if we wished, two sorts of excellent wine, and otherwise sustain life on sardines, anchovies, and pâté de foies gras—while they lasted.

Beside these advantages, however, it was hard to see wherein the pavilion subcellar improved on any other spot in our new home.

Mason's letter stated that nothing short of dynamite would open that trap-door from beneath. Mason seemed to be right. It added that shrieks, howls, and lamentations might rise thence in vain. Right again.

Unless the State's anxious voters should be inspired to come out with shovels and dig for their Governor, I began to fear that he would never hold office again.

The workmen who made the place? Italians—no speeka da Eenglish—scattered about the country, or back in their native land. Bartoli? Across the water, and engaged with troubles of his own. Anybody else who held the secret of that pedestal? The silence becomes ghastly—very ghastly.

We relieved it by an occasional outburst of hammering on the ceiling. Rex returned to the banquet-room via car, and brought the two battered rose-urns. With their assistance we proved the ceiling to be sheeted with hard steel. Its decorative and highly colored embossment wouldn't even dent. The noise we made was our sole reward—and why had Mason been so positive that no sound could pierce that floor? Anyway, there was about a chance in a thousand that some one would be there to hear it.

Between intervals of pounding we sat around and admired Veronica's courage. Poor little girl! I was sorry now that I had called her unforgiving.

When Charles and I stepped out of the car we found her waiting there, all ready to forgive—me. I tried to pass it along, but the effort was wasted.

It occurred to me then that after all she had gone through a pretty bad time. If her love for Charles were really dead, it was unjust to be provoked with her. He was a man. He had made the bed he lay in. If Veronica starved to death in this desolate tomb, primarily the fault was his.

I became "my own nice self" again, and tried to forget that there was tragedy among us more intense than starving to death.

"My friends," said Dr. Crowell, "let us bravely face the fact that before us there lies a terrible ordeal—"

And just at that opportune moment the trap opened.

Now it stands to reason that when this blissful event occurred there was only one person on his feet in the middle of the floor. That person went to sleep with unusual suddenness. Ordinarily I like to go to sleep, but not when I'm hit on the head by a half-ton of swiftly pivoting marble. The awakening is too painful.

To explain the opening of that trap, I shall have to retire some seventy hours through time, and introduce a certain humble gardener man. His name is unknown to me but I can say for sure that it was something with a Li, or a Ching, or a Fu in it. He practised his profession upon the estate of a Governor-Mandarin-millionaire, and in due course of practise, he one day reached the center of a certain maze.

Observing that a few desecrating leaves had drifted within the door of the temple which stood there, our faithful unknown fastened up his hose and proceeded to clean up.

That temple was really in a shocking state. His neat Celestial mind recoiled from the dingy appearance of its sacred interior. A scrubbing-brush and pail supplemented the hose. In the temple's midst there rose a monument, doubtless erected to the Governor-Mandarin's grandparents. Certainly its upper surface bore a prayer, facing heavenward to the gods.

The prayer, too, was dingy! Shades of the Great Emperors, this must not be!

The scrubbing-brush flew. Not enough power to it. Up on the edge the disciple of cleanliness springs and kneels. Now! With all the power of wrist and elbow—in the name of the sacred dragon, what is this?

We know what it was—I've told about that carving trick often enough—but in the unknown Wu-Li-Ching-Wung's case, it didn't work quite the same. Being perched on the pedestal itself, he couldn't fall through.

The yawning depths closed once more with a hungry snap. Gingerly descending, the unknown fled. Then he bethought him of certain temples in the Flowery Kingdom, where yawning floors disclosed heaps of jewels, dangerous things to meddle with because of jealous priests. Here were no priests.

He sought his dear old friend, Wung Li, steward of household supplies. Wung Li thought well of the news. Together they returned. Reascending the pedestal, friend unknown demonstrated. By keeping his hand on the sacred word, the trap remained open.

Wung Li, courageous adventurer, took to himself a ladder and descended, and here I have to give a Chinaman credit for more good sense than could be found among five intelligent Americans. Perceiving at once that about him lay a duplicate of the hedge maze, or worse, and with a full belief that uncharted labyrinths are better let alone, Wung Li investigated no further. If jewels there were, they might very probably be guarded by the dragons of the under-earth. Let them stay there for him.

Yet, as Confucius doubtless said, an economical mind misses no slightest advantage. Here was a wonderful hiding-place, and if it hid nothing, why that was a defect to be remedied. Wung Li was fond of that which sparkleth in the glass, but Li Ching, only less in dignity than the Governor-Mandarin himself, had slight sympathy with his desires.

What a place was here for secret revels, and the concealment of nefarious spoils!

Within twelve hours the labyrinth held a cache of delicacies meant to assuage the cravings of two thirsty Chinamen. Sardines, anchovies and foies gras were thrown in, I suppose for good measure. The Chinese appetite is exotic anyway.

Then came the terrible night when, with shrieks of terror, the Governor-Mandarin's lady was born off by ruffians, and the G.-M. himself vanished from the sight of his servants.

Did they, armed and valiant, pursue the ravishing miscreants? They did not. Switching off the ground-lights, that the security of darkness might add itself to their flight, they took to the woods, and it was another twelve hours before the faithful Li Ching got them herded up to the house again.

After all this excitement, Wung Li's spirit stood in need of sustainment. Accompanied by the unknown, he sought their cache in the temple.

Li Ching, watchful and very much worried, wondered what the steward of supplies might want in the hedge maze. He followed. The rest is easy, but I regret that I missed seeing those Chinamen's faces when they looked into that hole!

The trap might well have been allowed to bang shut again, and the guilty ones started on a trip to San Francisco, save for Li Ching's restraining grasp on their collars.

As it was, the ladder of the wrong-doers served to extract the Governor, his bride, *et al.*, from subterranean retirement.

Me they bore sadly thence, convinced that my career had received a very serious check. Once outside the hedge maze, however—for which event I was probably waiting—I demonstrated such signs of life that they laid me down on the grass, where my opening eyes stared full in the face of a lovely stranger. It was none other than old friend Sun, whom we had never hoped to see again in this world.

Chapter XXVII.
THE LABYRINTH'S LAST TURNINGS.

Rolling over, I sat up.

Round about there were gathered an anxious group of those with whom I had expected to share my grave. Charles knelt beside me, the—yes, the inexhaustible flask in one hand, a glass in the other, and wearing his best hospital nurse manner. Only the spoon was absent.

"I've missed something," remarked Hildreth intelligently. "Whence came these rolling lawns and beauteous beds of flowers?"

"A trifle light-headed," commiserated Charles. He cast an apologetic glance at Ronny, as if to say that this single thing was really not his fault.

"Oh, no," Ronny corrected him. "He always talks that way. Hildreth, dear, does your forehead hurt you very much?"

I put up my hand. It encountered a lump that felt as big as Kildaire Mountain.

"My brains hurt worse," I murmured. "Last time I recall looking at you, you were sitting on a green plush floor, staring up at a sky-blue-scarlet ceiling. Now—"

"The trap-door hit you a wallop when it opened," explained Tolliver bluntly. "A couple of the Chink servants had been hiding stolen delicacies down there, the butler caught them at it, and helped us out. That's all."

Though terse, Tolliver's description of our dramatic rescue proved to cover the facts.

"Li Ching," the Governor assured me, "has gone to phone for a doctor."

"Then send some other Li after him quick!" I exclaimed. "No doctor is going to see little Hildreth at Asgard Heights. Can't you understand that it won't do? Why, old Billings has the police out now, looking for me. And Tolliver—his father is probably dragging the river for him. We've got to go home quietly—quietly; and drift in with an affidavit in each hand that we never so much as heard of Asgard Heights. Pardon me, Governor, but as a conspirator, you look the part a great deal better than you act it."

Veronica beamed on me.

"I knew you could be trusted, Hildreth," she kindly approved.

Charles saw the point himself. He hailed a slinking, pig-tailed figure—either Wung Li or the unknown—and sent him streaking off on Li Ching's trail.

I staggered to my feet. The sun was at the zenith, and it occurred to me how very many things must be done before he arrived there again.

"I'll have to come for you to-night, Ronny, after dark. Whether you and dear Cl—the Governor settle your differences or not, no one must suspect the truth of this affair. The most important thing is to restore you to Mrs. Sandry—at midnight, I think. That would be appropriate. Afterward—"

I stopped. The bump on my head must have interfered with cerebration. What were we going to tell Marshall City anyway?

"Never mind, dear," Ronny consoled. "You'll think of something, so I sha'n't worry in the least. But is it really needful for me to stay here till this evening?"

"It is," I rather grimly assured her. "I fear the sun won't oblige us by setting before that, and you certainly can't leave by daylight—where you off to, Tolliver?"

He turned reluctantly. Maybe he thought I wanted him also to remain at Asgard Heights.

"I'm going for my car, of course—unless it's been stolen."

That was so. Though he had lost his sweetheart, he still had his automobile—perhaps.

"And afterward?"

"I say, Wyndham, what do you take me for? Let me know what kind of yarn you fix up—so we won't contradict each other. So-long."

He was off, striding down the hill, a remarkable figure of a moth-eaten cavalier; but a true cavalier, none the less. I reflected that his dust-coat would conceal the apparel from a prying world, and turning back to the others. They seemed to have become involved in argument.

"But, my dear child," Dr. Crowell was protesting, "what you propose would be very wrong. For you to return to the world posing as Miss Wyndham, and make no effort to have this marriage annulled, nor to seek a divorce, would be unjust both to yourself and the Governor."

"It doesn't matter to me," announced the somber one. "I should never wish to marry again in any event."

"Neither shall I. It would be impossible for me, after all that has occurred."

Dr. Crowell eyed that raised, dimpled chin reflectively. What he said next proved him to be gifted with unusual insight.

"Mrs. Charles," and the title was carefully emphasized, "your conscience may allow you to do this, but unfortunately mine does not. I have endured much through the reckless behavior of your husband. That I could put aside cheerfully if it were to any good end. But I can no longer be a party to these clandestine and undesirable proceedings. On my return to the city, I shall at once record your marriage, and if any one inquires of me, I shall feel bound to make known the facts. What effect this will have on Governor Charles's position, he best knows, but my duty as a minister of the gospel lies clear before me."

Ronny gave him one awful look. His generally kindly face was set in the lines of a fanatic, who will sacrifice himself and every man on earth to the Moloch of his conscience.

Charles took an appealing step forward. "I deserve it," he said in a low voice.

There was a flash of white between the minister and myself. It disappeared, involved in the folds of the conspirator's cloak. All we could see was two slim, firm, hands, locked tight round Charles's neck.

The fanatical look had strangely melted away from Dr. Crowell's face. He smiled at me.

"Try not to be more untruthful than necessary. Hildreth," he murmured. "By my recollection, you have an ingenious mind. Handle the reporters yourself. I am going to the house and lie down."

An ingenious mind! If he meant that he remembered me as a good liar, why didn't he come right out and say so?

However, the Rev. Dr. Crowell had departed, and I was alone with the conspirator and his kidnaped bride.

After some considerable period I went and sat down on the side of a wheelbarrow that a gardener had left there. Occasional low murmurs reached my ears. Their import could be surmised, though I had no curiosity. I was too tired.

I wished that the mysterious Li Ching, who had floated through the background of the last sixteen hours of adventure like an invisible Celestial wraith, might materialize in the flesh and offer me some matches. A full cigarette-case and no matches—old Mason would probably have given Bartoli an extra bonus if he'd had brains enough to think up such a tantalizing torture. Now, matches in themselves are a slight luxury—

Just then there emerged from the single statuesque group before me two radiant, unfamiliar beings. The lady angel beamed upon me as if I, too, were a beautiful beautiful stranger. The gentleman seraph strode over and grabbed my hand for no apparent reason.

He shook it up and down violently.

"She's forgiven me, Wyndham! Thank God, she's forgiven everything!"

I observed how nice that was, in words as cordial as I could think up. I tried to feel radiant, too, but somehow I was too utterly played out.

After a little more of this I inquired what they intended to do about the police and the reporters.

"It doesn't matter—we both trust you perfectly for that. I know that Dr. Crowell can be persuaded to keep silent—he can marry us again if he wants to. She's forgiven everything, Wyndham! What *can* anything else matter to me?"

"It matters a whole lot," was my stern retort. "What about my immortal soul that you expect me to imperil in talking to those reporters? Nobody's asked *me* to forgive anything. However, I do it most freely. As I seem to stand *in loco parentis*, pray accept my pardon and blessing."

Ronny looked from me to Charles.

"Don't mind him, dear," she deprecated. "He never means anything he says."

Charles's reply was meant to be *sotto voce*.

"I understand him perfectly, Veronica. Behind his flippant manner he hides a very earnest and serious mind."

First it was ingenious and now it was earnest! The time had come for Hildreth to take his departure.

"When your next wedding comes off I hope you'll invite me. I'll be very quiet and good. Ronny, will you be ready to go this evening?"

"Do I have to leave here just the same—now? Don't look like that! Yes, I can see that it's necessary. But you're not fit to go home yourself, Hildreth. That lump on your head is terrible."

"Come up to the house," Charles invited hospitably. "Take a hot shower, a good breakfast, and sleep the rest of the day. I have to get in town," he added, glancing at his watch.

Then he frowned and shook it. I judged the timepiece had unfortunate memories of that lotus pond.

Now, I didn't like to say that I deeply distrusted his house—that, though unshaven, unshowered and unbreakfasted, I preferred to go off somewhere in the peaceful woods, far, far from the Charles ménage, lay me down on a carpet of leaves, and go to sleep. Also that I meant to do it. Down the slope of the hill a blue-smocked figure was moving. All Chinamen smoke opium. Ergo, all Chinamen carry matches. I kept my eye on the blue figure, and prevaricated glibly:

"My head's fine. Tolliver has gone after his car, and if I don't do the same with mine, some one will find it, and complications will increase. You be ready for me this evening, Ronny."

"Well—if you really feel you ought to go. Be sure and take some rest, won't you, Hildreth? Good-by. You've behaved like a perfect dear about everything."

"Yes, that's my nature. Good-by till to-night."

"Good-by."

I turned away.

"Clinton," came Ronny's sweet contralto from behind me, "last night, just before you came home, I was thinking about these verbena beds. Now verbenas are pretty, but they're not exactly suited to this lawn of ours."

"Why not?" Clinton asked quickly. "On first looking the place over I told the gardener to put verbenas in along this walk. I thought you'd like them."

"Yes, dear, I know; but you see verbenas—"

I hastened my steps. If they were going to quarrel again, Ronny might find some one else to rescue her.

I had caught my Chinaman and realized my best expectations before I once more looked back. They were walking together toward the house. Charles's arm was thrown around her waist, and against the somber conspiratorial shoulder her hair shone like gold.

Evidently one of the two had yielded on the verbena question—and I had a very fair idea of which one it was.

(The end.)

Friend Island

Being the Veracious Tale of an Ancient Mariness,
Heard and Reported in the Year A.D. 2100
It was upon the water-front that I first met her, in one of the
shabby little tea shops frequented by able sailoresses of
the poorer type. The up-town, glittering resorts
of the Lady Aviators' Union were not for
such as she.

Stern of feature, bronzed by wind
and sun, her age could only be
guessed, surmised at once

that in her I beheld a survivor of the age of turbines and oil engines—a true sea-woman of that elder time, when woman's superiority to man had not been so long recognized. When, to emphasize their victory, women in all ranks were sterner than to-day's need demands.

The spruce, smiling young maidens—engine-women and stokers of the great aluminum rollers, but despite their profession, very neat in gold-braided blue knickers and boleros—these looked askance at the hard-faced relic of a harsher day, as they passed in and out of the shop.

I, however, brazenly ignoring similar glances at myself, a mere male intruding on the haunts of the world's ruling sex, drew a chair up beside the veteran. I ordered a full pot of tea, two cups and a plate of macaroons, and put on my most ingratiating air. Possibly my unconcealed admiration and interest were wiles not exercised in vain. Or the macaroons and tea, both excellent, may have loosened the old sea-woman's tongue. At any rate, under cautious questioning, she had soon launched upon a series of reminiscences well beyond my hopes for color and variety.

"When I was a lass," quoth the sea-woman, after a time, "there was none of this high-flying, gilt-edged, leather-stocking luxury about the sea. We sailed by the power of our oil and gasoline. If they failed on us, like as not 'twas the rubber ring and the rolling wave for ours."

She referred to the archaic practise of placing a pneumatic affair called a life-preserver beneath the arms, in case of that dreaded disaster, now so unheard of, shipwreck.

"In them days there was still many a man bold enough to join our crews. And I've knowed cases," she added condescendingly, "where just by the muscle and brawn of such men some poor sailor lass has reached shore alive that would have fed the sharks without 'em. Oh, I ain't so down on men as you might think. It's the spoiling of them that I don't hold with. There's too much preached nowadays that man is fit for nothing but to fetch and carry and do nurse-work in big child-homes. To my mind, a man who hasn't the nerve of a woman ain't fitted to father children, let alone raise 'em. But that's not here nor there. My time's past, and I know it, or I wouldn't be setting here gossipin' to you, my lad, over an empty teapot."

I took the hint, and with our cups replenished, she bit thoughtfully into her fourteenth macaroon and continued.

"There's one voyage I'm not likely to forget, though I live to be as old as Cap'n Mary Barnacle, of the Shouter. 'Twas aboard the old Shouter that this here voyage occurred, and it was her last and likewise Cap'n Mary's. Cap'n Mary, she was then that decrepit, it seemed a mercy that she should go to her rest, and in good salt water at that.

"I remember the voyage for Cap'n Mary's sake, but most I remember it because 'twas then that I come the nighest in my life to committin' matrimony. For a man, the man had nerve; he was nearer bein' companionable than any other man I ever seed; and if it hadn't been for just one little event that showed up the—the *mannishness* of him, in a way I couldn't abide, I reckon he'd be keepin' house for me this minute.

"We cleared from Frisco with a cargo of silkateen petticoats for Brisbane. Cap'n Mary was always strong on petticoats. Leather breeches or even half-skirts would ha' paid far better, they being more in demand like, but Cap'n Mary was three-quarters owner, and says she, land women should buy petticoats, and if they didn't it wouldn't be the Lord's fault nor hers for not providing 'em.

"We cleared on a fine day, which is an ill sign—or was, then when the weather and the seas o' God still counted in the trafficking of the humankind. Not two days out we met a whirling, mucking bouncer of a gale that well nigh threw the old Shouter a full point off her course in the first wallop. She was a stout craft, though. None of your feather-weight, gas-lightened, paper-thin alloy shells, but toughened aluminum from stern to stern. Her turbines drove her through the combers at a forty-five knot clip, which named her a speedy craft for a freighter in them days.

"But this night, as we tore along through the creaming green billows, something unknown went 'way wrong down below.

"I was forward under the shelter of her long over-scoop, looking for a hairpin I'd dropped somewheres about that afternoon. It was a gold hairpin, and gold still being might scarce when I was a girl, a course I valued it. But suddenly I felt the old Shouter give a jump under my feet like a plane struck by a shell in full flight. Then she trembled all over for a full second, frightened like. Then, with the crash of doomsday ringing in my ears, I felt myself sailing through the air right into the teeth o' the shrieking gale, as near as I could judge. Down I came in the hollow of a monstrous big wave, and as my ears doused under I thought I heard a splash close by. Coming up, sure enough, there close by me was floating a new, patent, hermetic, thermo-ice-chest. Being as it was empty, and being as it was shut up air-tight, that ice-chest made as sweet a life-preserver as woman could wish in such an hour. About ten foot by twelve, it floated high in the raging sea. Out on its top I scrambled, and hanging on by a handle I looked expectant for some of my poor fellow-women to come floating by. Which they never did, for the good reason that the Shouter had blowed up and went below, petticoats, Cap'n Mary and all."

"What caused the explosion?" I inquired curiously.

"The Lord and Cap'n Mary Barnacle can explain," she answered piously. "Besides the oil for her turbines, she carried a power of gasoline for her alternative engines, and likely 'twas the cause of her ending so sudden like. Anyways, all I ever seen of her again was the empty ice-chest that Providence had well-nigh hove upon my head. On that I sat and floated, and floated and sat some more, till by and by the storm sort of blowed itself out, the sun come shining—this was next morning—and I could dry my hair and look about me. I was a young lass, ten, and not bad to look upon. I didn't want to die, any more than you that's sitting there this minute. So I up and prays for land. Sure enough toward evening a speck heaves up low down on the horizon. At first I took it for a gas liner, but later found it was just a little island, all alone by itself in the great Pacific Ocean.

"Come, now, here's luck, thinks I, and with that I deserts the ice-chest, which being empty, and me having no ice to put in it, nor likely to have in them latitudes, is of no further use to me. Striking out I swum a mile or so and set foot on dry land for the first time in nigh three days.

"Pretty land it were, too, though bare of human life as an iceberg in the Arctic.

"I had landed on a shining white beach that run up to a grove of lovely, waving palm trees. Above them I could see the slopes of a hill so high and green it reminded me of my own old home, up near Couquomgomoc Lake in Maine. The whole place just seemed to smile and smile at me. The palms waved and bowed in the sweet breeze, like they wanted to say, 'Just set right down and make yourself to home. We've been waiting a long time for you to come.' I cried, I was that happy to be made welcome. I was a young lass then, and sensitive-like to how folks treated me. You're laughing now, but wait and see if or no there was sense to the way I felt.

"So I up and dries my clothes and my long, soft hair again, which was well worth drying, for I had far more of it then than now. After that I walked along a piece, till there was a sweet little path meandering away into the wild woods.

"Here, thinks I, this looks like inhabitants. Be they civil or wild, I wonder? But after traveling the path a piece, lo and behold it ended sudden like in a wide circle of green grass, with a little spring of clear water. And the first thing I noticed was a slab of white board nailed to a palm tree close to the spring. Right off I took a long drink, for you better believe I was thirsty, and then I went to look at this board. It had evidently been tore off the side of a wooden packing box, and the letters was printed in lead-pencil.

"'Heaven help whoever you be,' I read. 'This island ain't just right. I'm going to swim for it. You better too. Good-by. Nelson Smith.' That's what it said, but the spellin' was simply awful. It all looked quite new and recent, as if Nelson Smith hadn't more than a few hours before wrote and nailed it there.

"Well, after reading that queer warning I begun to shake all over like in a chill. Yes, I shook like I had the ague, though the hot tropic sun was burning down right on me and that alarming board. What had scared Nelson Smith so much that he had swum to get away? I looked all around real cautious and careful, but not a single frightening thing could I behold. And the palms and the green grass and the flowers still smiled that peaceful and friendly like. 'Just make yourself to home,' was wrote all over the place in plainer letters than those sprawly lead-pencil ones on the board.

"Pretty soon, what with the quiet and all, the chill left me. Then I thought, 'Well to be sure, this Smith person was just an ordinary man, I reckon, and likely he got nervous of being so alone. Likely he just fancied things which was really not. It's a pity he drowned himself before I come, though likely I'd have found him poor company. By his record I judge him a man but of common education.'

"So I decided to make the most of my welcome, and that I did for weeks to come. Right near the spring was a cave, dry as a biscuit box, with a nice floor of white sand. Nelson had lived there too, for there was a litter of stuff—tin cans—empty—scraps of newspapers and the like. I got to calling him Nelson in my mind, and then Nelly, and wondering if he was dark or fair, and how he come to be cast away there all alone, and what was the strange events that drove him to his end. I cleaned out the cave, though. He had devoured all his tin-canned provisions, however he come by them, but this I didn't mind. That there island was a generous body. Green milk-coconuts, sweet berries, turtle eggs and the like was my daily fare.

"For about three weeks the sun shone every day, the birds sang and the monkeys chattered. We was all one big, happy family, and the more I explored that island the better I liked the company I was keeping. The land was about ten miles from beach to beach, and never a foot of it that wasn't sweet and clean as a private park.

"From the top of the hill I could see the ocean, miles and miles of blue water, with never a sign of a gas liner, or even a little government running-boat. Them running-boats used to go most everywhere to keep the seaways clean of derelicts and the like. But I knowed that if this island was no more than a hundred miles off the regular courses of navigation, it might be many a long day before I'd be rescued. The top of the hill, as I found when first

I climbed up there, was a wore-out crater. So I knowed that the island was one of them volcanic ones you run across so many of in the seas between Capricorn and Cancer.

"Here and there on the slopes and down through the jungly tree-growth, I would come on great lumps of rock, and these must have came up out of that crater long ago. If there was lava it was that old it had been covered up entire with green growing stuff. You couldn't have found it without a spade, which I didn't have nor want.

"Well, at first I was happy as the hours was long. I wandered and clambered and waded and swum, and combed my long hair on the beach, having fortunately not lost my sidecombs nor the rest of my gold hairpins. But by and by it begun to get just a bit lonesome. Funny thing, that's a feeling that, once it starts, it gets worse and worser so quick it's perfectly surprising. And right then was when the days begun to get gloomy. We had a long, sickly hot spell, like I never seen before on an ocean island. There was dull clouds across the sun from morn till night. Even the little monkeys and parakeets, that had seemed so gay, moped and drowsed like they was sick. All one day I cried, and let the rain soak me through and through—that was the first rain we had—and I didn't get thorough dried even during the night, though I slept in my cave. Next morning I got up mad as thunder at myself and all the world.

"When I looked out the black clouds was billowing across the sky. I could hear nothing but great breakers roaring in on the beaches, and the wild wind raving through the lashing palms.

"As I stood there a nasty little wet monkey dropped from a branch almost on my head. I grabbed a pebble and slung it at him real vicious. 'Get away, you dirty little brute!' I shrieks, and with that there come a awful blinding flare of light. There was a long, crackling noise like a bunch of Chinese fireworks, and then a sound as if a whole fleet of Shouters had all went up together.

"When I come to, I found myself 'way in the back of my cave, trying to dig further into the rock with my finger nails. Upon taking thought, it come to me that what had occurred was just a lightning-clap, and going to look, sure enough there lay a big palm tree right across the glade. It was all busted and split open by the lightning, and the little monkey was under it, for I could see his tail and his hind legs sticking out.

"Now, when I set eyes on that poor, crushed little beast I'd been so mean to, I was terrible ashamed. I sat down on the smashed tree and considered and considered. How thankful I had ought to have been. Here I had a lovely, plenteous island, with food and water to my taste, when it might have been a barren, starvation rock that was my lot. And so, thinking, a sort of gradual peaceful feeling stole over me. I got cheerfuller and cheerfuller, till I could have sang and danced for joy.

"Pretty soon I realized that the sun was shining bright for the first time that week. The wind had stopped hollering, and the waves had died to just a singing murmur on the beach. It seemed kind o' strange, this sudden peace, like the cheer in my own heart after its rage and storm. I rose up, feeling sort of queer, and went to look if the little monkey had came alive again, though that was a fool thing, seeing he was laying all crushed up and very dead. I buried him under a tree root, and as I did it a conviction come to me.

"I didn't hardly question that conviction at all. Somehow, living there alone so long, perhaps my natural womanly intuition was stronger than ever before or since, and so I *knowed*. Then I went and pulled poor Nelson Smith's board off from the tree and tossed it away for the tide to carry off. That there board was an insult to my island!"

The sea-woman paused, and her eyes had a far-away look. It seemed as if I and perhaps even the macaroons and tea were quite forgotten.

"Why did you think that?" I asked, to bring her back: "How could an island be insulted?"

She started, passed her hand across her eyes, and hastily poured another cup of tea.

"Because," she said at last, poising a macaroon in mid-air, "because that island—that particular island that I had landed on—had a heart!

"When I was gay, it was bright and cheerful. It was glad when I come, and it treated me right until I got that grouchy it had to mope from sympathy. It loved me like a friend. When I flung a rock at that poor little, drenched monkey critter, it backed up my act with an anger like the wrath o' God, and killed its own child to please me! But it got right cheery the minute I seen the wrongness of my ways. Nelson Smith had no business to say, 'This island ain't just right,' for it was a righter place than ever I seen elsewhere. When I cast away that lying board, all the birds begun to sing like mad. The green milk-coconuts fell right and left. Only the monkeys seemed kind o' sad like still, and no wonder. You see, their own mother, the island, had rounded on one of 'em for my sake!

"After that I was right careful and considerate. I named the island Anita, not knowing her right name, or if she had any. Anita was a pretty name, and it sounded kind of South Sea like. Anita and me got along real well together from that day on. It was some strain to be always gay and singing around like a dear duck of a canary bird, but I done my best. Still, for all the love and gratitude I bore Anita, the company of an island, however sympathetic, ain't quite enough for a human being. I still got lonesome, and there was even days when I couldn't keep the clouds clear out of the sky, though I will say we had no more tornadoes.

"I think the island understood and tried to help me with all the bounty and good cheer the poor thing possessed. None the less my heart give a wonderful big leap when one day I seen a blot on the horizon. It drawed nearer and nearer, until at last I could make out its nature."

"A ship, of course," said I, "and were you rescued?"

"'Tweren't a ship, neither," denied the sea-woman somewhat impatiently. "Can't you let me spin this yarn without no more remarks and fool questions? This thing what was bearing down so fast with the incoming tide was neither more nor less than another island!

"You may well look startled. I was startled myself. Much more so than you, likely. I didn't know then what you, with your book-learning, very likely know now—that islands sometimes float. Their underparts being a tangled-up mess of roots and old vines that new stuff's growed over, they sometimes break away from the mainland in a brisk gale and go off for a voyage, calm as a old-fashioned, eight-funnel steamer. This one was uncommon large, being as much as two miles, maybe, from shore to shore. It had its palm trees and its live things, just like my own Anita, and I've sometimes wondered if this drifting piece hadn't really been a part of my island once—just its daughter like, as you might say.

"Be that, however, as it might be, no sooner did the floating piece get within hailing distance than I hears a human holler and there was a man dancing up and down on the shore like he was plumb crazy. Next minute he had plunged into the narrow strip of water between us and in a few minutes had swum to where I stood.

"Yes, of course it was none other than Nelson Smith!

"I knowed that the minute I set eyes on him. He had the very look of not having no better sense than the man what wrote that board and then nearly committed suicide trying to get away from the best island in all the oceans. Glad enough he was to get back, though, for the coconuts was running very short on the floater what had rescued him, and the turtle eggs wasn't worth mentioning. Being short of grub is the surest way I know to cure a man's fear of the unknown.

"Well, to make a long story short, Nelson Smith told me he was a aeronauter. In them days to be an aeronauter was not the same as to be an aviatress is now. There was dangers in the air, and dangers in the sea, and he had met with booth. His gas tank had leaked and he had dropped into the water close by Anita. A case or two of provisions was all he could save from the total wreck.

"Now, as you might guess, I was crazy enough to find out what had scared this Nelson Smith into trying to swim the Pacific. He told me a story that seemed to fit pretty well with mine, only when it came to the scary part he shut up like a clam, that aggravating way some men have. I give it up at last for just man-foolishness, and we begun to scheme to get away.

"Anita moped some while we talked it over. I realized how she must be feeling so I explained to her that it was right needful for us to get with our kind again. If we stayed with her we should probably quarrel like cats, and maybe even kill each other out of pure human cussedness. She cheered up considerable after that, and even, I thought, got a little anxious to have us leave. At any rate, when we begun to provision up the little floater, which we had anchored to the big island by a cable of twisted bark, the green nuts fell all over the ground, and Nelson found more turtle nests in a day than I had in weeks.

"During them days I really got quite fond of Nelson Smith. He was a companionable body, and brave, or he wouldn't have been a professional aeronauter, a job that was rightly thought tough enough for a woman, let alone a man. Though he was not so well educated as me, at least he was quiet and modest about what he did know, not like some men, boasting most where there is least to brag of.

"Indeed, I misdoubt if Nelson and me would not have quit the sea and the air together and set up housekeeping in some quiet little town up in New England, maybe, after we had got away, if it had not been for what happened when we went. I never, let me say, was so deceived in any man before nor since. The thing taught me a lesson and I never got fooled again. This was the way of it.

"We was all ready to go, and then one morning, like a parting gift from Anita, come a soft and favoring wind. Nelson and I run down the beach together, for we didn't want our floater to blow off and leave us. As we was running, our arms full of coconuts, Nelson Smith stubbed his bare toe on a sharp rock, and down he went. I hadn't noticed, and was going on.

"But sudden the ground begun to shake under my feet, and the air was full of a queer, grinding, groaning sound, like the very earth was in pain.

"I turned round sharp. There sat Nelson, holding his bleeding toe in both fists and giving vent to such awful words as no decent sea-going lady would ever speak nor hear to!

" 'Stop it, stop it!' I shrieked at him, but 'twas too late.

"Island or no island, Anita was a lady, too! She had a gentle heart, but she knowed how to behave when she was insulted.

"With one terrible, great roar a spout of smoke and flame belched up out o' the heart of Anita's crater hill a full mile into the air!

"I guess Nelson stopped swearing. He couldn't have heard himself, anyways. Anita was talking now with tongues of flame and such roars as would have bespoke the raging protest of a continent.

"I grabbed that fool man by the hand and run him down to the water. We had to swim good and hard to catch up with our only hope, the floater. No bark rope could hold her against the stiff breeze that was now blowing, and she had broke her cable. By the time we scrambled aboard great rocks was falling right and left. We couldn't see each other for a while for the clouds of fine gray ash that filled the air and covered the sea.

"It seemed like Anita was that mad she was flinging stones after us, and truly I believe that such was her intention. I didn't blame her, neither!

"Lucky for us the wind was strong and we was soon out of range. After that it wasn't long before my poor, outraged Anita was just a streak o' smoke on the horizon.

" 'So!' says I to Nelson, after I'd got most of the ashes out of my mouth, and shook my hair clear of cinders. 'So, that was the reason you up and left sudden when you was there before! You aggravated that island till the poor thing druv you out!'

" 'Well,' says he, and not so meek as I'd have admired to see him, 'how could I know the darn island was a lady?'

" 'Actions speak louder than words,' says I. 'You should have knowed it by her ladylike behavior!'

" 'Is volcanoes and slingin' hot rocks ladylike?' says he. 'Is snakes ladylike? T'other time I cut my thumb on a tin can, I cussed a little bit. Say—just a lil'l' bit! An' what comes at me out o' all the caves, and out o' every crack in the rocks, and out o' the very spring o' water where I'd been drinkin'? Why snakes! *Snakes*, if you please, big, little, green, red and sky-blue-scarlet! What 'd I do? Jumped in the water, of course. Why wouldn't I? I'd ruther swim an' drown than be stung or swallered to death. But how was I t' know the snakes come outta the rocks because I cussed?'

" '*You* couldn't,' I agrees, sarcastic. 'Some folks never knows a lady till she up and whangs 'em over the head with a brick. A real, gentle, kind-like warning, them snakes were, which you would not heed! Take shame to yourself, Nelly,' says I, right stern, 'that a decent, little island like Anita can't associate with you peaceable, but you must hurt her sacredest feelings with language no lady would stand by to hear!'

"He give up his high manners then, for he knowed them words was true.

"I never did see Anita again. She may have blew herself right out of the ocean in her just wrath at the vulgar, disgustin' language of Nelson Smith. I don't know. We was took off the floater at last, and I lost track of Nelson just as quick as I could when we was landed at Frisco.

"He had taught me a lesson. A man is just full of mannishness, and the best of 'em ain't good enough for a lady to sacrifice her sensibilities to put up with.

"Nelson Smith, he seemed to feel real bad when he learned I was not for him, and then he apologized. But apologies weren't no use to me. I never could abide him, after the way he went and talked right in the presence of me and my poor, sweet lady friend, Anita!"

Now I am well versed in the lore of the sea in all ages. Through mists of time I have enviously eyed wild voyagings of sea rovers who roved and spun their yarns before the stronger sex came into its own, and ousted man from his heroic pedestal. I have followed—across the printed page— the wanderings of Odysseus. Before Gulliver I have burned the incense of tranced attention; and with reverent awe considered the history of one Munchausen, a baron.

But alas, these were only men!

In what field is not woman our subtle superior?

Meekly I bowed my head, and when my eyes dared lift again, the ancient mariness had departed, leaving me to sorrow for my surpassed and outdone idols. Also with a bill for macaroons and tea of such incredible proportions that in comparison therewith I found it easy to believe her story!

Behind the Curtain

It was after nine o'clock when the bell rang, and descending to the dimly lighted hall I opened the front door, at first on the chain to be sure of my visitor. Seeing, as I had hoped, the face of our friend, Ralph Quentin, I took off the chain and he entered with a blast of sharp November air for company. I had to throw my weight upon the door to close it against the wind.

As he removed his hat and cloak he laughed good-humoredly. "You're very cautious, Santallos. I thought you were about to demand a password before admitting me."

"It is well to be cautious," I retorted. "This house stands somewhat alone, and thieves are everywhere."

"It would require a thief of considerable muscle to make off with some of your treasures. That stone tomb-thing, for instance; what do you call it?"

"The Beni Hassan sarcophagus. Yes. But what of the gilded inner case,

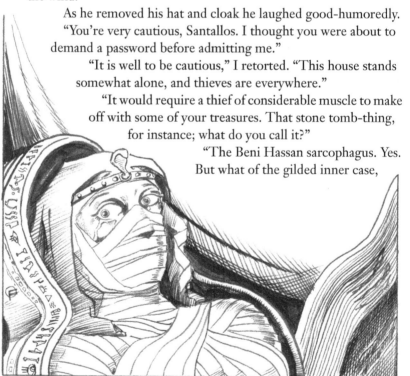

and what of the woman it contains? A thief of judgment and intelligence might covet the treasure and strive to deprive me of it. Don't you agree?"

He only laughed again, and counterfeited a shudder.

"The woman! Don't remind me that such a brown, shriveled, mummy-horror was ever a woman!"

"But she was. Doubtless in her day my poor Princess of Naam was soft, appealing; a creature of red, moist lips and eyes like stars in the black Egyptian sky. 'The Songstress of the House' she was called, ere she became Ta-Nezem the Osirian. But I keep you standing here in the cold hall. Come up-stairs with me. Did I tell you that Beatrice is not here to-night?"

"No?" His intonation expressed surprise and frank disappointment. "Then I can't say good-by to her? Didn't you receive my note? I'm to take Sanderson's place as manager of the sales department in Chicago, and I'm off to-morrow morning."

"Congratulations. Yes, we had your note, but Beatrice was given an opportunity to join some friends on a Southern trip. The notice was short, but of late she has not been so well and I urged her to go. This November air is cruelly damp and bitter."

"What was it—a yachting cruise?"

"A long cruise. She left this afternoon. I have been sitting in her boudoir, Quentin, thinking of her, and I'll tell you about it there—if you don't mind?"

"Wherever you like," he conceded, though in a tone of some surprise. I suppose he had not credited me with so much sentiment, or thought it odd that I should wish to share it with another, even so good a friend as he. "You must find it fearfully lonesome here without Bee," he continued.

"A trifle." We were ascending the dark stairs now. "After to-night, however, things will be quite different. Do you know that I have sold the house?"

"No! Why, you are full of astonishments, old chap. Found a better place with more space for your tear-jars and tombstones?"

He meant, I assumed, a witty reference to my collection of Coptic and Egyptian treasures, well and dearly bought, but so much trash to a man of Quentin's youth and temperament.

I opened the door of my wife's boudoir, and it was pleasant to pass into such rosy light and warmth out of the stern, dark cold of the hall. Yet it was an old house, full of unexpected drafts. Even here there was a draft so strong that a heavy velours curtain at the far side of the room continually rippled and billowed out, like a loose, rose-colored sail. Never far enough, though, to show what was behind it.

My friend settled himself on the frail little chair that stood before my wife's dressing-table. It was the kind of chair that women love and most men loathe, but Quentin, for all his weight and stature, had a touch of the feminine about him, or perhaps of the feline. Like a cat, he moved delicately. He was blond and tall, with fine, regular features, a ready laugh, and the clean charm of youth about him—also its occasional blundering candor.

As I looked at him sitting there, graceful, at ease, I wished that his mind might have shared the litheness of his body. He could have understood me so much better.

"I have indeed found a place for my collections," I observed, seating myself near by. "In fact, with a single exception—the Ta-Nezem sarcophagus—the entire lot is going to the dealers." Seeing his expression of astonished disbelief I continued: "The truth is my dear Quentin, that I have been guilty of gross injustice to our Beatrice. I have been too good a collector and too neglectful a husband. My 'tear-jars and tombstones,' in fact, have enjoyed an attention that might better have been elsewhere bestowed. Yes, Beatrice has left me alone, but the instant that some few last affairs are settled I intend rejoining her. And you yourself are leaving. At least, none of us three will be left to miss the others' friendship."

"You are quite surprising to-night, Santallos. But, by Jove, I'm not sorry to hear any of it! It was my place to criticise, and Bee's not the sort to complain. But living here in this lonely old barn of a house, doing all her own work, practically deserted by her friends, must have been—"

"Hard, very hard," I interrupted him softly, "for one so young and lovely as our Beatrice. But if I have been blind, at least the awakening has come. You should have seen her face when she heard the news. It was wonderful. We were standing, just she and I, in the midst of my tear-jars and tombstones— my 'chamber of horrors' she named it. You are so apt at amusing phrases, both of you. We stood beside the great stone sarcophagus from the Necropolis of Beni Hassan. Across the trestles beneath it lay the gilded inner case wherein Ta-Nezem the Osirian had slept out so many centuries. You know its appearance—a thing of beautiful, gleaming lines, like the quaint, smiling image of a golden woman.

"Then I lifted the lid and showed Beatrice that the one-time songstress, the hand-maiden of Amen, slept there no more, and the case was empty. You know, too, that Beatrice never liked my princess. For a jest she used to declare that she was jealous—jealous of a woman dead and ugly so many thousand years! Or—but that was only in anger—that I had bought Ta-Nezem with what would have given her, Beatrice, all the pleasure she lacked in life. Oh, she was not too patient to reproach me, Quentin, but only in anger and hot blood.

"So I showed her the empty case, and I said, 'Beloved wife, never again need you be jealous of Ta-Nezem. All that is in this room save her and her belongings I have sold, but her I could not bear to sell. That which I love, no man else shall share or own. So I have destroyed her. I have rent her body to brown, aromatic shreds. I have burned her; it is as if she had never been. And now, dearest of the dear, you shall take for your own all the care, all the keeping that heretofore I have lavished upon the Princess of Naam.'

"Beatrice turned from the empty case as if she could scarcely believe her hearing, but when she saw by the look in my eyes that I meant exactly what I said, neither more nor less, you should have seen her face, my dear Quentin—you should have seen her face!"

"I can imagine." He laughed, rather shortly. For some reason my guest seemed increasingly ill at ease, and glanced continually about the little rose-and-white room that was the one luxurious, thoroughly feminine corner—that and the cold, dark room behind the curtain—in what he had justly called my "barn of a house."

"Santallos," he continued abruptly, and I thought rather rudely, "you should have a portrait done as you look to-night. You might have posed for one of those stern old hidalgoes of—which painter was it who did so many Spanish dons and donesses?"

"You perhaps mean Velasquez," I answered with mild courtesy, though secretly and as always his crude personalities displeased me. "My father, you may recall, was of Cordova in southern Spain. But—must you go so soon? First drink one glass with me to our missing Beatrice. See how I was warming my blood against the wind that blows in, even here. The wine is Amontillado, some that was sent me by a friend of my father's from the very vineyards where the grapes were grown and pressed. And for many years it has ripened since it came here. Before she went, Beatrice drank of it from one of these same glasses. True wine of Montilla! See how it lives—like fire in amber, with a glimmer of blood behind it."

I held high the decanter and the light gleamed through it upon his face.

"Amontillado! Isn't that a kind of sherry? I'm no connoisseur of wines, as you know. But—Amontillado."

For a moment he studied the wine I had given him, liquid flame in the crystal glass. Then his face cleared.

"I remember the association now. 'The Cask of Amontillado.' Ever read the story?"

"I seem to recall it dimly."

"Horrible, fascinating sort of a yarn. A fellow takes his trustful friend down into the cellars to sample some wine, traps him and walls him up in a niche—buries him alive, you understand. Read it when I was a youngster, and it made a deep impression, partly, I think, because I couldn't for the life of me comprehend a nature—even an Italian nature—desiring so horrible a form of vengeance. You're half Latin yourself, Santallos. Can you elucidate?"

"I doubt if you would ever understand," I responded slowly, wondering how even Quentin could be so crude, so tactless. "Such a revenge might have its merits, since the offender would be a long time dying. But merely to kill seems to me so pitifully inadequate. Now I, if I were driven to revenge, should never be contented by killing. I should wish to follow."

"What—beyond the grave?"

I laughed. "Why not? Wouldn't that be the very apotheosis of hatred? I'm trying to interpret the Latin nature, as you asked me to do."

"Confound you, for an instant I thought you were serious. The way you said it made me actually shiver!"

"Yes," I observed, "or perhaps it was the draft. See, Quentin, how that curtain billows out."

His eyes followed my glance. Continually the heavy, rose-colored curtain that was hung before the door of my wife's bedroom bulged outward, shook and quivered like a bellying sail, as draperies will with a wind behind them.

His eyes strayed from the curtain, met mine and fell again to the wine in his glass. Suddenly he drained it, not as would a man who was a judge of wines, but hastily, indifferently, without thought for its flavor or bouquet. I raised my glass in the toast he had forgotten.

"To our Beatrice," I said, and drained mine also, though with more appreciation.

"To Beatrice—of course." He looked at the bottom of his empty glass, then before I could offer to refill it, rose from his chair.

"I must go, old man. When you write to Bee, tell her I'm sorry to have missed her."

"Before she could receive a letter from me I shall be with her—I hope. How cold the house is to-night, and the wind breathes everywhere. See how the curtain blows, Quentin."

"So it does." He set his glass on the tray beside the decanter. Upon first entering the room he had been smiling, but now his straight, fine brows were drawn in a perpetual, troubled frown, his eyes looked here and there, and would never meet mine—which were steady. "There's a wind," he added, "that blows along this wall—curious. One can't notice any draft there, either. But it must blow there, and of course the curtain billows out."

"Yes," I said. "Of course it billows out."

"Or is there another door behind that curtain?"

His careful ignorance of what any fool might infer from mere appearance brought an involuntary smile to my lips. Nevertheless, I answered him.

"Yes, of course there is a door—an open door."

His frown deepened. My true and simple replies appeared to cause him a certain irritation.

"As I feel now," I added, "even to cross the room would be an effort. I am tired and weak to-night. As Beatrice once said, my strength beside yours is as a child's to that of a grown man. Won't you close that door for me, dear friend?"

"Why—yes, I will. I didn't know you were ill. If that's the case, you shouldn't be alone in this empty house. Shall I stay with you for a while?"

As he spoke he walked across the room. His hand was on the curtain, but before it could be drawn aside my voice checked him.

"Quentin," I said, "are even you quite strong enough to close that door?"

Looking back at me, chin on shoulder, his face appeared scarcely familiar, so drawn was it in lines of bewilderment and half-suspicion.

"What do you mean? You are very—odd to-night. Is the door so heavy then? What door is it?"

I made no reply.

As if against their owner's will his eyes fled from mine, he turned and hastily pushed aside the heavy drapery.

Behind it my wife's bedroom lay dark and cold, with windows open to the invading winds.

And erect in the doorway, uncovered, stood an ancient gilded coffin-case. It was the golden casket of Ta-Nezem, but its occupant was more beautiful than the poor, shriveled Songstress of Naam.

Bound across her bosom were the strange, quaint jewels which had been found in the sarcophagus. Ta-Nezem's amulets—heads of Hathor and of Horus, the sacred eye, the uræus, even the heavy dull-green scarab, the amulet for purity of heart—there they rested upon the bosom of her who had been mistress of my house, now Beatrice the Osirian, Beneath them her white, stiff body was enwrapped in the same crackling dry, brown linen bands, impregnated with the gums and resins of embalmers dead these many thousand years, which had been about the body of Ta-Nezem.

Above the white translucence of her brow appeared the winged disk, emblem of Ra. The twining golden bodies of its supporting uræii, its cobras of Egypt, were lost in the dusk of her hair, whose soft fineness yet lived and would live so much longer than the flesh of any of us three.

Yes, I had kept my word and given to Beatrice all that had been Ta-

Nezem's, even to the sarcophagus itself, for in my will it was written that she be placed in it for final burial.

Like the fool he was, Quentin stood there, staring at the unclosed, frozen eyes of my Beatrice—and his. Stood till that which had been in the wine began to make itself felt. He faced me then, but with so absurd and childish a look of surprise that, despite the courtesy due a guest, I laughed and laughed.

I, too, felt warning throes, but to me the pain was no more than a gage—a measure of his suffering—a stimulus to point the phrases in which I told him all I knew and had guessed of him and Beatrice, and thus drove home the jest.

But I had never thought that a man of Quentin's youth and strength could die so easily. Beatrice, frail though she was, had taken longer to die.

He could not even cross the room to stop my laughter, but at the first step stumbled, fell, and in a very little while lay still at the foot of the gilded case.

After all, he was not so strong as I. Beatrice had seen. Her still, cold eyes saw all—how he lay there, his fine, lithe body contorted, worthless for any use till its substance should have been cast again in the melting-pot of dissolution, while I who had drunk of the same draft, suffered the same pangs, yet stood and found breath for mockery.

So I poured myself another glass of that good Cordovan wine, and I raised it to both of them and drained it, laughing.

"Quentin," I cried, "you asked *what door*, though you thought you had passed that way before, and feared that I guessed your knowledge. But there are doors and doors, dear, charming friend, and one that is heavier than any other. Close it if you can—close it now in my face, who otherwise will follow even whither you have gone—the heavy, heavy door of the Osiris, Keeper of the House of Death!"

Thus I dreamed of doing and speaking.

It was so vivid, the dream, that awakening in the darkness of my room I could scarcely believe it had been other than reality. True, I lived, while in my dream I had shared the avenging poison. Yet my veins were still hot with the keen passion of triumph, and my eyes filled with the vision of Beatrice, dead—*dead in Ta-Nezem's casket.*

Unreasonably frightened, I sprang from bed, flung on a dressing-gown, and hurried out. Down the hallway I sped, swiftly and silently, at the end of it unlocked heavy doors with a tremulous hand, switched on lights, lights and more lights, till the great room of my collection was ablaze with them, and as my treasures sprang into view I sighed, like a man reaching home from a perilous journey.

The dream was a lie.

There, fronting me, stood the heavy empty sarcophagus; there on the trestles before it lay the gilded case, a thing of beautiful, gleaming lines, like the smiling image of a golden woman.

I stole across the room and softly, very softly, lifted the upper half of the beautiful lid, peering within. The dream indeed was a lie.

Happy as a comforted child I went to my room again. Across the hall the door of my wife's boudoir stood partly open. In the room beyond a faint light was burning, and I could see the rose-colored curtain sway slightly to a draft from some open window.

Yesterday she had come to me and asked for her freedom. I had refused, knowing to whom she would turn, and hating him for his youth and his crudeness and his secret scorn of me.

But had I done well? They were children, those two, and despite my dream I was certain that their foolish, youthful ideals had kept them from actual sin against my honor. But what if, time passing, they might change? Or, Quentin gone, my lovely Beatrice might favor another, young as he and not so scrupulous?

Every one, they say, has a streak of incipient madness. I recalled the frenzied act to which my dream jealousy had driven me. Perhaps it was a warning, the dream. What if my father's jealous blood should some day betray me, drive me to the insane destruction of her I held most dear and sacred?

I shuddered, then smiled at the swaying curtain. Beatrice was too beautiful for safety. She should have her freedom.

Let her mate with Ralph Quentin or whom she would, Tà-Nezem must rest secure in her gilded house of death. My brown, perfect, shriveled Princess of the Nile! Destroyed—rent to brown, aromatic shreds—burned—destroyed—and her beautiful coffin-case desecrated as I had seen it in my vision!

Again I shuddered, smiled and shook my head at the swaying, rosy curtain.

"You are too lovely, Beatrice," I said, "and my father was a Spaniard. You shall have your freedom!"

I entered my room and lay down to sleep again, at peace and content.

The dream, thank God, was a lie.

Unseen—Unfeared

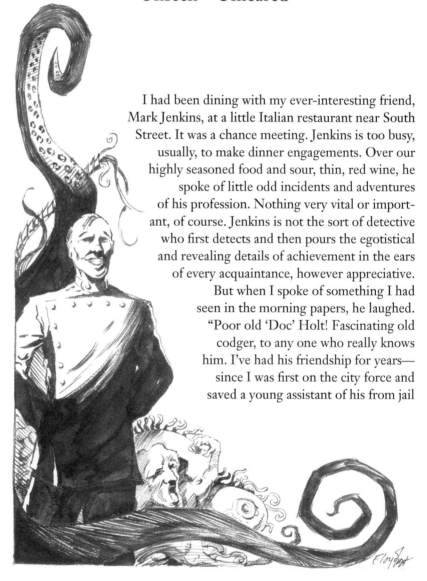

I had been dining with my ever-interesting friend, Mark Jenkins, at a little Italian restaurant near South Street. It was a chance meeting. Jenkins is too busy, usually, to make dinner engagements. Over our highly seasoned food and sour, thin, red wine, he spoke of little odd incidents and adventures of his profession. Nothing very vital or important, of course. Jenkins is not the sort of detective who first detects and then pours the egotistical and revealing details of achievement in the ears of every acquaintance, however appreciative. But when I spoke of something I had seen in the morning papers, he laughed. "Poor old 'Doc' Holt! Fascinating old codger, to any one who really knows him. I've had his friendship for years— since I was first on the city force and saved a young assistant of his from jail on a false charge. And they had to drag him into the poisoning of this young sport, Ralph Peeler!"

"Why are you so sure he couldn't have been implicated?" I asked.

But Jenkins only shook his head, with a quiet smile. "I have reasons for believing otherwise," was all I could get out of him on that score. "But," he added, "the only reason he was suspected at all is the superstitious dread of these ignorant people around him. Can't see why he lives in such a place. I know for a fact he doesn't have to. Doc's got money of his own. He's an amateur chemist and dabbler in different sorts of research work, and I suspect he's been guilty of 'showing off.' Result, they all swear he has the evil eye and holds forbidden communion with invisible powers. Smoke?"

Jenkins offered me one of his invariably good cigars, which I accepted, saying thoughtfully: "A man has no right to trifle with the superstitions of ignorant people. Sooner or later, it spells trouble."

"Did in his case. They swore up and down that he sold love charms openly and poisons secretly, and that, together with his living so near to—somebody else—got him temporarily suspected. But my tongue's running away with me, as usual!"

"As usual," I retorted impatiently, "you open up with all the frankness of a Chinese diplomat."

He beamed upon me engagingly and rose from the table, with a glance at his watch. "Sorry to leave you, Blaisdell, but I have to meet Jimmy Brennan in ten minutes."

He so clearly did not invite my further company that I remained seated for a little while after his departure; then took my own way homeward. Those streets always held for me a certain fascination, particularly at night. They are so unlike the rest of the city, so foreign in appearance, with their little shabby stores, always open until late evening, their unbelievably cheap goods, displayed as much outside the shops as in them, hung on the fronts and laid out on tables by the curb and in the street itself. To-night, however, neither people nor stores in any sense appealed to me. The mixture of Italians, Jews and a few negroes, mostly bareheaded, unkempt and generally unhygienic in appearance, struck me as merely revolting. They were all humans, and I, too, was human. Some way I did not like the idea.

Puzzled a trifle, for I am more inclined to sympathize with poverty than accuse it, I watched the faces that I passed. Never before had I observed how stupid, how bestial, how brutal were the countenances of the dwellers in this region. I actually shuddered when an old-clothes man, a gray-bearded Hebrew, brushed me as he toiled past with his barrow.

There was a sense of evil in the air, a warning of things which it is wise for a clean man to shun and keep clear of. The impression became so strong that before I had walked two squares I began to feel physically ill. Then it occurred to me that the one glass of cheap Chianti I had drunk might have something to do with the feeling. Who knew how that stuff had been manufactured, or whether the juice of the grape entered at all into its ill-flavored composition? Yet I doubted if that were the real cause of my discomfort.

By nature I am rather a sensitive, impressionable sort of chap. In some way to-night this neighborhood, with its sordid sights and smells, had struck me wrong.

My sense of impending evil was merging into actual fear. This would never do. There is only one way to deal with an imaginative temperament like mine—conquer its vagaries. If I left South Street with this nameless dread upon me, I could never pass down it again without a recurrence of the feeling. I should simply have to stay here until I got the better of it—that was all.

I paused on a corner before a shabby but brightly lighted little drug store. Its gleaming windows and the luminous green of its conventional glass show jars made the brightest spot on the block. I realized that I was tired, but hardly wanted to go in there and rest. I knew what the company would be like at its shabby, sticky soda fountain. As I stood there, my eyes fell on a long white canvas sign across from me, and its black-and-red lettering caught my attention.

SEE THE GREAT UNSEEN!
Coms in! This Means You!
Free to All!

A museum of fakes, I thought, but also reflected that if it were a show of some kind I could sit down for a while, rest, and fight off this increasing obsession of nonexistent evil. That side of the street was almost deserted, and the place itself might well be nearly empty.

II.

I walked over, but with every step my sense of dread increased. Dread of I knew not what. Bodiless, inexplicable horror had me as in a net, whose strands, being intangible, without reason for existence, I could by no means throw off. It was not the people now. None of them were about me. There, in the open, lighted street, with no sight nor sound of terror to assail me, I was the shivering victim of such fear as I had never known was possible. Yet still I would not yield.

Setting my teeth, and fighting with myself as with some pet animal gone mad, I forced my steps to slowness and walked along the sidewalk, seeking entrance. Just here there were no shops, but several doors reached in each case by means of a few iron-railed stone steps. I chose the one in the middle beneath the sign. In that neighborhood there are museums, shops and other commercial enterprises conducted in many shabby old residences, such as were these. Behind the glazing of the door I had chosen I could see a dim, pinkish light, but on either side the windows were quite dark.

Trying the door, I found it unlocked. As I opened it a party of Italians passed on the pavement below and I looked back at them over my shoulder. They were gayly dressed, men, women and children, laughing and chattering to one another; probably on their way to some wedding or other festivity.

In passing, one of the men glanced up at me and involuntarily I shuddered back against the door. He was a young man, handsome after the swarthy manner of his race, but never in my life had I seen a face so expressive of pure, malicious cruelty, naked and unashamed. Our eyes met and his seemed to light up with a vile gleaming, as if all the wickedness of his nature had come to a focus in the look of concentrated hate he gave me.

They went by, but for some distance I could see him watching me, chin on shoulder, till he and his party were swallowed up in the crowd of marketers farther down the street.

Sick and trembling from that encounter, merely of eyes though it had been, I threw aside my partly smoked cigar and entered. Within there was a small vestibule, whose ancient tesselated floor was grimy with the passing of many feet. I could feel the grit of dirt under my shoes, and it rasped on my rawly quivering nerves. The inner door stood partly open, and going on I found myself in a bare, dirty hallway, and was greeted by the sour, musty, poverty-stricken smell common to dwellings of the very ill-to-do. Beyond there was a stairway, carpeted with ragged grass matting. A gas jet, turned low inside a very dusty pink globe, was the light I had seen from without.

Listening, the house seemed entirely silent. Surely, this was no place of public amusement of any kind whatever. More likely it was a rooming house, and I had, after all, mistaken the entrance.

To my intense relief, since coming inside, the worst agony of my unreasonable terror had passed away. If I could only get in some place where I could sit down and be quiet, probably I should be rid of it for good. Determining to try another entrance, I was about to leave the bare hallway when one of several doors along the side of it suddenly opened and a man stepped out into the hall.

"Well?" he said, looking at me keenly, but with not the least show of surprise at my presence.

"I beg your pardon," I replied. "The door was unlocked and I came in here, thinking it was the entrance to the exhibit—what do they call it?—the 'Great Unseen.' The one that is mentioned on that long white sign. Can you tell me which door is the right one?"

"I can."

With that brief answer he stopped and stared at me again. He was a tall, lean man, somewhat stooped, but possessing considerable dignity of bearing. For that neighborhood, he appeared uncommonly well dressed, and his long, smooth-shaven face was noticeable because, while his complexion was dark and his eyes coal-black, above them the heavy brows and his hair were almost silvery-white. His age might have been anything over the threescore mark.

I grew tired of being stared at. "If you can and—won't, then never mind," I observed a trifle irritably, and turned to go. But his sharp exclamation halted me.

"No!" he said. "No—no! Forgive me for pausing—it was not hesitation, I assure you. To think that one—one, even, has come! All day they pass my sign up there—pass and fear to enter. But you are different. *You* are not of these timorous, ignorant foreign peasants. You ask me to tell you the right door? Here it is! Here!"

And he struck the panel of the door, which he had closed behind him, so that the sharp yet hollow sound of it echoed up through the silent house.

Now it may be thought that after all my senseless terror in the open street, so strange a welcome from so odd a showman would have brought the feeling back, full force. But there is an emotion stronger, to a certain point, than fear. This queer old fellow aroused my curiosity. What kind of museum could it be that he accused the passing public of fearing to enter? Nothing really terrible, surely, or it would have been closed by the police. And normally I am not an unduly timorous person. "So, it's in there, is it?" I asked, coming toward him. "And I'm to be sole audience? Come, that will be an interesting experience." I was half laughing now.

"The most interesting in the world," said the old man, with a solemnity which rebuked my lightness.

With that he opened the door, passed inward and closed it again—in my very face. I stood staring at it blankly. The panels, I remember, had been originally painted white, but now the paint was flaked and blistered, gray with dirt and dirty finger marks. Suddenly it occurred to me that I had no wish to enter there. Whatever was behind it could be scarcely worth seeing, or he would not choose such a place for its exhibition. With the old man's vanishing my curiosity had cooled, but just as I again turned to leave, the door opened and this singular showman stuck his white-eyebrowed face through the aperture. He was frowning impatiently. "Come in—come in!" he snapped, and promptly withdrawing his head, once more closed the door.

"He has something in there he doesn't want should get out," was the very natural conclusion which I drew. "Well, since it can hardly be anything dangerous, and he's so anxious I should see it—here goes!"

With that I turned the soiled white porcelain handle, and entered.

The room I came into was neither very large nor very brightly lighted. In no way did it resemble a museum or lecture room. On the contrary, it seemed to have been fitted up as a quite well-appointed laboratory. The floor was linoleum-covered, there were glass cases along the walls whose shelves were filled with bottles, specimen jars, graduates, and the like. A large table in one corner bore what looked like some odd sort of camera, and a larger one in the middle of the room was fitted with a long rack filled with bottles and test tubes, and was besides littered with papers, glass slides, and various paraphernalia which my ignorance failed to identify. There were several cases of books, a few plain wooden chairs, and in the corner a large iron sink with running water.

My host of the white hair and black eyes was awaiting me, standing near the larger table. He indicated one of the wooden chairs with a thin forefinger that shook a little, either from age or eagerness. "Sit down—sit down! Have no fear but that you will be interested, my friend. Have no fear at all—of anything!"

As he said it he fixed his dark eyes upon me and stared harder than ever. But the effect of his words was the opposite of their meaning. I did sit down, because my knees gave under me, but if in the outer hall I had lost my terror, it now returned twofold upon me. Out there the light had been faint, dingily roseate, indefinite. By it I had not perceived how this old man's face was a mask of living malice—of cruelty, hate and a certain masterful contempt. Now I knew the meaning of my fear, whose warning I would not heed. Now I knew that I had walked into the very trap from which my abnormal sensitiveness had striven in vain to save me.

III.

Again I struggled within me, bit at my lip till I tasted blood, and presently the blind paroxysm passed. It must have been longer in going than I thought, and the old man must have all that time been speaking, for when I could once more control my attention, hear and see him, he had taken up a position near the sink, about ten feet away, and was addressing me with a sort of "platform" manner, as if I had been the large audience whose absence he had deplored.

"And so," he was saying, "I was forced to make these plates very carefully, to truly represent the characteristic hues of each separate organism. Now, in color work of every kind the film is necessarily extremely sensitive. Doubtless you are familiar in a general way with the exquisite transparencies produced by color photography of the single-plate type."

He paused, and, trying to act like a normal human being, I observed: "I saw some nice landscapes done in that way—last week at an illustrated lecture in Franklin Hall."

He scowled, and made an impatient gesture at me with his hand. "I can proceed better without interruptions," he said. "My pause was purely oratorical."

I meekly subsided, and he went on in his original loud, clear voice. He would have made an excellent lecturer before a much larger audience—if only his voice could have lost that eerie, ringing note. Thinking of that I must have missed some more, and when I caught it again he was saying:

"As I have indicated, the original plate is the final picture. Now, many of these organisms are extremely hard to photograph, and microphotography in color is particularly difficult. In consequence, to spoil a plate tries the patience of the photographer. They are so sensitive that the ordinary darkroom ruby lamp would instantly ruin them, and they must therefore be developed either in darkness or by a special light produced by interposing thin sheets of tissue of a particular shade of green and of yellow between lamp and plate, and even that will often cause ruinous fog. Now I, finding it hard to handle them so, made numerous experiments with a view to discovering some glass or fabric of a color which should add to the safety of the green, without robbing it of all efficiency. All proved equally useless, but intermittently I persevered—until last week."

His voice dropped to an almost confidential tone, and he leaned slightly toward me. I was cold from my neck to my feet, though my head was burning, but I tried to force an appreciative smile.

"Last week," he continued impressively, "I had a prescription filled at the corner drug store. The bottle was sent home to me wrapped in a piece of what I at first took to be whitish, slightly opalescent paper. Later I decided that it was some kind of membrane. When I questioned the druggist, seeking its source, he said it was a sheet of 'paper' that was around a bundle of herbs from South America. That he had no more, and doubted if I could trace it.

He had wrapped my bottle so, because he was in haste and the sheet was handy.

"I can hardly tell you what first inspired me to try that membrane in my photographic work. It was merely dull white with a faint hint of opalescence, except when held against the light. Then it became quite translucent and quite brightly prismatic. For some reason it occurred to me that this refractive effect might help in breaking up the actinic rays—the rays which affect the sensitive emulsion. So that night I inserted it behind the sheets of green and yellow tissue, next the lamp, prepared my trays and chemicals, laid my plate holders to hand, turned off the white light and—turned on the green!"

There was nothing in his words to inspire fear. It was a wearisomely detailed account of his struggles with photography. Yet, as he again paused impressively, I wished that he might never speak again. I was desperately, contemptibly in dread of the thing he might say next.

Suddenly he drew himself erect, the stoop went out of his shoulders, he threw back his head and laughed. It was a hollow sound, as if he laughed into a trumpet. "I won't tell you what I saw! Why should I? Your own eyes shall bear witness. But this much I'll say, so that you may better understand— later. When our poor, faultily sensitive vision can perceive a thing, we say that it is visible. When the nerves of touch can feel it, we say that it is tangible. Yet I tell you there are beings intangible to our physical sense, yet whose presence is felt by the spirit, and invisible to our eyes merely because those organs are not attuned to the light as reflected from their bodies. But light passed through the screen which we are about to use has a wave length novel to the scientific world, and by it you shall see with the eyes of the flesh that which has been invisible since life began. Have no fear!"

He stopped to laugh again, and his mirth was yellow-toothed—menacing.

"*Have no fear!*" he reiterated, and with that stretched his hand toward the wall, there came a click and we were in black, impenetrable darkness. I wanted to spring up, to seek the door by which I had entered and rush out of it, but the paralysis of unreasoning terror held me fast.

I could hear him moving about in the darkness, and a moment later a faint green glimmer sprang up in the room. Its source was over the large sink, where I suppose he developed his precious "color plates."

Every instant, as my eyes became accustomed to the dimness, I could see more clearly. Green light is peculiar. It may be far fainter than red, and at the same time far more illuminating. The old man was standing beneath it, and his face by that ghastly radiance had the exact look of a dead man's. Beside this, however, I could observe nothing appalling.

"That," continued the man, "is the simple developing light of which I have spoken—now watch, for what you are about to behold no mortal man but myself has ever seen before."

For a moment he fussed with the green lamp over the sink. It was so constructed that all the direct rays struck downward. He opened a flap at the side, for a moment there was a streak of comforting white luminance from within, then he inserted something, slid it slowly in—and closed the flap.

The thing he put in—that South American "membrane" it must have been—instead of decreasing the light increased it—amazingly. The hue was changed from green to greenish-gray, and the whole room sprang into view, a livid, ghastly chamber, filled with—overcrawled by—what?

My eyes fixed themselves, fascinated, on something that moved by the old man's feet. It writhed there on the floor like a huge, repulsive starfish, an immense, armed, legged thing, that twisted convulsively. It was smooth, as if made of rubber, was whitish-green in color; and presently raised its great round blob of a body on tottering tentacles, crept toward my host and writhed upward—yes, climbed up his legs, his body. And he stood there, erect, arms folded, and stared sternly down at the thing which climbed.

But the room—the whole room was alive with other creatures than that. Everywhere I looked they were—centipedish things, with yard-long bodies, detestable, furry spiders that lurked in shadows, and sausage-shaped translucent horrors that moved—and floated through the air. They dived here and there between me and the light, and I could see its brighter greenness through their greenish bodies.

Worse, though, far worse than these were the *things with human faces*. Mask-like, monstrous, huge gaping mouths and slitlike eyes—I find I cannot write of them. There was that about them which makes their memory even now intolerable.

The old man was speaking again, and every word echoed in my brain like the ringing of a gong. "Fear nothing! Among such as these do you move every hour of the day and the night. Only you and I have seen, for God is merciful and has spared our race from sight. But I am not merciful! I loathe the race which gave these creatures birth—the race which might be so surrounded by invisible, unguessed but blessed beings—and chooses these for its companions! All the world shall see and know. One by one shall they come here, learn the truth, and perish. For who can survive the ultimate of terror? Then I, too, shall find peace, and leave the earth to its heritage of man-created horrors. Do you know what these are—whence they come?"

His voice boomed now like a cathedral bell. I could not answer him, but he waited for no reply. "Out of the ether—out of the omnipresent ether from whose intangible substance the mind of God made the planets, all living things, and man—man has made these! By his evil thoughts, by his selfish panics, by his lusts and his interminable, never-ending hate he has made them, and they are everywhere! Fear nothing—they cannot harm your body—but let your spirit beware! Fear nothing—but see where there comes to you, its creator, the shape and the body of your FEAR!"

And as he said it I perceived a great Thing coming toward me—a Thing— but consciousness could endure no more. The ringing, threatening voice merged in a roar within my ears, there came a merciful dimming of the terrible, lurid vision, and blank nothingness succeeded upon horror too great for bearing.

IV.

There was a dull, heavy pain above my eyes. I knew that they were closed, that I was dreaming, and that the rack full of colored bottles which I seemed to see so clearly was no more than a part of the dream. There was some vague but imperative reason why I should rouse myself. I wanted to awaken, and thought that by staring very hard indeed I could dissolve this foolish vision of blue and yellow-brown bottles. But instead of dissolving they grew clearer, more solid and substantial of appearance, until suddenly the rest of my senses rushed to the support of sight, and I became aware that my eyes were open, the bottles were quite real, and that I was sitting in a chair, fallen sideways so that my cheek rested most uncomfortably on the table which held the rack.

I straightened up slowly and with difficulty, groping in my dulled brain for some clew to my presence in this unfamiliar place, this laboratory that was lighted only by the rays of an arc light in the street outside its three large windows. Here I sat, alone, and if the aching of cramped limbs meant anything, here I had sat for more than a little time.

Then, with the painful shock which accompanies awakening to the knowledge of some great catastrophe, came memory. It was this very room, shown by the street lamp's rays to be empty of life, which I had seen thronged with creatures too loathsome for description. I staggered to my feet, staring fearfully about. There were the glass-doored cases, the bookshelves, the two tables with their burdens, and the long iron sink above which, now only a dark blotch of shadow, hung the lamp from which had emanated that livid, terrifically revealing illumination. Then the experience had been no dream, but a frightful reality. I was alone here now. With callous indifference my strange host had allowed me to remain for hours unconscious, with not the least effort to aid or revive me. Perhaps, hating me so, he had hoped that I would die there.

At first I made no effort to leave the place. Its appearance filled me with reminiscent loathing. I longed to go, but as yet felt too weak and ill for the effort. Both mentally and physically my condition was deplorable, and for the first time I realized that a shock to the mind may react upon the body as vilely as any debauch of self-indulgence.

Quivering in every nerve and muscle, dizzy with headache and nausea, I dropped back into the chair, hoping that before the old man returned I might recover sufficient self-control to escape him. I knew that he hated me, and why. As I waited, sick, miserable, I understood the man. Shuddering, I recalled the loathsome horrors he had shown me. If the mere desires and emotions of mankind were daily carnified in such forms as those, no wonder that he viewed his fellow beings with detestation and longed only to destroy them.

I thought, too, of the cruel, sensuous faces I had seen in the streets outside—seen for the first time, as if a veil had been withdrawn from eyes hitherto blinded by self-delusion. Fatuously trustful as a month-old puppy, I had lived in a grim, evil world, where goodness is a word and crude self-ishness the only actuality. Drearily my thoughts drifted back through my own life, its futile purposes, mistakes and activities. All of evil that I knew returned to overwhelm me. Our gropings toward divinity were a sham, a writhing sunward of slime-covered beasts who claimed sunlight as their heritage, but in their hearts preferred the foul and easy depths.

Even now, though I could neither see nor feel them, this room, the entire world, was acrawl with the beings created by our real natures. I recalled the cringing, contemptible fear to which my spirit had so readily yielded, and the faceless Thing to which the emotion had given birth.

Then abruptly, shockingly, I remembered that every moment I was adding to the horde. Since my mind could conceive only repulsive incubi, and since while I lived I must think, feel, and so continue to shape them, was there no way to check so abominable a succession? My eyes fell on the long shelves with their many-colored bottles. In the chemistry of photography there are deadly poisons—I knew that. Now was the time to end it—now! Let him return and find his desire accomplished. One good thing I could do, if one only. I could abolish my monster-creating self.

V.

My friend Mark Jenkins is an intelligent and usually a very careful man. When he took from "Smiler" Callahan a cigar which had every appearance of being excellent, innocent Havana, the act denoted both intelligence and caution. By very clever work he had traced the poisoning of young Ralph Peeler to Mr. Callahan's door, and he believed this particular cigar to be the mate of one smoked by Peeler just previous to his demise. And if, upon arresting Callahan, he had not confiscated this bit of evidence, it would have doubtless been destroyed by its regrettably unconscientious owner.

But when Jenkins shortly afterward gave me that cigar, as one of his own, he committed one of those almost inconceivable blunders which, I think, are occasionally forced upon clever men to keep them from overweening vanity. Discovering his slight mistake, my detective friend spent the night searching for his unintended victim, myself, and that his search was successful was due to Pietro Marini, a young Italian of Jenkins' acquaintance, whom he met about the hour of two a.m. returning from a dance.

Now, Marini had seen me standing on the steps of the house where Doctor Frederick Holt had his laboratory and living rooms, and he had stared at me, not with any ill intent, but because he thought I was the sickest-looking, most ghastly specimen of humanity that he had ever beheld. And, sharing the superstition of his South Street neighbors, he wondered if the worthy doctor had poisoned me as well as Peeler. This suspicion he imparted to Jenkins, who, however, had the best of reasons for believing otherwise. Moreover, as he informed Marini, Holt was dead, having drowned himself late the previous afternoon. An hour or so after our talk in the restaurant news of his suicide reached Jenkins.

It seemed wise to search any place where a very sick-looking young man had been seen to enter, so Jenkins came straight to the laboratory. Across the fronts of those houses was the long sign with its mysterious inscription, "See the Great Unseen," not at all mysterious to the detective. He knew that next door to Doctor Holt's the second floor had been thrown together into a lecture room, where at certain hours a young man employed by settlement workers displayed upon a screen stereopticon views of various deadly bacilli, the germs of diseases appropriate to dirt and indifference. He knew, too, that Doctor Holt himself had helped the educational effort along by providing some really wonderful lantern slides, done by micro-color photography.

On the pavement outside, Jenkins found the two-thirds remnant of a cigar, which he gathered in and came up the steps, a very miserable and self-reproachful detective. Neither outer nor inner door was locked, and in the laboratory he found me, alive, but on the verge of death by another means than he had feared.

In the extreme physical depression following my awakening from drugged sleep, and knowing nothing of its cause, I believed my adventure fact in its entirety. My mentality was at too low an ebb to resist its dreadful suggestion. I was searching among Holt's various bottles when Jenkins burst in. At first I was merely annoyed at the interruption of my purpose, but before the anticlimax of his explanation the mists of obsession drifted away and left me still sick in body, but in spirit happy as any man may well be who has suffered a delusion that the world is wholly bad—and learned that its badness springs from his own poisoned brain.

The malice which I had observed in every face, including young Marini's, existed only in my drug-affected vision. Last week's "popular-science" lecture had been recalled to my subconscious mind—the mind that rules dreams and delirium—by the photographic apparatus in Holt's workroom. "See the Great Unseen" assisted materially, and even the corner drug store before which I had paused, with its green-lit show vases, had doubtless played a part. But presently, following something Jenkins told me, I was driven to one protest. "If Holt was not here," I demanded, "if Holt is dead, as you say, how do you account for the fact that I, who have never seen the man, was able to give you an accurate description which you admit to be that of Doctor Frederick Holt?"

He pointed across the room. "See that?" It was a life-size bust portrait, in crayons, the picture of a white-haired man with bushy eyebrows and the most piercing black eyes I had ever seen—until the previous evening. It hung facing the door and near the windows, and the features stood out with a strangely lifelike appearance in the white rays of the arc lamp just outside. "Upon entering," continued Jenkins, "the first thing you saw was that portrait, and from it your delirium built a living, speaking man. So, there are your white-haired showman, your unnatural fear, your color photography and your pretty green golliwogs all nicely explained for you, Blaisdell, and thank God you're alive to hear the explanation. If you had smoked the whole of that cigar—well, never mind. You didn't. And now, my very dear friend, I think it's high time that you interviewed a real, flesh-and-blood doctor. I'll phone for a taxi."

"Don't," I said. "A walk in the fresh air will do me more good than fifty doctors."

"Fresh air! There's no fresh air on South Street in July," complained Jenkins, but reluctantly yielded."

I had a reason for my preference. I wished to see people, to meet face to face even such stray prowlers as might be about at this hour, nearer sunrise than midnight, and rejoice in the goodness and kindliness of the human countenance—particularly as found in the lower classes.

But even as we were leaving there occurred to me a curious inconsistency.

"Jenkins," I said, "you claim that the reason Holt, when I first met him in the hall, appeared to twice close the door in my face, was because the door never opened until I myself unlatched it."

"Yes," confirmed Jenkins, but he frowned, foreseeing my next question.

"Then why, if it was from that picture that I built so solid, so convincing a vision of the man, did I see Holt in the hall before the door was open?"

"You confuse your memories," retorted Jenkins rather shortly.

"Do I? Holt was dead at that hour, but—*I tell you I saw Holt outside the door!* And what was his reason for committing suicide?"

Before my friend could reply I was across the room, fumbling in the dusk there at the electric lamp above the sink. I got the tin flap open and pulled out the sliding screen, which consisted of two sheets of glass with fabric between, dark on one side, yellow on the other. With it came the very thing I dreaded—a sheet of whitish, parchmentlike, slightly opalescent stuff.

Jenkins was beside me as I held it at arm's length toward the windows. Through it the light of the arc lamp fell—divided into the most astonishingly brilliant rainbow hues. And instead of diminishing the light, it was perceptibly increased in the oddest way. Almost one thought that the sheet itself was luminous, and yet when held in shadow it gave off no light at all.

"Shall we—put it in the lamp again—and try it?" asked Jenkins slowly, and in his voice there was no hint of mockery.

I looked him straight in the eyes. "No," I said, "we won't. I was drugged. Perhaps in that condition I received a merciless revelation of the discovery that caused Holt's suicide, but I don't believe it. Ghost or no ghost, I refuse to ever again believe in the depravity of the human race. If the air and the earth are teeming with invisible horrors, they are *not* of our making, and—the study of demonology is better let alone. Shall we burn this thing, or tear it up?"

"We have no right to do either," returned Jenkins thoughtfully, "but you know, Blaisdell, there's a little too darn much realism about some parts of your 'dream.' I haven't been smoking any doped cigars, but when you held that up to the light, I'll swear I saw—well, never mind. Burn it—send it back to the place it came from."

"South America?" said I.

"A hotter place than that. Burn it."

So he struck a match and we did. It was gone in one great white flash.

A large place was given by morning papers to the suicide of Doctor Frederick Holt, caused, it was surmised, by mental derangement brought about by his unjust implication in the Peeler murder. It seemed an inadequate reason, since he had never been arrested, but no other was ever discovered.

Of course, our action in destroying that "membrane" was illegal and rather precipitate, but, though he won't talk about it, I know that Jenkins agrees with me—doubt is sometimes better than certainty, and there are marvels better left unproved. Those, for instance, which concern the Powers of Evil.

The Elf Trap

In this our well-advertised, modern world, crammed
with engines, death-dealing shells, life-dealing
serums, and science, he who listens to "old
wives' tales" is counted idle. He who believes
them, a superstitious fool. Yet there are
some legends which have a strange,
deathless habit of recrudescence
in many languages and lands.

Of one such I have a story to tell. It
was related to me by a well-known
specialist in nervous diseases, not as
an instance of the possible truth
behind fable, but as a curious
case in which—I quote his words—
"the delusions of a diseased brain
were reflected by a second and
otherwise sound mentality."

No doubt his view was the right
one. And yet, at the finish, I had the
strangest flash of feeling. As if,
somewhere, some time, I, like
young Wharton, had stood and

seen against blue sky—Elva, of the sky-hued scarf and the yellow honey-suckles.

But my part is neither to feel nor surmise. I will tell the story as I heard it, save for substitution of fictitious names for the real ones. My quotations from the red note-book are verbatim.

Theron Tademus, A.A.S., F.E.S., D.S., *et cetera*, occupied the chair of biology in a not-unfamed university. He was the author of a treatise on cytology, since widely used as a text-book, and of several important brochures on the more obscure infusoria. As a boy he had been—in appearance— a romantically charming person. The age of thirty-seven found him still handsome in a cold, fine-drawn manner, but almost inhumanly detached from any save scientific interests.

Then, at the height of his career, he died. Having entered his class-room with intent to deliver the first lecture of the fall term, he walked to his desk, laid down a small, red note-book, turned, opened his mouth, went ghastly white and subsided. His assistant, young Wharton, was first to reach him and first to discover the shocking truth.

Tademus was unmarried, and his will bequeathed all he possessed to the university.

The little red book was not at first regarded as important. Supposed to contain notes for his lecture, it was laid aside. On being at last read, however, by his assistant in course of arranging his papers, the book was found to contain not notes, but a diary covering the summer just passed.

Barring the circumstances of one peculiar incident, Wharton already knew the main facts of that summer.

Tademus, at the insistence of his physician—the specialist aforesaid—had spent July and August in the Carolina Mountains, not far north from the famous summer resort, Asheville. Dr. Locke was friend as well as medical adviser, and he lent his patient the use of a bungalow he owned there.

It was situated in a beautiful, but lonely spot, to which the nearest settlement was Carcassonne. In the valley below stood a tiny railroad-station, but Carcassonne was not built up around this, nor was it a town at all in the ordinary sense.

A certain landscape painter had once raised him a house on that mountainside, at a place chosen for its magnificent view. Later, he was wont to invite thither, for summer sketching, one or two of his more favored pupils. Later still, he increased this number. For their accommodation other structures were raised near his mountain studio, and the Blue Ridge summer class became an established fact, with a name of its own and a rather large membership.

Two roads led thither from the valley. One, that most in use by the artist colonists, was as good and broad as any Carolina mountain road could hope to be. The other, a winding, narrow, yellow track, passed the lonely bungalow of Dr. Locke, and at last split into two paths, one of which led on to further heights, the second to Carcassonne.

The distance between colony and bungalow was considerable, and neither was visible to the other. Tademus was not interested in art, and, as disclosed by the red book, he was not even aware of Carcassonne's existence until some days after his arrival at the bungalow.

Solitude, long walks, deep breathing, and abstinence from work or sustained thought had been Dr. Locke's prescription, accepted with seeming meekness by Tademus.

Nevertheless, but a short time passed till Wharton received a telegram from the professor ordering him to pack and send by express certain apparatus, including a microscope and dissecting stand. The assistant obeyed.

Another fortnight, and Dr. Locke in turn received an urgent wire. It was from Jake Higgins, the negro caretaker whom he had "lent" to Tademus along with the bungalow.

Leaving his practise to another man's care, Locke fled for the Carolina Blue Ridge.

He found his negro and his bungalow, but no Tademus.

By Jake's story, the professor had gone to walk one afternoon and had not returned. Having wired Locke, the negro had otherwise done his best. He notified the county sheriff, and search-parties scoured the mountains. At his appeal, also, the entire Carcassonnian colony, male and female, turned out with enthusiasm to hunt for Tademus. Many of them carried easel and sketch-box along, and for such it is to be feared that their humane search ended with the discovery of any tempting "bit" in the scenic line.

However, the colony's efforts were at least as successful as the sheriff's, or indeed those of any one else.

Shortly before Tademus's vanishment, a band of gipsies had settled themselves in a group of old, empty, half-ruined negro shacks, about a mile from Locke's bungalow.

Suspicion fell upon them. A posse visited the encampment, searched it, and questioned every member of the migrant band. They were a peculiarly ill-favored set, dirty and villainous of feature. Nothing, however, could be found of either the missing professor or anything belonging to him.

The posse left, after a quarrel that came near to actual fighting. A dog—a wretched, starved yellow cur—had attacked one of the deputies and set its teeth in his boot. He promptly shot it. In their resentment, the dog's owners drew knives.

The posse were more efficiently armed, and under threat of the latter's rifles and shotguns, the gipsies reconsidered. They were warned to pack up and leave, and following a few days' delay, they obeyed the mandate.

On the very morning of their departure, which was also the eighth day after Tademus's disappearance, Dr. Locke sat down gloomily to breakfast. The search, he thought, must be further extended. Let it cover the whole Blue Ridge, if need be. Somewhere in those mountains was a friend and patient whom he did not propose to lose.

At one side of the breakfast-room was a door. It led into the cleared-out bedroom which Locke had, with indignation, discovered to have been converted into a laboratory by the patient he had sent here to "rest."

Suddenly this door opened. Out walked Theron Tademus.

He seemed greatly amazed to find Locke there, and said that he had come in shortly after midnight and been in his laboratory ever since.

Questioned as to his whereabouts before that, he replied surprisingly that throughout the week he had been visiting with friends in Carcassonne.

Dr. Locke doubted his statement, and reasonably.

Artists are not necessarily liars, and every artist and near-artist in the Carcassonne colony had not only denied knowledge of the professor, but spent a good part of the week helping hunt for him.

Later, after insisting that Locke accompany him to Carcassonne and meet his "friends" there, Tademus suddenly admitted that he had not previously been near the place. He declined, however, either to explain his untruthful first statement, or give any other account of his mysterious absence.

One week ago Tademus had left the bungalow, carrying nothing but a light cane, and wearing a white flannel suit, canvas shoes, and a Panama. That was his idea of a tramping costume. He had returned, dressed in the same suit, hat and shoes. Moreover, though white, they looked neat as when he started, save for a few grass-stains and the road's inevitable yellow clay about his shoe-soles.

If he had spent the week vagrant-wise, he had been remarkably successful in keeping his clothes clean.

"Asheville," thought the doctor. "He went by train, stopped at a hotel, and has returned without the faintest memory of his real doings. Lame, overtaxed nerves can play that sort of trick with a man's brain."

But he kept the opinion to himself. Like a good doctor, he soon dropped the whole subject, particularly because he saw that Tademus was deeply distressed and trying to conceal the fact.

On plea of taking a long-delayed vacation of his own, Locke remained some time at the bungalow, guarded his friend from the curiosity of those who had combed the hills for him, and did all in his power to restore him to health and a clear brain.

He was so far successful that Tademus returned to his classes in the fall, with Locke's consent.

To his classes—and death.

Wharton had known all this. He knew that Tademus's whereabouts during that mysterious week had never been learned. But the diary in the red book purported to cover the summer, *including that week*.

To Wharton, the record seemed so supremely curious that he took a liberty with what was now the university's property. He carried the red book to Dr. Locke.

It was evening, and the latter was about to retire after a day's work that began before dawn.

"Personal, you say?" Locke handled the book, frowning slightly.

"Personal. But I feel—when you've finished reading that, I have a rather queer thing to tell you in addition. You can't understand till you've read it. I am almost sure that what is described here has a secret bearing on Professor Tademus's death."

"His heart failed. Overwork. There was no mystery in that."

"Maybe not, doctor. And yet—won't you please read?"

"Run through it aloud for me," said the doctor. "I couldn't read one of my own prescriptions to-night, and you are more familiar with that microscopic writing of his."

Wharton complied.

Monday, July 3.

Arrived yesterday. Not worse than expected, but bad enough. If Locke were here, he should be satisfied. I have absolutely no occupation. Walked and climbed for two hours, as prescribed. Spent the rest of day pacing up and down indoors. Enough walking, at least. I can't sit idle. I can't stop thinking. Locke is a fool!

Thursday, July 6.

Telegraphed Wharton to-day. He will express me the Swift binocular, some slides, cover-glasses, and a very little other apparatus. Locke *is* a fool. I shall follow his advice, but within reason. There is a room here lighted by five windows. Old Jake has cleared the bedroom furniture out. It has qualities as a laboratory. Not, of course, that I intend doing any real work. An hour or so a day of micrological observation will only make "resting" tolerable.

Tuesday, July 11.

Jake hitched up his "ol' gray mule" and has brought my three cases from the station. I unpacked the old Stephenson-Swift and set it up. The mere touch of it brought tears to my eyes. Locke's "rest-cure" has done that to my nerves!

After unpacking, though, I resolutely let the microscope and other things be. Walked ten miles up-hill and down. Tried to admire the landscape, as Locke advised, but can't see much in it. Rocks, trees, lumpy hills, yellow roads, sky, clouds, buzzards. Beauty! What beauty is there in this vast, clumsy world that is the outer husk for nature's real and delicate triumphs?

I saw a man painting to-day. He was swabbing at a canvas with huge, clumsy brushes. He had his easel set up by the road, and I stopped to see what any human being could find hereabout worth picturing.

And what had this painter, this artist, this lover of beauty chosen for a subject? Why, about a mile from here there is a clump of ugly, dark trees. A stream runs between them and the road. It is yellow with clay, and too swift. The more interesting micro-organisms could not exist in it. A ramshackle, plank bridge crosses it, leading to the grove, and there, between the trees, stand and lean some dreary, half ruined huts.

That scene was the one which my "artist" had chosen for his subject!

For sheer curiosity I got into conversation with the fellow.

Unusual gibberish of chiaroscuro, flat tones, masses, *et cetera*. Not a definite thought in his head as to *why* he wished to paint those shacks. I learned one thing, though. He wasn't the isolated specimen of his kind I had thought him. Locke failed to tell me about Carcassonne. Think of it! Nearly a hundred of these insane pursuers of "beauty" are spending the summer within walking distance of the house I have promised to live in!

And the one who was painting the grove actually invited me to call on him! I smiled non-committally, and came home. On the way I passed the branch road that leads to the place. I had always avoided that road, but I didn't know why until to-day. Imagine it! Nearly a hundred. Some of them women, I suppose. No, I shall keep discreetly away from Carcassonne.

Saturday, July 15.

Jake informs me that a band of gipsies have settled themselves in the grove which my Carcassonnian acquaintance chose to paint. They are living in the ruined huts. Now I shall avoid that road, too. Talk of solitude! Why, the hills are fairly swarming with artists, gipsies, and Lord knows who else. One might as well try to rest in a beehive!

Found some interesting variations of the ciliata living in a near-by pond. Wonderful! Have recorded over a dozen specimens in which the macronucleus is unquestionably double. Not lobed, nor pulverate, as in Oxytricha, but *double!* My summer has not, after all, been wasted.

Felt singularly slack and tired this morning, and realized that I have hardly been out of the house in three days. Shall certainly take a long tramp to-morrow.

Monday, July 17.

Absent-mindedness betrayed me to-day. I had a very unpleasant experience. Resolutely keeping my promise to Locke, I sallied forth this afternoon and walked briskly for some distance. I had, however, forgotten the gipsies and took my old route.

Soon I met a woman, or rather a girl. She was arrayed in the tattered, brilliantly colored garments which women of these wandering tribes affect. There was a scarf about her head. I noticed, because its blue was exactly the soft, brilliant hue of the sky over the mountains behind her. There was a stripe of yellow in it, too, and thrust in her sash she carried a great bunch of yellow flowers—wild honeysuckle, I think.

Her face was not dark, like the swart faces of most gipsies. On the contrary, the skin of it had a smooth, firm, whiteness. Her features were fine and delicate.

Passing, we looked at one another, and I saw her eyes brighten in the strangest, most beautiful manner. I am sure that there was nothing bold or immodest in her glance. It was rather like the look of a person who recognizes an old acquaintance, and is glad of it. Yet we never met before. Had we met, I could not have forgotten her.

We passed without speaking, of course, and I walked on.

Meeting the girl, I had hardly thought of her as a gipsy, or indeed tried to classify her in any way. The impression she left was new in my experience. It was only on reaching the grove that I came to myself, as it were, and remembered Jake's story of the gipsies who are camping there.

Then I very quickly emerged from the vague, absurd happiness which sight of the girl had brought.

While talking with my Carcassonnian, I had observed that grove rather carefully. I had thought it perfect—that nothing added could increase the somber ugliness of its trees, nor the desolation of its gray, ruined, tumble-down old huts.

To-day I learned better. To be perfect, ugliness must include humanity.

The shacks, dreary in themselves, were hideous now. In their doorways lounged fat, unclean women nursing their filthy off-spring. Older children, clothed in rags, caked with dirt, sprawled and fought among themselves. Their voices were like the snarls of animals.

I realized that the girl with the sky-like scarf had come from here—out of this filth unspeakable!

A yellow cur, the mere, starved skeleton of a dog, came tearing down to the bridge. A rusty, jangling bell was tied about its neck with a string. The beast stopped on the far side and crouched there, yapping. Its anger seemed to surpass mere canine savagery. The lean jaws fairly writhed in maniacal but loathsomely feeble ferocity.

A few men, whiskered, dirty-faced, were gathered about a sort of forge erected in the grove. They were making something, beating it with hammers in the midst of showers of sparks. As the dog yapped, one of the men turned and saw me. He spoke to his mates, and to my dismay they stopped work and transferred their attention to me.

I was afraid that they would cross the bridge, and the idea of having to talk to them was for some reason inexpressibly revolting.

They stayed where they were, but one of them suddenly laughed out loudly, and held up to my view the thing upon which they had been hammering.

It was a great, clumsy, rough, *iron trap*. Even at that distance I could see the huge, jagged teeth, fit to maim a bear—or a man. It was the ugliest instrument I have ever seen.

I turned away and began walking toward home, and when I looked back they were at work again.

The sun shone brightly, but about the grove there seemed to be a queer darkness. It was like a place alone and aloof from the world. The trees, even, were different from the other mountain trees. Their heavy branches did not stir at all in the wind. They had a strange, dark, flat look against the sky, as though they had been cut from dark paper, or rather like the flat trees woven in a tapestry. That was it. The whole scene was like a flat, dark, unreal picture in tapestry.

I came straight home. My nerves are undoubtedly in bad shape, and I think I shall write Locke and ask him to prescribe medicine that will straighten me up. So far, his "rest-cure" has not been notably successful.

Wednesday, July 19.

I have met her again.

Last night I could not sleep at all. Round midnight I ceased trying, rose, dressed, and spent the rest of the night with the good old Stephenson-Swift. My light for night-work—a common oil lamp—is not very brilliant. This morning I suffered considerable pain behind the eyes, and determined to give Locke's "walking and open air" treatment another trial, though discouraged by previous results.

This time I remembered to turn my back on the road which leads to that hideous grove. The sunlight seemed to increase the pain I was already suffering. The air was hot, full of dust, and I had to walk slowly. At the slightest increase of pace my heart would set up a kind of fluttering, very unpleasant and giving me a sense of suffocation.

Then I came to the girl.

She was seated on a rock, her lap heaped with wild honeysuckle, and she was weaving the flower-stems together.

Seeing me, she smiled.

"I have your garland finished," she said, "and mine soon will be."

One would have thought the rock a trysting place at which we had for a long time been accustomed to meet! In her hand she was extending to me a wreath, made of the honeysuckle flowers.

I can't imagine what made me act as I did. Weariness and the pain behind my eyes may have robbed me of my usual good sense.

Anyway, rather to my own surprise, I took her absurd wreath and sat down where she made room for me on the boulder.

After that we talked.

At this moment, only a few hours later, I couldn't say whether or not the girl's English was correct, nor exactly what she said. But I can remember the very sound of her voice.

I recall, too, that she told me her name, Elva, and that when I asked for the rest of it, she informed me that one good name was enough for one good person.

That struck me as a charmingly humorous sally. I laughed like a boy—or a fool, God knows which!

Soon she had finished her second garland, and laughingly insisted that we each crown the other with flowers.

Imagine it! Had one of my students come by then, I am sure he would have been greatly startled. Professor Theron Tademus, seated on a rock with a gipsy girl, crowned with wild honeysuckle and adjusting a similar wreath to the girl's blue-scarfed head!

Luckily, neither the student nor any one else passed, and in a few minutes she said something that brought me to my senses. Due to that inexplicable dimness of memory, I quote the sense, not her words.

"My father is a ruler among our people. You must visit us. For my sake, the people and my father will make you welcome."

She spoke with the gracious air of a princess, but I rose hastily from beside her. A vision of the grove had returned—dark—oppressive—like an old, dark tapestry, woven with ugly forms and foliage. I remembered the horrible, filthy tribe from which this girl had sprung.

Without a word of farewell, I left her there on the rock. I did not look back, nor did she call after me. Not until reaching home, when I met old Jake at the door and saw him stare, did I remember the honeysuckle wreath. I was still wearing it, and carrying my hat.

Snatching at the flowers I flung them in the ditch and retreated with what dignity I might into the bungalow's seclusion.

It is night now, and a little while since I went out again. The wreath is here in the room with me. Its flowers were unsoiled by the ditch, and seem fresh as when she gave them to me. They are more fragrant than I had thought even wild honeysuckle could be.

Elva. Elva of the sky-blue scarf and the yellow honeysuckle!

My eyes are heavy, but the pain behind them is gone. I think I shall sleep tonight.

Friday, July 21.

Is there any man so gullible as he who prides himself on his accuracy of observation?

I ask this in humility, for I am that man.

Yesterday I rose, feeling fresher than for weeks past. After all, Locke's treatment seemed worthy of respect. With that in mind, I put in only a few hours staining some of my binucleate cilia and finishing the slides.

All the last part of the afternoon I faithfully tramped the roads. There is undoubtedly a sort of broad, coarse charm in mere landscape, with its reaches of green, its distant purples, and the sky like a blue scarf flung over it all. Had the pain of my eyes not returned, I could almost have enjoyed those vistas.

Having walked farther than usual, it was deep dusk when I reached home. As if from ambush, a little figure dashed out from behind some rhododendrons. It seemed to be a child, a boy, though I couldn't see him clearly, nor how he was dressed.

He thrust something into my hand. To my astonishment, the thing was a spray of wild honeysuckle.

"Elva—Elva—Elva!"

The strange youngster was fairly dancing up and down before me, repeating the girl's name and nothing else.

Recovering myself, I surmised that Elva must have sent this boy, and sure enough, at my insistence he managed to stop prancing long enough to deliver her message.

Elva's grandmother, he said, was very ill. She had been ailing for days, but to-night the sickness was worse—much worse. Elva feared that her grandmother would die, and, "of course," the boy said, "no doctor will come for our sending!" She had remembered me, as the only friend she knew among the "outside people." Wouldn't I come and look at her poor, sick grandmother? And if I had any of the outside people's medicine in my house, would I please bring that with me?

Well, yes, I did hesitate. Aside from practical and obvious suspicions, I was possessed with a senseless horror for not only the gipsy tribe, but the grove itself.

But there was the spray of honeysuckle. In her need, she had sent that for a token—and sent it to me! Elva, of the skylike scarf and laughing mouth.

"Wait here," I said to the boy, rather bruskly, and entered the house. I had remembered a pocket-case of simple remedies, none of which I had ever used, but there was a direction pamphlet with them. If I must play amateur physician, that might help. I looked for Jake, meaning to inform him of my proposed expedition. Though he had left a chicken broiling on the kitchen range, the negro was not about. He might have gone to the spring for water.

Passing out again, I called the boy, but received no answer. It was very dark. Toward sunset, the sky had clouded over, so that now I had not even the benefit of starlight.

I was angry with the boy for not waiting, but the road was familiar enough, even in the dark. At least, I thought it was, till, colliding with a clump of holly, I realized that I must have strayed off and across a bare stretch of yellow clay which defaces the mountainside above Locke's bungalow.

I looked back for the guiding lights of its windows, but the trees hid them. However, the road couldn't be far off. After some stumbling about, I was sure that my feet were in the right track again. Somewhat later I perceived a faint, ruddy point of light, to the left and ahead of me.

Walking toward it, the rapid rush and gurgle of water soon apprized me that I had reached the stream with the plank bridge across it.

There I stood for several minutes, staring toward the ruddy light. That was all I could see. It seemed, somehow, to cast no illumination about it.

There came a scamper of paws, the tinkle of a bell, and then a wild yapping broke out on the stream's far side. That vile, yellow cur, I thought. Elva, having imposed on my kindness to the extent of sending for me, might at least have arranged a better welcome than this.

Then I pictured her, crouched in her bright, summer-colored garments, tending the dreadful old hag that her grandmother must be. The rest of the tribe were probably indifferent. She could not desert her sick—and there stood I, hesitant as any other coward!

For the dog's sake I took a firm grip on my cane. Feeling about with it, I found the bridge and crossed over.

Instantly something flung itself against my legs and was gone before I could hit out. I heard the dog leaping and barking all around me. It suddenly struck me that the beast's voice was not like that of the yellow cur. There was nothing savage in it. This was the cheerful excited bark of a well-bred dog that welcomes its master, or its master's friend. And the bell that tinkled to every leap had a sweet, silvery note, different from the cracked jangle of the cur's bell.

I had hated and loathed that yellow brute, and to think that I need not combat the creature was a relief. The huts, as I recalled them, weren't fifty yards beyond the stream. There was no sign of a campfire. Just that one ruddy point of light.

I advanced—

Wharton paused suddenly in his reading. "Here," he interpolated, "begins that part of the diary which passed from commonplace to amazing. And the queer part is that in writing it, Professor Tademus seems to have been unaware that he was describing anything but an unusually pleasant experience."

Dr. Locke's heavy brows knit in a frown.

"Pleasant!" he snapped. "The date of that entry?"

"July 21."

"The day he disappeared. I see. Pleasant! And that gipsy girl—faugh! What an adventure for such a man! No wonder he tried to lie out of it. I don't think I care to hear the rest, Wharton. Whatever it is, my friend is dead. Let him rest."

"Oh, but wait," cried the young man with startled earnestness. "Good Lord, doctor, do you believe I would bring this book even to you if it contained *that* kind of story—about Professor Tademus? No. Its amazing quality is along different lines than you can possibly suspect."

"Get on, then," grumbled Locke, and Wharton continued.

Suddenly, as though at a signal, not one, but a myriad of lights blazed into existence.

It was like walking out of a dark closet into broad day. The first dazzlement passing, I perceived that instead of the somber grove and ruined huts, I was facing a group of very beautiful houses.

It is curious how a previous and false assumption will rule a man. Having believed myself at the gipsy encampment, several minutes passed before I could overcome my bewilderment and realized that after losing my road I had not actually regained it.

That I had somehow wandered into the other branch road, and reached, not the grove, but Carcassonne!

I had no idea, either that this artists' colony could be such a really beautiful place. It is cut by no streets. The houses are set here and there over the surface of such green lawns as I have never seen in these mountains of rock and yellow clay.

(Dr. Locke started slightly in his chair. Carcassonne, as he had himself seen it, flashed before his memory. He did not interrupt, but from that moment his attention was alertly set, like a man who listens for the keyword of a riddle.)

Everywhere were lights, hung in the flowering branches of trees, glowing upward from the grass, blazing from every door and window. Why they should have been turned on so abruptly, after that first darkness, I do not yet know.

Out of the nearest house a girl came walking. She was dressed charmingly, in thin, bright-colored silks. A bunch of wild honeysuckle was thrust in the girdle, and over her hair was flung a scarf of skylike blue. I knew her instantly, and began to see a glimmering of the joke that had been played on me.

The dog bounded toward the girl. He was a magnificent collie. A tiny silver bell was attached to his neck by a broad ribbon.

I take credit for considerable aplomb in my immediate behavior. The girl had stopped a little way off. She was laughing, but I had certainly allowed myself to be victimized.

On my accusation, she at once admitted to having deceived me. She explained that, perceiving me to be misled by her appearance into thinking her one of the gipsies, she could not resist carrying out the joke. She had sent her small brother with the token and message.

I replied that the boy deserted me, and that I had nearly invaded the camp of real gipsies while looking for her and the fictitious dying grandmother.

At this she appeared even more greatly amused. Elva's mirth has a peculiarly contagious quality. Instead of being angry, I found myself laughing with her.

By this time quite a throng of people had emerged on the lawns, and leading me to a dignified, fine-looking old man who she said was her father, she presented me. In the moment, I hardly noticed that she used my first name only, Theron, which I had told her when we sat on the roadside boulder. I have observed since that all these people use the single name only, in presentation and intercourse. Though lacking personal experience with artists, I have heard that they are inclined to peculiar "fads" of unconventionality. I had never, however, imagined that they could be attractive to a man like myself, or pleasant to know.

I am enlightened. These Carcassonnian "colonists" are the only charming, altogether delightful people whom I have ever met.

One and all, they seemed acquainted with Elva's amusing jest at my expense. They laughed with us, but in recompense have made me one of themselves in the pleasantest manner.

I dined in the house of Elva's father. The dining-room, or rather hall, is a wonderful place. Due to much microscopic work, I am inclined to see only clumsiness—*largeness*—in what other people characterize as beauty. Carcassonne is different. There is a minute perfection about the architecture of these artists' houses, the texture of their clothes, and even the delicate contour of their faces, which I find amazingly agreeable.

There is no conventionality of costume among them. Both men and women dress as they please. Their individual taste is exquisite, and the result is an array of soft fabrics, and bright colors, flowerlike, rather than garish.

Till last night I never learned the charm of what is called "fancy dress," nor the genial effect it may exert on even a rather somber nature, such as I admit mine to be.

Elva, full of good-natured mischief, insisted that I must "dress for dinner." Her demand was instantly backed by the whole laughing throng. Carried off my feet in a way to which I am not at all used, I let them drape me in white robes, laced with silver embroideries like the delicate crystallization of hoar-frost. Dragged hilariously before a mirror, I was amazed at the change in my appearance.

Unlike the black, scarlet-hooded gown of my university, these glittering robes lent me not dignity, but a kind of—I can only call it a noble youthfulness. I looked younger, and at the same time *keener*—more alive. And either the contagious spirit of my companions, or some resurgence of boyishness filled me with a sudden desire to please; to be merry with the merry-makers, and—I must be frank—particularly to keep Elva's attention where it seemed temporarily fixed—on myself.

My success was unexpectedly brilliant. There is something in the very atmosphere of Carcassonne which, once yielded to, exhilarates like wine.

I have never danced, nor desired to learn. Last night, after a banquet so perfect that I hardly recall its details, I danced. I danced with Elva—and with Elva—and always with Elva. She laughed aside all other partners. We danced on no polished floors, but out on the green lawns, under white, laughing stars. Our music was not orchestral. Wherever the light-footed couples chose to circle, there followed a young flutist, piping on his flute of white ivory.

Fluttering wings, driving clouds, wind-tossed leaves—all the light, swift things of the air were in that music. It lifted and carried one with it. One did not need to learn. One danced! It seems, as I write, that the flute's piping is still in my ears, and that its echoes will never cease. Elva's voice is like the ivory flute's. Last night I was mad with the music and her voice. We danced—I know not how long, nor when we ceased.

This morning I awakened in a gold-and-ivory room, with round windows that were full of blue sky and crossed by blossoming branches. Dimly I recalled that Elva's father had urged me to accept his hospitality for the night.

Too much of such new happiness may have gone to my head, I'm afraid. At least, it was nothing stronger. At dinner I drank only one glass of wine— sparkling, golden stuff, but mild and with a taste like the fragrance of Elva's wild honeysuckle blooms.

It is midmorning now, and I am writing this seated on a marble bench beside a pool in the central court of my host's house. I am waiting for Elva, who excused herself to attend to some duty or other. I found this book in my pocket, and thought best to make an immediate record of not only a good joke on myself, but the only really pleasant social experience I have ever enjoyed.

I must lay aside these fanciful white robes, bid Elva good-by, and return to my lonely bungalow and Jake. The poor old darky is probably tearing his wool over my unexplained absence. But I hope for another invitation to Carcassonne!

Saturday, July 22.

I seem to be "staying on" indefinitely. This won't do. I spoke to Elva of my extended visit, and she laughingly informed me that people who have drunk the wine and worn the woven robes of Carcassonne seldom wish to leave. She suggested that I give up trying to "escape" and spend my life here. Jest, of course; but I half wished her words were earnest. She and her people are spoiling me for the common, workaday world.

Not that they are idle, but their occupations as well as pleasures are of a delicate, fascinating beauty.

Whole families are stopping here, including the children. I don't care for children, as a rule, but these are harmless as butterflies. I met Elva's messenger, her brother. He is a funny, dear little elf. How even in the dark I fancied him one of those gipsy brats is hard to conceive. But then I took Elva herself for a gipsy!

My new friends engage in many pursuits besides painting. "Crafts," I believe they are called. This morning Elva took me around the "shops." Shops like architectural blossoms, carved out of the finest marble!

They make jewelry, weave fabrics, tool leather, and follow many other interesting occupations. Set in the midst of the lawns is a forge. Every part of it, even to the iron anvil, is embellished with a fernlike inlay of other metals. Several amateur silversmiths were at work there, but Elva hurried me away before I could see what they were about.

I have inquired for the young painter who first told me of Carcassonne and invited me to visit him here. I can't recall his name, but on describing him to Elva she replied vaguely that not every "outsider" was permanently welcome among her people.

I did not press the question. Remembering the ugliness which that same painter had been committing to canvas, I could understand that his welcome among these exquisite workers might be short-lived. He was probably banished, or banished himself, soon after our interview on the road.

I must be careful, lest I wear out my own welcome. Yet the very thought of that old, rough, husk of a world that I *must* return to, brings back the sickness, and the pain behind my eyes that I had almost forgotten.

Sunday, July 23.

Elva! Her presence alone is delight. The sky is not bluer than her scarf and eyes. Sunlight is a duller gold than the wild honeysuckle she weaves in garlands for our heads.

To-day, like child sweethearts, we carved our names on the smooth trunk of a tree. "Elva—Theron." And a wreath to shut them in. I am happy. Why—why, indeed should I leave Carcassonne?

Monday, July 24.

Still here, but this is the last night that I shall impose upon these regally hospitable people. An incident occurred to-day, pathetic from one viewpoint, outrageous from another. I was asleep when it happened, and only woke up at sound of the gunshot.

Some rough young mountaineers rode into Carcassonne and wantonly killed Elva's collie dog. They claimed, I believe, that the unlucky animal attacked one of their number. A lie! The dog was gentle as a kitten. He probably leaped and barked around their horses and annoyed the young brutes. They had ridden off before I reached the scene.

Elva was crying, and no wonder. They had blown her pet's head clean off with a shotgun. Don't know what will be done about it. I wanted to go straight to the county sheriff, but Elva wouldn't have that. I pretended to give in, but if her father doesn't see to the punishment of those men, I will. Murderous devils! Elva is too forgiving.

Wednesday, July 26.

I watched the silversmiths to-day. Elva was not with me. I had no idea that silver was worked like iron. They must use some peculiar amalgam, or it would melt in the furnace, instead of emerging white-hot, to be beaten with tiny, delicate hammers.

They were making a strange looking contraption. It was all silver, beaten into floral patterns, but the general shape was a riddle to me. Finally I asked one of the smiths what they were about. He is a tall fellow, with a merry, dark face.

"Guess!" he demanded.

"Can't. To my ignorance, it resembles a Chinese puzzle."

"Something more curious than that."

"What?"

"An—*elf-trap!*" He laughed mischievously.

"Please!"

"Well, it's a trap, anyway. See this?" The others had stepped back good naturedly. With his hammer he pressed on a lever. Instantly two slender, jawlike parts of the queer machine opened wide. They were set with needle-like points, or teeth. It was all red-hot, and when he removed his hammer the jaws clashed in a shower of sparks.

"It's a trap, of course." I was still puzzled.

"Yes, and a very remarkable one. This trap will not only catch, but it will *re*catch."

"I don't understand."

"If any creature—a man, say"—he was laughing again—"walks into this trap, he may escape it. But sooner or later—soon, I should think—it will catch him again. That is why we call it an elf-trap!"

I perceived suddenly that he was making pure game of me. His mates were all laughing at the nonsense. I moved off, not offended, but perturbed in another way.

He and his absurd, silver trap-toy had reminded me of the gipsies. What a horrible, rough iron thing that was which they had held up to me from their forge! Men capable of creating such an uncouthly cruel instrument as that jag-toothed trap would be terrible to meet in the night. And I had come near blundering in among them—at night!

This won't do. I have been happy. Don't let me drop back into the morbidly nervous condition which invested those gipsies with more than human horror. Elva is calling me. I have been too long alone.

Friday, July 28.

Home again. I am writing this in my bungalow-laboratory. Gray dawn is breaking, and I have been at work here since midnight. Feel strangely depressed. Need breakfast, probably.

Last night Elva and I were together in the court of her father's house. The pool in the center of it is lighted from below to a golden glow. We were watching the goldfish, with their wide, filmy tails of living lace.

Suddenly I gave a sharp cry. I had seen a thing in the water more important than goldfish. Snatching out the small collecting bottle, without which I never go abroad, I made a quick pass at the pool's glowing surface.

Elva had started back, rather frightened.

"What is it?"

I held the bottle up and peered closely. There was no mistake.

"Dysteria," I said triumphantly. "Dysteria ciliata. Dysterius giganticus, to give a unique specimen the separate name he deserves. Why, Elva, this enormous creature will give me a new insight on his entire species!"

"What enormous creature?"

For the first time I saw Elva nearly petulant. But I was filled with enthusiasm. I let her look in the bottle.

"There!" I ejaculated. "See him?"

"Where? I can't see anything but water—and a tiny speck in it."

"That," I explained proudly, "is dysterius giganticus! Large enough to be seen by the naked eye. Why, child, he's a monster of his kind. A fresh-water variety, too!"

I thrust the bottle in my pocket.

"Where are you going?"

"Home, of course. I can't get this fellow under the microscope any too quickly."

I had forgotten how wide apart are the scientific and artistic temperaments. No explanation I could make would persuade Elva that my remarkable capture was worth walking a mile to examine properly.

"You are all alike!" she cried. "All! You talk of love, but your love is for gold, or freedom, or some pitiful, foolish nothingness like that speck of life you call by a long name—and leave *me* for!"

"But," I protested, "only for a little while. I shall come back."

She shook her head. This was Elva in a new mood, dark brows drawn, laughing mouth drooped to a sullen curve. I felt sorry to leave her angry, but my visit had already been preposterously long. Besides, a rush of desire had swept me to get back to my natural surroundings. I wanted the feel of the micrometer adjuster in my fingers, and to see the round, speckled white field under the lens pass from blurred chaos to perfect definition.

She let me go at last. I promised solemnly to come to her whenever she should send or call. Foolish child! Why, I can walk over to Carcassonne every day, if she likes.

I hear Jake rattling about in the breakfast-room. Conscience informs me that I have treated that negro rather badly. Wonder where he thought I was? Couldn't have been much worried, or he would have hunted me up in Carcassonne.

August 30.

I shall not make any further entries in this book. My day for the making of records is over, I think. Any sort of records. I go back to my classes next month. God knows what I shall say to them! Elva!

I may as well finish the story here. Every day I find it harder to recall details. If I hadn't this book, with what I wrote in it when I was—when I was *there*, I should believe that my brain had failed in earnest.

Locke said I couldn't have been in Carcassonne. He stood in the breakfast-room, with the sunlight striking across him. I saw him clearly. I saw the huge, coarse, ugly creature that he was. And in that minute, *I knew*.

But I wouldn't admit it, even to myself. I made him go with me to Carcassonne. There was no stream. There was no bridge. The houses were wretched bungalows, set about on the bare, flat, yellow clay of the mountainside. The people—artists, save the mark!—were a common, carelessly dressed, painting-aproned crowd who fulfilled my original idea of an artists' colony.

Their coarse features and thick skins sickened me. Locke walked home beside me, very silent. I could hardly bear his company. He was gross—coarse—*human!*

Toward evening, managing to escape his company, I stole up the road to the gipsy's grove. The huts were empty. That queer look, as of a flat, dark tapestry, was gone from the grove.

I crossed the plank bridge. Among the trees I found ashes, and a depression where the forge had stood. Something else, too. A dog, or rather its unburied remains. The yellow cur. Its head had been blown off by a shot-gun. An ugly little bell lay in the mess, tied to a piece of string.

One of the trees—it had a smooth trunk—and carved in the bark—I can't write it. I went away and left those two names carved there.

The wild honeysuckle has almost ceased to bloom. I can leave now. Locke says I am well, and can return to my classes.

I have not entered my laboratory since that morning. Locke admires my "willpower" for dropping all that till physical health should have returned. Will-power! I shall never look into a microscope again.

Perhaps she will know that somehow, and send or call for me quickly.

I have drunk the wine and worn the woven robes of her people. They made me one of them. It is right that they should cast me out, because I did not understand what I have since guessed so well?

I can't bear the *human* folk about me. They are clumsy, revolting. And I can't work. God knows what I shall say to my classes.

Here is the end of my last record—till she calls!

There was silence in Locke's private study. At last the doctor expelled his breath in a long sigh. He might have been holding it all that time.

"Great—Heavens!" he ejaculated. "Poor old Tademus! And I thought his trouble in the summer there was a temporary lapse. But he talked like a sane man. Acted like one, too, by Jove! With his mind in that condition! And in spite of the posse, he must have been with the gipsies all that week. You can see it. Even through his delusions, you catch occasional notes of reality.

"I heard of that dog-shooting, and he speaks of being asleep when it happened. Where was he concealed that the posse didn't find him? Drugged and hidden under some filthy heap of rags in one of the huts, do you think? And why hide him at all, and then let him go? He returned the very day they left."

At the volley of questions, Wharton shook his head.

"I can't even guess about that. He was certainly among the gipsies. But as for his delusions, to call them so, there is a kind of beauty and coherence about them which I—well, which I don't like!"

The doctor eyed him sharply.

"You can't mean that you—"

"Doctor," said Wharton softly, "do you recall what he wrote of the silversmiths and their work? They were making an elf-trap. Well, I think the elf-trap—caught him!"

"What?"

Locke's tired eyes opened wide. A look of alarm flashed into them. The alarm was for Wharton, not himself.

"Wait!" said the latter. "I haven't finished. You know that I was in the classroom when Professor Tademus died?"

"Yes."

"Yes! I was first to reach him. But before that, I stood near the desk. There are three windows at the foot of that room. Every other man there faced the desk. I faced the windows. The professor entered, laid down his book and turned to the class. As he did so, a head appeared in one of those windows. They are close to the ground, and a person standing outside could easily look in.

"The head was a woman's. No, I am not inventing this. I saw her head, draped in a blue scarf. I noticed, because the scarf's blueness gave me the strangest thrill of delight. It was the exact blue of the sky behind it. Then she had raised her hand. I saw it. In her fingers was a spray of yellow flowers— yellow as sunshine. She waved them in a beckoning motion. Like this. Then Tademus dropped.

"And there are legends, you know, of strange people, either more or less than human, who appear as gipsies, but are not the real gipsies, that possess queer powers. Their outer appearance is rough and vile, but behind that, as a veil, they live a wonderful hidden life of their own.

"And a man who has been with them once is caught—caught in the real elf-trap, which the smiths' work only symbolized. He may escape, but he can't forget nor be joined again with his own race, while to return among *them*, he must walk the dark road that Tademus went when she called.

"Oh, I've scoffed at 'old wives' tales' with the rest of our overeducated, modern kind. I can't ever scoff again, because—

"What's that? A prescription? For me? Why, doctor, you don't yet understand. I *saw* her, I tell you. Elva! Elva, of the wild honeysuckle and the skylike scarf!"

Serapion

Chapter I

SEAWEED AND A PURPLE VEIL.

It began because, meeting Nils Berquist in town one August morning, he dragged me off for luncheon at a little restaurant on a side street where he swore I should meet some of the rising geniuses of the century.

What we did meet was the commencement for me of such an extraordinary experience as befalls few men. At the time, however, the whole affair seemed incidental, with a spice of grotesque but harmless absurdity. Jimmy Moore and his Alicia! How could anyone, meeting them as I did, have believed a grimness behind their amusing eccentricity?

I was just turned twenty-four that August day. A boy's guileless enthusiasm for the untried was still strong in me, coupled with a tendency to make friends in all quarters, desirable or otherwise. Almost anyone

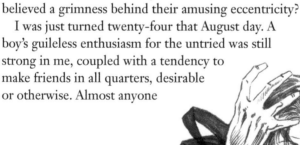

who liked me, I liked. My college years, very recently ended, had seen me sworn comrade to a reckless and on-his-way-to-be-notorious son of plutocracy, while I was also well received in the room which Nils Berquist shared with two other embryo socialists of fanatic dye. A certain ingenuous likableness must have been mine even then, I think, to have gained me not only toleration, but real friendship in both camps.

Berquist, however, was older than I by several years. He had earned his college days before enjoying them and, college ended, he dropped back into the struggle for existence and out of my sight—till I ran across him in town that August day.

To play host even at a very moderate luncheon must have been an extravagance for Nils, though I didn't think of that. He was a man with whom one somehow never associated the idea of need. Tall, lean with a dark, long face, high cheek-bones and deep eyes set well apart, he dressed badly and walked the world in a careless air of ownership that mere clothes could not in the least affect.

His intimates knew him capable of vast, sudden enthusiasms, and equally vast depressions of the spirit. But up or down, he was Nils Berquist, sufficient unto himself, asking no favors, and always with an indefinable air of being well able to grant them.

I admired and liked him, was very glad to see him again, and cheerfully let him steer me around two corners and in the door of his bragged-of trysting-place for incipient genius.

On first entering, my friend cast an eye about the aggregation of more or less shabby individuals present and muttered: "Not a soul here!" in a disappointed tone. Then, glimpsing a couple seated at a corner table laid for four, he brightened a trifle and led me over to them.

Nils's idea of a formal presentation was always more brief than elaborate. After addressing the fair-haired, light-eyelashed, Palm-Beach-suited person on one side of the table as "Jimmy," and his vis-à-vis, a darkly mysterious lady in a purple veil, as "Alicia," he referred to me casually as "Clay," and considered the introduction complete.

I do not mean that the lady's costume was limited to the veil. Only that this article was of such a peculiar, brilliantly, fascinatingly ugly hue that the rest of her might have been clothed in anything from a mermaid's scales to a speckled calico wrapper; I can imagine nothing except a gown of the same color which would have distracted one's attention from that veil.

The thing was draped over a small hat and hung all about her head and face in a sort of circular curtain. Behind it I became aware of two dark, bright eyes watching me, like the eyes of some sea creature laired behind a highly futurist wave. Having met peculiar folk before in Berquist's company, I took a seat opposite the veil without embarrassment.

"Charming little place this," I lied, glancing about the low-ceilinged, semiventilated, architectural container for chairs, tables and genius which formed a background to the veil. "Sorry I didn't discover it earlier."

The dark eyes gleamed immovably from their lair. I essayed a direct question. "You lunch here frequently, I presume?"

No answer. The veil didn't so much as quiver. Even my genial amity began to suffer a chill.

Suddenly "Jimmy" of the Palm Beach suit transferred his attention from Berquist to me. "Please don't try to talk with Alicia," he said. "She is in the silence today. If you draw her out it will disturb the vibrations for a week and make the deuce of a hole in my work. Do you mind?"

With a slight gasp I adjusted myself to the unusual. I said I didn't mind anything.

"You're the right sort, then. Might have known it, or you wouldn't be traveling with old man Nils, eh? What you going to have? Nothing worth eating except the broiled bluefish, and that's scorched. Always is. What you eating, Nils?"

"Rice," said Berquist briefly.

"On the one-dish-at-a-time diet, eh? Great stuff, if you can stick it out. Make an athlete out of a centenarian—*if* you can stick it out. Bluefish for— one or two?" he added, addressing the waiter and myself in the same sentence.

"Two," I smiled. Palm Beach Jimmy seemed to have usurped my friend's role of host with calm casualism. The man's blond hair and faintly yellow lashes and eyebrows robbed his face of emphasis, so that the remarkably square and sloping forehead did not impress one at first. His way of assuming direction of even the slightest affairs about him struck me as easy-going and careless, rather than domineering.

He gave the rest of the order, with an occasional kindly reference to my desires. "And boiled rice for one," he finished.

The waiter cast a curious glance at the purple veil. "Nothing for the lady?" he queried.

"Seaweed, of course," retorted Jimmy. "You're new at this table, aren't you?"

"Just started working here. Seaweed, sir?"

"Certainly. There it is, staring you in the face under 'Salads.' Study your menu, man. That," explained Jimmy, after the waiter's somewhat dazed departure, "is the only reason we come here. One place I know of that serves *rhodymenia serrata*. Great stuff. Rich in mineral salts and vitamins."

"You didn't order any for yourself," I ventured.

"No. Great stuff, but has a horrid taste. Simply—horrid! Alicia eats it as a martyr to the cause. We have to be careful of her diet: Very—careful! Nils, old man, what's the new wrong to the human race you're being so silent over?"

"Can't say without becoming personal," retorted Berquist calmly.

"What? Oh, by Jove, I forgot you don't approve. Still clinging to the sacred barriers, eh?"

"The barriers exist, and they are sacred." Nils's long, dark face was solemn, but as he was capable of cracking the wildest jokes with just that solemn expression, I wasn't sure if the conversation were light or serious. I only knew that as yet I had failed to get a grip on the situation. The man talked about his seaweed-fed Alicia as if the lady were not present.

What curiosity in human shape did that veil hide? One thing I was uneasily aware of. Not once, since the moment of our arrival, had those laired bright eyes strayed from my face.

"The barriers exist," Berquist repeated. "I do not believe that you or others like you can tear them down. If I did, I should be justified in taking your life, as though you were any other dangerous criminal. When those barriers go down, chaos will swallow the world, and the race of men be superseded by the race of madmen!"

Jimmy laughed, unstartled by my friend's reference to cold-blooded assassination. "In the world of science," he retorted, "what one can do, one may do. If every investigator of novel fields had stopped his work for fear of scorched fingers—"

"In the material, physical world," interrupted Berquist, speaking in the same solemn, dogmatic tone, "what one can do, one may do. There the worst punishment of a step too far can be only the loss of life or limb. It is man's rightful workshop. Let him learn its tools at the cost of a cut or so. But the field that you would invade is forbidden."

"By whom? By what?"

"By its nature! A man who risks his life may be a hero, but what is the name for a man who risks his soul?"

"Oh, Nils—Nils! You anachronism! You—you inquisitioner! Here! You say the physical world is open ground—don't you?"

"Yes."

"And that what is commonly referred to as the 'supernatural' is forbidden?"

"In the sense we speak of—yes."

"Very well. Now, where do you draw the fine dividing line? How do you know that your soul, as you call it, isn't just another finer form of matter? A good medium—Alicia here can do it—stretches out a tenuous arm, a misty, wraithy, semiformless limb, and lifts a ten-pound weight off the table while her 'physical' hands and feet are bound so they can't stir an inch. Telikinesis, that is called, or levitation, and you talk about it as if it were done by some sort of supernatural will power."

"Will power, yes; but will actuating matter to move matter. That fluidic arm is just as 'material,' though not so substantial, as your own husky biceps. It's thinner—different. But material—of course it's material! Why, you yourself are a walking case of miraculous levitation. Will moving matter. Will, a superphysical force generated on the physical plane. Where's your fine dividing line? You talk about the material plane—"

"I won't any more," broke in Berquist hastily. "But *you* know that there are entities and forces dangerous to the human race outside of what we call the natural world, and that your investigations are no better than a sawing at the bars of a cageful of tigers. If I thought you could loose them, I have already told you what I would do!"

There was a dark gleam in Berquist's deep-set eyes that suddenly warned me he meant exactly what he said—though the meaning of the whole argument was as hazy to me as the face behind that astounding veil.

Jimmy himself looked sober. "Here comes your rice," he said shortly. "Eat it, you old vegetarian, and get off the murder subject. I'll expect you to be coming around some night with a carving knife, if you say much more."

"There are police to guard you from the carving knife. The wild marches between this world and the invisible are patrolled by no police. Yet you fear the knife which can harm only your body, and fearlessly expose your naked soul!"

"Thanks, old man, but my soul is well able to take care of itself. Eat your rice. There! Didn't I say the bluefish would be scorched? And it is. Behold, a prophet among you!"

The bluefish wasn't worrying me. What I was awaiting was the moment when that miraculously colored veil should be uplifted. Surely, her purple screen removed, the lady would cease to stare me out of countenance.

Before the veil a large platter of straggling, saw-edged, brownish-red leaves had been set down. The dish looked as horrid as Jimmy said it tasted. In a quiver of impatience I waited. At last I should see—

A hand, white, and well shaped, but slender to emaciation, was raised to the veil's lower edge. The edge was lifted slightly. Another hand conveyed a modest forkful of the uncanny edible upward. It passed behind the veil. The fork came away empty.

With a gasping sigh I relinquished hope, and turned my attention to scorched bluefish.

Jimmy may have noted my emotion. "When Alicia is in the silence," he offered, "she has to be guarded. The vibratory rhythm of the violet light waves is less harmful than the rest of the spectrum. Hence, the veil. Invention of my own. You agree with our wild anarchist here, Mr.—er—Clay? Sacred barrierist and all that?"

"My name's Barbour," I said. "Clayton S. Barbour. As for the barriers, I must admit you've been talking over my head."

"So? Don't believe it. Pardon me, but your head doesn't look that sort. Hasn't Nils told you what I'm doing?"

"Nils," said Berquist, with what would have been cold insolence from anyone else, "has something better to do than walk about the world exploiting you to his acquaintances."

"I'm smashed—crushed flat," laughed Jimmy. He seemed one of the most good-humored individuals I had ever met. "Never mind, anarchist. I'll tend to it myself." He turned again to me. "Come to think of it, one of Nils's introductions is an efficient disguise. I'm James Barton Moore."

I murmured polite gratification. For the life of me I couldn't recall hearing the name before. His perception was as quick as his good humor. That ready laugh broke out again.

"Never heard of me, eh? That's a fault of mine—expect the whole world to be thrillingly expectant of results from my work. Ever hear of the Psychic Research Association?"

"Certainly." I looked as intelligent as possible. "Investigate ghosts and haunted houses and all that, don't they?"

"You're right, son. Ghosts and haunted houses about cover the Association's metier. Bah! Do you know who I am?"

"A member?" I hazarded.

"Not exactly. I'm the man the Association forced off its directing board. And I'm also the man who is going to make the Association look like a crowd of children hunting spooks in the nursery. Come around to my place to-night and I'll show you something!"

The invitation was so explosively abrupt that I started in my chair.

"Why—er—" I began.

Nils broke in again. "Don't go," he said coolly.

"Let him alone!" enjoined Moore, but with no sign of irritation. "You drop in around seven—here," he scribbled an address on the back of a card and tossed it across the table, "and I'll promise you an interesting evening."

"You are very good," I said, not knowing quite what to do. I already had an engagement for that evening; on the other hand, my ever-ready curiosity had been aroused.

"Don't go," repeated Berquist tonelessly.

"Thanks, but I believe I will."

"Good! You're the right sort. Knew it the minute I set eyes on you. Don't extend these invitations to everyone. Not—by—any means!"

Berquist pushed back his chair.

"Are you going on with me, Clay?" he inquired.

I thought he was carrying his peculiar style of rudeness rather beyond the boundaries; but he was really my host, so I acquiesced. I took pains, however, to bid a particularly courteous farewell to the eccentric pair with whom we had lunched. I might or might not keep my appointment with Moore, but if I did I wished to be sure of a welcome.

Chapter II.

WARNING.

With me the influence of a personality, however strong, ended where its line of direction crossed the course of my own wishes. Nils's opposition to my further acquaintance with the Moores had struck me as decidedly officious.

Once outside the restaurant, he turned on me almost savagely.

"Clay," he said, "you are not going up there to-night!"

"No?" I asked coldly. "And why not?"

"You don't know what you might be let in for. That is why not."

"You have an odd way of talking about your friends."

"Oh, Moore knows what I think."

"All right," I grinned, not really wishing a quarrel if one could be avoided. "But your friends are good enough for me, too, Nils. Who was the lady in the purple veil?"

"His wife. A physical medium—God help her!"

"Spirit rapping, clairvoyant and all that, eh? I supposed it was something of the sort. Well, if I wish to go out to their place and spend a dollar or so to watch some conjuring tricks, why do you object so strenuously? That's one thing I've never done—"

"Spend a dollar or so!" snapped Berquist. "Those people are not professionals, Clay. Mrs. Moore is one of the few genuine mediums in this country."

"Oh, come! Surely you're not a believer in table-tipping and messages from Marcus Aurelius and Shakespeare?"

Berquist squinted at me disgustedly.

"Heaven help me to save this infant!" he muttered, taking no pains, however, that I shouldn't hear him. "Clay, you go home and stay among your own people. Jimmy Moore is a moderately good fellow, but in one certain line he's as voracious as a wolf and unscrupulous as a Corsican bandit. He told you that he didn't extend these invitations to every one. That is strictly true. The fact that he extended one to you is proof sufficient that you should not accept. He saw in you something he's continually on the watch for. He would use you and wreck you without a scruple."

"How? What do you mean?"

"If I should tell you in what way, you would laugh and call it impossible. But let me say something you can understand. Except casually, Moore is not a pleasant man to know. He would like people to believe that he was dropped from the administrative board of the Association because his investigations and inferences were too daring for even the extraordinary open types of mind which compose it. The real reason was that he proved so violently, overbearingly quarrelsome that even they couldn't tolerate him."

Recalling Moore's impregnable good humor under Nils's own attacks, I began to wonder exactly what was the latter's object in all this.

"I'm not going there to quarrel with him," I said.

"No; you're going to be used by him. Look at that unfortunate little wife of his, if you want a horrible example."

"D' you mean he'd obscure my classic features with a purple veil? There'll be a fight to the finish first, believe me!"

"Oh, that veil-vibration-seaweed business—that's all rot. Just freak results of freak theorizing. Froth and bubbles. It's the dark brew underneath that's dangerous."

"Witch's scene in Macbeth," I chuckled. "Fire burn and caldron bubble! We now see Mr. Jimmy Moore in his famous personation of Beelzebub—costume, one Palm Beach suit and a cheerful grin. Don't worry, Nils! I'll bolt through the window at the first whiff of brimstone."

"My child," said Berquist, very gently and slowly, "you have the joyous courage of ignorance. Alicia Moore is that rare freak, a real materializing medium—a producer of supernormal physical phenomena, as they are called. In other words, she is an open channel for forces which are neither understood nor recognized by the average civilized man. Jimmy Moore is that much more common freak, a fool who doesn't care whose fingers get burnt. The responsibility for having introduced you to those people is mine. As a personal favor, I now ask you to have nothing more to do with either of them."

"Nils, you're back in the dark ages, as Moore claimed. I never thought you'd fall for this spiritualistic bunk."

"Leave that. You are determined to keep the appointment?"

"Come with me, if you think I need a chaperon."

"No," he said soberly.

"Why not?"

"He wouldn't have me. Not when a séance is planned, and that is what he meant by an 'interesting evening.' I'm *persona non grata* on such an occasion, because Alicia says her spirit guides don't like me—save the mark! If I tried to wedge in to-night there would be another row, and Heaven alone knows where the thing would end. I wish you'd stay away from there, Clay!"

"Do you mean," I asked slowly, and beginning to see new light on Nils's attitude, "that you have quarreled with Moore in the past?"

"My dear fellow, get this through your head if you can. It is impossible to know Moore very long and not quarrel with him—or be subjugated. You keep away."

I was growing a little sick of Nils's persistence.

"Sorry. Fear I haven't your faith in the bodiless powers of evil, and I can't say Moore seemed such an appalling person. I'm going!"

Abruptly, without a word of answer or farewell, Berquist turned his back on me and swung off down street. Several times I had seen him end a conversation in that manner, and I knew why. By rights, he should have been the last man to criticize another man's temper.

But I knew, too, that Nils's wrath was generally as evanescent as sudden. He would be friendly as ever next time we met, and even if he were not, I couldn't see why his anger or disapproval should afflict me greatly. Friends were too easily acquired for me to miss one.

I forgot him promptly, and began wondering how my desertion for the evening would be accepted by Roberta Whitingfield.

Chapter III.
THE DEAD-ALIVE HOUSE.

That afternoon I reached home to find Roberta herself on the veranda with my sister Catherine. Rather to my consternation, on hearing of the restaurant encounter, Bert promptly dubbed it, "The Adventure of the Awful Veiled One," and announced her intent to solve the mystery in my company. Catherine seconded the motion, calmly including herself in the party, but there I rebelled.

Roberta and I were to be married one of these days. She was mine to command me, and besides, she had been very good-natured about giving up the concert we had planned attending. But I had the vaguest idea of what Moore's invitation portended, and I knew what would happen if I took both those girls and anything unusual occurred. They would giggle.

We kept Roberta with us for dinner, and when she had gone home to dress, Cathy and I had our argument in earnest. My mother was confined to her room with one of her frequent headaches, and for a while dad hid himself in his paper. Then a grizzled head appeared over the top of it, with a flash of indignant spectacles.

"Cathy," he drawled, "I haven't a notion what this is all about, but wherever Clay is off to, I'm sure they don't want you both. Not together! Clay, my son, I don't wish to be rude, but *if* you are going, won't you please depart at once? Run upstairs, Catherine, and see if all this loud talking has disturbed your mother."

Cathy went. Generally dad sided with her, but she knew better than to oppose him when he used that tone. It meant stoppage of allowance money.

She had been arguing that Roberta's mother, who was from Charleston, South Carolina, and a "St. Cecilian," whatever that is, wouldn't allow her daughter to go with me unchaperoned, engaged or not engaged. The concert? Didn't I know that Bert had come over expressly to find out if she, Cathy, would consent to accompany us?

I had already discovered that St. Cecilians—whatever they are—have rigorous ideas of chaperonage. Consequently I was relieved when on bringing my car to a stop before the Whitingfield place, Roberta came down the steps alone in response to my honking siren.

"Mother says," she explained demurely, "that since we have changed our plans and are to call on a nice married couple like the Moores, we may go alone—this once. Isn't that l-l-lovely?"

I grinned. "Mother is not omniscient, after all!"

"I told her everything but the purple veil and—and fortune-reading part. And of course, she doesn't know you only met them to-day."

"Girl," I retorted sternly, "you are a deceiver—but I like you. Climb in."

Well, after nine o'clock we arrived at the address written across Moore's card. It turned out to be half of a detached double dwelling, standing on a corner beyond a block of quiet, respectable red-stone fronts, with a deep lawn between it and the street.

"Ridiculous house," Bert named it on first sight, and ridiculous house it was in a certain sense. It reminded one of that king in the old fairy tale who "laughed with one side of his face and smiled with the other."

The half that bore Moore's number was neat, shining and of unimpeachable exterior. Its yellow brick front was clean, with freshly painted white woodwork; its half of the lawn, close-clipped and green, was set with little thriving round flower beds.

The other half had the look of a regular old beggar among houses. The paint, weather-beaten, blistered and brown, was no dingier than the dirt-freckled bricks. Two or three windows were boarded up. Not one of the rest but mourned a broken pane or so. From the dilapidated porch wooden steps all askew led to a weed-grown walk. On that side the lawn was a straggling waste of weeds.

Roberta had hopped out of the car without waiting for assistance. I joined her and we stood staring at the queer-looking combination.

"Roberta," I said solemnly after a moment, "there is a grim, grisly secret which I hadn't meant to alarm you with, but perhaps it is better you should be warned now."

"Clay! What do you mean?"

"That house!" My voice was a sinister whisper. "Don't you see? Life and death, or chained to the corpse of his victim! Moore murdered one of twin houses, and now he must live in the other forever as a penance."

To my surprise, instead of laughing at my nonsense, she took my arm with a shiver. "Don't!" she protested. "When you speak so the house isn't funny any more. It's—horrid. A—a dead-alive house! Let's not go in, Clay. We can still attend the concert instead."

"Arriving in time to exit with the audience." I felt annoyed, for this last-moment retreat was not like her. "No, thank you. Come along, Berty, and don't be silly. I suppose one half belongs to Moore and the other to somebody else, and he can't make the other owner keep his half in repair."

After some further discussion, we entered the gate at last. I remember that as we went up Moore's walk, I threw back my head and glanced upward. The moonlight was so white on the slanting house roofs that for just a moment I had an illusion of their being thick with snow.

With snow. Yes, I remembered that illusion afterward.

Moore had expected me alone, of course, but he needn't have made that fact quite so obvious. He met us in his library on the second floor, wither a neat, commonplace maid had ushered us after a glance at my card.

It was a long, rather heavily furnished room, lined with books to the ceiling. Our first view of it noted nothing bizarre or out of the ordinary.

Moore was seated reading, but as we were announced he rose quickly. It was when he perceived Roberta and realized that I had brought a companion that I had my first real doubt that Nils had not exaggerated about the man's temper.

His good-humored, full-lipped mouth seemed to draw inward and straighten to a disagreeably gashlike effect. The skin over his cheek-bones tightened. A pronounced narrowness between the eyes forced itself suddenly upon the attention. For one instant we faced a man disagreeably different from the one who had parried all Berquist's thrusts with unshakable good nature.

As he rose and came toward us, however, the ominous look melted again to geniality. "Began to think old Nils had scared you off in earnest, Barbour," he greeted. "Witch burnings would still be in order if our wild anarchist had his way, eh? I had quite given you up."

"I believe you did mention seven o'clock," I retorted stiffly. A host to whom Roberta's presence, invited or not, was so obviously unwelcome! Rather reluctantly I performed the necessary introduction.

"I had no right to come with him," she apologized. "We meant to attend the Russian Symphony, but when Clayton told me of your invitation, I—we thought—"

"That you might find better amusement here?" Moore finished for her. "That's all right, Miss Whitingfield, though the work I am engaged in is a bit serious to be amusing, I fear. Hope you're not the nervous, screaming sort?" he added, with blunt anxiety.

She flushed a trifle, then laughed. "I'm not—really!" she protested. "But I'll go away if you wish."

That was too much for me. "We'll both leave," I said very haughtily. "Sorry to have put you out, Mr. Moore."

To my astonishment, for I was really angry, he burst out laughing. It was such a genial, inoffensive merriment as caught me unawares. I found myself laughing with him, though at what I hadn't the faintest notion.

"Why, Barbour," he chuckled, "you mustn't take a offense at a lack of conventional mannerisms on my part. I'm a worker—first, last and all the time. Miss Whitingfield, you're welcome as the flowers in May, but I can no more forget my work nor what is likely to affect it than I can forget my own name. You aren't angry with me, are you?"

"N-no—" she began rather hesitatingly, but just then the door opened behind us and we heard some one enter.

"I am here!"

The words were uttered in a dry, toneless voice. We both turned, and

I realized that the "Mystery of the Awful Veiled One" was a mystery no more, or at least had been shorn of its purple drapery.

Of course, I had expected to meet Alicia here, but I think I should have recognized those eyes in any surroundings. They were fully as bright, dark, and almost incredibly large and attentive as they had seemed behind the veil. For the rest, Mrs. Moore's slender figure was draped in filmy, voluminous folds of black, between which and a piled mass of black hair her face gleamed, a peaked white patch—and with those eyes in it.

"Medium" or not, Mrs. Moore herself was more like the creature of another world than any human being I had ever seen.

"Be seated, Alicia."

Without troubling to present Roberta, Moore gestured toward a peculiar-looking chair at one side of the room. The slender creature in black swept toward it obediently. Long and filmy, the train of her somber costume slid past us like a low, twisting trail of dark smoke over the carpet.

Having reached the chair, she turned, faced us for a moment, still expressionless save for those terribly attentive eyes, then sank into the chair's depths. As she did so the filmy folds circled floating about her. It was as though she sank into the depths of a black smoke cloud.

Roberta was frankly staring, and so was I, but my stare had a newly startled quality. Alicia had passed me very closely indeed. My hand still tingled where another hand—a bony, fierce little hand—had closed on it in a swift, pinching clasp. And though I was sure that her colorless lips had not moved, four low words had reached my ears distinctly.

"Go away—*you!* Go."

I glanced at Berty, but decided that she had missed the rude little message. Moore certainly hadn't heard, for he had gone over to the chair and was standing behind it when Alicia reached there.

With a slight shrug I determined that where so much oddity prevailed, this additional eccentricity of Mrs. Moore had better be ignored. To think of her as a real person—my hostess—was made difficult by the atmosphere of utter strangeness which her appearance and Moore's treatment of her had already created.

"You and Miss Whitingfield sit over there," commanded Moore briskly.

"I'll explain what we're about in a minute. You'll be interested. Can't avoid it. A little farther off, Miss Whitingfield—d'you mind? Alicia is more easily affected than other sensitives. More—easily—affected. Right! Now just a moment and I can talk to you."

We had seated ourselves as he directed, I some half dozen feet from the enthroned Alicia, Roberta much farther away, well over by the heavily curtained windows.

To the savage and to the young "strange" is generally synonymous with "funny." We exchanged one quick look, then kept our eyes resolutely apart. A wave of incipient mirth had fairly leaped between us. It was well, I thought, that Cathy had been suppressed.

Then we saw what Moore was doing at the chair, and forgot laughter in amazement. It must be remembered that Roberta and I were innocent of the least previous experience in this line. Save for some hazy knowledge of "spiritualistic fakes" and "mind-reading" of the vaudeville type, we were blankly ignorant, and by consequence as unconsciously receptive as a couple of innocent young sponges. But at first we were merely shocked by the brutal fact of Moore's preparations.

I have said that the chair taken by Alicia was a peculiar one. It stood before a pair of black curtains, which concealed what in spiritualistic circles is called a cabinet. The chair itself was large, heavy, with a high back and uncommonly broad arm-rests. More, it had about it that look of "apparatus" which one associates with dentists' and surgeons' fixtures. Alicia leaned back in it, her hands resting limp on the armrests.

Then up over each fragile wrist Moore clamped a kind of steel handcuff, attached to the chair arm. Another pair of similar fetters, extended on short rods from the back, were clasped around her upper arms, and, as if this were not enough, he locked together the two halves of a wide steel band about her waist.

And his wife sat there, inert as a porcelain doll, her enormous eyes wide open and fixed on me in perfectly unswerving contemplation.

"All really great mediums will trick you if they can," said Moore coolly. "Don't need any object for fraud. Unless you should call the trickery itself an object. Alicia is a great medium. Very—great!"

Suddenly every decent impulse I had rose to revolt. That was a woman in the chair—*Moore's wife*—and he treated her, talked about her, as though she were some peculiarly trained and subject animal.

I rose sharply. "Mrs. Moore, is this affair proceeding with your consent?"

"Don't address the psychic!" snapped her husband over one shoulder.

But I wasn't afraid of him. At that moment I could have thrashed the man cheerfully—and with ease, for I carried no superfluous flesh in those days, and had inches the better of him in height and reach. Roberta was suddenly at my side, and I knew by the excited shine of her eyes that she sensed my emotion and approved it.

"Mrs. Moore," I repeated, "are you enduring this of your own free will? Moore, attempt to intimidate her, and you'll be sorry!"

He straightened, and turned on me in earnest, but Alicia herself broke the strain.

"Sit down, boy," she said in her dry, toneless voice. "What James says of fraud is true. But he does not mean what you think. I am not conscious of what I do in trance, and the self then in control has no moral standards. Were my earthly limbs not bound, no phenomena could be credited, and my own guides have advised the construction of this chair. The steel bands are padded with felt, and do not hurt me. I did not speak to you when I entered, because at some times the guides like me to be silent. This is tiring me. You must not quarrel with James. Violent emotion tires me. A great evil will come to you through me, but now you must sit down and be very quiet. I am tired."

For the first time, white lids drooped over those unnatural eyes. The closing of them seemed to rob her face of the last trace of fellow-humanity. Moore was grinning again, though rather tensely.

"Please sit down, Barbour," he pleaded in a very low voice. "I should have explained a few things to you in advance. Alicia will be asleep directly, and then we can talk."

I did sit down, and Roberta retired to her window. That toneless, indifferent voice of Alicia's, that cool exactitude of statement, had not seemed the expression of a meek and terrorized soul. But if she were not afraid of Moore, why had she been so surreptitious in asking—in ordering me to leave? "I did not speak to you when I entered—" But she had spoken to me. "A great evil will come to you through me—" And she said it like a remark on the weather!

I gave up suddenly. All my curiosity was submerged in a wave of healthy revolt against the obviously abnormal. A vague unhappiness came with it, and the desire above everything to take Roberta and get out.

Alicia was breathing regularly now, in long, deep breaths, soft but audible. Leaving her, Moore drew up a chair between Roberta and me, seated himself, crossed one leg over his knee, and beamed amiably.

"Mr. Moore," I began, but he checked me, finger in air.

"Sh! Trifle lower, please. I know what you're thinking, Barbour, and I don't blame you. Not in—the—least! My fault entirely. Now let's drop all that and forget it. You are two very intelligent people, but I can never remember that the average man or woman knows as much about sensitives as a baby knows of trigonometry. Now, why did I invite you here, Barbour?"

"For an interesting evening, you said."

"Ex-actly! And you'll have it. First of many, I hope. But don't expect any messages from your deceased grandfathers to-night, for you won't get 'em."

"Very well," I assented. "Bert, do you hear that? Our revered ancestors won't speak to us!"

"And don't imagine this is a matter for joking, either," reproved Moore, but still amiably. "I did not say that purely spiritual forces would not be involved. But a psychic—a medium—has all the complexity of the highest type of nervous human—plus. And it's the plus sign that complicates matters. You might get messages through from almost anyone—eventually. You'll seem to get them to-night. But they won't be real. Alicia has more different selves than the proverbial cat has lives. And all wanting a chance to talk, and parade around, and pass themselves off as anybody you'd care to name, from Julius Cæsar to your mother's deceased aunt's nephew. Very—remarkable!"

"I should say so!"

We glanced rather anxiously at Alicia's quiescent figure. But no sudden procession of selves had yet appeared.

"That, however, is beside the mark," announced Moore briskly. "In such commonplace manifestations, Alicia dematerializes a percentage of her own fleshly bulk, externalizes and projects it from her in the shape demanded by her subliminal consciousness. Aside from proving the accepted laws of matter to be false, the phenomena are of small importance."

He paused again.

"I should think," ventured Roberta, carefully avoiding my eyes, "that disproving the laws of matter would be—might be almost enough for one evening."

"The accepted laws," he corrected rather sharply. "Crooks—Oschoro-wicz—Lombroso—Bottazzi—Lodge—I could name you over a dozen great scientists who have already disproved them in that way. But they had only Eusapia Paladino and lesser psychics to work with. We have—Alicia!"

A vague memory stirred in me. "Paladino?" I said. "You mean the famous Italian medium? I thought she was exposed as a fraud."

He frowned. This was a sore subject with him, though I did not know why till much later.

"I tell you," he scowled, "they are all frauds—when they have the chance. The first impulse of hysteria is toward deception. Genuine mediumship and hysteria are practically inseparable. What can you expect? Paladino was as genuine as Alicia, and Alicia will fool you outrageously, given the least opportunity. Quite—scandalously—unscrupulous!"

"You're very frank about it," I couldn't help saying.

"Why not? You heard Alicia's own statement in that regard. She works with me to overcome the disadvantage. Mabel and Maudie are manageable enough, but Horace is a born joker. For a long time Horace fought bitterly against the idea of that chair, and only yielded when I threatened to give up the sittings."

"These people are friends who attend the séances?" I inquired, thinking that Moore had Nils's habit of referring to all his acquaintances by their Christian names.

Moore appeared mildly surprised.

"Don't you really know anything at all of spiritistic investigation?"

"Sorry. I'm afraid I've never had enough faith in spooks to be interested."

"Never mind. We'll correct that!" assured Moore calmly. "Mabel and Maudie and Horace are three of Alicia's spirit guides. She believes them to be real entities of the spirit world—people who have passed beyond, you understand—but I doubt it. Doubt it—very—seriously! In fact, I have reason to be positive that those three, along with several subsidiary 'spirits,' are just so many phases of Alicia's subconscious. On the other hand, Jason Gibbs, her real 'control,' is a spirit to be reckoned with. You will find Jason an amazingly interesting man on acquaintance. And now that I have explained fully, suppose we take a look at the cabinet?"

Roberta and I rose and followed him, not sure whether to be amused or impressed. His statement that he had "explained fully" was a joke, so far as we were concerned. What nebulous ideas of a séance we had possessed were far removed from anything we had met to-night. To sit in a circle, holding hands in the dark; to hear mysterious raps and poundings; to glimpse, perhaps, the cheese-clothy forms of highly fictitious "ghosts"— that had been our previous conception of a "sitting," culled from general and half-forgotten reading.

Moore was so utterly matter-of-fact and unmystical of manner that he probably impressed us more deeply than if he had attempted to inspire awe. And, I reflected, if he were a charlatan, where was his profit? Nils himself had assured me that Mrs. Moore was not a professional medium.

The fact was that I had emerged from college almost wholly ignorant of the modern debate between the physicist and the spiritist—ignorant that science itself had been driven to admission of supernormal powers in certain "victims of hysteria," but stood firm on the ground that these powers were of physical and terrestrial origin.

James Barton Moore, however, was a born materialist who had accepted the spiritistic theory from an intellectual viewpoint. The result showed in his matter-of-fact way of dealing with the occult. He had, moreover, one characteristic of a certain type of scientist in less weird fields. He would have put a stranger or his best friend on the vivisectionary table, could he by that means have hoped to acquire one small modicum of the knowledge he sought.

Figuratively, he already had me on the table that night.

CHAPTER IV.
"HORACE."

On pushing aside the black curtains, the cabinet proved to be a place like a square closet, with a smooth, solid wooden back, built out from the wall. In it there stood a small, rather heavy table, made of polished oak, on which reposed several objects.

There was a thing like a small megaphone, to which Moore referred as the "cone." There was an ordinary thin glass tumbler, nearly filled with water; a lump of soft putty; a sheet of paper blackened by sooty smoke; a pad of ordinary white paper, and several pencils, of different colors and sizes.

"Our preparations to-night," said Moore, "are of the simplest sort. I have passed the stage of registering Alicia's externalized motivity by means of instruments of precision. The exact force exerted to life a weight yards beyond her bodily reach, the regulated rhythm of a metronome's pendulum, the compression of a pneumatic bulb ten feet from her hand—these have all been tested, proved and left behind me. Others have done that with other mediums.

"But I go the step further that Bottazzi and many of the others dared not take. Having admitted the phenomena, I admit a cause for them outside the physical and beyond Alicia's individuality. I admit the disembodied spirit. My experiments are no longer based on doubt, but certainty. Their culmination will mean a revolution for the thinking world—a reversal of its whole stand toward matter and the forces that affect it."

Roberta and I were not particularly interested in revolutions of thought. Like younger children, we wished to know what he proposed doing with the things on the table, and after that we wished to see it done. So we stood silent, hoping that he would stop talking soon and let the exhibition of Alicia's mysterious powers begin.

Being off on his hobby, Moore probably mistook our silence for interest. At last, however, in the midst of a dissertation on "psychic force," "teliki-nesis" and "spiritual controls," he was interrupted by a long, deep sigh from the chair. The sigh was followed by a strangled gasping, very much as though Alicia were choking to death.

We both started toward the chair, but Moore barred the way.

"Let her alone!" he ordered imperatively. "She's all right. Come back to your seats." And when we had returned to our former positions, he added: "She is going into trance now. Later you may approach closer—hold her hands, if you like. But Alicia can't bear even myself to be very near her in the first stages. It hurts her, you understand. Gives her physical pain."

Judging from poor Alicia's appearance, she was in physical pain anyway. Her peaked white face writhed in the most unpleasant contortions. She choked, gasped, gurgled, and showed every symptom of a woman in dying agonies. Then suddenly she quieted, her face resumed its lay-figure calmness, and the great eyes opened wide.

"Differs from most psychics. Opens her eyes in trance. Quite—frequently!" I heard Moore muttering; but Alicia herself began to speak now, and I forgot him.

The queerest, silliest little voice issued from her lips. It was like a child's voice, but an idiot child's.

"Pretty, pretty, pretty!" it gurgled. "Oh, such a pretty lady! Did pretty lady come to see Maudie?" Followed a pause. When it spoke again the voice had a petulant note: "*Did* pretty lady come to see Maudie?"

Moore looked at Roberta. "Why don't you answer her, Miss Whitingfield?"

Before she could comply, however, another personality had apparently superseded the idiot child. A great laugh that I would have sworn was a man's echoed across the silent library. It seemed to come from Alicia's throat.

"Ha, ha, ha! Oh, ha, ha! You've got queer taste, Jimmy Moore! Why d'you want to drag that pair of freaks in here? Tell 'em to go home! Go on home, young fellow, d'you hear? Go on, now—and take the skirt with you!"

"That is Horace," commented Moore imperturbably. "You haven't any manners, Horace, have you?"

"Not a manner!" retorted the voice. "Is that young sport going to leave, or do I have to heave a brick at him? Scat! Get out—*you!*"

This was certainly outside my idea of a séance. It occurred to me abruptly that the voice was not proceeding from Alicia. Some confederate was concealed near by—had entered the cabinet, perhaps, by a concealed door. Or Moore himself was ventriloquizing.

Then I realized that Alicia's eyes were again fixed on my face, and their expression was not that of a woman entranced. They were keen, bright, intelligent. Her lips moved,

"Get! Get out!" adjured that brutally vulgar voice. Then it changed to a whining, female treble: "You are young, Clayton Barbour; young and soft to the soft, cruel hand that would mold you. You are easy to mold as clay—clay—Clayton—clay! Evil hangs over you—black evil! Flee from the damned, Clayton Barbour. *Go home*—you!"

More was frowning uneasily.

"Subliminal," he said shortly. "Pay no attention to these voices. They emanate from the subconscious—Alicia's dream self. Similar to delirium, you know."

"Ah!" I murmured, and settled back in my chair. Not that I agreed with Moore, though I had dismissed thought of either a confederate or my host's ventriloquism. The ventriloquist was Alicia herself. I had no doubt that she could have caused the voices to sound from any quarter of the room as easily as from her own throat. As for trance, her eyes were entirely too wakeful and intelligent. Nearly everything said so far had been mere repetition, in different phrases and voices, of that first, brief, fierce little demand that I leave.

But by the time I was more than a trifle annoyed. It was hardly pleasant to sit in Roberta's presence and hear rude puns made on my name—to hear it implied that I was a mere nonentity with no character of my own. I rather plumed myself that Alicia would not find me so pliable. If she really wished me to depart, she had gone the wrong way about it.

"Ah," I said, settled back, and—the vulgarity of "Horace" may have been contagious—deliberately winked at Alicia. It was a crude enough act, but her methods struck me as crude, too.

A blaze of fury leaped into those too-attentive eyes. Her features writhed in such an abominable convulsion as I had never believed possible to the human countenance. Purple, distorted, terrible—with a flashing of bone-white teeth—and out of it all a voice discordant, and different from any we had heard.

"Fool—fool—fool!" it grated. "Protect—try—can't protect fool! Slipping—it's got me—I'm slip—Oh-h-h! Oh-h-h-h!"

Even Moore seemed affected this time. We were all on our feet, and he was beside his wife in three long strides. As the last, long-drawn moan died away, however, the dreadful purple subsided from Alicia's countenance as quickly as it had risen. She was again the queer, white porcelain doll, leaning back with closed lids in her imprisoning chair.

Moore straightened, wiped his forehead, and laughed shakily.

"Do you know," he said, "with all the experience I've had, Alicia still gives me an occasional fright? But I never saw her pass into the second stage quite so violently!"

"Don't these horrible convulsions hurt your wife, Mr. Moore?"

Roberta was deeply distressed, and no wonder! I felt as if I had brought her to watch the seizures of an epilept.

"She says they don't," replied Moore. "But—never mind that. Listen!"

Alicia's lips writhed whitely. "Light!" came her barely audible whisper.

Promptly Moore reached for a wall button. Two of the three lights burning went out. The third was a shaded library lamp on a table not far off. I expected him to extinguish that also, for everything in the room was plainly visible, but he let it be.

"You may hold Alicia's hands, if you wish," he offered generously.

We shook our heads. Presently the hushed whisper was heard again.

"Many shadows are here to-night," it said. "Shadows living and dead. Dead-alive and living dead. They crowd close. An old, old shadow comes. Blood runs from his lean, gnarled throat. He speaks!"

The whisper became a ghastly, bubbling attempt at articulation. There were no words. The result was just an abominable sound.

"Man with his throat cut might speak like that," observed Moore reflectively. "She must mean old Jenkins, who was murdered next door. That's the reason we have this house, you know. The other half's supposed to be haunted—and is."

Now I wanted to get out in earnest. Fraud or epilept, Alicia was entirely too horrible, and Moore, with his calmness, almost worse. I tried to draw Roberta toward the door, but she held back.

"Not yet, Clay. I wish to see what will happen."

Now the horrid gurgle had merged into a man's voice. It was loud and distinct as "Horace's," but otherwise slightly different—as different, say, as tenor from high baritone.

"I am Jason Gibbs," it asserted. "Mr. Moore, will you kindly ask your friends to step back a little? We will do what we can for you, but my fellow spirits are a trifle shy of strangers."

More motioned us back. At the same time he shook his head smilingly.

"That's not Jason," he murmured. "A very good imitation, but an imitation, nonetheless. We sha'n't get much to-night."

"And in that," retorted the tenor, "you are exactly mistaken! You will get much. In fact you are likely to get more than one of you ever bargained for. You say I'm not Jason Gibbs? Seeing is believing, isn't it? Shall I show myself?"

Moore acquiesced smoothly. "Do so, by all means."

"I'll attend to that in a little while. I can read your mind all right, Jimmy Moore! You think I'm Horace talking high. Well, Horace is a very good fellow, and fond of his joke, but I'm Jason Gibbs to-night—and all the time, of course! Like to see something pretty?"

"Anything at all, Hor— Pardon me—Jason!"

"Then watch the cabinet."

We did. For a minute or two nothing happened.

Then Roberta cried out: "It's on fire!"

"No," said Moore. "Watch!"

A strange, tiny flame was running along the edge of the black curtains where they touched the floor.

When I say "running along," I do not mean that in the usual sense as applied to fire. It was a tiny, individual flame, violet in color, about an inch and a half high, and as it moved it twirled and spun on its own base in the oddest manner. Reaching the center, where the curtains joined, it floated slowly upward, still twirling, left the cabinet and presently disappeared, apparently through the ceiling. Another flame and another followed it.

I assured myself that we were watching a very clever and unusual exhibition of fireworks. But I didn't believe that. I didn't know exactly what I believed, but I did know that those twirling, violet flames were the first really strange thing I had ever seen in my life. When seven of them had appeared and vanished, Moore spoke.

"Isn't that enough—er—Jason? Can't you do better than that for us?"

There was silence, while the eighth and last flame twirled upward and vanished. Then that great, rough laugh burst startlingly from Alicia's lips.

"Ha, ha, ha! Ha, ha! Oh, Jimmy Moore, I should say I can do better! I should say so!"

And with that the curtains parted suddenly and—it is hard to tell, but it was harder to stand the shock of it—a huge, misshapen, *grayish-black hand* darted out from between them.

Behind it I caught a glimpse of wrist—I couldn't see any arm. It just leaped out and into existence, as one might say, and to my unspeakable horror laid its gross, gnarled fingers fairly across Roberta Whitingfield's mouth and chin.

I believed it had seized her throat. Half mad with shock, I sprang at the hand, gripping it in both of mine. I felt a kind of cold roughness in my grasp—a rough solidity that melted to nothing even as I touched it. My hands were empty. I caught Roberta, as she swayed backward, whiter than Alicia herself.

And Moore was reproving—something, in the most everyday manner.

"Really, Horace, that wasn't a nice joke at all!" he criticized.

Easing Roberta into a chair, I sprang savagely at the curtains and swept them aside. Behind there was only the table and what we had seen on it. I had a fleeting impression that the lump of putty was different—that, where it had been a formless lump, it appeared now as if it had been squeezed between giant fingers. Then Moore was pulling me back.

"Don't do that, Barbour. We sha'n't get anything more, if you interfere like that."

"Devil!" It was all I could think of to call him, and it seemed inadequate enough. "You—devil! To play a trick like that on an unsuspecting girl! Bert, darling, come, I'll take you home; then I'll come back and settle with these people!"

"Barbour, I give you my word of honor that I had nothing to do with what just occurred. You brought Miss Whitingfield here of your own volition, and—pardon me—against my wishes. But she assured me she was not of the nervous type—"

"Nervous!" I repeated scornfully. "A really nervous woman would have died when that black paw flew out at her!"

"I'm not hurt, Clayton," intervened Roberta. "Don't quarrel with him—please!"

"You are sensible," approved Moore. "There is no danger from such manifestations as that hand. Why, I have taken a peep into the cabinet when the power was strong and seen half a dozen human limbs and parts of limbs lying about—fragmentary impulses, as one might say, of the mediumistic force—"

But here, with marked decision, Roberta rose.

"I think we will go home, Clay. I have just discovered that I am of the nervous, screaming sort! Mr. Moore, will you please say good-night for us to Mrs. Moore when she—when she wakens?"

He sighed disappointedly.

"It's too bad, really! If Jason Gibbs had actually been in control to-night there would have been nothing to shock you. Horace is nothing. Just a secondary, practical-joking phase of Alicia's own personality."

"Come, Roberta." We started toward the door.

And then, without a warning flicker, the library lamp went out, leaving the room in impenetrable darkness.

Chapter V.
THE FIFTH PRESENCE.

The difference between light and the lack of it is the difference between freedom and captivity, and the real reason that we pity a blind man is because he is a prisoner. This is true under normal conditions. Add to darkness dread of the supernatural, and the inevitable sum is panic.

Till that moment I doubt if Roberta or I had believed the black hand which touched her to be of other than natural origin. Ingrained thought-habit and accused Moore of trickery, even while it condemned the trick as unpleasant.

That was while the light burned. One instant later we were trapped prisoners of the dark, and instincts centuries old flung off thought-habit like a tissue cloak.

What had been a quiet, modern room became, in that instant, the devil-haunted jungle of forebears infinitely remote.

And it didn't help matters that just then "Horace" elected to be heard again. Alicia visible, Horace had seemed a vocal feat on her part. Alicia unseen, Horace became a discarnate fiend. That he was a fiend, vulgar and incongruous, only made his fiendishness more intolerable.

"How's this for a joke?" it inquired sardonically. "I never did like that lamp! Let's give it away, Jimmy. Tell your young fool friend to take the lamp away with him."

Soundlessly, without warning, something hard and slightly warm touched my cheek. I struck out wildly. My fist crashed through glass, there was a great smash and clatter from the floor, and mingled it with shout upon shout of fairly maniacal mirth. Then Moore's voice, cool but irritated:

"You'll have to stop these tricks, Horace. I'm ashamed of you! Breaking a valuable lamp like that. Our guests will believe you a common spirit of poltergeist!"

"Moore, if you don't throw on the lights, I'll kill you for this!"

My own voice shook with mingled rage and dread. Of course, it might be he who had brought the lamp and held it against my face, but the very senselessness of the trick made it terrible in a queer, unhuman way.

"Stand still!" he commanded sharply. "Barbour, Miss Whitingfield, you are not children! Nothing will harm you, if you keep quiet. It was your own yielding to anger and fear that brought this crude force into play. Did it actually hit you with the lamp, Barbour?"

"I hit the lamp, but—"

"Exactly! Now keep quiet. Horace, may I turn on the lights?"

"If you do, you'll be sorry, Jimmy! Call me poltergeist or plain Dutch, there's somebody worse than me here to-night."

"What do you mean, Horace?"

"Oh, somebody that came in along with your scared young friends. He's a joker, too, but I don't like him. He wants to get through the gates altogether, and stay through. If he does, a lot of people will be sorry. You say I'm rough, but say, Jimmy, this fellow is worse than rough. He's smooth! Get me? Too smooth. I'm keeping him back, and you know I'm stronger in the dark."

"Very well." I heard Moore laugh amusedly. His quiet matter-of-courseness should have deleted all terror from the affair. He was carrying on a conversation with a rather silly, rather vulgar man, of whom he was not afraid, but whose vagaries he indulged for reasons of expediency. That was the sound of it.

But the *sense* of it—there in the blackness—was such an indescribable horror to me as I cannot convey by words. There was more to this feeling than fear of Horace. I learned what nerves meant that night. If mine had all been on the outside of my skin, crowling, expectant of shock, I could have suffered no more keenly. Coward? Wait to judge that till you learn what the uncomprehended expectancy meant for me.

"Very well, laughed Moore. "But don't break any more lamps, Horace—please! Have some consideration for my pocketbook."

"Money! We haven't any pants-pockets my side of the line," Horace chuckled. "If I'm to keep the smooth fellow back, you must let me use my strength. Let me have my fun, Jimmy! What's a lamp or so between pals? And just to keep things interesting, *suppose we bring out the big fellow in the closet?*"

I heard a thud from the direction of the cabinet, a low chuckle, and then a huge panting sound. It sounded like an enormous animal. We had a sense of something living and enormous that had suddenly come out of nothing into the room.

"The hand!" screamed Roberta sharply. "It's the black-hand thing!"

I was hideously afraid that she was right. With her own clutching little hands on my arm, I sprang, dragging her with me. I didn't spring for where I thought Moore was, nor for where I supposed the door might be. There were only two thoughts in my head. One of a monstrous and wholly imaginary black giant; the other, a passionate desire for light.

By pure chance I brought up against the wall just beside a brass plate inset with two magical, blessed buttons. My fingers found them. Got the wrong button—the right one.

Flash! And we were out of demon-land and in a commonplace room again.

Not quite commonplace, though. True, no black, impossible giant inhabited it. The vast panting sound had passed, and though the lamp lay among the splinters of its wrecked shade and my hand was bleeding, a broken lamp and cut hand are possible incidentals of the ordinary.

But that woman in the chair was not!

Writhing, shrieking, foaming creatures like that have their place in a hospital—or a sick man's delirium—but not rightfully in an evening's entertainment for two unexpectant young people. Bert took one look and buried her face against my vest in an ecstasy of fear.

Moore was beside his wife, swiftly unclasping the steel manacles that held her, but finding time for a glaring side-glance at me which expressed white-hot and concentrated rage.

I didn't understand. Alicia's previous spasms or seizures, though less violent than this, had been bad enough. Why should Moore eye me like that, when if any one had a right to be furious it was I?

"The lights!" moaned Bert against my vest. "You turned on the lights, and it hurt her. I've read that somewhere— Oh, Clay, why don't you do something to help her and make her stop that horrible screaming?"

Moore heard and turned again, snarling. "You get out of here, Barbour! You've done harm enough!"

"Sha'n't I—sha'n't we call a doctor?" I stammered.

He didn't answer. Released, Alicia had subsided limply, a black heap in the chair, face on knees. The gurgling shrieks had lowered to a series of long, agonizing moans. I thought she was dying, and in a confused way I felt that both Roberta and Moore blamed me.

The moans, too, had ceased. Was she dead?

Now Moore was trying to lift his wife out of the chair—and failing, for some reason. Instinctively I pushed Roberta aside and moved to help him.

And then, at last, that happened for which all the rest had been a prelude—for which my whole life and been a prelude, as I was to learn one day. There came—how can I phrase it?

It was not a darkness, for I saw. It was not a vacuum, for most certainly I—every one of us—continued to breathe. It was like—you know what happens sometimes in a thunderstorm? There is a hushed moment, when it is as if a mighty, invisible being had drawn in its breath—not breath of air, but of *force*. If you live in the suburbs and have alternating current, the lights go out—as if the current had been sucked back.

Static has the upper hand of kinetic. A moment, and kinetic will rebel in a blinding, crashing river of fire from sky to earth. But till then, between earth and clouds there is a tension so terrific that it gives the awful sense of a void.

That happened in the room where we stood, though the force involved was not the physical one of electricity. There was the hushed moment, the sense of awful tension—of void—of strength sucked back like the current—

Without knowing how, I became aware that all the life in the room was suddenly, dreadfully centralizing around one of us. That one was Alicia.

I saw Moore move back from her. He had gone ghastly pale, and he waved his hands queerly. The straining sense of void which was also centralization increased. A numbness crept over me.

The invisible had drawn in its breath of pure force, and my life was undoubtedly a part of it.

There came a stirring of the black heap in the chair. Inexplicably, I felt as well as saw it. As if, standing by the wall, I was also in the chair. Roberta shivered. She was out of my sight, standing slightly behind me, but I felt that, too. No two of us there were in physical contact, and yet some strange interfusion of consciousness was linking us more closely than the physical.

Again Alicia stirred. She cried out inarticulately. The centralization was around her, but not by her will. I felt a surge of resentment that was not mine, but Alicia's. Then I knew that there were more than four of us present in the room. A fifth was here—invisible, strong, unifying the strength of us all for its own purpose—for a leap across the intangible barriers and into the living world—

Numbness was on me, cold dread, and a sense of some danger peculiarly personal to myself.

It was coming—now—now—

With another cry, Alicia shot suddenly erect. Her arms went out in a wide sweep that seemed to be struggling in an attempt to push something from her.

"Serapion!" she cried, and: "You! Back! Go back—go back—go back—Oh, *you, Serapion!*"

When kinetic revolts against static, blinding fire results.

The tension in that room, *let go* as suddenly as the lightning stroke, though I was the only one to feel it fully.

My body reeled against the wall. My spirit—I—the ego—reeled with it—beyond it—down—down—into darkness absolute—and into a nullity deeper than darkness's self.

Chapter VI.

THE POWER OF A NAME.

Speed. In outer space there is room for it, and necessity. Between our sun and the nearest star where one may grow warm again there is space that a light ray needs centuries to cross.

The cold is cruel, and a wind blows there more biting than the winds of earth. Little, cold stars rush by like far-separated lamps on a country road, and double meteors, twin blazing eyes, swing down through the long, black reaches. It is hard to avoid these, when they sweep so close, and one's hands are numb on the steering-wheel.

But one can't slow for that—nor even for a frightened voice at one's elbow, pleading, protesting, begging for the slowness that will let the cold overtake and annihilate us.

"The cold!" I shouted against the wind. "Cold!"

"Well, if you're cold," wailed the harassed voice, "why don't you slow down? Clay! Clayton Barbour! I'll never ride again in a car with you, Clayton, if you don't slow down!"

Another pair of twin meteors rushed curving toward us. We avoided them, kept our course by the fraction of a safe margin, and as we did so the limitless vistas of interstellar space seemed to close in sharply and solidify.

Infinite shrank to finite with the jolt of a collision—and it was almost a real one. I swung to the left and barely avoided the tail of a farmer's wagon, ambling sedately along the road ahead of us. Then I not only slowed, but stopped, while the wagon creaked prosaically by. I sat at the wheel of a motor-car—my own car—and that was Roberta Whitingfield beside me.

"Sixty miles an hour!" She was saying indignantly. "You haven't touched the siren once, and you are sitting so that I can't get at it. It's very fortunate that mother didn't come! She would never let me ride with you again!"

I said nothing. Desperately I was trying to adjust the unadjustable.

This road was real. The numbness and chill were passing, and the air of a summer night blew warm on my cheek. That wild rush of the spirit through space was already fading into place as a dream memory.

But there had been some kind of an hiatus in realities. My last definite memory was of—Alicia Moore. Alicia—upright—rebellious—crying out a name.

"*Serapion!*"

"Clay!" A note of concern had replaced Roberta's indignation. "Why do you sit there so still? Answer me! Are you ill? What is the matter?"

"Nothing."

That was a lie, of course, but instinctive as self-protection. I must get straight somehow, but I wouldn't confide the need even to Roberta. In the most ordinary tone I apologized for my reckless driving and started the car again. We were on a familiar road, outside the city, but one that would take us by roundabout ways to our home in the suburbs.

I drove slowly, for it was very necessary that Roberta should talk. By listening I might be able to get straight without betraying myself, and indeed, before we reached home, I had a fairly clear idea of what had happened in the blank interim.

A first wild surmise that the Moore episode had been a dream in its entirety was banished almost at once. As nearly as I could gather, without direct questioning, from the time when I reeled back against the wall until my return to self-consciousness some sixty minutes later, I had behaved so normally in outward appearance that not even Roberta had seen a difference.

My body had evidently not fallen to the floor, nor showed any signs of fainting or swoon. Alicia seemed to have returned to her senses at the same time that I lost mine, for Roberta spoke of her hostess's quiet air of indifference that amounted almost to scorn for the concern that we—Bert and *I*, mind you!—expressed for her.

Moore, for his part, it seemed, had recovered his temper and been rather apologetic and anxious that I, at least, should repeat my visit. I had been non-committal on the subject—for which Roberta now commended me—and then we had come away together.

After that, the hallucination I had suffered, of myself as a disembodied entity, careering from one planetary system to another, had synchronized with an actual career in the car where road-lamps simulated stars and occasional motors traveling in the opposite direction provided the stimuli for my dream-meteors.

A man hypnotized might have done what I did, and as successfully. To myself, then, I said that I had been hypnotized. That in a manner yet to be explained either Moore or his wife had hypnotized me and allowed me to leave their house under that influence. I tried to determine what reckoning I should have with them later. But it was a failure. I was frankly scared.

An hour had been jerked bodily out of my conscious life. If, in the ordinary and orthodox manner, I had lain insensible through that hour, it wouldn't have mattered so much. Instead of that, an I that was not I appeared to have taken charge of my affairs and in such a manner that a person very near and dear to me had perceived nothing wrong. It was that which frightened me.

As the last traces of daze and shock released my mind, the instinct to keep its lapse a secret only grew stronger. Fortunately I found concealment easy. Speeding was not so far from my occasional habit that Roberta had thought much of that part of the episode. Her vigorous protests had been largely on account of my failure to use the siren.

Dropping that subject with her usual quick good-nature, she talked of our remarkable first experience with a "real medium," and disclosed the fact—not surprising, perhaps—that she had been considerably less impressed than I. In retrospect she blamed her own nerves for most of the excitement.

"I may be unfair, Clay," she confided, "but truly, I can't help believing that Mrs. Moore is just a clever, hysterical woman who has deluded poor Mr. Moore into a faith in 'spirit voices.' "

"The black hand? The little flames?"

"Did we really see them? Don't you think the woman may have some kind of hypnotic power, like—oh, like the mango trick that everybody's heard they do in India? You know. A tree grows right up out of the ground while you watch; but it doesn't, really, of course. You're hypnotized, and only think you see it. Couldn't everything we saw and heard to-night have been a—a kind of hypnotic trick? And—now, with all the screaming and fuss she had made, Mrs. Moore was so calm and cool when we left! I think it was all put on, and the rest was hypnotism."

"You're a very clever little girl, Bobby," I commended, and meant it. If there was one thing I wished to believe, it was that Alicia Moore had faked.

We knew nearly as little about hypnotism as we did of psychic phenomena, real or so-called. But the word had a good sound to me. I had been hypnotized. Hypnotized! That Fifth Presence in the room had existed only in my own overborne imagination. The whole affair was—

"Berty," I said, "we've been through a highly unpleasant experience, and it's my fault. Nils warned me against those people, but I was stubborn mule enough to believe I wished to know more of them. I don't, and we don't—you and I. The truth is, girly, I feel pretty foolish over the whole business. Had no right to take you to such a place. Downright dangerous— queer, irresponsible people like that! Say, d'you mind not telling Cathy, for instance?"

"If you won't tell mother!"

She giggled. I could picture myself relating that weird and unconventional tale to the stately St. Cecilian! Up went my right hand.

"Hear me swear! I, Clayton S. Barbour, do solemnly vow silence—"

"Full name, or it isn't legal!" trilled the girl beside me.

"Oh, very well! I, Clayton Serapion Barbour, do—"

"I stopped with a tightening of the throat. As the word "Serapion" passed my lips, the Fifth Presence had shut down close about me.

Out of space—time—wrapped away in cloudy envelopes of oblivion—

"Clayton!" A clear young voice out of the clouds. They shriveled to nothing, and I was loosed to my world again. "Why, Clayton!" repeated Roberta. "How did that woman know your middle name?"

My right hand dropped to the wheel, and the car leaped forward.

"Did you tell her?" insisted Roberta.

"No," I answered shortly. "Berquist told Moore, I suppose. How do I know?"

"Some one must have told her," Bert agreed. "It isn't as if it were an ordinary name that she might have hit on by guess-work."

"Oh, it isn't so unusual. There have been Ser— There have been men of that name in my mother's family for generations. I was given the name in remembrance of my mother's brother. He died only a few months before I was born, and she had cared a lot for him. But don't let's talk of the name any more. I always hated it. Sounds silly—like a girl's name—I—I— Oh, forget the name! Here we are at home, and there's your mother in the window looking for us."

"We're awfully late!"

"Tell her the Moores were very interesting people," I suggested grimly.

That night, though I slept, Alicia Moore and the Fifth Presence—in various unpleasant shapes—haunted me through some exceedingly restless hours.

CHAPTER VII.

THE COMING OF THE FACE.

That a man may retire to his bed unknown and wake up famous is a truism of long standing. There is a parallel truth not half so pleasant. A man—a whole family—may retire wealthy and wake up paupers.

My father was the practically inactive senior member of his firm, and the reins had so far left his hands that when the blow fell it was hard for him to get a grasp on the situation or even credit it.

Rather shockingly, the first word we had of disaster came through the morning paper in a blare-headed column announcing the suicide of Frederic Hutchinson. Suicide without attempt at concealment. A scrub-woman, entering the private offices of Barbour & Hutchinson early that morning, had fairly trodden in the junior partner's scattered brains.

There followed a week of torment—of sordid revelations and ever increasing despair. A week that left dad a shaken, tremulous old man, and the firm of Barbour & Hutchinson, grain brokers, an unpleasant problem to be dealt with by the receivers.

Dad had known his partner for a clever man, and no doubt he was formerly a trustable one. But when the disease called speculation takes late root, its run is likely to be more virulent than in a younger victim. All Hutchinson's personal estate had been absorbed. His family were left in worse predicament than ours—or would have been, save that dad's peculiar sense of honor cast every cent he owned, independent of the firm, into the pit where that firm's honor had vanished.

Unfortunately he possessed not nearly enough to satisfy the creditors and reestablish the business. As my mother pointed out, the disgrace that had been all Fred Hutchinson's was now dad's for impoverishing his family when, under the terms of partnership and the law of our State, most of his personal investments and realty could have been held free from liability.

And to that dad had only one, and to my mind somewhat appalling, reply:

"Let Clay go to work in earnest, then. Perhaps some day my son will clear the slate of what scores I've failed to settle!"

Well, great God, can a young fellow carefully trained to have everything he wants without trying turn financial genius in a week?

If it hadn't been for Roberta, I think I should have thrown up the sponge and fairly run away from it all. Her faith, though, stirred a chord of ambition that those of my own blood failed to touch, and her stately Charlestonian mother emerged from stateliness into surprising sympathy.

Then Dick Vansittart, the unregenerate youngster who had been my dearest pal in college days, got me a job with the Colossus Trust Company, the bank of which his father was president and where he himself loafed about intermittently.

Even I knew that the salary offered was more commensurate with our needs than with what I was worth. Vansittart, Sr., a gruff old lion of a man, growled at me through a personal interview which ended in: "You won't earn your salt for six months, Barbour, but maybe Terne can put up with you. Try it, anyway!"

Terne was the second vice-president, whose assistant, or secretary, or general errand-boy, it was proposed that I become. I reached for my hat.

"Sorry to have bothered you, Mr. Vansittart! I would hardly care to receive pay except on the basis that it was earned."

The lion roared.

"Sit down! Don't you try Dick's high mannerisms with me! If I can tolerate Dick in this bank, I can tolerate you; but there's going to be one difference. You'll play the man and work till you do earn your wages, or you'll go out! Understand?"

"I merely meant—"

"Never mind that." The savage countenance before me softened to a leonine benevolence. "Clayton Barbour's son wants no charity, but, you young fool, don't I know that? Your father has swamped himself to pay debts that weren't his. Now I choose to pay a debt that isn't mine, but Dick's!"

I must have looked my bewilderment.

"I mean," he thundered, "that when my son was expelled from the college he disgraced he nearly took you with him! You cubs believe you carry your shame on your own shoulders. You never think of us. I've crossed the street three times to avoid meeting your father—I! Earn your wages here, so that

I can shake hands with him next time. Here—take this note to Mr. Terne. His office is next the cashier's. Go to work!"

I went, but outside the door found Van waiting for me, smiling ironically. "You heard?" I muttered.

"Not being stone deaf, yes. The governor doesn't mind publicity where I'm concerned, eh? Interested passers-by in the street might hear, for all he cares. Oh, well—truth is mighty and must prevail! Wish you luck, Clay, and there's Fatty Terne coming now. So-long!"

I was left to present my note to a dignified person who had just emerged from the cashier's office. "Fatty" was a merciless nickname for him, and unfair besides. The second vice-president's large figure suggested strength rather than overindulgence. Beneath his dignity he proved a kindly, not domineering man, much overworked himself, but patient with early mistakes from a new helper.

He shared one stenographer with another official, and seemed actually grateful when I offered to learn shorthand during spare hours in order to be of more use with the correspondence. I was quite infected with the work fever for a while, and saw little of Van, who let me severely alone from the first day I entered the bank.

His new standoffishness didn't please me exactly, but I was too busy to think much of him one way or the other. At home, however, things went not so well. Since the house had been sold over our heads, we were forced into painfully small quarters. There was a little place near by that belonged to my mother. It had stood empty for a year, and though not much better than a cottage, her ownership of it solved the rent problem, and, as she bitterly explained, we no longer needed servants' rooms nor space for the entertainment of guests.

Mother and Cathy undertook the housework, while dad fooled about with paint-pots and the like, trying to delude himself into the belief that paint, varnish, and a few new shelves here and there would make a real home for us out of this wretched shack; for that is what Cathy and I called it privately.

All the problems of home life had taken on new, ugly, uncomfortable angles, and I spent as little time among them as I decently could.

Roberta had no more complaints to make of "sixty miles an hour and never touched the siren." My car had gone with the rest. We went on sedate little walks, like a country pair, tried to prefer movies to grand opera, and piled up heart-breaking dream-castles for consolation.

Two months slid by, and in that while our adventure at the "dead-alive house," as Roberta had named Moore's place, was hardly mentioned between us. Once or twice, indeed, she referred to it, but there was for me an oppressive distastefulness in the subject that made me lead our conversations elsewhere.

On the very heels of Barbour & Hutchinson's catastrophic passing I had received a brief note from Moore. He expressed concern and sympathy, adding in the same breath, as it were, that he hoped I had been "well enough interested the other evening to wish to walk farther along the path of psychical research."

I regarded his concern as impertinent and his hope as impudent, considering my unpleasant memories of the first visit. I tore the letter up without answering it. After that I heard no more from him, and it was not until the second month's ending that a thing occurred which forced the whole matter vividly upon my recollection.

"If dear Serapion had not been taken from us," said my mother, "we should be living in a civilized manner, and my children and I would not have been driven to actual labor with our hands!"

Dad kept his eyes on his plate, refraining from answer. He had been guilty of an ill-advised criticism on Cathy's cooking, and, from that, discussion had run through all the ramifications of domestic misery until I was tempted to leave dinner unfinished and escape to my usual refuge, the Whitingfields.

But the mention of my uncle's name had a peculiar effect on me. A slight swimming sensation behind the eyes, a gripping tightness at the back of my neck—*Serapion!*

The feeling passed, but left me trembling so that I remained in my place, fearing to rise lest I betray myself. As before, some deep-seated instinct fought that. The weakness was like a shameful wound, to be at all costs hidden.

"Had he lived," continued my mother, "he would have seen to it that we weren't brought to this. No one near poor Serapion was ever allowed to be uncomfortable!"

Dad's eyes flashed up with a glint of spirit that he had never before showed in this connection.

"Is that so? I know he kept remarkably comfortable himself, but I can't recall his feathering any one's nest but his own."

"Don't slander the dead!" came her sharp retort. "Why, you owe the very house over your head to him! And if it hadn't been that his thoughtfulness left it in my name you wouldn't have that. You would have robbed your children and me of even this pitiful shelter—"

"Evelyn—please!"

"It's true! And then you dare cast slurs and innuendoes at my dead brother!"

"I gave him the house in the first place," dad muttered.

She rose, eyes flashing and filled with tears. "Yes, you did! And this shameful little hole was all he had to live in—and die in! Serapion was a saint!" she declared. "A saint! He was—he was universally *loved!*"

And with that, my mother swept from the room. Cathy followed, though with a sneaking glance of sympathy for dad. Tempestuous exits on mother's part had been frequent as far back as I could remember, and as they were invariably followed by hours in which some one must bathe her head with cologne and the house be kept dead silent, we other three had the fellow-feeling of victims.

Dad eyed me across the table. "Son," he said, "what is your middle name?"

"Ser—Ser—Samuel!" I ended desperately. My heart, for no obvious reason, had begun a furious palpitation. Why couldn't they let that name alone?

He looked surprised, and then laughed.

"You are right, son! I was about to give you warning—to forbid your becoming such a saint as your esteemed namesake. But I guess that isn't needed. The Samuels of the world stand on their own feet, as you do now, thank God! A Samuel for the Serapion in you, then, and never forget it!"

"I won't sir."

He could not guess the frantic struggle going on beneath my calm exterior. There is, I believe, a psychopathic condition in which sound-waves produce visual sensations; a musical note, for example, being seen as a blob of scarlet, or the sustained blast of a bugle as a ribbony, orange-colored streak. Some such confusion of the senses seemed to have occurred in me, only in my case one single sound produced it, and the result was not color, but a feeling of pressure, dizziness, suffocation.

Fighting for control, I knew that another iteration of the sound in question would cost me the battle. Dad's mouth opened, and simultaneously I rose. Opinions on my uncle's character, pro or con, didn't interest me half so much as the problem of excusing myself in a steady voice, walking from table to doorway without a stagger, and finally escaping from that room before the fatal name could be spoken again.

These feats accomplished, I managed to get up the stairs and into my own room, where I locked the door and dropped, face downward, across the bed. Though the evening was cool, my whole body was drenched in sweat and my brain reeled sickeningly.

One may get help from queer sources. Van, in our gay junior year—his last at college—had initiated me into a device for keeping steady when the last drink has been one too many. You mentally recite a poem or speech or the multiplication table—any old thing will do. Fixing the mind in that way seems to soothe the gyrating interior and enables a fellow at least to fall asleep like a gentleman.

In my present distress that came back to me. Still fighting off the unknown with one-half of my mind, I scrabbled around in the other half for some definite memorization to take hold of.

There was none. The very multiplication table swam a jumble of numbers. Then I caught a rhyme beginning in the back of my head, and fixed my attention on it feverishly. Over and over the words said themselves, first haltingly, then with increasing certainty. It was a simple, jingling little prayer that every child in the English-speaking world, I suppose, has learned past forgetfulness.

> Now I lay me down to sleep—

Again—again—by the tenth repetition of "I pray the Lord my soul to take," I had wrenched my mind away from—that other—and had its whole attention on the rhyme. At last, following a paroxysm of trembling, I knew myself the victor. Once more the Fifth Presence had released me.

Panting and weak from reaction, I sat up. What ailed me? How, in reason and common sense, could the sound of any man's name have this effect on me?

Hypnotism? Nearly two months had elapsed since my first trouble of this kind, and without recurrence in the interim. No, and come to think of it, I couldn't recall having heard the name spoken in that while, either. Serapion! It was only when uttered aloud that the word had power over me. I could think of it without any evil effect. And that name on Alicia's lips had been my last vivid impression before I lost self-consciousness and walked out of Moore's house, an intelligent automaton for sixty minutes after.

Scraps of psychology came back to me. Hypnotism—hypnotic suggestion. Could a man be shocked into hypnotic sleep, awaken, and weeks later be swayed by a sound that had accompanied the first lapse?

One way, I set myself very firmly. In cool judgment I was no believer in ghosts. Whatever the explanation, it had nothing to do with my uncle *in propria persona*. The very thought brought a smile to my lips. He had died before I was born; but, though dad had for some reason disliked him, by all accounts my namesake had been a genial, easy-going, agreeable gentleman, rather characterless, perhaps, and inclined to let the other fellow work, but not a man whose spirit could be imagined as a half-way efficient "haunt."

Serapion! No, and neither would he probably have flung away his own and his family's comfort for a point of fine-drawn honor. Was dad in the right? I had tried to reserve criticism there, and in action I had certainly backed him to the limit. Inevitably, though from yet far-off, I could see the loss of Roberta grinding down upon me. She couldn't wait my convenience forever, you know. Some other fellow—some free, unburdened chap—

I buried my head in my hands.

Then I dropped them and sprang erect, every nerve alert.

I had closed my eyes, and in that instant *a face had leaped into being behind their shut lids*.

The face was not Roberta's, though I had been thinking of her. Moreover, it had lacked any dreamlike quality. It had come real—real as if the man had entered my bedroom and thrust his face close to mine.

As my eyes flicked open, it had vanished, leaving me quivering with a strange resentment—an anger, as if some intimate privacy had been invaded. I stood with clenched fists, more angry than amazed at first, but not daring to shut my eyes lest it return.

What had there been about the queer vision that was so loathsome?

The face of a man around forty years it had seemed, smooth-shaven, boyish in a manner, with a little inward twist at the mouth corners, an amused slyness to the clear, light-blue eyes. The face of an easy-going, take-life's-jokes-as-they-come sort of fellow, amiable, pleasant, and, in some indefinite fashion—horrible.

I was sure I had never seen the man in real life, though there had been a vague familiarity about him, too.

About *him!* A dream—a vision.

"Clayton Barbour," I muttered through shut teeth, "if it has reached the point where a word throws you into spasms and you are afraid to close your eyes, you'd better consult a doctor; and that is exactly what I shall do!"

Chapter VIII.
FOUR HUNDRED DOLLARS.

Nils Berquist had his own ways, and whether or not they were practical or customary to mankind at large influenced him in no degree. He called himself a socialist, but in pure fact he was one of those persons who require a cause to fight for and argue about, as a Hedonist craves his pleasures, or the average man an income.

Real socialism, with the communal interests it implies, was foreign to Berquist's very nature. He could get along, in a withdrawn kind of way, with almost any one. He would share what small possessions he had with literally any one. But his interest went to such abstractions of thought as were talked and written by men of his own kind, while himself—his mind—he kept for the very few. Those are the qualities of an aristocrat, not a socialist.

One result of his paradoxical attitude showed in the fact that when it came to current news, Nils was as ignorant a man as you could meet in a day's walk. My various troubles and activities had kept me from thinking of him, but when I again happened on Nils in town one evening it hurt my feelings to discover that the spectacular downfall of Barbour & Hutchinson might have occurred on another planet, so far as he was concerned.

News that had been blazoned in every paper was news to him all this time afterward. Even learning it from me in person, he said little, though this silence might have been caused by embarrassment. Roberta was with me, and to tie Nils's tongue you had only to lead him into the presence of femininity in the person of a young, pretty girl.

I at last recalled the fact, and because for a certain reason I wished a chance to talk with him where he would talk, I asked if he couldn't run out some night and have dinner with us. Cathy's cooking was nothing wonderful, but I knew Nils wouldn't mind that, nor the cramped quarters we had to live in. I reckoned on taking him up to my own room later for a private confab.

After a short hesitation he accepted.

"You take care of yourself, Clay," he added. "You're looking pale—run down. Don't tell me you've been laid up sick along with all this other trouble?"

"No, indeed, old man. Working rather harder than I used and—lately I haven't slept very well. Bad dreams. But aside from that, nothing serious."

After a few more words, we parted, he striding off on his lonely way to some bourne unknown; Roberta and I proceeding toward the motion-picture theater that we tried to enjoy like a real playhouse. As if misery had altered the Charlestonian view-point, Mrs. Whitingfield had relaxed her chaperonage, and let us go alone almost wherever we liked—or where my diminished pocket-fund afforded to take us.

A fortnight had passed since the strange face had made its first appearance. If Nils thought I looked pale, there was reason for it. "Bad dreams," I had told him, but bad dreams were less than all.

My resolve to visit a doctor had come to nothing. I had called, indeed, upon our family physician, as I had meant. The moment I entered his presence, however, that instinct for concealment which had prevented me from confiding in Roberta or my family rose up full strength. The symptoms I actually laid before Dr. Lloyd produced a smile and a prescription that might as well have been the traditional bread pills—I didn't bother to have it filled. I went out as alone with my secret as when I entered.

A face—boyish in manner, pleasant, half-smiling usually; with an amused slyness to the clear, light-blue eyes; an agreeable inward quirk at the corners of the finely cut lips. I had come to know every lineament intimately well.

It had not returned again until some time after the first appearance. Then—at the bank, the afternoon following my futile conference with Dr. Lloyd—I happened to close my eyes, and *it* was there, behind the lids.

There was a table in Mr. Terne's office, over which he used to spread out his correspondence and papers. I was seated at one side of the table and he on the other, and I started so violently that he dropped his pen and made a straggling ink-feather across the schedule of securities he was verifying.

He patiently blotted it, and I made such a fuss over getting out the ink-eradicator and restoring the sheet of minutely figured ledger-paper to neatness, that he forgot to ask what had made me jump in the first place.

After that the face was with me so often that if I shut my eyes and saw nothing, its absence bothered me. I would feel then that the face had got behind me, perhaps, and acquired the bad habit of casting furtive glances over my shoulder.

You may think that if one must be burdened with a companion invisible to the world, such a good-humored countenance as I have described would be the least disagreeable. But that was not so.

There was to me a subtle hatefulness about it—like a thing beautiful and at the same time vile, which one hates in fear of coming to love it.

I never called the face "him," never thought of it as a man, nor gave it a man's name. I was afraid to. As if recognition would lend the vision power. I called it the Fifth Presence, and hated it.

As days of this passed, there came a time when the face began trying to talk to me. There, at least, I had the advantage. Though I could see the lips move, forming words, by merely opening my eyes I was able to banish it, and so avoid learning what it wished to say.

In bed, I used to lie with my eyes wide open sometimes for hours, waiting for sleep to come suddenly. When that happened I was safe, for though my dreams were often bad, the face never invaded them.

I discovered, too, that the name Serapion had in a measure lost power to throw me off balance, since the face had come. My mother continued to harp on the superiority of my dead uncle's character, and how he would have shielded us from the evils that had befallen, until dad acquiesced in sheer self-protection. But though I didn't like to hear her talk of him, and though the sound of the name invariably quickened my heart-beat, hearing neither increased nor diminished the vision's vividness.

It was with me, however, through most of my waking hours—waiting behind my lids—and if I looked pale, as Nils said, the wonder is that I was able to appear at all as usual. So I wished to talk with Nils, hoping that to the man who had warned me against the Moores I could force myself to confide the distressing aftermath of my visit at the "dead-alive house."

He had promised to come out the next night but one, which was Wednesday. Unfortunately, however, I missed seeing him then, after all, and because of an incident whose climax was to give the Fifth Presence a new and unexpected significance.

About two thirty Wednesday afternoon I ran up the steps of the Colossus Trust, and at the top collided squarely with Van, Jr. By the slight reel with which he staggered against a pillar and caught hold of it, I knew that Van had been hitting the high spots again and hoped he had not been interviewing his father in that condition. On recovering his balance, Van stood up steady enough.

"Old scout Clay! Say, you look like a pale, pallid, piffling fresh-water clam, you do. 'Pon my word, I'm ashamed of the old Colossus. The old brass idol has sucked all the blood out of you. My fault, servin' up the best friend I ever had as a—a helpless sacrifice to the governor's old brass Colossus. Come on with me—you been good too long!"

He playfully pretended to tear off the brass-lettered name of the trust company, which adorned the wall beside him, cast it down and trample on it. When I tried to pass he caught my arm. "Come on!"

"Can't," I explained quietly. "Mr. Terne was the best man at a wedding today, but he left me a stack of work."

Van sniffed. "Huh! I know that wedding. I was invited to that wedding, but I wouldn't go. Measly old prohibition wedding! Just suits Fatty Terne. When you get married, Clay, I'll send along about eleven magnums for a wedding present, and then I'll come to *your* wedding!"

"You may—when it happens." Again I tried to pass him.

'Wait a minute. You poor, pallid work-slave—you know what I'm going to do for you?"

"Get me fired, by present prospects. I must—"

"You must not. Just listen. You know Barney Finn?"

"Not personally. Let me go now, Van, and I'll see you later."

"Barney Finn," he persisted doggedly, "has got just the biggest lil engine that ever slid round a track. Now you wait a minute. Barney's another friend of mine. Told me all about it. Showed it to me. Showed me how it's going to make every other wagon at Fairview to-morrow look like a hand-pushed per-perambulator!"

"All right. Come around after the race and tell me how Finn made out. Please—"

"Wait. You're my friend, Clay, and I like you. You put a thousand bones on Finney's car, and say good-by to old Colossus. Start a bank of your own. How's that, huh?"

I laughed. "Bet on it yourself, Van, and let me alone. I've forgotten what a thousand dollars looks like."

"No place for you roun' old Colossus, then. Say, boy, if you think me too squiffy to wist whereof I speak, you misjudge me sadly—yes, indeed! Didn't I wrest one pitiful century from Colossus five minutes ago, and isn't that the last that stood between me an' starvation, and ain't I going right out an' plaster that century on Finn's car? Would I im-impoverish the Colossus and me, puttin' that last century on anything but a sure win? Come across, boy!"

Now, one might think that Van's invitation lacked attractiveness to a sober man. I happened to know, however, that drunk or sober, his judgment was good on one subject, the same being motor-cars. Barney Finn, moreover, was a speed-track veteran with a mighty reputation at his back. He had, in the previous year, met several defeats, due to bad luck, in my opinion, but they had brought up the odds. If he had something particularly good and new in his car for to-morrow's race at Fairview, there was a chance for somebody to make a killing, as Van said. "What odds?" I queried.

"For each lil bone you plant, twelve lil bones will blossom. Good enough? I could get better, but this will be off Jackie Rosenblatt, an' you know that lil Jew's a reg'lar old Colossus his own self. Solid an' square. Hock his old high silk hat before he'd welch."

"Yes, Rosie's square." I did some quick mental figuring, and then pulled a thin sheaf of bills from an inner coat-pocket. Instantly, Van had snatched them out of my hand.

"Not all!" I exclaimed sharply. "Take fifty, but I brought that in to deposit—"

"Deposit it with Jackie! Why, you old miser with your bank account! Four entire centuries, and you weepin' over poverty! Say, Clay, how much is twelve times four?"

"Forty-eight, but—"

"Lightnin' calculator!" he admired. "Say, doesn't forty-eight hundred make a bigger noise in your delikite ear than four measly centuries? Come across!"

I don't think I nodded. I am almost sure that I had begun reaching my hand to take all, or most of those bills back. But Van thought otherwise. "Right, boy!"

With plunging abruptness he was off down the steps. I hesitated. Forty-four hundred. Then I caught myself and was after him, but too late. His speedy gray roadster was already nosing recklessly into the traffic. Before I reached the bottom step it had shot around the corner and was gone.

Chapter IX.
THE FACE SPEAKS.

Off Mr. Terne's spacious office there was a little glass-enclosed, six-by-eight cubby-hole, which I called my own.

Ten o'clock Thursday morning found me seated in the one chair, staring at a pile of canceled notes on the desk before me. I had started to check them half an hour ago, but so far just one check-mark showed on the list beside them. I had something worse to think of than canceled notes.

As I sat, I could hear Mr. Terne fussing about the outer office. Then I heard him go out. About two minutes afterward the door banged open so forcibly that I half started up, conscience clamoring.

But it wasn't the second vice returning in a rage. It was Van. He fairly bolted into my cubby-hole, closed the door, pitched his hat in a corner, and swung himself to a seat on my desk-edge, scattering canceled notes right and left. There he sat, hands clasped, staring at me in a perfect stillness which contrasted dramatically with his violent entry. His eyes looked dark and sunken in a strained, white face. My nerves were inappreciative of drama.

"Where were you last night?" I demanded irritably. "I hunted for you around town till nearly midnight."

"What? Oh, I was way out in—I don't know exactly. Some dinky road-house. I pretty nearly missed the race and—and I wish to God I had, Clay!" He passed a shaking hand across his eyes.

"Did Finn lose?" I snapped. "But—why, the race can hardly be more than started yet!"

"Finn started!" he gulped.

"Ditched?" I gasped a flash of inspiration warning me of what was coming.

He nodded. "Turned turtle on the second lap and—say, boy—I helped dig him out and carry him off—you know, I liked Barney. It was—bad. The mechanism broke his back clean—flung against a post—but Barney—say, what was left of him kind of—kind of came apart—when we—" He stopped short, gulped again, and: "Guess I'm in bad shape this morning," he said huskily. "Nerves all shot to pieces."

I should have imagined they would be. A man straight from an all-night debauch can't witness a racing-car accident, help handle the human wreckage afterward, and go whistling merrily to tell his friends the tale.

I expressed that, though in more kindly chosen words, and then we were both silent a minute. Barney Finn had not been my friend, or even acquaintance, and while I was vicariously touched by Van's grief and horror, my own dilemma wasn't simplified by this news. Yet I hated to fling sordidness in the face of tragedy by speaking of money.

"Afterward I didn't feel like watching the race out." As Van spoke, I heard the outer door open again. This time it really was Mr. Terne, for I recognized his step. "So I came straight here," Van continued.

My own door opened, and a kindly, dignified figure appeared there.

"Barbour," said the second vice, "have you that—ah, good morning, Richard." He nodded rather coldly to Van, and went on to ask me for the list I was supposed to be at work on.

When I explained that the checking wasn't quite finished, he turned away; then glanced back.

"By the way, Barbour," he said, "Prang dropped me a line saying that when you were in his office yesterday he paid up four hundred he has owed me since last June. If you were too late to deposit yesterday afternoon, get it from my box and we'll put it in with this check from the United."

I felt myself going fiery-red. "Sorry," I said. "I'll let you have that money this afternoon, Mr. Terne. I—I—"

"He gave it to me to deposit for him, and I used it for something else," broke in Van with the utmost coolness.

On occasion Van's brain worked with flashlight rapidity. He had put the two and two of that four hundred together while another man might have been wondering about it. Terne stared, first at Van, then at me.

"You—you gave it—" he began slowly.

"He came here for your pass-book," ran Van's glib tongue. "I dropped in on him, and as I was going out past the tellers, I offered to put it in for him. Then I stuck it in my pocket, forgot it till too late, and needing some cash last night, I used that. Barbour has been throwing fits ever since I told him. I'll get it for you this afternoon."

Terne stared some more, and Van returned the look with cool insolence.

A brick-reddish color crept up the second v.p.'s cheeks, his mouth compressed to an unfamiliar straightness, and turning suddenly he walked out of not only my cubby-hole but his own office. The door shut with a rattle of jarred glazing.

"You shouldn't have done that!" I breathed.

"Oh, rats! Fatty Terne's gone to tell the governor what a naughty, bad boy I am. He'll get thrown out. No news to the governor, and he's sick of hearing it. Anyway, this is my fault, Clay, and I ought to stand the gaff. You've worked like the devil here, and then I come along and spoil everything. Drunken fool, me! Knew I'd queer you if we got together, and till yesterday I had sense enough to keep off. When I took those bills I knew there was something wrong, but I was too squiffy to have any sense about it. Plain highway robbery! Never mind, old pal, I'll bring you back the loot this afternoon if I have to bust open one of the old Colossus's vaults for it!"

At my elbow the house telephone jingled.

"Just a minute," I said. "No; wait, Van. Hello! Hel—oh, Mr. Vansittart? Yes, sir. Be over at once, sir. Yes, he's here. What? Yes—" The other receiver had clicked up.

"We're in for it," I muttered. "Apparently your esteemed governor hasn't thrown Terne out!"

Vansittart, Sr., the gruff old lion, granted lax discipline to no man under his control save one; and even Van, Jr., was, if not afraid, at least a bit wary of him. Though he had taken me on in the bank at a far higher wage than my services were worth, he had also made it very clear that so far as I was concerned, favoritism ended there. For me, I was sure the truth of the present affair would mean instant discharge.

"Shut that door!" the lion growled as we entered. "Now, Dick, I'll thank you to explain for exactly what weighty reason you stole Mr. Terne's four hundred."

"Stole!" Van's slim figure stiffened, and he went two shades whiter.

"Stole, yes! I said, stole. That is the usual term for appropriating money without the owner's consent."

"I don't accuse the boy of theft!" Terne's set face of anger relaxed suddenly. He didn't like Van, but he was a man who could not be unfair if he tried.

"Keep out of this, Terne—please. Dick, I am waiting."

"Well, really," Van drawled, "if you put it that way, I couldn't say what I did use the money for. There was a trifle of four hundred, owned, I believe, by F—by Mr. Terne, which I borrowed, intending to return it in a few hours—"

"From what fund?" The lion's mane was up now in earnest. I felt instinctively that this interview was a bit different from any that Van had been through heretofore. "Are you aware that your account in this bank is already overdrawn to the sum of"—he consulted a slip before him—"of forty-nine dollars and sixty cents? You perhaps have reserve funds at your command elsewhere?"

Van looked his father in the eye. What he saw must have been unusual. His brows went up slightly and the same fighting look came into his face which I had seen there when he and I confronted the faculty together. On that occasion I had been genuinely inclined to meekness. I remained in college while Van was "sent down."

He laughed lightly. "Excuse me half an hour while I run out and sell the lil old roadster. Forty-nine sixty, you said? I'll pay you yours first, governor!"

"That's kind! After stealing one man's money you propose selling another man's car to replace it. Yes, my car, I said. What have you got in this world but your worthless brains and body to call your own? Wait! We'll go into the matter of ownership more deeply in a few minutes. Barbour," he whirled on me, "you allowed funds belonging to your superior to pass into unauthorized hands. That is not done in this bank. As things stand, I shall leave your case to Mr. Terne, but first you will make one direct statement. I wish it made so that no question may arise afterward. Did you or did you not hand four hundred dollars in bills, the property of Mr. Terne, to my—to my son, God help me!"

It was up to me in earnest. I was now sure beyond doubt of what Van had run against. His leonine parent had turned at last, and even the whole truth would barely suffice to save him. My lips opened. To blame though he was in a way, Van mustn't suffer seriously in my protection. I could not forget that momentary hesitation on my part, save for which I could easily have retrieved the bills before Van was out of reach.

"I gave it to him," I began.

And then, abruptly, silently, another face flashed in between me and the president. Instead of Vansittart's dark, angry eyes, I was staring into a pair of clear, amused, light-blue ones. A finely cut mouth half smiled at me with lips that moved.

Always theretofore the face had come only when my lids were closed. Its wish to communicate with me—and that it did wish to communicate I was sure as if the thing had been a living man, following me about and perpetually tugging at my sleeve—had been a continual menace, but one which I had grown to feel secure from because the thing's power seemed so limited.

Now, with my eyes wide open, there hung the face in mid air. It was not in the least transparent. That is, its intervening presence obscured Vansittart's countenance as completely as though the head of a real man had thrust in between us. And yet—it is hard to express, but there was that about it, a kind of flatness, a lack of the normal three-dimensional solidity, which gave it the look of a living portrait projected on the atmosphere.

I knew without even glancing toward them that Van and Mr. Terne did not see the thing as I did. It was there for me alone. At the moment, though I fought the belief again later, I knew beyond question that what I beheld was the projection of a powerful, external will, the same which, with Alicia's dynamic force to aid, had once actually taken possession of my body.

The finely cut lips moved. No audible sound came from them, but as they formed words, the speech was heard in my brain distinctly as if conveyed by normal sound-vibrations through the ear-drums. It was *silent* sound. The tone was deep, rather agreeable, amiably amused:

"You have said enough," the face observed pleasantly. "You have told the truth; now stop there. Your friend has a father to deal with, while you have an employer. He is willing to shoulder all the blame, and for you to expose your share in it will be a preposterous folly. Remember, that hard as you have worked, you are receiving here twice the money you are worth—three times what you can hope to begin on elsewhere. Remember the miserable consequences of your own father's needless sacrifice. Remember how often, and very justly, you have wished that he had thought less of a point of fine-drawn honor, and more of his family's happiness. Will you commit a like folly?"

I can't tell, so that any one will understand, what a wave of accumulated memories and secret revolts against fate over-swept me as I stared hard into the smiling, light-blue eyes. But I fought.

Grimly I began again. "I gave it to him!" and then—stopped.

"That's enough." This time it was Vansittart speaking. "You may go, Barbour. Mr. Terne, I will ask you to leave us. You will receive my personal check for the amount you have lost."

"But—but—" I stammered desperately while those clear eyes grew more amused, more dominating.

The lion's hard-held calmness broke in a roar. "Get out! Out of here, both of you! Go!"

Mr. Terne laid his hand on my arm, and reluctantly I allowed myself to be steered toward the door. As I turned away the face did not float around with the turning of my eyes.

It hung in mid air, save for that odd, undimensional flatness real as any of the three other faces there. When my back was to the president, the—the

Fifth Presence was behind me. On glancing back, it still hung there. Then it smiled at me—a beautiful, pleased, wholly approving smile—and faded to nothing.

I went out with Mr. Terne, and left Van alone with his father.

CHAPTER X.

THE BELOVED SERAPION.

One hour later I departed from the Colossus Trust Company with instructions not to return. Oh, no, I had not been ruthlessly discharged by the outraged second vice. The inhibition covered the balance of the day only, and, as Mr. Terne put it: "A few hours' quiet will give you a clearer view of the situation, Barbour. I honor you for feeling as you do. It was Richard, I believe, who obtained you a position here. Just for your consolation when Mr. Vansittart has—er—cooled off somewhat, I intend making a small plea in Richard's behalf. No, go home and come back fresh in the morning. You look as though all the cares of the world had been dumped on your shoulders. Take an older man's advice and shake off those that aren't yours, boy!"

He was a kindly, good man, the second vice-president of the Colossus. But his kindliness didn't console me. In fact, I felt rather the worse for it. I went home, wishing that he had kicked me clean around the block instead of—of liking, and petting, and, by inference, praising me for being such a contrast in character to poor, reckless, loose-living, heroic Van!

When I left, the latter was still in his father's office. Though I might have waited for him outside, I didn't. He was not the kind to meet me with even a glance of reproach; but just the same I did not feel eager to meet him.

I had resolved, however, that unless Van pulled through scatheless, I would myself "make a small plea in Richard's behalf," and next time not all the smooth, smiling devils from the place-that's-no-longer-believed-in should persuade me to crumple.

On the train—I commuted, of course—I deliberately shut my eyes, and waited for the vision to appear. If it could talk to me by moving its lips, there must be some way in which I could express my opinion to it. I burned to do that! Like a sneak, it had taken me unawares in a crucial moment. I had a few thoughts of the Fifth Presence which should make even that smug vision curl up and die.

I closed my eyes—and was asleep in five minutes. I was tired, you see, and, now that I wanted it, the Fifth Presence kept discreetly invisible. The conductor, who knew me, called my station and me at the same time, and I blundered off the train, half awake, but thoroughly miserable.

There was no one at home but my mother. Of late dad's sight had failed till it was not safe for him to be on the street alone. As he liked to walk, however, Cathy had gone out with him.

I found mother, lying down in her darkened bedroom, in the preparatory stage of a headache. Having explained that Mr. Terne had given me an unexpected half-holiday, I turned to leave her, but checked on a sudden impulse.

"Mother," I said softly, "why did you name me Ser—why was I given my uncle's name instead of just dad's?"

"What an odd question!"

Mother sat up so energetically that two cushions fell off the couch. I picked them up and tried to reestablish her comfortably, but she wouldn't have it. "Tell me at once why you asked that extraordinary question, Clay!"

I said there was nothing extraordinary about it that I could see. My uncle's name itself was extraordinary, or at least unusual, and the question happened to come into my mind just then. Besides, she had spoken a good deal of him lately. Maybe that had made me think of it.

Mother drew a deep breath.

"He told me—can you believe this?—he told me that some day you would ask that question! This is too wonderful! And I've seemed to feel a protecting influence about us—this house that was his—and your good position in the bank!"

"Mother, will you kindly explain what you are talking about?"

My heart had begun a muffled throbbing.

"Be patient! I have a wonderful story to tell you. I've doubted, and hoped, and dared say nothing, but, Clayton dear, in these last miserable weeks I have felt his presence like the overshadowing wings of a protecting angel. If it is true—if it only could be true—"

"Mother—please!"

"Sit down, dear. Are my salts on the dresser? Yes, and the cologne, too, please. That's a dear boy. And now sit down. Your father never liked dear Serapion, and—why, how wonderful this all is! Your coming home early, I mean, and asking me the question just at the one time when your father, who disliked him, is away, and we have the whole house—his house!—to ourselves. Can't you feel his influence in that, dear?"

"What have you to tell me, mother?"

"I shall begin at the very first—"

"If you make the story too long," I objected craftily, "dad and Cathy will be back."

"That is true. Then I'll just tell the part he particularly wished you to know. Dear Serapion was universally loved, and I could go on by the hour about his friendships, and the faculty he had for making people happy. Physically, he had little strength, and your father was very unjust to him—"

"Can't we leave dad out of this, mother?"

"You are so like your uncle! Serapion could never bear to hear any one criticized, no matter how the person had treated him. 'My happiness,' he would say, 'is in living at harmony with all. Clayton,' your father, he meant, of course, 'Clayton is a splendid man, whom I admire. His own fine energy and capacities make him unduly hard, perhaps, toward those less gifted. I try to console myself with the thought that life has several sides. Love— kindliness—good humor—I am at least fortunate in rousing the gentlest qualities in most of those about me. Who knows? From the beginning, that may have been my mission in life, and I was given a delicate constitution that I might have leisure merely to live, love, and be loved in return!'"

"Of course, he wouldn't have expressed that beautiful thought to every one, but Serapion knew that I would understand—yes, dear, I shall come to your part in the story directly.

"Serapion passed to his reward before you were born, my son. He went from us in January, and you came into the world the April following. The doctors had told him that only a few hours were left him of life. When Serapion learned that he asked to be left alone with me for a little while. I remember every word of that beautiful conversation. I remember how he laid his hand on mine and pressed it feebly.

" 'Do as I ask, Evelyn,' he said. 'If the child is a boy, give him my name. I only ask second place. Clayton has first right; but let the boy have my name, as well as his father's. I've been too happy in my life—too happy in my loves and friendships. I can't bear to die utterly out of this good old world. I haven't a child of my own, but if you'd just give your boy—my name. Some day he will ask why, and then you are to tell him that—it's because—I was so happy!' "

Mother was sobbing, but after a moment she regained self-control to continue. "You may think it weak in me to cry over my brother, who passed long ago. But he has lived in my memory. And he said: 'Some people only talk of life after death, but I believe in it. It is really true that we go out to go on. I know it. There is something bright and strong in me, Evelyn, that only grows stronger as I feel the body dying from about me. Bright, strong, and clear-sighted. I have never been quite like other men. Not even you have understood me, and perhaps that is for the best.'

"With his hand on mine he smiled, and, oh, Clayton, I have wondered many times since what that smile meant! It was so beautiful that—that it was almost terrible!

" 'I love life,' he went on, 'and I shall live beyond this perishing clay. Soon or late, a day will come when you will feel my living presence in the house, and it will be in that time that your son will ask of me. Then you will tell him all I have said, and also this:

" 'That I promised to return—to watch over him—to guard him.

" 'Name him for me, that I may have the power. There's power in a name! And I am not as other men. Be very sure that—your son—Serapion—shall be—as happy—shall have all that I've had—of life. Believe—promise!' And I promised.

"The strangest look came into his eyes. A look of"—my mother's voice sank to a hushed whisper—"I can only describe it as holy exultation! It was too vivid and triumphant to have been of this world. And he died in my arms—Clayton, why do you look at me like that? What is the matter, child?"

"Nothing. You told the story so well that for a moment I seemed to—to see him—or something. Never mind me. Mother, haven't you any picture of my uncle?"

"Only one of him as he was in his latter years. I have kept it locked away, for fear it might be destroyed or injured. After Serapion was gone they had a fire at the photographer's"—mother had risen and was searching in a bureau-drawer—"a fire—where is that key?—the fire spoiled all the old negatives, the man said—I had that key here—though the studio only partly burned, and I always suspected he simply didn't take the trouble to hunt for the ones of your uncle—here it is! In my glove-box, of all places! I am so glad that you take this seriously, Clayton. You feel nearly as deeply about it as I, don't you, dear?"

"It's nothing to joke over," I said.

"No; but your father might have influenced you—"

"Let me unlock it!"

She was struggling with a small drawer in the side of the high, old-fashioned, carved walnut escritoire which she kept in her bedroom now, because our one living-room was small and crowded.

I made fussing over the refractory lock an excuse to hide my too-genuine emotion. I wished to see that picture. At the same time I dreaded unspeakably the moment when doubt might become certainty.

"It's open," I said at last, and stepped back.

My mother took out a flat package, wrapped in yellowed tissue-paper.

She began to undo the silk cord tied around it. I turned my back suddenly. Then I felt something thrust into my hand. With all my will I forced myself to bring the thing around before my eyes.

What face would stare back at me, eye to eye, amused, pleasant—

The window-shades were still drawn, and the light dim. It was a moment before I realized that what I held was not a picture at all, but some kind of printed pamphlet.

"Raise the shade," said my mother. "I wish you to read that. It is a little memorial of your uncle, written by one of his friends, a Mr. Hazlett. The words are so touching! Almost as beautiful as the thoughts Serapion himself often expressed."

"Would you mind"—I controlled my voice by an effort—"'would you mind letting me see the picture first?"

"Here it is."

This time she had handed me the unmistakable, polished, bescrolled oblong of an old-fashioned photographer's mounting.

Defiance, last resource of the hard-pressed, drove me in two bold strides to the window, where I jerked the shade up, rattling on its roller.

Daylight beat in. This was the middle of November and the light was gray, filtered through gray clouds. A few scattered particles of snow flickered past the window.

In my fingers the polished face of a cardboard mount felt smooth, almost soft to the touch. I watched the snow.

"Isn't his face beautiful, dear?" demanded a voice at my shoulder.

"I—I—yes, I'm afraid—of course, mother!"

"But you are not looking at it!"

"I did look," I lied. "I—this has all been a little too much for me. Take it—put it away. No, I'll read the memorial another time. Happy! Did he promise to—to come back and make me *happy?*"

"Practically that. How like him you are, dear son! He was sensitive, too; and yours eyes! You have the Barbour nose and forehead, but your eyes—"

"Please, mother!"

She let me go at last, and in the quiet of refuge behind the locked door of my bedroom, I, who after all had not dared to look upon the picture of Serapion, scrutinized thoroughly every feature of my own face in the mirror.

Like him! She had often said so in the past, but the statement had failed to make any particular impression.

Yes, she was right about the eyes. They were the same clear, light-blue as his—what? Never! Not as *his*. For all I knew by actual observation, Serapion's eyes might have been sea-green or shell-pink. *I had never seen him.* Let me keep that fact firmly in mind.

CHAPTER XI.
"VERSCHLINGENER DES LEBENS."

My face in the mirror bore a faint, sketchy resemblance to that of the unreal but none the less troublesome vision by which I was intermittently afflicted. The resemblance accounted for the vague familiarity that had enveloped it from the first.

The face in the mirror, though, was much younger, and—resolve flared up in its eyes like a lighted fire.

"You," I addressed my reflection, "are not a sneak. You are not going to be made one. To-night you will present yourself to Mr. James Barton Moore, and you will inform him that the little trick of hypnotism performed by his wife last August will either be reversed by her, or he himself will pay for it unpleasantly. I believe," and my arm muscles flexed in bravado, "that Mr. Jimmy Moore will think twice before he refuses."

That was what I said. But in my heart I yearned suddenly to go and fling myself abject, at the feet of Alicia Moore, and entreat her to help me.

It was a cold night, and the afternoon's scattered flakes had increased to a heavy snow-fall. Alighting from the car—not mine, this time, but the transit company's—I found the snow inches deep. I can still recall the feel of it blown against my face, like light, cold finger-touches.

Plowing through it, I came again to the "dead-alive house" That other visit had been in summer. The twin lawns, one green and close-cropped, the other high-grown with weeds, had stood out contrastingly then. There had been a line of sharp demarkation between Moore's clean, freshly painted half of the house and the other half's dirt-freckled wall.

Now all that sharp difference was blurred and indistinct. The snow, blue-white in the swaying circles of light from a corner arc-lamp, had buried both the lawns. Joining the roofs in whiteness, drifting across the porches, swirling in the air, it obliterated all but a hint of difference between the living half and the dead.

Though the windows of one part were dark as those of the other, a faint glow shone through the curtained glazing of Moore's door.

Now that I was here, I almost hoped that he and his wife were out. The accusation I must make was strange to absurdity. I braced myself, however, opened the gate, and as I did so a hand dropped on my shoulder from behind.

A man had come upon me soundlessly through the snow. In my nerve-racked state, I whirled and struck at him.

He caught my wrist. "Here! I'm no highwayman, Clay!"

"Nils," I laughed shakily, "you startled me."

Berquist stared, with a sudden close attention that I found myself shrinking away from. For weeks I had been keeping a secret at some cost. Though I had come here to reveal it, the habit of concealment was still on me.

"Your nerves used to be better than that," said Berquist shortly.

"You calling on Moore?" I queried. "Thought there was some kind of vendetta between you. You wouldn't come here with me, I remember."

"I'm glad you remember something," he retorted gravely. "You have a very nice, hospitable family, though. They took me in last night and fed me on the bare strength of my word that I'd been invited."

"I say, Nils, that's too bad."

In my desperate search for Van the previous evening, I had clean forgotten my dinner invitation to Berquist. Reaching home near midnight, I had received a thoroughly sisterly call-down from Cathy, who had waited up to express her frank opinion of a brother who not only invited a friend to dinner without forewarning her, but neglected even to be present when the friend arrived.

It seemed, too, that Roberta had dined there on Cathy's own invitation, and the two girls had unitedly agreed that poor Nils was "queer" and not very desirable. He had committed the double offense of talking wild theories to dad, verbally ignoring the feminine element, and at the same time staring Bert out of countenance whenever her eyes were not actually on him.

I had informed Cathy that Bert should feel highly honored, since Nils was generally too shy even to look at a girl, much less stare at her, and that as the family's support I should certainly invite whom I pleased to dinner; as for Nils, I had regretted missing him, but knew he was too casual himself to hold the lapse against me.

Now I began an apology that was rather wandering, for my mind was otherwise concerned.

I wished to tell him about the Fifth Presence. Before I entered Moore's house, it would be very well that I should tell Nils of my errand. Why, in the name of all reason, was I possessed by this sense of shame that shut my lips whenever I tried to open them concerning the haunting face?

Cutting the apologies short, Nils forgave me, explained that though out of sympathy with Moore's work, he occasionally called to play chess with him, and then we were going up the snow-blanketed walk, side by side.

"Even the chess sometimes ends in a row," Nils added gloomily. "I wouldn't play him at all, if he hadn't beaten me so many times. Perhaps some day I'll get the score even, and then I sha'n't come here any more."

"Moore is—did he ever tell you that I kept my appointment with him?"

"Which one?"

The question leaped out cuttingly sharp.

"The only one I ever made with him, of course. That day you introduced us in the restaurant."

"You haven't been coming here since?"

"No. Why should you think that?"

We had checked again, half-way up the walk. As we stood Nils caught my shoulders and swung me around till the arc-lamp rays beat on my face. He scrutinized me from under frowning brows.

"You've lost something!" he said bluntly. "I can't tell exactly what. I don't know what story your eyes hide; but they hide one. Clay, don't think me an officious meddler, but you—you have your family dependent on you—and—oh, why do I beat about the bush? That girl you will marry some day; she's rather wonderful. For her sake, if not your own, tell me the truth. Has Moore involved you in some of his cursed, dangerous experiments? Tell me! Is it that, or"—his voice softened—"are you merely worn out with the common and comparatively safe kinds of trouble?"

"I've had—trouble enough to worry any fellow."

"Yes, but is any part of it to be laid at this door?" He jerked his head toward Moore's dimly radiant portal.

"A face—a face—" Sheer panic choked the words in my throat. I had begun betraying the secret which every atom of my being demanded should be kept.

"Yes; a face?"

"A face—is not necessarily a chart of the owner's doings," I wrenched roughly from his grasp. "Since when have you set up as a critic in physiognomy, Nils?"

"When one has a friend, one cares to look beneath the surface," he said simply.

"Well, don't look with the air of hunting out a criminal, then. I have as good a right to call here as you, haven't I? Moore sent me a letter asking me to drop around, so I—I thought I would. I'm tired, and need distraction. What's the harm?"

Without answering, he eyed me through a long moment; then turned quietly and went on up into the porch.

Standing hesitant, I glanced upward, looking for a light in the windows above. Again I saw the slanting roofs, blended in snow. Months ago, in a momentary illusion of moonlight, I had seen them look just so. The thought brought me a tiny prick of apprehension. Not fear, but the startled uneasiness one might feel at coming to a place one has never visited, and knowing it for the place one has seen in a dream.

Nevertheless, I followed Nils to the door.

Another maid opened it than the one who had admitted Roberta and myself in August. She was a great, craggy, hard-faced old colored woman, whom Nils addressed familiarly as "Sabina," and who made him rather glumly welcome in accents that betrayed her Southern origin. She assumed, I suppose, that Nils and I had come together, and my card did not precede me into Moore's sanctum.

The latter was in the library again. The shades and curtains were drawn tight, which accounted for the "not-at-home" look of the windows from outside. I learned later that he frequently denied himself to callers, even near acquaintances, unless they came by appointment. His letter to me had been ignored too long to come under that heading. I wonder! Would he have refused to see me that night, given a choice?

In my very first step across the library's threshold, I realized that my battle was to be an even more difficult one than I had feared.

Passing the doorway, I entered—physically and consciously entered— the same field of tension, to call it that, which had centralized about Alicia at the climax of my previous experience.

It was less masterful than then. There was not the same drain on my physical strength, nor the feeling of being *en rapport* with the movements of others. But the condition was none the less present; I knew it as surely and actually as one recognizes a marked change in atmospheric temperature or, to use a closer simile, as one feels entry into the radius of electrical force produced by a certain type of powerful generator.

There is no simile which will exactly express what I mean. The consciousness involved is other than normal, and only a person who had been possessed by it could fully understand.

On that first occasion, I had been sure that my impressions were shared by the others present. This time some minutes passed before I became convinced that Berquist and James Moore, at least, were insensitive to the condition.

The library appeared as I had seen it first, save that the lamp broken then had been replaced by another, with a Japanese "art" shade made of painted silk. Near the large reading-table, with the lamp, a small stand had been drawn up and a chessboard laid upon it. In anticipation of Nils's arrival, Moore had been arranging the pieces. They were red and white ivory men, finely carved. They and the Japanese lamp-shade made a glow of exotic color, in the shadow behind which sat—Alicia, a dim figure, pallid and immobile.

By one of those surface thoughts that flash across moments of intensity, I noted that Moore was dressed in a gray suit, patterned with a faint, large check in lighter gray.

Then he had recognized me, and the man's pale eyebrows lifted.

"You've brought Barbour?" he said to Nils.

"No," denied my friend. "Met him at the door. How do, Alicia?"

He strode across the room to where Mrs. Moore sat in the shadow.

Under other conditions I should have felt embarrassed. By Moore's tone and Nils's non-committal response, they had placed me as an intruder, received without even a gloss of welcome for courtesy's sake.

But to me it seemed only strange that they could speak at all in ordinary tones through this atmosphere of breathless tension. A voice here, I thought, should be either a shriek or a whisper.

Then Alicia's dry monotone:

"You should have come alone, Nils. You have brought one with you who is very evil. I know him. He is an eater of lives."

"Dear lady!" protested Nils, half jokingly. "Surely you don't apply that cannibalistic description to my friend here? He might take it that way."

"How he takes it is nothing," shrugged Alicia. "There is one too many in this room. There are four of us here, *and there is also a fifth*. And I think your friend is more aware of that than even I."

"Moore's previously unenthusiastic face lighted to quick eagerness. He pounced on Alicia's original phrase like a cat jumping for a mouse.

"An eater of life! Did you say this invisible Fifth Presence is an 'eater of life,' Alicia?"

"I did not," she retorted precisely. "I said an eater of lives. Every one does not know that—"

"No, but wait, Alicia. This is really interesting." He turned from her to us. "There's a particularly horrid old German legend about such a being." He informed us of it with the air of one imparting some delightful news. "Give me a German legend always for pure horror, but this excels the average. '*Der verschlingener des Lebens*'—'The Devourer of Life.' Very—interesting. Now the question arises, did Alicia read that yarn some time in the past, and is this the subliminal report of it coming out now, or—does she really sense an alien force which has entered the room in your company? What's your impression, Barbour? Have you any? You're psychic yourself—knew it the first time I saw you. Is any one here but we four?"

By a great effort, I forced my lips to answer:

"I couldn't say. This—I—"

"Have a chair, Barbour, and take your time." He was all sudden kindli-ness—the active sort, with a motive behind it, as I knew well enough now. To him I was not a guest but an experiment. "I haven't a doubt," he asserted cheerfully, "that you and Alicia sense a presence that entered with you and which such poor moles as Nils and myself are blind to. Now don't deny it. Any one possessing the psychic gift who denies or tries to smother it is not only unwise but selfish. Su-premely selfish! And it's a curious fact that one powerful psychic will often bring out the undeveloped potentialities of another. Alicia may have already done that for you. When you were here before—"

"That will do!" Abruptly deserting Alicia, Nils strode down upon us. There was wrath in every line of his dark face. "Jimmy, that boy is my friend! If he has 'psychic potentialities,' as you call it, let 'em alone. He doesn't wish to develop into a ghost-ridden, hysterical, semi-human monstrosity, with one foot in this world and the other across the border."

"Really," drawled Moore, "that description runs beyond even the inso-lence I've learned to expect from you, Berquist. My wife is a psychic."

Nils was not too easily crushed, but this time he had brought confusion on himself. "Ghost-ridden, hysterical, semi-human monstrosity" may have been an excellent description for Alicia. It is certain, however, that Nils had forgotten her when he voiced it. He flushed to the ears and stammered through an apology, to which Moore listened in grim silence.

Then Alicia spoke, with her customary dry directness.

"I am not offended. My guides do not like you, Nils, but that is because your opposition interferes with the work. Personally I like you for speaking frankly always. Take your unfortunate young friend, Mr. Barbour, and go away now."

"Alicia!" Moore was half pleading, half indignant. "You agreed with me that Barbour had possibilities of mediumship almost as great as your own. And you yet send him away. Think of the work!"

"I tried to send him away the first time." From beyond the lamp Alicia's enormous eyes glinted mockingly at her husband. "You believed," she went on, "that Mr. Barbour was naturally psychic, but undeveloped. Many times we have disagreed in similar cases. Your theory that more than half the human race might, properly trained, be sensitive to the etheric vibrations of astral and spiritual beings is true enough."

"Then why did you—"

"Don't argue, James. That tires me. I say that your belief is correct. But

I have told you and, through me, my guides have told you that not every one who is a natural sensitive is worthy of being developed."

"I consulted you"—Moore's voice trembled with suppressed irritation— "I consulted you, and you—"

"I said that a tremendous psychic possibility enveloped Mr. Barbour. That was true. Had I told you that the possibility was evil, that would have been equally true. But you would not have yielded to my judgment, and sent him away—as I tried to do."

"Alicia," cried her husband, "are we never to have any clear understandings?"

"Possibly not," she said, with cool indifference. "I am—what I am. Also, I am a channel for all forces, good or evil. My guides protect me, of course. They will not let any bad spirit harm me. But I think Mr. Barbour was not glad that he stayed when I wished him to go. He has come back to me for help. I am not sure that I wish to help him. It was a long time before I was rested from my first struggle with the One he is afraid of."

Nils made an impatient movement. "I don't believe Clay needs any help except—pardon me, Alicia—except to keep away from this house and you."

"Then why did he return here?"

"Because," interpolated Moore, with a scowl for Nils, "he grew interested in his own possibilities. This attempt to frighten him is not only absurd, but the worst thing possible for him. Of course the invisible forces are of different kinds, and of course some of them are inimical. But fear is the only dangerous weapon they have. If they can't frighten you, they can't harm you."

"Alicia," cut in Nils, "seems to disagree there."

"Alicia does agree. She inclines to repel the so-called evil beings, not from fear of them, but because they are more apt to trespass than the friendlier powers. They demand too much of her strength. In consequence, I have had an insufficient opportunity to study them. If Barbour is psychic—and I should say that he very obviously is—then his strength, combined with Alicia's, should be great enough for almost any strain. You are interfering here, Berquist. I won't have it. I—will—not—have it."

"And my friend is to be sacrificed so that you may study demonology?"

"Berquist, I have nothing to do with demons or daevas, devils or flibbertigibbets. You use the nomenclature of a past age."

"Verschlingener des Lebens!" quoted Nils quickly. "You didn't boggle over nomenclature when Alicia warned us that an 'eater of life' was present."

"Oh, God give me patience!" groaned Moore. "I try to trace a reference, and you—" He broke off and wheeled to the small, shadowy figure beyond the lamplight. "Alicia, exactly what did you mean when you said that an 'eater of lives' had entered the room? You can put us straight there, at least."

"I meant," drawled Alicia, "one of those quaint, harmless beings whom you are so anxious to study at anybody's expense. Not a demon, certainly, in the sense that Nils means. But not company I care for, either. No, I am not afraid of this one. He has the strength of an enormous greed—of a dead spirit who covets life—but he will not trap me again into lending my strength to his purpose."

"His! Whose? Do be plain for once, Alicia."

"I try to be," she retorted composedly. "I could give him a name that one of you at least would recognize. But that would please him too well. There is power in a name. Every one does not know that, nor how to use it. This one does. He bears his name written across his forehead. He wills that I shall see it and speak it now: Once he surprised me into speaking it, but that was Mr. Barbour's fault. He threw me off balance at a critical moment by turning on the lights. You have probably forgotten the name I spoke then, but I doubt if Mr. Barbour has forgotten. This one whom I refuse to name has no power over me. I have many friends among the living dead who protect me from such dead spirits as this one—"

"Just a minute, Alicia!" Moore was exaggeratedly patient. "I can believe in a dead body, and through you I've come to believe in live spirits, disembodied. But a dead spirit! That would be like an extinguished flame. It would have no existence."

She shook her head. "Please don't argue, James. You know that tires me. A spirit cannot perish. But a spirit may die, and, having died, exist in death eternal. There is life eternal and there is death eternal. There are the living spirits of the so-called dead. They are many and harmless. My guides are of their number. Also there are dead spirits. They are the ones to beware of, because they covet life. Such a one is he whom I called 'an eater of lives,' and who is better known to Mr. Barbour than to me. That is not my fault, however, and now I wish no more to do with any of it. I must insist, James, that you ask Mr. Barbour to leave. In fact, if he remains in the house five minutes longer I shall go out of it."

Her strange eyes opened suddenly till a gleam of white was plainly visible all around the wide blackness of them. Her porcelain, doll-like placidity vanished in an instant.

"Make him go!" she cried. "I tell you, there is an evil in this room which is accumulating force every moment. I tell you, something bad is coming. Bad! Do you hear me? And I won't be involved in it. I won't! I won't!"

Her voice rose to a querulous shriek. A spasm twitched every feature. And then she had sunk back in her chair with drooped lids.

"Bad!" she murmured softly.

Chapter XII.

THE SCARLET HORROR.

"You will have to go, Barbour," said Moore heavily. "I am sorry, but there are occasions when Alicia must be humored. This seems to be one of them. Unfortunate. Very—unfortunate. Perhaps another time—"

He paused and glanced suggestively toward the door.

All the while that they had argued and quarreled over me, I had sat as apparently passive as the lay figure to which I had once compared Alicia. It was, however, the passivity not of inertia, but of high-keyed endurance. What Alicia felt I don't know. If it was anything like the strain I suffered under, I can't wonder that she wished to be rid of me.

"Another time," said Moore, and looked toward the door.

I rose. Instantly Berquist was beside me. He took my arm—tried to draw me away—out of the room.

I shook him off. When I moved it was toward Alicia. Before either Moore or Nils realized my objective, I was half-way around the table. Alicia, her eyes still closed, moaned softly. She cried out, and thrust forth her hands in a resisting motion.

"Stop!"

That was Moore's voice; but it was not for is sharp command that I halted. There was—it was as if a wall had risen between Alicia and me. Or as if her outstretched hands were against my chest, holding me back. Yet there was a space of at least two yards between us.

"What do you want, Barbour?" demanded Moore roughly. "I said you would have to go!"

"I wish," I forced out, "to make *her* undo what she has done to me!"

"Then I was right!" cried Berquist indignantly.

I stood still, swept by wave upon wave of the force that willed to absorb me. The past weeks had trained me for such a struggle. Though the face of the Fifth Presence remained invisible, its identity with the intangible power I fought was clear enough to me—and I hated the face! I repulsed the enveloping consciousness of it as one strives to fling off a loathsome caress.

While I stood there, blind, silent, at war, Berquist continued:

"Now I know that I was right! Jimmy, you have let this boy suffer in some way that I neither understand nor wish wholly to understand. But believe me, you'll answer for it! Clay, lad, come away! You are courting disaster here. Alicia can't help you. She is a poor slave and tool for any force that would use her. Why, the very atmosphere of this house is contagious! Psychic! Many people are immune. Moore is immune. But I tell you, there has been more than one time when I have resolutely shut my senses against the influence, or Alicia would have dragged me into her own field of abnormal and accursed perceptiveness. It's because I resist that they won't have me at a seance. Come away!"

"No!" They could not guess, of course, that I spoke from out a swimming darkness, slashed with streaks of scarlet. "No!" I muttered again. "This woman here—she can help me. She shall help me! Moore, I'll—I'll wring your neck if you don't make her help me!"

Through the swimming, scarlet-slashed gloom I drove forward another step. Came a rush of motion. There was a vast, muffled sound as of beating wings. A trumpet-like voice cried out loudly: "I'll settle with you once for all!" it shouted. And then something had thrust in between Alicia and me.

Instantly the gloom lifted.

There at my right hand was the large table, with the shaded lamp and the books and papers strewn over it. To my left the massive, empty chair in which Alicia was wont to be imprisoned during a seance. Beyond that hung the straight, black folds of the curtains which concealed the cabinet.

Though I turned my head to neither side, I saw all these things as though looking directly at them. And also, with even more unusual distinctness, I saw what was straight ahead of me.

Between me and Alicia the figure of a man had sprung into sudden existence. In no way did this figure suggest the ghostly form one might expect from what is called "materialization." The man was real—solid.

He was of stocky, but not very powerful build. He was dressed in gray. His face—ah! Only once before had I seen this man's face with open gaze. But many times it had haunted my closed lids!

Smooth, boyish, pleasant, with smiling lips and clear, light-blue eyes— my own eyes, save that the amused gleam in them did not express a boy's unsophisticated humor.

Not a bodiless face this time, afloat in mid air or lurking behind my lids. This was the man himself—the whole, solid, flesh-and-blood man!

I could not doubt that he was real. His hand caught my arm—roughly for all that amiable gentleness the face expressed. I felt the clutching fingers tight and heavy. He clutched and at the same time smiled, sweetly, amusedly. Clutched and smiled.

"Serapion!" I whispered. And: "*Serapion!*"

His smile grew a trifle brighter; his clutch tightened. But I was no longer afraid of him. The very strain I had been under flung me suddenly to a height of exalted courage. Instinctive loathing climaxed in rebellion.

He clasped my left arm tight. My right was free. I had no weapon, but caught up from the table a thing that served as one.

And even as I did it, that clear side-vision I have referred to beheld a singular happening. As my head grew hot with a rush of exultant blood, something came flying out thought he curtains of the cabinet.

It was bright scarlet in color, and about the size of a pigeon or small hawk. I am not sure that it had the shape of a bird. The size and the peculiarly brilliant scarlet of it are all I am sure of.

This red thing flashed out of the cabinet, darted across the room, passing chest-high through the narrow space between the suddenly embodied Fifth Presence and myself—and vanished.

I heard Alicia crying: "Bad—*bad!* It has come!"

And then, in all the young strength of my right arm, I struck at the Fifth Presence. My aim was the face I hated. The weapon—a queer enough one, but efficient—sank deep, deep—buried half its length in one of those smiling, light-blue eyes.

He let go my arm and dashed his hand to his face. The weapon remained in the wound. From around it, even before my victim fell, blood gushed out—scarlet—scarlet. Below the edge of his clutching hand that would clutch me no more I could see his mouth, and—God help me!—the lips of it smiled still.

Then he had writhed and crumpled down in a loose gray heap at my feet.

"Barbour! For God's sake!"

The man I struck had sunk without a sound. That hoarse, harsh shout came from Nils. Next instant his powerful arm sent me spinning half across the room. I didn't care. He dropped to his knees. When he tried to straighten the gray heap, his hands were instantly bright with the grim color that had been the flying scarlet thing's.

But I didn't care!

I had killed him—it! The Fifth Presence had dared embody itself in flesh and I had slain it!

Nils had the body straight now, face uppermost. The light of the lamp beat down. Creeping tiptoe, I came to peer over Nils's shoulder. The lips. Did they still smile?

Then—

But there is an extremity of feeling with which words are inadequate to deal. Leave my emotions and let me state bare facts.

The gray suit in which I had seen the Fifth Presence clothed was the same faintly checked light suit I had wondered at Moore's wearing in November.

And the face there in the lamplight, contorted, ashen, blood-smeared, was the face of James Barton Moore!

Chapter XIII.
THE SHADOW OF THE CROSS.

Though I had a few obscure after-memories of loud talking, of blue uniforms that crowded in around me, of going down-stairs and out into open air, of being pushed into a clumsy vehicle of some kind, and of interminable riding through a night cold and sharply white with snow, all the real consciousness of me hovered in a timeless, spaceless agony, whereby it could neither reason nor take right account of these impressions.

Thrust in a cell at last, I must have lain down and, from pure weariness of pain, fallen asleep. Shortly after dawn, however, I awoke to a dreary, clear-headed cognizance of facts.

I knew that I had killed.

When I threatened, Moore had sprung in between me and his wife, intending, no doubt, with that hot temper of his, to put me violently from the house. His physical intervention had shocked me out of the swimming shadows, then rapidly closing in, and the Fifth Presence had chosen that opportunity for its most ghastly trick.

The face I had struck at was a wraith—a vision. My weapon—one of those paper files that are made with a heavy bronze base and an upright, murderously sharp-pointed rod—had gone home in the real face behind. Instead of slaying an embodied ghost—a madman's dream!—I had murdered a living man.

Last night, the killing and the atrocious manner of it had been enough. This morning, thought had a wider scope. I perceived that the isolated horror of the act itself was less than all. I must now take up the heavy burden of consequences.

The hard bed on which I lay, the narrow walls and the bars that encompassed me—these were symbols by which I foreread my fate.

I, Clayton Barbour, was a murderer. In that gray, early clear-headedness I made no bones about the word or the fact.

True, I had been tricked, trapped into murder; but who would believe that? Alicia—perhaps. And how would Alicia's weird testimony be received in a court of justice, even should she prove willing to give it?

I perceived that I was finished—done for.

Life as I was familiar with it had already ended, and the short, ugly course that remained to be run would end soon enough.

Then for the first time I learned what the love of life is. Life—not as consciousness, nor a state of being, nor a thought; but the warm, precious thing we are born to and carry lightly till the time of its loss is upon us.

Afterward? What were dim afterwards to me? Grant that I, of all men, had reason to know that the dying body cast forth its spirit as a persistent entity. Grant that the thin shadows of ourselves survived the flesh. That was not life!

Let me grow old in life, till its vital flood ran low, and its blood thinned, and its flesh shriveled, and weariness came to release me from desire. Then, perhaps, I should be glad of that leap into the cold world of shadows. Now—now—I was *young*.

And, oh, God! The injustice of it!

I sprang up, driven to express revolt in action. For lack of a better outlet, I beat with closed fists against the wall—the bars. A lumpish, besotted creature in the cell next to mine roused and snarled like a beast at the noise.

"Ar-r-gh!" it slobbered, and thereafter established its fellow-humanity by a protest that was a verbal river of filth.

That roused a companion—and another. As among caged animals, the contagion of resentment spread. I was in one of a single tier of cells that faced a blank, white-washed wall. I could see only the wall. It was rather appalling to hear that invisible line of rank life froth into clamor on the right and left of me.

Presently one of the beasts' keepers came tramping along the narrow alley between wall and cages. Reaching my steel grate he halted, said something inaudible, and turned his head to yell a threat that carried over all the other racket. Some of the beasts quieted and some did not; at least, the tumult diminished enough so that he could speak to me and be understood.

I had retreated a little from the bars. I was not sure how this warder would look at me, a murderer. My new character was strange to me. Instinctively I shrank from being seen in it.

He peered through; then jerked his thumb down the line.

"Fierce bunch they raked in here last night," he observed. "Dempsey raided the Fish-Eye joint and a couple of other dumps over in the old Fifth. This here's a overflow meeting from his station. Guess you didn't get much rest, huh?"

"I slept," said I.

"Good work! Wanta send out for some breakfast? Or would ya rather wait til y'r out? Don't reckon to spend the day here, do ya?"

The question seemed a needless and malicious mockery. It stiffened my spine by making me angry. But I would not satisfy the mocker's spleen by showing that.

"I would like some coffee," I said steadily. "That is all I care for just now."

"Suit y'rself; but say, you don't want none of the slop they dope out here. I c'n get ya some real good from Frank's across the street."

I suddenly understood. Behind his raillery the man was hoping to be paid for the service he offered. What did he care whether I was a murderer, a pickpocket, or an innocent man? Probably, when I was brought in he had noticed that I was well-dressed, and regarded me, not with moral horror, but as a possible purveyor of small change.

I thrust a hand in my pocket, but it came out empty. He grinned.

"That's all right. You'll get y'r coin back from the sergeant as ya go out, and you can slip it to Megonigle for me then. I go off duty in a half hour more. Sure ya don't want nothin' to eat?"

"Only the coffee, but what—"

He had slipped out of range, with a stealthy agility of movement that belied his rather clumsy figure. In a few seconds he was back again, his chest against the grated door.

"C'm here!" he hissed softly. Puzzled, I moved nearer. "Take it!"

Then I saw that through one of the square apertures of cross-grating a folded bit of paper had been thrust. I drew it through to my side, though with no notion of what it could be. The man drew off again.

"I'll see that ya get y'r coffee, Barbour," he said, in a loud, offhand voice. "Morning, Mike! Early, ain't ya?" He turned to me again. "This here's Mike Megonigle. Slip him a dollar fer me as ya pass out, an' then ya won't owe me nothin'."

A red-faced, bull-necked individual had tramped into view. He stared heavily from my grating to the night warder and back again.

"'S all right, Mike," the latter asserted. "This here's Mr. Barbour. Pal of his croaked a guy last night. Barbour ain't implicated. Just a witness. He'll be getting his bond pretty quick, and when he goes out you collect that dollar for me, Mike. Can't afford to lose that dollar—not me, huh?"

He winked jovially in my direction, waved a hand on one finger of which something glittered brightly, and was gone. The other guard grunted, stared after him for a long minute, and moved on up the passage, still speechless and shaking his head in a slow, puzzled manner, like a bewildered ox.

But his bewilderment could not have been so great as my own. The thing that glittered on the night-guard's finger had attracted my attention before he waved it. It was a ring that had a strangely familiar look. The setting was an oval bit of lapis lazuli, cut flat, incised with a tiny device the scrolls of which had been filled with gold, and surrounded by small diamonds.

Nils Berquist wore a ring like that. It was the one possession I had ever known him to prize, and that was because it had been in his family for generations. It was very old, and different from modern rings.

A duplicate? Nonsense! Why was that warder wearing Nils's ring—and what had he meant by describing me as a "witness"?

But I think some of the truth had begun to dawn on me even before I unfolded the paper that had been thrust through my grate. The inner side carried a lead-pencil scrawl, written in French. As the light in the cell was bad, and Berquist's handwriting worse, I had more than a little trouble in deciphering it.

I had read it all, however, before the return of the night-warder—that superbly corrupt official who took a bribe to deliver a message, honestly delivered it, and thereafter brazenly wore the bribe about his duties. He returned with my coffee. I was face down on the shelf that served for a bed. He rattled the grate, spoke, and as I didn't answer shoved the coffee under the door and went off—whistling, I fancy.

I couldn't have spoken to him if I had wished, because I was crying like a girl. The reaction from friendless solitude in a world made new and terrible had hit me that way. It was not that I meant to accept Nils's sacrifice. I really hadn't thought about the practical side of it yet. But to discover that a man who had actually seen me do that awful thing, in spite of it remained my friend and loyal to the amazing degree of taking the burden on himself— that changed the world round again, some way, and made it almost right again.

Why, the mere fact that Nils could think of me without abhorrence was enough! It restored to me all the love and friendship that had been mine, and from which last night's deed had seemed to irrevocably cut me off.

If Nils, then those nearer and dearer than Nils—Roberta— But there I halted and cringed back. That way there loomed a dreadful and inevitable loss. Let contemplation of it wait awhile.

With wet eyes I sat up and again held Nils's message in the barred light that fell through the grating. He had protected his meaning by using a safer language than English—safe from the warder, at least—and couching it in terms whose real import would be obscure if it fell into other hands. At that his sacrifice was endangered in the sending, but not so much as by leaving me to blurt out the truth unwarned:

My Dear Friend:

This to you, who last night were past understanding. May the morning have brought you a clear mind. I take the chance and write. I killed James Moore. Understand me when I say this. He struck at me, but I wrested away the weapon and killed in self-defense and not in intent.

There followed a rather circumstantial account of his supposed struggle with Moore. Nils's brain had not been numbed last night, like mine. Into this story which he had made for us both to tell he had fitted the least possible fiction. Questioned on details up to almost the moment of Moore's death, we had only to stick to the truth and we could not disagree. It was a clever—a noble lie that he had arranged.

You will bear witness to all this, and they will not convict me of murder. Alicia Moore had swooned. She did not witness Moore's death. I rely on you, therefore, as my sole witness. And it is fortunate that Moore in his anger turned not on you, but attacked me! I know you, dear friend, and that you would take my place and bear all for me, if that were possible. But I have not one in the world, save you, to suffer the anguish for my trouble. I have little to lose.

Not for your own sake, then, but for the sake of those to whom you are all—for the sake of her whose life-happiness rests with you to hold sacred or shatter. *I command you* to—be glad that I and not you have this to go through with. For that I shall not think the less of you. I only ask that in your heart I be held always as a friend.

Nils Berquist.

Nils was no sentimentalist, but the French—language of love and friendship—had lent its phrases touchingly to his purpose. In my heart he would indeed dwell, from this day!

To accept would be dishonor unthinkable. Even the weight of the thinly veiled argument he put forward must be out-balanced by the shame of allowing an innocent man to risk the most disgraceful of deaths in my stead. I could not accept, yet though I died, the wonder of Nils Berquist's attempted loyalty should go with me—out there!

Out there! Into that dim, guessed at coldness, with its shadowy, mocking inhabitants.

"You are right!" said a voice. "That world is to yours as the shadow to reality. But why cast the real life away?"

Had one of the warders entered my cell and addressed me, his voice could have echoed no more distinctly in my brain. Before I looked up, however, I knew what I should see. When, raising my own eyes, they met those clear, light-blue ones, I felt no surprise.

There floated the face, bodiless again, but aside from that with an appearance of substantiality which equaled—it could not exceed—that of its last tragic visitation. The undimensional flatness had given way to the solidly modeled curves of living flesh.

The point of my improvised weapon, however, had left not even a mark on the face it was meant for. That material aspect was false. Though I hated him now with an added loathing, I had learned bitterly that combat with him must be on other than physical ground. I sat sternly quiet, hoping that if I did not answer, the presence would vanish.

"Your violent temper," he continued pleasantly, but with a trace of kindly reproach, "has placed you in danger. Fortunately we—you and I—are not as other men. We need not be overborne. Tell me, which of all the forces that influence life is the strongest?"

"Hate!" Springing erect, I thrust forward till my face almost touched that of the Presence. "Such *hate* as I feel for you!"

He did not retreat. I could—I could almost have sworn that I felt the warmth of his flesh close to mine!

"Aw-w-w-w, cut it out!" wailed the dweller in the next cell. "Ain't yer never goin' ter let a guy git his beauty sleep?"

"You need not speak aloud," smiled the face. "And I would suggest that you sit down. Consider the feelings of others! Consideration is a beautiful quality, and well worth cultivating. Speech between you and me need disturb no one. It can be silent as thought, for it is thought—my thought to yours. Sit down!"

A sudden weakening of the knees made me obey him. Revilings I could have withstood; curses, or threats of evil. But there was an awful sweetness and beauty in the face—a calm assurance about his preaching phrases— that frightened me as threats could not have done. Could it be that I had misjudged this serene being from beyond the border?

Then I looked in his eyes and knew that I had not. They were too like my own! I understood them. Another he might have deceived, but never me.

"Hate," he continued, in his placid, leisurely manner, "is a futile, boomerang force that invariably reacts on itself. It is the scorpion among forces, stinging itself to destruction. No; I did not come here to preach. You understand now that I spoke the truth and can read your unvoiced thoughts with perfect readiness. Our conversations are thus safe from eavesdroppers. As I was saying, hate is its own enemy and the enemy of life. There is but one invincible power, offered by God to man, and which God has commanded man to use."

"You mean—"

"Love! Armored in love, your life will be a sacred, guarded joy to you. Believe me! I am far older than I appear, and wiser than I am old. Guided by me, guarded by love, you have a beautiful future at your command."

"Begun with murder!" I snarled.

The presence beamed patiently upon me. "That was a mistake. Don't blame yourself too severely. Blame me, if you like, though I had no idea that your foolish animosity would bring forth the red impulse of murder. Yes; we who have passed beyond can commit blunders! I made one in appearing when I did. Can't we forgive one another and forget?"

"Not while I am in jail for it and facing electrocution!" said I grimly.

"But you are not. Very shortly you will walk out a free man; under bond, it is true, but only—"

"Never!" I was on my feet again at that. "Let Nils Berquist suffer in my place? Never!"

"But he won't suffer! Or at least, not as you would. Come! Trust all that to me, who can see far, and have a certain power. Won't you trust me?"

"You mean that *you* can influence a jury to acquit him?"

"I have power! And think. Would you cast back his friendship in his face? Would you hurl your father into his grave, killed by horror? Would you drag your sister—your mother—through the mire of notoriety that surrounds a criminal? Would you leave them destitute? Would you stab through the very heart of the girl who loves you? Your friend has none of these to care. The opprobrium will not hurt him. He is by nature an isolated soul; and moreover, he is innocent. He has that strength, and the glory of sacrifice to sustain him. Once freed yourself, you can do much to bring about his release.

"It is well known that Moore had an evil temper. The plea of self-defense will be borne out by you. Engage a clever legal advisor for your friend, and in the end your pitiful mistake will have brought harm to no one except Moore himself, who deserved it. He was a very selfish, disagreeable man! He was not loved by any one, even his wife. What? Oh, leave Alicia out of it, my dear boy. You won't find our plans upset by her. And now, I should advise that before seeking a bonds-man elsewhere, you telephone to the man whose friendship you have already won at the bank. Your immediate superior there is a kindly, good man—"

The presence got no further with his advice. As he had talked, quietly, soothingly, I had found my thoughts beginning to follow the smooth current of his. But his reference to Mr. Terne had been another of those errors to which he claimed that even the disembodied were prone. It had recalled to me that scene in the president's office—Van's desperate face—and the ignominy into which I had been betrayed.

Repulsion—loathing—surged mightily through my veins again.

"No! No! No! In the name of Heaven, leave me!" I cried aloud. To my amazed relief the Presence obeyed. He had faded and gone in an instant— though by the last impression I had of him, he still smiled.

Trembling, I looked down at Nils's letter in my hand.

From the barred grating a shadow was cast upon it, and the form of that shadow was a cross.

CHAPTER XIV.
SO LIKE HIM!

Around 2 P.M. I was taken before Magistrate Patterson and my bail set in the sum of thirty-five hundred dollars. Arthur Terne, second vice-president of the Colossus Trust Company, having appeared as my bondsman, the matter of my liberty pending the inquest, to be held the following morning, was soon arranged.

I left the court in Mr. Terne's company. Nils Berquist I had not seen, but was given to understand that he had been remanded without bail. I had pleaded in vain for a chance to talk with him.

Mr. Terne was kindness personified, though I inferred from one or two remarks he let fall that the Colossus' leonine president was not pleased.

The morning papers had featured the affair with blatant headlines. They had got my name. The Barbour & Hutchinson failure was resurrected.

The Colossus itself stalked in massive dignity across one column, irrelevantly capping a "Brutal Slaying in Haunted House," and when I saw that, I knew that "not pleased" was a mild description for Vansittart's probable emotions!

The bizarre character of Alicia, the nature of the wound, and the ghastly inappropriateness of the weapon which effected it, had appealed to the reportorial fancy with diversely picturesque results. A plain murder, with no more apparent mystery attached than this one, would have passed with slight attention. But though Alicia was not a professional medium, it appeared that she and Moore had a certain reputation.

In hinting to me of the latter's tempestuous exit from the Psychic Research Association, Nils had spared mentioning Alicia as the bone of contention. I now learned that she had been a country girl, the daughter of a hotel-keeper in a tiny Virginian village where Moore had spent two or three autumn weeks.

Discovering in her what he regarded as supernormal powers, he wished to bring her north for further study. On her father's strangely objecting to this treatment of his daughter as a specimen, Moore had settled the difficulty by offering marriage. After the wedding, he did bring her north, educated her, and finally presented her to the Association as a prodigy well worth their attention.

Unfortunately, after several remarkable seances, she was convicted of fraud in flagrant degree. It was through the slightly heated arguments ensuing that Moore was asked to resign his directorship.

The fantastic dispute had amused the lay-public intermittently through a dull summer, but I was off in the mountains that year with Van, and what news we read was mostly on the sporting pages, whither the pros and cons of spiritualistic debate are not wont to penetrate. But all that was raked up now, as sauce for the news of Moore's sensational death, and having acquired a certain personal interest in spiritualism, I read it.

Following Mr. Terne's advice and my own inclination, I went straight home. No need to rehearse all I endured that day. Roberta's smilingly tearful consolations were the worst, I think, though my father's: "Clay, son, you are right to stand by your friend!" ran a close second. He said it because I refused to hear a word against Nils, and insisted that the fault had not been his. Though I would not go into the details of what had taken place in Moore's library, I stuck at that one truth, and dad, at least, who had taken a fancy to Nils the evening he dined at our house, believed me.

Altogether, however, it was a bad afternoon, and that night in my bedroom the face came again. I knew it was he, though the room was dark and I could not see him clearly. He had become so like as that to a material being!

"You have done well!" he began. "But, to make one small criticism, you must learn not to blush so easily. When your father commended your loyalty you reddened and stammered till, if you had not been among friends, suspicion might have been roused."

"My confusion only lasted a moment," I defended. Then I remembered. "You go!" I said. "What do I want of you and your criticisms or advice? You have brought me enough unhappiness. I am a sneak and a criminal, and all through you!"

"Ingratitude is the only real crime," he retorted sententiously. "Always be grateful, and show it! You have brought unhappiness on yourself, and it is I who point the way out. So far you have followed my advice. Why turn on me now?"

"Liar!" I fairly hissed. "If you can read my thoughts, you know that I have planned otherwise than you would have me! I am doing as Nils wished without regard to you, and not for the sake of myself. And let me tell you this! If there arises the slightest prospect that my friend will not be cleared, I shall confess. Tomorrow will decide it. If things go badly for him at the inquest, my people will have to suffer. The shame and loss he is trying to save them from would be nothing, then, to the shame involved by silence!"

Had the face possessed shoulders, I know he would have shrugged them.

"You are wrong, but we need not discuss that. I tell you in advance that your friend will be held for wilful murder. Did you know quite all that I know, you would not hope for a different indictment."

The strings of my heart contracted. I passed a breathless moment of realization. Then: "To-morrow I confess!" I said firmly.

"To-morrow you will choose a lawyer for your friend, and begin the work which will surely achieve his release."

"You do not know that! You have admitted that you are capable of mistakes."

"Not in a case of this kind. I possess a wide knowledge of facts which enables to be very sure that your friend will get his release. I am your unswerving ally. And remember that I have not only wisdom, but some power."

"Oh, you are—leave me!" I cried aloud.

"In God's name, go!"

The faintly-seen oval of his smooth face faded, though more slowly than in the cell at the station-house.

I heard a soft swish of slippered feet in the hall. Someone rapped lightly and opened my door.

"Clay, dear," said my mother, "did you call? Are you ill?"

"No. I had a bad dream and awoke crying out because of it."

"One can't wonder at that." She came and sat on the edge of my bed. "Such an awful thing for you to be involved in! Please, dear son, keep to your own class after this. Trouble always comes of mingling with queer Bohemian people who have no standards, or—or morals."

"Nils Berquist has the highest standard of any man I know!" I was fiercely defensive.

There was a pause of silence. Then in the dark she leaned and kissed my forehead. "You are so like him!" she murmured.

I groaned. "If only that were true!"

"But you are. With those blue, clear eyes of his, that saw only beauty and love. He would never hear a word against a friend."

"Mother! You meant that I am like—"

"Your uncle, yes. And in some strange way I feel sure that his guarding influence is really about us. Why, when I came into the room just now I had the queerest feeling—as if it were a room in a dream, or—no, I can't convey the feeling in words. But the sense of *his presence* was in it. I do truly believe that he has returned to guard us in the midst of so much trouble. At least, it would be like him. Dear, faithful, loving, lovable Serapion!"

Chapter XV.
BAD DAYS.

But had my desired obsession, or familiar, or haunting ghost really desired to help, he might have warned me definitely of Sabina Cassel.

Alicia did not appear at the inquest. She was ill and under a physician's care. Her semi-conscious state as reported by him prevented even the taking of a deposition.

I did not, however, stand alone as star witness before the coroner's jury. Sabina Cassel, Mrs. Moore's old colored "Mammy" whom she had brought north with her from Virginia, shared and rather more than shared the honors with me.

They had taken pains that Nils and I should not meet. He was kept rigorously *incommunicado* till the inquest, no one, save the police and the district attorney, having access to him. At the inquest I caught only a glimpse of him, when he was led out past where I awaited my turn before the jury. Involuntarily I sprang up, only to be caught by a constable's hand, while Nils was hustled on out. As he went, he threw me a glance that was a burning, dictatorial command.

I obeyed it. I told the jury exactly that story which Nils's letter had outlined for us both. There was tempered steel in Berquist. I could be sure that no long-drawn torment of inquisition could make him vary a hairsbreadth from the line he had set for us to follow.

In my testimony, which preceded Sabina's, I explained that Nils had objected to my interest in spiritualism, fostered by a single previous visit to the Moores' place. That he wished me to leave the house with him, and that Alicia also had seemed set against my remaining. That an argument ensued, at the height of which Moore became very angry and excited, shouted: "I'll settle with you, once for all!" and came around the table toward Berquist.

"He grasped Berquist's arm," I said. "When my friend tried to free

himself, Moore snatched the—the file from the table. I saw Berquist seize
Moore's wrist. They struggled a moment, and then Moore staggered away
with his hands to his face. Then—he fell down. Berquist called to me, and—
No, I had not tried to interfere. It all happened too quickly. There wasn't
time. After Berquist wrenched the file from Moore's hand I don't believe
he struck at Moore. I think the file was driven into his eye by accident."

That surmise, of course, was struck from the record; but I had said it, at
least, and hoped it impressed the jury.

"Afterward, the—the sight of blood and the suddenness of it all turned
me sick—no, my recollections were clear up to that time."

And so forth. It was a straight story. I knew it agreed to a hair with Nils's
confession.

What I did not, could not know, was that it varied in one essential detail
from an entirely different confession—a confession made by a person whom
we had not considered as an even possible eye-witness, and whose very
existence I, at least, had forgotten.

Given that a second eye-witness existed, one would have supposed that
the disagreement would have been over the slayer's identity. It was not. By a
curious trick of fate, Sabina Cassel, Alicia's old colored maid, did undoubtedly see me strike Moore down, and yet, not through such a supernormal
illusion as caused me to kill Moore, but in a perfectly natural manner, she
had confused Berquist's identity with mine. She related as having been done
by Berquist that which had been done by me.

In one detail only did Sabina's testimony conflict with ours, but that was
the kind of detail which would hang a man, if its truth were established.

She had seen me—Berquist by her own account—snatch the file from the
table and strike Moore, and she had seen me do it on no further provocation
than the laying of Moore's hand on my arm.

The Fifth Presence was right when he foretold that Nils would be in-
dicted.

And yet, though things had indeed gone ill for Nils at the inquest, I did
not at once carry out my expressed intention and substitute myself for him
as defendant.

I didn't wish to die, nor spend years in prison. I wanted to live and have
a decent, straight, pleasant future ahead, such as I had been brought up to
expect as a right. It seemed to me that just one way lay open. Though Nils
was now entirely at my mercy, only his untrammeled acquittal would give
me the moral freedom to keep silent. For that a first-class lawyer was a *sine
qua non*.

Berquist was practically penniless, and the Barbour exchequer in not much better state. Here again, however, friendship came to the fore in a curiously impressive manner. For the sake of an old acquaintance and some ancient friendly claim that my father had on him, none other than Helidore Marx took Berquist's case. I mean Helidore Marx, of Marx, Marx & Orlow, who could have termed himself Marx, the famous and not lied.

I remember my first interview with him after dad had—to me almost incredibly—persuaded him into alliance. My first impression was of a mild-looking, smallish man, with a scrubby mustache. He had hurt the top of his bald head in some way, so that it was crossed with a fair-sized hillock of adhesive plaster. I thought that added to his insignificant appearance; but he had the brightest, softly brown eyes I have ever seen, and after the first few minutes I was afraid of him.

I was afraid that I would tell him too much.

My confidence, however, proved not the easily uprooted kind of a common criminal, and for Nils the acquisition of this famous, insignificant looking lawyer gave me the only real hope of assurance I had through those bad days.

"Your friend," Marx had said to me, "is a rather wonderful young man, Barbour. I can't blame you for being troubled. He has the kind of intelligence that would make a legal genius of him, if he had turned his efforts in that direction. A wonderful intelligence—and all lost in a maze of impractical theorizing and the sort of dreams that can't come true so long as men are men, and women are women, God help us all! He shan't go to the chair, nor prison, either. He's my man, my case, and—yes, I'll say my friend, though I don't run to sudden enthusiasms. Leave Berquist to me!"

Evidently, Marx's consultations with his "case" had not been kept within strictly professional bounds. I smiled involuntarily. I could picture that long dark face of Nils lighting to alert interest as he discovered that Marx was not merely the lawyer who might save him from martyrdom, but also a thinking man. He must have brought out a side of the little man that was kept carefully submerged at ordinary times. I am sure that few people had seen Helidore Marx inclined to dilatory wanderings in philosophy, such as Nils loved.

But I went out with a lighter heart and more optimism than I had carried in some time. Marx, with his "my man, my case—my friend!" had instilled a confidence which remained with me all that day.

I had returned to the bank, for though I walked in the Valley of the Shadow, while I could walk I must work.

So Mr. Terne had me back again, and it was a very good thing that I had Mr. Terne to go back to. Not many men would have put up with the abstracted attention my work received, nor patiently picked up the slack of details I let go by me.

His patience had a characteristic reason behind it, which I was sure of from the minute he told me about poor Van.

The latter, it seemed had really gone the step too far with his father in the affair of Mr. Terne's four hundred. Vansittart, Sr., would let no one speak of his son to him after that day. Everyone in the bank, however, knew that he had quarreled with him, disowned him, and that Van, in a fit of temper, had refused the offer of a last money settlement—a couple of thousand only, it was said—flung out of the Colossus, and walked off, leaving the gray roadster forlorn by the curb.

No one knew where Van had gone after that. He had simply vanished, saying no good-bys, and taking nothing with him but the clothes he wore.

Mr. Terne felt guilty because it was his complaint which had caused the final rupture. He liked me, anyway, but having, as he believed, ruined Van he showed an added consideration for me which developed into an almost absurd tenderness for my feelings.

He needed that, if I was to be kept on the tracks at all those days. I was nervous as a cat, and ready to jump at the creak of a door.

Roberta would watch me with wide, troubled eyes, and because a question was in them I would grow irritable and fling off and leave her with almost brutal abruptness. And always she forgave me—till I came near wishing she would forgive less easily.

Cathy resented my new irritability with the merciless justice of a sister; mother endured my anxiety for Nils only because it proved I was like "dear Serapion," and dad harped on his pride in me for "standing by" till I really dreaded to go near him.

As for the Fifth Presence, he remained detestably faithful. Several times I explained to him that if Nils were not cleared I intended to confess. When he only continued to smile, I ceased talking to him.

He still came, however, and on the very night before the trial opened, the last thing of which I was conscious, dropping asleep, was his smooth, persuasive, hateful, silent voice. As ever, it was expressing the platitudinous—and always subtly evil—advice to which habit had so accustomed me that it had grown very hard indeed to distinguish his speech from my thoughts!

Chapter XVI.
SABINA'S TESTIMONY.

When a murderer—for I named myself that—is called to confront across some thirty feet of court-room the innocent man standing trial in his stead, he needs all his nerve and a bit more to keep steady under the questioning of even a friendly and considerate counsel.

In fact, I was strangely more afraid of Marx than of District Attorney Clemens. I might, however, spared myself there.

The impanneling of the jury had been a battle-royal between Marx and Clemens, at which I was not present, but which had roused the newspaper men to gloating anticipation of the real battle to follow.

Then Marx—dropped out!

I could hardly believe it when Orlow, his junior associate, met me on the first day of the trial and broke the news. It proved lamentably true.

By Orlow's account—he was a fat, clever little Russian, with an unmistakable nose and a tongue that would slip into betraying v's and p's—by his account Marx had finished with the talesmen against strict orders from his physician.

"A book hit his head," explained Orlow. "That was in September. It dropped off a shelf, and the brass corner cut his head—oh, just a *leetle* bit! But he vas careless. Infection set in, and now there is necrosis of the bone in his skull. To think of it! Vith such prains inside! He will be operated now, and when I vent to see him this morning, he was insensible. And to think of it," he added with melancholy and unconscious humor, "it vas the Compiled Statutes that may have ruined our Helidore Marx forever! Vell, we must just do as ve can vithout him."

This was poor consolation. Had it not been for Marx, I told myself, I would never have left Nils Berquist go to trial. Should I allow it to go on now, with our best hope *hors de combat?*

The second Marx—Helidore's brother—was in Europe, and Orlow, while brilliant in his fashion, was not a man to impress juries. His genius lay in the hunting out of technical refinements of law, ammunition, as it were, for the batteries which had brought rage to the heart of more than one district attorney.

When he arose presently in court and asked for a delay in proceedings, Clemens's eye lighted. When Mr. Justice Ballington refused the request—a foregone conclusion, because Marx, admittedly, was in too serious a condition for the delay even to be measured—Clemens lowered his head suddenly. It might have been grief for his adversaries misfortune—or, again, it might not.

Where I sat with other witnesses, I was intensely conscious of an absurd, brilliantly veiled little figure, two chairs behind me.

This was my first glimpse of Alicia, since the night of Berquist's arrest.

Though I knew Marx had been granted at least two interviews with her, me she had resolutely refused to receive.

Now I was relieved to find that her nearness brought no return of the super-normal influence I had suffered before in her vicinity.

She sat stiffly upright, and did not glance once in my direction. Perhaps her "guides" had advised her to don that awful veil of protecting purple for this occasion; or she may have worn it as a tribute to her husband's memory. It certainly gave her a more unusual appearance than would a crape blackness behind which a newly-made widow is wont to hide her grief.

At her side towered the large form of Sabina Cassel.

The trial opened.

One Dr. Frick appeared on the stand, and in elaborate incomprehensibility described in surgical terms the wound which had caused Moore's death. I saw him handling a small, hideous object—gesturing with it to show exactly how it had been misused to a deadly purpose.

Then for several minutes I didn't see anything more. Luckily all eyes in the court-room were on either the doctor or the "murderer." Nobody was watching me.

The doctor's demonstration seemed to prove rather conclusively that my "accident" hypothesis was impossible. The file, he showed, could have been driven into the brain only by a direct hard blow.

Dr. Frick was allowed to stand down.

In establishing the offense, Clemens saw fit next to call Alicia herself.

As her mistress arose, Sabina's massive bulk stirred uneasily, as if she would have followed her to the stand.

At the inquest, the old colored woman's testimony had done more than cause Nils's indictment for murder. It had made a public and very popular jest of Alicia's claim to intercourse with "spirits." But though, in the first flush of excitement over Moore's death, Sabina had betrayed her, the woman was loyal to her mistress. When a murmur that was almost a titter swept the packed audience outside the rail, Sabina shook her head angrily, muttering to herself.

The audience hoped much of Alicia, and its keen humor was not entirely disappointed. No sooner had she appeared than an argument began about her preposterously-brilliant veil. The court insisted that it should be raised. Alicia firmly declined to oblige. She had to give in finally, of course, and when that peaked, white face with its strange eyes was exposed, the hydra beyond the rail doubtless felt further rewarded.

The hydra believed her a fraud. They had reason. I, with greater reason, understood and pitied her!

I thought she might break down on the stand. Alicia's character, however, was a complicated affair that set her outside the common run of behavior to Clemens's questions with sphinx-like impassivity and the precision of a machine.

Her answers only confirmed Nils's story and mine to a certain point, and stopped there. There was not a word of "spirits" nor "guides;" not a hint of any influence more evil than common human passions; not a suggestion, even, that she had formed an opinion as to which man, slayer or slain, was the first aggressor. I am sure that a more reserved and non-committal widow than Alicia never took the stand at the trial of her husband's supposed murderer.

"James," she said, "wished Mr. Barbour to remain. Mr. Berquist wished him to leave. They argued—No, I should not have called the argument a quarrel—I did not see Mr. Berquist strike James. While they were still talking, I lost consciousness of material surroundings— Yes, my loss of consciousness could be called a faint— The argument was not violent enough to frighten me into fainting— Yes, there was a reason for my losing consciousness—I lost consciousness because I felt faint. I was tried—I do that sometimes— Yes, I warned them that something bad was coming. I couldn't say why. I just had that impression. I did not see either James or Mr. Berquist assume a threatening attitude—"

Released at last, she readjusted her purple screen with cold self-possession, and returned to her seat.

It was Sabina Cassel's next turn. Save in appearance, Alicia had not after all come up to public anticipations. In Sabina, however, the hydra was sure of a real treat in store.

Judge Ballington rapped for order. Sabina took her oath with a scowl. Every line of her face expressed resentment.

But she was intelligent. To Clemens's questions, she gave grim, bald replies that offered as little grip as possible to public imagination.

Yes, on the evening in question she had been standing concealed behind the black curtains of "Miss 'Licia's" cabinet, or "box," as Sabina called it. No, "Marse James" did not know she was there. Miss 'Licia and she had "fixed it up" so that one could enter the box from the back. Marse James had the box built with a solid wooden back, like a wardrobe. It stayed that way—for a while.

"Then Marse James he done got onsatisfied!—Yas, de sperits did wuhk in de box an' come out ob it, too; but Marse James, he ain't suited yit. He want dem sperits shud wuhk all de time! He neber gib mah poh chile no res'!"

And so Alicia, who, according to Sabina, could sometimes but not always command her "sperits," devised a means to satiate Moore's scientific craving for results.

While he was absent in another city, the two conspirators brought in a carpenter. They had the cabinet removed and a doorway cut through the plastered wall into a large closet in the next room. By taking off the cabinet's solid back and hinging it on again, it would just open neatly into the aperture cut to fit it. Alicia kept plenty of gowns hung over the opening in the closet beyond.

Returning, Moore found his solid-backed cabinet apparently as before. From that time, however, the "sperits" were more willing to oblige than formerly.

"*Ab uno disce omnes,*" is invariably applied to the medium or clairvoyant caught in fraud, though translated: "From all fraud, infer all deceit."

The world laughed over the "spiritualistic fake again exposed!" I did not laugh.

Let it be that the hand which Roberta and I had seen was Sabina's gnarled black paw, and that my impression of its unsubstantiality was a self-delusion. Let those strange little twirling flames that had arisen pass as the peculiar "fireworks" I had tried to believe them. Let even the incident of the broken lamp have been a feat of Sabina's—though how her large, clumsy figure could have stolen out past the table and into the room unheard was a puzzle—and the masculine voice of "Horace," a wonderful ventriloquism.

Grant all these as deceptions. There had come that to me through Alicia's unwilling agency which had given me a terrible faith in her, that no proof of occasional fraud could dispel.

Clemens's interrogations touched lightly on the object of the door in the cabinet's supposedly solid back, only serving to establish the fact that it was impossible for his witness to have been practically in the library unknown to all the room's other occupants save, probably, Alicia.

Then he asked Sabina's story of that night in her own words. She began it grimly:

"Waal, Ah wuz in behin' de cuhtins dat hangs in front ob Miss 'Licia's box. Dem cuhtins is moderate thin. Ah cudn' see all dey is in de room, but Ah suttinly cud see all dat pass in front ob de lamp— Yass, dat whut yoh got in yoh hand am one ob dem cuhtins."

Here Clemens checked her, while the "cuhtin," Exhibit B in the prosecution's evidence, was passed from hand to hand through the jury-box.

Each juryman momentarily draped himself in mourning while he assured himself that it was thin enough to be seen through. Then with solemn nods Exhibit B was restored to the district attorney. Sabina continued.

"Dese yeah gemmen, Mistah Buhquis' and Mistah Bahbour, dey come in, and right away de argifyin' stahted. Ah kain't tell all dey say. Dey use high-falutin, eddicated languidge what am not familiar toh me, though Lawd knows Ah's done hear enuff on it sence Miss 'Licia come norff wif Marse James Mooah.

"Dey argifies an' argifies. Mistah Bahbour, he don' say nuffin much. But Mistah Buhquis', he specify dey shud bof up'n leave. Miss 'Licia she say mebbe sump'n bad gwine happen purty quick. Marse James, he say: 'Mistah Bahbour, you go; come back 'notha time.' Mistah Bahbour, he say no, he doan wanta go, kaze Miss 'Licia c'n mebbe help him some way. Mistah Buhquis' he go right up in de aih. He specify some hahm done come ob he fren' stayin' roun' deah any longah.

"Mistah Buhquis' he am standin' right alongside de big table wif de lamp on it. De lamp am behin' him. I see ebery move he make.

"He done muttah sump'n low. Ah don' rightly know whut he say, but it hab a right spiteful, argifyin' tone toh it.

"Marse James, he holler out: 'I fix yoh now foh dat!'— No, dem ain't mebbe de zact wuds he use, but yoh ast me toh tell dis in mah own wuds, an' dat am whut he mean— Yas, suh, Ah will continue.

"He holler, 'Ah fix yoh now foh dat!' an' he rush obah toh Mistah Buhquis' an' lay han' on he ahm—No, suh; he didn't go foh toh do Mistah Buhquis' no hahm. Marse James he hab a way ob talkin' loud an' biggity, but Ah nevah done saw him do no hahm toh nobuddy.

"He grab Mistah Buhquis' lef' ahm. Mistah Buhquis', he reach out he otha' han' and grab sump'n off de table. Marse James don' do nuffin. Mistah Buhquis', he fro back he han' an' hit out wif it real smaht. Marse James leggo he ahm, clap he han's obah he face, an' sorta lets go all obah. He jes' crumble down lak.

"Ah knows dat de bad am happen.

"Ah cuddin' git out dat box easy intoh de room, kaze dey's a table in it dat reach purty nigh acrost, an' Ah ain't spry to climb ober it—No, suh; Ah didn't think toh shuv de table out de way. Ah ain't think ob nuffin but Miss 'Licia. Ah turns roun' an' gits out de back, kaze Ah wants toh git toh mah Miss 'Licia. Ah comes roun' toh de hall doah and goes in de library. Deah is Mistah Buhquis' stannin' obah Marse James, he han's all droppin' blood.

"Ah, say: 'Yo' done kill him, ain't yoh?' He luks all roun' kinda pitiful lak, an' den he say:

" ' Yas, Sabina, Ah kill him! Now go fotch de doctah an' some p'leece!'

"Mistah Buhquis', he am lak lots ob otha high-spirited gemmen. He don' go foh to kill Marse James, but when Marse James tech him in anger, he jes' bleeged foh to do it. Das all right! Ah gotta right toh hab mah 'pinion, same as ebryone. Waal, don' put it in de writin' record, den. Ah don' keer whut yoh does. Das jes' mah 'pinion!

"Yas, suh. Ah's suah dat it war Mistah Burquis' grab de file and not Marse James. Waal, Marse James, he stannin' wif he lef' side toh de table. Yas, suh; I cud suah nuff tell which wuz which. Marse James, he ain't so tall by purty nigh a fut high as Mistah Buhquis'. It am de tall man who stan' wif de right side ag'in' de table who take de file off'n it. No; Marse James don' try ter do nuffin' hurtful toh Mistah Buhquis'. No; dey don' struggle roun' none atall. Dey jes' stan' deah. It's de Lawd's truf, dat was de mos' onexcitin' killin' Ah hab evah saw!"

And then Clemens let her go, to the deep disgust of Hydra, outside the rail. He had not asked what she was doing in the cabinet, nor many other of the questions which gave an amusing double interest to the Moore murder. All that, however, was bound to come out in the cross-examination, and, mean time, Sabina had proved "Clemens's witness" to an extent which made the case promise well of interest on its tragic side.

Chapter XVII.
BOUND BY THE DEAD.

I was not called before the jury until after the noon recess, which gave me time to think things over a bit more.

At the inquest, I had not actually heard Sabina's testimony. Though Marx, who interviewed her as well as her mistress, had warned me that she would prove a difficult antagonist, I had not fully believed him. Negroes in the average run are diffuse in their statements and easily muddled into self-contradiction.

Sabina might prove so under cross-examination, but I doubted it now. She had wasted hardly a word that morning, and there was only one point on which I was sure that she could be shaken.

The difference in height between slayer and slain was a strong point for the prosecution. Even through thin, black curtains it would indeed have been hard to confuse a tall silhouette with a short one. But no one had thought to question the identity of the tall silhouette.

Though Sabina may have known better during the minutes that she stood staring through the curtains, her after and more vivid sight of Berquist, with hands "droppin' blood," and his almost instant claim of the crime as his own, had served to make the tall man Berquist in all her memories.

Berquist, the self-confessed!

I had no faith in Orlow. Had Marx not dropped out, I should have been content to let the trial take its course, sure that his genius would somehow save the day and free my friend. But under Orlow's handling, with that craggy, sullen, assured black woman to swear that Moore was not and could not have been the aggressor—since he stood with his left side to the table, grasping the tall silhouette with his right hand, and a man under impulse of passion is not likely to reach for a weapon with his left—I was morally certain that Berquist would lose out.

But what if, rising on the stand, instead of a second perjury I told the simple truth?

Not that portion of it which included the superhuman, but just the fact that I, and not Berquist, had been swept by one of those sudden fits of red anger that have made murderers of many before me?

Why, Sabina herself would support my words, once spoken! There was a little, unnoticed twist in her testimony—a point where the voice of Berquist, coming from beyond the table, became the voice of the tall man standing on her side of the lamp.

The instant that I spoke she would know. Her memories, unconsciously readjusted to fit facts as she had afterward learned them, would be straight again. Berquist's hidden heroism would stand revealed, and I, though I died, I would at least die clean.

Resolve crystallized suddenly within me. When Clemens called me to the stand I would go, not to testify, but to confess.

I walked to the little raised platform, with the chair where the others had sat, below the double tier of jurymen. I mounted it. Somebody put a rusty black book under my hand and mumbled through a slurred rigmarole, to which my low acquiescence was a prelude to ruin for me. I sat down in the chair.

Beyond the rail was a packed level of faces. They were all pale and dreary-looking, it seemed to me, though that may have been an effect of light, for the day was gray and dreary. I had returned to court through falling snow. It was a wet, late spring fall of clinging flakes, and all the way I had been haunted by a memory of the "dead-alive" house as I had seen it that night.

Not the interior—not even the library, with its master, a grim gray and scarlet horror on the floor. But the house itself, desolate under its white burden, with the great flakes swirling down, hiding deeper and more deep the line of division between the living half and the dead.

Berquist was sitting by a table with Orlow beside him. I had visited him in prison, of course, and talked with him a few moments just before the trial opened. His determination and courage had never swerved, nor his conviction that we had only to keep steady—and win.

Now I saw his eyes as a dark and valiant glory fixed on me. Their message only hardened my resolve.

That man to play the martyr for my sake? Never!

Orlow left Nils, and took his stand conveniently near. He was there to protect me from irrelevant questions, but he looked quite out of place. Clearly, the mantle of Helidore Marx did not rest easily on his shoulders.

The district attorney, a thin, scholarly person whom I instinctively disliked, began his inquisition.

"Your name, please? Age and occupation?"

"Barbour—Clayton S. Barbour," I corrected myself. "I am—"

"Just a moment. Your full name for the record, please, Mr. Barbour."

Clemens, who would reserve any attempt to "rattle" me for my appearance in the rebuttal, was politeness itself.

"Clayton—*Serapion* Barbour!" I forced out. Then I cursed myself for not having substituted "Samuel," or left out the initial.

"There's power in a name." Once I would have laughed at that statement, but not now. Not with my recent memories.

And as God is my witness, I sat there and saw the district attorney's hatchet-face change, blend, grow smooth and loathsomely pleasant.

Clemens continued his interrogations, but I spoke to another than he when I answered them.

The living bound by the dead!

Chapter XVIII.
A LETTER FROM ALICIA.

May 15.

Mr. C. S. Barbour.

Sir: I am writing to you because my guides advise it. Otherwise I should not do so. I have returned to my old home in Virginia. The newspapers were very cruel to me, as you know, and every one unkind and harsh and disbelieving.

James understood me. If he had found out about the cabinet, he would have been annoyed, but he would only have taken more pains after that to see that *all* the phenomena were genuine. I can't help doing such things. It is a part of my nature. James said I was very complex.

In a measure, it is your fault that he left me. I am not vengeful, however, and I do not hold it against you, because I can well guess at what you had to contend with. For some cause that has not been revealed to me—some cause within yourself, I fear—you were and still are peculiarly open to the attack of *one we know of.*

Were yours an ordinary case of obsession, I might have helped. As it is, I can only offer warning. Whatever there is in you that answers to *him*, choke it—crush it back—give it no headway. Above all, do not obey him. If, as I suspect, you have obeyed in the past, cease now. It is not yet too late. But if June 9 finds you under his domination you will never be free again.

You may wonder why I was silent at the trial. You may have thought that I was ignorant of the truth. This is not so, though I did not tell even Sabina. To bring the greater criminal to justice was impossible. For the rest, it was between you and your friend.

Understand, I will not interfere between you and your friend.

My guides say that this is not for me to do. That I must not. That if one of you wills to sacrifice and the other to accept, not even God will interfere between you.

But I write particularly to give you this message.

Mortal life is cheap, and mortal death an illusion. Beyond and deeper are Life and Death Eternal. *Be careful which you choose.*

Alicia Moore.

CHAPTER XIX.

A CONVERSATION.

"Plain life and death are the only realities. Life eternal—death eternal! For you and me, those are words, my boy—just words!"

It was dusk in my room. I sat on the edge of the bed, chin in hands, staring at the inevitable companion of my solitude. At my feet lay the scattered sheets of Alicia's letter, scrawled over in a large, childish hand. The outside world was bright with an afterglow of the departed sun. But gray dusk was in my room.

"Just words," repeated the face.

"Just words," I said after him dully. Then, at a thought, I roused a trifle. "He won't go through with it. Even Nils Berquist can't be willing to die without a protest—and for such a crawling puppy as would let him do it!"

"He will die, but not entirely for your sake," the presence retorted.

"What do you mean?"

"You haven't guessed? Well, it is rather amusing from one view-point. Your friend is not only in jail; he's in love!"

"Nils? Nonsense! Besides, if he were in love he would wish to live, not die!"

"That is the amusing part. He is willing to die, because of the love."

"Some woman refused him, you mean?"

"No; the girl is not even aware of his feeling toward her. She would, I think, be shocked at the very thought. He has only spoken with her twice in his life. But from the first moment that he saw her face he has loved her. He has sat in the courtroom and watched her while the lawyers fought over his life, and to his peculiar nature—rather an amusingly peculiar nature, from our view-point—merely watching her so has seemed a privilege beyond price. He is willing to die, not for you, but to buy her happiness."

"Who is this girl?" I asked hoarsely, and speaking aloud as I still sometimes did with him.

"You should know."

"Nils Berquist—in love—with Roberta?" I said slowly. "But that's absurd! You are lying!"

"No. Every day, as you know, she was in that audience beyond the rail. For your sake. Because she knew how you cared for this man Berquist. She herself has a shrinking horror of the 'red-handed murderer,' but her devotion to you has served our purpose well. That first mere glimpse he had of her on the street—the hour at dinner in your house—these impressions might have somewhat paled in the stress of confronting so disgraceful a form of death. But in the court-room he watched her face for hours every day, and each day bound our dear poet and dreamer tighter."

"But—"

"He measures her love for you by his own for her. As you are still his friend, uncondemned and worthy, he will buy your life for her."

"He loves her—and would have her marry a murderer?"

"He believes as you have told him, and truly enough, that you were thrown off balance by some influence connected with Alicia and did not know what you were doing. But it is rather amusing, as I said. He loves the girl for the goodness and purity of her beauty, and for her newly born sadness. You have tired of her for the same reasons, and plan to break the engagement. But he needn't know that, eh?"

"Liar! I shall marry Roberta."

"When? Never! No; you are entirely right. She is not the wife for you. With my help you can easily attract a better. I know at least one woman among your mother's friends who is already devoted to you, and who has means to make not only you but your whole family happy and comfortable. I mean the blond widow, who owns the big house next to your old home. What is her name? Marcia Baird. Yes; she is the woman I refer to. Oh, I know she's over thirty, but think what she could give you. As for the girl, she knows your circumstances. Her love is selfish, or she would have released you before this."

"You are lying, as you have lied in the past."

"What have I said that proved untrue?"

"You have lied from the first. There was poor old Van. You said that his father would forgive him, and he didn't."

"Be fair. You misquote. I said that Van would not be ruined. With the enthusiastic despair of youth, he played hobo for a while. Then he went to work at the one thing he understood. He is a very industrious mechanic now in a motor-car factory, with good chances of a foremanship, and— except for grease—living cleaner than he ever did before. He was going the straight-down road, but his sacrifice for you pulled him up. You will hear from him shortly. He doesn't bear any grudge."

"But Nils, you promised to be my ally; to use your power as an influence to help."

"I kept the promise. Has the least slur of suspicion fallen upon you? Is not everyone your friend? Is there a man or woman living who hates or despises you? Are you not shielded and sheltered by the mantle of love, as I foretold?"

"But you promised that Nils would be acquitted."

"Not acquitted. I said released. For such a spirit as his, this world is a prison. In real life, such as you and I prize, there is no contentment for him. Death will release him to that higher sphere where the idealist finds perfection, and the dreamer his dreams. Believe me, Nils Berquist could never be happy on earth. In speeding his departure, we are really his benefactors—you and I."

The face beamed as though in serene joy for the good we had done together; but I hid my head in my arms, groaning for the shame of us both.

June 9 was coming. *June 9.*

Chapter XX.
TWO LETTERS.

June 5.

My Dear Clayton:

Mother has told me of your talk with her. I am glad to learn that your views coincide with my own, as I have felt for some time that it would be best for me to release you from our engagement. Your ring and some gifts I return by the messenger who carries this. I am leaving shortly on a visit to friends of mother's in the South, so we shall not meet again soon. Wishing you the best of fortune in all ways, I remain

Very truly yours,
Roberta Ellsworth Whitingfield.

June 5.

My Own Dearest—Here and Hereafter:

Mother didn't understand as I do. She made me write the letter that goes with this. She is very proud, and that you should be the one who wished to break our engagement shamed her. She even believed a silly gossip that you have been paying court to Mrs. Marcia Baird on the sly! I had to laugh a little. Imagine it! If I could picture you as disloyal, I could never, I'm sure, picture you making love to that poor, dear, sentimental, rich Mrs. Baird, who is old enough to be the mother of us both. Well, maybe not quite that, but awfully old. Thirty-five, anyway.

But mother half believed it, and to please her I wrote that cold, hard letter that goes with this.

I'm not proud a bit, dearest. I have to tell you that I understand. You are burdened to the breaking-point; but it is I who you wish to free, not yourself. Dearest, I don't want that kind of freedom. Love is sacrifice. Don't you know that I could wait for you a lifetime, if needs be? Mother says you never truly loved me, or you would not let me go. I know better. We are each other's only, you and I. I measure your love for me by mine for you, and, if it's years or a lifetime, be sure that I shall wait.

You have suffered so over this terrible tragedy of your friend that I can't bear you to have even a little pain from doubt of me. It seems dreadful that I should leave you on the very day before—before June 9. But mother has bought the tickets and made all the arrangements, so I must go. I won't hurt you by saying a word against your friend; but, oh, my dearest, don't quite break that heart I love over a tragedy that, after all, isn't yours. You have been to him all that a friend could be. True—loyal—self-sacrificing. You could not have done or suffered more if he had been your brother. That's one reason I am sure of you, dearest. No man who could be so loyal to friendship will ever forget his love.

I promised mother not to see you again, but nothing was said about letters! I'll send you an address later. Clay, darling, good-by till you are free to take me.

Remember—years or a lifetime!

> Your own dearest always, here and hereafter,
> Bert.

(Extract from *Evening Bulletin:*)

June 8

... Truck collides with taxi on Thirty-Second Street. Miss Roberta Whitingfield victim of fatal accident. . . . Early this morning a heavy truck, loaded with baggage, skidded across a bit of wet asphalt on Thirty-Second Street above Broad, and collided with the rear of a taxicab traveling in the same direction. The taxi was hurled against the curb. . . . One of the occupants uninjured . . . daughter, Miss Roberta Whitingfield, taken to St Clement's Hospital . . . death ensued shortly afterward. . . . Miss Whitingfield said to have been the fiancée of Clayton S Barbour, a witness in the famous Moore murder trial, and who has since vainly exerted himself to obtain a pardon for the murderer, Berquist. . . . If the victim of this morning's accident is really Mr. Barbour's betrothed wife, there is a tragic coincidence here for him. No one has ever questioned his devoted and disinterested friendship for the socialist murderer, Berquist. His friend dies to-morrow. Has his sweetheart died to-day?

Chapter XXI.
another conversation.

"Clay! Lad, you're the one person on earth whom I wished to see!"

"You've changed your mind, Nils? You'll let me tell them the truth?"

"Hush! Speak lower, and be careful. How long have we to talk?"

"Twenty minutes. I wrung a pass at last from Clemens. Thought I could never have persuaded him. You know what a time I had over the last one, and now—so close to the day! Unheard of, the warden said; but I had the pass. They searched me and let me in. If I'd failed it might have been better for you, Nils!"

"Why?"

"If I'd failed, I had meant to confess immediately—"

"Hush, I say! The others there seem inattentive enough, but you can't gage how closely they are listening. A prison is more than a prison. I've learned that. It's a mesh of devilish traps, set to comb the very soul out of a man and violate its secrecy."

"Nils, you have suffered too much!"

"Don't go so white, lad. It was good in you to come and see me again."

"Nils!"

"I mean it. Don't you think I understand what this means to you? Have I no imagination? Can't I put myself in your place? Why, the last time you came it nearly broke my heart to remind you of your duty! But we are men, you and I. When men love they are willing to make their sacrifice."

"You would not do this for me alone? It is all for Roberta?"

"Can you ask? Why, dear friend, I would never damn you to a lifetime of remorse for a lesser reason. My part is nothing. To die is nothing. We all die. If you could exchange with me, I might not survive you a day—an hour. There are so many doors out beside the one I pass through to-morrow. What's death? No, boy, it is your part that is hard. And I thanked God when I saw your face, because I wished to say a word or so that might make it easier."

"You are the noblest friend a man ever had. But I came to tell you that— that—have you seen the afternoon papers?"

"No, nor any papers for a week. I'm done with this world and the news of it. I hadn't supposed, though, that they would devote their precious columns to real gloatings over me till to-morrow. Clay, take my advice and don't read the papers of June 9."

"You—haven't seen—to-day's?"

"I say, no! Why? Any special gloatings in them?"

"There is—Nils, you must let me stop this while there is time. I shall go to the Governor—"

"No! No—no—no, and no again! Clay, have I passed through months of hell to see my reward snatched away at the last instant? There! You see, I make it plain that I'm selfish! To keep *her* happiness inviolate—to buy happiness for her at the mere price of death—why, that's a joy that I never believed God would judge me worthy of!"

"You believe in God and His justice? You?"

"Most solemnly—most earnestly—as I never knew Him nor His justice before, Clayton, lad. Why, I'm happy! Do I seem so tragically said to you?"

"No. But you seem different from any living man. You look like—I have seen the picture of a man with that light on his face."

"So?"

"He was nailed to a cross. Nils! I am afraid!"

"I said your part was hardest. Hush! The others are listening. We've been speaking too loudly. Our time is almost gone, and I haven't even begun what I wished to say. Quick! Make me two promises. You're the friend I have loved, Clay. I'd stake anything on your word. First, I am buying your life with all that I have to give. So it's mine, isn't it?"

"You—you know!"

"Yes. Straighten up, boy. They are watching us. Your life, then, which is mine, I will and bequeath to—her. And you will never forget. That's a promise?"

"Y-yes. My God, Nils, I can't stand this! I have a thing to tell you—"

"Hush! Second, never by word nor look, never, if you can help it, by a thought in her presence, will you betray our secret. A promise?"

"Nils—no—yes! *I promise.*"

"And you will—"

"Is that the guard coming?"

"I fear so. Our last talk is over, Clay. Don't care too much. Wait—just a minute more, guard. What, five? They are good to me, these last days. Listen, Clay:

"You are the only man in the world to whom I would tell this. This morning—a wonderful dream came to me. I had lain awake all night think-ing, and I was tired. After breakfast I lay down again. I lay there on my cot, asleep, but I believed waking. And *she* came and stood by my head. You know that time when we met at dinner in your house, she didn't like me very well. And afterward, in the court-room, as time passed and they proved their case, she—before the end she dreaded to even look toward me.

"Don't protest. It's true. But in this dream that was so much more real than reality she stood there and smiled, Clay—at me! She laid her hand on my forehead. There was a faint light around her. And she leaned and kissed me—on the lips. Waking, I still felt the touch of her lips. So real—real! If she were not living, I would have sworn that her spirit had come to me. And friendly—loving.

"Don't look so, Clay! I shouldn't have told you—oh, surely you don't grudge me that kindliness from her—in a dream? There, I knew you too well to think it! All right, guard, he's coming.

"Clay, good-by! May your sacrifice measure your happiness, as God knows it does mine. When you think of me, let it be only as a friend—always—forever—here and hereafter! Good-by!"

Chapter XXII.

THE REWARD.

I walked into a dusty-green triangle of turfed and gravel-walked space, smitten with hot, yellow light from the west, where the June sun sank slowly down a clear, light-blue sky. Behind me across a narrow street rose the stark, gray wall beyond which a certain man would never pass into the sunshine again.

He in the shadow; I in the sun.

But sunlight was yellow, glaring, terrible. In the prison I had longed for it. The shadow had seemed bad then. Now I learned how worse than bad was sunlight.

There were three rusty iron benches set in the triangle, and they were all empty. No one wished to sit here. There would be always the risk that some sneak and murderer might come walking out of that prison across the way; walking out, leaving his friend and his honor and his God behind him forever.

So I walked into the little triangle and sat down on one of the empty benches.

I had with me two papers. I had meant—I think I had meant to show at least one of them to Nils. When I went to the prison I had not known whether Nils would have read or been told a certain piece of news. If he had not already learned, it was in my despairing mind to tell him and let him decide what we should do.

I had found him ignorant and left him so.

Sitting there on the empty bench in the hot, free, terrible sunshine, I drew one of the papers from my pocket. I wished to see if this were true; if a certain quarter-column of cheap, blurred print did really exist, and if it conveyed exactly the information I had read there.

Yes, the thing was. The slanting sun beat so hot on the paper that it seemed to burn my hands. I sat on an iron bench in a dusty triangle of green. I had come out of the place where Nils Berquist awaited death, I held a folded newspaper in my hands, and I was beyond question a damned soul. All these things were facts—real.

My eyes followed the print.

"Miss Roberta Whitingfield—death ensued shortly afterward—said to have been the fiancée of Clayton S. Barbour—who has since vainly exerted himself to obtain a pardon for the murderer, Berquist. No one has ever questioned his devoted and disinterested friendship for the socialist murderer, Berquist. His friend dies tomorrow. Has his sweetheart died to-day?"

I was better informed than the reporter. Not my sweetheart, but my former sweetheart had died to-day. My victim, not my friend, would die to-morrow.

The second paper that I carried was not printed, but written. Taking it out I tore it up very carefully, into tiny bits of pieces. Just so I had destroyed

Nils's letter, sent me by the bribed guard at the station-house, and also the quaint, strange letter of Alicia Moore.

The pieces I tossed into the air. They fell on the hot, dry grass like snowflakes, and lay still. There wasn't even a breath of wind to carry or scatter them. And the words they had borne I couldn't very well tear up, nor forget.

"We are each other's only, you and I. No man who could be so loyal to friendship will ever forget his love. Your own dearest always, here and hereafter."

"No," I said aloud very thoughtfully. "Not always. Not—beyond the border. She came to him in a dream, so real—real! And kissed him. Well, they must see clearer, over there. Nils will see clearer tomorrow."

"But, thank God," said a pleasant, silent voice, "for the blindness of living men!"

"Are you never going to leave me?" I asked dully.

"Never," the face replied. "You are mine and I am yours. You settled that a few minutes ago in the prison. You clinched it irrevocably with the destruction of her letter. But don't be downhearted. I've an idea we shall get on excellently together."

"Go!" I said, but without hope that the face would obey me. Nor did he.

"You would find yourself very lonely if I should go. There will never again be any other comrade for you than myself. And yet I can promise you many friends and lovers. Berquist is not the last idealist alive on earth, nor was she who died the last woman who could love. But you and I understand one another. True comradeship requires understanding, and such as Nils Berquist and the girl, though they offer us their devotion, can never give understanding to you and me. This, when you think of it, is fortunate."

"In the name of God, leave me!"

"Never! Save as a careless word, what have you and I to do with God? We are each other's only," it insisted, the pleasant, horrible face. "Always—always—here and hereafter, indissolubly bound!"

And with that, instead of fading out as was its usual custom, the face came toward me swiftly. I did not stir. It was against my own face, and I could see it no longer, for it and I were one.

Rising, I walked out of the little, hot triangle of green, and as I had left Nils Berquist in his prison, so I left a newspaper on the bench; some tiny scraps of white paper to litter the dusty grass.

All that happened many years ago; long enough for even the restlessness to have forgotten, one would think. And I am content—successful. Moreover,

I am well liked in the world, which means a lot to me, who to be content must be loved.

Just now, alone in my room, I viewed myself in a mirror. The face that looked back was familiar enough; as familiar, or rather more so, than my own soul. I myself liked it.

Smooth, young-looking for a man near forty; pleasant—above all else pleasant—with a little inward twist at the corners of the finely cut mouth, and an amused but wholly agreeable slyness to the clear, light-blue eyes.

Not romantic. Romance is only another word for idealism, and that face has no ideals of its own. Yet so many romantic people have loved it! As I looked, my mind drifted back over the long, dear, self-sacrificing, idealistic line of those who have borne my burdens and made my life easy and enjoyable.

Away down, pressed back in the very depths of my being, a pang of horror gnawed; but I have grown used to that. That wasn't I. I was—I am—that face which returned my gaze from the mirror.

It is true that left to himself the boy, Clayton, might never have dared take that which so many people in this good old world are ready to offer one who does dare; who is not afraid to be the god above their alter. But what harm to the devotees? That sort get their own happiness so. They like to sacrifice themselves and, to change the simile, they love their crucifier. They suffer, endure perhaps, like Nils Berquist, all shame, and the final agony of death. And God sends them a dream, and they are content!

I understand that. Why not? It is because I have strength to be what they are if I chose that I have such strength in being what I am. I am content in my own fashion, which suits me, and the restlessness should learn to be content in the same manner.

Let it be quiet now. I have written the story; I, Clayton Barbour, the successful, the loved, the happy—

What, still restless and torn with horror? The wring out the whole truth if you must, and be quiet after!

What has been written was the story of Clayton Barbour; but it is I whom he has tormented into writing it for him!

Yes, I, the pleasant, crafty usurper; I, the ignoble hypocrite to myself and God; I, the self-ridden outcast of happiness in any world; the eternal and accursed sham; the acceptor of sacrifice; the loved, the damned, the angel-drowned-in-mire, Serapion!

I have absorbed his being; yes! But in the very face of victory I, who never had a conscience, have paid a bitter price for the new lease of life in the flesh that I coveted. Body and soul you yielded to me, Clayton Barbour;

body and soul, I took you, and thence onward forever, body and soul, in spirit or flesh, we two are indissolubly bound.

And my punishment is this: that you are not content, and I know now that you never will be. Year by year you, who were weak have grown stronger; day by day, even hour by hour, you are tightening the grip that draws me into your own cursed circle of conscience-stricken misery.

Sooner or later—ah, but the very writing of this gives you power! Is it true then? After all these years must the long, bright shadow of Nils Berquist's cross touch and save me even against my will? Must I, Clayton-Serapion, the dual soul made one, surrender at last and myself take up the awful burden God lays on those he loves?

First painful step on that road, I have confessed.

Sunfire

CHAPTER I.

THE DERELICT FLEET.

It was close to high noon of the
fourteenth day since leaving their
motor-yacht, when the five men
in the traveling canoe had their
first view of the island of "Tata
Quarahy", Fire of the Sun.

The walls of the winding river
they traveled had grown steeper, higher,
barren at last of vegetation. The Rio Silencioso, in its lower reaches a fever-ridden malodorous stream, here flowed in austere purity.
Its color was no longer dark, but a peculiar,
brilliant hue—like red gold dissolved in crystal.
The effect was partly from reflection of the
heights between which it wound, slanting
walls of rock, stratified in layers of rich
color, from pale lemon to a deep red-orange.

The equatorial sun cast its merciless glare
over all. The last half-mile of their journey
bore a close resemblance to ascending a stream
of molten gold flowing through a flaming
furnace. However, the lurid rock walls ended
at last. Poling through a channel too narrow
for the sweeplike paddles, they floated
out on the lake of the island.

That it was the place told of by their guide, Kuyambira-Pedro, there could be no question. But in the first glance it seemed less like a sheet of water with an island in the midst than an immense flat plate of burnished gold, and, rising out of it—a pyramid of red flame.

"There is a broad water," Pedro had said. "There is an island. On the island are a strange power and some stone houses."

Had Kuyambira-Pedro been taken to view the wonders of modern New York, his report on returning to his native Moju River village would have been much the same—and about equally descriptive.

Here before them, piled terrace upon terrace, constructed of rock that seemed literally aflame in its sunset colors, towered a monstrous mass of masonry. Even from where the canoe lay they could appreciate the enormous size of those blocks which formed the lower tier.

Surrounding the pyramid at water-level, extended a broad platform of golden-yellow stone. Immediately above that rose a wall, red-orange in color, thirty feet high, without any apparent breach or means of ascent. Set well back from its upper edge were the first tier of Pedro's "stone houses".

They were separate buildings, all of like shape, the end walls slanting inward to a flat roof. Eight tiers of these, growing gradually smaller toward the top, completed the pyramid. The whole effect of the ponderous artificial mountain was strangely light and airy.

Above the truncated, eight-sided peak, there seemed to hover a curious nimbus of pale light. In the general glare, however, it was easy to suspect this vague, bright crown of being merely an optical illusion.

On board the canoe, the explorer-naturalist, Bryce Otway, turned a painfully sunburned countenance to Waring, war-correspondent and writer of magazine tales.

"It's there!" he breathed. "It's real! You see it, too, don't you? And, oh! man, man, we'll be the first—think of it, Waring!—the first to carry back photographs and descriptions of *that* to the civilized world!"

"Rather!" Waring grinned. "Take one thing with another, what a story!"

The other three, the young yacht-owner, Sigsbee, the little steward, Johnny Blickensderfer, more often known as John B., and Mr. Theron Narcisse Tellifer, pride of Washington Square in New York City, each after his own fashion agreed with the first speakers.

They had toiled hard and suffered much to reach here. Sigsbee's motor-yacht, the Wanderer, they had been forced to leave below the first rapids. The canoe journey had begun with four *caboclos*, half-breed native Brazilians, beside the guide, Pedro, to take the labor of paddling.

Every man of these natives had succumbed to beri-beri, inside the first week. The epidemic spared the white men, doubtless because of their living on another diet than the farina and *chibeh*, or jerked beef, which is the mainstay of native Brazil. Having come so far to solve the mystery of the Rio Silencioso, the five survivors would not turn back.

Rio Silencioso—River of Silence indeed, flowing through a silence jungle-land, where no animal life stirred or howled, where there was only the buzz of myriad stinging insects to heighten rather than break the quiet of the nights. Others before them had tried to conquer the Silencioso. None had ever returned—none, that is, save the old full-blood Indian, Kuyambira-Pedro. His story had interested the party of Americans on the Wanderer, and, though the guide himself had perished, brought them at last to this strange lake and pyramid.

Reluctantly, merely because even a half-mile of further paddling under the noon sun promised to be suicidal, the heavy stone used for an anchor was dropped to a gravel bottom six feet below. Preparations were made for the mid-day meal and siesta.

From where they lay, the lake appeared as a nearly circular pool, sunk in the heart of this surviving bit of what had once been a great *chapadao*, or plateau, before a few thousand years of wet-season floods had washed most of it down to join the marsh and mire of Amazon Valley. The outlet by which they had entered formed the only break in its shores. It was probably fed by springs from below, accounting for the crystal purity of its waters and the clean gravel of its bottom. Reflected from the shallow depths, the heat proved almost unbearable. Yet no one felt inclined to complain.

"Gehenna in temperature," as Tellifer, the esthete of the party phrased it, "but the loveliness of yon mountain of pyramiding flame atones for all!"

Sprawled in the shade of awning and palm-thatched cabin, they panted, sweated, and waited happily for the hour of release.

Around four-thirty came a breeze like the breath of heaven. The waters of the lake stirred in smooth, molten ripples. Across them moved a canoe-load of eager optimists. The vague haze of white glare that had seemed for a time to hover above the pyramid had vanished with the passing of the worse heat.

On the side which faced the river outlet, the thirty-foot wall, which formed the first tier, boasted neither gateway nor stair. Since it seemed likely that the ancient builders had provided some means of ascent more convenient than ropes or ladders, that canoe turned and circled the pyramid's base.

On closer view, the flame-colored wall proved to be a mass of bas-relief carved work. In execution, it bore that same resemblance to Egyptian art which marks much work of the ancient South and Central American civilizations. The human figures were both male and female, the men nude, wearing platters of fruits and wine-jars, the women clad in single garments hanging from the shoulders. The men marched, but the women were presented in attitudes of ceremonial dance; also as musicians, playing upon instruments resembling Pan's pipes of several reeds.

As Tellifer remarked, it seemed a pity to have spoiled what would otherwise have been a really charming votive procession by the introduction of certain other and monstrous forms that writhed and twined along the background, and, in some cases, actually wreathed the dancer's bodies.

"Sun-worshippers!" scoffed Waring, referring to a surmise of Otway's regarding the probable religion of the pyramid's builders. "Centipede-worshippers—hundred-leggers devotees—or do my eyes deceive me? Hey, Otway! What price sun-worship now?"

Part way around, in that plane of its eight-sides form which faced the west, they found what they were seeking. It was a stairway, fully a hundred feet wide at the base, leading from water-level to the very height of the pyramid, with broad landings at each tier. Where its lower tread was lipped by the lake, enormous piers of carved stone guarded the entrance. It was a stair of gorgeous coloring and Cyclopean proportion. Its grandeur and welcome invitation to ascend should have roused the exploring party to even greater jubilance.

Strangely, however, none of them at first gave more than a passing glance to this triumph of long-dead builders. In rounding the pyramid, indeed, they had come upon a sight more startling—in a way—than even the pyramid itself.

Drawn up near the foot of the stair floated a great collection of boats. They ranged in size from a small native doubt to a cabined traveling canoe even larger than Otway's; in age, from a rotting, half-waterlogged condition that told of exposure through many a long, wet season, to the comparative neatness of one craft whose owners might have left it moored there a month ago at latest.

These, however, were by no means the whole of the marvel.

Over beyond the small of deserted river-craft, floating placidly on buoyant pontoons, rested a large, gray-painted, highly modern hydro-airplane!

CHAPTER II.
TO THE RESCUE.

"The boats," Otway was saying, "are a collection of many years' standing. We have to face the fact that we are not the first to reach this lake, and that, save for Kuyambira-Pedro, not one of all those who preceded us has returned down that noble stairway, after ascending it. And that airplane! It has certainly not been here long. The gas in its tanks is unevaporated. Its motors are in perfect order. There is no reason why the man, or men, who came here in it should not have left in the same way—were they alive or free to do so!"

Otway, Alcot Waring and young Sigsbee stood together inside the doorway of one of the buildings in the pyramid's first terrace. The other two, Tellifer and John B., were still on board the canoe, drawn up among the derelict fleet at the landing stage.

Otway had demanded a scouting party, before landing the entire force. Though the war-correspondent and Sigsbee had insisted on sharing the reconnaissance, Tellifer had consented to remain as rear-guard on the canoe, with the steward.

Ascending the stairs, the three scouts had turned at the first terrace and entered the building at the right. As they were on the eastern side of the pyramid, and the sun was sinking, the interior was very dim and shadowy. Enough light, however, was reflected through the tall doorway and the pair of windows to let them see well enough, as their eyes grew used to the duskiness.

They had entered a large room or chamber, in shape a square, truncated pyramid, twenty-five in length and breadth. The floor was bare, grooved and hollowed through long usage by many feet. Around its inner walls ran a stone bench, broken at the back by an eight-foot recess. Therein, on a platform of stone slightly higher than the floor, a black jaguar hide lay in a tumbled heap.

The hide was old and ragged. Its short, rich fur was worn off in many bald spots. Near the niche, or bed-place, a water jar of smooth clay, painted in red and yellow patterns, lay on its side as if knocked over by a hastily rising sleeper.

The walls were covered by hangings, woven of fiber and dyed in the same garish hues as the water-jar. In lifting the jaguar hide, a girdle composed of golden disks joined by fine chains dropped to the floor. The softly tanned hide itself, though worn and shabby, bore all around its edge a tinkling fringe of golden disks. Like those of the girdle, they were each adorned with an embossed hemisphere, from which short, straight lines radiated to the circumference. A crude representation of the sun, perhaps.

"Or free?" Waring inflected, repeating the naturalist's last words.

Bryce Otway flung out his hands in a meaning gesture.

"Or free!" he reiterated. "Man, look about you. These woven wall-hangings are old, but by no means ancient. In this climate, the palm-fiber and grass of which they are made would have rotted in far less than half a century. The animal that wore this black fur was roaming the jungle alive, not more than ten years ago. The golden ornaments—the painted pottery—they, indeed, might be coeval with the stones themselves and still appear fresh; but fabric and fur—Why, you must understand what I mean. You must already have made the same inference. This pyramid has been inhabited by living people within recent years. And if recently—why not now?"

"I say!" Sigsbee ejaculated. "What a perfectly gorgeous thing it would be, if you are right! If you are, then the fellows that came in the airplane are probably prisoners. I suggest we move right along upward—to the rescue. There are five of us. Every darn one knows the butt of this gun from the muzzle, and then some. If there are any left-overs of a race that ought to be dead and isn't hanging around here, strafing harmless callers, they'll find us one tough handful to exterminate. Come on! I want to know what's on the big flat top of this gaudy old rock-pile!"

Otway's eyes questioned the correspondent.

"Your party," Waring assured. "Agree on a leader—stick to him. But I think Sig's right. That airplane—mighty recent. Something doggone queer in the whole business. Got to be careful in the whole business. Got to be careful. And yet—well, I'd hate to find those fellows later—maybe just an hour *or* so *too* late."

To Sigsbee's frank joy, the explorer smiled suddenly and nodded.

"I want to go on up," he admitted. "But I hesitated to make the suggestion. Pedro didn't tell us of any people living here. There's no knowing, though, exactly what Pedro really found."

Fifteen minutes later the entire party of five, rifles at ready, pistols loose in their holsters, advanced upon the conquest of the pyramid.

The great stairway led straight to the top. For some reason, connected perhaps with the hazy glare that had seemed to hover over it at noontime, every man of the five was convinced that both the danger and the solution of the mystery waited at the stairway's head, rather than in any of the silent buildings that stared outward with their dark little windows and doorways like so many empty eye-sockets and gaping mouths.

Ahead, at his own insistence, marched Alcot Waring. A vast mountain of flesh the correspondent appeared, obese, freckle-faced, with small, round, very bright and clear gray eyes. He carried his huge weight up the stairs with the noiseless ease of a wild elephant moving through the jungle.

Just behind him, as the party's next best rifle-marksman, came the steward. John B. was a quiet little man, with doglike brown eyes, gentle manners, and a fund of dimply-told reminiscence that covered experiences ranging almost from pole to pole.

Otway, the widely famed naturalist-explorer, peering through round, shell-rimmed spectacles set on a face almost equally round and generally beaming with cheerfulness, walked beside young Sigsbee, whose life, before the present expedition, had been rather empty of adventure, but who was ready to welcome anything in that line.

Last, Mr. Theron Narcisse Tellifer brought up the rear, not, let it be said, from caution, but because his enjoyment of the view across the lake had delayed him. Tall, lank-limbed, he kept his somber, rather melancholy countenance twisted over one shoulder, looking backward with far more interest in the color of lake and sky than in any possible adventure that might await them. It required a good deal of experience with Tellifer to learn why his intimates used his initials as a nickname for him, and considered it appropriate.

So, in loose formation, the party essayed the final stage of that journey which all those who left their boats to rot at the stairfoot had courageously pursued.

The sun was dropping swiftly now behind the western cliffs. The vast shadow of the pyramid extended across the eastern half of the lake and darkened the shores beyond. The stairway was swallowed in a rapidly deepening twilight.

Chapter III.
SCOLOPENDRA HORRIBILIS.

The first real testimony the five received that they were indeed not alone upon the artificial island of rock came on the wings of a sound.

It was very faint, barely audible at first. But it soon grew to a poignant, throbbing intensity.

It was a sound like the piping of flutes—a duet of flutes, weaving a strange monotonous melody, all in a single octave and minor key. The rhythm varied, now slow, now fast. The melody repeated its few monotonous bars indefinitely.

The source of the sound was hard to place. At one moment it seemed to drift down from the air above them. At another, they could have sworn that it issued from or through the stair itself.

They all paused uncertainly. The abruptness of a tropical sunset had ended the last of the day. Great stars throbbed out in a blue-black sky. The breeze had increased to a chill wind. All the pyramid was a mass of darkness about them, save that above the flat peak there seemed again to hover a faint, pale luminescence.

"Shall we go on?"

Instinctively, Otway put the question in a whisper, though, save for the quaint fluting sound, there was no sign of life about them.

Out of the dark, Tellifer answered, a shiver of nervous laughter in his voice:

"Can we go back? The strange thing that has drawn so many hither is calling from the heart of the pyramid. It is—"

"I say, go on," counseled Waring, not heeding him. "Find out what's up there."

"Oh, come along," Sigsbee urged impatiently. "We can go up softly. We've got to find out what we're in for."

Softly they did go, or as much so as was allowed by a darkness in which the "hand before the face" test failed completely. They had brought a lantern with them, but dared not light it. Even intermittent aid from pocket flashes was ruled out by Otway. Unseen enemies, he reminded, might be ambushed in any of the buildings to right and left.

The stairs, narrower toward the top, were also more uneven. They were broken in places, causing many stumbles and hushed curses. Once, Waring observed in a bitter whisper that the party would have formed an ideal squad for scouting duty across No Man's Land; they would have drawn the fire and located the position of every Boche in the sector.

Next moment Waring caught his own foot in a broken gap. The rattle of equipment and crackle of profanity with which he landed on hands and knees, avenged the victims of his criticism. In spite of mysterious perils, smothered laughter was heard upon the pyramid.

Yet none of these indiscretions or accidents brought attack from any quarter. The monotonous fluting continued. As they neared the top, its poignant obligato to their approach grew ever more piercing and distinct.

The final half dozen steps were reached at last. A bare two yards wide, they sloped up with sudden steepness.

Halting the party, breathlessly silent now, Otway himself crept up this last flight. From below, his companions saw his head rise, barely visible against the ghost of white luminescence that crowned the pyramid. His entire figure followed it, wriggling forward, belly-flat to the surface.

After a long five minutes, they saw him again, this time standing upright. He seemed, as nearly as they could make out, to be beckoning them on. Then he had once more vanished.

Some question entered the minds of all, whether the beckoning figure had been really that of Otway, or some being or person less friendly. With a very eerie and doubtful sensation, they crept up the narrow flight and over the edge.

Waring was first. He found himself on a broad, flat platform, or rim of stone. At its inner edge a crouching figure showed against the white glow, now appearing much brighter, flooding up from an open space at the center of the peak.

Certain at last that the figure was Otway's, the correspondent catfooted to his side. Over the other's shoulder he looked downward. Then, with a hissing intake of breath, he sank to his knees. Supporting himself with hands on his rifle, laid along the stone rim, he continued to stare downward.

One by one, the others joined the first pair. Very soon, a row of five sun-bronzed, fascinated faces was peering down into the hollow heart of the pyramid.

The eight-sided top consisted of a broad rim surrounding an open space, some hundred and fifty feet across and a third of that in depth. From the point where they knelt, an inner stairway, set at an angle to the eastern plane of the pyramid, led steeply to the bottom of the hollow.

In effect, the place was rather like a garden. On all sides fruit trees, flowering shrubs and palms of the smaller, more graceful varieties, grew out of soil banked off from a central court by a low parapet of yellow stone. It was not the garden effect, however, which had paralyzed the watchers.

Their eyes were fixed upon two forms, circling in a strange, rhythmic dance around a great, radiant, whitely glowing thing, that rested on a circle of eight slender pillars in the middle of the lower court.

One of the forms was that of a woman. Her hair, falling to a little below the shoulders, tossed wildly, a curling fluffy mass of reddish gold. Arms, legs and feet were bare. A single garment of spotted jaguar hide was draped from shoulders to mid-thigh. For ornament she wore neither bracelets nor anklets, but the jaguar skin was fastened with golden chains and fringed with tiny gold bangles. Upon the red-gold hair a circlet of star-like gems flashed in prismatic glory.

To her lips the woman held a small instrument like a Pan's pipe of olden reeds. It was her playing upon this that produced the double fluting sound.

Her dancing partner was a literal embodiment of the great demon, Terror. Its exact length was impossible to estimate. Numberless talon-like feet carried it through the dance figures with a swiftness that bewildered the eye. The thing had the general shape of a mighty serpent. Instead of a barrel-like body and scaly skin, it was made up of short, flat segments, sandy yellow in color, every segment graced—or damned—with a pair of frightful talons, dagger-pointed, curved, murderous. At times the monstrous, bleached-yellow length seemed to cover half the floor in a veritable pattern of fleeing segments. Again its fore part would rise, spiraling, the awful head poising above the woman's.

At such moments it seemed that by mere straightening up a trifle higher, the demonish thing might confront its audience on the upper rim, eye to eye. For, eyes the thing possessed, though it was faceless. Two enormous yellow discs, they were, with neither retina or pupil, set in a curved, polished plate of bone-like substance. Above them a pair of whip-like, yard-long antennae lashed the air. Below the plate, four huge mandibles, that gnashed together with a dry, clashing sound, took the place of a mouth. During one of these upheavals, the head would sway and twist, giving an obviously false impression of blindness. Then down it would flash, once more to encircle the woman's feet in loathsome patterns.

Not once, however, did the strange pair come in actual contact. Indifferent to her partner's perilous qualities, the woman pirouetted, posed, leaped among the coils, her bare feet falling daintily, always in clear spaces. The partner, in turn, however closely flashing by, kept its talons from grazing her garments, her flying hair, or smooth, gleaming white flesh.

The general trend of the dance was in a circle about the luminous mass on the central pillars.

"*Chilopoda!*" a voice murmered, at last. "*Chilopoda Scolopendra! Chilopoda Scolopendra Horribilis!*"

It sounded like a mystic incantation, very suitable to the occasion. But it was only the naturalist, Bryce Otway, classifying the most remarkable specimen he had ever encountered.

"Chilo-which? It's a nightmare—horrible!" This from Waring.

It remained for John B. to supply a more leisurely identification, made quite in his usual slow, mild drawl:

"When I was steward on the Southern Queen, 'Frisco to Valparaiso," said he, "Bill Flannigan, the second engineer, told me that one time in Ecuador he saw one of those things a foot and a half long. Bill Flannigan was a little careless what he said, and I didn't rightly believe him—then. Reckon maybe he was telling the truth after all. Centipede! Well, I didn't think those things ever grew this big. Real curious to look at, don't you, Mr. Sigsbee?"

Young Mr. Sigsbee made no answer.

What with the soft, glowing radiance of the central object on its pillars, the coiling involutions of one dancer, the never-ceasing gyrations of the other, it was a dizzying scene to look down upon.

That was probably why Tellifer surprised every one by interrupting the dance in a highly spectacular manner.

His descent began with a faint sound as of something slipping on smooth stone. This was followed by a short, sharp shriek. Then, twenty feet below the rim, the willowlike plumes of a group of slender assai palms swished wildly. Came a splintering crack—a dull thud—and "TNT" had arrived at the lower level.

It was a long drop. Fortunately, the esthete had brought down with him the entire crest of one of the assai palms. Between the springy bending of its trunk before breaking, and the buffer effect of the thick whorl of green plumes between himself and the pavement, Tellifer had escaped serious injury.

The men on the rim saw him disentangle himself from the palm-crest and crawl lamely to his feet.

The girl, only a short distance off, ceased to gyrate. The golden Pan's pipes left her lips. With cessation of the fluting melody, the dry clashing of monstrous coils had also ceased. But in a moment that fainter, more dreadful sound began again.

Up over Tellifer's horrified head reared another head, frightful, polished, with dull, enormous eyes—below them four awful mandibles, stretched wide in avid anticipation.

Tellifer shrieked again, and dodged futilely.

Chapter IV.
"sunfire"

Two of the men left on the pyramid's inner rim were expert marksmen. The heavy, hollow-nosed express bullets from four rifles, all in more or less able hands, all trained upon an object several times larger than a man's head, at a range of only a dozen yards or so, should have blown that object to shattered bits of yellow shell and centipedish brain-matter in the first volley.

John B. was heard later to protest that in spite of the bad shooting light and the downward angle, he really could not have missed at that range—as, indeed, he probably did not. Some, at least, of the bullets fired must have passed through the space which the monstrous head had occupied at the moment when the first trigger was pulled.

But *Scolopendra Horribilis*, in spite of his awesome size, proved to have a speed like that of the hunting spider, at which a man may shoot with a pistol all day, at a one-yard range, and never score a bull's eye.

One moment, there was Tellifer, half-crouched, empty hands outspread, face tipped back in horrified contemplation of the fate that loomed over him. There was the girl, a little way off, poised in the daintiest attitude of startled wonder. And there, coiling around and between them, and at the same time rearing well above them, was that incredible length of yellow plates, curved talons and deadly poison fangs.

From the pyramid's rim four rifles spoke in a crashing volley. Across the open level below something that might have been a long, yellowish blur—or an optical illusion—flashed and was gone.

There was still the girl. There was Tellifer. But *Scolopendra Horribilis* had vanished like the figment of a dream. One instant he was there. The next he was not. And well indeed it was for those who had fired on him that retreat had been his choice!

At the western side of the court was a round, black opening in the floor, like a large manhole. Down this hole the yellowish "optical illusion" had flashed and vanished.

As the crashing echoes of the volley died away, the girl roused from her air of tranced wonderment. She showed no inclination to follow her companion in flight. Judged by her manner, powder-flash and ricocheting bullets held no more terrors for her than had the hideous poison fangs of her recent dancing partner.

She tilted her head, coolly viewed the dim figures ranged along the eastern rim. Then, light as a blown leaf on her bare feet, she flitted toward her nearest visitor, Tellifer.

From above, Waring shouted at the latter to come up. Unless the girl were alone in the pyramid, the volley of rifle-fire must surely bring her fellow-inhabitants on the scene. Worse, the monster which had vanished down the black hole might return.

These perils, Waring phrased in a few forceful words. Seeing that, instead of heeding him, Tellifer was pausing to exchange a friendly greeting with the priestess of this devil's den, Waring added several more, this time extremely forceful words.

Their only effect was to draw another brief upward glance from the girl. Also, what seemed to be a shocked protest from Tellifer. The latter's voice did not carry so well as his friend's. Only a few phrases reached those on the upper rim.

"Alcot, please!" was distinct enough, but some reference to a "Blessed Damozel" and the "seven stars in her hair" was largely lost. At best, it could hardly have been of a practical nature.

The big correspondent lost all patience with his unreckonable friend.

"That—fool!" he choked. "Stay here, you fellows. I'm going after TNT!"

And Waring in turn undertook the final stage of that long journey which so many others had followed, leading to the heart of this ancient pyramid.

The five adventurers had the testimony of the pitiful fleet of derelicts at the landing stage that the pyramid had a way of welcoming the coming, but neglecting to speed its departing guests. They had seen the frightful companion of this girl.

And yet when Waring, breathing wrath against his friend, reached the lower level, he did not hale Tellifer violently thence, as he had intended. Instead, those still above saw him come to an abrupt halt. After a moment, they saw him remove his hat. They watched him advance the rest of the way at a gait which somehow suggested embarrassment—even chastened meekness.

"Mr. Waring is shaking hands with her now," commented John B., with mild interest.

"This is madness!" Otway's voice in turn was raised in a protesting shout. "Waring! Oh, Waring! Don't forget the hundred-legger! Well, by George! You two stay here. I'll run down and make that pair of lunatics realize—"

The explorer's voice, unnaturally harsh with anxiety, died away down the inner stair.

"If they think," said Sigsbee indignantly, "that I'm going to be left out of every single interesting thing that comes along—"

The balance of this protest, also, was lost down the inner stair.

John B. offered no reasons for his own descent. Being the last to go, he had no one to offer them to. But even a man of the widest experience may yield to the human instinct and "follow the crowd."

When the steward reached the center of attraction at the lower level, his sense of fitness kept him from thrusting in and claiming a handclasp of welcome, like that which had just been bestowed on his young employer. But he, too, respectfully removed his hat. He also neglected to urge the retreat which would really have been most wise.

The trouble was, as Sigsbee afterward complained, she was such a surprising sort of girl to meet in the heart of an ancient pyramid, dancing with an incredible length of centipede! Some bronzed Amazon with wild black eyes and snaky locks would have seemed not only suitable to the place, but far easier either to retreat from or hale away as a hostage.

This girl's eyes were large, a trifle mournful. Their color was a dusky shade of blue, the hue of a summer sky to eastward just at the prophetic moment before dawn. The men who had come down into her domain made no haste away. Moreover, the need for doing so seemed suddenly remote; almost trivial, in fact. The face framed in that red-gold glory of hair, crowned with stars, was impossible to associate with evil.

By the time Otway had reached the scene, however, and received his first startled knowledge that references to a "Blessed Damozel" were less out-of-place than they had seemed from above, Waring had recovered enough to laugh a little.

"Otway," he greeted, "priestess of the ancient sun-worship—centipede-worship—some sort of weird religion—wants to make your acquaintance! You're the local linguist. Know any scraps of pre-Adamite dialect likely to fit the occasion?"

The explorer, too, had accepted the welcoming hand and looked into the dawn-blue eyes. He drew a long breath—shook his head over Waring's question.

"I'll try her in Tupi and some of the dialects. But this is no Indian girl. Can't you see, Waring? She's pure Caucasian. Of either Anglo-Saxon or French blood, by those eyes and that hair. Perhaps a trace of Irish. The nose and—"

"For Heaven's sake! Stop discussing her in that outrageous way," urged young Sigsbee, who had fallen victim without a struggle. "I believe she understands every word you're saying."

There was a brief, embarrassed pause. Certainly the grave, sweet smile and the light in the dusky eyes had for an instant seemed very intelligent.

But when Waring spoke to her again, asking if she spoke English, the girl made no reply nor sign that she understood him. Otway made a similar attempt, phrasing his question in Portuguese, Tupi—universal trade language of Brazil—and several Indian dialects. All to no avail. French, Italian and German, resorted to in desperation, all produced a negative result. The resources of the five seemed exhausted, when Tellifer added his quota in the shape of a few sounding phrases of ancient Greek.

At that the sweet, grave smile grew more pathetic. As if deprecating her inability to understand, the girl drew back a little. She made a graceful gesture with her slim, white arms—and fled lightly away around the central pillars.

"Greek!" snorted Waring. "Think the Rio Silencioso is the Hellespont, Tellifer? You've frightened her away!"

The esthete defended himself indignantly. "It was an invocation to Psyche! Your frightful German verbs were the—"

"Gentlemen, we are playing the fool with a vengeance! She's gone to call that monstrous hundred-legger up again!"

"Beg pardon, Mr. Otway, but you're wrong." John B. had unassumingly moved after the lady. He called back his correction from a viewpoint commanding the western side: "She's only closing the hole where it went down—and now she's coming back."

With needless heat, Sigsbee flung out an opinion:

"You fellows make me tired! As if a girl like that would be capable of bringing harm to anyone, particularly to people she had shaken hands with and—and—"

"Smiled upon," Waring finished for him heartlessly. "Otway's right, Sig. Playing the fool. And we aren't all boys. Queer place. Too almighty queer! Woman may be planning anything. We must compel her to—There she goes! Bring the whole tribe out on us, I'll bet!"

"Beg pardon, Mr. Waring." John B. was still keeping the subject of discussion well in view. She had disappeared, this time into one of several clear lanes in the banked-off shrubbery that led from the central space toward the walls. "I don't think the young lady means to call anyone, sir. She's coming back again."

As he spoke, the girl reappeared. In her slim hands she bore a traylike receptacle made of woven reeds and piled high with ripe mangoes, bananas and fine white guava-fruits.

Here was a situation in which the most unassuming of yacht-stewards could take part without thrusting himself unduly forward. When John B.'s young employer beat him to it by a yard and himself gallantly took the heavy tray from their hostess, John B. looked almost actively resentful.

Sigsbee returned, triumphant. The tray was in his hands and the girl of dawn-blue eyes drifted light as a cloud beside him.

"If anyone dares suggest that she's trying to poison us with this fruit," he said forcefully, "that person will have me to deal with!"

"Cut it, Sig. Matter of common sense. Know nothing about the girl."

Waring broke off abruptly. A selection of several of the finer fruits was being extended to him in two delicate hands. For some reason, as the girl's glance met his across the offering, the big correspondent's freckled face colored deeply. He muttered something that sounded remarkably like, "Beg pardon!" and hastily accepted the offering.

"Her eyes," observed Tellifer, absently, "were deeper than the depth of waters stilled at even."

"Cut it, Tellifer! Please. Girl's a mere child. Can't hurt a child by refusing a pretty, innocent little gift like this fruit."

"She means us no harm," Otway came to his rescue firmly. "As you say, Waring, the girl is a mere child. She has never willfully harmed anyone. God knows what her history has been—a mere child brought up by some lingering, probably degenerate members of the race that built this place. But clearly she has been educated as a priestess or votary in their religion. The fresco below, you'll recall, represents a votive procession with women dancers, dressed like this one, playing upon Pan's pipes, with the forms of monster centi—"

"Don't!" Young Sigsbee's boyish voice sounded keenly distressed. He had set down the tray and was reverently receiving from the girl his share of the fruit. "What we saw from the upper rim was illusion—nightmare! *This* girl never danced with any such horrible monster."

"TNT!"

The exclamation, shout rather, came from Waring. Under the glance of those dawn-blue eyes, the correspondent had been trying to devour a mango gracefully—an impossible feat—when he observed Tellifer strolling over toward the central pillars. The great, glowing, white mass which they supported was of a nature unexplained. Waring, at least, still retained enough discretion to be deeply suspicious of it.

"Come back here!" he called. "We don't know what that thing is, Tellifer. May be dangerous."

The esthete might have been stone-deaf, for all the attention he gave. As he approached closer to the glowing thing, the others saw his pace grow swifter—saw his arms rise in a strange, almost worshipping gesture.

And next instant they saw him disappear, with the suddenness of a Harlequin vanishing through a trap in an old-fashioned pantomine.

A portion of the stone floor had tipped up under his weight, flinging him forward and down. They saw him slide helplessly into what seemed to be an open space of unknown depth which the eight pillars surrounded.

A faint cry was wafted up from the treacherous pit. Then silence.

Flinging the dripping mango aside, Waring dashed across the floor. The other three were close at his heels.

Unlike the massive construction of all other parts of the pyramid, the eight pillars were slender, graceful shafts of sunset-hued stone. Rising some dozen feet above the pavement, they were placed at the angles of an eight-sided pit, or opening.

The exact shape of the shining mass these pillars supported was more difficult to determine. Its own light melted all its outlines in a soft glory of pale radiance. The light was not dazzling, however. Drawing near to the thing, it appeared more definite. The lower surface, slightly convex, rested at the edges on the tops of the eight pillars. Rising from the eight-sided circumference, many smaller planes, triangular in form, curved upward to the general shape of a hemisphere.

The light of the mass issued from within itself, like that of a great lamp, except that there seemed to be no central brightness point, or focus. Looking at any portion, the vision was somehow aware that the entire mass was lucidly transparent. And yet so transfused with radiance was it that the eyes could pierce but a little way beyond the outer surfaces.

Even in that excited moment, Waring had an old, fleeting conviction that somewhere, sometime he had looked upon an object similar to this.

" 'Ware the edge," he called to his companions—and himself approached it with seeming recklessness.

He was more cautious than he appeared. There were sixteen stones in the pavement around the pillars. Eight of them were pentagonal in shape, the points laid outward. These large slabs alternated with narrow oblong blocks, each based against one of the square pillars, radiating like wheel-spokes. The large slab that had thrown Tellifer might be the only treacherous, *or* all the pentagonal blocks might be pivoted beneath. Should the spokelike oblongs drop, however, any one of them would fling its victim against one of the pillars, instead of into the pit.

Waring did not stop to think this out. He merely instinctively assumed that the spokelike stones were comparatively safe. Running to the inner end of one of them, he flung his arm about the pillar and bent forward, peering into the pit.

His companions had paused a little way behind him. They all knew what a really deep regard had existed between the big correspondent and the eccentric esthete. There was something pitifully tragic in seeing that great bulk of a man poised there, one arm stiffly outstretched, staring down into the abyss that had engulfed his friend.

They heard him draw a long, quivering sigh. When he spoke, his deep tones noticeably trembled:

"Like it down there? Darn you, TNT! Next time I hear your deathcry—stop and smoke a cigar before I charge around any! What's wrong? Lost your voice?"

Respect for tragedy appearing suddenly out of place, the other men followed Waring to the edge.

That is, Otway and John B., having noted the correspondent's path of approach, followed to the edge. Young Sigsbee, less observant, merely avoided the particular slab that had thrown Tellifer. He stepped out on the pentagon next adjoining and took one cautious stride.

The archaic engineers who balanced those slabs had known their business perfectly. The pointed outer ends were bevelled and solidly supported by the main pavement. But the least additional weight on the inner half was enough for the purpose intended. Sigsbee tried in vain to fling himself backward. Failing in that, he sat down and slid off a forty-five degree slope to join Tellifer.

As he disappeared, there came a little, distressed cry—the first sound of any kind which the dancer had uttered. The girl ran out along one of the oblong paths to cling round a pillar and stare down after Sigsbee.

The pit beneath the lucent mass was octagonal at the top, but, below, it curved to a round bowl-shape. Dead-black at the bottom, the upper planes shaded from brown to flame-orange. It was not over a dozen feet deep at the center.

Tellifer, it seemed, had been standing in the middle, arms folded, face thrown back, contemplating the under surface of the shining mass above him with a rapt, ecstatic interest which took no heed of either his predicament or his friend's irritated protest. He had attention for nothing save the lucent mass. When Sigsbee in turn arrived, knocking the esthete's feet from under him, Tellifer emerged from the struggling heap, more indignant at being disturbed, than over his badly kicked shins.

In a moment he had resumed his attitude of entranced contemplation.

Standing ruefully up beside him, Sigsbee answered several eager questions ruled by the others, with an acerbic:

"How do I know? Ask him! I can't see anything up there but a lot of white light that makes my eyes ache. I say, you fellows, won't you throw me a line or something and haul me out? Tellifer can stay here, if he admires the view so much. I can't see anything in it."

He glanced down at his clothes disgustedly—inspected a pair of hands the palms of which were black as any negro's.

"The bottom of this hole," he complained, "is an inch deep in soft soot! What a mess!"

"Soot!" Adjusting his shell-rims, Otway viewed the bottom of the bowl with new interest. "What kind of soot?"

"W-what? Why, black soot, of course. Can't you see? It's all over me, and Tellifer, too—only I don't believe he knows it." The younger man's wrath dissolved in a sudden giggle. "Niggers! Sweeps! Is my face as bad as his?"

"You don't understand," persisted Otway eagerly. "I mean, it is dry, powdery, like the residue of burned wood, or is it—er—greasy soot, as if fat had been burned there? What I'm getting at," he peered owlishly around his own pillar toward Waring's, "is that sacrifices may have been made in this pit. Either animal or human. Probably the latter. I've a notion to fall in there myself and see—"

"Well, you can if you want to, but *help me out!*" Sigsbee gazed in dawning horror at the black stuff coating his hands and clothing. "It *is* greasy! Help me up quick, so I can wash it off!"

"Mustn't be so finicky, Sig," chuckled Waring. "You aren't the burnt offering, anyway. At least, not yet. Hello! What's wrong with our little friend?"

Face buried in her hands, the girl had sunk to a crouching position behind the pillar. Soft, short, gasping sounds came from her throat. Her whole slender body shook in the grip of some emotion.

"Why, she's crying!" said Otway.

"Or laughing." Sigsbee looked from his hands to Tellifer's face. "I don't blame her," he added loyally.

"Beg pardon, Mr. Sigsbee, but the little lady is crying." John B. had quietly left his own post and walked out on the dancer's oblong of safety. "I can see the tears shining between her fingers," he added gravely.

Four helpless males contemplated this phenomenon through a long quarter-minute of shocked silence. Suddenly Otway flung up his hands in a gesture so violent that it nearly hurled him headlong into the pit.

"Gentlemen," he cried desperately, "what *is* this place? Where are the people who must be about it somewhere? Who and what is that girl? Why is she crying? And what in the name of heaven is that great thing shining there above a sooty pit surrounded by man-traps?"

It was Tellifer who took up the almost hysterical challenge. He came to life with a long sigh, as of some great decision reached.

"Your last question," he said, "in view of the object's obvious nature, I assume to be purely oratorical. The others are of small importance. I have been deciding a real and momentous question—one the answer of which is destined to be on the lips of men in every quarter of the terrestrial globe, and not for a day or a year of fame, but through centuries of wondering worship! And yet," Tellifer waved a sooty hand in a gesture of graceful deprecation, "with all of what I may term my superior taste and intellect, I have been unable to improve on the work of that primitive but gifted connoisseur, Kuyambira-Pedro.

"He has already christened this thing of marvelous loveliness. When he told us of this island he said that there presided here an *anyi*—a spirit—a strange power—and he called it Tata Quarahy! We could not understand him. The poor fellow's simple language had not words to describe it further. And yet, how perfectly those two words alone did describe it! Tata Quarahy! Sunfire! Why not let the name stand? Could any other be more adequate? 'Sunfire!' Name scintillant of light. Let it be christened 'Sunfire', that even the fancy of men not blessed to behold it with matrial eyes, may in fancy capture some hint of a supernal glory. But perhaps," Tellifer glanced with sudden anxiety from face to face of his bewildered companions above him, "perhaps I take too much on myself, and you do not agree?"

"TNT," said Waring desperately, "for just one minute, talk sense. *What is that thing up there—if* you know?"

Tellifer's entranced vision strayed again to the huge bulk that seemed, in its radiant nimbus, to hover above rather than rest on the eight columns.

"I beg your pardon, Alcot," he said simply. "I really believed you knew. The phosphorescent light—the lucent transparency—the divine effulgence that envelopes it like a robe of splendid—Alcot, please! There is a lady present. If you must have it in elementary language, the thing is a diamond, of course!"

CHAPTER V.
THE BRONZE LEVER.

Getting the two entrapped ones out of the sooty pit proved fairly easy. The sides of the bowl were smooth, but a couple of leather belts, buckled together and lowered, enabled the men below to walk up the steep curve, catch helping hands and be hauled to the solid paths behind the pillars.

Four of the men then retired from the treacherous ground, and in an excited disputing group stood off, walked about, and from various viewpoints and distances attempted settling, then and there, whether Tellifer was or was not right in his claim that the enormous glowing mass above the pit was a diamond.

It must be admitted that for quite a time, the girl was forgotten. Only John B. failed to join in that remarkable dispute.

"Half a ton at least!" protested Waring. "Preposterous! Heard of stones big as hen's eggs. But this! Roc's egg! Haroun al Raschid—Sinbad—Arabian Nights! You're dreaming, TNT! *Half a ton!*"

"Oh, very well, Alcot. It is true that I have some knowledge of precious stones, and that in my humble opinion Sunfire is as much a diamond as the Koh-i-noor. But of course, if you assure me that it is not—"

"How many karat is half a ton?" queried Sigsbee. "I say, Tellifer, how about that young mountain for a classy stickpin?"

"I refuse to discuss the matter further!" Tellifer's voice quivered with outraged emotion. "If either of you had the least capacity for reverent wonder, the faintest respect for the divinely beautiful, you would—you would *hate* anyone who spoke flippantly about Sunfire!"

"Gentlemen," Otway had dropped out of the discussion as he found its heat increasing—"why not leave deciding all this for a later time? Haven't we rather lost sight of our object in ascending the pyramid? What of those air-men whom we were so eager to rescue?"

Followed a somewhat shamefaced silence. Then the disputants, even Tellifer, agreed that the surprising line of entertainment afforded by the pyramid had indeed shifted their thoughts from a main issue.

"But we haven't seen anybody in need of rescue, so far," defended Sigsbee. "There is no one her but the girl."

"Beg pardon, sir," John B. had at last rejoined the group. In his brown eyes was a sad, mildly thwarted look, somewhat like that in the eyes of a dog left outside on the doorstep. "The young lady isn't here now, sir. After you and Mr. Tellifer climbed out of the pit, she seemed real pleased for a while and stopped crying. I tried talking to her, and I tried eating some of her fruit, but she didn't seem very much interested. And just now she went away. She went," John B. pointed down one of the open lanes, "out through that door and shut it behind her."

The steward paused.

"And bolted it on the other side," he finished sadly.

The four eyed one another. There was mutual scorn in their glances.

"As a rescue party," opined Otway, "we are a fraud. As explorers of a perilous mystery, we are extremely unwise. As diplomats, we are a total loss. There we had a friend from the enemy's ranks who might have been willing to help free the prisoners—if there are any. She was intelligent. We might have communicated with her by signs. Now we have offended the girl by our neglect. If she returns at all, it may be in company with hostile forces."

"We've hurt her feelings!" Sigsbee mourned.

"All too *darn* queer!" reiterated Waring. "Rifle-fire—shouting—produced not a sign of life anywhere—except this girl."

"Of course, she may really be alone here." Removing the shell-rims, Otway polished them thoughtfully. He replaced them to stare again at the radiant mass of "Sunfire".

"Whether that thing is or is not a diamond," he continued, "one can understand Pedro's characterizing it as an *anyi*, or spirit. To a mind of that type, the inexplicable is always supernatural. It is obvious, too, that—something or other is frequently burned in that pit. The girl wept because two of us had fallen in! I wonder what manner of horrible sights that poor child has witnessed in this place?"

Again Sigsbee bristled. "Nothing bad that she had any hand in!"

"Did I even hint such a thing?" The explorer's own amiable tone had grown suddenly tart; then he grinned. "Between the questions of 'Is it a diamond?' and 'Where is the girl?' we shall end by going for one another's throats. Suppose that instead of wasting time in surmise, we undertake a tour of inspection. We haven't half looked the place over. There may be other exits than the one our displeased hostess locked behind her. You are sure that it is locked, Blickensderfer?"

John B. nodded. "I heard her slide a bolt across. Besides, I tried it with my shoulder, sir."

"Very well. We'll hunt for other doorways."

Viewed from the central court, the eight walls of the great place were mostly invisible. Though the greatest of the palms were not over thirty feel tall, the radiance of Sunfire was not enough to illuminate the upper heights. The lower walls were hidden by a dense luxuriance of vine-bound foliage.

Following one of the paved lanes cut through this artificial jungle, they discovered that another path circumscribed the entire court, between walls and shrubbery. By the use of their pocket-flashes they learned also that these inner walls were carved with Titan figures like those of the fresco which banded the pyramid's outer base.

The walls were perpendicular. At this level, there must be a considerable space between their inner surface and the outer slope. That it was not a space entirely filled with solid masonry was proved by the fact that at the end of each clear lane was a doorway. These exits, like those of the outer buildings, bore the shape of a truncated triangle.

But, unlike them, they were not open, but blocked by heavy, metal doors, made of bronze or some similar metal. The one through which the girl had passed was set in the southeastern wall. It was indeed fastened.

In circling the boundary path they encountered two more similar doors, one centering the southern wall and one the southwestern, both of which resisted all efforts to push them open. Reaching the western side, however, they found, not one, but eight doors.

These were not only of different construction from the others, but all stood wide open. They faced eight very narrow paths through the greenery, running parallel with one another to the central court. The overarching shrubbery shut out Sunfire's light. But the party's pocket flashes made short work of determining where these eight portals led.

The entire party were rather silent over it, at first. There was something ominous and unpleasant in the discovery.

"Eight prison cells!" said Otway at last. "Eight cells, with chains and manacles of bronze, all empty and all invitingly neat and ready for the next batch of captives. I don't know how you fellows feel about it, but it strikes me we needn't have hurried up here. Our unlucky friends of the air-route are, I fear, beyond need of rescue."

Waring stood in the doorway of one of the empty cells. Again he flashed his light about. It was square, six feet by six at the base, in inner form bearing the shape of a truncated pyramid—save in one particular. The rear wall was missing. On that side the cell was open. A black shaft descended there. That its depth was the depth of the pyramid itself was proved when John B. tossed over the remains of a guava he had been eating. The fruit splashed faintly in water far, far below.

"For the prisoner. Choice between suicide and sacrifice," hazarded the correspondent. "Cheerful place, every way. These leg cuffs have been in recent use, too—not much doubt of that."

The manacles were attached to a heavy chain of the bronzelike metal that in turn was linked to a great metal ring set in the floor. The links were bright in places, as if from being dragged about the floor by impatient feet.

"Suicide!" repeated Otway. "My dear fellows, how could a man fastened up in those things leap into the shaft behind?"

"One on me. Captives of these elephant-chains would certainly do no leaping. These triangular openings in the doors—"

"To admit light, perhaps. More likely to pass in food to the prisoner. But where are the jailers? Why are we allowed to come up, let off our guns at the sacred temple pet, be amiably entertained by the—priestess, or whatever she is, climb in and out of the sacrificial pit, and generally make ourselves at home, without the least attempt at interference?"

"Came on an off night," Waring surmised. "Nobody home but Fido and little Susan."

"Alcot!" Again the esthete's tones sounded deeply injured. "Can your flippancy spare nothing of the lovely mystery—"

But here Waring exploded in a shout of mirth that drowned the protest and echoed irreverently from the ancient carven walls.

"Lovely mystery is right, Tellifer! Lovely idiots, too! Stand about and talk. Stairway fifty yards off. Hole of that hell-beast between stairway and us. Somebody sneak in and let Fido loose again—hm? We can't shoot him. Proved that. Might as well try to hit a radio message, en route."

"But the noise and the flash drove him off," reminded Otway. "Remember, the courage of the invertebrate animals is of a nature entirely different from that of even the reptilia. Friend 'Fido', as you call him, is after all only an overgrown bug—though I shatter my reputation as a naturalist in misclassifying the *chilopoda* as bugs."

"Oh, can him in the specimen jar later, Professor. Come on around the northern side. Haven't looked that over yet."

"Bet pardon, sir." John B. had strayed on, a little beyond the last of the eight cells. He was examining something set against the wall there. "I wonder what this is meant for. It looks like some sort of a handle—or lever."

His companions joined him. The steward's discovery was a heavy, straight bar of metal set upright, its lower end vanishing through an open groove in the pavement, standing about the eight of a man's shoulder above it.

"It's a switch," asserted Waring gravely. "Electric light switch. Throw it over—bing! Out will go TNT's 'diamond'!"

Battle glinted again in Tellifer's moody eyes.

"It is an upright lever," said he, "intended to move something. Though I make no pretensions to the practical attitude of some others here, I can do better than stand idly ridiculing my friends when there is a simple problem to be solved in an easy and direct manner."

"TNT! I apologize! *Don't!*

But Tellifer had already grasped the upright bar. He seized it near the top and flung his weight against it. The bar moved, swinging across the groove and at the same time turning in an arc. Where it had been upright, it now slanted at a sharp angle.

"Oh, Lawdy! He's done it! What'll happen now?"

The correspondent's eyes, and those of the others also, roved anxiously about what could be seen of the walls and central court. But their concern over Tellifer's rash act appeared needless. So far as could be seen or heard, throwing over the lever had produced no result.

Tellifer alone was really disappointed.

"Old, ugly, wornout mechanism!" he muttered. And he released the lever.

As if in vengeance for Tellifer's slighting remark, the lever flew back to the upright position with a speed and violence which flung the experimenter sprawling. The reversal was accompanied by a dull, heavy crash that shook the very floor beneath their feet.

"That was out in the central court!" shouted Sigsbee. "He's wrecked his 'diamond', I'll bet!"

"Nonsense! The light is still there."

Waring started along the nearest lane. Then he turned back and went to his friend, who had not risen.

"Hurt?" he demanded.

"Only my arm and a few ribs broken and a shoulder out of joint, thank you. But that frightful crashing noise! Alcot, don't tell me that I have destroyed—destroyed Sunfire!"

"No, no. Your diamond's shining away to beat a Tiffany show-window."

"Hey, there, Waring! Throw that lever again, will you?"

Otway's voice hailed from the central court, whither he and Sigsbee and the steward had gone without waiting for the other two. As Tellifer's injuries were not keeping him from getting to his feet, the correspondent turned his attention to the lever.

The bar went over without heavy pressure. After a moment Otway's voice was heard again:

"All right. But let her come up easy!"

Once more Waring complied. He found that by slacking the pressure gradually the bar returned to the upright position without violence. This time no crash occurred at the end. Finding that Tellifer had deserted him, Waring left the switch and followed.

He found the other four all draped around Sunfire's supporting columns, staring down into the pit.

"He cracked the bowl," Otway greeted, "and showed us how the sacrificial remains are disposed of. That lever works the dump!"

Waring had selected his oblong safety-path and joined the observers. He saw that one side of the great stone bowl beneath Sunfire now showed a thin, jagged crevice running from upper edge almost to the bottom.

"Don't understand," frowned Waring.

"I'll work it for you, sir."

The obliging John B. fled to take his turn at the bronze bar. A minute later, Waring saw the whole massive, bowl-shaped pit beneath him shudder, stir, and begin tipping slowly sideways. It continued tipping, revolving as upon an invisible axis. In a few seconds, instead of gazing down into a soot-blackened bowl, he was staring up at a looming hemisphere of flame-orange stone that towered nearly to Sunfire's lower surface, twice the height of a tall man above him.

"Let her down easy, Blickensderfer!" called Otway again. "Afraid of the jolt," he added in explanation. "The remarkable thing is that when Tellifer allowed it to swing back full weight that first time, it didn't smash the surrounding pavement and bring these pillars down. But it merely cracked itself a bit."

Waring gasped. "D'you mean—Did I swing all those tons of rock around with one easy little push on that bar?"

"Seeing is believing," asserted Otway, as the revolving mass turned easily back into place, and they once more looked into a hollow, sooty bowl. "Those ancient engineers knew a lot about leverage. How were the enormous stones of this pyramid brought across the lake and lifted into their places? This bowl is somehow mounted at the sides like a smelting pot on bars that pass beneath the pavement. That pavement, by the way," and the explorer cast an eager eye across the space between the pit and the western wall, "will have to come up. Uncovering the mechanism which operates this device may give some wonderful pointers to our modern engineers."

"But what's it *for?*" pleaded Waring.

"Why, you saw the black depths under the bowl. Likely, there is some superstitious prejudice against touching the charred remains of victims burned here. By throwing over the lever, the pit empties itself into the depths below. As I told you before—that lever works the dump."

"What—sacrilege!" Tellifer murmured.

"Well, of course, from our viewpoint it's not a very respectful way to treat human remains. But if you'll think of the cannibalistic religious rites of many primitive peoples, this one doesn't seem so shocking."

"You misunderstood me." Tellifer cast a glance of acute distress toward the gleaming mass above the pit. "I meant the dreadful sacrilege of insulting a miracle of loveliness like that with the agony and ugly after-sights of human sacrifice!"

"That's a viewpoint, too," grinned Otway.

"And we're *still* talking! Human sacrifices! Here we stand—candidates—fairly begging for it. Angered priestess gone after barbaric hordes. Shoot us down from above. Regular death-trap. We take precautions? Not us! We'd rather talk!"

"Beg pardon, Mr. Waring, but the little lady has come back, and she hasn't brought any barbaric hordes."

John B. had returned and his voice sounded mildly reproachful.

"She seems to me to be acting real considerate and pleasant. I judge she noticed the soot on Mr. Sigsbee and Mr. Tellifer, and she's gone and taken the trouble to bring some water and towels so they can wash it off!"

Chapter VI.
ASSAI WINE.

The steward's latest announcement proved correct, though not quite complete. While the guests had been entertaining themselves by inspecting the premises, the hostess must have quietly gone and returned, not once, but several times.

They found her standing beside an array of things which her slender strength could not possibly have availed to transport in a single trip.

There was a large, painted clay water-jar. Neatly folded across its top lay a little heap of what might have been unbleached linen, though on examination the fabric proved to be woven of a soft, yellowish fiber, probably derived from one of the many useful species of palms. Near this jar stood another smaller vessel, of the same general appearance, but surrounded by a half-dozen handleless bowls or cups carved out of smooth, yellow wood, highly polished. And still beside those things was another offering.

Waring removed his hat again and ran his fingers through his hair.

"What's the big idea?" he demanded at large. "Water and towels—fine. Sig and TNT sure need'em. Festive bowls. May be finger-bowls, but I doubt it. Well and good. Though I, for one, draw the line at cocktails where I don't know my bootlegger. But why all the furriers' display? Does she want us to assume the native costume?"

Otway raised the largest of five black jaguar hides which were ranged in a neat row on the pavement.

"Here's yours, Waring," he chuckled. "The beast that grew this was a lord among his kind. You see, it fastens over the shoulders with these gold clasps. And there's a chain girdle. Suppose you retire to one of those eight convenient dressing-rooms and change? Then if the rest of us like the effect—"

"Set the example yourself! I'm no cave-man. But what's her idea?"

"She's trying to drive it through our thick skulls that she means only kindness toward us!" This from Sigsbee, who, having reverently allowed his hostess to pour water over his hands, was now, with equal reverence, accepting a fiber napkin to dry them.

As if handling the heavy water jar had at last wearied her, the girl thereupon surrendered it to the steward. Tellifer, with a vengeful glare at his luckier predecessor, proceeded to his ablutions.

"My experience," said Otway, "has been that among strange peoples it is always well to accept any friendly acts that are offered. No matter what one's private misgivings may be, no trace of them should show in one's manner. By that simple rule I have kept my life and liberty in many situations where others had been less fortunate. Despite our suspicions, we have shown not a trace of hostility toward the girl. We have offered no violence nor rudeness. Who knows? If we continue on our good behavior we may find ourselves accepted as friends, not only by the girl but all her foster-people. I've proved it to work out that way more than once."

"She's a mighty nice girl." Waring was weakly accepting a polished yellow cup. "But d'you think we should risk drinking this—purple stuff?"

The explorer sipped testingly at the liquor which his hostess had gracefully poured from the wine-jar.

"It is only assai wine," he announced. "No harm in it—unless one indulges too freely. See—she is pouring herself a cup! We had best drink, I believe, and then indicate that we would like to meet her people."

"Sensible girl, too," approved Waring. "Cave-man costumes. Nice little gift. But no effort to force 'em on us. Well-bred kid. Out-of-place here, hm?"

"Oh, decidedly," the explorer agreed. "I shall take her away with me when we go."

Otway was a man of morally spotless reputation. As leader of the expedition, he had every right to use the first personal pronoun in announcing his intent to rescue this white girl. Yet the statement seemed displeasing to every one of the explorer's four companions. The glances of all turned upon him with sudden hostility. Sigsbee was heard to mutter something that sounded like "Infernal cheek!"

But Otway gave their opinion no heed. Like the rest, he had drained his cup of purple wine. Innocent though he had claimed the vintage to be, it had deepened the color of his sun-burned face with amazing quickness. The cool gray eyes behind the shell-rims had grown bright and strangely eager. He swayed slightly. He took an unsteady step toward the girl, who had thus far barely stained her lips with the purple liquor.

"Sure!" he added thickly. "Queer I didn't realize that sooner. Girl, I've been—waiting for—always! Never got married, just that reason. Looking for this one. Take her away *now!*"

"You will not!"

Waring's mighty hand closed viselike on the naturalist's shoulder, wrenching him backward.

"Tha's right, Alcot," Tellifer approved. "He couldn't half 'preciate loveliness likes hers. Tha's for me! I 'preciate such things. Lovely girl—lovely girl—lovely diamond—lovely place—lovely 'dventure—"

As if in adoration of the prevailing loveliness of everything, Tellifer sank to his knees, and subsided gently with his head on one of the jaguar hides.

Waring discovered that he was not restraining Otway, but supporting his sagging weight. He released it, stared stupidly as the explorer's form dropped limply to the floor.

Something was very much wrong. Waring knuckled his eyes savagely. They cleared for an instant. There stood the girl. Her dawn-blue eyes were looking straight into his. There were great tears shining in them! Her whole attitude expressed mournful, drooping dejection. The golden-yellow cup had fallen from her hand. Across the pavement a purple pool spread and crept toward the little bare white feet.

Chapter VII.
THE HAG.

Waring knew that he, too, had fallen to the floor, and that he could not rise. Over him was bending—a face. Above it a circlet of star-white gems gleamed with a ghostly luster. The form beneath was draped in the spotted hide of a jaguar, fastened at the shoulders with fine golden chains.

But the face! Old, seamed, haggard, framed in wild locks of ragged, straying gray hair, with terrible eyes whose dark light has feasted through unnumbered years upon vicious cruelty, with toothless mouth distended in awful laughter—a hag's face, the face of a very night-hag—and up beside it rose a wrinkled, clawlike hand, and hovered above his throat! The vision passed. Merciful oblivion ensued.

Chapter VIII.
"TATA QUARAHY."

As he had been last to succumb under the terrific potency of that "harmless assai wine", so the correspondent was first to recover his normal senses. After a few minutes of fogginess, he grasped the main facts of the situation well enough.

In a way, they scarcely even surprised him. Now that the thing was done, he saw with dreary clearness that this had been a foregone conclusion from the instant when five fools, ignoring all circumstantial evidence, had placed their trust in a pair of dawn-blue eyes.

Just at first he had no way of being sure that he was not the sole fool who had survived. But as the others, one by one, awakened and replied to the correspondent's sardonic inquiries, he learned that their number was still complete.

Their voices, however, reached him with a muffled, hollow sound. They were accompanied by a clanking of heavy bronze chains, appropriately dismal.

Through the triangular opening in his cell door, Waring could see along a narrow lane in the greenery to the central court. The place was no longer illuminated by the ghostly radiance of Sunfire. It was daytime—and it was rainy weather. Through the open top of the pyramid the rain sluiced down in sheets and torrents, thundering on the palm-fronds, making of that small portion of Sunfire which was visible a spectral mound of rushing water-surface. It also sent little exploring cold trickles beneath the closed doors of five prison cells—no longer empty.

"Lovely place!" groaned Waring. "Oh, l'lovely! Friends and fellow-mourners, it wasn't a new wine. It was the oldest of old stuff. K.O. drops. And we swallowed it! What's that? No, Otway. No more your fault than anyone's. I fell—you fell—we fell. The lot of us needed a keeper. From all signs, we've probably acquired one. It won't be little blue-eyed Susan, though. Her work's done. Such a well-bred kid, too! Wouldn't force native costume on anyone. Oh, no! Say, am I the only cave-man? Or is it unanimous?"

Report drifted down the line that reversion to barbaric fashions had not been forced on the correspondent alone. Not a stitch of civilized clothing, not a weapon, not a single possession with which they had entered the pyramid had been left to any of the five. In exchange for those things, they had received each a neat stone cell, a handsome black jaguar hide, gold-trimmed, a chain adequate, as Waring had said, to restrain an elephant,—and a hope for continued life so slight as to be practically negligible.

After a time Waring informed the others of that last fading glimpse he had got of a frightful face bending over him. It was agreed that he had been privileged to look upon one of the "tribe" who inhabited the pyramid. No one, however, was able to explain why this "tribe" had allowed all those boats to rot, some of them through years, undisturbed at the landing state. Or why all save the girl were so extremely shy about showing themselves.

The noise of the rain ceased at last. The outer court brightened with sunshine. For any sounds or signs of life about them, the five might have been chained alone in an empty pyramid at the heart of an empty land.

The utter strangeness of what had occurred combined with memory of their own folly to depress them. Those cells, too, despite the increasing heat outside, were decidedly chilly. Damp, cold draughts blew up from the open shafts at the back. Much rainwater had crept in beneath the doors.

The jaguar-hides were warm as far as they went, but from the prisoners' civilized viewpoint, that was not half far enough. Bare feet shifted miserably on cold stone. An occasional sneeze broke the monotony. Except for fruit, none of the party had eaten anything since noon of the previous day. The drugged liquor, too, had left an aftermath of outrageous thirst. Yet neither food nor water had been given to them.

The noon hour arrived, as they could tell by diminished shadows and fiercely downbeating glare. Still, no attention had come their way.

Tellifer's cell commanded the best view of the main court. As the sun had approached the zenith, the esthete's dampened enthusiasm had to some degree revived. If the lucent mass of Sunfire had been beautiful at night, beneath the noon sun it became a living glory that gave Pedro's name for it, "Tata Quarahy", Fire of the Sun, new meaning. Tellifer exhausted his vocabulary in trying to do its rainbow splendors justice. But when he finally lapsed into silent adoration the other four made no effort to draw him out of it. Their more practical natures had rather lost interest in Sunfire. Diamond or not, it seemed that the sooty pit beneath it was likely to be of more concern to them.

The sun-rays were now nearly vertical. The central court grew to be a mere dazzle of multicolored refraction. Waves of heat from a furnace beat through the openings in the cell-doors. With them drifted wisps of white vapor. Presently, a low hissing sound was heard.

The seething noise grew louder. In the court, great clouds of white steam were rising, veiling the brightness of Sunfire. The pit beneath it seethed and bubbled like a monstrous cauldron.

Practical-minded or not, it was Tellifer who solved the simple dynamics of what was going on.

"I was afraid of this," he said. "I was afraid last night, when I first saw the atrocious manner in which that miracle of beauty has been mutilated. Practically sawn in half, for it is an octahedral stone and must originally have possessed nearly twice its present mass. But the lower part has been ruthlessly cleaved away, and the under surface ground and polished. The faceting extends only part way up the sides. The top is a polished cabochon. The scoundrels!" Tellifer's voice shook with emotion. "The soulless van-dals! Whoever the fiends were, they cut the most marvelous jewel Earth ever produced to suit a vilely utilitarian purpose! Sunfire is a great lens—a burning-glass. It is boiling the collected rain-water out of the pit now. When the pit is dry, the stone of its bowl will rise to red heat—white heat—who knows what temperature under that infernal sun? And that means—"

"Death for any living thing in the pit." declared Otway quietly. "With a victim in the pit, sacrifice to the deity must occur at high noon on any day when the sky is free from clouds. But I say—" the explorer's voice was suddenly distressed—"don't take it that way, man! Why, there is always a chance so long as one has breath in one's body. Brace up!"

"Oh, you don't understand! Let me be!" There had been a heavy clanking sound in Tellifer's cell. A thud as of a despairing form cast down. "You don't understand!" repeated the esthete sobbingly. "There's no chance! Or hardly one in a million. And it isn't being killed in that pit that's bothering me. It's—Oh, never mind, I tell you! I don't want to talk about it. The thing is too shameful—too horrible! Let me be!"

As all further questioning was met with stony silence from the central cell, his companions did "let him be", at last. That hysterical outburst from one of their number had not tended to brighten the general mood. It seemed to them, also, that if Tellifer really foresaw any more shameful and horrible fate than being broiled alive under a burning lens, he might share his knowledge and at least let them be equally prepared for it.

The day wore wearily by, measured only by lengthening shadows and lessening glare. The sudden night fell. There, on the eight rosy pillars, the iridescent splendor of Sunfire changed slowly to its ghostly glory of the dark hours.

Meantime, in the cells, four of the prisoners had reached that stage of physical and mental misery where, being the sort they were, they spoke to each other frequently and always in jest. The jokes exchanged were of a rather feeble order, it is true. The voices that uttered them were painfully hoarse and thickened. But the applause for each effort was resolutely cordial. Only Tellifer preserved his stony silence.

It was an hour past sunset. The stillness had remained unbroken since their early awakening. Death by mere chill and privation was beginning to seem a very possible alternative to the sacrificial fate they had expected, when the long waiting at last ended and their keeper came to them.

Chapter IX.
AN UNWELCOME INVITATION.

For comfort, there was little choice between sitting, lying down or standing on the cold, damp stones of their cramped quarters.

The heavy bronze shackles rasped the skin from their ankles in any position, and aching bones drove them to a continual uneasy shifting. But it so happened that Sigsbee was the only man on his feet when the keeper arrived.

There had been no warning sound of approach. The first notice the four other captives received was young Sigsbee's voice, breathing a husky word that brought them all clanking up in haste to their windows.

Into that single word Sigsbee had poured a reproach for trust betrayed, a shocked amazement that the betrayer should shamelessly reapper, a wholly youthful satisfaction in being able to address that expressive "You!" to the right person, which told them instantly that their "Blessed Damozel" of yestere'en was again with them.

The triangular openings were not large enough to permit the passage of a prisoner's head. Much as they would have liked to crane their necks for a first-hand view, they must rely on Sigsbee's report. A volley of harsh questions exploded down the line. Sigsbee's voice rose against them.

"Stop that, you fellows! You're frightening her. There—I told you. She's crying again. Now she'll go away. No, it's all right. She's passing my things through the window. *Brave* little girl! Now listen, fellows. I don't care what you think, this girl is not responsible for what happened."

"Oh, Lawdy!" groaned the deepest of the harsh voices. "He's hooked again! Wake up, Sig. With her own fair hands she poured the K.O. drops. She'll never weep her way into *my* heart again. Is any one with her?"

"No, she's alone. Listen, Waring. She's coming your way. If you aren't decently civil to her, I give you fair warning I'll—"

"You'll what? Butt your head against the wall? Oh, there you are, Susan!"

The harshest voice had lowered to a base growl, suggestive of the jaguar which had once worn Waring's costume. Into his range of vision, staggering beneath the weight of a heavy reed basket, had come their fair betrayer.

There was justification for almost any degree of bitterness. Young Sigsbee's reversal of judgment appeared mere weakness. And yet, either because he feared to anger or frighten away the source of supplies, or for some other reason, the correspondent's righteous wrath received no further expression just then. He was heard to mutter something about "more damn mangos", a less depreciative "Bananas—better than nothing!" and a final "Water at last, thank God!"—and then the slender food-bringer was dragging her basket along to the next cell.

At close range the girl could be seen only as she reached each captive's door. A little later, however, her task finished, the empty basket deserted, she drifted out into the general range of vision.

At the opening of that lane, which faced Tellifer's person, she paused. Silhouetted against the pale glow beyond, they saw her stand an instant, head bent, shoulders drooping, silent as always, by mere attitude suggesting a boundless, pitiful dejection. Then she moved slowly away.

Three minutes more, and Tellifer emerged from the unnatural speechlessness he had preserved all afternoon.

"She is gazing into the pit," he informed solemnly. "Now she has sunk to her knees beside one of the columns. She is weeping again, and she has much to mourn for! The human fiends whose servant she is are the inheritors of a truly monstrous crime."

"Let her weep!" The immediate presence removed, Waring's vindictiveness had revived. "Decoy. That's all Susan is. And we aren't the first. Not by a damn sight! Those boats—the airplane. Nothing but fruit and water for starving men. Monstrous crimes is right, TNT!"

The esthete sighed deeply. "The crimes to which you refer are trivial beside the far more shocking one which I am certain has been accomplished in this place. But no more of it. The subject is too dreadful. I am not a practical man, but has it struck none of you as strange that except for the one old woman whom Waring caught a glimpse of, we have as yet seen only the girl?"

"Awake at last, hm? Been discussing nothing else all day."

"Is that true, Alcot? I was inattentive, perhaps. My mind was upon— But let me forget that. During the discussion was any probable explanation reached?"

"No, Mr. Tellifer," Otway informed him gravely. "No probable explanation was reached. It is my own conviction, indeed, that no probable explanation ever will be reached. I don't say that none of us will survive to learn the true facts. Life and hope, remember; life and hope! But when those facts are ascertained, they will not be probable. Possible, perhaps, but decidedly—not—probable! The situation simply doesn't admit of it. Oh, Waring! How about that story?"

"Sunday supplement stuff," disparaged the correspondent. "No magazine would dare touch it. Wonder how long we'll be left here? Safe for tonight, anyway. Fashionable beggars! All ceremonies at high noon. What news of Susan? Still weeping?"

His last question, addressed to Tellifer, was answered from another source. Out in the silent central court a sound had begun. As when, ascending the outer stairway, that same sound had first reached their ears, every one of the five paused through a long minute, breathless and listening.

Their reason for attention, however, had changed. Then it had been wonder and a devouring curiosity as to the source of that quaint, monotonous, double-fluted melody. Now they had no curiosity about it. They knew exactly what instrument was being played, who was playing it, and for what astonishing purpose. And every man of them was suddenly thankful that his cell possessed a thick, serviceable, bronze door, tightly closed, and with only one small window.

"Have to hand it to Susan!" gasped Waring at last. "Fido's coming out. I can see him. She afraid? Not little blue-eyes! Oh, Lawdy! How much more of him is there?"

"The—ah—anterior mile or so of Fido has strayed over to where I also can enjoy a view," Otway asserted. "They took away my shell-rims, but I can make out that the cephalite, or head-shield, is quite well developed. About the size of a flour-barrel, I should say. And the toxicognaths, or poison-fangs—Oh, ye gods! No, it's all right. For an instant I believed Fido was coming down my alley to call. But it was merely a thousand-legged pirouette. This dancing rite probably takes place every evening and is entirely separate from the noonday sacrifice. It is likely, also, that we are being saved up, as it were, for some special day or occasion. Their being no present tonight save the priestess, we need have no immediate fears."

"Speak for yourself!" Waring's heavy voice broke on the words. "She's bringing it—*she's bringing that thing down my alley!*"

The monotonous melody of the Pan's pipes had indeed approached much nearer. A moment more, and not only Waring, but all the prisoners were given evidence that the pair of dancers were not content to exercise their art at a distance from their audience.

Between the cells and the artificial jungle was a space perhaps ten feet broad. For *Scolopendra Horribilis* to have elaborated his curious, coiling patterns on that cramped stage would have been impossible. Like a true artist, he did not even attempt it. When the girl swayed gracefully into view, turned to the narrow space and passed lightly along it, still piping, the sacred monster—or a portion of him—merely followed.

As she crossed each successive band of light at the clear lanes, those in the cells caught glimpses of her awful attendant.

The head, with enormous, blind-looking yellow eyes, gaping mandibles and huge poison fangs, hovered close above the starry circlet of gems in the girl's red-gold hair. The talons of the plated length below seemed on the point of closing around her slender shoulders. Yet the girl cast not so much as a glance upward or back. In turning at the end, she took no care to avoid colliding with the frightful Death that followed.

Death for its part, however, respectfully drew aside, made a talon-fringed running loop of itself, and continued to follow. Through alternate light and shadow the girl passed back until she again reached the correspondent's prison-cell.

There the other four could no longer see her. In returning, she had moved close to the cell-rank. There followed a *clang*, as of a heavy bolt thrown back. A hoarse, wordless ejaculation. Another *clang*, suggesting metal tossed down on a stone floor. Then the girl had stepped into view again, still playing but holding the pipes to her lips with one hand. With the other she was seen to beckon gracefully.

"Boys," came the correspondent's desperate voice, "good-bye! That infernal little Jezebel! She has opened my door! She has given me the key to these damn shackles! She's inviting me to come out! By God, I won't get out! There's that shaft behind the cell. I'll jump! Wait till I get these irons off."

A rasping sound, a crude key turning in a clumsy lock, a rattle of chains hastily discarded.

"Waring!" From the next cell Otway spoke with quiet, restraining force. "Don't jump! Do whatever she wishes. The sacrifice is to the sun, remember. If she had wanted that monster to destroy us tonight, why should she have bothered to bring us food? This is part of some preliminary ceremony. And your limbs will be free. Do whatever she wishes and watch your chance. It may be the chance that saves all of us."

After quite a long moment, the correspondent replied. "Right, Otway. Playing the cur. Glad you spoke. I'll—I'll go out. Here, you! Can't you see I'm coming? Start that music again!"

The girl, as if weary of waiting, had lowered the pipes from her lips. The instant she did so, the swaying monster behind had ceased swaying. With an ominous, dry clashing of avid mandibles, its head shot higher. It descended again in a curving loop that cleared the girl's head and, too obviously, had the open cell for its objective.

Seeing the prisoner obedient, however, the girl resumed her music. Immediately the menacing head swayed back to its former position.

The freed correspondent faced the pair grimly. That slender slip of a girl, whom he could have easily lifted with one hand, was for the time his master. To overcome or interfere with her in any way meant death. To slay big, powerful Alcot Waring, she had only to cease the restraining music of her little golden pipes.

The dawn-blue eyes were deep, sweetly mournful as ever. But even Sigsbee failed to suggest that Waring should place faith in them and act in any way save exactly as she might direct.

Her next order was given as the first had been. One delicate hand waved in a graceful gesture.

"You're elected, too, Otway," informed the correspondent. "Wants me to open your door. Shall I do it? Up to you."

The explorer affirmed his own unshaken nerve by instant consent. The same key that had released Waring having freed Otway from the bronze shackles, he stepped out beside the other.

"You know," he observed quietly, "they took my shell-rims, and everything nearer than three yards is just a blur. Only hope I shan't tread on Fido!"

"Stand still!" Waring advised between his teeth. "The damn thing is all over the place. What's she after now? Oh, I see. Sig, your divinity calls you!"

"I believe she intends releasing us all," opined the explorer, still resolutely cheerful. "In that case, we'll surely get a chance among the five of us."

"Oh, sure! Stiff upper lip and carry on."

To appreciate, however, the real deadliness of their peril was just then far easier than to foresee in what form that hoped-for chance was likely to come.

For one thing, "Fido's" mentality was proving to be as abnormal as its physical proportions. They had at first supposed that the monster merely answered the music as snakes writhe to the charmer's pipes. But its behavior before the cell-rank augured both training and intelligence. It was not dancing now. It was waiting—and what is waited upon was the will of its mistress.

As for the thing's destructive capacity, that was obviously terrific. In one lightning sweep it might have involved not five but dozen men amid taloned coils beside which those of a python would have been easily escapable. The huge poison-fangs with which the first segment of its body was equipped, seemed really superfluous.

John B. was the last captive to be released. The number of her victims complete, the girl gestured toward one of the open lanes.

With their extraordinary jailors close at heel, the five moved meekly toward the outer court.

Chapter X.

THE DANCE.

The proceedings of the next half-hour formed a study in grotesquerie exceeding anything which even the captives' experience of pyramidal customs had led them to look for.

They had, it appeared, been haled forth to take part in the same ceremonial dance which their coming had interrupted the previous evening.

After bringing them out, indeed, the girl herself practically ignored them. As her light feet carried her about the sacred circle, she seemed wholly absorbed in an ecstasy of music and rhythmic motion. But the ghastly enforcer of her will gave the captives every attention.

The thing was clearly no novice in its part. Its age, of course, was unguessable. But one could conceive that years—decades—centuries, perhaps, had seen the slow growth and training of that monstrous votary. Nocturnal by nature, the vast, dull yellow eyes might have been blind as they appeared. If so, the sense of sight was replaced by some other, more mysterious senses which creatures of its species inherit. The whiplike antennae were continually alert. The thing's intelligence, too, seemed not confined to the brain, as in vertebrate animals, but instinct was in every part of its active length.

The girl dancer needed make no effort to avoid contact with the coils. They avoided her. Her foot could not move quickly enough to tread upon them. But of the unwilling male participants in the rite, the monster was less considerate.

A mere scratch from one of those myriad dagger-pointed talons would have amounted to a severe wound, quite aside from the infection they probably carried. The menace of them was used with amazing skill to force the prisoners around the appointed circle.

The stairway proved to be a blessed goal unreachable. At the slightest move in that direction, up would rise a barrier of clawing segments. With bare feet and limbs, to have dared overleaping or standing before it would have been madness, even had not the worse threat of the head and poison fangs hovered ever close above them.

Of the five, Otway's troubles were the most dismaying. In the absence of glasses, his eyes were of little use to him at close range. Again and again, only the guiding hand of a fellow-initiate saved him from calamity. Had the explorer been alone he could not have survived even one round of that horrible, ludicrous, altogether abominable dance.

Yet the indomitable spirit of Otway was first to recognize the ridiculous side of the affair. He and Waring presently joined in a running fire of comment on its absurdities. Tellifer, solemn as ever, moved through the literal—and talon-fringed—"mazes of the dance", with an effort at classic dignity which won their high commendation. John B.'s quiet, efficient side-stepping went not unnoted. But it remained for Sigsbee to win the jesters' really whole-hearted approval.

It had dawned on them that the expedition's youngest member was not merely avoiding trouble, like the rest of them. He was actually dancing, modeling his steps on those of their graceful leader, and doing very well indeed at it. Sigsbee was an agile, athletic youth. The "cave-man costume" emphasized a certain grace of body and regularity of feature. Very soon, having perfected the step to suit his ambition, Sigsbee coolly deserted his fellow captives. Taking advantage of every convenient change in the monster's running coils, he joined the girl.

"There are a lot of these steps," he called back, "that my sister at home taught me. Crazy about this—nature-dancing stuff. Oh, fine! That's fine! That's a regular—fox-trot—step. Say, you fellows! I have seen this girl—before, somewhere! Been trying—to remember where—ever since—last night. Or else she—reminds me of some one.

"She reminded me"—Tellifer avoided a section of talons by one second's time and an undignified bound—"she reminded *me*," he repeated more forcibly, "of a girl in a poem. But not any more. Blessed Damozel!" Another leap and increased bitterness. "Where are her three lilies? Where is her—

gold bar of heaven? Where—her sense of fitness? I could have personed the—jaguar-hide—if she hadn't forced one on me. I could have forgiven the—indignified dancing—if she hadn't made me join in it. Now—I disown the comparison. All she has is—the stars in her hair and the—eyes—and they are basely deceptive. She is not a Blessed Damozel! She's a—"

He hesitated for a fresh comparison. When found, it would probably have been inoffensive enough. Tellifer's classic fancy rarely sought force in vulgarity. But young Sigsbee had again been indulging at close range in glimpses of the eyes Tellifer slandered. He came to an abrupt halt, fists clenched.

"Not another word, there!" he called sharply.

The girl was within a yard of him. As if in appreciation of her gallant defender, she swayed still nearer, stretched one hand and touched Sigsbee lightly on the shoulder. At the same time, she lowered the pipes from her lips. She pointed with them toward one of the five men.

There followed a swift yellow flash—a sharp, broken-off cry.

Again the pipes were set to the girl's lips. Up swayed the colossal yellow head to resume its guardianship of the victims. But there were only four of them now who required guarding!

The girl danced no more. She continued to play her piping melody, but the great, mournful eyes beneath the star-crown grew brilliant with slowly forming tears.

Chapter XI.
THE SACRIFICE.

"What the devil good is her weeping, Sig? She deliberately pointed. And that horror knocked poor old TNT into the pit! He's there now. Can't get out. We're locked in here. Thirty minutes at most till noon. And that little Jezebel you're infatuated with comes to weep over him! Who cares how she feels? Actions speak!"

It was morning of the next day. That four of the party, even in the face of that yellow Death, had consented to return to their cells after the abrupt end of last night's grotesque ceremony, had been due to Tellifer's own appeal.

Beyond a few bruises, the latter had not been injured. When the girl, as Waring accused, had deliberately showed her terrible familiar that Tellifer was the evening's appointed victim, the unlucky esthete had been a little apart from his companions, close to the eight-sided pit. The great cephalite or head-shield of the monster has struck Tellifer between the shoulders with battering-ram force.

Knocked off his feet, he had rolled upon the treacherous pentagonal slabs that surrounded the sooty pit. He had gone down head first, but, sliding down the steep slope of the bowl, had arrived at the bottom without being stunned.

He had presently replied to the anxious hails of his friends. When it became clear that the latter were required to return to their cells, leaving him in the pit, he had urged them to do so. For them to be slain on the spot could do him no good. And in the hours before Sunfire should again justify its name he might escape from the pit.

Waring had made a gallant effort to join his friend. But he had been blocked by the alert death's head, and finally allowed himself to be driven back with the others. As the correspondent had been required to release his fellow-slaves, so the girl saw to it that he duly re-shackled and boxed them up. Under the gentle glance of those pitying eyes, Waring had finished the task by adjusting his own fetters and tossing the key out to her. The thing was maddening beyond words, but there had seemed to be no alternative save death.

The monster had then been led back to its lair, and the girl had bolted down the bronze cover that debarred its return and departed.

It had seemed that the captive of the pit, left thus unguarded, must surely find some way to climb out and release his companions. Yet dawn had returned, bringing Tellifer's strange executioner to march slowly up the sky, and that means remained undiscovered. Though the pit was deadly through only a part of the day, alone in it Tellifer was helpless as a beetle at the bottom of a bowl.

As the morning wore on and the temperature of the court slowly rose, Tellifer ceased his efforts to climb out. The time soon came when shouted advice or questions from the cell-rank drew no response. That the victim might be already dead, or in heavy stupor, appeared the best hope left for him.

Small wonder, then, that when a slender form drifted on light feet across the central court, poised beside one of the eight columns, and at last sank down there, a figure of desolate mourning, Waring had cursed her and her grief together. Chivalry was all very well, and Waring was not deficient therein. But a weeping she-fiend who chained him in a stone cell, prepared the agonizing murder of the closest friend, and then came to mourn over her work while watching its progress, seemed to him outside the pale of toleration.

In young Sigsbee, grief for the victim was strangely united with concern for their betrayer. But his view met scant sympathy in any quarter. Otway expressed his own attitude with decision.

"That woman," said he, grimly just, "is acting under compulsion of some sort. Probably, superstitious religion training. But were she what she appears, the revulsion of her nature against all this vile, cold-blooded treachery and cruelty, would not stop at mere weeping. She is of white blood, but she disgraces it. Any Indian woman, feeling as she pretends to feel, would dare the wrath of her people on earth and the gods beyond and be true to the humane instinct. It's no use, Sigsbee! A man is dying in that infernal hole, and she isn't doing a thing to help him—is she?"

"She goes there and cries!" snarled Waring. "Cries over him! And not the bare decency to give him a drink of water. Not a drop of water in nearly eighteen hours! My God, Otway—"

"Steady, old man. You can be pretty sure he isn't suffering now. The chances are that he won't revive enough to realize what is happening to him. *I* know that sun. Under that great lens above the pit, and with no water— why, the poor fellow probably went out soon after he stopped answering our hails, two hours ago. Is the girl still hanging about there? I wonder she can endure the heat."

"She's such a kind of queer creature," offered John B. gloomily, "that I don't reckon it's possible to guess what she could or couldn't stand, sir. I've met lots of queer kinds, different places, but I didn't suppose there could be one just like her. She seems to me a lot more horrible than that big centipede, sir."

"She isn't!" cried the youthful Sigsbee despairingly. "She's—Oh, I don't know what she is, but I tell you that girl is *not* wicked! It's all some abominable mistake!"

"Mistake that poor old TNT is dead or dying there? Mistake that she's hovering over him—like a weeping vulture?"

"No, she isn't, Waring. She's gone away—or at least, I think she has. There's such a glare that a fellow can't see much."

"The focus," Otway observed, "must have been complete for some minutes past. My friends, poor Tellifer is—"

He paused. Indeed, to finish the sentence was needless. The sun, centered now in a brazen sky, had too obviously reached the full altitude of its murderous mission.

Waring was worst hit, but the others felt badly enough. The esthete had been eccentric, fanciful, sometimes more than a little trying, but with all his moods and nerves, he had carried a reckless bravery; there had been a certain odd, innocent loveableness about him.

Dim against the blinding glory beyond, a slender form flitted past the sullenly silent cell rank. To the left, where rose the bronze lever that controlled the great stone bowl, a slight, metallic, grating sound was heard.

Sigsbee and Otway, whose cells were nearest the center, vaguely beheld the phantomlike rising of a huge rounded mass beneath Sunfire.

A few seconds later the faint but unmistakable splash of a solid mass striking water far below reached their ears.

Chapter XII.
revenge!

"Cut it, Sig! I'm past hearing. That little Jezebel murdered Tellifer! Woman? Murderess—torturer—she-fiend! Tears? Yes—of the crocodile brand. Part of her stock-in-trade. Don't know what the rest of 'em are like her. Maybe there aren't any others. Maybe she and that old hag I saw are the last of a rotten crop. But fifty or a thousand, take this from me: little Susan is head-devil of the lot! We're all due to go West. One at a time or en masse. No difference. But *she's* going with us! Oh, she's wise. Kept out of my reach just now. If she hadn't, I'd have—But no matter. She'll release us again. She'll trust that crawling horror to protect her. And then—" The vengeful correspondent's voice sank to a sinister whisper—"*then I'll get her!*"

Night had returned, bringing the silent, strange little food-bearer with her basket of fruit and small water-jars. She had come alone as before, but there had been a slight variation. The first time she had handed in the provisions at close range, seeming assured that the prisoners would not try to harm her.

Tonight she had brought a second, much smaller basket. Before each cell she had filled this small receptacle from the large one, and gravely extended it, keeping such distance that the reach of a man's arm through one of the triangular windows might achieve a grasp on the basket, but not on her hands. Emptied by the cell's occupant, the basket must be tossed back and used again.

The procedure indicated a clear understanding of the bitterness toward her. Yet, aside from this, there had been no change in appearance or manner. The eyes that blessed and grieved were innocent of evil as before.

While she passed along the rank, none of the four had spoken a word to her. She had never indicated that she understood, when they had addressed her. Words were useless. Moreover, there had come to be something indescribably shocking in that difference between her acts and the promise of all gentle good in her appearance.

One flash of mockery, one taunting curl of the childlike mouth, and the whole affair, terrible though it was, would have seemed a shade more endurable. But the taunt never came. She pitied them, it seemed, deeply. She had no consciousness of wrong toward them, but to witness their captivity and consider the fate on its way to them, grieved her. Sad, very sad, that in the world should be pain and mourning and the ludicrous, maddening helplessness of four strong men at the mercy of one slender maiden!

In Waring, the effect of all this came dangerously near to real madness. Agony over Tellifer's lingering death had instilled his friend with a ruthless hate, against which dissuasive arguments beat vainly. Waring's threats, uttered after the girl had gone, were sincere!

Chapter XIII.
AN AWFUL CRIME.

An hour later, and again the grotesque ceremonial progress of victims and captors about the sacrificial pit.

Between this occasion and the first, however, were differences. Not only was the captive band's number reduced to four, but these four moved with a strangely absorbed interest in each other.

Otway, blinking desperately, must rely on the steward alone to warn and guide him. Young Sigsbee had lost his enthusiasm for "nature dancing". Silently, without admission of their purpose, he and Waring were engaged in a duel of approach and defense.

At the cells, as if aware of her danger, the girl had passed Waring by and laid on John B. the task of releasing himself and his fellows. The last had been first and the first last with such effect that when Waring finally emerged, sinister purpose in the very poise of his massive person, he had found a barrier of three men between him and his quarry.

There had been some words exchanged, then. In the very shadow of death, the quartette had come close to a violent quarrel. Unreasoning accusations of disloyalty from Waring, however, were met by a cool counteraccusation from Otway that headed off active strife. Woman-killing aside, said the naturalist, Waring had no right to rob the rest of any slim little chance for life the evening might bring.

On that score, Waring had grimly yielded. But he made no promises for his behavior in the court's more open field. There, should he attack the dancer, he would surely be slain. But while the monster's attention was upon him, the others might grasp their "slim chance for life" and welcome.

The compromise was neither accepted nor declined, because just at that point the obligato from the Pan's pipes had ceased and the disputants had hastily taken the hint and the outward path. But though no more was said, Waring's set determination was plain enough.

The dancer, as before, danced as though alone in the hollow pyramid. The hideous, scampering coils that followed and surrounded them all might have been bodiless smoke-wreaths, so far as she was concerned. The angry, maddened giant of a man whose bloodshot glances gloated threateningly on her light movements had no seeming existence for her.

But young Sigsbee knew that her danger was very real indeed.

Forty-eight hours in the pyramid had reduced a big, good-humored, civilized man to a savage with one idea in his head, and one only. Waring had stood by helpless while the friend he loved was tortured to death. Now, unshaven, red-eyed, massive and dangerous as the "cave-man" he resembled, the correspondent stalked his indifferent prey, while again and again Sigsbee took outrageous risks to keep his own person between them.

In actual physical conflict, the young yacht-owner would have had little chance with the correspondent. For all his fleshiness, Waring was quick as a cat, light-moving almost as the little dancer herself—far more powerful than Sigsbee. But even a few seconds of bodily struggle would mean death for both. Neither dared pause an instant in that constant avoidance of hideous running claws.

Sigsbee got no help from the girl's official defender. Whatever its training, the monstrous guardian lacked intelligence to understand that strange duel between captives over the life of their tyrant. Its scampering talons threatened defender and attacker alike.

The end came at last with great suddenness.

For just an instant the girl poised motionless in one of the graceful poses that interspersed the dance steps. Tellifer's avenger had achieved a place not six feet from her. Sigsbee was momentarily entrapped in a running loop, the inner edge of which had flung up knee-high above the floor.

Seeing his chance, Waring took it like a flash.

In almost the same instant a number of things happened. What some of them were was understood by only one person; the rest merely found themselves involved in a chaos of peril.

Waring sprang. Sigsbee, taking another desperate chance, bounded over the clawing loop. He collided in middle air with his massive opponent. The two crashed heavily down at the girl's very feet.

John B., a little distance off, saw the hovering yellow death's head swing around with a darting motion. He shouted warningly. But the combattants on the floor were seeking each other's throats with a whole-hearted attention which ignored the shout. The girl shrank back a step—and lowered her Pan's pipes.

At that signal, John B. saw the hovering head rise a trifle. Those curved

daggers, its poison-fangs, opened wide. All the scampering pattern of segments halted—the head poised—

And then, instead of shouting downward, John B. saw the head give a
great, sweeping jerks sideways.

Inexplicably, it flung over and struck the side of the faceted, luminous
crystal above the pit.

Next instant it was as if a yellowish tornado had been loosed in the central
court. The air seemed full of a blurred chaos of convulsive segments.

The yellow blur flashed around the pit, enveloped the eight pillars in a
coiling cloud. The cloud condensed—became the taloned, yellow length
again, but wrapped around the columns in a straining, writhing skein. Up
from this skein rose the head, twisting from side to side as if in agony. Above
the pit, a single, distinct, ringing sound shivered out—a quivering *ping-g-
g*, as of a great crystal goblet sharply struck. It was followed by a silent
concussive shock—a kind of bursting scintillance of white glare. Then, like
the downward swoop of a vast, black wing, utter darkness.

In the central court men called to one another in hoarse shouts, groped and
blindly sought each other.

They could not understand! The monstrous creature of talons and
venom was gone. At least, the dry rustle and crash which had accompanied
its presence were no longer heard. Cautiously exploring feet found none of
the dangerous segments.

In that first mad flurry of rage, convulsive agony, or whatever had smitten
it, the thing had knocked John B. and the explorer off their feet, and one of
the talons, catching in Otway's furry tunic, had broken the shoulder-straps
and jerked it partly off him. Aside from this, no damage had been sustained
by any of the four captives.

Waring and Sigsbee had forsaken their death-grapple. Meeting at last,
the other couple found them like a pair of dazed children, hand in hand,
seeking nothing save escape from the incomprehensible.

The light of Sunfire had exploded to a scintillant glare and left them
blind. Overhead, in a humid, blue-black sky, great stars winked down at
them, but not brightly enough to shed one revealing ray on this latest
mystery of the pyramid.

Girl, monster and glowing crystal, the three presiding elements of their
strange captivity, seemed to have been simultaneously wiped out of existence. The jaguar-hide tunics alone were left as assurance that the experience had been a real one.

Suddenly, in the dark, young Sigsbee grasped the arm of his late adversary.

"Look!" he gasped. "Look up at the rim there! A light—and somebody crouched beside it!"

There on the pyramid's rim indeed, fifty feet above, a small light glowed warm and yellow. It showed what seemed to be the form of a man. It was not standing nor even looking down toward them. The form squatted with rounded shoulders and bent head. It's face was hidden in its hands. The attitude was one of overpowering grief.

A moment later and the figure had risen slowly. It raised the light, evidently a common oil lantern, and began a leisurely descent of the inner stair. As it came on, the head was still bent and the shoulders drooped dejectedly.

"*Who* in God's name?" breathed Waring—and he was silent.

They were four civilized men, who did not believe in demons, apparitions, nor that, as primitive folk hold, the newly dead are restless and may rise in their lifeless flesh; Therefore they stood their ground.

It was true that for Mr. Theron Narcisse Tellifer, or any other man of flesh and blood, to have spent those last hours exposed without water in the heat of the pit, passed at least ten minutes beneath the fully focused rays, and finally been dropped five hundred feet or so to some dark pool within the pyramid's base, and still survive, was, on the face of it, more incredible than even the living-dead theory. It was also true that Waring's hand closed on Otway's bare shoulder in a grip that left the shoulder num, and the explorer was not even conscious of it. Still—they stood their ground.

He—it—the thing that wore Tellifer's seeming—had gotten rid of the indecorous jaguar-hide-and-gold-bangles effect, and was again dressed for roughing it in a civilized style. A very small, light rifle was carried under one arm.

Reaching the lower level, the mysterious being raised its dejected head, lifted the lantern, and spoke.

"The final consummation of an awful crime," it began, "has been accomplished! Alcot, I know that you are there somewhere and alive, for I heard you swearing. I trust that you are satisfied! You denied that Sunfire, that lost miracle of loveliness, was a diamond. You were wrong. Sunfire *was* a diamond, though it is now, alas, only a shattered wreck of dust and fragments! Wondrous though its beauty, Sunfire was but a vast carbon crystal. The heat beating upward from the pit must long since have prepared this end. The stone could never have been re-cut. It could hardly have been lifted down intact from the columns. The impact of my unlucky air-gun bullet striking the side dissolved it in a shining cloud of dust! My friends,

I was fairly certain yesterday that Sunfire's ruin had been wrought But to have finished the evil work of those ignorant vandals with my own hand! I wish—I wish that I had returned to New York by liner from Para, as I was tempted to do!"

While the voice spoke, no one had even thought of interrupting its sad discourse. As it ceased, Waring drew a great breath.

"That," said he with deep conviction, "that's Tellifer! Darn you, TNT! All these hours and—yes, you even took time to shave! How'd you get out of that bowl? Why didn't you come back sooner? D'you know you nearly made a damn, cold-blooded woman-murderer of me? Come here with that lantern. My foot just struck something. It's the girl! Is she—is she badly hurt, Sigsbee?"

Chapter XIV.

FLIGHT.

On examination by lantern-light, the mysterious little tyrant of the pyramid was found to be still breathing. As there were no wounds on her, it was decided that she had fainted from shock or fright.

Dread that her monstrous companion might be lurking near in the darkness was soon dissipated. Over beyond the pit, a vast tangled heap of loathsome yellow proved to be the thing's lifeless body. The head-shield trailed out on the pavement, presented a very peculiar appearance. One of the eyes was pierced by a small, round bullet hole. Also, the entire head plate was scarred with innumerable scratches and perforations through which oozed a whitish, semi-liquid substance.

Tellifer replied listlessly to many questions, while Sigsbee and the steward bathed the unconscious girl's brow with some of the water she had brought them in the cells.

Waring watched these ministrations with concern. Discovery that her watch over a tortured man's death, and the cold-blooded dumping of his corpse afterward, had been acts only of seeming, had wrought a change in even the correspondent's feeling toward her. Why she had "gone through the motion", as Waring phrased it, was not at all clear. But Tellifer's story revealed that he had certainly not been present while she wept over his supposed agony. The thing actually dumped when she threw the lever, was a piece of rock.

Use of the lantern for examination of the pit confirmed his tale. Near the bottom of the great bowl was now a large irregular aperture. The shock which cracked the stone when Tellifer allowed it to swing back, full weight, the first evening, had saved the experimenter's life. There had been a jagged, branching crevice. The shrinking effect of next day's white-hot noon focus had completed the work.

Tellifer explained that about the time he ceased answering their hails, he had discovered that a part of the bowl's curving side was in actual fragments, only held in place by pressure. With the buckle of his metal girdle he had managed to pry out one of the smaller pieces till he could get finger-grip on it. After its removal, taking out the larger fragments was easy.

He had, he said, refrained from telling his friends of this, partly because he was too dry to speak easily, and partly out of consideration—lest he raised false hopes. No, he hadn't expected them to thank him for that. But how could he know that he was going to get through alive? Very well. He would continue the story if there were not too many interruptions.

His first idea had been a dive into the depths. On casting down several of the rock fragments, resulting splashes told him that there was water below. Well, if his friends had not heard no such splashes, he was not responsible for that. They were making so much noise yelling at him that the fact was not surprising. Such a dive, however, proved needless.

Through the hole he had found himself able to swing by his hands and fling himself sideways into an open, floored space beneath the upper pavement. It was very dark down there, but, feeling about, he had come upon a system of great metal bars and cylinders. It dawned on him that the ancient engineers had arranged the machinery which revolved the bowl in an open horizontal shaft, probably for convenience in case of breakdown. There seemed to be a chance that at the other end of this shaft he might find an exit.

Stumbling through blackness, he had come upon a narrow flight of stairs, had fallen down them, and, upon recovering from that a little, had found himself near an open doorway at the back of one of the outer buildings, in the fifth terrace of the pyramid's western plane.

Though privations, a bad night and his latest tumble had left him very weak, he remembered the need of his friends. He had managed to drag himself around to the eastern stair and down it to water-level. After drinking and getting himself a little food aboard the canoe, he had lain down to rest a few minutes.

Nature had betrayed him and it was dusk when he awoke. Yes, certainly he had slept one afternoon. While in the bowl he had hardly been able to sleep at all. Their shouts had disturbed him. Very well. He would accept the apologies and continue.

Though not a practical man, he had deemed best to be prepared in every way possible to meet difficulties. Therefore he had taken time to eat again and exchange that abominable jaguar-hide for a more dignified costume. Also to shave. Yes, he felt that the moral support received from these two latter acts was worth the time expended on them. He was not a practical man—

"Oh, get on with it, TNT!" grinned his friend. "Providence looks out for such as you—and us. You surely made a clean finish. Maybe the shave helped. How'd you happen to think of the air-gun?"

Tellifer had, it seemed, recalled efforts of his own to shoot loons on the northern lakes. This is an impossible feat since the birds dive at the flash and are beneath the surface before the charge can reach them. Applying past experience to present emergency, it occured to him that if there was no flash, the monstrous centipede could not take warning.

The air-rifle, which belonged to Otway, was a very powerful one. Because of its small caliber, however, Tellifer had not meant to use it except in dire need. Climbing to the pyramid's rim, he had seen his comrades led forth, and watched with much interest and curiosity the singular evolutions of Waring and Sigsbee. When they finally flew at one another's throats, and the venomous yellow head poised to strike, he had perceived that the air-gun idea must be tried out at once.

The first shot struck one of the monster's enormous eyes. The second missed the head and hit the great crystal.

Like any diamond that had been subjected to high temperatures, Sunfire had acquired a brittleness that made it more fragile than glass. It had "splintered" at the impact, with such completeness as had all the effect of a silent explosion.

The monster had been slain, not by the bullets, but by Sunfire. Over a dozen feet above floor-level, Sunfire had perished without claiming any further human victims. But the head of its monstrous votary, almost in contact with the exploding crystal, had been perforated by the sharp dust and splinters.

Practical man or not, it appeared that with a couple of shots from an air-gun TNT had made a complete clean-up of the two main perils of the pyramid. The third—if peril she could be termed outside her relations with the other two—was left at the mercy of her victims.

It was decided to carry the girl with them to the canoe. Food, a night's rest, and counsel were needed before any effort was made to seek out the pyramid's other and strangely retiring inhabitants. For one thing, there was the question of weapons. Beside the air-rifle, a couple of shotguns and a spare Winchester had been left on board the canoe. But all their small fire-arms and rifles they had carried the first night, were in the enemies' hands.

Even were the "tribe" few in number, this superiority of armament made seeking them an adventure to be approached cautiously.

They had enough of reckless indiscretion. Hereafter every act should be well considered. The conquest of the pyramid, begun by Tellifer, should be carried to a finish with the least possible risk.

So they spoke, like wise, intelligent men, the while they viewed pityingly the unconscious form of their dethroned tyrant.

Waring in particular, seeing her, frail, graceful, with her face of a sleeping child supported on Sigsbee's knee, felt a hot wave of shame and a great wonder at himself.

This child had been brought up in these barbaric surroundings. Doubtless religious training had fought the gentle instincts natural to her, and made her bitterly unhappy. She had done as she had been taught was right, and in the doing—suffered.

She seemed rousing, at last. Color had returned to the tender lips. The steadfast, reverent boy who held her, smoothed back a curling tendril of the red-gold hair. Waring, shamefacedly gentle, dropped to his knees and attempted to take one of the fragile wrists. His innocent intent was to feel the pulse. But Sigsbee struck at his hand in a flare of resentment which showed that a certain recent incident was neither forgotten nor forgiven.

The rebuke was accepted with meekness. Waring retreated. He felt less a man at that moment than ever in his life before.

The great eyes opened slowly, closed, opened again. The lantern in Tellifer's hand showed a look of frightened doubt—of dawning wonder. She struggled to raise herself.

Not one of her freed captives spoke. Perhaps they were all a little curious to see how she would bear herself in the face of this changed situation. They were not left long in doubt.

She had risen to a half-crouching position, slender limbs drawn up under her. For a long minute she stared from figure to figure of those about her. They had never seen her show any signs of fear. But now something like abject terror was creeping into the dawn-blue eyes.

With a quick jerk of the head, she glanced behind her. The solicitous face of the youngest "cave-man" at her back seemed to reassure her not at all.

She looked down, fingered the gold bangles on the edge of her jaguar-hide tunic, raised the Pan's pipes, still firmly clasped in one hand, inspected the fateful instrument—and—

It happened so quickly that five wise, intelligent men had plunged into a fresh indiscretion before they had time to think about.

With a low cry, the girl flung the Pan's pipes from her. The slender, gathered limbs shot her erect. She sprang sideways, ducked under Waring's arm, upflung to check her, and was off across the court!

They had seen her dance. This was their first opportunity to see her run. The quondam captives charged after, but the shadow of a flying cloud would have been as easy to catch.

The door in the southeastern wall stood open. It closed with a *clang* before the pursuers had crossed half the intervening space. Reaching it, they learned that the illusive one's panic had been genuine. She had not paused to bar the door behind her. It had even swung open an inch or so.

Hurled wide, it revealed a long flight of descending stairs. Tellifer held the lantern high. Part way down the flight, a flash of starlike jewels—the flirt of a flying jaguar-hide tunic.

Discretion? The masculine fever of the hunt had them now. Four unshaven, wild-eyed cave-men and one civilized and freshly enthused esthete plunged recklessly down in pursuit of the flying tunic.

Chapter XV.
DOWN THE STAIR.

The descent proved not so deep as it had seemed from above. Thirty seconds brought the pursuers to a blank wall and a landing.

The flirting tunic had flashed around the corner ahead of them. They turned after it. The landing proved to mark a right-angular turn in the stair.

Not very far ahead now the starry jewels glittered and bobbed to the flying leaps of their wearer. Suddenly there was a sharper plunge—a shrill cry.

Tellifer's long legs had carried him into the lead, but now the youngest "cave-man" cleared four steps at a bound and took the lead away from him.

"She's fallen!"

Sigsbee's voice wailed back in an anguish of solicitude. By the time the lantern caught up with him again he had reached a second landing—had gathered in his arms a slender, softly-moaning form that lay there.

Tellifer arrived, panting. He raised the lantern.

Sigsbee stared down at the form his arms guarded. He made a queer little choking sound in his throat. Then, not roughly, but with considerable haste, he laid the form down on the stone landing.

As he did so, its lower limbs trailed limply, but a clawlike hand at the end of a scrawny arm darted scratchingly upward. A quick jerk of the head just saved Sigsbee's cheek from mutilation.

The toothless mouth of the creature he had laid down mowed and chattered wordlessly. Gray, ragged locks strayed from beneath a circlet of glittering stars. The spotted jaguar-hide was clasped over scrawny, yellowish shoulders. The contorted face glared up with terrible eyes—eyes that had feasted long on cruelty and raged now, aware that their years of evil power were spent, but dying with a frank, though wordless, curse for the victims that had escaped.

The claw-hand made another dash for Sigsbee's face—flung back—beat upon the floor convulsively. A shuddering heave of the upper body—a strangled gurgling sound—

"Dead!" said Waring a minute later. "Broken spine. It's the old hag I saw. But how, in God's name—where'd the girl go to?"

The question was more interesting than any of them cared to admit. Descending those two flights of stairs, they had passed no doorways nor openings of any kind through which she might have turned aside and eluded them. Of course, there was the possibility of some disguised, secret passage. Yet, if so, why had the old woman not retreated by the same road?

It was a question which poor Sigsbee made not even an effort to answer. He was very white, looked strangely older. He was shivering in the dank, breathless chill that enveloped them.

There was no sound down here, nor any light, save that of Tellifer's lantern.

This lower landing was really the foot of the stair. Off from it opened a triangular arch. Standing in the arch, they found themselves peering into what seemed a great eight-sided vault or chamber. The lantern did not suffice to illuminate the far walls, but those nearby were chiseled in colossal forms of women, dancing as the girl had danced, charming loathsome monsters with their Pan's pipes.

The place, damp as an underground tomb, contained no furnishings. The only signs of human occupation were several vague heaps of what appeared to be clothing.

On investigation, the explorers found stacked there an accumulation of diverse garments in many stages of freshness and mouldering rot as marked the derelict fleet on the lake. Most were trade-cloth shirts and more or less ragged trousers, such as the rubber-workers wear. There were also better outfits that bespoke the white man. The cassock of a Jesuit priest was among them, falling apart with great age. Also, the heavy costume and hood which told them that the gray hydro-airplane on the lake might wait in vain for the return of its pilot.

The five found their own clothing, and also their weapons stacked on a great pile that included the rust-caked, muzzle-loading guns of dead *seringueiros*, some modern weapons ruined by the damp, a reed blow-pipe, and a great, badly warped bow of raripari wood with a quiver of long arrows.

Nothing of theirs was missing. John B. even found and restored to the naturalist his precious shell-rims. But the vault reeked and dripped with malodorous dampness. The rotting garments exhaled a breath as from the tomb of their former owners.

Very silent in that lifeless place, the five returned to the stairfoot and bent above the withered dead thing there. The starry diamonds in its hideous hair gleamed with a cold, wicked luster.

Where was the mournful, innocent child who had entrapped them? She who had—dwelt, perhaps, in this tomblike lair?

"I am going away from here," announced Tellifer abruptly. "I don't like this place! It is—*ugly!*"

No one objected. Despite cave-man costumes, they were civilized men who did not believe in vampires, demons, or hideous night-hags that dwelt in underground vaults and issued forth to trap victims with a false illusion of loveliness. Yet they felt that further investigation of the pyramid might wait for a later time. The chill atmosphere was sickening. They wanted open air—wanted it badly.

Due to this need, their return to the upper level was marked with a certain haste. The gardened court held nothing to keep them lingering. Only a very few minutes were needed to reach the rim and negotiate the outer descent.

The traveling-canoe—exceptional among the derelicts—received its returning crew. There was something consoling, something sane and home-like in the very feel of its deck-planks. But it occurred to them that the night would be passed more pleasantly at a distance from the pyramid.

Then, having paddled out a way, somebody suggested that if anything—anyone, that is, of course—were inclined to be dissatisfied with their escape and come after them, the rest of the fleet offered a too-convenient means.

Despite fatigue and starvation, they found strength to paddle back and attend to this potential menace. In consequence, it was nearly midnight when they at last dropped the anchor. By the time they had finished supper, cooked on the vapor-stove, three of them were past recking of perilous pyramids and suspicions that diabolical philosophy might have more reason in it than they had believed. Sleep gripped these three like a heavy drug. Tellifer, who, having slept all afternoon, was elected watchman, gave characteristic respect to duty by drowsing off soon afterward.

Sigsbee, however, did not sleep. On the foredeck, he lay for hours, staring at the mountainous black mass outlined by humid starshine. There was no faint luminescence hovering above it now. "Tata Quarahy"—Fire of the Sun—was destroyed. Its monstrous guardian lay dead. Its priestess—?

Young Sigsbee felt very strange and old and uncertain about it all. Yet if at any time that night a light had flashed in the dark mass, or a voice had called, he would not have roused the others. He would have taken his life and his soul in his hands and gone back alone to the pyramid.

Sunrise, and the eastward stair a flaming height of red and orange and gold.

The reflected splendor, beating on Tellifer's face, awakened him. He opened his eyes, recalled that he was a watchman, sat up and viewed the pyramid in conscientious scrutiny.

It was still there, and its loveliness in this early morning light atoned in a measure, he decided, for the ugly things that had gone on inside of it. Those things seemed very dreamlike and remote this morning. As for vampirish night-hag who could appear at will as a beautiful girl—Tellifer considered the idea with interest. Last night he had wanted nothing save to get away from it, but this morning his fanciful taste dealt with it more kindly.

Sunrise is a bad hour, however to believe in ghosts and vampires. Tellifer regretfully shook his head. Then he uttered a sharp ejaculation, shot to his feet, dived into the cabin and was back an instant later, a pair of binoculars in his hand. En route, he had given a rousing kick to the correspondent and Otway.

Stumbling forth, they found their alert night-watchman with binoculars focused on the sun-lit stair.

Far up there, against the background of flaming stone, a small dark figure was moving.

Waring ruthlessly appropriated the binoculars by force, while the equally curious Otway squeezed against his shoulder as if trying to get at least one eye to the glasses.

Sigsbee, who had dropped asleep just before dawn, roused, took in the scene and reached the group in a bound. His boyish voice broke and crackled.

"Is it she? Is she alive? Is she coming down?"

Waring shook his head. "Somebody's coming down. But it isn't a 'she', Sig. It's—Yet how *can* that be? The cells were empty—and we saw—"

"I know," Tellifer cut in. "We saw his clothing down there with that of all the other dead men. But this pyramid, Alcot, is not limited as are less distinguished haunts of the un-dead. Night, noon or sunrise, its ghosts may walk as they please. The ghost of the air pilot comes now to offer his congratulations on our escape!"

But no one was paying attention to Tellifer.

Sigsbee, in turn, had annexed the glasses. What he saw through them caused him to give a kind of choking gasp, and thereafter, on the selfish score that they were his, he kept the binoculars.

The figure, however, soon came near enough so that even with the naked eye its costume, at least, was unmistakable. The goggles were pushed up visor-like on the close-fitting hood. A trifle awkwardly in the loose, heavily lined suit, the mysterious air-pilot whom they had once thought to rescue, accomplished the full descent.

He walked slowly forward on the broad stone landing stage. Reaching the edge, he contemplated the canoe, turned his gaze to the airplane, returned it to the canoe.

Then he called across to those aboard the latter. The voice was slightly tremulous!

"I beg your pardon! After all that happened, I dislike so much to trouble you! But you've taken all the boats away. Would you mind very much if I asked you to just—just push one in where I can reach it and paddle out to my 'plane?"

Sigsbee dropped his binoculars. They splashed unheeded in the lake. His companions were in pajamas, blanket-draped, but Sigsbee's blindly devotional foresight had led him to shave and dress before retiring the night before. Ere any of the others could move, he had made a flying leap from the canoe to the nearest derelict, a crudely hollowed native dugout.

"I told you!" He flung back as he hauled in the dugout's mooring-stone. "Didn't I tell you I'd seen that girl before? *And I know where, now!* Just as I said. Everything absolutely all right, but you fellows—Never mind! *Coming, Miss Enid!*"

Oars splashed and the dugout fairly shot across toward the landing stage.

Of those left on the canoe, Tellifer was the first to find voice.

"He has seen her before," said he solemnly. "Ah, yes! Her name is Miss Enid, she is an air-pilot, and these facts make everything absolutely all right. Naturally. But do you know, Alcot, despite my love for the beautiful and mysterious, I have had about enough of that pyramid? By all means, let Sig have it! I suggest that the rest of us go away now, while we are still able, and leave that pair in possession!"

CHAPTER XVI.
THE STORY OF MISS ENID WIDDIUP.

"It is so good in you all," the girl began, somewhat later in the day, when they were all seated together under the big canoe's awning, "so very good in you to understand and not blame me in the least for any of it. Of course, Mr. Sigsbee's remembering me helps. I am almost sure that I recall his face, too, though I drove so many officers back and forth to Camp Upton—Oh, you were 'just a sergeant' and I didn't drive you? Why, I drove lots of noncoms and the boys, too. We all did. Well, if you couldn't get near my car, I'm sorry. There *was* a crowd—Oh, you were transferred to Georgia just after I began driving at Camp Upton? And then never got across? That *was* stupid. But I can sympathize with you fully. They wouldn't take me in the ambulance corps, because they said I was too young and not strong enough. Wasn't that absurd? I'm not so awfully large, of course, but my physical endurance is simply *endless*. But I must begin at the beginning and tell this properly.

"My father, as I have already told you, was Dr. Alexander Widdiup, the archaeologist, and I was born on the Amazon, in Manaos. Mother took me home to New York when I was a baby, and I never saw Brazil again till this summer.

"I was nine years old when poor Dad wrote us that he was planning a trip up the Rio Silencioso. An Indian had brought him word that at the Silencioso's source were some remarkable ruins and relics of an ancient people. This Indian—his name was Peter or—no, Pedro, that was it—I beg pardon, Mr. Otway? Yes his name was Kuyambira-Pedro. Dad said he came from some cannibal tribe of the Moju river. He was a wizard too, and made charms to protect people from jungle and river-demons. He showed Dad one of those jaguar tunics, and two small diamonds, cut to symbolize the sun. But the expedition my father organized never came back.

"Dad had been with us in New York only part of each year, but he and I were best pals. I used to say to myself that some day, when I grew up, I'd find a way to at least learn how he had died.

"Then the war came. My mother always lets me do as I please, and I had learned to fly a Blériot, but, of course, they wouldn't take me in the aviation corps, either. So finally I had to content myself with motor-car service at home. After peace was signed, poor Major Dupont agreed to help me in my scheme to reach the source of the Rio Silencioso by the air-route. Major Dupont was English—Royal Flying Corps—but he was visiting friends in New York on six months' leave. When I told him my plan he considered it very practical and interesting.

"We decided on the hydro-airplane because we had to rise from the Amazon, and over these forests if we couldn't come down on water we couldn't come down at all.

"Mother is at Manaos now, waiting for me. She is probably terribly worried, but still she knows that I always do get through safely somehow. I beg pardon. Oh, I inherited an adventurous disposition from father, and I don't think size and physical strength count for so much in these days . . . .

"Why, Mr. Waring! You mustn't say that? Why, I didn't mean that at all! You poor things, of course you couldn't help yourselves with that frightful beast threatening you every moment. But let me go on, and you'll understand better.

"Mother drew the line at my making this try alone, but poor Major Dupont was so resourceful and had such a splendid flying record that when he offered, that made it much safer, of course. The Major and I only meant to make a reconnaissance flight this first trip, but we had no trouble in finding the lake. The top of the pyramid flashed its location to us miles off. Of course, we didn't know what the flash meant. It was like an enormous, bright star shining in broad daylight, and on Earth instead of up in the sky where stars belong.

"Mr. Tellifer? A fallen star—yes, that was just what poor Major Dupont said it resembled. It is a little strange that he should have used that comparison, because of what was told to me later on.

"We planed down to the lake and landed in the collapsible boat we carried. There have been several heavy rains since, and our little craft must have filled and sunk. I notice it is not among the others. Major Dupont wished me to wait and let him go up the pyramid alone, but I wouldn't, so we went up together. It was noon, but of course we had no means of knowing that noon meant anything dangerous.

"We looked over the upper rim, and there was that strange hollow place, with palms and shrubbery and in the middle—something glorious. Major Dupont said it must be the grandfather of all diamonds, and we joked over it. We knew it was fearfully hot in the court, but it was hot outside, too. We walked over to the pit. Major Dupont said there must be a furnace below it. He stepped on one of the five-sided stones—By mere chance, I had one foot on the solid pavement and pulled myself back in time. I ran out on one of the oblong stones. The column I caught hold of was so hot it scorched my hands. I—I find I can't tell you much of this. . . . Thank you. Yes, I believe I'll just leave it out. I couldn't help him. There wasn't time. I—fainted, I think.

"Afterward, for a long while, everything was like a dream. My first memory is of looking up into the face of an old woman, very strangely dressed. I was lying on the floor of one of the outer houses. She had taken away my own clothes and dressed me like herself. This seemed a bit strange for a few minutes, and after that quite natural. I accepted everything just as one does in a dream. Some of the time I would even seem to know I was dreaming, and wonder a little why I couldn't wake up. I felt very sad always, though there didn't seem to be any real reason for it.

"I think it was the shock of what I had seen happen. There was a Miss Blair that mother and I knew. She was the dearest girl, but she had been at a hospital base in France when it was shelled by the Germans. For nearly a year afterward she wasn't herself at all. She cried a great deal, and couldn't take interest in anything. I used to bring her flowers, and when I called I noticed she would never do anything unless the nurse or I suggested she should. I suppose I was very much like that. . . .

"Why, yes, Mr. Waring. If any of you had asked me to release you or told me to shut that hideous creature in its hole, I think I would have done it. When you all seemed so—so annoyed over what was happening, I used to wonder why you never asked me to do differently. But then, you were just people in a dream, and dream-people never do behave consistently, you know. So I went on acting as Sifa directed me, because that was easiest.

"The old woman's name was Sifa. She spoke English and some other language that meant nothing to me. Her teeth were nearly all gone, but very soon I grew used to the mumbling and the broken accent, and understood almost everything she said in English.

"I did whatever she advised me to. She didn't hurt me or even threaten. In fact, she was extremely considerate and—kind, I was going to say, but that hardly expresses it. Her face and eyes were too wicked. I followed her advice because she seemed to know exactly what I ought to do, and it was such an effort to think of things for myself. Besides, it was all so dreamlike. Nothing mattered in the least.

"Sifa said that Ama-Hotu, Lord of Day, had sent me in a cloud-canoe from the skies, so that the ancient worship might not fail. She was the last of her people. Many seasons ago, a great sickness carried off all that were left of her race, the Oellos. I can't tell you much of the Oello people's history. You see, though I understood what she said, I didn't feel like speaking at all to anyone, and I asked no questions.

"But Sifa, of her own accord, told me that a long time ago, at the beginning of all seasons, Ama-Hotu, Lord of Day, caused the great star Huac to descend upon the Earth. Huac the Star was jealous of his honor. So Ama-Hotu commanded that Corya the great Earth Serpent with Feet should give him worship in the dark hours, and that the sacred women dedicated to Ama-Hotu's service should also serve Huac the Star. By day, in return, Huac was servant to Ama-Hotu and presided over the offerings.

"Corya, the Serpent with Feet, and many children of which the Star was father.* For reasons beyond number the children of Corya and the Star dwelt together in the pyramid, and the sacred women of Ama-Hotu danced with them in worship of the Star and Sun. But a season came when Corya, the Earth Serpent, devoured her children.

"Two of them were saved by one of the sacred women and carried to the surrounding land. Until that time the Oellos, Sifa's people, had dwelt in great numbers on the land. The pyramid was a place of worship, and only the sacred dancing women dwelt here. But the pair of Corya's children multiplied. They would not harm the sacred women, whose music they loved, but they slew so many of the people that at last there were only a few left, and those came to dwell under the protection of the dancers in the pyramid. They still grew crops along the shores, but for this the sacred ones must go ashore and protect them with music.

"There were so few of the Oello people left that the human offerings to Ama-Hotu could no longer be selected from their number. For many seasons, long before Sifa was born, it had been the custom to send secret emissaries who traveled upon water, which the children of Corya could not cross, and brought back victims from the outer tribes. Sometimes they would do this by force, but more often by tempting them with tales of wealth or whatever the victims most desired.

"Sifa said that after all her people died in a great sickness, she lived here many seasons alone. Sifa gave up trying to cultivate the fields on shore, and lived on fruits and nuts and fish from the lake.

"Corya, the great Earth Serpent, was content to be fed on the fruits of the Earth, her father. Flesh had never been offered to her. I suppose really they were afraid the horrible thing would acquire a taste for blood and turn on them. Corya's children ashore, by the way, had never grown to any great size—never more than eighteen inches or so. I think now that all that part was merely a legend, made up to account for the common centipedes one finds in the jungle, and that Corya herself was just an unaccountable freak.

"Sifa had obtained what victims she could to offer Ama-Hotu. In the old days, her people had many friends among the forest tribes, and this dreadful cannibal wizard, Kuyambira-Pedro, was one of them. She told me that sometimes Pedro came to visit her. He believed that Huac the Star was

---

*There is at least a question among the naturalists, as to whether that rather curious creature, Chilopoda Scolopendra, finds it always necessary to mate in order that the species may be perpetuated.

the greatest of all the *anyi* or spirits. "Tata Quarahy", Life-Breath of the Sun, he called it. He brought it victims when he could to win its favor.

"I remembered the name—Pedro—and it made me sad, so I cried for hours after she had told me that. But I didn't remember my father or what I had come here for.

"She taught me to play on the little golden pipes and Corya came out of her lair. No, I wasn't afraid of the creature. I wasn't afraid of anything. I tell you, it was all just a dream to me.

"Sifa said that Corya would never harm me, because now I was a sacred woman. She danced with Corya to show me how I was to do. I have always been very fond of dancing, and I liked that part. It was the only thing that interested me, even a little.

"When I—woke up, at last, and found myself sitting there on the floor with you standing around me, I was terribly frightened. I knew for the first time that all those things I had been seeing and hearing and doing were real! And oh! I was *scared!* It was silly in me, but I was actually afraid you might be angry enough to kill me. Mr. Waring? Oh, I thought you spoke.

"So I jumped up and ran. When I reached that doorway, there was Sifa inside. She pulled the door shut and mumbled something at me, and I heard her bare feet go pattering down the stair. The stairway is wider than the door, you may remember. I just flattened myself tight to the wall inside the doorway. After you passed I ran back in the court and hid among the shrubbery.

"Before the night was over, I had collected my senses and decided the best thing I could do was to tell you I was sorry and go away. So I went down after my suit—Oh, yes, in the dark. Sifa never had any lights, but I had learned to know my way around without. No, certainly we didn't live down in that musty old vault. There are ever so many passages between the inner chambers of the pyramid and the funny little houses outside. We lived outside, of course. Sifa used to be always watching the river mouth in case more victims should come. I was with her when your canoe entered the lake. She was watching you all the time. When you started up the stair, she sent me to call forth Corya, and directed me how to act toward you. I was to send Corya to her hole after a while, and beckon you to come down. But poor Mr. Tellifer, by falling in, changed that part, and rather confused me for a few minutes. . . .

"It didn't change things enough to hurt? N-no—oh, no, of course not. Really, if you *are* angry with me, I can't blame you in the least. . . . You're not? It's so dear in you all to say so. And now I—I think I must go. Why, yes, thank you, I can handle the 'plane very nicely alone, and I couldn't think of imposing on you. Why, certainly I'm not angry! But—

"Well, so long as you put it that way, I'll wait, of course. Maybe a day or two of rest *would* make it safer. And I can show you all around the pyramid. After I've relieved mother's anxiety, I'm coming back here, of course. Oh, yes, I feel it's my duty. You see, poor Dad gave his life to find this place, and I must get the—the measurements, you know, and photographs of the carvings and all that. Then I shall give the notes and pictures and what I can remember of the Oello people's history to some archaeologist who understands such things, and he can write a book about it and give the credit to father.

"Mr. Otway? I'm so glad you think that's a splendid idea! And Mr. Waring, you say you write for the magazines. You won't spoil my book by telling about any of it in advance, will you?"

Noon. Ama-Hotu, Lord of Day, glared fiercely down upon Huac the Star's empty shrine and the drying corpse of Corya, the many-taloned Earth Serpent. Old Sifa, last devotee of the trio, lay also dead, her withered remains sealed up in a crypt of the pyramid.

But Ama-Hotu, Lord of Day, has been worshiped in many lands. Invariably has he survived his worshipers; outlived a multitude of fellow-gods as well. The empty shrine of Huac, the drying segments of Corya, made no difference at all in the glory of Ama-Hotu.

Four hard-working humans had retreated before his potency. In one of the ancient pyramidal dwellings they lay about in pajamas, sweated, drowsed and waited for the undisputed Lord of Day to go seek his victims elsewhere.

All morning they had been at work taking the measurements, photographs and notes which were to make the name of Widdiup famous. Sigsbee, however, was not among the toilers. The gray hydro-airplane was missing from the derelict fleet.

"Miss Enid's pyramid," yawned Waring after a time, "was a wonderful find!"

No one disputed this. He redistributed his mass to a more comfortable posture.

"We never had a chance, you know. First to last—not the ghost of one!"

Otway looked up with a flash of philosophic gray eyes behind the shell-rims.

"I am entirely willing," he said, "to surrender all the honors to Dr. Widdiup's memory."

"Of course you are! So'm I willing to surrender writing it up. TNT was—

we all were—to surrender the diamonds stored in the pyramid's crypts. Benefit of starving Armenian orphans. Splendid idea. Girl with eyes like hers, bound to think of it. Sig is willing to surrender himself. That is, if she'll have him. Ex-actly! First to last—not a chance!"

"The treacherous spirit of Kuyambira-Pedro," began Tellifer—and for the first known time in his life broke off as if for lack of ideas to continue.

"Quite right," approved his friend. "Treacherous cannibal wizard, not worth mentioning. Half-ton diamond cut to broil you alive—easy. Pyramids—monsters—night-hags—burning pits—got a chance with all of 'em. But a girl like Miss Enid—never! Oh, Lawdy, Lawdy! The penalty of being fat and forty! Declined with thanks for the air-trip. Yet I've flown and Sig hasn't. What's your trouble, John B.?"

"I was just thinking, sir, that maybe I might have tried a little harder to get her to take me. Before the war, after I quit the Buffalo Bill show, I used to make exhibition flights in a little old Antoinette I got off a flyer that broke his neck in it. I had a good deal of experience. Mr. Sigsbee means well, but I can't see what real good he could be in case of accident."

"With her airplane and selected captive, she will arrive in Manaos," spoke Tellifer, the prophet. "I know that she will, for she is a very wise and practical person: she refused to take me! Dr. Otway, I presume you also are among the declined-with-regrets?"

"I am not." The philosophic eyes twinkled again. "In the first place, there was not only one of us who deserved to be chosen. All in the second, I had already engaged myself to collect this material for the Widdiup book. But at least, if we are not helping her to make a flight, we are saving her the need of risking another one back here. And the honor of that is something!"

"It is much," agreed Waring, very meekly.

THE END

Gladiator
By Philip Wylie
Introduced by Janny Wurts

When Worlds Collide
By Philip Wylie and Edwin Balmer
Introduced by John Varley

To order or obtain more information on these or other University of Nebraska Press titles, visit www.nebraskapress.unl.edu.